Matthew Condon was born in Brisbane in 1962 and has lived in the UK, Germany and France. He is the author of several novels and short story collections, including *The Motorcycle Café*, *A Night at the Pink Poodle*, *The Pillow Fight* and *Lime Bar*. He is also the recipient of two Steele Rudd awards for short fiction.

The Trout Opera

Matthew Condon

BLACK SWAN

TRANSWORLD PUBLISHERS
61–63 Uxbridge Road, London W5 5SA
A Random House Group Company
www.rbooks.co.uk

THE TROUT OPERA
A BLACK SWAN BOOK: 9780552775120

First published in Australia in 2007 by Vintage, Random House Australia Pty Ltd
First published in Great Britain
in 2010 by Doubleday
an imprint of Transworld Publishers
Black Swan edition published 2011

This project has been assisted by the Australian Government through the
Australia Council, its arts funding and advisory body.

Addresses for Random House Group Ltd companies outside the UK
can be found at: www.randomhouse.co.uk
The Random House Group Ltd Reg. No. 954009

Penguin Random House is committed to a sustainable future for
our business, our readers and our planet. This book is made from
Forest Stewardship Council® certified paper.

MIX
Paper from
responsible sources
FSC
www.fsc.org   FSC® C018179

Printed and bound in Great Britain by Clays Ltd, Elcograf S.p.A.

Typeset in 12/14pt Bembo by Falcon Oast Graphic Art Ltd.
2 4 6 8 10 9 7 5 3 1

For my darling wife, Kate, with all my love

Whatever lies under a stone
Lies under the stone of the world

THE GREEN CENTIPEDE by Douglas Stewart

ON THE VERANDAH of the Buckley's Crossing Hotel, reclining in dimpled leather armchairs, Judges Carrington and Thorpe observed in silence the giant trout shuffling across the bridge.

It was almost dusk, and the two elderly men, nursing malt whiskies after a day's fishing, said nothing of the apparition, just as they would have said nothing, impassive beneath horsehair, in their courtrooms back in Sydney on the hearing of evidence. They largely worked in silence, listening, day after day, to the human story, and their identical blankness of face at the appearance of the outsized trout indicated there was very little in the world that surprised Judges Carrington and Thorpe.

A light breeze pushed up from the river, bringing with it the tinkling of the trout's scales. Both men heard it, tangled in the roar from the Snowy, and if the slow-moving trout, rocking on the points of its tail fin, had disturbed their recollections of the day's fishing – silken lines looping, stones pressing at the soles of their boots, the silent nodding of bulrush heads – they did not show it. Watching it, they felt a chill rise up from their feet and through their legs and a rash of goose bumps from their memory of the early morning wading. As unlikely as the sight of the tin and hessian fish was, they could not help recalling the icy waters of the river.

With the apparition defining itself as it hobbled closer to the bridge's westernmost span, the judges – almost brothers, really, and law school chums – each recalled the respective specimens they had mounted under glass in their chambers back in Macquarie Street. Two rainbows, fixed against a hand-painted riverbank scene, caught on the same trip, transported in ice and preserved with the same loving care and attention by Mr Smiggett Junior of The Rocks. (Poor Smiggett Senior, dead the previous year from arsenic asphyxiation.) Two rainbows, high up on the wood-panelled walls facing their desks. Two rainbows, in which the men often lost themselves, dreaming of clear streams and distorted stones when they should have been dismantling the great and complex machinery of the criminal mind. If only the truth could be pulled from the water as readily, and mounted, they often said. How much less complicated their lives would have been.

The dinner gong sounded inside the hotel, yet the two judges were loath to leave the verandah and the spectacle of the giant trout, now clambering with difficulty onto the wooden end rail of the bridge.

'A brown, do you think?' Thorpe inquired.

Carrington leaned forward in his chair and adjusted his spectacles.

'Of sorts, yes. A brown of sorts.'

They chuckled at the thought of their discussion a half-hour earlier: James Arndell Youl's feat of delivering salmon ova from the other side of the world. And a gift of brown trout. After hatching and on release, the salmon swam straight out into the ocean and were never seen again. As for the trout, the ova afterthoughts, they headed up the streams, and survived. The two judges had agreed there was a 'lesson' in Youl's experiment. One they could apply to life. Or to their work in the Darlinghurst courts. It was the nature of fishing. All things garnered an almost religious significance and transformed, between the opening of the creel and the recollection of the day, into the metaphorical. Outside the recreation – as it was with the courthouse's bloody narratives; the foreign language of that elusive muscle, the human heart; the maps of jealousy, revenge, greed that could be read four ways, the compass point-less, beyond those sandstone walls – there was no sense to it.

It was why they waited for the giant trout on the bridge. It could become a talisman, an omen, for the next day's fishing on the Snowy.

Encased in the hessian trout was Wilfred Lampe, aged six, who finally, after a few false starts, managed to balance on the bridge rail's middle rung and peer over into the swift-running river. He slipped down into the suit momentarily, the mouth hole rising above his fore-head. Once firmly balanced, he tugged the head down and had a clear view through the padded velvet-lipped slit.

They must be there, the boy thought. The water roared. They must be there, facing upstream, waiting for the fall of white moths. For the brush of insect leg and wing on the surface of this trembling plate of melted ice. He knew them better than anyone on the Monaro. Had names for them. Talked to them, for heaven's sake.

But what would they have made of him now? This giant trout, one of their own, yet not, looming over them high up on the bridge. Suspended in the dryness of the sky – out there in the mirror world that was both life and death for them – where there had only ever been the needle legs of their prey, a madness of flying ants and dragonfly, or the exotic, feathered, often brilliantly plumed morsels that fooled many of them and failed to fool just as many others. Its huge eyes wild and googly and tenuously attached to an ill-shaped head. The flanks vibrating. (Could they hear it, down through the jade green water to the rocks and wild streamers of reed?) The tail ragged. The side fins abnormal. This, some god of trout. A king of trout. Watching over them.

In an hour Wilfred Lampe would take to the stage of the Imperial Hall as star of *The Trout Opera*. He had known his lines off by heart for a fortnight. This, he realised, would be his last rehearsal. Gripping the rail tighter, he leaned out even further and told them, I am King Trout of the Monaro. I am your guardian, your protector, here to ensure that your spirit will forever travel through the rivers and creeks of this country, into the lakes and the pools and the hollows.

He was distracted by the special string of light bulbs at the front of the Imperial Hall which suddenly crackled to life. He thought he could hear the bulbs humming, just as a filament of excitement had vibrated within him for days. He momentarily lost his lines, thinking of the bulbs.

Oh yes, he went on. However many of you may disappear from the waters, however many of you are lifted into heaven by the pretty fly, there are multitudes more who will grow older and older, and pass on their secrets, and . . . and . . .

He heard a bell ringing deep inside the hotel, looked up momentarily, then squinted again into the darkening waters of the river. Are you there? He thought he saw a flickering, a scissoring of trout shapes across the constellation of stones. At this time of day, at dusk, you could not be sure of anything. He liked to think – as he did at night on his cot on the verandah of the house – the trout were always there somewhere, just as clouds continued their business, easing across the sky while he was asleep.

And never forget your eye, he resumed, sweating inside the blunt head of the fish costume. The eye of all trout. Where you can see through the surface of the water, to the world, to the future, and at the same time see your own world, your home, your past, reflected off the water's skin. Believe in me. I am your King. The King Trout of the Monaro.

His parents had told him not to go into town so early. To wait for the cart. But he had shuffled off anyway, down the track to the gate, and onto the road into Dalgety. He could hear the rumble of the river even as he started off. (Like the ocean, he imagined, having never seen the ocean. Wasn't it why they called the stone church on the hill Our Lady Star of the Sea?) The tin can lids of his scales occasionally caught the setting sun, sending discs of orange light through the lucerne stalks. He slipped once in a cart rut and fell with a clang into the dust.

For once, in the suit, he was big – this narrow boy with his elongated torso and broom-handle arms and splashings of freckles across not just his face but his ears and eyelids as well. They had always called him Trout anyway.

And here he was, Wilfred Lampe, aged six, looking over the bridge rail for his obedient subjects. Me lady, he said croakily. Me lady. But the lines had gone from him, lost in the sighs from the willows and the honking of ducks, an arrowhead of them rising at the river bend. So the giant trout finally came down off the rail and progressed towards the hotel. Horses and carts began arriving from all directions – the cricket oval, the blacksmith shop, the police station and lockup east of the town. The giant trout, disoriented, almost stumbled into the path of one, the horse shying.

'My word,' said Carrington, enjoying the show.

'Bound to be an accident with big fish like that allowed to wander freely,' said Thorpe.

'The litigation would be terribly complicated,' Carrington added.

The traffic was of the most extraordinary kind, and it would be something the judges would recall fondly – in the confines of their chambers, and on occasion in their sleep – for years. For in each and every cart and sulky were children dressed in costume. Whole transports of frogs and birds and insects. (One particular flying ant, on passing, had waved vigorously and emitted a distinct 'gidday'.) There were trout flies, drab in the torso but bearing spectacular tendrilled headdresses. There was an entire flatbed dray of muddy browns, rocking with the gait of a Clydesdale. Not to mention an assortment of

16

yabbering bulrushes and reeds. And a single flame robin, alone amongst a cluster of crows, wailing inconsolably.

Wilfred Lampe continued his slow progress up the rutted road in front of the hotel, his wide trout eyes spinning wildly through a veil of dust, his small freckled fingers occasionally emerging from a gill in recognition of the shouts of his schoolfriends. His excitement now was so great he felt, for a moment, he might faint. He stopped, rested against the verandah railing of the hotel, and caught his breath.

The judges instantly took pity on the hot and heaving fish.

'May we be of assistance in any way?' Thorpe inquired, his whisky now empty.

A small, muffled voice said through the gill: 'No thank you, sir.'

'Are you sure?' asked Carrington, indicating a small blue jug on their drinks table. 'A little water, perhaps?'

'Thank you all the same,' the boy said. 'I must be getting on.'

'Very well,' said Carrington.

With that the trout – watched paternally by the judges – shuffled over to the Imperial Hall and entered the mad, skittering maelstrom of plant and fish and horse and parent and dust beneath the sagging string of glass bulbs. Outside the hall they poked and prodded Wilfred Lampe and rattled his scales and shouted 'Trout! Trout! Trout!' and he turned again and again on his heels but it was difficult to recognise anyone through the thick velvet lips. In yellow light the judges could just read the sign nailed to the wall of the hall: DALGETY SCHOOL PRESENTS *THE TROUT OPERA*. ONE

PERFORMANCE ONLY. AN UNFORGETTABLE EVENING.

And for a brief moment, perhaps a historic one – although history is never made that easily, and would come, to some, decades later behind the wheel of a tractor, or at the fall of a hat in the town cemetery – the world of Dalgety and the river and the whole Monaro was there, alive, in the main street.

Only the judges could hear the hotel dinner gong being struck with some urgency.

'I believe it is Trout Amandine this evening. With Sauternes,' said Carrington.

Thorpe leaned forward and squinted at the sign across the street. 'The show,' he finally said. 'Are we taking it in?'

And Carrington sniffed. 'No seats left, I'm afraid.'

The street suddenly emptied and the night fell quiet. Everything – the cattle and sheep in the dark hill folds, the tips of poplar trees, the wheel of stars – seemed to pull tight, to hold breath.

The cast of *The Trout Opera* assembled behind the heavy curtains at the front of the Imperial Hall, tittering and whispering and waiting for their cue – the slow lilt of a violin. It came at last, the single note as thin and graceful as a freshly cast silk line. Wilfred Lampe heard his Queen, Her Majesty the Lure, clear her throat beside him, her feathered rainbow headpiece reaching high up towards the tongue-and-groove wooden ceiling of the hall. The muddy browns muttered incessantly despite a repeated 'Ssshhh!' from the wings. And the willows, ahead of time, began their ghostly humming.

They were making history. And while he wasn't sure what history felt like, Wilfred sensed something, there, behind the slow ocean roll of the ancient curtains, with the living, quick-breathing, eye-glinting, shadowy entity of the cast – the reeds, the willows, the damsel and caddis flies, the bogong moths and fingerlings – ready to spill onto the stage. They would, they had been promised, draw the attention of the world.

Wilfred Lampe suddenly felt cold inside the hessian. The sounds of footsteps and the barking of chairs thrummed in his suit. The violin note lifted through the heat, through the scent of rosewater and hair oil and a trace of sheep dung and the whole sticky breath of the Imperial Hall.

Then the curtains opened.

PART I

ONE

SHEEP ON THE hills froze and stared in the direction of the car, and for a moment the distant passage of the white sedan reflected across the watery films of their eyes like a parasite.

It was early spring, and snow clung to the mountains, and was still deep inside the mistrals that came down into the valley. The wind flowed from the stands of snow gums high up and through the blue eucalypts and then over blankets of buttercups and billy buttons until it poured into the bowl of the Monaro. It ruffled the long fleece of the sheep.

The sheep carpeted the valley and the lower terraces of the hills above the white car. They twitched and ticked and tore at the grass to the drone and crank of blowfly and grasshopper, and the gunshot-cracking of the giant boulders wrapped in lichen. They were sheep like all sheep throughout the High Country, dulled and sleepy and unthinking until those startling eruptions of life – fox fang to underbelly, thunder or fire across the ranges, a car crackling its way up a dirt road through the middle of a valley.

They stood motionless now on the tiers of this

amphitheatre, mouths locked and holding clods, pink tongues soiled and wet and twinkling with quartz. They trembled slightly. Some urinated. The car crept past, and by the time the sheep had bowed their heads again to graze, they had forgotten what had happened.

The two men in the car had read the name – LAMPE – painted on a piece of tin on the gate down by the main road, and driven cautiously into the valley, through sudden carousels of grasshoppers.

'This has to be it,' said the driver, his right foot tentative on the accelerator, his city shoes at sea in the country.

His passenger looked out to the swarms of sheep easing up the foothills. They were the same russet brown as the grass, and for a moment it seemed the earth itself was alive and moving.

Hoppers clung to the bonnet and windshield and side mirrors and when the driver slowed down still more of them attached themselves to the car, giddy and drunk in the pale light, their spiny legs awkward and wings half unsheathed. Some were already cooking on the radiator grille.

'Plague,' the passenger said.

The driver was silent.

'Thought it was supposed to be quiet, the bush. This is like George Street at peak hour.'

The driver looked for signs of human life.

'Like a bloody horror movie. Blood and guts. The boys are going to be real happy back at the garage.'

⤙

They had left Sydney just before dawn in the government-issue car and eaten bacon and eggs in a roadhouse halfway to Canberra. At the small formica-topped table in the diner they had studied the files again and compared notes.

In the folder was a single photograph of Wilfred Lampe taken in the 1930s or '40s. He was dressed in work shirt and trousers and braces and boots and wore a battered hat. In the picture he was sitting on the running board of a car with his chin in his hands, and he was as dirty as the soil in which his heavy boots were planted.

'We can get there two ways,' said the driver, finishing his coffee. His uncapped pen was poised over a photo-copied map. 'Via Jindabyne. Or the back way, out of Cooma.'

'You decide,' the passenger said.

'You could show some interest.'

The passenger mopped the egg yolk off his plate with a piece of toast and looked out to their car. Two identical grey suit coats rested on hangers in the back seat.

'What is it, another three hours' drive? Maybe an hour there, do what we have to do, and four or five hours back.'

'About that.'

'That's a half-day's overtime,' the passenger said, dabbing his mouth with a serviette.

The driver stared at him across the table. Adjusted his tie. Returned to the maps and the paperwork.

'We've got to get this right,' he said.

'And I've got to get back for dinner by eight tonight. Rock-pool. You ever been? There's a week's pay right there, but what can you do?'

The coats rocked gently on their hangers as the car passed Lake George. The driver turned the radio off as they entered Canberra. They passed through the capital, down towards the skeletal flagpole of Parliament House, then south-west, to the Monaro Highway and Cooma.

The driver decided they would take the back road into Dalgety. An element of surprise, he thought. He did not share his strategy with his passenger.

The driver had been instilled with a sense of mission, despite the indifference of his colleague, as they drove through the order and alignment of Canberra. That feeling did not leave him all the way to Cooma. But it began to fall away when he turned the car onto the arterial road towards Jindabyne.

It was the thousands of ancient boulders scattered across the hills and fields, the remnants of volcanic eruption. The driver could not connect with the randomness of it all, and how the weird configurations of granite bore the vague shapes of things he knew and yet didn't know.

He saw the reclining bodies of goddesses and dinosaurs and Etruscan columns and temples, galleons and bridges and lighthouses and battalions of warriors. It was the picture books of his childhood when the world was fresh, and something never seen before not only held the eye but lit the heart. Then there were the silhouetted faces he may have recognised, and those of great figures in history – pioneers, bushrangers, prime ministers – and kilometre after kilometre of misshapen breasts and cracked heads and other dismembered body parts. In the rocks he saw everything and nothing, and it disturbed a distant part of him. The driver felt pangs of nausea, and attributed it to the settling of the diner eggs.

'Weird, eh,' was all the passenger said.

The sheep were omnipresent. Thousands of them. Eating and shitting around the monuments, their tiny minds unendingly registering the shift from shadow to sunlit grass and gravel.

It felt cold in the cabin of the vehicle on the drive to Dalgety. The men could hear the grinding of the coat hangers in the back seat.

They arrived at the village before they realised they were in it. The car had rounded a stand of pines when the road narrowed suddenly and they were there; an abandoned garage and fuel pump, an empty tourist park that backed onto the Snowy River, a closed community hall. The driver stopped outside the Buckley's Crossing Hotel.

They stepped out of the car, relieved by the solid forms of the scattered town. The bricks and faded timbers. Glass and lacework. Even the geometrics of an abandoned tennis court down by the community hall, its old clay surface bearded with weed shoots. They saw no people.

The passenger stretched, looked down to the span bridge across the Snowy, the sports oval and stockyards that reared onto the riverbank. A few bluestone and weatherboard houses hunkered behind trees on the low rise at the back of the hotel.

'This is it?' he said.

'This is it,' said the driver.

The driver went into the pub and bought pies and sausage rolls and the two men went down to the river's edge and ate their lunch. They studied the river, silted with algae collecting in rustcoloured skirts at both banks. Further down, beyond the bridge, it forked around deposits of sand and pebble and disappeared into a tangle of blackberry bushes at the first bend. The tea-hued water did not appear to move. Its surface, from where they sat, was covered in rainbowed isobars of oil.

The driver looked at the near-stagnant water and thought of the old photographs on the wall of the pub. The grey men in hats holding up clusters of trout.

'You're telling me this is the Snowy River?' said the passenger, his mouth half full of pastry, his bottom lip crumbed.

The driver chewed methodically and stared straight ahead. 'The one and only,' he finally said.

They both thought of the poems and pictures from schoolbooks and the hides of rearing horses dark with mountain rain and a cavalcade of other images and sounds and words learned in another part of the country where great rivers did not exist. It was what made the Snowy so important to them as children, just to know they had a great river, flowing, roaring, some-where. A country had to have a great river. One that coursed and carved through their stories and imagin-ings. A great river gave strength to a country. Someone had told them that. Or written it. Who knew? History was the rickety house of such platitudes.

'It's dead,' the passenger said.

They sat by the river for another quarter of an hour, locked in the same confused silence, their imagined picture not matching the strangled stretch of water before them. The passenger felt he had been tricked, made a fool of by a long line of conspirators stretching back into his boyhood. He was momentarily angry at being fooled. Not at the sad state of the river. He had no concept of permanence.

'Who cares,' he said at last. 'It's all shit.'

The publican at the Buckley's Crossing, Jim Mitchell, observed the two men through the front windows of the hotel. In Dalgety they were used to public servants passing through. It'd been happening since the early 1900s, when the town was inspected and surveyed as the nation's potential capital. So much for that.

They were regulars again during the construction of the hydroelectric scheme. Now, ironically, they'd blow in once a year to meet with the Snowy River protest groups who wanted them to give back the water they took away for the scheme. The world, Mitchell often said, was arse-up.

The men down by the river, though. It was the first time Jim Mitchell had seen an official Sydney Olympics tie. The little coloured worm of the logo. It reminded him of a Dingo trout fly.

He mentioned the tie to Larry Brindlemere, who popped into the pub for a slab of beer. Larry dropped by the general store for some fuse wire, and told Bill and Meredith Haskell that the logo apparently looked exactly like a Dingo fly. When Mrs Peat telephoned the store about refreshments for the weekend's performance of *Sleeping Beauty* in the community hall, she was told of the two men beside the river below the bridge, the ties, and the Olympics logo. By the time Larry had delivered the warming beers to his fence workers, farmers and their wives from Berridale to Paupong knew of the visitors.

Back in the car, the driver studied another smaller, hand-drawn map, and they drove out of town, across the wood-slat bridge, towards the ranges.

A few kilometres later they found the gate.

'You know what sort of shape he's in?' the passenger asked.

'They didn't say.'

'Does he know we're coming?'

'Why the questions all of a sudden?'

'I'm interested. I'm showing interest.'

The driver drummed on the wheel with his fingers. 'Not that I'm aware of. This is a get-to-know-you visit, that's all.'

'Don't want the old boy to have a heart attack or something.'

'Wilfred Lampe has a heart attack,' the driver said, 'and we're out of a job.'

They drove for two minutes through Lampe's valley before they broached a rise and saw the house. The car idled and dropped air-conditioning fluid onto the dirt road. A smudge of smoke issued from the chimney at the side of the shack.

For several moments they looked down at Lampe's home. It was ramshackle, the core of the house lost behind decades of additions, of verandahs and sheet-tin lean-tos and tacked-on wash-houses and storage rooms of different materials, all this furred and spiked with stands of cut timber, pipes, guttering, old insulation batts and clutches of homemade fishing rods leaning higgledy-piggledy against the sprawling structure.

Scattered out from the dwelling were piles of blue-stone riddled with weeds and rotting tyres and concrete laundry tubs and abandoned machinery. They could hear from inside the closed cabin of the car the tongue-click of a generator in a nearby shed.

The shells of several old cars were parked beneath a huge pepper tree thirty metres from the house, models that stretched back to the 1920s. A tomato bush flowered up through the flooring and around the steering wheel of a Plymouth. The roof of a black, tyreless Humber Vogue was tickled by the furthest overhang of the pepper tree.

'He lives here?' the passenger said.

'He was born here.'

'His whole life he's lived here?'

'He left once as far as we know,' said the driver. 'To Sydney, in the 1930s, to find his missing sister.'

The passenger shook his head. 'And that's it? Once? In a lifetime?'

'That's it.'

'Ever married?'

'No.'

'Brothers? Sisters?'

'All dead,' said the driver.

'There's nobody? No next of kin?'

'One. A great-niece. Twenty-six years old. I doubt he even knows she exists. We can't find her, anyway.'

The driver edged the car towards the house.

It had been a month since the committee appointed the two men to find the perfect candidate. Both thought the job would take little more than a week. But they had travelled to every capital city on the east coast of

Australia then to Fremantle and the Dandenongs and Eden and Wauchope and Emerald, visited dozens of nursing homes, hospitals and rural homesteads, one-bedroom flats overlooking the ocean, caravans on patches of scrub. They had come up with nothing. No one.

They had investigated personal connections, family and friends, and when that was exhausted, gambled on neighbourhoods close to home, eyed old men and women in supermarkets, took notes in the bars of lawn bowling clubs.

Then someone found Lampe. An old clipping, yellowed, from a rural newspaper, cut out by the aunt of a staff member, sent in the post. Lampe, only five hours' drive from the office, down in sheep country, snow and ice country, trout stream country.

They stopped the car near the house.

'And nobody's spoken to him,' said the passenger, straightening his tie.

'Correct.'

'He might be out.'

'Ninety-nine-year-old men don't get out that much.'

They sat in silence in the car for a few moments, daunted by the grand disorder, and the driver wondered if this was how life unravelled itself; if Old Man Lampe and all men were like the house; the original little homestead of clean lines and fresh timbers obscured, slowly, by decades of accretion, until it all disappeared. Not raw and exposed at the end, life, but buried into oblivion.

They wondered if their search was over, here, in a low valley on the Monaro. If the weeks of expeditions into the country of the elderly – wafer-thin skin, the open mouths of the sleeping, the perfume of sour antiseptic and, inside it, death, that shape beyond the veil of everything – was done.

It was Lampe, now, that they feared. Not who he was, but what he represented. He was their immediate future.

'Let's get this over with,' the driver said.

They stepped out of the white car. They opened the rear passenger doors, removed the identical coats from their wire hangers, and reached for their briefcases.

Both men automatically adjusted their Sydney Olympics ties with their free hand.

The driver, out of habit, activated the car alarm, and its quick double beep sent grasshoppers wheeling.

'Mr Lampe?'

They stood on the verandah of the house, peering through the gauze of the flyscreen. The driver tapped on the doorframe.

'Hello?'

Beyond the flywire they could see the outline of a wooden table, a single chair, and the black curves of a kettle in the fireplace. A handful of coals glowed in the grate.

They opened the door and stepped inside. The room was rank with wood smoke and food smells and they could hear a permanent buzzing somewhere in the gloom. Flies, or bees, or the muffled static of a radio.

Their eyes adjusted to the lack of light and suddenly the room appeared to them. A small gas camp cooker on a timber bench to the left, and a tin sink filled with dishes and cutlery. Beside the sink an old-fashioned meat safe. The four panes of the small window above the sink were sealed with sheets of newspaper.

To the right was a wooden sideboard with leadlight in the doors. In the centre of the leadlight were two frosted diamonds. Inside the cabinet, behind the diamonds, was a porcelain ballerina, a butter dish, and faceted rose-glass salt and pepper shakers. Above the sideboard was a photograph of a faded Merino wearing a wreath, a ribbon. It was freckled with fly spots.

At the end of the room stood the fireplace. Its sooted mantel was decorated on each side with hand-carved chickens. On top of the mantelpiece was a squat twin-key clock. From the far end of the room the clock resembled the wigged silhouette of a judge.

Slivers of light appeared between the wide slabs of hardwood that constituted the walls.

The buzzing got louder. It was stuffy inside the house, and the coals flared at the base of the kettle, rasping and clawing at the shifts in the air. The men's hands sweated around their briefcase handles.

'Jesus,' the passenger whispered.

On the kitchen table was a single cream-coloured plate, and on the plate three slices of corned beef, bleeding beetroot, lettuce and a mound of chutney. A knife and fork rested on the food. To the right of the plate was a small teapot. Steam eased from the spout. Just beyond the teapot was an open jar of sugar, a tin of jam with the serrated lid pulled back, and a bread plate.

The driver flicked his head slightly and they moved through the living room to the bedroom doorway. Sheets of newspaper were laid out on the bare wooden floor around the bed. They could see the shape of a human being in the old mattress, and the indentation of a head on the single pillow. Above the iron bedhead, looking out into the room, was the framed photograph of a woman. Her hair was pinned in a bun, her eyes large and dark and almost without whites, her mouth a line of pale pencil. The pink of the lips had faded away.

It was the eyes that held the two men at the doorway of the room. The eyes of a hard, plain woman looking into a future of physical labour, possibly tragedy. Eyes unsoftened by firelight, alert to the crazed stitching of sheep tracks in dew all the way to the distant mountains, to the onset of snow. Pioneer eyes that were prepared for everything, out there, in the world, beyond the slab house in the valley. Or was it the same with all these early photographs, rendered cold and featureless at the studio assistant's hand, character extinguished by a miniature bushel of horsehair, a real life somewhere behind the template of eye shells and mouth brackets.

The stench in the room was almost unbearable.

'Let's try out the back.'

The buzzing had entered their heads and they could feel flies or bees brushing their suit jackets and the hair of their wrists, and their skin crept at the touch, real or imagined. They passed down a narrow hall to a wash-room at the back of the house then re-entered the blinding light of early afternoon.

'He's not here,' the passenger said, breathing deeply. 'Let's go.'

'But the fire. The tea.'

They stood together on the back staircase and when their eyes adjusted again they looked over a waist-high

35

field of weeds and grasses. The sunlight illuminated hundreds of tiny dandelion globes. From the stairs the driver could see the end of the valley, a pinched cul-de-sac of boulders and dead timber and what appeared to be the charred remains of a hut, its long-rotted roof struts and slab walls fallen in around a corrugated-iron chimney.

This place, the driver thought. It was too lived in. As with people, places had a finite life. Lampe's valley, the soil, the car bodies and the trees, were at the end of a long cycle. The driver could feel it, and smell it in the air. A decay that attached itself to the fine fibres of his suit.

'He's not here,' the passenger repeated.

But neither of them could escape the fact of the meal on the kitchen table. And the steam. There was the life of the steam.

'I'll check in the shed,' the passenger said.

He disappeared around the side of the house. The driver didn't move. He could feel sweat collecting under his arms. Up on the hill to the east, he saw a handful of sheep looking down at him. A sudden breeze rattled the dandelions and he felt a coldness working its way inside his suit. Then he heard a moan.

'Lampe?' he said, almost to himself.

He stepped down into the yard where the weeds reached up to his black leather belt.

'Mr Lampe?'

He waded through the weeds. Spore clung to his trousers and unseen nettles bit his socks and cuffs. The weed stalks hissed with his movement.

A flash of colour. Red. Ten metres away. He walked faster, towards the flecks.

He saw the old man, lying on his side, a spotted hand clutching at weed stalks and grass. Lampe's eyes were open and milky at the rims. His white hair was dishevelled and sprinkled with seeds. One of his braces had slipped from his shoulder. His red checked shirt, buttoned at the neck, pulled tightly at his throat. A dark line of beetroot juice stained a deep wrinkle that ran down the left side of the old man's mouth.

'Christ.' The driver dropped his briefcase and knelt down beside Wilfred Lampe. He put a hand on Lampe's arm and brushed the hair off his forehead. Then, without understanding why, he nursed the old man's head.

'Get a fucking ambulance!' the driver shouted into the valley.

When the helicopter lifted from the earth, hovered above his property and then moved out across the Monaro, Wilfred Lampe knew two things: that he was dead, finally, and that he had at last solved the greatest riddle of his life.

That death and the solving of the riddle should coincide came as no surprise. They were a single occurrence. It was as it should be.

He was, at last, inside the mind of his beloved trout. A place he had tried to enter for almost a century. With this, the rising from the earth, he was seeing with their eyes.

Lampe registered patches of blue sky and felt a strong vibration running through his body, but he could hear nothing. He felt very cold. He was rising. Seeing, as he knew trout did, through the surface of the water to the outside world. And seeing, simultaneously, the river stones, the reeds, the submerged logs, even a clear picture of himself, reflected back off the underside mirror of the river.

Shadowy figures hovered over him, blocking and unblocking the sky, and he knew immediately these were little puffs of cloud crossing the sun, or pieces of timber rushing down the river with the snow melt, or maybe the odd specimen of human detritus that occasionally found its way into the Snowy. He had, as a boy, seen a steamer trunk sail under the Dalgety Bridge.

He watched himself interrupting his lunch of corned beef and beetroot. Remembering an old washing machine motor out by the back fence, he had risen with the aid of his cane and set out to find it. Might yield a part or two, he thought, to fix that dodgy generator. He caught a toe in some undergrowth, and had gone down into the weeds.

I feel no pain, he thought, looking up into the luminescent cathedral of arced stalks. They always said the Lampes were made of wire, didn't they? But he was so tired, as wire, too, gets tired, and as he lay there in the grass, he thought of his tea getting cold on the table. The sweet hot tea cooling inside the teapot, and then the metal of the pot cooling down, and the fire in the grate sputtering to nothing, then the coals fading, and the big black kettle cold as the granite in the fields at night.

Wilfred Lampe could see all this as his body vibrated and he rose higher.

He was happy to be dead, having solved the riddle.

For years he had gone to bed each night not knowing if he would wake up. He was comfortable with that. In the room he had been born in, with his mother looking over him.

How they had pushed him to go into the nursing home at Berridale. Wilfred Lampe had not been to Berridale since his grandfather had died and they had gone to bury him, and sell the orchard, and remove the remnants of his giant hives of Cyprus bees. They told him he had a friend in the nursing home in Berridale. Cecil Sweetwater. Do you remember Cecil? You were quite a duo. But he didn't remember Cecil Sweetwater. Only lying on his back in the orchard when he was a boy, his belly filled with raspberries and plums, looking up into the ripe trees, the fruit like carnival globes.

I'll die at home, he told them. I don't want to drop off the perch sitting in an armchair with Cecil Sweetwater in my ear. Who's Cecil Sweetwater?

They came out to the valley to check on him. In 1983 the area constable restricted his licence to a twenty-kilometre radius from Dalgety. They reduced it to ten kilometres in 1993. That just got him from his front gate into town, to the general store or the Buckley's Crossing Hotel, or Our Lady Star of the Sea church on the hill. They had joked with him that if Haskell's store was a bit further up the main street, Wilfred Lampe would starve to death. He hadn't turned over the motor of the Humber Vogue in a year.

He caught glimpses of the sky and could see everything reflected back to him. He saw Dorothea's face. You said you'd come back. He had asked her this, in his head, forever. And I waited, didn't I? Now I can see you clearly, just when it's all over.

The rising. Wilfred Lampe was rising to the surface.

The old man's body vibrated as the helicopter peeled away from the property and threw wave after wave of warm air at the earth, sending grasshoppers into violent and unfamiliar patterns of flight, throwing phantoms through the sheep flocks, shaking the house, the china ballerina trembling in its cabinet, rusted nails aching in the roof, the smoke from the dying fire a mad dance. The pepper tree was lashing itself, cutting itself up, and the smell of pepper infused the air. The whole valley beat like a heart.

Across the ridge Tom and Peter Crank were the first to hear and then see the helicopter sink down towards the Lampe shack and scream back into the sky. They had no immediate thoughts on it, because they could not comprehend it. They stood as silent and dumb-faced as their sheep.

Larry Brindlemere and his fence workers were sitting on bales of wire, finishing their beers – it was the last Friday of the month, and early knock-off time – when they heard the thud of the rotors. They stared in the direction of the sound, unmoving.

Mrs Peat heard it also, taking a tray of scones from her Kooka. She was pleased with the golden hue of the scone tops, and could already see them neatly arranged in their wicker basket during the interval at the performance of *Sleeping Beauty*. She placed the hot tray on a bench and cocked an ear. She didn't remove her hen-faced mittens.

Jim Mitchell was halfway through fitting a new keg

when he heard the helicopter. He stepped out onto the verandah of the hotel, leaned on the railing and checked the sky. He saw nothing but clouds as thin and ordered as fish bones.

Down on the river, a few kilometres from Dalgety Bridge, Ed Hourigan had just found a nice spot where the Snowy fluted into a narrow pool. He had fished the river all his life, had never seen it so anguished. It was harder to find the pools. The whole river was being squeezed out, to the sea. He knew on this day he would catch nothing. He hadn't landed a decent trout in several years. But he loved working the rod and line, he loved the rhythm of it, now that he was alone and getting old and the children had moved away.

Hourigan checked the flies he had made at the kitchen table that morning and had just begun casting, his shoulders and arms and wrists aching, not yet used to the action, when he heard the helicopter and, looking over his right shoulder, saw it lift into the air above what must have been the old Lampe place.

He stopped casting, let the fly drift on the water's surface, and watched as the helicopter banked and headed towards the south of the town and right over him, over the sole fisherman beside the pool. The shadow of the helicopter darted over the silt and pebble and pool and then it was gone.

The old man woke up in a white bed with white sheets tucked up across his chest in a small white room. It was night and the room was dark. There was one window on the right wall.

He knew he was dead. That this was death, this feeling of being half asleep, and half awake. He could smell citrus.

A pale, milky light reflected through the window and onto the white wall in front of him. Sometimes, long ripples of sharper light moved down off the ceiling and across the wall. Wilfred Lampe recognised them. They were ribbons of sunlight through the water of the river. He was in the cool waters of the river, and he could see everything and everyone reflected back on the silver plate of the surface.

He closed his eyes.

TWO

WILFRED LAMPE, DEEP inside the trout suit, shut his eyes tightly as he had been told to do when he forgot something and needed to dredge it from memory. He had been inched forward onstage by the little pulsating amoeba of the cast, and there the limelight had bleached his memory.

He shut his eyes so tight he could feel the globes of his eyeballs, and he tumbled back through the events of the past few weeks, his mind snagging on the wire and kindling of the trout suit, and the labour of its making. He started there, with his mother by the fire in their house on the plain, and he wasn't sure, blind and immobile onstage in front of the entire township, if it was this recollection of the fire that made him run with sweat.

He could see himself sitting in the house, watching his mother make the suit. On a stool beside her chair was a white china plate, and on the plate a brown trout, caught by his father just that morning at the deep hole up from the Dalgety Bridge.

As his mother cut and stitched, glancing at the dead trout as she worked, Wilfred marvelled at how her hands costumed the shape of the fish from the small bolt of hessian she'd brought back from the general store. The scratchy sacking slipped and slid across her knees, as dun-coloured as the paddocks that stretched out from the woodslab house, all squat and temporary and riddled with gaps and cracks which whistled when the wind came down from the mountains. And here was his mother, taking instruction from the rotting fish, its stiff body arced head to tail in the warmth of the fire. Wilfred Lampe tried to avoid its shrivelled eye.

It was six days before the suit had enough shape to be tried on. He slipped into it there in front of the hearth, and scraped his arms on its scaffolding of wire and pine. Eventually, he could see, through its incomplete mouth, his mother's creased brow, her own mouth spiked with bead-headed pins. Amber firelight teased at the gills.

'Is he almost finished, Mama?' He had lost count of how many times he had asked.

'Patience,' she said through the pins.

At dusk, when his father came in from the property, the boy, standing silently inside the hessian during the attachment of the scales, heard him washing up on the verandah, the sway and slop of the water in the tin bowl, the rasping of his father's large calloused hands beneath the water. It was all as familiar as the clock chime.

The ritual, too, at this time of year, was accompanied by the thud of the fat bogongs against the flyscreen door, the moths trying to get in to the light, urgent for the fire and the kerosene lanterns, for the source of death and delirium – the sooted wicks themselves. Then the boy waited for his father's clean sigh, the thud of his

44

boots, and the tongue-clicking that signalled his official homecoming. Wilfred heard the flyscreen door squeak open and close, the clicking, and the whirr of a moth brushing the hessian near his right ear.

Everything in the world was right, then, and in its place.

When he put on the suit the sniggerings of his little sister Astrid scratched around him like mice. Everything that Wilfred thought he knew – the voices of his family, the sounding of the old clock, the wooden mantelpiece decorated with carved chickens, the spit of the fire, the cooling of the boulders out in the paddock – became, for a moment, fresh and strange, and the boy trembled inside the body of the trout. It was like those times when, as his mother told him, someone walked over your grave.

'He's a good fifty pounds, wouldn't you say, Mother?' his father said.

'He's good enough to eat,' said Astrid, repeating her new nightly mantra. 'Ma, will we get out the pan?'

'What a beaut idea, and I'm starved,' he heard his father say. 'Mother, where is it? I'll grease it up.'

Astrid issued a gentle stream of giggling.

That summer Wilfred slept on a cot on the verandah. After prayers, he recited his lines from *The Trout Opera*, and regularly lifted his head from the pillow to check the suit was still there, standing in the corner by the wash bowl, and beyond it the ragged flywire decorated, here and there, with the husk carcasses of wasps or flies, or the dismembered wing of a bogong floating with the stars. He had once been afraid to sleep alone on the verandah, but with the dark shape of the trout nearby, he felt comforted.

On a clear night he could hear the Snowy River from the cot and he thought of the families of trout sleeping in their hollows, and of his trout, the guardian trout, forever awake and vigilant, a sentry looking over not just Wilfred Lampe under the embroidered coverlet on the cot, but all the trout of the Snowy, millions of them nestled down in the great river that wound its way past the hulls of grazing cattle near the Dalgety cricket oval and the huddled boulders that diamond-winked in the sun and the Chinaman's cabbage and rhubarb patches that ran in neat lines to the river's edge out of town and even further down, through the rolls of wild blackberry trees and gangly willows and into the gorges of the mountains near the border with Victoria.

Some nights, when the river was so loud it shook the trees of their cicadas and herded sheep to the far corners of paddocks and loosened a chime from the old clock on the mantelpiece, he tried to imagine the source of it, high in the mountains above Jindabyne, where he had never been.

He saw himself tiptoeing across pillows of sponge moss and into a chilly rivulet, dressed in the trout suit, then taking to the cold water and floating swiftly at first beneath a canopy of snow gums, shooting over lichened rock like a sliver of soap, dropping down from one eddying pool to another until he approached the town. There he would pass scores of fishermen on the banks of the river, and they would wave to him inside the giant trout boat, and Wilfred Lampe would continue on beneath the criss-cross of their silken and catgut lines and slip under the steel-rivet bridge and through the canyons of granite and finally be coughed into the sea. Then he would sail the currents of the great oceans.

Wilfred Lampe, aged six, was beginning to see the shapes of the world. Ancient church spires and clock towers woolly with ivy; pyramids and lions rising from the desert; ocean liners. And the scarlet plumes of light-horse brigades and Chinese junks fat and spiky and volcanoes shooting stars of lava. Distorted and jumbled and soft-edged as these images were, taken from picture book to memory, he prickled pleasurably with the coming together of it all.

There was his own immediate universe. Frost on grass. River roar. Cattle honking and creaking. The currents of sheep, like little metal filings under magnet, shifting across the bare hills. Tick of clock. Boot weight. The feather snore of his sister. These ran through him day and night, like the river. Not to mention all the things in the habitat of a boy: favourite tree; deepest waterhole; most secret of secret caves; collection of pink granite stones like jewels in hand under water; toe stubs; bumps and dips of the dirt road into town; the person-alities of marbles. These were all contained within his freckled frame.

All this, and the round spectacles of his school teacher and principal Mr Schweigestill, whose lenses were so thick his eyes appeared huge, like those of some foreign fish dragged onto the bank and heaving for life.

Mr Schweigestill was tall and stooped and dis-appeared when he turned sideways (or so said Wilfred's father). His clothes billowed around him like the coat

47

and trousers of the scarecrow down in the vegetable patch by the river. The skin on his face and hands was stretched white, thin as paper, almost translucent, his fingers spidery, the machinery of the bones so close, the knots of cartilage and veins so horribly near the surface that the children pulled away from them, leaned back as the fingers skittered towards blackboards and chalks or crept across the backs of chairs. He had no lips and, as far as they could tell, no teeth. His mouth was a quick gutting with a fish knife. On top of his narrow, elongated head was a small thatch of oily black hair divided down the centre by a part so exact and brilliant white it hurt to look at it.

Yet everything about Mr Schweigestill was loud. The thud and tremor of his hobnailed boots in the tiny schoolhouse. The tapping of his pointer. Books snapped shut. His voice of greater volume and timbre than fat Mr Eales, the last schoolmaster, whom they'd buried not long ago in Paupong. Mr Eales had simply died, dressed in his hat and suit, at the annual fair on the edge of the oval in town, sitting with his back against the base of a tree, amidst spread blankets and wicker baskets and shattered eggshells from the spoon races. Everyone thought he was sleeping, and there he stayed, his hat tilted over his face in the shade of the gum, for the rest of the afternoon. Wilfred Lampe, dripping after several leaps into the river from the new bridge, had passed the resting Mr Eales and bid him good day.

They had all liked Mr Eales. Meat and potato, they said.

Even before the funeral – a matter of course to Wilfred, really, for his days were punctuated with death:

48

sheep ripped and torn by the razor-teeth of foxes, the bloated ships of drowned cattle, bloody explosions of feather and flesh in the hen house – had come Mr Schweigestill. A committee of parents and the local constable had greeted his coach on its arrival from Cooma and witnessed the suited stranger's awkward extraction from the cabin, like some black insect pulling out of a cocoon. His eyes – well – so large and watery behind the spectacles they travelled ahead of him, or so reported Mrs Corcoran.

'*Guten Tag*,' he had boomed, forgetting himself, this flat, animal utterance so at odds with the spring air thick with dandelion and the perfume of eucalyptus and wattle that it stamped him for all time as just a visitor to the Monaro.

In the first few weeks his every move was scrutinised. That he received, once a fortnight, strange sausages and pastries by post did not escape a single person in the region. That he read books in the corner of the Buckley's Crossing Hotel, sitting for hours, *hours*, on a single ale, somehow told the community all they needed to know about Mr Schweigestill. Oh yes, the funny gentleman of the books and the sausages. And the one beer.

In class, he held up an atlas and showed the children where he had come from and they crowded around him to get a closer look (careful of the spider hands) and there, at the tip of his long index finger, just above the perfect nail, was a small town in southern Germany, a dot of ink beside a river. It meant nothing to them, this little green paddock on a map. What was a fly speck compared to this, *their* paddock, warted with boulders and criss-crossed by fences that disappeared over hills which gave way, eventually, to the shoulders of the Snowy Mountains, the biggest mountains in the whole wide world?

It was Wilfred Lampe who knew, looking at the map, that the two of them would get along. They had both been brought up beside a great river.

THREE

AT 6.17 AM Aurora Beck was woken again by the dream, and had cocaine for breakfast.

Moments before, in sleep, she was back on the same limb of the pine tree, its bark gnarled and sharp, and through a cross-hatch of needles she saw a woman kneeling beside the hole in the ground, lowering a small blanket-wrapped bundle into the damp earth.

Then Aurora was in the grave itself, accepting the body from the hooded woman, gathering in the bundle of child wrapped in a blue woollen blanket patterned with white prancing horses, the horses fluffy at the edges, of frayed mane and hoof where the white fused with the blue. As Aurora took the child her hands and wrists were tickled by whiskers of straw and thin severed roots deep in the freshly dug grave, and pine needles came down from the sky and caught in her hair. Under the thin crescents of her fingernails were dirt and seed and spore.

From the grave Aurora could see herself perched on the branch, but as a girl, swinging her feet without fear as the giant arrow's tail of a pine swayed with the gait of aeons. She brought the bundle to her face and the world grew darker and the horses reared and threshed and Aurora smelled talcum powder and the overwhelming infusion of pine oil and it made her dizzy and scratched at the back of her throat. She unfolded the blanket, and the baby was so small now, a shell, a conch, resting in the open palm of her hand. That's when Aurora Beck stopped breathing, and woke gasping for air.

She lay motionless on her back in the ochre light of morning. In the bedroom crowded with packing cases. The walls were bare, except for two brass picture hooks. Through the window, frosted at the edges with her night breath, she heard a cold, single loop of birdcall.

In her half-sleep she went into the kitchenette and had two lines of cocaine straight off the knife-cut linoleum.

She lived alone in this one-bedroom apartment on the third floor of a building at the edge of Rushcutters Bay Park. She'd moved in six weeks earlier, and had only unpacked her clothing. She had met no one in the apartment building. Sometimes she heard muted laughter through the plaster and brick or the cry of a chair leg from upstairs. She had two new Lockwood deadlocks fitted on the inside of her front door. The conversation she had with the locksmith was the longest she had had with one person since she'd been in Sydney, except her dealer.

As she prepared the cocaine at the kitchen bench she looked down into the park and saw the giant trees quivering. Hundreds of bats dangled like black earrings in the canopies. The grass of the park was dusted white with dew. The dew was stitched with the tracks of running shoes and dog paws.

She had spent so many hours staring into the park she had begun to sense the patterns of life in its scalloped wedge of grass and path and figs and sandstone, heaving day and night, an entity. The early morning joggers and power walkers. The dog owners and the giant poodles, the whippet with nails painted with pink polish, the shivering silky terrier in its navy cardigan, the young women with babies and prams meeting for lattes in the park cafe mid-morning, their suited husbands over there in the CBD, beyond the great crowns of the figs, the sunbathing men in G-strings, the footballers and the cricketers, the dealers in the evening, lonely men waiting on the park benches late at night, and the sleeping bats rousing at dawn.

She watched the park sometimes for ten minutes, other times for hours, sitting on unpacked cardboard boxes with her back to the deadlocks. It held her like a view of the ocean, or an open fire.

That morning Aurora took the two lines of cocaine, one after the other, closed her eyes and tilted her head back. The shapes of molluscs spun across the deep red of her eyelids. It was exactly 6.35 am.

Unwillingly, she was thinking back to dark rooms in motels where the bed trembled at passing semitrailers and the bar refrigerator shuddered and rattled its water glasses and loose shelves, and things out of place came at her from the stucco ceiling. When a baby's whimper became the cry of a wolf. When the venetian blinds turned into the gills of a sea monster. The ashtray swarming with scarlet maggots. Her hand and fingers a dead tree. And, near the end, the baby's eyes were so dull they no longer held her reflection. It had been a memory, all of it, not so long ago, and now it was passing into dream.

She knew about things out of place. It was what she had known best for years, being with Wynter. She had lost the rules of normal life, just as you lost a language if you didn't use it.

She could sense a momentum she had within herself, something that moved her relentlessly, railed through her, swept her to places in life she could barely imagine from one day to the next. She wanted to stop it. Paddle against it. She always made it to the side shoals, to the warmer water at the edge, the tobacco-stained water and the submerged rocks, only to be pulled, suddenly, back to the central current. For the first time, Aurora Beck wanted to find the source of that river inside her.

Now, with the cocaine coursing through her blood, standing naked at the kitchen window, a chill travelled through her and she rubbed her arms vigorously, warming the fading bruises and the pale scars.

She looked back through the flat to the front door, to the two silver barrels of the deadlocks. She was now Aurora Beck. He would never find her, here, in the most densely populated postcode precinct in Australia. Not here, with its layers of human beings, its back lanes and hidden courtyards and fire escapes. She was Aurora Beck who worked only at night. Moved swiftly in and out of the rose haze of streetlights. Ate sparingly. Paid for everything in cash. Hardly slept. Changed the style of her make-up every time she ventured out. Altered the length and colour of her hair. Knew nobody, except the other girls she worked with, and her dealer. And the locksmith.

She went out onto her small balcony to look at the park. The bats were stirring in the trees, baring their teeth at each other, pushing and shoving with leathery wings. She closed her eyes, opened them, and the entire park tilted up to the left, and the curve of the bay shifted up to the right, and she gripped the rail with its bubbles of rust and the world was level again. She moved inside and drew a bath.

Naked in front of the mirror as the water roared into the lion-footed tub, she stared at the fine, high, pitted cheekbones framed by her raven-black bob. The small, narrow nose and her nostrils, pitched slightly upward, impossibly small apertures, yet the left slightly smaller than the right. Her eyes those of a cat, shaped as if permanently drifting into sleep. The right iris tethered, on this morning, to her tear duct by a bright red vein. The lips those of another face, of a larger head, the top swollen and bowed perfectly, the bottom a smooth neat palette for the work of the top lip. She opened them slightly, and through the gathering milky steam on the surface of the mirror still saw clearly the two top canines, a fraction longer than the line of her other teeth, pressing gently into her soft bottom lip, the impressions as delicate as the buttons on a silk cushion. The mirror fogged over.

She sat on the rim of the tub as it filled and could see in her mind a small wooden box with compartments, and in the compartments beautiful bright feathers and copper hooks and cotton. She could not recall what they were, these brilliant explosions in their tiny rooms in the wooden case. She rubbed her forehead, trying to draw them out in her mind, as the water crept up to the middle of her ankles.

Suddenly she was cold again, dropped into the green snow melt, and goose bumps rashed her body. She couldn't stop looking at them, these constellations on her flesh. She caught sight of her tattoo, the very ink of it lifted with the chill. It was supposed to be the symbol of an ancient Egyptian cat. That's what she was told. They took it from a book on ancient Egypt. But it had changed over the years, and kept changing. Now it had turned into – what? A hook. An old, hand-hewn fish hook. A large, growing, tempered metal hook.

Below the hook was the scar. Through and around the pink keloids from the digging of the penknife, she could still read it, his name, Wynter.

The roar of the bathwater filled the small room. Shook it. She put both hands to her ears and rocked on the enamel lip of the bath.

Aurora Beck turned off the taps and eased into the water. The door to the bathroom was open. She could see the two barrels of the deadlocks. She closed her eyes and the child of the dream came back to her. Was in front of her. Its eyes lifeless. Its legs and arms useless. She was holding it around its tiny ribcage. She was moving the baby up and down, its legs dangling, its head lolling. She was trying to make it dance. Aurora Beck was trying to make the baby dance.

She slipped into the water. The warmth ate her, swallowed her alive. And she slid down beneath the surface. Gone.

FOUR

ONSTAGE AND FACING the entire town at the premiere of *The Trout Opera*, with a rivulet of sweat meandering towards his buttocks cleft, Wilfred ached for the cool waters of the Snowy. He was convinced that if they dipped him in the river there and then he would hiss and issue steam.

As the willows and bulrushes that surrounded him started to warble and hum, their breaths smelling variously of fruit and lamb leg and quite possibly, in one instance, aniseed, Wilfred caught the silhouette of Mr Schweigestill in the stage wing, and was returned to that fateful Saturday, not so long ago.

Wilfred had headed cross-country to his secret trout hole early that day, and clearly remembered tapping his satchel and smiling at the thought of the fly box. His father had prepared it the night before at the kitchen table, having returned mid-evening from the Buckley's Crossing Hotel after a few 'quiet jars, Mother', and set out the hand-tied flies for the boy. It was a ritual. A way his father could be there in the morning with Wilfred, by the river, without being there. And it was the gamble of the flies. An operational strategy, taking into account time of day, cloud, wind, water flow, shadow. They huddled together, a war cabinet.

'Chin's Choice,' his father said, presenting a hook that looked like it had been swallowed by a wasp. Although the wasp was made of chicken feather and possum fur. It trailed three thin black whiskers. 'Doctor Alfred. Bonza Bluey. Constable Wetherill. Corcoran's Corker.'

He placed each fly side by side in a line. The boy put a hand to his mouth to muffle his laughter. Astrid, watching quietly, rolled her eyes.

'Miss White,' his father continued.

'Whoo hoo,' said the boy.

'Whoo hoo,' his father said, raising his eyebrows. Miss White was a sleek, compact fly of white rabbit fur.

'That's enough,' Wilfred's mother said from behind her old copy of the *Town and Country*.

'Whoo hoo,' the father mouthed silently to the boy.

Finally, he held up to the light a squat brown fly, slowly turning it around between thumb and forefinger, as if examining the facets of a jewel. 'The Sour Kraut,' he whispered. And Wilfred spluttered into his hand.

Each fly his father tied he had named after someone from Dalgety or the surrounding properties of the Monaro. It was their secret. Something that never left the house. And as he placed his choice for a day's fishing in Wilfred's little fly box, bedding each fly in its own compartment, he gave the boy a rundown of their characteristics.

'Now Chin's Choice,' he said. 'A deceptive little morsel. Promises more than it delivers. Dry to taste. Once you're hooked . . .'

'Will charge you to the blazes,' the boy said.

'Will charge you to the blazes, correct,' said his father, silently dispatching the Chin.

'Wilfred, I'll not hear that word from you again,' his mother said, not looking up from the magazine. 'Or you know what to expect.'

The father looked at the boy, winked, and asked: 'Which word might that be, Mother?'

'You know.' The magazine shadowed her face.

'Miss White,' he continued quietly. 'Sleek. Compact. As you can see. Everything in the right place, Miss White. Very, very—'

'Bill. That's enough.'

'The boy must know the rudiments, dear. The finer points . . .'

She glanced at, then lingered over, the picture of father and son, both suppressing delight, carrying cowlicks, stamped with identical half-grins, two figures drawn by the same hand in the lamplight, and held her tongue.

William carefully put Miss White to rest in the wooden box. He coughed, and said loudly: 'There you are, lad, a couple of Constables and a Corcoran's Corker should do the trick.' He closed the lid of the fly box, and winked again.

Wilfred tapped the satchel the next morning and remained amused that he had people from the town inside his fly box, even though he could never share the family secret. He would stand behind Mrs Corcoran in the general store, dwarfed by the buttress of her backside, and make a mental note to his father about the width of the corker. He became transfixed by the long, wriggly whiskers that grew out of an island mole on

Chin the vegetable gardener's left cheek. He'd giggle and have to run away.

On this Saturday, however, as he headed for the waterhole, his head full of flies, he emerged from his tunnel in the lantana and blackberry bushes two miles south of the Dalgety Bridge and caught a trace of movement through the foliage. He stopped and gripped the satchel.

He was not unused to finding strangers on the river. They were becoming more frequent, these gentlemen in their tweeds and newfangled waders and pipe tobacco which he could smell way before he saw the smouldering source. They drank liquor from silver flasks.

But here. One of them had stumbled across his secret trout hole, and was standing in the nest he had fashioned amongst the heavy-headed bulrushes where the river swept, suddenly, to the north, and created a small but deep little crescent bay, full of detritus from higher in the mountains.

Wilfred crept closer and could see, up the bank, an open canvas carry bag on the grass and, around it, a neatly placed pair of shoes, a book, a cheap fly tin, a folded coat and a small bottle of Haig whisky.

Clearing the lantana and blackberry, and at the base of the bulrushes, he recognised Mr Schweigestill. He crouched and watched as the teacher repeatedly snagged his line on the hidden logs in the trout hole. His teacher had a stiff, mechanical cast, and raised his thin body onto the balls of his feet each time the fly hit the surface of the water. Reeling in, he would emit a staccato whistling until the job was done. He wore strange leather britches and braces.

Wilfred observed the man for several minutes. The tall German's face displayed a multitude of comic configurations during the act of fishing, but always returned to a doughy desperation. The boy did not laugh at the funny faces. It was something that belonged only to fishing.

The following Monday, Wilfred Lampe presented his teacher with a tobacco tin of flies — several Bonza Beauties and two Sour Krauts — made by his father. Mr Schweigestill carefully examined each one, sitting at his desk after class, turning them over with an almost reverential care. He brought them flush to his spectacles with his spidery fingers.

'Ohhh,' he said, studying the flies.

'That's a Bonza,' said Wilfred. 'And that there's a Sour Kr . . . umm . . . Sou'wester.'

'A sour . . . ?'

'Keep 'em,' said Wilfred Lampe. 'I got plenty.'

After the gift of the flies, Mr Schweigestill started attending evenings of card games at the Buckley's Crossing Hotel. He abandoned his dark woollen suits for light tweed and was observed strolling, with difficulty, in a new pair of boots with elasticised sides. Virtually overnight he appeared in public chewing on pieces of straw, yarning outside the blacksmith's after school and overstaying his welcome at the post office. Local graziers were frequently startled by him striding out of nowhere across their paddocks, seeking out anyone for a chat on local affairs.

He had started wearing a huge tan bushie's hat, its shade as big as a cartwheel, on the dirt streets of Dalgety. The sausages and pastries stopped coming in the mail.

Mr Schweigestill began landing trout with Wilfred Lampe's flies. So many, in fact, that on his domestic errands he regularly distributed them, wrapped in sheets of old copies of the *Bulletin* and the *Town and Country*, as gifts to the people of the town. (Wilfred was one of the first recipients, and the whole family had studied the phenomenon of a partial stanza of Banjo's 'It's Grand' left printed in reverse on the skin of a brown trout.)

Schweigestill left them on the bar at the hotel without a word, beside the glass display cabinets in the general store, anonymously on verandahs and back steps, and in the garden of Miss Amelia White, the only single woman aged under thirty in Dalgety. She had been the recipient of gifts from suitors all over the district. Flowers. Lace doilies. Even a young bull, tethered to her front gate. But never trout, lovingly smoked and placed gently in her window box of dahlias.

The teacher would stand at the head of the bridge and tip his hat to the horsemen who brought their animals through town – for years one of the only Snowy River crossings. The stock crossing had been an amusement, once, to boys like Wilfred. The great streams of sheep and cattle flowed in from Cooma, took a left through Dalgety's main street and caught their own reflections in the shop windows. The earth tingled with hoof beat as they turned sharp right at the Imperial Hall, and onto the long bridge across the Snowy, not a hundred yards away, and shivered at the glittering of the river through the slats in the bridge, then onto secure earth on the other side, away to the mountains and over them to the western slopes, or down into the meadows of Victoria.

It soon lost its excitement for Wilfred Lampe, but to Mr Schweigestill it was an essential part of opening himself to the country now that the vial of him, of his Europeanness, had split open.

'The bloke's cracked,' Wilfred's father said. 'Dippin' his lid to cows and sheep.'

But the boy knew that the gift of the flies had somehow snagged something deep within Mr Schweigestill, and brought it to the surface. He knew, too, that his teacher had come to the other side of the world for reasons beyond curiosity. He could see it when he watched Mr Schweigestill fish at his secret trout hole. The German was still a young man, and though ancient to Wilfred, the boy caught glimpses of *him* as a boy, too, by the edge of the river. There were moments when Wilfred could almost hear Schweigestill the fisherman think, and alter his bearing, and become his age, and put into action casting and reeling that had been taught to him, perhaps by his own father. Then Wilfred could see for an instant a much older Mr Schweigestill, twice the age he was, standing in his peculiar trousers and boots. At that moment, the German's face would glow: when everything he knew synchronised, and he wasn't working at his fishing but just fishing effortlessly, and he was in another place. When he was just Mr Günter Schweigestill, his own man, a pioneer and explorer, forging his own way at the bottom of the world.

When the boy witnessed these moments, he thought that the thick ribbon of the Snowy now stretched all the way to Mr Schweigestill's river back home in Germany, that the two rivers had joined, and that the trout the teacher remembered from his old life had connected with the trout here, and swam with each other, and passed on stories, and that the Snowy trout, although they didn't know it yet, were turning themselves into new silvery memories for Mr Schweigestill.

It was only later that Wilfred Lampe wondered if the tobacco tin of flies hadn't given birth to *The Trout Opera*.

In that spring of 1906 – seven weeks before the holidays – Mr Schweigestill announced to the class that the annual Christmas pageant, an institution in Dalgety as fixed as the birthday of Christ, would this year be something 'a little special' for everyone. Something educational and profound, that would 'echo into the century' and into the lives of the children and even *their* children.

Wilfred thought of the story of baby Jesus and couldn't imagine what sort of spectacular Mr Schweigestill could create that was bigger.

He raised his hand to remind the teacher of the manger and donkey suit stored in the back room of the Imperial Hall, but Mr Schweigestill was oblivious of his pupils, and the shadows of chair legs and swinging feet across the floor of the classroom, and the crack of a whip and muffled dog barks down by the Snowy.

It will, he said, be an opera.

Wilfred noticed, through the schoolhouse window, that the low hills of the valley had lost their wintry blue stubble, and the poplars, wiggling at their apex, seemed fluffed and overweight and relieved now that the dawn frosts had gone for another year. He saw little maggot sheep on the rump of hillocks across the river, and the rare tick of cattle.

An opera, children. A pageant that will take in all of life.

The teacher had extended his arms, so thin and winter twig-like he nearly touched the side walls of the schoolroom. His face beamed and the beaming produced fine wrinkles from the corners of his eyes. And two deep grooves, like parentheses, on the sides of his mouth. His eyes, of course, were horribly magnified through his thick spectacles. And Wilfred saw, for the first time, way back in the mouth as if in a cave, teeth that were moist and shaped like almond crumbs. His gums were the deep red of flyblown meat, and the children who cared to look puckered their own mouths in revulsion.

A story, he said, of how trout were brought to this wonderful country of Australia. These magnificent creatures, he said, and their journey to a strange land.

'Like you, sir,' interjected Tom Hackett. 'Comin' over here from a strange land.'

'Correct, Herr Hackett.'

'Maybe youse is a magnificent creature too, sir.'

'Maybe I *am* a magnificent creature, Herr Hackett.'

'That's what I said, sir.'

'Herr Hackett, may I continue?'

'Sorry, sir.'

Our opera will be the story of the brave Mr J. A. Youl, and the gentlemen of the Australia Association, and the journey of the trout ova in their breeding boxes on board the clipper ship *Norfolk*. And after eighty-four days the ship arrives in Melbourne, and the little ova are taken to Tasmania for hatching.

'Me new sister's name's Eva,' said John Corcoran without raising his hand for permission to speak.

'Ova, Herr Corcoran. *Ova*.'

And then the trout are released into the river and streams of the country, and especially here, at Dalgety, not far from where the politicians bathed together naked when they were considering making the town the capital of Australia.

Wilfred had heard his mother and father talk about this, and the men in the Buckley's, and the ladies in the general store. It was capital this and capital that. His father said the 'capital' talk was 'bunkum', and Wilfred had even souvenired a survey peg the 'capital' people had left behind.

The children were bored. Mr Schweigestill, so caught up in the excitement of his opera, lowered his arms and stared at the class. His arms tingled with an exertion he could not recall having made.

Of course the real heart of the story, said the teacher, will be the King and Queen Trout of the Monaro.

Wilfred turned his attention away from the neighbouring hills, and listened.

This is their story too, boys and girls. Together they travel from England to Australia in their little wooden boxes. They are not even born then, Schweigestill continued. They are hatched, together, when they arrive. And they are the first trout ever to be seen on the Monaro. And they will rule the Snowy River for years. For this is their new kingdom, and they oversee all the families of trout for miles around, and for many decades to come.

'So, so, so . . .' said little Patrick Corcoran, '. . . when do the animals come round and stare at the baby Jesus in the manger—'

'Please, sshh.'

'—and, and look into the manger and the star comes down over the manger and—'

'There is no manger, Herr Corcoran. Please pay attention.' He brought down his blackboard pointer on the edge of his desk.

Wilfred Lampe raised his hand.

'*Yes*, Wilfred.'

'The breeding boxes of your opera story, sir. The breeding boxes could be the mangers, and the trout could be the little Jesuses.'

Mr Schweigestill stood motionless, the pointer half raised, and stared at Lampe without blinking.

'*Jaaaaaa*,' he said softly. 'The breeding boxes are the mangers. *Jaaaaa. Gut*, Wilfred. *Sehr gut.*'

That evening over dinner the boy Lampe tried to explain *The Trout Opera* to his parents. They sat together around the old dining table, made out of mountain ash by Uncle Berty. They very rarely discussed Uncle Berty, even though he lived alone half a mile away, across the hills at the end of the valley. Some nights Wilfred was kept awake by the steady ring of an axe through the dark. It was Uncle Berty, striking out ferociously in the pitch-black, taking to the snow gums during an 'unhappy moment', bringing down tree after tree into the early hours of the morning. He never came to the house. Uncle Berty was just there, somewhere, always, like a hint of movement in the corner of your eye.

'I don't get it,' said his father, sucking on a rabbit leg. 'The bloke's cracked.'

'What about when the animals look into the manger?' said Astrid. 'What about the baby in the manger?'

Wilfred shook his head. 'There isn't no real manger.'

'I'll tell you one thing,' his father said, scrutinising the small bone knots. 'There's no baby in a manger come concert time and they'll fair dinkum throw him in the river.'

The boy felt sorry for Mr Schweigestill and wanted to warn him about the dangers of staging the opera. It would be the end for Mr Schweigestill, his fishing by the river on Saturdays, his wooing of Miss White, his card evenings in the hotel.

But Wilfred was caught up in events, in the great creation of the opera, and at first rehearsals was told that he would have one of the starring roles in the production. He would be King Trout of the Monaro alongside Maggie Corcoran, his Queen Lure. He. Wilfred. Herr Lampe. He. Beside Maggie Corcoran, daughter of the district's second-largest property owner, and the only child in the area to be delivered to school and retrieved by sulky. She, who lived in a homestead so big you could see it from Our Lady Star of the Sea church, on the hill.

He noticed, within days, that Maggie had taken the regal manners of Queen Lure beyond the perimeters of the classroom. She got in and out of the sulky with a previously unseen delicacy and confidence, and had taken to waving dismissively at passers-by.

As for Wilfred, he felt awkward and embarrassed rehearsing the imperious gestures of King Trout. He was a boy with manure beneath his nails. A boy of nettle wounds and fence-post splinters and dust on the rims of his ears. He peed behind trees and broke wind. His music was the exhalations of dawn cows and crows on a fence and the snoring of his father and the thud of bumble-footed sheep. It was the crackle of pan-fried fish. The tearing of melted ice. This was the boy's opera.

It would all change later, once he was inside the trout suit. Yet on those many afternoons, when it was so hot in the Imperial Hall that children fainted, and Mr Schweigestill became so pale you could almost see the shift of his wiry muscles and foreign organs beneath that tissue skin, and the only music you could hear was the drone of blowflies or the occasional overriding performance of a wasp, Wilfred Lampe saw only disaster, and the minutes became hours, and he could picture nothing of the grand opera, no grace or elegance or even the fairytale story itself. He could picture nothing but the waterhole down from the bridge which, the second rehearsals ended, he and several others raced for, tripping in their eagerness, rolling in dust and lucerne, discarding their clothes on the run as they approached the willows where they would dive into cool water, disappear into it, washing off all thoughts of violin and dance, harmony and waltz, losing the heat from their bodies, the friction of history, as they paddled deeper and deeper to the stones and sand on the floor of the Snowy River.

FIVE

HER HEART BEAT like the pounding on a door and she surfaced from the bathwater and it swayed and slapped over the lip of the bath and, gasping, she looked to the twin deadlocks through her wet fringe.

Aurora's skin was pale in the greenish water and she examined the scars of her life that the paleness and the lens of the water drew out. There were scratches from barbed wire and neat Swiss Army knife cuts hatched and equidistant across her thighs and she noticed for the first time and without interest that the freckles flecked through the scar hatching could have been some crazy musical composition. Three ancient cigarette burns cratered her abdomen. A small knife puncture wound to her left breast had healed with a scar that resembled a failed third nipple. The needle wounds on her arms were gone, but through the water she saw a sepia shadowing where she had, once, mined her veins.

She had been on the run from him now for more than two months. Since the day she fled from the country town down in the Alps with his car and the money and the pretty little balloons of heroin she had been secreting from him. Had they been Alps? Was there snow? Or was it ash? She remembered something – ice or ash – falling from the sky, and blue along the edge of somebody's lips, a lake, the guttural voices of sheep, a graveyard, and the eyes and ears and mouths and hair of angels clotted with dirt. Then the flight on the highway, her head and the cabin of the car and the blackness outside filled with sliding discs of light, pinpointed the size of coins then plates then tunnels, expanding so fast and edged with rainbows – behind her in the rear-vision mirror, coming towards her out of the darkness, and over and in and out of the car, shaking it, and she fighting the wheel, her hands trembling even with her knuckles white.

As the breakfast cocaine faded in the stillness of the bathroom she could hear a bird calling the same note over and over, and she continued to stare at the deadlocks as the water dripped from her fringe. The bathwater cooled and she leaned forward and turned on the hot water faucet until she could feel the heat travelling towards her, then she turned it off. Drips echoed in the tiled room. She could hear the drips and the morning bird through a pounding in her ears.

She saw at the end of the bath the large black shampoo bottle. She had emptied it somewhere, in some hotel, a long time ago, rinsed and dried it, and neatly cut the bottom out an inch from the base to fit into it, nice and snug with wads of plastic shopping bags cut into strips, a similarly altered soft drink can, then slotted the bottom back on, painting a near-perfect red strip over the seam with nail polish. The money was in the can inside the shampoo bottle. Nobody would look for money in a girl's cheap, bulk-sized supermarket shampoo. She kept the drugs in the conditioner.

The money was getting low. She'd been good at managing money. It was like she kept ledger columns in her head. But Tick's drugs were expensive, and the drugs would be the last thing to go.

In the early part of the second month, and in an effort to ration the drugs, she lived for days on satchels of soup and two-minute noodles until they ran out. Later, too afraid to leave the apartment, she ate rice and vegemite mixed with boiling water.

Aurora kept the blinds drawn and grew listless and exhausted with the effort of keeping herself still and listening for signs of Wynter. It was tiring to listen. But her dealer's methamphetamines kept her awake, and she needed to be awake.

'It's the next big thing, darling,' Tick told her of crystal meth. 'A little birdie in New York put me onto it. They call it biker's coffee, isn't that cute? Or *redneck* cocaine, which has its own appealing ring. It's recommended by some gentlemen truck drivers I know.'

He was her only real human contact in the city underneath the everyday layer of perfunctory half-sentences to shopkeepers and neighbours in the building, and so their meetings, from the outset, had an unexpected warmth. Tick, older, cannier, and an expert in the nature of need, came to her from the outset as a sister, or a girlfriend, and folded her into titter and gossip and confidences, that little pilot light of friendship. So their exchanges quickly took the form of meetings for coffee and pastries, or a short wander through the Saturday markets by the fountain, and their roles of vendor and buyer were lost. They had become, as some people do, accidental siblings.

After years with Wynter, Aurora knew to be on guard with Tick. But when she found no ulterior motives, despite her vigilance, she slowly gave over to the friendship and began to rely on their intimacies. If it hadn't been for her new role – as prey to Wynter – she might have been very surprised by it all. Rules changed when you feared for your safety.

For a week, a man and a woman next door had been continuing a rolling argument that began very loudly and then went through days of tense silence, then slowly built and ruptured and went quiet again. In the peaceful stretches the banging of a saucepan on the stove top or the clang of cutlery thrown into the sink released staccatos of abuse which always ended neatly with the slamming of a door. An increase in volume of the stereo or the television always pushed either the man or the woman out of the flat. Sometimes she heard either the man or the woman sobbing through the old plaster walls.

Upstairs they held a party during her isolation at the start of the second month, and the deep tribal thud of dance music reverberated through her hollow apartment and skittering around the beat were the sounds of stiletto heels on the wooden floor and smashed glasses and, looking out the sliding doors to the bay, she could see all night the dull shooting stars of flicked cigarette butts.

Sometimes she heard the long wail of the container ships coming in and out of the harbour. It made her think how big the world was with its ocean traffic of ships full of cars and furniture and timber and coal and wool and sugar and shoes and handbags and washing machines and DVD players. When she thought this her head ached and she craved more of Tick's crystal meth. It made her feel bigger. Without it she was small and weak and the flat pressed in on her and she got headaches.

After several days locked in the flat, with the man and woman yelling at each other and the picture on her wall shifting millimetres out of alignment with every slam of their door, she found a plain envelope slipped beneath her front door. Inside was one of Tick's sachets of biker's coffee, and a pressed flower. She smoked the meth and opened the blinds and in the bathroom mirror could see that some blood had leached onto her tongue from the back of her throat and had turned her front teeth pale pink.

Aurora discovered the high of Tick's new drug seemed to last forever, that two smokes could take her through twenty-four hours, and she paced the small flat and talked to herself and relayed to the empty rooms what seemed to be the diary of her life. It was all there, on her tongue, and she heard the story as if someone else was reading it to her. In the end she didn't have to speak at all. Another voice simply took over.

The voice told her she had to get out, into the world, that this was fucking ridiculous and if he found her and killed her, then so fucking what, you had to die sometime. You've known him for nine years and you know what? You know what? Those nine years were no different from hiding here in this fucking shitbox of a flat. You never had any friends, a proper place to live, a bedroom with your own bed and a garden out the back and a dog and a cat. You never had anyone you could call for a coffee or someone to laugh and cry with or just to sit with, someone you could trust, someone normal, because that's the way he wanted it. That's the way he had to live. Now you're here with four million people in a box in the city and you may as well be out in the middle of the fucking outback, it's the same thing.

For years she'd been living inside Wynter's head. It was small and cramped and lonely and she'd been inside his head since the moment he found her at Central Railway Station. She still had the warmth of the train compartment inside her that night after the trip down from Murwillumbah, and her hair still carried the stale cigarette smoke from the cabin, and she'd barely alighted from the train when he had taken her hand and walked her straight into the dark room of his head. Later, it didn't matter if they were in Goondiwindi or Bourke or Adaminaby, it was always the same dark room.

She decided not to inhabit it anymore. And if he found her and killed her, at least she was free of that room. You don't have to live in that place anymore, the voice said.

Only after several days did she realise the voice she was hearing in her own head was a male voice. It was not Tick's or Wynter's or her father's, but a stranger's. It was like the voice on her bedside radio.

As the methamphetamines slowly wore off she'd see she was in different clothes, and that someone had moved her sparse furniture and boxes around, and that her bedhead was against a different wall.

She knew, too, she had to work. Was Tick's envelope

a gift, or a debt? He was still her dealer, at the heart of everything. It could unfold as it always did. He would deliver more meth, and her debt would deepen. He would arrange work for her, and lend her some money so she could get by in the meantime, and there'd be more drugs, and he would encase her in tabs, favours, loans, moments of apparent generosity and kindness, then pity, and then he would own her, and her thoughts of a normal life and a friend to have coffee with and a garden to tend would fade.

Then she smoked more crack and none of it mattered.

It was a Saturday, and she sat on her small balcony that overlooked the bay and beyond it the rarefied hilly spine of Darling Point with its millionaires and movie stars. Through its thin canopy of gums and palms and figs she could see the old terraces along the foot of the ridge and, higher up, the old red brick flats and Spanish-style villas and, breaking through the top of the canopy, the gangrenous spire of an ancient church.

She could hear its bells, the bells of a Saturday wedding, and she turned Tick's pressed flower around and around by its dry stem.

They continued to ring inside her for a long time, as perfect as the click of a metronome, and she was on her father's shoulders in Murwillumbah, holding on gently with her small hands, his hair tawny reins for little Aurora, riding through that peculiar white light of a Saturday morning when time stretched forever and everything was so clear and detailed it took an age to travel from the drapery to the Regent Cinema, from the river to the rotunda. Then, life to her was of the second

– one moment she was marvelling at the blood-red poppies splayed across a woman's dress, and the heads of pens in a man's shirt pocket, and the spots of discarded chewing gum down on the footpath, the next at the infinity of space on a movie poster, and the shaved patch and stitched cut on the crown of a passing boy's head, and the fuse-wire hairs that sprouted from her father's ears.

Aurora spun the dried flower and wondered what had happened to that girl.

She was only twenty-six years old and she believed she had lived an entire life. Wynter had removed the middle of it, cut it out of her, and hooked her childhood onto early middle age. She had spent an eternity in motel rooms and in cars and in the unending stupors they had experienced together where it was always dusk or dawn, where there was always new and old light, fresh yellow and old yellow, clear and blurred shadows, but never a moment without a trace of the night.

The metronome continued its clicking. Her poor, mad mother had one of polished red wood on the old piano. She never played the little cottage upright. Didn't know how to play it. Just had it there, dusted daily, as if she expected someone to come up the front stairs and into the house and sit down on the fringed stool and start making beautiful music.

Who was she waiting for? Who was it that never came to play the piano?

Not long before Aurora left home she would tiptoe into the house late at night and hear the metronome in the dark. Sometimes it was ticking in the morning. Near the end, she rarely saw the lead weight motionless.

Her mother sat and listened to it, and Aurora knew she was dying even then, had been dying most of her adult life, because that's the way it was with some families, with some family lines, dying while they were living. Her mother. Face creased with herringbone lines. Eyes alert, anticipating something. A bullet, fired a long way away, heading for her, just for her, this small casing of spinning brass that would eventually find its target.

Aurora's mother was old before she had a chance to be young, just like her daughter. Aurora only remembered it and pieced it together later. Aches, pains, fussing, pottering. There were always things to do, which were never done, because her mother was dying, and there was no point in doing anything.

She wasn't the type of mother who threatened confiscation, or brandished the wooden spoon. She just said: you'll be sorry when I'm gone. Or, I won't be here for much longer, so do as you wish. Or, I'll no longer be a nuisance to you in five years, and you'll have to cope on your own.

It took Aurora a long time to see that hers was a family tethered to death. It was in the cane setts in the late afternoon, crouching in the fields. It was embedded like dust in the lace curtains. It was in the retreat of the kettle whistle after the gas jets were turned off.

It dulled Aurora's father. Wore him down. The ticking entered him and he couldn't get it out. He set the cane fields ablaze and stood back and watched rats and snakes and mice and lizards flee, expunged from the cane, but nothing could cleanse the ticking from him.

It had to come from somewhere, Aurora thought. This waiting for death, while living. From somewhere

78

upriver. Things that float down to you. They have to come from somewhere.

Bury me, her mother always said. I don't want to be burned.

❦

Just before noon on the thirteenth day of her fasting Aurora finally left the apartment. She wore cheap mules and jeans and a peasant blouse and carried her suede shoulder bag with the suede fringes. She felt, negotiating the hill up Greenknowe Avenue, that she had somehow lost the ability to walk properly. The sloping footpaths seemed to tilt her off balance.

By the time she got to the T-junction with Macleay Street she felt an odd tension of fear inside her – not of being spotted by Wynter, but from being out and amongst other human beings. She clutched the strap of the suede bag and sweat from her hand stained the suede dark.

This is where Wynter had brought her several years before; straight out of the great womb of Central Station to Kings Cross. To a second-floor apartment that overlooked an alley and the blue and red and orange glow of a drycleaners and a tattoo parlour and a kebab shop. If she hung out the window as far as she could and looked over to her right she could see the illuminated aura of the city as huge and imposing as Mount Warning.

As she walked down Macleay Street she recognised nothing. The fish bowl cafes of modular stools and chrome. The 7-Elevens. The new apartment buildings with brass door handles and potted palms in the foyers. The boutique furniture stores displaying wicker chaises longues like distorted and oversized cannoli beans. Everything was shiny and ill-shaped and round-edged.

She continued towards the harbour, past the naval base, and crossed over to the long fence that guarded the military wharf and stretched all the way to Harry's Cafe de Wheels.

A third of the way along the fence she stopped in front of a memorial, open to the thundering traffic of the street, and so gritty and fouled by vehicle exhaust that it was almost impossible to read. It was a shrine to the men and women who had left to fight in the First World War. There was a little red flame. She read that this was the wharf from which they had sailed for Gallipoli and France. In the heat she heard the ticking of insects in the soiled shrubbery.

Aurora flanked the fence and passed the Finger Wharf then followed a group of people up the steps at the back of the Art Gallery. From the steps she looked over and saw two giant matches in a park. She had never seen these matches. One with its red head intact. The other singed and twisted. She thought of Wynter and the menace of his smile and the burn of his eyes and she became afraid again.

She hurried up the stairs, avoiding eye contact with anyone, and looked for somewhere to shelter, to get out of the open, and she quickly crossed the bridge over the Cahill Expressway and cut into the Botanical Gardens.

Before they had to flee Sydney, before they broke out for the west and breached the Blue Mountains and then ran north, tucking into towns and hamlets off the high-way, stealing bread from the open back doors of country bakeries, she had lived only fifteen minutes' walk from the gardens, up on the foul spine of Darlinghurst Road. Sometimes the view to the city had stopped her and held her, and she was back home, in Murwillumbah, smoking weed in the park on the Tweed River, the great looming mountain across the river catching threads of cloud at its peak just as Centrepoint caught the clouds. It frightened her to see the city. The sunlight coming through it at dusk. The thick columns of sunlight between the skyscrapers, the columns hitting the river of trees and shattering into millions of shards.

She had never been awake to see it in the morning when the streets and footpaths were black and fresh-washed by the street cleaners and the tyres of the delivery trucks hissed over the wet tarmac. The city out of sleep, warming up for the day, the warm steam exhaling from silver coffee machines, the warm-glassed streetlights flicking off and letting the sun take over. The big and little fountains all over the city clicking on and the sound of the rushing water in concert for a while with the wet black bitumen. The features of statues returning after a long dark night strafed by the blue of police lights and the red of tail-lights and the yellow of the council cleaning trucks. Fresh fish, swimming in their vast, beating universe just hours before, ferried on pallets of ice into window displays and restaurant cool rooms. The cleaners sprinkled throughout the office blocks out of breath amongst the acres of desks and computers and the thousands of tableaux of yesterday's abandoned work. The thousands of desk photographs unmoved, the little creamy thumbnail faces of men and women and children staring out into the empty offices.

Aurora Beck had never seen this. Wynter had ensured

her addiction kept her within the small grid of Darlinghurst Road and Victoria Street. She had drifted in this small, foul pond of his design.

Was Tick now gently reeling her in after all? At first using the finest grade line. Then thicker and unbreakable, later, when she was past caring. And the biker's coffee, which had hooked her firmly through the lip. She didn't feel a thing.

Aurora wandered down the bitumen paths of the gardens. The rich, unexpected rush of oxygen, of plant air, hit her and made her light-headed. It overwhelmed her and she suddenly felt cold in the changed atmosphere and became aware of an extreme hunger within her.

Stopping to sit on a bench, she felt at once light and heavy, and the sounds of the gardens became very loud. She felt she could identify the noise of leaves scratching against each other and the groan of trunks and the opening of buds and the hum of incessant bat chatter, their millions of throaty growls entering the cool air. She could hear teeth grinding up against the shells of her ears.

She staggered off the bench and tried to retrace her steps to the anchor of some familiar landmark but she took a wrong turn and entered deeper into the gardens.

She felt pure panic at having lost her bearings, at a bore having unexpectedly been sunk to the centre of her loneliness, and she emitted a rhythmic whimper as she strode drunkenly beneath the dark canopy of trees. She shook violently and was on the edge of breaking into a run when she saw, in the distance, what she thought was a bright red coat disappear to the left, and she followed the colour, knew instinctively the square of colour was not part of the gardens, and when she reached the junction of the path she looked to the left and saw the fernery.

She walked towards it and her heart slowed. She dried her eyes with a tissue. She entered and heard human voices somewhere behind the ancient interlocking fronds, and she smiled to herself and checked herself and gathered herself and became, again, just another person in the world beneath the green canopies. Amongst the prehistoric plants she felt warm and safe. Studying the plants she was filled with admiration for them, for the perfect order of the spores, and the little curled tails of the new shoots. Her tears then were not born of fear but of wonder. She thought once more of the child and of her nightmare. And she had the need, there, to talk to it. She hummed nursery rhymes to it, and whispered to it, and could see the white fluffy horses of its blanket lift off the blue cloth and prance amongst the brilliant green plants.

Aurora cried and laughed at the horses in this place where there was no dawn or dusk, where the baby shoots unfurled around her, and for the first time since she could remember she felt the cool air rush in and out of the tree of her lungs.

SIX

AT THE SQUEAK of the curtain pulley inside Dalgety's Imperial Hall, Mrs Eloise Corcoran, fidgeting with her new spectacles, fumbled them onto the bridge of her nose and found she could only see out of one eye.

The glasses had arrived two days prior, from Williams & Sons in Pitt Street, Sydney, the name imprinted in copper-coloured serif on the inside lid of the maroon case, and she had yet to 'find her way around them', as she put it. When the curtains parted, she was cleaning the right lens with a special cloth, smudging the left with her thumb. She did not want to miss a minute.

Her daughter, Maggie, was Our Lady of the Lures, the Queen of the production, a child destined for limelight, for *The Mikado* and *Madama Butterfly* and Juliet balconies finished in gold leaf. Not this impossible landscape of snow gum and thistle. Not this vista of sunburnt hillocks warted with granite, melancholy willow, ice that bit the skin.

So the spectacles were ear-hooked unevenly at the signal of the squeak, and for several minutes Mrs Corcoran saw nothing but a blurred and moving splash of blood through her left eye, and through the other the awkward tug of the old curtain which, at each foot of laboured travel, launched ghostly whorls of dust motes.

In the end it mattered little. It was so humid that early evening inside the hall, the wooden seats in tight and crooked rows, the centre and side aisles so choked with farmhands still wearing saddles of horse sweat, and lice-flecked siblings of the cast, and crazed uncles and grandfathers physically there but still at camp in Ladybird or Potfontein in their flushed heads, and even two old ladies in camphored bustles pulled from the cupboard of the last century, that Mrs Corcoran's glasses, both lenses, very quickly steamed over, despite the energies of a busy Foy's paper fan guttered with mother-of-pearl.

When the curtain finally parted, the audience – an amalgam of fidgety relatives, glass-eyed dignitaries, stockmen and herders still hypnotised by the straw-coloured horizons of their daily lives, and children feverish with the heat and the prospect of colour – saw that the stage was empty, except for a garnish of waver-ing blue cloth just above the wooden boards, an uneven rippling of lake surface or sea, its tremoring accom-panied by a rapid sawing of bass and violin from the minute orchestra down the side of the stage by the refreshment counter.

Mrs Corcoran hefted her considerable buttocks slightly off her seat, the left cheek higher than the right, her balance now skewed to one side courtesy of the smudged lens. The hefting revealed only to her a damp patch on her dress, and she discreetly lowered herself.

The cool blue cloth was one moment tempest, one moment mill pond. Then slowly, from the right, nosed the prow of a little ship. To a smattering of applause, it rocked onto the stage, revealing a black hull and three broom-handle masts. Beneath the waves the audience could see the ship propelled by three small sets of legs.

A ship? thought Mrs Corcoran. Maggie mentioned nothing of a ship.

The thin music – what else could it be but thin under the guidance of Mr Schweigestill? – looped about the hall, and the sawing, the friction of bow on string, increasing, building to the end of the overture, seemed to make the hall even hotter, and all the while the cackle of fans underscored it. Mrs Corcoran's fan was beginning to wilt, damaged at the hinge by a growing patch of sweat that had passed from her thumb on the handle to the paper.

The awkward ship dropped anchor in the centre of the stage and the music too dumped its intensity to the spotted boards, and a single note streamered off the walls and a child, Spud Baker, dressed as an urchin (not unlike his day-to-day demeanour) was pushed out amongst the waves. He put his hands on his hips, looked dramatically from left to right, and sang in a crackly voice: 'Set sail have we/to the South Seas/with this preshuss cargoo of ours/to the land of the freeeee.'

The boy could have been calling the cows in. A few snickers scuttled around the legs of the audience chairs. Spud hesitated and squinted into the crowd, looking for the anchor of parent or aunt. His bladder tingled.

'From London to Australeeyaa/bring we the eggs of the trout/where they will sprout/and one day swim in schools/thanks to Mister Youllll.'

At that the boy froze, and the waves ceased to move.

Not even Mr Schweigestill, striding onto the stage in what appeared to be an undertaker's suit and stove-flue top hat, could dislodge the boy from his fright, his fear a tick pinned to the boards. The principal nudged him with a spidery hand, smiling into the audience, then prodded, and Spud shuffled into the wings.

Mrs Corcoran took the time now to properly clean her glasses. There was no sign of her Queen, and she rubbed the spectacles with something approaching disgust.

Wilfred Lampe's father, meanwhile, back in the seventh row, developed an involuntary tic in the right corner of his mouth at the sight of the deathly Schweigestill. He was already lost by the production. He liked things simply explained, as farm work simply explained itself. His thoughts ran not to the appearance of Wilfred, King Trout of the Monaro, or whatever that elaborate suit deemed him, but to how and when they would fit the baby and the manger into this peculiar spectacle. Sight of the sea had ignited hope of an ark, and a potato-sacked Noah – anything he might remember from the Good Book. In an instant it was snuffed.

'I am Youllllll/James Arndell Youllllll,' the principal sang, so suddenly and gratingly that it frightened the children crouched at the front of the stage, his extended right hand reaching over them like a blackened tree branch. Mrs Corcoran winced and her powdered jowls contracted, as if at the taste of a wild lemon.

The orchestra, too, mistimed Schweigestill's operatic debut, and their notes tumbled before recovering and catching up with the high-pitched voice. They did not know the German well enough to notice the peculiar tonal disparity between his deep speaking timbre and the almost metallic galah-fright of his singing.

The ship in the background had grown restless and was beginning to list and drift. The stern appeared to be taking water.

'To this new country/we bring the trout/never seeeeen/in the rivers and streaaamms/a new race/in this special place/for generations to commme.'

Schweigestill held the final note so long its twig-like trembling became a hiss and finally a strangulated gurgle, reminiscent to the farmers in the audience of the moment you ran the blade across a sheep's throat.

Miss White, in row four, scrunched her nose as if she had smelled something distasteful. She was still perplexed by the handwritten invitation from the teacher to join him for tea the following evening, and she thought of the card in its envelope, still lodged between her sugar and flour canisters in the kitchen, and imagined those long porcelain fingers holding the pen over the expensive paper, those digits creeping ever closer, and an involuntary shudder travelled up her spine.

'These eggs/transpooorted on ice and charcoal,' he continued, 'destined for the creeks and waterholes/of this vast land/whence they will happily create/a coloneee/as God intended/for eterniteee.'

Bill Lampe harrumphed, and leaned forward at the mention of God. Now, he thought, must come the baby and the manger. The Virgin Mary and the hessian-wrapped Joseph and the ratty donkey. But no. The cumbersome ship sailed off, the waves vanished, and Schweigestill, his pipe-thin arms spread wide, slowly stepped backwards to the rear of the stage.

Suddenly a profusion of green poured from both sides of the stage, a quivering wilderness of reeds and bulrushes and willows, gums and wildflowers, all ghostly and bulb-lit, wrapped in the humid and feathery steam of their own humming.

This humming, whether by accident or design, fell in harmony with the distant gurgling bass of the nearby river. Layers of it rose and fell, surged and retreated, eased around the smooth heads of the people of Dalgety, and it became an almost living thing, an approaching blanket of locusts, a curlicue of bees.

Mrs Corcoran, having smudged the right lens in haste at the unexpected wash of green, felt a stab of nausea at the blurred effusion, and large beads of sweat, as perfect as the heads of pins, rashed her cleavage, clotting into globules of baby powder. She dabbed them with a hand-kerchief. Her fan had gone limp.

The reeds shifted in figures of eight with the willow branches. The willows entwined with the bulrushes. But nothing shifted on the Monaro. The fields of granite. The low, bare hills that ran up to the mountains. Our Lady Star of the Sea, fat with local bluestone, that surveyed the town. Even the sheep were still from a distance and the colour of the stubbled hills and fields. Only the river had propulsion, and the things it some-times shunted unexpectedly through the middle of town – logs, once a picnic basket, human bodies, hats, and the odd canoe of the adventurous.

The audience could have been explorers, training their eyeglasses on a foreign shore, on this scissoring green.

It was the rush of familiar colour that launched

thoughts of the day's residue for several of the audience, shoulder to shoulder inside that brick of heat. Hubert Johnson had been slicing sheep dags just hours before, wrestling lambs into the crutching saddle and snipping the extrusions as neatly as he would trim his gardenia buds in retirement, which was many decades away. He was brought back to the jets of blood arcing through the air, splashing wrists and boots.

John 'Flint' O'Hagan closed his eyes and returned to the kiss he had snatched from Louise Emerson under the empty grandstand at the racetrack that afternoon. His first with mouth open, with taste of another's tongue, and she smelling of bread and poppy seeds, the aroma not caught in her pinafore and hair, but exuding from her pores.

Mrs Muggeridge, for no reason, was back in her kitchen that overlooked the bare paddocks of Paupong, a black stitching of fence to break the view, and was calculating ingredients for Christmas luncheon, counting currants for the pudding, potatoes that would corral the lamb leg in a baking tray, sifting all of this through her mind. If she had ever thought of life, it would be as fluid in a measuring cup.

Jimmy Haskell, whose child was about to flutter onstage as a mayfly – he had fashioned the sturdy wings himself – tried to imagine what Judges Carrington and Thorpe were doing now in the Imperial Hotel. He had taken them that morning to a bend in the river, just ahead of the rash of gorges, that was profuse with rainbow, and had arranged that two of their finest specimens be iced with an eye to mounting. He was wondering if the performance would finish in time for him to take up their offer of brandy and gin rummy.

The blacksmith, Gordy Thomas, hardly perspired in the hot hall and reminisced, as he did at least a dozen times a day, of the family cottage in Strathblane when he was a wee boy, and the many happy hours he had spent wandering the Campsie Fells, and he explored the range again and again in his mind, though he was tethered to an anvil on the other side of the world. In each child onstage he saw himself, and a few noticed the melancholy Gordy's eyes well with tears, but could not know they were for something lost a long time ago, not for the spectacle before him.

And Mrs Lampe, beside her big, sweaty husband, as lumpy as a fleece bale, waited for her boy to appear from this willy-willy of plant and leaf. The sustained humming somehow relieved her, like unseasonal mistrals that rushed down from the mountains and across the Monaro and strained through the narrow cracks in the walls of the timber house.

'Where the hell is he?' her husband half-whispered.

'Ssshhh.'

'I can't make head or tail,' he said. 'Can you make head or tail?'

'*William*,' she hissed, squeezing his knee.

Old Alf Brindlemere erupted in a deep, guttural coughing fit, and on cue it seemed to rattle the stage, sending out a cavalcade of insects, as if shaken from a tree.

First came what appeared to be thin-legged larvae, followed by a handful of nymphs, a pair of gangly pupae, and the imago. They joined hands in a circle and danced in a clockwise direction, alternately spinning a member

91

of each evolutionary stage in the centre. It was the life cycle of the insect, spinning in Mrs Corcoran's steamed spectacles, skipping to each phlegmatic roar from Brindlemere ahead of the orchestra, all of its orgiastic delight caught in the saucer eyes of Wilfred's sister Astrid, who was shaking like a wet dog in winter at the front of the stage.

There was an exasperated wheeze from the audience as the grown insects filed on stage and formed larger rings around the nymphs and pupae and imago, whirling in the opposite direction, forming ever-widening pools – sandflies, mayflies, cicadas, bees, butterflies, moths, dragonflies, damsel flies and caddis.

It was at this precise moment that Judges Carrington and Thorpe, having decided on a stroll through Dalgety after their evening meal in the Buckley's, and attracted like bogongs to the yellow light and sounds from the hall, ambled over to a side window and peered in.

They had, during dinner, discussed the two specimens of rainbow that would soon be added to their growing collection of trophies back in Sydney, preserved for all time and mounted on the walls of their chambers. And again of the opera unfurling a stone's throw away without them. When their main dishes arrived conversation automatically returned to the giant giddy trout. And stepping into the dark and empty street, their bellies straining vest buttons, they couldn't resist, and snuck a peek at *The Trout Opera*.

In the pale light through the window of the hall the two elderly men lost all thought of creaking buttons and fish eyes in ice and the flutter and finger-crack of cards that awaited them in the hotel's smoking room, for here was a glimpse of life in all its delicious chaos.

No matter that the insects onstage butted and buffeted each other's wings, knocked pinchings of still freshly adhered gold and silver glitter to the floor. No matter that a few antennae clunked into the front row, and that tissuey exoskeletons were punctured. For some minutes Judges Carrington and Thorpe stood on the dry grass in a crooked square of yellow light as dumb-struck as children.

In the hall, Mrs Corcoran dabbed at the puffy sediments of skin beneath her eyes, and men who worked all day with the dirtied cauliflower of sheep fleece felt a softness break open inside them, and mothers stiffened with pride at not only the magic of the costumes but the tiny, squirming pink-skinned children embedded in them, for it was a drama of indefinable beauty, touching a dormant part of them, forgotten from birth, the truth of being, and the weight, both infinite and nothing, of in turn having the capacity to create, and it affected all of them in different ways.

'Oh my,' said Wilfred's mother.

William Lampe, for once, had no thoughts of mangers, and licked his dry lips at the richness of the shining insect bait, wet with new life, made for the hook, and his simple, methodical mind began constructing, piece by piece, new combinations for trout flies.

The stage insects sang a nursery rhyme foreign to the ear, yet still recognisable in its gay lilt as a child's nursery rhyme. Then the circles broke, one by one, and the insects, some damaged, some having caught foreign wing dust, moved to the perimeter of the stage.

'From the hatcheeng ponds they come/after a journey of eighty dayyys,' boomed Youl, fists clenched like creamy anvils.

But *The Trout Opera* had reached such a point of tension that his words were nothing but a fly in the ear, the story of transportation to Australia and hatching and the growth of colonies like cow pats out of which something beautiful might grow, a bloom, perhaps, from an undigested seed. The hall held its breath.

Down the front Astrid Lampe stood and swayed and trembled in anticipation. The spectacle had totally consumed her, and touched something in her, a feeling that she had seen this before, that it was a part of her. The curve of the insects' wings. The glittering costumes. The slippers that jutted out from the base of cocoons and plant stalks. And the dance. The slide of the slippers, the taking of hands, the hands alighting on waists, the waists turning and the hands gently taking flight, and then the fingers dancing. Astrid Lampe knew they were performing *The Trout Opera* just for her.

When Maggie Corcoran took to the stage there was an audible 'ohhh' from the town.

Her headdress rose her body length again, a plumage of iridescent feathers that quivered with each step as gently as the gossamer fins of a goldfish. Beginning at the golden skullcap with a sturdy tussock of black and brown, the edifice gave way to a vivid turquoise then reds and fiery oranges and, finally, a hint of daffodil at the crown that, even through her fugged glasses, extracted tears of recognition from Mrs Corcoran.

Maggie's face was as stiff as a mannequin's, with the

concentration of each step and the burden of the head-dress's weight.

In the stiffness of concentration it was possible, for those who looked carefully enough not at the explosion of feathers but at the child's face, to see her at forty, at fifty, a faint pencilled template of her mother.

The girl's narrow torso, draped in a chenille fairy dress covered in over a thousand crowded, hand-stitched beads, sucked in the sepia bulb-light of the hall.

It was so quiet, except for an occasional faint nostril whistle and a deep, purring rattle from the chest of old Alf Brindlemere, that you could hear the swish of rubbing beads.

She stopped near the centre of the stage but was supposed to keep moving, Our Lady of the Lures, to weave her way amongst the reeds, around the insects, with the delicacy of flight. She was to dance, to entice Wilfred Lampe, King Trout of the Monaro, from the dark folds of the side curtains, to draw him out of his hollow, to bring him up from the cool lower waters of the river and tempt him towards the warmth and light of the world.

But she stood immovable as a pylon of the Dalgety Bridge.

'Maggie,' Mr Schweigestill whispered from one side of his mouth. '*Gehen Sie*, Maggie.'

For he, too, had been transfixed by her appearance, and for a moment was not in the hall in the town but in an opera house in Berlin. The hint of dung and sweat had been replaced by rolling waves of perfume and sweet tobacco breath off the tongue, and statesmen and artists filled rows and balconies, and he could hear them talking about the opera in coffee houses and the backs of leather-rich carriages. And the clop of hoof on cobble brought him back to the Imperial Hall. '*Gehen Sie!*'

Wilfred, stage right, was counting a slow thirty seconds before shuffling to Maggie's side.

'. . . twenty-seven . . . twenty-eight . . . twenty-nine . . .'

Wilfred looked up at the high-pitched screaming, and saw a blur of rainbow and an explosion of stardust.

And Astrid held her small chubby arms outstretched as Maggie and the headdress tumbled off the stage towards her, welcomed them with a joy that was like nothing she had ever felt in her short life, and was eaten by a tongue of feathers and millions of little glass teeth.

SEVEN

THE DRIVER AND the passenger stood in the doorway to the white room at the hospice in Darlinghurst and looked at the old man.

It was mid-afternoon and yet the room was silent and dark, barely illuminated by a tiny child's night-light that one of the nurses must have installed. The glow of the lamp made shadowed valleys across the sheet that covered Wilfred Lampe. They could not see the features of his face but presumed he was asleep.

In the bed, the old man looked shorter than when they had seen him lashed to the stretcher in the helicopter just two days earlier.

'What will we tell them?' the passenger whispered.

'That he's doing well. Under the circumstances.'

The men could both detect a tang of citrus in the antiseptic that filled the room.

'I feel sorry for him,' the passenger said. He fingered some loose coins in his suit trouser pocket.

'Yeah.'

'Taken away from his home and all that. It must be hard for him.'

'I doubt he knows where he is. At the moment.'

The passenger sighed and said, 'How's he going to understand all this? Who could? I'm not sure that *I* do.'

'When he's back to full health, they'll have a word with him.'

'You found him. You saw what he was like.'

'Yes,' said the driver, seeing in the gloom the distant globes of feathered dandelion in the old man's over-grown yard back in Dalgety. Seeing them explode under the beat of the helicopter rotors.

'You have to tell them,' said the passenger.

'What? That our perfect candidate for the ceremony of a lifetime would rather be dead?'

'Yes. Exactly. You felt that, didn't you? You told me that.'

The driver stared at the shape under the white sheet.

'Yes. I did.'

'You said it. That when you found him, he was ready to die.'

'Yes.'

'Do you still believe it?'

'Yes.'

'You have to tell them.'

The driver said nothing.

The passenger went on: 'We'll find someone else, for Christ's sake. There's time.'

'They won't buy it. He's perfect. Anything else is a waste of resources.'

'Stuff the resources. We have this poor bugger who wants to die, and we have to keep him alive for some silly ceremony?'

'I don't need to remind you that this is in the national interest.'

'National interest, my arse. It's just a sporting carnival.'

'It's big business.'

'I can't look at him anymore. Let's go.'

They closed the door. Somewhere, a long way away, Wilfred Lampe heard the click of a latch and it carried to him across the hills like a distant rifle shot.

And then he heard rushing water getting closer, a sigh at first, and then a hiss, and then a roar, and for a moment he was right there, where the river coursed through the ancient gorges of the High Country, and he could feel it wearing away the granite.

Hours later, partially opening his eyes, he detected the amber glow from the night-light and for a moment was sitting beside a campfire at Ingeegoodbee, and around the fire he could see the moist nose of his sleeping collie, and the boots of his father, his legs crossed at the ankle, the boots at odd angles, the heads of each nail in the sole black and clear in the leather, and he was reminded of the ochre dots around the heads of gods or spirits the Aborigines had painted under the rock over-hangs up in the Thredbo Valley. Beyond his dog and his father he could hear the cattle and the soft chafing of their hides and their breathing and the gurgle of their bellies in the dark.

And the bogongs, racing in and out of the flames, the heat searing off legs and wingtips, and still they came back.

Wilfred Lampe, on the roof of the world, protected by rings of brown cattle, next to a fire with his father.

It was pleasant, he decided. To be dead.

EIGHT

ASTRID LAMPE WENT missing for the first time on the night of *The Trout Opera*.

They initially blamed the shock of being struck down by Queen of the Lure Maggie Corcoran's monstrous beaded headdress. The effect of a galaxy of glass beads, some of which broke off on impact and scattered over the uneven boards of the Imperial Hall, lodging in cracks in the hardwood, a few somehow negotiating their way to the back of the hall, and to the feet of the chest-rumbling Alf Brindlemere, who stooped with effort to retrieve one ruby specimen, amazed at how perfectly the colour matched the blood he hacked from himself every morning and evening.

Children in the vicinity of the wreckage wailed in chorus with Maggie Corcoran who, without her head-piece, stood in the stage light like a pale silkworm, too soon out of the chrysalis.

In the audience, suddenly spotted with open mouths, Mrs Corcoran stood, revealing an odd wet patch on the bottom of her dress, opened her own mouth, the teeth strung with saliva, and emitted a squeak of horror, her palms pressed to her jowls.

Parents rushed to the engulfed Astrid, carefully hefted the headpiece from her, and found her there, wide-eyed and delirious, still not back in the world even with the weight of bead, feather and cloth removed. A small duck feather was caught in the corner of her mouth.

Wilfred had shuffled onto the stage at the sound of disaster, saw the back of Maggie Corcoran's hair-netted head, her small shoulders shaking with deep inner sobs, and could not comprehend the scene.

Several of the willows and bulrushes had collapsed and entangled themselves in laughter. The swallows, wagtails and robins, having yet to catch up with the moment, scratched and flapped, but hesitantly, sensing the shift in the room, perhaps the onset of a storm. Wilfred stood centre stage peering through his velvet lips.

'Me lady,' he whispered, to himself. 'Me lady . . .'

Above the hubbub, someone let out a cough that sounded like a rifle shot.

Mr Schweigestill emerged from the gloom of the wings, bereft, signalled the tiny orchestra to continue playing, something upbeat, something vaudeville, to buffet the confusion and embarrassment of the children, to deflect the growing anarchy in the hall. 'Ooom-pah, ooom-pah!' he whispered loudly to the players, then surveyed the wreckage of his opera. Something had collapsed inside him though he had yet to feel the full force of it. A concertina-ing of his positive self, his disposition to dreams, the whole tenuous network of connections to this foreign community he'd been trying to build. It all fell in on itself like Maggie's headdress.

The wheezing Maggie was nursed offstage, the bees and mayflies and caddis following the flora helter-skelter, and a murmur issued from those left in the audience. Only Wilfred Lampe remained, a bemused old trout, stunned and silent between the open red felt drapes.

He could see his mother and father, still seated halfway down the hall, and Astrid, curled in her mother's lap, sucking pleasantly on a thumb.

'Me lady,' he said into the suit.

The hall slowly emptied, and a cool breeze came up from the river, allowed entry, at last, through the open doors of the hall. It flowed through the auditorium and up and over the footlights and even flued into Wilfred's suit, and for a moment he could smell moss and scud and cut timber and blackberries. Someone drew the old curtains closed.

The crowd, and the children, gathered in the dirt street outside the Imperial Hall, across from the Buckley's Crossing Hotel, and milled and mumbled the way people do around a motor vehicle accident, scratching chins and folding arms in an effort to pinpoint the trajectory of impact, the geography of human error.

Already there were exclamations of the opera's brilliance, of the colour and entertainment leading to the point of collapse, and whooping and backslapping and hair-ruffling of congratulation as if nothing had gone wrong at all.

There were several confirmations that the show was much better than the recent performance of *Tom, Dick and Harry* by the Cooma Amateur Dramatic Company. Their measure of matters in life was anything that happened in Cooma. Yes, *The Trout Opera* was infinitely superior.

The contagion riffled through the townspeople gathered in the street, was blown like spore across the verandah and into the open doors and slide-up windows of the hotel. It was the good and warm connective of a close community. It was what forced Mitchell, the publican, to step out onto the verandah, lean on the rail with both muscularly knotted arms, and shout a free keg for everyone, and fizzy drinks for the children.

Thus Dalgety celebrated its one and only opera in the warm air of that mid-December night, in the street, under the great black scoop of night sky, the stars as if shot out of the peaks of the Snowy Mountains, the electric lights allowed to burn, the filaments singing with the afterglow of the children's pageant. An explorer, drifting on the river at this moment, would have cause to come ashore at the warm glow of electric light and lantern, at the burble of voices, and think he had stumbled upon a great civilisation.

The Judges Carrington and Thorpe – they had missed the calamity, lured by thoughts of brandy in the smoking lounge – and other guests were drawn out of the hotel and into the street life, where they mingled and conversed with the locals, shared the keg, and were consumed by another opera, one of froth and hops, of skirts trailing in dust, calloused hands, children shedding wings and fairy dust, bawdy jokes whispered, fishing tips and gossip, all a murmur that rose and fell like the river.

Wilfred had extricated himself from the trout suit, which he laid out gently on the back of the family cart down by the cricket oval. He returned to being just a boy, and he stood for some minutes in the shadows of the eucalypts that ringed the oval, and saw the trout as a great and noble warrior who had died in battle, and been brought home.

The suit looked smaller on the back of the cart. Wilfred felt a sharp sorrow looking at it resting on its side, shivering, occasionally, to the tics and heavy sighs and tail switch of the harnessed horse. The pupils of the trout's large, googly eyes were trained sideways, and to Wilfred, in the dimness, it was a look of deep disappointment. He headed up to the pub, where he learned they had taken Astrid into the hotel to be examined by Dr Fingal.

In town on his fortnightly visit, Fingal used the kitchen of the hotel as a surgery, his exploration of the recesses of the people of Dalgety conducted to the backdrop of bottled peaches and plums, and the occasional hooked duck. Dr Fingal had stayed for the performance of *The Trout Opera*, but had not made it beyond the workers' side of the public bar.

Farmhands or squatters, it made no difference to Dr Fingal. He was as shambolic and weathered as the fence repairers and sorghum stookers and sheep herders of the Monaro. He treated humans and animals alike, when called upon, and did so with the most delicate and scrubbed hands. They were freckle-free, unscarred and completely smooth, the black hairs of his arms ceasing miraculously at the bones of the wrist, retreating, it seemed, or stopping short at the border of these valuable instruments.

He was one of them, except for the hands. And was able to mingle freely on the workers' side of the curtain that separated the bar, and over the other side, in the squatters' and visiting dignitaries' lounge, occasionally glimpsed through the shift of thin muslin. This other world of fireplace and ottomans, a rug and drinks trolley. Two continents, between which Dr Fingal drifted.

It was at the curtain that the worlds of the men mingled in an earthy verbal gruel, the talk of stock prices and European vacations and grain returns scratching against whispers of unwanted pregnancies, slaughtered vermin and the fleshy textures of timber. Sometimes, but rarely, the dialogues coalesced – the Saturday race meet, an accidental death, a cataclysm out in the greater world beyond Dalgety. It was so on this night, with Schweigestill's calamity still crackling in the air, when they carried Astrid Lampe into the kitchen, cleared the large wooden table of fish scales and potato peelings and lamb blood, and laid her down on the surface.

'Well, what do we have here?' said Dr Fingal, his eyes already alert to injury, the clean white fingers limbering. 'A little angel, perhaps, who fell off her cloud? Hmm?'

He had last seen the child at her birth.

Within ten minutes Astrid Lampe was out in the street pirouetting, and tugging at the remnants of costumes, souveniring paper stars and insect antennae. She even ate a wet forefinger of glitter off a bemused fry.

In a cage of shadow through the verandah railing slats, Judges Carrington and Thorpe were unwittingly drawn into a debate about the recent decision to pass over Dalgety as the choice for the nation's capital. The town had it in the bag, they said, until Premier Carruthers had gotten a darned bee in his bonnet and pushed for a stretch of sheep pasture south of Yass.

'Because of the bloody hills around it,' said Alf Brindlemere, spitting quietly into a handkerchief. 'They think it's bloody Rome.'

'Like we ain't got hills,' added Hubert Johnson. The crown of his battered hat was tall and craggy in the half-light. 'Got the highest hill in 'Stralia, eh. Now they want a friggin' ballot, a *ballot*, mind, when all they need is a friggin' measurin' stick. We'll see who's got flamin' hills, eh.'

Judges Carrington and Thorpe said nothing of their acquaintance with Premier Joseph Carruthers. In their handful of meetings over the past two years they had followed the royal commission into the selection of a federal capital site with more than a cursory interest. A house of parliament on the Snowy at Dalgety would certainly mean the end of their fishing and, as they were not getting any younger, the end of a profound portion of their retirement. They were cautious with the locals, and carefully considered the evidence that spilled forth through often blackened teeth and punctuated with spittle.

'They been stickin' their surveyor pegs around here for years, like we were a pin cushion,' continued Johnson. 'And nothin' but flamin' promises all the while.' He sipped his beer. 'Eh.'

'You remember,' said Alf, with a gravelly underscore, 'when they turned up all spit an' polish to have a gander at us the first time, like they was comin' to a funeral? 'Member? What a laugh.'

'Night of the big storm, eh.'

'That's it. All these pretty pollies in their city suits and a flamin' 'lectrical storm peels off half the bloody roof of the hotel. They weren't too pleased.'

They had told, and heard, this story more times than they could count, and it came to them this evening like a lovely worn stone. Washed with water, or beer, it still yielded interesting facets.

'Tha's right, Emelia's pa brought 'em in the mail cart. Had to farm 'em out to the Jockey Inn and the school. Important ones stayed in the Jockey, 'course. Rest on the school floor.'

Alf continued. 'Had a good sniff around they did. Ooh, 'ow loverly. What a wonnerful place for the capital of 'Stralia, they said. What a loverly river. But this were in the spring. Snowy runnin' like a mad woman with the snow melt. All sparklin' for 'em she was, all prettied up for the pollies. In her Sundee best ya might say.'

'Cleaned us out of grog too, eh,' said Johnson, looking into his jar scudded with rings of beer froth.

'Next mornin', after the storm, they want to take a dip in the river. Let's have a bloody splash in the grand ole Snowy. Readin' too much Banjo, you know? Bloody Banjo Paterson in their back pockets. Let's 'ave a soap up in Banjo's Snowy.'

'Twits, eh.'

'Just down there,' said Alf, pointing into the dark. 'Off with the clobber and in they go, washin' themselves with Banjo. A sorrier sight you never seen, if you never seen a bunch o' city blokes playin' in a river. White as ghosts. Splashin' like children. Took Inglis's two boys to

107

pull out the fat one who got washed down past the oval.'

''E'd 'ave been spat out at Marlo if those boys hadn't grabbed 'im.'

After the laughter subsided Judge Carrington gently interrupted. 'The visit was obviously favourable. The Act of only two years ago . . .'

'My oath,' said a heated Alf Brindlemere. 'We was the bloody capital. Hold yer horses, some of us said. It ain't done yet. Don't go hoistin' the flag. Old man Crank goes makin' plans for one of them deepartment stores, right 'ere in town . . .'

'That's right, eh. Old Cranky says he seen the future, better get crackin'.'

'And suddenly the town's full o' strangers, see? Trudgin' through paddocks, strollin' down the street like they was on the booleevards of Paris. Comin' to buy land, grab a slice of the capital of 'Stralia.'

'A good thing, surely, for Dalgety,' said Judge Thorpe.

'Your honour,' said Brindlemere, 'them parcels o' nettle been waitin' around close on two years, now Carruthers come along and look where we are. Rooted.'

The rabbiters amongst them readjusted their hats and nodded.

'Too cold for Carruthers, eh. Too close to the border. But he's still scratchin' a road out from Jindabyne to the top of the mountains and buildin' his fancy hotels.'

Alf said, 'Openin' up the place, that's the words they use. We're goin' to open it up. Wouldn' mind doin' the same to the good Premier . . .'

Wilfred Lampe, still numb from his experience,

wandered silently from group to group in the street between the hotel and the Imperial Hall.

Alf Brindlemere drew him into the circle.

'If it ain't the King of the Monaro.'

Wilfred found it difficult to recognise anyone in the group.

'We don't need no capital,' said Johnson, 'when we got the King right 'ere, eh. Waddya say, Wilfred?'

He noticed the arcing gold chains of the judges' watch fobs and wanted to respond but couldn't. He was still full of his rehearsed opera lines, the ones never permitted to be spoken, and could not get any of his normal speech past the barrier of them. He swallowed and chirruped, thinking of the trout suit laid to rest on the back of the cart in the dark beneath the gum trees.

'Anyways,' said Alf. 'Who gives a stuff if we're the capital or no? What we need with a fancy empoorium? We got all we need 'ere.'

'Too right.'

The judges raised their beers in a silent toast.

'Sandwiches, boys? We got plenty.' It was Mrs Muggeridge with a tray of food brought from the hall. Miss White followed in her substantial wake, with a small pile of serviettes which, on the men's side of the festivities, she knew would not be needed.

'Ta, Mabe.'

'Yeah, ta.'

'Mitchell!' someone yelled. 'Whack some steaks on too, will ya. Take what you need out of the fishin' club kitty.'

Their club, the Dalgety Anglers' Society, had its monthly meetings in the front bar of the Buckley's and

109

the slatted walls carried the beginnings of what would, over the decades, become a version of their history. Three photographs: the club members; a huge brown still heaving on a mat of crushed reeds; and their politicians, bathing in the Snowy River, their various pale torsos shiny with river water, their heads damp and beards bristling.

'Thank you, gentlemen,' said Miss White, and the men partially doffed their hats, and a few looked after her, and squeezed the handles of their steins, and the creaminess of imagined flesh flickered beneath those wide oiled brims.

Alf Brindlemere let out a deep, almost imperceptible whinny.

The men were momentarily silent.

'Three gangs of roadworkers already on their way from Sydney, you heard? For the Premier's road to Kosciusko,' said Brindlemere.

After further silence, they began discussing the Dalgety Annual Races and the Peach Blossom Ball.

Wilfred disappeared from the ring of men and looked for Mr Schweigestill. The boy still needed the residue of the opera, a line to it, and longed for the teacher's bony fingers resting, no matter how briefly, on his narrow shoulder. He could not, at that moment, face the emptiness of the hall. Drifting between the little clusters of local society – the Lady Mayoress of Berridale, the undertaker, an unsteady Dr Fingal, J. L. Stark, reporter, from the *Monaro Mercury*, wealthy Crank and his sons Tom and Donald, and Chin and his family – he found no anchor, and wandered down to the edge of the river.

He sat on the rounded head of a huge granite

boulder and watched the dark flow. Where the water rose and bubbled over a hidden rash of clustered rock, the surface threw off reflections. Wilfred could see the gullied, uneven surface of the river by an underlying, unceasing rush of noise that was movement over rock and against bank and tangled in it duck honks and willow whispers from upstream, and a hollow splashing from downstream. In this part of the river's voice he imagined the minute plonking of crickets and other insects on the surface right along its reach, and the shift of logs on the river bed, and the echoes from the surrounding paddocks – mewling, bawling, bird call, rabbit skitter – all drawn into and pulled along by the swift flow of the Snowy.

For a while the music from the hall had become part of the river's voice. Now it was already way downstream, probably past Dead Horse Gap by now. He had not been a part of the voice tonight. But Wilfred Lampe was always going to be a part of the river. This was where he lived. This was his home forever.

He felt cheered by it. One day, when he was bigger, he'd go find the source of the Snowy. He was smiling, thinking of this, when he heard his sister Astrid's name called. Turning, he saw the group of townspeople break up, their figures dim in the lamp and electric light, some running towards the river, others striding over to the oval ringed by eucalypts, and others heading up the hill past the school and the police station. Lamps were lit, one by one, and the groups moved off in deliberate directions.

Astrid, they shouted as they walked off with their lamps. Astrid. Astrid. It sounded mournful and odd and became another word and formed an unknown meaning to him when it was sung long and low into the night. Small coins of lantern light moved up the sides of the hills behind the town.

Wilfred ran back to the hotel. His mother and father had already gone. He looked around, and saw more flickering lanterns in the bush beyond the oval and along the river's edge south of the bridge.

And there, confused, he saw her, the girl in the white dress and red shoes, standing on the wooden steps of the Imperial Hall, a ghost, a spirit from the mountains and snow, staring at him.

NINE

SOMETIMES, WHEN HE had the strength and his nurse allowed it, they took the short walk along Onslow Avenue to the fish pond in the park that overlooked Sydney Harbour, and he caught his reflection in the dark water. If he leaned over the pond long enough, the orange and cream fish eased through his thinning hair and the hollows of his cheeks and eye sockets.

He had been pondering his reflection a lot lately, with the change, and realised he had reached the point where what he saw looking back at him in mirrors and shop windows and pond surfaces was, finally, the true him, and not how he had imagined himself. For a while it shocked him, this forty-nine-year-old self, just as it is shocking to hear your own voice. Somewhere, he had stepped over that line, with the reflection, in the march towards death.

Before the onset of the sickness, Tick had been a local identity. The vital young man – beautiful, some said – in a velvet cape, the escort of gentlemen poets and painters who vied for his attention. A young man of infinite guises – one week the thug boxer, the next a Cuban-heeled cowboy, another a mysterious European androgyne in outfits always a half-year ahead of the boutiques. Then he became Juliet and nobody recognised him and he lost himself. There had been something frightening about him, even as Juliet, but it was not dread of the sort he possessed now, where you could see the death in him.

He became like a beast from a children's book of fables; a big, furred half-animal half-human that had somehow been jilted from the pages and, once free, skittered into the darkness under the bed, or out into the city. Regardless of season he wore a monstrous fur coat that he had stitched and lined himself, the fur so long he brushed it like someone would brush their hair. And at night, when he moved in and out of cones of streetlight, the coat threw a giant, wobbling egg-shaped shadow on the footpath.

His evening walks often took him as far as Circular Quay, across the bridge into Pyrmont and Darling Harbour and Chippendale, or as far as Bondi Beach and Watsons Bay and Vaucluse. And he thoroughly worked his own neighbourhood – Rushcutters Bay, Elizabeth Bay, Kings Cross. The egg shadow followed him, or preceded him, or disappeared altogether in the alleyways and passages and stairwells that he haunted. And his eyes were open to everything.

He felt a peculiar satisfaction peering into ground-floor apartment windows in the middle of the night. He would squint, concentrate, his short, dainty fingers around cold steel security bars, and see – through the cracks in blinds and curtains – the green and red filaments of clock radios, and the shapes of people under blankets and sheets. All the little children asleep. He would smile and touch the window glass with his fingertips. Kill her, kill him.

He liked the name they had given him, Tick, and he had several of them, life-sized and engorged with blood, tattooed across his body, deep under the fur of the coat. Tick, tick, tick.

Only a few months earlier, before his illness took hold, Tick trawled Elizabeth Bay, his home suburb. It never failed to yield, so high-density, so compressed. He searched for street detritus, for items lost, dropped, misplaced, tipped from the sills of high-rise apartments. For goods abandoned during a move, or redecoration, or a break-up. For clothes and books and CDs and jewellery and shoes tossed from windows in a rage, for make-up and wallets and sentimental objects ejected to the music of raised voices. Even for underwear returned to the gutter, where it belonged, with the owners, the philanderers, the secret lovers fleeing on detection. The ones who left a piece of themselves behind in the panic of discovery. These were Tick's favourites. The casualties of war.

In the last week he had recovered a broken yet majestic neon Buddha shrine, a carton of old bowling trophies with little chipped gold bowlers on their wooden pedestals, a birdcage with a boot-shaped dent above the door, a gentleman's wig, a formica-topped table, an amateur painting of Mount Kosciusko, and a rubber vagina.

One wall of his small apartment was papered with notes and envelopes and shopping lists and love letters he found on streets or pinned under windscreen wipers or crumpled in garbage cans. He called it his Wall of

Lost Souls. There was one: *Thanks for parking me in. Bring a can opener next time, you fucking Dwaf.* There were pleas torn in half or disintegrated by rain: *Josie please forgive me I . . .; am going to kill myself tonight; . . . can't live without you Rabbit. Buy BHP . . .*

Interspersed with the notes were his photographs of toilet wall graffiti and drawings and invitations. *Carrie sucks cock. For a good time. Midnight every Saturday by the Wall. Lonely. Blowjob. Lonely. There was a young man from Nantucket. Suck. Eat. Lonely.*

Tick lived in a one-bedroom apartment in Onslow Avenue, a leafy ribbon of road halfway between the high spine of the hill that was Macleay Street and the more rarefied mansions of Billyard Avenue, on the harbour foreshore. There were two entrances to his apartment. The street-level lobby where, under apartment 7, he went by one of his many other aliases – Peter David. And the side door at the back of the flats which was, as Tick, his primary passageway. He gained access to it via a forgotten path, overgrown with ferns. A path, an artery of old bitumen, that had been overlooked in decades of development. A path that had once had a function in the architecture of a sandstone mansion long disappeared. A gardener's walkway, perhaps. A servant's thoroughfare, between house and tennis court, once maintained, once catching grass clippings and splashes of fruit punch on the perimeter of wealthy lives. Now scratched only by the feet of Tick.

He often thought of those glory days of stone and pillar and shutter and slate, the sandstone facades brushed by salted breezes that funnelled through the Heads. Perhaps young men and women kissed here in the forgotten lane, Tick thought, their bodies still quivering with the rattle of the tram home from work. And with the quivering, and the kiss, and the aroma of freshly cut grass and the perfume of jasmine, maybe the lovers felt that momentary invincibility of a grand life stretching out before them.

Most of the mansions were gone now. The breezes still barrelled through the Heads, squeezing between high-rise apartment blocks, picking up the whimpering of women and men and children and the wail of car alarms and police sirens and the scales of trainee opera singers and the snores of drunks and the monologues of addicts and piano notes and dog barks. There were movie stars on the foreshore with their ratty palms and trickling fountains, the backs of their mansions turned firmly to the hill that ran down from Macleay Street, to the glacier of the commoners that inched towards the foot of their security gates. And there was Tick, embedded firmly in the ice.

It was 1.17 am when one of Tick's three mobiles, his customer phone, rang. He had just returned to the apartment with two hubcaps and a soiled brassiere. He checked the screen of the phone. It read: L'il Sister. His codename for Aurora.

'Yes, darling, yes, of course. Naturally, darling. Thirty minutes. Ta-ta.'

The thought of her made him happy. He had not expected this, to be instantly touched by somebody at his age, and in his state of health. The illness had separated him from affection. It had halted physical contact. Embedded a large chip of dry ice inside him. Yet, as sometimes happens, or so he read in the love

117

stories he enjoyed, certain people clicked at first sight. It was how he felt about Aurora. She possessed pain he recognised, and the early stages of a vulnerability that would eventually cost him his life. With Aurora, he found he wanted to cut through the preambles of friendship, to rush to it, fully formed. He was running out of time, and she had come along at the precise moment that his need for love had decided to stage one last fightback. The second they first met in the darkened street near his flat, he decided he was going to love Aurora Beck.

He opened the central cabinet of his imitation French bureau, retrieved two small plastic sachets of cocaine from a nest of more than fifty sachets, and secreted them in the hidden internal pocket of the giant bear coat.

He caught his reflection in the large, gilt-edged mirror above the bureau. It had become a child's lucky dip to him. He never knew who he would find in the mirror, the change was coming on so rapidly. Who are you today? he thought.

Tick had a face like an inverted teardrop – narrow at the chin, wide at the brow. His eyes were now distinct globes, fierce, hard, with the sinking of flesh around the orbs. The cheekbones were precariously sharp, cheekbones he had always cooed over in magazines, but subsiding quickly, slipping down against bone. His lips remained full, top and bottom, but were now approaching the obscene against the collapse of the face, not erotic any longer, but exposed and vulnerable. He had long, yellowing teeth and ulcerated gums.

He brushed his thinning, shoulder-length hair and then brushed the coat. Miss Aurora could wait. He had other deliveries, from three am, on the half-hour, up to seven o'clock. He prepared a pot of herbal tea and sat at his antique writing desk – retrieved, inexplicably, from beneath a fig tree in Rushcutters Bay Park. He switched on the desk lamp, a beautiful piece, its base a brass gathering of three fish – were they dancing, or dying? – their heads meeting at the bulb fixture, poured his tea and looked at the music box in the centre of the desk. He had found it, several months prior, on the median strip in Challis Avenue.

He had completed the repairs on the box that same afternoon. It was decorated with yellow flowers of no identifiable genus, and he had touched them up with a little brush and paint pots he had shoplifted for the purpose. It had taken him a month to calculate and repair the worn-out mechanics of the box. He had surgically removed the tiny, exhaust-soiled ballerina from the centre of the box, laid her down gently on a piece of black velvet, stripped her and hand-sewn a new, miniature outfit.

As he performed the delicate work on the redressing, he clicked his tongue and gently shook his head. What dreams you had promised to little girls, he thought, in your vivid pinkness, your satin and tulle. With your painted eyelashes and dot eyes and nub of a hair bun. Oh sweetness, he whispered. He replaced her slippers, patched her thin legs, replaced a missing finger so small he had to work with a magnifying glass. And when she was naked and restored, he dressed her in navy sailor's shorts, and an open sailor's shirt, and stitched a tiny white sailor's hat on her pea head. When she danced again, she went about her old routine, her Swan Lake,

119

but this time she grinned cheekily – thanks to Tick's artistry – and exposed her small breasts throughout the routine. He had painted red fly-speck nipples on her tiny twin breasts.

He took the cocaine sachets from his coat and placed them inside the music box. A gift, to his sweet customer, Aurora Beck.

He made a fresh pot of tea and went out onto the small Juliet balcony at the back of his flat and looked down into the blocks of flats below him, in the shadow of the giant hoop pine that obstructed his view of the harbour.

Voices and music and the clinking of glasses and cutlery drifted up to him from the mansions of the movie stars and property developers and media moguls – a party to which he would never be invited, but which he penetrated through his drugs, ferried in little designer handbags and small beaten-silver pill boxes and wallets into the glamour of the city, the society set. Three of his buyers there, perhaps four, in the milieu of the rich, all hooked to Tick, belonging to Tick.

He sighed a breath soured with Russian Caravan, then telephoned Harold.

'Now don't be late, Harold, don't leave me sitting there alone,' he said into the phone. 'You what? Say that to me again. Say it, Harold. Yes? Good. My favourite table. Correct. That's right, Harold.'

He thought, as he dressed for a very late dinner, or extremely early breakfast, how essential it had always been to him to have a friend like Harold. A person at whom to vent things. To vent. Yes. Harold was his apparatus for venting.

They had known each other since Tick first moved to Sydney and within moments of meeting had established their respective roles. Tick, the smaller man, would vent. And Harold, a tall, round-shouldered man whose face, no matter what age, betrayed the baby photographs of his mother's sideboard, would be the recipient of venting. The dry ice in Tick, when it came, was by and large reserved for poor Harold.

As Tick dressed, he was warmed with the wisdom that in life there were people who chose and others who were chosen. That people secured around them others who could nurse those undeveloped, tender inadequacies within themselves. People shed friends not as a snake threw off skin, but because the wound had been healed, or could never be healed. In either case, the chosen became irrelevant.

Towards Harold, more and more as the years moved on, Tick felt a deep disconcertedness that he tried to ignore. Fearing that to Harold, Tick was in fact becoming his own father. Screaming at Harold, as his father had at him.

When he thought of his father, he thought of the evenings when he was very young, in a dim kitchenette in Murrumbeena, where he was made to stand at the end of the room naked and covered in honey that had been spatulaed onto him with a bread knife, while his father and drunken friends played game after game of euchre. Looking over at the naked boy, at the flies that gathered on his face, in the corners of his eyes, between his legs on those summer evenings. And he, Tick, trembling as if it was mid-winter, kept his eyes fixed on the beaded bottles of beer, the tears that would build and run, and stop, and build and run again.

The flies caught on him. Struggled to pull their legs from the honey. They buzzed with the effort. The buzzing filled his head, hot sparks that fought to break out of his skull, and he stood straight as a lead soldier because he had been told not to move, and he pissed sweet urine straight onto the linoleum without blinking, and the card players pointed at him and held their bellies with laughter and spat frothy beer at the sight.

Later, when the men were gone, his father would roar and rage, and still he didn't move, this pale-skinned boy freckled with dead flies. And he was only free when his father fell unconscious, and he could hear the great ship-like wail of his snoring from another room.

Tick fixed his cravat and adjusted his shirt's frilled white sleeves. He put on his African beads and his gold cross, and buffed the tips of his pointed snakeskin boots on the backs of trousered legs. He secured his ponytail with a navy velvet hair tie and checked both profiles in the mirror. My pathetic Harold, he said to himself. I shall try to be nicer to you.

Tick put on the heavy fur coat, slipped the music box into an inner pocket, checked the secret lining for its sachets of cocaine and ice, ran his thumb around the compartment in the collar for his small, perfectly prepared little coloured balloons of heroin, looked at himself one more time in the mirror, sighed, winked at himself, and went to work.

TEN

SOME DAYS AURORA sat on her concrete balcony that overlooked the bay and chain-smoked and stubbed the butts into a small pot plant forgotten by the previous tenant.

In the brown plastic pot there was a handful of pale soil and the whiskery strands of a dead plant. She quickly filled the pot with butts and was surprised to find sometimes she had accidentally set alight one of the straw whiskers.

She remembered the smell of burning straw.

A few weeks after she'd been at the apartment she noticed one morning that the light slanting through the glass balcony door was different. It was an odd mustard light that made everything familiar look alien and set her heart beating, and when she stepped onto the balcony she could see great wheeling sheets of birds in the sky. She looked for the sun but could not find it beyond the dome of filtered light that pressed down on the city.

At the back of her throat she tasted scorched eucalypt seeds and gum leaves, and even when she closed all the windows and the curtains it was still with her, so familiar, the burning of the Australian bush.

She had no television and didn't know where the bushfires were, but took a long shower and scrubbed herself until her skin was rashed pink and washed her hair until her scalp hurt. In bed she could still smell the burning through a veil of apple and aloe vera, and when she shut her eyes she saw the men again, the shapes of them, dark monsters with stalks for hands and flames licking from the stalks, walking towards her, forever, since she was a child.

They came out in the early evening in their overalls with their metal kerosene lighting cans and their worn hats, and paced the edges of the great square oceans of cane, and every two steps, or three, pressed a lick of flame to the dry setts.

When the cane fields burned, the whole of Murwillumbah was cupped in amber, the lava light reflected back off plates of low cloud. It was like switching on a huge orange-shaded reading lamp.

In the town, late at night, the glow sketched out the wood and vinyl booths and sugar jars and serviette canisters through the windows of the cafe, and teased at diamantés and beads on the shop dummies in the dress shop, and outlined Victa mowers and rows of secateurs in the hardware store. It caught the cellophane of the rows of cigarettes behind the counter in the petrol station at the bend of the river, and made sinister the faces of movie stars on posters in the cabinets at the front of the Regent Cinema.

Down Cane Road, the mill where her father worked never slept, and the field fires gave shape to the billowing steam from the primary funnel, and in the semi-dark the trucks, with their round headlights and long-nosed bonnets, looked like giant dogs banished to the corners of the yard.

And in a street just down from the mill and its general store, framed in a clear louvred window at the back of the house that overlooked the river, the distant fires illuminated the small, creamy oval face of a six-year-old girl – Aurora – her eyes moist and her bottom lip puckered at an odd angle as she bit it with her small front teeth. There were several smudges on the louvre in front of her face where she had pushed forward and touched the glass with the tip of her nose. Every August, she looked out to the fields of hell.

For here, the girl, and all the cane burners and cutters, and the whole town, lived near the middle of the ancient volcanic caldera, the cauldron, the rim more than forty kilometres in diameter, worn and softened with figs and brush box and booyongs and rainforest, threaded with the call of whippoorwills and bowerbirds. Mount Warning. The giant, seething caldera, now cradling dairy farms and the patchworks of sugar cane.

From their back verandahs and milking sheds and the little grid of the town with its red iron roofs clustered together like match heads, they couldn't know the dimensions of the cauldron inside which they made their lives. But they could see, for as long as they lived, the monolith of their volcano's plug, grey-green and hunched against future heat. It was there, always, a benign growth in the mind of every inhabitant.

During the nights of the cane burning, Aurora prayed to the mountain for the safety of her father.

In this place of violet jacaranda blooms and feathered

rain and the hulk of Mount Warning, where it snowed ash in the spring and the air was sometimes so thick with molasses you could almost taste it on your lips, the cane burning was the backdrop to the child's nightmare. Her father always volunteered for the burning and was out there, at the edge of the three-metre cane setts, lighting the walls of dry grasses two steps at a time with his kerosene can, running from the apocalypse with the rats.

She tried to hold him back each night of the burning. She tugged on his arm, or his trouser leg, afraid he would never come home.

At night the glow from the field fires flickered across the ceiling of her bedroom, and through her window she watched great monsters heave up together and fight and wrestle and roll over and into each other and spit sparks, and sometimes she could feel the heat of their battle on the glass.

And each morning she woke with swollen eyes and rushed to her parents' bedroom and her father would be there asleep, his face sooted, his hair flecked with husks and grey with ash, snoring and exhaling burnt breath. She'd squeeze his hand, the creases and pores etched with charcoal, and skip into the yard that backed onto the river, just north of the sugar mill. Often, steam gathered around the mill's huge central flue just the same as her Mount Warning had clouds huddled around its summit.

She had a crayon drawing of the mountain pinned to the wooden tongue-and-groove wall of her bedroom, like every six-year-old in Murwillumbah, with a few little pademelon wallabies grazing at its foot. All the other children drew the mountain's crooked head with eyes and a mouth and a big smiling face. But Aurora had sketched it veiled in cloud, which it often was, because her father had told her its secret name was Wollumbin, or the Cloud Catcher, and she liked to think of it snatching those clouds before they scuttled to the sea.

'It's all yours,' her father had told her one day, on the way to the Regent in town.

'What?'

'The mountain.' He pointed above the flaking tin rooftops and jacaranda crowns to Mount Warning.

'All of it?'

'Yep.'

'How come, all of it?'

'You go up there and on a clear night you can see the Aurora.'

'What's the Roarer?' she asked.

'The southern lights, waves of them. Like the sky's on fire.'

'Can we see them?'

'One day, maybe.'

'I'd like to see them.'

'Sure, one day.'

And he laughed that afternoon, and carried her into the dark cool of the cinema.

It was more than just the place where her name came from, this mountain. She talked to it. Told it things. Asked it questions. It watched her from every part of the town. It cleared of clouds and she'd say, there you are, where you been hiding? Or, 'bout time you woke up, sleepy head. She watched the summer electrical storms roll in and strike its flanks, and she'd put her hand over her mouth, her eyes wide with fear for her mountain.

On a school excursion into the big billowing rain-forest skirts at its base, she became mother to it, ordering the teacher and other children to speak quietly, not to scare the lyrebirds and bush turkeys, not to break off tree branches or pull away leaves. She was the last back on the bus. Thank you, she said to the mountain. See you tomorrow.

When she was a teenager she made the climb. Five of them went up. She said nothing of the secret of her naming. She was starting to hate many things and her name was one of them; and sometimes she even admonished the mountain, because it was a hulking lava core, this unchanging, unwavering, twenty-million-year-old monster that never moved, was always there, would always be there, and it made the whole town seem so small, and made her feel like nothing, and no matter how many times she wailed at it, cried to it that she was growing, and changing, and wouldn't be staying in this shit hole forever, it just stared back at her.

There were clouds the morning of her climb. There was no golden sunrise. Instead, on her descent she looked over to the little town on the bend of the river, and the smouldering, blackened cane fields that surrounded it, and she knew she'd been named right. Fire was the colour of Aurora.

One day I'm just gonna leave, she told the silent mountain. Just like that, I'll be gone.

On weekends she worked in the general store across from the sugar mill. She served chipped cups of caffeine to the truck drivers. When the mill was processing, the shredders crushing the cane and the rollers extracting the sugar juice, her father feeding the boiler furnaces with bagasse, facing the flames again, half of him bleached of features in the white light of the boilers, a man always at the edge of intense heat, of his own personal hell, day after day, Aurora could smell nothing after working in the store. Her olfactories saturated with sugar, with the stench of bitter molasses. Her head and her body filled with it and sickened by it. It was the flavour of her life – raw, unrefined sugar.

Early one Saturday morning at the store, after she'd switched on the single petrol bowser, and sorted Friday's mail for the store's fifteen post office boxes, before she'd opened up proper, a white Valiant four-door had stopped on the gravel out front. She saw the car through the front windows of the store, and the two men come up the three wooden stairs onto the verandah and peer in past the CLOSED sign and the home-printed notification of the union delegate's arrival in a fortnight.

One of the men tapped on the old door. The sky behind the strangers was clouded with mill steam.

'Morning, sweetheart,' one of them said to her. 'Get some smokes?'

She could tell they were not from the town. They were in their twenties, wore dark suits and open-necked business shirts and scuffed black shoes. They smelled of alcohol inside the molasses. Aurora had grown to recognise that smell.

The man who spoke had short dark hair, rumpled with awkward sleep, and when he smiled at Aurora she noticed a gap between his front teeth. The other man sat at a table and held his head in his hands.

'Peter Jackson, love, ta. And a coffee, I think. A coffee?'

he said over his shoulder. 'Two coffees, love, white, two sugars.'

'Take a seat,' she said.

'That's a good girl, ta,' he said, and glanced at her breasts beneath her pink and white striped top and pushed a furred tongue against his top teeth and sucked in air through the gap. His eyes were dull and bloodshot and the glance he gave her made her shiver. 'You're orright,' he said, nodding, sucking through his teeth, and he turned and sat down at the table.

Aurora switched on the coffee maker and prepared fresh grinds and saw, outside, a woman emerge from the Valiant. She pulled herself unsteadily from the rear passenger's door, a bare foot first and then the second shod in a bright red stiletto. As she came out of the door well her ball gown bloomed around her, a flower too quick to open in sudden heat, ragged and lopsided. She held herself against the car door, her bare foot suspended above the grey gravel, and appeared stranded. Her face tweaked at the smell of the mill, and she lowered herself back onto the car seat.

Aurora took the coffee to the two men.

'From round here, are ya? Course you are, silly question,' said the man with the gap in his teeth.

'Yes, not far,' she said. She wanted to talk to them, because they were not truck drivers and mill workers. They were from outside.

'Good on ya.'

'Passing through?'

'Aren't we all, one way or another?' He sipped the coffee loudly and smarted at the heat of the cup on his bottom lip. 'Oi, dopey. Have your coffee.'

Aurora stood and watched them and was not afraid anymore.

'Big night?' she asked.

'Been on the town, so to speak. Made some donations to the casino up the coast. You know what I mean?'

'Yeah.' She knew nothing of casinos and the lights of cities at night and coloured cocktails in elegant glasses and men in suits and women in gowns. What she knew about was the lonely lives of her truck drivers and the dim lights of their truck cabins and the silent mountain that was sometimes blacker than night.

'What's that godawful stink?'

'Sugar. The mill.'

'Sugar,' he said, taking the sugar canister and pouring some into his half-empty coffee. 'Knew I forgot something. Sitting on top of a friggin' sugar mill and I forget me sugar. That'd be right, eh?'

He stared at Aurora as he sipped the rest of the coffee. She went back behind the counter.

'We'll be off then,' he said, standing, and his partner rose and walked straight out to the car.

'Here,' he said on his way out, and he leaned over and tucked a ten-dollar bill into the top of her blouse. He winked, put his hands in his pocket, and left the store. The bell over the door tinkled once.

She went to the window and watched him get into the car. The woman in the back was staring at her, her face pale and her lips smudged pink. Eyeliner had run from her left eye. Aurora thought the woman was wearing a tiara.

Nobody came into the store for an hour. She sat at the formica table where the men had been and slowly twirled the sugar canister and looked out to the bowser and the gravel. The steam lugged from the mill, and the muted sounds of machinery, and the human labour inside that sound, filled the interior of the store and dulled the counters and food warmers and checked linoleum floor. In her daydream she remembered everything about the strange man – the three pierced holes in his right earlobe, the streak in both irises as pale as dead cane husks, the wiry black chest hair that spidered out of his open-necked shirt, the cat's eye dress ring, the square-toed shoes, the fur of his tongue in the gap between his teeth.

She recalled the wink he gave her, and how the wink had slightly lifted the corner of his mouth, and at that moment she felt a charge run through her, a feeling she had never experienced, and now that she had felt it, could not describe. She tucked that feeling inside her, just as he had slipped the note into her blouse.

Another hour later she heard the first reports of the robberies in town – the service station before the bridge across the river, Costa's milk bar and the Returned Servicemen's Club, where a cleaner was shot in the thigh. Two men and a woman in a white Valiant. A random raid. Professional. All happened in forty minutes. Roadblocks were being put up. Forensics left with nothing but the bullet in the cleaner's leg, and a fresh pool of vomit in the car park where a woman in a tiara was witnessed throwing up out the window of a white Valiant. The criminals absconded.

Every potential witness in the town was interviewed by local police and later the city detectives. Had Aurora seen anything unusual out at the general store that morning? The vehicle? Two men in black suits, and a woman? Could she remember anything?

I didn't see a thing, she said.

They published black ink sketches of the suspects in the local newspaper. She kept a clipping of the man who had winked at her, though it looked nothing like him, folded in her purse.

It was the biggest news in Murwillumbah since the runaway petrol tanker demolished Choy's service station and Holiday Park on the other side of the river. The wounded cleaner became a hero. He wore the cast on his leg for over a year, and commandeered a corner of the Royal, where beer and meals were bought for him, and a fluffy blue pouf was provided by the publican's wife for his comfort. He was the first local to be shot – not by his own hand – since the Second World War.

Aurora sat at her place around the kitchen table in the evenings and instead of the machinations of the mill and the annual Banana Festival and the hippies, as colourful as rainbows from up in the ranges, starting to appear in the town, they talked of the robbery and attempted murder of the cleaner.

'Are we going to have to lock up now? The house? The car? Is that what we're going to have to do?' Her mother had, in recent years, become skeletal, the dry skin a sudden palette for fine knife-cut wrinkles, drawn close to the bone, which had thrown out the look of her, the balance of her frame. Her eyes had become rounded and penetrating in a setting of shadowed skin. She appeared pinched, and winced at each action of the everyday that had before never warranted thought – the lifting of a kettle, sitting down, rising from a chair,

133

pegging clothes in the yard. The wasting of her body had made her head look larger, the brown bobbed hair kinked at odd angles and dry and sharp at the ends, like the hard foliage of a native plant, and not something that belonged to her, to a mother who not long ago still possessed soft edges. Who naturally smelled of something like raspberries. A woman who had radiated life, and now hardened herself against it.

For Aurora it was like having two mothers – the soft, milky, corpulent one of childhood, and this, the one of wire, weathered and flaky and alert to the closing of a door.

'What steps are being taken?' Aurora's mother went on. She had recently become convinced that everything had to follow proper procedure, that everything was the product of *steps*. Since the beginning of winter she had taken umbrage at how the world worked. She became incensed at the service and attention she received at the local supermarket, and had initiated *steps* to rectify the slight, writing a formal letter to the on-duty manager, a faintly whiskered nineteen-year-old who, after the letter, and a public stripping down near the meat coolers, had taken to hiding in the stockroom when she appeared. The supermarket letter had burst a levee, and soon her complaints and suggestions for correct steps had reached into every corner of town, from the local council to the letterbox of the parents of a nine-year-old who had poked out his tongue at her one afternoon near the bandstand in the square.

In the cinema the air-conditioning was too cool, or not cool enough. Lamb loins at the butcher were bulked up with too much fat, or were too small. Over at the service station they were fiddling the pumps. The haberdashery had switched good local fabric for inferior foreign bolts.

She began penning letters to the local newspaper, and was published, unabridged, the first few times. A new dissenting voice was welcome. Then they baulked at her lengthy treatise on the town's half a dozen traffic lights which, as she wrote, she had made the effort to time, and found no evidence of synchronisation.

Her world was contracting.

'We have a teenage *daughter*,' she said, shrilly, fussing around the kitchen as if Aurora wasn't there. 'This sort of thing shouldn't *happen* where . . . where . . . there are *children*. We shall have to organise a meeting, with the *police*, and that *buffoon* of a local member . . .'

She had, to her husband, started to disappear. He sat at the table and said nothing.

'Is anybody *listening* to me? Am I the only one who can see the *gravity* of this situation? A man *shot* in town. People threatened with *guns*. Are we safe anymore? Are we?' She closed the kitchen window over the twin stainless steel sinks and reefed the cafe curtains shut against the threat of the world.

After dinner her father walked into town and drank at the Royal. Aurora, too, had begun disappearing from the house. There was not enough air left in it for all of them.

A peculiar axis of evening began: Aurora sitting and smoking with friends under the rusted rotunda in the park. Her father, only a few hundred metres away in a window seat at the Royal, sometimes alone, sometimes with a companion, looking out to the brown river whose flow they studied in silence, the current at the bend providing just enough spectacle to preclude talk. And her mother, scratching around the small house, alert to each creak of nail and joint, to the ping of raindrop on the corrugated-iron roof, the tip of a poinciana branch tapping on glass.

Theresa had spun around, as easily as flipping from her front and onto her back in her sleep. Her focus now was not looking ahead to the rituals of her daughter's expected engagement and marriage, and grandchildren, and their retirement, but back. She had stepped away from Aurora and now watched her, removed, a spectator. She surveyed each step that had brought her to latter middle-age, and judged herself, and everyone around her, and what she saw was pointless and a sequence of disappointments, each as perfectly shaped as pearls. And in that great aching cumulus of disappointment, she began to waste away.

Some nights, when she broke through the fug of her obsessions, and realised she was alone, the thoughts of her own mother slipped in beneath the front and back doors, and it made her feel colder. Aurora won't be like you, she sobbed at the shadow of her mother. She won't be. I will take *steps* to make sure she isn't. Do you *hear* me, you monster? You will never touch her.

Since Aurora's birth she had discarded everything from her past. There was nothing; no photographs, treasured porcelain figurines, rolling pins and cooking bowls, vases, dulled rings. Just her flesh and blood, crying at the kitchen table in a small louvred house behind the cane fields in the middle of the ancient caldera.

She traced the withering of herself, of her soul, to the afternoon the envelope arrived following the death of her mother in a Sydney nursing home. She had known the old woman was dying. She had spoken to a sequence of day and night nurses on the telephone. But she found she was unable to leave the house. To step out the front door. To find a way through the thick green cane fields and into the world where her mother was dying.

When the envelope arrived she took it down the yard to the edge of the river, where she sat on the bank and, after a long time, finally read its contents. She didn't want to open it inside the house. Didn't want to let any ghosts out of the envelope.

The legal documents and letters and jottings were yellowed and coming apart at the folds and were brittle to the finger yet they hit her with such force that they turned her around, shifted her focus, and on the bank of the river she could smell the foul mud of ages and decaying fish and she went to throw the papers into the water but something stopped her. She immediately felt old.

A week before her mother's death she'd had a short telephone conversation with the night nurse.

'My mother is what?'

'She's dancing,' the nurse said. 'Astrid is dancing.'

To music in her mind, the nurse said without surprise. An opera, she says. She's dancing to her favourite opera.

One night at the end of spring, with her husband and daughter still not home, she sensed the storm from several kilometres away and checked all the latches on the windows and stuck crosses of masking tape on each window pane and turned off the power at the fuse box and waited in the dark.

It swept across the cane fields, and the setts swayed madly, and the rain and fragments of hail pounded on the iron roof, and she held her hands against her ears but it grew louder and louder, and the fields thrashed in the blue lightning.

She went out onto the verandah and gripped the railing. The rain stung her face and drenched her and the flashing light worked on her like an X-ray and she was skin and bone in the face of the storm. She struggled to keep her eyes open and she looked for the great dark monolith of Mount Warning beyond the mill and the town.

You will *never* take her, she howled at the storm and the mountain. You will *never* take my daughter.

ELEVEN

FOR TWO DAYS the men of Dalgety searched the valley and along the river for Astrid Lampe.

The entire district ceased its normal functioning. The general store closed. The perennial fires of the blacksmith cooled. The hotel served no beer or meals across the counter. Sheep ready for dipping were left waiting in their paddocks. Ploughs remained embedded in fields where they had last been worked, the leather reins and harnesses dropped to the soil. The school year was terminated early. The doors to the Imperial Hall were closed, the stage still bearing beads of glass and sprays of tinsel and the hand-made mandibles and eyes of unidentified insects.

Something unseen had broken, something vital to the mechanics of Dalgety and the community, stretching right through the Monaro to the mountains and all the way to Cooma.

A little girl was missing.

And as the men searched, women came and went at Our Lady Star of the Sea on the hill behind the town, and a month's candles were burned in forty-eight hours, and faint wisps of incense gathered in sickly clouds amongst the roof beams of the old church.

Over at the Lampe property, the timber shack became a whirlpool of grief, drawing in carts and sulkies and people on foot bearing consolation and gifts. Trays of fresh fish. The elongated torsos of skinned rabbits. Potatoes. Loaves of bread. Cans of fresh water. Bundles of kindling. It was as if life for the Lampes had been temporarily emptied out, in their grief, and the community, by instinct, delivered the basic building blocks of survival.

Women filled the house with their gentle rustling and fussing, and the constant unspoken labour of cleaning, washing, polishing and ordering. They came in groups of two and three, and just as one set left, another appeared, so there was never a moment in the house when movement lapsed, when the warm air inside was not shifted by a passing skirt, or the scissor action of elbows or flash of fingers. Already clean plates were washed and rewashed. Blankets were aired. Socks and shirts mended.

The fire in the hearth was maintained at the same size and intensity, and the water boiled continuously in the black kettle, ready, as for a birth. They did everything they could, in those crucial hours, to keep out death. They swept it away, and closed the windows against it, and what few words they said were carefully chosen. Though it was out there, they knew, in the Lampe valley.

In the centre of this great silent industry was the still figure of Mrs Lampe. She sat at the edge of great loss and grieving. She knew how it went. She had been in other women's houses in similar moments, and this time alone, but not, was to give her an opportunity to meditate on her missing child. With Wilfred, she knew she'd never be in this position. She understood that from his birth. He had arrived in the world alert and diffident, the neck strength immediate, the eyes rarely blinking. He was slow and quiet and fitted like a worn key into an old clock cabinet. Wilfred was comfortable in his place. With Astrid, the opposite. She had fought at birth, tearing with her tiny shoulder, and had announced her life with a wail and eyes that didn't want to open. She sketched out her early years with noise and action, and never crawled, but sat unhappily then suddenly stood and took flight. Invisible tendrils pulled at her, drew her away at any hour of the day from hearth and home. Restrained, she bawled and frightened the sheep. So it was that Mrs Lampe sat in the busy house with her hands not clenched but gently clasped, with a degree of resignation. She had, in a way, been waiting for this for years.

The men hoped to find the girl soiled and bedraggled in the hills and paddocks surrounding the town. It was early summer, and a child could comfortably survive the overnight temperatures at that time of year.

But they did not want to think of the river, rising sporadically, swift with the snow melt, because the river meant the end of the Lampe girl, and it meant a small rough-hewn coffin courtesy of Pendergast & Sons of Cooma, and a procession to the cemetery out of town, where the sheep grazed freely amongst the headstones, and a Christmas and New Year shadowed by death.

On that first day, as the search parties scoured the hills both east and west of the town, they tried not to catch a glimpse of the Snowy River. But it intruded without warning, a silver tail of it through a fold of paddock, a diamond wink catching the eye, a V of ducks overhead, their underbellies and feet dripping with water lifted from its surface.

By dusk of the first day's search the men repaired to the rear yard of the Buckley's Crossing Hotel to be fed by Mitchell and his wife. Some made crude beds on the verandah or unfolded their swags down on the oval. They spoke of small things in small voices, in the dark. Of machinery and fences, brumby breaking and rabbit traps. Or the approaching cattle musters down into Gippsland. They continued this talk as a way of warding off the sound of the river. Or avoiding the moment when they had to put their heads down, and knew it would be the last thing they heard prior to entering sleep.

Wilfred Lampe and his father were accommodated in the gentlemen's smoking room, and both lay awake in the stale odour of forgotten cigars and gentlemen's hair oil. It was one of those rooms that was usually filled with talk, warm with tales of fish caught or lost, and the tiny adventures of men together, striking out to the fishing holes, returning in the half-light. Rooms like that, when they have no talk, are as silent as a tomb.

At about midnight they rose silently and, hand in hand, made their way down to the oval and settled with the other men of the district.

'We'll find her,' Wilfred whispered to his father.

'Go to sleep, boy.'

In the blue morning Mitchell dished out bacon and eggs, ferrying steaming plates of them from the hotel kitchen to a trestle table on the oval, and the men sat, dotted across the finely dewed grass, and ate and stared just beyond the rims of their plates.

When Cecil Freebody and his sons brought armfuls of scythes and poles and machetes from the general store to the oval near the end of breakfast at the beginning of the second day, the men rose and went quietly to the implements, and selected the one of their choice, and proceeded in ordered groups to the bridge. Nobody needed to tell them what they had to do. The Monaro was their country, and they knew its shape and temperament like they knew their wives.

In the group at the bridge were the Judges Carrington and Thorpe, distinctive in their expensive fishing clothes and galoshes, but a part of the search team.

Wilfred clung to his father.

'Stay here, son,' he said to the boy. 'It's for the best. Do as I say now.'

Wilfred stood on the dirt road between the hotel and the Imperial Hall and observed the men at the bridge.

He watched them swarming beneath the bridge pylons and noticed the awkwardness of the judges, carried along with the local men, and couldn't under-stand why the judges, who didn't know Astrid from Adam, were allowed to look for her, and not he, her very own brother.

'Me lady,' he said to himself, for no reason.

He spent the morning climbing the willows a little way upriver, roping their long green boughs and swing-ing out over the rushing water.

He was a boy happy to be alone, but as he flung him-self through the air above the Snowy, he wondered where all the other boys from the district were, and why some of them were not here, swinging with him, through the sudden mists and whirligigs of new summer insects. And he realised that with the men combing the riverbanks, they would be at their properties, in charge in the absence of their fathers and mothers during this emergency.

Emergency. He had heard that word for the first time in the last day. But was it? He knew Astrid. She was a scallywag. He had seen her often wandering the paddocks and the low hills of their valley in the early hours before sunrise, a dim white ghost in her nightdress. She was a scallywag who liked to wander. She went to check on the sheep, and the calves, and the hens. She worried about them in the dark. He never told his parents.

He wished he had the trout suit so he could set sail on the Snowy and find Astrid.

Later that day, after he had wandered through all the streets of the town, he found Mr Schweigestill sitting at his desk in the schoolhouse. The teacher wore the same undertaker's suit in which he had taken to the stage during *The Trout Opera*. His sad, scuffed top hat rested on a chair at the front of the room. He looked out the window, and Wilfred could see his eyes were red-rimmed and hugely swollen behind the thick spectacles.

'Sir?'

The long opaque fingers were knitted in front of him.

'Mr Schweigestill, sir?'

The boy took his familiar seat. He could tell by the light on the hills and the shadows at the base of the granite outcrops that it was close to mid-afternoon.

It was two nights before but it seemed years ago, *The*

Trout Opera, its colours and lights already retreating for Wilfred, sliding away behind the new daily operas of his life.

'Sir?'

The teacher still did not respond.

To Wilfred he appeared tight and coiled. An insect girding itself under threat. Only his rheumy eyes, at that point, revealed that he was human.

'They'll find her, sir,' the boy said. He, too, clasped his hands on the desk, in empathy with the teacher.

But there were far more complex pageants unfolding in Schweigestill's mind. The opera, the failure of it, he knew he could reconcile and move beyond. He had tried to present them with a soufflé, when bread would have sufficed. A chandelier too big and bright for the room.

It wasn't that. It was his shambolic, ordinary inner self he had shuffled and shooed onstage that night, his own emptiness dressed up in baubles and glitter but transparent nonetheless, affixed with weak glue and cheap string. That it ended as it did was, he saw now, *die Bestimmung*. It was destined to shatter. Because the backbone of it, the core of it – he – was brittle. I am a man of brittle stuff.

He knew, too, that this country, this place, only made his brittleness more obvious. It was the backdrop to his emptiness and fragility. What did he know of this country? He had marvelled at the sculptures of granite in the coach ride from Cooma on that first day. He had wound through them agape at their newness. But they were not new. The newness of everything had disappeared, risen from him, been burned off, the way the

145

sun burned off the mist that hovered over the river in the mornings. This was a hard country. It seared through your affectations, your accent, the ornaments of your past. It left you bare.

And where could you go here? Where could you hide, at the moment of exposure? In this valley of thousands of acres of dry stubble?

Schweigestill looked out to the boulders dotting the hills across the river. Bare souls, all of them, open to the elements. It was his inherent romanticism again, as silly, here, as a heart-shaped cushion on the moon. He pondered the little Lampe girl. She tripped and scratched her way through the briars of his troubled mind.

Deep in these thoughts, he did not see the boy. His vision had darkened around the edges, narrowed, and he looked at the hills through the schoolhouse window as if through a coin-sized aperture.

'. . . and we could go fishing, sir, if you wanted,' Wilfred said. 'I still got some Bonzas . . .'

Mr Schweigestill's eyes watered heavily with his minimal blinking.

'She ain't lost, sir,' the boy added, then corrected himself, in the cocoon of the classroom. 'Isn't lost. She'll be collectin' flowers, sir. She likes the wildflowers. She don't eat much anyway. One night she wandered halfway to Berridale. I followed her. Kids always getting lost out here, Mr Schweigestill.'

The teacher appeared to tremble. Wilfred Lampe kept talking. Perhaps it would stop the trembling.

'My father? He says she been like it since she was born. She couldn't wait to be born, he says. That young girl's in a rush, he says. She's just a little kid to me, sir. She's my little sister, you know? But she done some dumb things.

'She tries to see how long she can hold her breath? She goes a funny colour and drops to the floor, I've seen her do that lots of times. Some nights, she goes to the end of the valley and sits with Uncle Berty. He's my father's brother. He was in the war. That's the Boer War. He's been living out the back forever. That's what my mother says. Berty? He's been here forever.

'No one goes out back to see Uncle Berty 'cause that's the way he likes it. But Astrid goes out there a lot. I've seen her there at night, just sitting in his shack. He makes furniture and stuff out of the trees around the shed. There ain't many left. Trees, that is. He's made a lot of things. We got a nice dresser in the house that Uncle Berty made, with glass and everything and two diamonds in it. Not real diamonds but in the glass, you know what I mean?

'Sometimes he takes his axe out in the middle of the night. He likes to chop. 'Cause of the war, that's what my mother says. It was the war that made him like chopping. Astrid, she'll sit right down and watch him chop in the dark.

'She yells out things to him. More! when he done chopped a tree down. More! She's like that. She's a girl in a rush . . .'

Schweigestill was thinking of the men trawling the edges of the river. He could hear the suck of their boots in the muddy reeds. See them dipping their hats in the river to keep cool. Working down the river, observing things in its surface he would never understand, scouring for tracks, broken brambles, pieces of cloth on nettles. He was not a man like they were men. He could not read the elements. He and the earth had no attachment.

He was the person who had brought his strange foreign affectations to Dalgety, which had led to a little girl being lost. He embodied the blame now on behalf of the town. It was how it worked with him. It was what he had tried to get away from by travelling halfway around the world. This capacity to see himself, in good times and ill, at the centre of everything.

But nothing had changed. He was a man who still checked his silhouette, be it on the paving stones of Leopoldstrasse or the dirt thoroughfares of Dalgety.

'. . . anyway, Moses, he went missing for forty days and nights, isn't that right, sir?'

Wilfred Lampe left the schoolhouse and, as he closed the door, he heard the teacher sob. It prickled the boy's neck. He had never heard a grown man do that before, except maybe Lenny Black the brumby breaker. Wilfred knew then, before he left the schoolyard, they'd have to find another teacher before the start of next year.

He wandered up to Our Lady Star of the Sea, along the carriageway of pines, and sat on a nest of needles at a spot that looked over the town. There was the school-house, and inside poor Mr Schweigestill shaking like a lamb before crutching. There was the oval, where they would soon be playing cricket, and beyond that, across the ridge, the horse track, waiting for the Dalgety Races at the end of January, with the silks of the jockeys as fine and slippery as fish skin. To the east he could see the police station and courthouse, where Spud Baker's mother was fined by a visiting magistrate for not making him come to school enough. He could see Miners Forest. He could see the body of the river stretching back up towards Jindabyne, and his view of it from here was sometimes broken by the hills, and it was like bits of an ever-narrowing snake. He could see fold after fold of hills – his house was behind one of them – all the way to the Alps.

But within this expanse, he was the only one who knew where he had secretly hidden the surveyor's stake he'd treasured from when the politicians came to town and wanted to make Dalgety the capital of Australia. Or what Miss White sang in her bathtub at two pm every Saturday. Or what the Crank boys got up to in the granite caves across the river from Chin's vegetable gardens. He knew the best fishing holes. Fox holes. Rabbit holes. He knew Louise Emerson had received three letters from Flint O'Hagan and he knew where she kept them, because in class he sat next to Harry Emerson who had seen them with his own eyes, even if he couldn't read much of them, and one had at the bottom Flint's perfect thumbprint in blood. He knew that some nights when he came to get his father from the Buckley's he'd find Lenny Black curled up like a baby down on the oval, all full of grog and wailing for his mama, and yet the next week there he'd be at the saddler or chewing the fat at the general store, as right as rain with that big ruddy grin on his face, and he'd ruffle Wilfred's hair and say howdy do, and not know the boy had heard his cries and seen him in pissed pants. He knew Astrid collected glass and other shiny things like a magpie. He knew it was not true that Uncle Berty never talked, for he had heard him many times through the rough-hewn slats of his shed, and that he mainly talked about dead horses, horses shot through the head, the bodies of shot horses, the poor horses.

Wilfred looked down over Dalgety. It was deserted. A ghost town. He saw it without the distraction of life. Maybe this is what it'll be like when I'm old, he thought.

He would never leave the place. He was not in a rush, like Astrid. He would stay forever.

It was just after four pm when he heard the approaching herd. The faint thud of hooves came to him through the hissing of the pine needles. He stood and looked towards the sound. From near the church portico he could see a column of dust dirtying the horizon to the east.

He had seen more cattle pass through Dalgety than he could remember. But they usually came mid-morning, and took water at the river, and moved off towards the mountains by sunset. Never this late in the day.

The boy ran down from the church on the hill to the main street and waited.

It took almost two hours from when Wilfred Lampe first saw the columns of dust for the team to reach Dalgety. He could hear the hundreds and hundreds of hooves, the whip crack, whistling, and snapping of dogs, as the carnival of it hit the dogleg and entered the main street. He stood at the bottom of the hotel steps, rocking from side to side in his lace-up boots. His hands were deep in his trouser pockets. He suddenly needed to pee.

The music of the muster rolled down over the main street and bounced off palings and buildings and sheet glass as the moist-nosed cattle, their heads rocking, filed haphazardly into Dalgety. It was all overlapping bawls and thud and soft drop of cow pat and chafing hides and wet snorts, looped together by the dogs and the men's whistles and the snap of plaited leather.

Smelling the river, tongues lolling pink and long in the herd, the cattle seemed to lift their pace, and the tight column began to fray at the front and they half trotted down the grass bank by the bridge to the water. Before even a third of the herd had passed through the main street Wilfred could hear loud sucking noises along the banks of the Snowy.

At the back of the herd he saw his sister Astrid, high in a stockman's saddle.

'Blow me down,' Wilfred said, imitating his father.

As the stockman approached the hotel where Wilfred stood, she squirmed and was lowered to the road. She was filthy and her hair was tangled and flecked with burrs. There were old tear tracks on her dusty cheeks.

They stood facing each other. She was suddenly shy in front of her brother, and looked down to the ground and swivelled her small hips from one side to the other.

'Where you been, Astrid?' he asked.

And she held out to him a posy of battered wildflowers.

TWELVE

TICK'S USUAL TABLE was just inside the Bourbon and Beefsteak in front of the fibreglass statue of Marilyn Monroe.

From there, from his poop deck, he could survey the bar clientele to his left and the street population ahead and right. He could sit with Marilyn and her raised and frilled white skirt protected his back. He could study the El Alamein Fountain, a globe of spiked green water pipes. When it was not operating it looked like some giant sea mine that had found its way up the hill from the navy wharves at Woolloomooloo and become stranded.

Tick and Harold sat at an imbalanced table draped in a red and white checked plastic tablecloth outside the bar, separated from the sidewalk by a small picket fence. Tick hated the strip of tables outside, hemmed in by the fence and a low, gnarled hedge, decorated like disfigured Christmas trees with cigarette butts and dried vomit and sometimes splashes of blood.

'I'm sorry, Juliet,' Harold said. 'About the table.'

Tick seethed within reach of the pickets. He couldn't explain to Harold that the hedge disturbed him because lately it felt like he had swallowed a part of it, that its sooted limbs and deformed buds sat inside him, and he felt the fist of it scratching the tender tissue of his throat. But he was containing his anger towards his Harold, this last friend, in his grey taxi driver's shirt, as sorry as a schoolboy.

Tick sighed the sigh of a person disaffected by his age. He was convinced he had been born in the wrong era. Belonged in one far more graceful and attuned to his sensitivities. To his style. One, at least, with some sartorial standards.

It was a game of his, to study faces and slot them into their proper eras. Only this morning he had seen a delightful young boy operating a jackhammer halfway down Macleay Street. How perfectly he would have suited the trenches of Gallipoli. The natty slouch hat, hollowed cheeks and rifle. It was not difficult, too, to see the Edwardian nanny in the girl at the ice-cream and waffle emporium, her bloomers around her ankles and she being ridden, *ridden*, by the Master of the House.

Since they had again changed Tick's medication he experienced extreme surges of energy and depletion, a crazy tide he could never measure, and he would be propelled or apprehended without warning, a wind-up toy with unpredictable innards. He had lost all interest in the meal with his friend Harold and his delivery run by the time he had walked the half-kilometre from his flat to the El Alamein Fountain.

His legs heavy, he had skirted the fountain, and for a second thought back to one of his other lives, when he was not Tick, when Tick wasn't even born. The evenings here, the same spray brushing his make-up, his long,

153

curled fake eyelashes, and droplets catching the fox fur of a stole or a white kid leather glove.

Much later he realised how vulnerable he had been when he was Juliet. The mini-skirts and brief tops in autumn. His legs a constant rash of goose bumps, his lower back aching in the cold. She, Juliet, huddling out of the rain in bus shelters on William Street. She, Juliet, pressing against the luxury car showroom windows out of the winds that tore up from Rushcutters Bay, silhouetted against German and Italian roadsters and convertibles. Always vulnerable and exposed to the wind and the cold and serious damage. A damage, Tick now knew, he had wanted to bring upon Juliet, the street-walker that tore away inside him. With those perfect nails she was scratching to get out.

It was how he had met Harold. When he was Juliet, fishing for clients.

And in that early morning, in the little picketed garden area with its hideous hedge, he resented that Harold had, as he invariably did, dared mention her name in front of him, and the odd new gruel of drugs in him momentarily flared, and he wondered if he should punish his friend.

Poor, confused Harold. He wanted the woman in Tick, and could not understand where she had gone.

'Let me buy you a drink,' Harold said.

Tick adjusted the frilled cuffs of his shirt. 'Considering I didn't bring any money with me, it's a rather lame offer.'

'Are we going to have one of those nights?'

Tick chortled without looking at Harold. 'For fuck's sake, you sound like a little '50s hubby with his hat and raincoat on a hook in the *vestibule*, Harold. A petty clerk denied his conjugal rights. But it is *Wednesday*, darling. Is it *women's things*? Are we going to have one of *those* nights? Sometimes, Harold, you tell me more than I need to know about your mummy and daddy.'

Tick sniffed and adjusted his coat. He was instantly regretful. This death thing. It walked arm in arm with sentimentality. He felt the shape of the music box for his special new friend Aurora Beck in one of the pockets.

He delicately waved Harold away, again without looking at him. 'Toddle off to the bar, Harold. You reek of the taxi cabin.'

Sitting alone in the raw bulb light, he found from his street-level position that his thoughts turned not to the passers-by – the strangers whose lives he played with in his imagination, and many of his clients, the night crabs, who scuttled by more urgently than the strangers, with purpose, although Tick knew they had no purpose and nowhere to go, except perhaps a rendezvous with him, later, at an assigned time and place – but to himself, to his own past.

Suddenly he was again in Broken Hill, or Bourke, towing a 1950s caravan he had dubbed Lucy, its narrow open wardrobe a jangle of hangers and fishnets and teddies and sequined dresses.

What worked for Juliet late at night on William Street, what lured those lonely judges and television presenters and bankers and investment advisers and commercial real estate hawkers, also worked out bush in the mining towns. It was, for Juliet, a sort of annual holiday, and she and Lucy would settle on the periphery of the towns and she would seduce the miners and a few

155

of the local dignitaries and Chamber of Commerce underlings and Rotarians until word leached out, and the wives of the towns gathered, and then Juliet and Lucy moved on. It was a licence to print money for Juliet, the country.

And in the country she could acquaint herself with the lost days of pioneering, with barter and trade, and feel she was connected to her own history. Hadn't there been a great-grandfather at Gallipoli? A story of his jaw, shattered by a bullet. Later, in England, he'd been one of the first in the world to undergo the new science of plastic surgery. Dearest Grandpop.

Trade and barter. Out in the bush Juliet could get a flat tyre fixed for a blowjob, a radiator belt repaired for a handjob. One service for another. And the big road trains would pull away and signal their air horns for her and she would know that traces of her perfume would linger for hours in their truck cabins, even be carried interstate.

She could have lived this way forever. Hauling Lucy back and forth across Australia like a celebrated explorer, a Burke, Wills or Leichhardt, opening the frontier.

But the country was dying. The new generations gravitated to cities where everyone wore the same clothes and had the same mobile phones and shared cocaine and needles in the convivial way of the new standardised young and looked for excitement not on a weekend, but every five minutes.

The bright, feathery lures were the cities, and Juliet understood this. Now and again, though, she took her own little knot of colours out into the flaxen fields and bulldust, to touch what was disappearing. She did this for years, until a gaggle of incensed wives in Cobar burned down Lucy one evening, and that was the end of that.

Harold returned with two glasses of dry white wine but Tick was still out west, thinking of the boy Juliet had taken under her wing in Dubbo. The look on the boy's face when Juliet had first injected him with heroin. The Christ-like calm and innocence of that alabaster face.

He had never, until now, been able to see his role in the trajectory of these many lives. He had caught them, yes, at vulnerable moments. But his source, back then, was his own pleasure, and their pleasure, and he had merely accelerated something in them that he saw as inevitable.

With the illness, he was beginning to understand the true meaning of inevitable.

'Tick?'

They had run into each other on a street in Sydney once, Tick and the Dubbo Christ. The boy was plying the Wall. Wore a designer singlet and black tracksuit pants with white stripes down the outside leg.

Tick observed him from a distance. Watched him wait in line for coffee and a sandwich at the charity food truck under the great Moreton Bay figs in the park in front of St Vincent's Hospital. He was hard-edged now, his whole body tuned to take flight, or brace itself for danger. He was, like every other boy on the street, combustible.

Tick had been there. He knew the chafe of monstrous self-hate and the need to be gentle and sub-servient with clients. They came, wave after wave of them, in the dark interiors of their vehicles, in the toilet cubicles and cheap motel rooms, and it hollowed you out, this duty of care, when nobody had ever touched your own face with love, or desire born of love. This chafing, it started fires.

Tick had worked the Wall himself when he arrived from Melbourne as a fifteen-year-old. A runaway. His skin as yet unblemished with tattoos. Not a single burrowing tick on his pale skin. And when he became Juliet, he often cut across to Oxford Street via the Wall to see how many of his old friends were still there, this gang of lost children. The few he knew he brushed close to in his high heels and tight skirts, whispered their names, and they would look around, confused at this voice, unsure if they had heard correctly, or if it had come from inside their heads.

Then he saw the Dubbo Christ, the boy he had delivered here with a single shot of heroin, and one evening his curiosity got the better of him, and he offered Christ a cigarette sitting on a bench under one of the fig trees. The seat, he remembered, was sticky from the breath and pores of the tree. Tick wore a base-ball cap, a sweatshirt and sneakers. Juliet was far, far away.

'Why do you do this?' Tick asked, after small talk.

The Christ took long draws on the cigarette. His fingers were stained with nicotine. He was pretty. But it was the prettiness of a new knife.

'What's it to you?'

'I was interested, that's all.'

'You're like them journalists up here every six months, when some judge or celebrity gets nicked and they come up here tiptoeing around like they know what you're going through.'

'I'm not pretending to understand. I was just interested. How people get where they are, you know?'

Christ turned and looked at Tick. He stared for a few moments, a pale curlicue of smoke leaking from his nostrils, and looked back over to the sandstone blocks of the Wall.

Tick handed him another cigarette, which the boy tucked behind his ear.

'Nothing new. Bored in the country. Bored wherever I am. Came to the city and that's it.'

'How much you using?'

The boy snorted.

'Oi. You a cop?' he asked, smiling.

'Do I look like a cop?'

'You look like shit, man.' He laughed. He stamped the butt of his cigarette beneath his left sneaker, pulled the spare from behind his ear and lit it.

'Got a good dealer?'

The boy's hand trembled as he pulled the fresh cigarette from his mouth and exhaled a perfect column of white smoke.

'I am a fucking dealer, scumbag.'

Tick smiled and lit his own cigarette. He knew the Dubbo Christ was not a dealer, but a small-time delivery boy for some bigger, unknown strong-arm fresh out of Long Bay, who was beholden to an even bigger and more powerful supplier. We all have our rings of power, he thought. Rings within rings. This was one part of life that was intricately connected. The sudden idea gave him some satisfaction.

'I know where you're at, kid. I've been here before,' said Tick.

'You have, have ya? You fucking been here before. What a big cunt you are.'

He looked at Tick again and he was no longer pretty with his hatred ignited and the muscles in his face drawn against bone and his eyes so narrowed Tick could see no whites, and suddenly the Christ looked unearthly.

'How long you been HIV?' Tick asked, casually flicking ash from his cigarette.

The boy turned away and Tick could see in his profile he was just a country kid again and the tension had snapped cleanly like a tendon and all that was left after the snapping was a nauseous wave of pain and a hurried accumulation of events that mounted so quickly they were too much for the boy's face to carry and hide. The Dubbo Christ's eyes welled with tears.

'You should be looking after yourself now,' Tick said, with the tenderness of Juliet. 'Not working the street.'

'And what the fuck do you care?' the boy said. His voice shook on that narrow span bridge between being an adolescent and a man, between the need for a mother, and the need for a flick-knife in his back pocket. 'This shitty fucking world that did this to me? I'm going to give as good as I got.'

'You're happy to infect other people?'

'I'm going to fuck it over, what it did to me. Fuck it right up, man.'

'You're God now, are you, kid?'

The boy turned to Tick, cuffed his cap off with the heel of his left hand, and stood. 'Fuck you too, cocksucker,' he said, and walked away and into the rose halo of the streetlights.

'Tick?' Harold said. 'Are you hungry?'

That was years ago, and he had looked for the boy again in the shadowed edges of those pools of light by the Wall and never found him. He liked to think of him out west, getting drunk for the first time in the local pubs, sleeping in the tray of his ute with a strange girl after a Bachelors and Spinsters Ball, she running her hand through his tousled hair at dawn, his black tie and dinner jacket rolled into a pillow. Running his own property. Dressed up for the stock sales in his pale blue shirt and khaki trousers. Measuring his life by the seasons. The long measure of the seasons.

'Tick?'

And in this season of his own, where he was no longer afforded his favourite table in a saloon bar high on a hill above the harbour, this place built for resting soldiers and sailors between wars, or threats of war, with his mouth and tongue ulcerated, and his daily drugs changing in colour and shape, altering him at whim, altering his own colour and shape and how he saw the world and moved within it, one minute wanting to tear himself out of his skin, and the next listless, and quiet, and able to feel his own heart slow to almost nothing, he knew the warm, sour breath of Juliet was with him always.

He kept a lock of Juliet's hair, pressed under glass in a frame on the wall of his bathroom. It was the one thing he had left of her. And what she had put in his blood. It was Juliet in his veins now, and she had come back to kill him.

Tick adjusted his cuffs and straightened his African beads and crucifix necklace and as he felt himself

161

weaken inside, collapse, he hoped that dignity would hold him up for a while.

'Just another wine, thank you, Harold. Nothing to eat.'

His old friend went into the bar and Tick looked down the row of tables inside the picket fence, at the wide-eyed tourists and the drunken young men who had come into Kings Cross for some adventure and the hookers drinking milky cocktails before a shift.

Juliet had dined at only the best places. She liked the Bayswater Brasserie, and its little table lamps, and the oysters – Pacific, madam? Manning River? Coffin Bay? – and the fine and educated gentlemen she dined with, men of an age and confidence who ordered for her, and on inspecting a wine bottle label could tell you the soil composition of the vineyard.

One of the last of them, before Juliet disappeared, had appropriated her as a part-time wife, a fantasy that began with courtship, a pretend marriage and honeymoon, and on to compressed years of mundanity which, to Juliet, he seemed to relish the most. At their final dinner, in which he pronounced his desire for divorce, she snapped her silver cigarette case with mock indignation.

'Do you have to do that, Juliet?' he had asked.

She opened and closed it, over and over, to thrill him.

'Well, you gave it to me, darling, don't you remember?'

Who was he, this man? Tick wondered, staring across the hedge to the traffic. What was his name? This person who had taken Juliet to a boutique hotel in Darlinghurst Road and, opening the curtains, had insisted that they were in the Crillon, and wasn't springtime in Paris beautiful?

A diplomat. Was he a visiting, homesick diplomat?

Tick squeezed the music box in his jacket pocket and felt nauseous.

'Two white wines,' said Harold, placing the glasses on the table and pulling up his chair.

'I'm sorry, Harold. Next time. I'm not feeling well.'

He left Harold on the terrace and made his way with effort back to his apartment. He took the shortcut, down the alley opposite Challis Avenue and the long stone stairs into Billyard Avenue. His fur coat felt very heavy and he stopped to rest in the fingernail of park, his favourite, opposite Elizabeth Bay House.

He had decided he liked the park best at night, rather than the daytime with the nurse, because at night he could not see his own reflection.

It was the best-tended park in the area. The grass trimmed with nail scissors. The flowers large and fleshy, the goldfish pond in the centre bordered by succulent cannas. Across the oblong pond was a small stone bridge, a replica of some arched masterpiece in Scotland or Wales, built and maintained by a group of locals whose gardenless apartments overlooked the park.

Tick sat by the pond in the dark. The water hid what he knew was there – fish splotched and speckled, some with hideous growths around their eyes or out the sides of their heads. Tails like old rotted flags. But he adored them. They were Tick's fish. There's Jimmy. There's Carl. There's Harold. And look – Aurora. He came often and sprinkled little fish delicacies onto the surface of the pond, and watched them rise for the morsels, rise and fight and thrash for what Tick had to give them. They were Tick's hungry little children.

He took the music box out of his coat. He put it in his lap and opened the lid, and the tinny notes of *Swan Lake* flowed over the cold body of water and through the cannas and around the long dusted stems of the hibiscus. The box thrummed gently in his hands, and he could feel the fire that was Juliet, fanned by a sudden gust off the harbour, sucking oxygen from him, and it tore through his veins.

THIRTEEN

'AND WHAT HAVE you found out about her?' the ceremonies official asked.

'Her name's Aurora Beck. Twenty-six. Born in Murwillumbah, far northern New South Wales. Mother deceased. Suicide. Father works in the sugar mill up there, or did, for most of his adult life. She left home at seventeen – family problems, adolescent angst. Call it what you like. Then disappeared.'

'More cowpokes and hayseeds. We've got an old man from the Snowy River – what is he? A sheep farmer? – and now we've got cane cutters and the traditional troubled youth. How do you mean, disappeared?'

'They just do. There are thousands of people like her. They go off the radar. Your guess is as good as mine.'

'How'd you find out about her in the first place?'

'Classifieds. All the dailies on the eastern seaboard and retirement magazines, grey nomad and genealogy journals, nursing home pamphlets, church newsletters. Very discreet. Did anyone know of the descendants of Mr Wilfred Lampe, late of the Dalgety region, Snowy Mountains? That sort of thing. Family tree research. You'd be amazed the number of people that read that classified shit. Pore over it. A few days and a couple of letters later we find the girl's old man up north. The police gave us the rest. This country is smaller than you think.'

'Can we assume she's alive, this girl?'

'She's alive. According to police she went on a – how would you describe it – a *spree* with her boyfriend, a Wynter Craig Thomas, through western New South Wales and down to the border.'

'A spree? What do you mean, *spree*? Shopping?'

'Very funny. More serious than that, I'm afraid.'

'Who uses the word *spree* these days? What sort of spree? Drugs?'

'Correct.'

'What sort of drugs?'

'Heroin. Thomas is known to police. Armed robbery. Drug use. A substantial record.'

'How long ago was this?' asked the ceremonies official.

'Six months or so.'

'So where are they now?'

'They separated at some point. Both are missing.'

'Terrific.'

'She could be anywhere.'

'Terrific.'

'We need to get professionals onto this. They're going to have to start from scratch.'

'Yes.'

'Ask around. Pick up the trail. That sort of thing.'

'Can we secure the authority to do this?'

'That's up to you.'

'As next of kin to, what's his name, Wilbur?'

'Wilfred. Wilfred Lampe.'

'As next of kin to Mr Lampe, we'll need her, obviously. The consent, you understand. We can't involve him without formal consent.'

'I understand.'

The ceremonies official removed his spectacles and rubbed his eyes with the heels of his hands.

'This is supposed to be fun,' he said, half smiling. 'This is *entertainment*. Not Alice in fucking Wonderland. Down the fucking rabbit hole. All we needed was a pleasant old man from a nursing home, some old bloke from Restful Palms or Serenity Glade or whatever, our quiet centenarian, who turned a hundred on show day. Was it too much to ask? The human race is living longer, isn't it? Modern science? Fifties are the new forties. Seventies are the new sixties. All that shit. How many people do we have to choose from? Nineteen million? Just one ordinary Australian. A big ask? You wouldn't think so. There's letters from the Queen going out every day, turning up in letterboxes. Dear Ordinary Australian, Congratulations, blah blah blah. And what do you dingalings bring back? Some sheep farmer who doesn't want his letter from the palace, some moron country bumpkin who, at the *exact* moment we find him, not the week before mind you, not the day before, but the precise *hour* we pay him a visit, wants to buy the farm, *literally*, and is now, unbelievably, in our care, is now our responsibility, and the only family we can find, or in this case *can't* find, to clean up this unholy fucking mess is some spaced-out junkie kid on the loose with a wanted *felon*. Do I have this straight? Am I on the right track here? Am I in the right *hole*? We're tinsel and glitz, for

Christ's sake. We're the *fluff* merchants. We're not the federal fucking police.'

The ceremonies official ran a hand through his copper-dyed hair. 'This isn't happening. It was fun in LA. Even Atlanta. Do you know how hard it is to have fun in Atlanta?'

He stopped, looked up, and slapped an open palm on the table.

'We'll just put him back. Can we? Back where he came from. Why not? We'll scrub that bit from the show. Who needs it? It's only a couple of minutes. Sentimental hogwash. We've already got the horses, haven't we? At the start? The Man from Snowy River rubbish? You didn't hear that. That's confidential. Stuff it. We'll wipe it. I'll make a formal submission. Trim the fat, I'll say. How many heartstrings do you need to pull? I'll say. And the insurance. Christ. Think of the *insurance* on him if anything happens. Can we do that? Let's do that. Take him home, for Christ's sake, and none of this ever happened.'

'It's too late.'

'It's too late? What do you mean it's too late?'

'He's been formally reported missing.'

'Of course he's formally fucking missing – we've got him in a hospital stuffed with drips and wired up to monitors, haven't we?'

'To his local police.'

'And?'

'And people have started to worry.'

'So?'

'So that worry, so to speak, has entered the system. The old bird who wrote to us from Paupong. Yeah, she

168

knew the Lampes, but did we know he was *missing*. It's out there, and spreading.'

'So fucking what?'

'A pebble has been dropped in the pond.'

'What is this, fucking Philosophy 101? What do you mean a pebble has been dropped in the fucking pond?'

'We dropped the pebble. We made him go missing. That single act is having ramifications. Those ramifications are now growing every day. We arrived at a moment in a man's life when a decision had to be made. In Mr Wilfred Lampe's case it was a medical decision. These decisions are made every day, all over the world. In our case, we had an imperative that collided precisely with – call it what you will – an act of God.'

The ceremonies official was momentarily silent. 'Tell me you're joking,' he said finally.

'We did what we did. He was dying.'

'What's that got to do with it?'

'We are still human beings, in the end.'

'We're fucked in the end, that's what we are.'

'The pebble was dropped. The ramifications are widening. We are now open to things like abduction, holding a person against their will . . .'

'He was *dying*, for Christ's sake. We *saved* his life.'

'That could be argued. In court.'

'I can't believe I'm hearing this.'

'The blessing of the next of kin, however, could solve many of these problems. Which brings us back to Aurora Beck.'

'Aurora Beck,' the ceremonies official said, shaking his head, chortling. 'This isn't happening.'

'I suggest we locate Ms Beck as quietly and expediently as possible.'

'Yes,' the ceremonies official said, 'let's just do that. Give her and the killer boyfriend anything they want. Buy them a poppy farm in Afghanistan. Whatever. Jesus Christ. Use whatever resources you need. Go and be expedient.'

'All right.'

'Just find her.'

FOURTEEN

WILFRED WALKED BESIDE his grandfather through the fruit groves.

Callistus Lampe was tall and had bandy legs. His long grey beard dangled from his jaw like a weathered beehive. Wilfred often studied the beard, the way it moved in a single mass, and appeared heavy. The boy had seen things caught in it – seeds, strands of tobacco, droplets of black ink.

As they strolled side by side through the orchard they both studied the ground and held their hands behind their backs. They walked at the same pace – old man and child.

The boy waited for his grandfather to talk. He glanced at him as they entered the shadows of the fruit trees. Beyond the craggy profile and beard he caught sight of the bright globes of grapefruit and orange and mandarin. They were heavy on their branches. Insects clicked inside the dark canopies.

It was early January. The boy had ridden his pony to Berridale for his first visit in a month. He usually arrived around midday on a Saturday. Never earlier. On a Saturday morning, his grandfather was locked in his study, writing his articles for the *Australasian Bee Keeper* and the *American Bee Journal*.

'Tell me of the Christmas pageant,' Callistus Lampe said.

Wilfred described the opera, and the journey of James Arndell Youl and the trout ova, all the way from England to Melbourne to Hobart and finally up to the Snowy River. He told of the giant trout costume, the King Trout of the Monaro, and the calamity of his Queen.

His grandfather showed little facial expression, or none that Wilfred could ever see behind the hive of beard. They reached a wall of blackberry bushes at the bottom of the property. His grandfather gently touched leaves and traced an ink-stained forefinger around the berries.

Callistus Lampe was the father of blackberries on the Monaro. He had introduced them.

'Continue,' he said. 'I'm listening.'

Wilfred went on to recount the accident Astrid had suffered, and her later disappearance, and the subsequent vanishing of the school principal, Mr Schweigestill.

'Father says he cracked,' the boy said.

'Cracked, eh? Like dry earth.'

'Father says more like a nut.'

'Good gracious.'

'And that he won't get far without his clothes, 'cause he left them all behind, and his watch too.'

'Did he now?'

'It was a big crack Mr Schweigestill suffered. That's what Father says.'

Wilfred kept a careful eye out for the bees. His grand-father had had them brought over from a place called

Cyprus. They were sent through the postal service just like you'd send a letter. The Cyprus bees caused a ruckus when they got to Berridale, but then, much of what Callistus Lampe did sparked gossip and chatter. He had a heat about him, even as an old man, perhaps more so than when he was younger, and they often shook their heads at this, the Callistus in his prime, the Callistus of another time whom they had not met but could still feel, railing behind the beard and the braces and the baggy dungarees.

After the transaction of business, or simply in his silent wake, the women of Berridale shook their heads and said of Callistus's wife, and Wilfred's grandmother, Alice: 'That poor woman.'

The Cyprus bees were special bees with a shield of gold between their wings. The old man had trained them to attack, or so the boy had heard from some of his own classmates in Dalgety, for news of his grandfather had even swarmed over the sheep paddocks and into the bluestone schoolhouse, miles away. The bees protected the orchard.

Special or not, they were still bees. Wilfred imagined he could hear them, across the creek, deep in the stand of eucalypts. Or inside the voice of Callistus Lampe. They had never once stung his grandfather.

'We didn't have no bees in the opera,' Wilfred said suddenly.

'Understandable,' Callistus said.

The old man stopped at a lemon tree and examined the underside of the waxen leaves. He carefully removed a bright, fat lemon and handed it silently to the boy.

'But we did have a Queen, I suppose,' Wilfred said,

holding the globe in both hands. 'For a little while, anyway.'

They continued their walk towards the mandarins.

'Youl, you say,' Callistus said.

'Yes. J. A. Youl.'

'How peculiar. I met him once, back home.'

Wilfred had no thoughts of his grandparents' life 'back home'. He knew they had come from a place called Essex across the sea, but when he looked at them he thought of the deep roots of the fruit trees and the old beehives with their queens deep inside, and the sea, then, was not like the Snowy, sometimes flat, sometimes bubbly, but an enormous, endless silver blue sheet that was not horizontal but rose up and was a wall to 'back home'. It was not real. A bee sting was real. Not a place called Essex. Though the boy had looked into their bedroom once or twice from the hallway, and across the room was an old darkwood dresser, and on it an arrangement of silver and ivory brushes and combs and a hand mirror, and he presumed these treasures had come from 'back home', because he'd never seen anything like them anywhere else, and they looked like they didn't quite belong on the Monaro.

They were like some of the saddles and strange riding trousers and boots that Mr Crank showed up in, in town sometimes, which caused the men at the Buckley's to whisper and sometimes laugh. Once, waiting to bring his father home, Wilfred had stood with two other boys in the stable out the back, and studied one of Crank's special saddles from 'back home', and been entranced by the warm flame in the leather.

But Wilfred couldn't see his grandparents 'back

home', because he didn't know what it looked like. He had only known them here, and they were a part of Berridale with their front gate an archway of white roses and their fifty-one acres of fruit trees and shrubs and natives, and the shed at the back of the house out of which his grandfather ran the Monaro Seed and Plant Nursery, and the Singer sewing machine on the two-horse cart kept at the side of the shed which serviced the area three days a week, the horses Doug and Dale plodding their way through paddocks and the shadows of boulders and herds of sheep to the steaming tea and warm damper of welcoming farmhouses.

While Alice mended breeches, made curtains, and summoned fine dresses for the races or the Peach Blossom Ball out of bolts of cloth, Callistus wandered the paddocks, studying soils and frilled algae in the dams, or quietly sucked on his pipe while sizing up various pieces of farm machinery, his thoughts moving through the apparatus, reworking the individual components towards something more efficient.

'Mr Youl's head,' Callistus said, 'was like a perfectly polished duck egg.'

The boy walked silently, feeling the pitted skin of the lemon.

'I had been invited to the room of the Australia Association, in Northumberland Place.'

The old man stroked his beard as he spoke, gently tugging the whiskers, as if to extract the recollections.

He continued. 'I had begun thinking of emigration and had some queries. I was most interested in the flora, you see. What it was possible to grow. I had had these thoughts for some time. Could I take an English oak and

175

graft it to foreign soil? Is this uninteresting, Wilfred?'

'No, sir.' The boy was familiar with the situation. They would walk until the story was done. This one, he could feel, would take them beyond the orchard and the nursery, and way into the grazing paddocks.

'It was Darwin, you see. *On the Origin of Species*. It got a tremendous number of men rather overexcited. Your Mr Youl was one of them.'

Wilfred was certain he could hear the bees. He kept alert.

'You are correct in a rudimentary fashion. Youl had a vision to bring salmon to Australia. The trout, goodness gracious, were a comical afterthought. They would have had Mr Youl committed, you see, if it hadn't been for Darwin. The thought of shipping fish eggs across the world, let alone hatching them at the other end, would have been a sign of madness. But Darwin. It wasn't just what he had proposed, as crazy as that may have been in itself. He had opened a door to another way of looking at things. How they rushed for that door. They fell over themselves trying to get through it. Such was our Mr Youl.

'We met before a large fire at the Association. I quizzed him on soils and weather conditions and, as a farmer first and foremost, he was particularly knowledgeable. Most helpful.

'He had yet to make his famous journey. The one your Mr Schweigestill found fit to be the centrepiece to his opera. So many failed attempts. And then the breakthrough. In Paris.'

They had reached the grazing paddocks, separated from the orchard and nursery by a low wall of neatly placed river rocks. It was the only stone fence on the Monaro and stretched up and over a low rise.

Callistus and Alice could see it from the back verandah of the main house, a rope of stone that wound and wavered over mustard stubble, above the dense and dark green foliage of the orchard. They often sat there for hours and looked to the wall.

'Youl had, he told me, dined with some fellow enthusiasts in Paris,' his grandfather continued. 'And it was suggested to him, there, how he could transport his ova to the southern hemisphere. The use of charcoal, I recall, and moss, and chilled water.

'It excited him wholeheartedly.'

They stopped at the first rise. Callistus clawed at his large breeches and lowered himself slowly onto a boulder beside a thread of sheep track. The boy imitated him.

'Hmmph,' he grunted, amused by his memories, his entire upper body shifting with the effort of the mirth which had come to him from almost half a century ago.

They studied the quilt of orchard from the boulders. Even at that distance, and in the almost phosphorescent light of high summer, they could see lemons and mandarins in the foliage, and the blooms in the nursery were like soft and coloured stuffing from a torn mattress.

The old man saw the tall, thin poplars that lined the main road into Berridale sway in unison, and he remembered his first sight of Sydney as their ship inched into the harbour, and the huge and splendid view of the Garden Palace that rose like a mirage from the strange trees.

He had been told of the International Exhibition at

177

the Garden Palace during their journey, but nothing prepared him for this show of opulence, and he felt, staring at the building as they approached the quay, that they had left an old, decaying civilisation and arrived at the birth of a new one.

Callistus did not know, then, that the palace had been built in the grounds of the Botanic Gardens, where he hoped to have some fruitful discussions with the director, Charles Moore, about acclimatisation.

On his second day in Sydney he had gone to see Mr Moore, but was drawn into the exhibition, and spent hours wandering through the countries of the world, peering into display cabinets from Rome to Japan.

It had all set a fire beneath him, and he had landed in Berridale with the work and words of Charles Moore in his mind. He would create his own botanic gardens. Make new discoveries. Grow things on this hard, baked plate of a continent that nobody thought possible.

The orchard and the homestead came into focus for him again. To the west of the worked land was a narrow rectangular strip of flinty soil that was Callistus Lampe's 'experimental earth', the horticultural laboratory where he perfected his irrigation methods, and insect control. Here, too, he tested whether new species would graft. He took prodigious notes, the writings in and around drawings of root systems and stems and shoots, the words as small and busy as aphids.

He was not as far away in mind and ambition as J. A. Youl.

Wilfred wriggled his toes inside his lace-up boots. Only since Christmas had his boots begun to feel tight and uncomfortable.

'Your Mr Youl,' his grandfather continued, 'could see the glint of a knighthood in all that charcoal and moss. I can see him now, rocking on the balls of his feet in front of that open fire.

' "What of the soils of New South Wales, Mr Youl? What is the state of honey production?"

'But he was gone, you see. Lost. Back in that restaurant in Paris on that evening which was to become, well, historic. The ordinary men who blunder into history's pages, Wilfred. So very ordinary.'

Callistus produced a handkerchief and blew loudly, then futtered for a long time into the soiled cloth. The action seemed to draw up another clear picture from the past.

'He said there was a great trough of shaved ice outside the restaurant that night,' he added. 'Oysters. Lobster. And three rows of trout, side by side. He said they were arranged like notes of sheet music.'

The old man shook his head slightly then stared into the mid-distance.

'It was a very strange thing for a Tasmanian farmer to say. Yet I have never forgotten it. See? Art can spring from the most unlikely sources. Hmmph. A poet with fishy hands, Wilfred. And his knighthood came to pass.'

He ended the story musically like the conclusion of a fairytale, his voice higher, lighter. And it was over, with their buttocks resting against warm boulders.

'Come,' Callistus said, slapping his knees. 'Time for tea.'

As they made their way down the sheep track Wilfred noticed in the distance a caravan of several horses and carts with a tail of men inching along the yellow road

179

that led through Berridale. Dust lifted and smudged the poplars.

'Grandfather,' he said, pointing.

The old man looked up.

'So they're here at last,' he said. He had only glanced at the visitors.

'Who?'

'The Premier's axemen.' He spat unexpectedly into the clover and old sheep dags.

At the house they sat in wicker chairs on the front verandah, bathed in the perfume of roses from the gable. It was the only time Wilfred ever had tea, and when he sipped his, cooled prior by his grandmother, he believed he was drinking roses and they tasted white, if white was a taste, on his small tongue.

Grandmother Alice brought out a plate of warm scones and touched the boy's shoulder before disappearing inside the house. She had always looked old, even in the photographs of herself in Essex, and kept to the cool shadows of the house and the canopy of the Singer wagon. Her transplanting from Essex to the Monaro had been, Wilfred's father said, 'not a happy one'. Her years of discomfort had not been assuaged by liberal quantities of Seigel's Syrup and the 'women's friend', Madame Kurtz Pills.

The source of her fear, it transpired, was the sunlight. She complained repeatedly of its inescapability in Australia, how it glanced off every surface. As if the entire continent was a prism. How it came at her, attacked her, off water and rocks, off leaves and grass. From late August through to the middle of April she felt besieged, and became known in the district for her peculiar habit of wearing a widow's veil on her rounds with the Singer.

Callistus, in turn, made notes of his wife's condition and potential solutions to her light sensitivity, and had discovered several similarities with assorted plants and flowers of his acquaintance in the northern hemisphere. He wrote, in smaller handwriting than the rest of his journal, that his wife's face, neck and hands had seemingly suffered a premature ageing whilst the rest of her person, pale and concealed, had escaped such ravaging. An article he had published in the *Monaro Mercury* on the skin conditions of immigrants had caused some unseemly gossip.

Wilfred took a scone, and asked of the axemen.

'The fool Carruthers,' Callistus said, sucking the name through his whiskers. 'Our idiot Premier. Only at the pulpit because men better than he joined the gold rush for federal representation.'

Wilfred comprehended nothing. He rarely did on his Saturday visits. But Callistus Lampe chose to unload a week's raft of ideas on the boy each time they sat together, or walked the hills, and Wilfred could only presume that he was still bubbling from his morning's writing for the bee journals, and that the writing of bees triggered something within him, a ferment, a stirring of the hive, and that it could not be contained by a single afternoon, just as an attempt to dam the Snowy River would be impossible, and the effluvia washed over and kept running, and it was into this that Wilfred stepped.

'He was here just a few weeks ago with his Minister for Lands,' Callistus continued, turning the teacup in his hands. 'Sniffing around Kosciusko, our mountain, as if it were born inside him. How many have followed the same path of self-importance. Leaders, attaching themselves to oceans, and mountains. Our Carruthers is no different.

'The axemen, Wilfred. Here to cut a road from Jindabyne to the mountain itself. There'll be another gang tomorrow. And the day after. Out from Cooma. Carruthers' battalions. Come to open up the country. How they love that phrase. To open up.'

He had written a letter of protest to the *Mercury* in Cooma, and it had not been published. He wrote another. And another. Nothing. Then, at the offices of the *Mercury*, he had caused 'a scene' and been shown the door. They would get no further articles or correspondence from Callistus Lampe.

'This country,' he went on, to himself. 'So vast, and with so many different climates. Is it why no cohesive thought can take root? People close together, Wilfred, they can almost think as one. Why? Because they can feel the same things, together – injustice, hunger, death. One thing affects all. Together they can take measures. But here? Thought can't come together. It's jolted off the cart with these endless distances. There is no hope of collective thinking.'

He dangled the empty teacup off his right forefinger.

'This. Carruthers. It is not a road to the future, Wilfred,' he said, writing in his head an article that would never be published. 'It is a road to disaster.'

Wilfred thought he might like to see the road builders. He remembered from school the road builders of Rome and Mr Schweigestill's talk of other roads as wide as a paddock and all the busy and important things that happened on roads, and he thought he might like to see how you make a road.

His bladder tingled with excitement at the thought of his first cattle muster in ten days' time, with his father through the Alps and down into Victoria, and it struck him that he might see the road builders along the way.

'Father said we're going to Gippsland with a mob,' Wilfred said.

But Callistus had closed his eyes tight, and deep wrinkles fanned down into his whiskers, and his right fist was clenched on his thigh, the teacup rocking, its mouth cast down to the rough verandah boards.

After a long while the old man said, 'The affairs of men.'

Wilfred, sitting and watching the nodding heads of roses in the front garden, could not have known his grandfather was forming tomorrow's sermon, extracting the pain of it from himself there, before the cold scones, on the verandah. Sermons he gave each Sunday, in the homestead dining room, not as a formal man of the cloth, but as a small voice for God, in a house shuttered from the sun, in a tiny settlement in a vast continent. He was a man with faith and opinions and a voice, in a place where the gusts that came down from the mountains took your words away, or didn't. Where opinions were cause for suspicion. Where they fell on barren soil.

Callistus Lampe, though, was an old oak here, strong of trunk and branch, steady and sturdy season after season in a place that should not have supported an oak. He would continue his sermons, even if he delivered them to no one.

Callistus had forgotten about the boy, swinging his tight boots on the edge of a wicker chair.

'How is your father?' he said suddenly.

'Father says we're taking a mob to Victoria.'

'Does he?'

'Yes, sir. Father says it's time the boy learned something about the mob. That's me who's learning. The boy.'

'Yes.'

'Mr Crank, the boss, he wants that mob taken to Gippsland by the end of the month, next month that is, and Father says it's time I did some learning.'

The old man played with his whiskers. Wilfred was wiggling his legs more excitedly with talk of the mob.

The boy continued. 'I wanted to do some more fishing before school starts. But the learning is the thing to do, Father says. I like fishing. One day I want to fish all the way along the river. Up to the top, where it starts.'

The grandfather smiled but it was so slight behind the veil of whiskers that only his wife would have detected it.

'I would like to do that myself,' Callistus said.

'You would? We could do it one day, Grandfather, together.'

The old man was silent.

'To the source. Yes, Wilfred. We'll do that one day.'

And he closed his eyes again. He closed his eyes for a long while. He could hear the Cyprus bees down in the stand of eucalypts, a low hum at first, and then the full thrum of angry swarms, hovering, swirling galaxies of them alert to some as yet undetectable danger.

When Callistus woke, the boy was gone, except for the tiny frilled indent of his teeth in the side of a scone.

FIFTEEN

IN THE EARLY morning, when Aurora Beck could not sleep, she listened to the sad comforting monotony of talkback on her small transistor radio.

She had found the radio in the glove compartment of the car when she sold it on Parramatta Road after she fled Wynter. He had stolen it from his father the last time they visited the caravan park in Kiama – it was the old man's fishing radio, the dial ingrained with slime and blood spots – and as they wandered aimlessly through western New South Wales, Wynter became fanatical about tuning in to news bulletins on local stations. He searched for news of himself, modern bushranger, squeezed through the pinprick speaker perforations, and giggled at mention of the fires he left in their wake.

Aurora had missed her rendezvous with Tick. She waited for the filtered bushfire light to disappear, and when the sun set she was left with the smell, and it was this, her changing relationship with her dealer – his odd affection towards her; was it a trap, a sophisticated big city ploy she'd never encountered? – and the omnipresent threat of Wynter that kept her in her room.

She telephoned Tick but his mobile was switched off. Later, she opened the door to the apartment and found a small music box. Inside her flat, the deadlocks bolted, she opened it and smiled at the partially naked ballerina dancing to *Swan Lake*. The ballerina pirouetted around two clip-seal sachets of cocaine.

She saved the drugs and sat in the lounge room in the dark and rested the radio on a packing case.

With the curtains open, in the dark, she stared at the small red pinpoint of light on the console of the radio. She liked to watch the world through the windows when she listened to the voices. The distant streetlights twinkling through the shift of the tree foliage. The tail-lights of traffic on New South Head Road.

'. . . and nobody did anything,' a man said. 'They just walked straight past like nothing was happening, you know? That's the sort of society we—'

'Including you,' the host interrupted.

'Pardon?'

'Including you. You also walked past and did nothing.'

'It was four blokes on this one bloke, in broad daylight.'

'But you didn't intervene, Frank. You observed this but didn't feel you could do anything to help the victim.'

'I . . . well, I didn't think there was anything I could do, they could have had knives, or a gun, you know? Knives and guns today. You got schoolkids carrying them, you know what I mean?'

'Unfortunately I do.'

'Kids murdering for a mobile phone. You know?'

'I do.'

'Something's gotta be done.'

'You're right, Frank. Something has got to be done.'

'I keep a baseball bat in the truck. For me own personal safety, like, but I've never had to use it, you know, touch wood . . .'

'Thank you Frank. Touch wood indeed. If only your humble servant had a dollar for every time he'd heard that phrase. Touch wood. Some of us have handy resources, like Frank. Frank, touch your head, you lucky son of a gun. But what will happen to that phrase when the world runs out of wood? Thought of that, have you? What will our unborn generations be touching for luck? I've never had to use it, you know, touch titanium. Doesn't have the same ring to it, does it? Next we have Deirdre on the line. Go ahead, Deirdre . . .'

'Hello?'

'Yes. Deirdre, go ahead.'

'Hello?'

'You're on the air, Deirdre.'

'Oh, hello . . . yes. Let me say I love your show . . .'

'Thank you. You're the one who listens to it.'

'Oh, I do, yes. Since my husband passed away I . . . it . . .'

'I understand.'

'. . . gives me comfort, when I can't sleep.'

'Of course. What would you like to talk about, Deirdre?'

'Well, I was at the Olympics in Melbourne in 1956 . . .'

'Is that right?'

'Oh yes. It was marvellous. John and I decided it was a once in a . . . in a . . .'

'An experience.'

'That's right, yes. So down we went to Melbourne and we had a wonderful time . . .'

'Hmm. We don't hear that too often, do we, folks?'

'. . . wonderful time. But it wasn't as big then, do you understand my meaning? Not as . . . I don't know how to say it . . .'

'. . . as commercial.'

'Well, yes . . . not as commercial . . . but everything was not in . . . such a *rush*. It's all such a rush now, and so big and . . . I mean, I remember when Homebush was an abattoir – an *abattoir* – and now . . .'

'Progress, unfortunately, Deirdre. They call it progress. No abattoir is safe in these modern times.'

'That's *right*! I mean . . .'

'This is our opportunity to show who we are to the world, Deirdre. A sports carnival. The biggest school sports day on earth. No abattoirs here, Deirdre. No homeless people on the streets of Sydney. Truck 'em out. Put a hose through Redfern. But let's make sure we relocate that colony of frogs out at dear Homebush. Heaven forbid we render the Homebush frogs homeless. Homeless at Homebush. At least we have clean streets with pretty flowers. I feel for the florists of Sydney, I really do. Bouquets all over town, for *free*, mind. Is there a florists' union? I'd be onto the union. It's a disgrace. There must be legislation. Homeless frogs, free daffodils. The city's been turned *upside down* . . .'

'. . . the flowers, yes. John loved . . . loved daffodils . . .'

'Thank you, Deirdre, always good to talk to you . . . We have another caller . . .'

The host. His name was Graham Featherstone. He called himself the Friend of the Sleepless.

'Featherstone, friend of the sleepless, go ahead caller,' he said.

People telephoned him to speak about anything and everything. Their love lives, or absence of love, dogs with depression, the state of the nation, the reduced amount of ink in ballpoint pens, death, the weather, the lifespans of light bulbs, the Prime Minister, the disappearance of Christmas beetles, money, violence, depression, football, service in restaurants, sleeplessness.

He talked to shift workers, truck and taxi drivers, the bereaved, the drunk and drugged, the insomniacs, the maniacs, the old and the addled. In the night hours he was their company, their only friend, someone they could count on being awake and ready to listen.

Aurora liked the night talking. It was a different language to that spoken during the day. It was like listening to voices in your head.

'If it isn't my old friend William. How could we pass the early morning without a call from you?'

'Hello, Mr Featherstone.'

'How have you been, William? The last time we spoke you had moved out of the hospital and into your own flat. How are you settling in, William?'

'I'm fine, sir.'

'Got the bachelor pad all set up?'

'I don't know what that is, sir, they said there was no room in the hospital for people like me, sir, and I got this flat where I have a refrigerator and a bed.'

'That sounds very nice, William.'

'Yes, sir, and during the day I get the train into the town where I sit and watch people in the mall.'

'You like to sit and watch people in the mall, don't you, William?'

'Yes, sir. And when I'm at home I like to draw pictures at the kitchen table.'

'Draw pictures, that's right.'

'That's right, sir. And today two ladies knocked on my door.'

'Did they? And who were they?'

'They was two ladies from the Salvation Army come to see if I was happy, sir.'

'Did you make them a cup of tea, William?'

'I don't have a teapot, sir. But I asked them in and then they ran away.'

'And why was that, William?'

'I pulled down my trousers, sir.'

Voices in your head. Thousands of them, scudding across the city and up and down the coast and over the Blue Mountains and out west. Like the voices of her parents in their bedroom next to hers, in the wooden house in Murwillumbah, where the cane fires threw shadows across her ceiling, and the shadow play sometimes worked in tandem with her mother's sobbing, or the long discussions she had with herself in her room at night, waiting for her husband to return from the mill.

When Aurora was a girl, the voice of her mother through the tongue-and-groove timber sent her off to sleep. As a teenager, it kept her awake. Her mother was wasting away, only in her late fifties, and the wasting sharpened her voice like a knife.

She would hear her mother foraging through

drawers in the middle of the night. Could hear the shift of floorboards as she moved about the house in the dark. Dalgety, she said over and over.

Aurora's father had taken to sleeping on a camping stretcher on the front verandah. The more his wife spoke to herself, the less he had to say. She was filling the house with a strange language that came from somewhere else, and was bringing the words, fresh and peculiar, into their lives.

Crankcrankcrank, she mumbled. It was crankcrankcrank.

Shortly before Aurora left home she had returned one night from the rotunda in the park to the dark house. She walked quietly up the back stairs and eased the latch shut, a velvet click, and heading to her bedroom heard a voice speak her name from the lounge room. Aurora went into the room. She could see the outline of her mother's head against the lace curtains of the front window, the patterns in the old dusted lace etched by the streetlight.

'You are her,' her mother said.

'What?'

'You are her. There is nothing I can do. I *realise* that now. Her. Herherher.'

'What are you talking about?'

'I smell smoke.'

'They're burning the fields.'

'Sit down.'

'I'm going to bed.'

'My mother's dead.'

'What?'

'My *mother*. Is *dead*.'

'Grandma Gladys?'

'Astrid.'

'Astrid? Who's Astrid? What are you talking about?'

'Astrid was dancing.'

'As usual, I don't know what you're talking about.'

'You met her once, do you remember?'

'Grandma?'

'We took a trip. To Sydney. Then we drove her out to Dalgety.'

'I'll get you a glass of water.'

'Sit down.'

Aurora sat on the edge of the couch opposite her mother.

'Dalgety. Where it all started. This long dark walk of ours.'

Everything was beginning to scare Aurora. She had seen her father still drinking through the window of the Royal on her way home. Should she get him? Or call the doctor? The weary doctor, losing patience with each visit.

'Astrid was dancing.'

'I think you should lie down, Mum.'

'Astrid was dancing before she died. How she loved to dance, apparently. She'll take you. I've waited for this. She didn't get *me*, but even in death she'll take you. I can feel it.'

'Take me where?'

'Astrid went missing, you see. Long time ago. From Dalgety. Dalgety. Went missing from Dalgety when she was just a girl. Astrid went missing and never saw her family again. Started the long dark walk.'

'I'm getting Dad.' She rose and went into the kitchen

to the phone. She turned on the fluorescent light, and saw the number for the Royal sticky-taped on the wall.

'Long dark walk. To here. The black line. Black line of the family, all the way from Dalgety. To here. Black line, black line . . .'

Aurora held the phone receiver but didn't dial. She listened to the voice in the other room. Like a voice in the back of her head.

'Astrid had to dance. She couldn't help it. Danced away from everything, from her family. Danced from me and my father and kept dancing. Danced into other people's lives and twirled them around and danced away from them. Now she's got you, too, Aurora. Dancing with my Aurora. What can I do? What can I do? Tell me what I can *do*.'

Aurora sat at the kitchen table and listened.

'Poor brother. Poor Astrid's brother. To Sydney on the train, he did. To the morgue. Is this your sister Astrid? Do you think this is her? She'd been gone so long. Anybody not identified for years, decades, is this your sister? No. Not her. Nonono. Astrid's out there somewhere, dancing. The Crank boy. Dalgety Cranks. The sheep kings. That was him. Away she ran. Ashamed. Astrid ashamed. Just your age, Aurora, your age, pregnant to a Crank. Did the music in her start before then? Must have started. Never stopped. Just like you, Aurora . . .'

Aurora put her hands to her ears. She was fed up. First the strange looks from people she'd known all her life in town. Then the visits from the police. And finally the hallucinations. The gunmen hiding in the fields. Mental institution officials disguised as postmen and water

193

meter readers and junk mail deliverers, preparing to take her away. Now the phantom dancer, Astrid. And the name, so similar to Aurora's. She was confused and drained by the madness.

'Big long dance. In a dark room. Dead now. But I can still hear the music, oh yes, hear it now in the dark empty room still playing away, echo, echoed, echoing . . .'

Aurora started to cry. She found it difficult to breathe, and didn't know if it was the aftereffects of the speed she had taken in the rotunda, or the cigarettes, or the ash in the air over Murwillumbah and Mount Warning, the ash fall in the heart of the great volcano's caldera, the opposite of snow, the other, darker face of snow here at the end of the earth.

'That you, Gavin?' she heard her mother say. 'That you? Gavin? That you?'

The kitchen had gone very cold and Aurora shook and then in an instant it was furnace hot. She stood and turned off the light and crept down the hall to her room.

'That you?'

She lay on her stomach on the bed and put the pillow over her head and tried to escape the hot and cold of the house by thinking of her afternoon with Travis up on the mountain.

They had entered the speckled shade of the base of Mount Warning and started the walk to the summit, through the sclerophyll forest, the grand Bangalow palms stilted through the foliage like foundation stumps, the mountain's footings. The floor of the rainforest was a rustic carpet of leaves and curls of bark and palm fronds, and through it rummaged the bush turkeys, their bruise–blue undercarriages dusted with the muck of their raking, their ceaseless scavenging for their giant nests of mulch.

They were silenced by the rainforest, by the freakish acoustics of it, and only a few hundred metres into their walk, hand in hand, they could hear each other breathing.

Half a kilometre up they stopped and looked at each other, and turned back down silently, as if the summit held some truth about themselves that they did not wish to face, or were too young to understand. Instead, they returned to the car park at the beginning of the trail and took a side path.

They crossed a creek and saw the boulders as big as houses and cars strewn upstream. Here, under the canopy, the tear of turkey claws seemed as loud as 'dozers. The giggle of a child dropped down out of the trees. There were murmurs from down the creek. They were alone on the trail.

Within ten minutes they stood on a wooden lookout platform, high above the creek and the boulders and the turkey nests, surrounded by the pale trunks of the Bangalow palms, as if in another, rarer atmosphere, and they felt simultaneously the exhilaration of height and the pinch of insignificance.

They held each other and kissed in the way of teenagers, their mouths wet and clumsy as if rehearsing for a greater pleasure.

It was late afternoon and the car park had emptied and they sat and smoked a joint in their roost. The forest became dark very quickly and under the cloak of it they felt each other and kissed some more and tasted the burnt marijuana heads on each other's tongues.

'The gear's gas,' said Travis.

Aurora laughed out loud. The whip crack of the laugh echoed through the trees.

'I'm gassed,' he continued. 'You're gas.'

She roared again.

When the echo fell to the thick leafy floor, to the skeletons of dead palm fronds that, in the fading light, looked to them like dinosaur bones scattered all around them, they both froze.

'Did you hear something?' Aurora whispered.

'Yeah.'

'What was it?'

'Dunno.'

Aurora giggled and he put his hand over her mouth. A few moments later, down below the lookout perch, they heard someone else giggling.

'Oi,' Travis said, to himself. 'It's underneath.'

'What?'

'Someone's underneath. Oi!'

They got on their stomachs and peered down through the slatted timber.

'Oi,' someone said.

They looked into the mulch and bones.

'Hello?' Aurora asked.

They waited. They heard, then, a feeble, 'Lo.'

'What the fuck?' Travis said.

'Uck.'

They saw nothing in the gloom. The plane of the sun's rays was tilting quickly now.

'Let's get out of here,' he said.

They moved quietly down the path, stumbling on rocks and exposed roots, glancing back at the lookout for the source of the voice.

'Fucking weird, man,' Travis said, holding Aurora's hand, trying to steer her through the dark. 'You think they saw what we were up to back there?'

'Ghost,' she said. 'The turkey spirit, wounded by a warrior's spear. That's why they can't fly. Whoooo.'

'Shut up, will ya?'

'Whoo hooo.' She laughed.

They heard a voice again. This time in front of them. 'Whooo,' it said.

'It's those fucking drongos from school. Come out, you bastards!' Travis shouted.

They were close to the car park entrance when Aurora stopped, broke away from Travis's hand, and crouched by the path.

'What?' he said.

'Whaa.'

She pointed a few metres off the track. He squatted and followed the direction of her pointed finger.

It was an Albert lyrebird that had strayed from the thicker undergrowth, and was trying, in vain, to hide behind the shoot of a young fern half its size.

'Fuck me.'

'Kmee,' the bird said.

'Imitators,' Aurora said quietly.

It was replicating them in its fright. With no place to hide.

'That's gas,' Travis whispered.

'Ssss.'

She rose and pulled Travis away. He kept staring back

at the bird even when he could no longer see it in the gloom, and they stumbled to the car park like children.

❧

'That you? Gavin? That you?' Aurora's mother asked, alone in the dark.

Aurora lay with the pillow over her head. She did not know, even then, that in less than a week she would be walking to school, down Cane Road, on a morning thick with flurries of ash, and instead of taking the right turn past the park to the back of the school ovals, she would cross the bridge just past the Royal, and take the short walk up to the Pacific Highway, and to the railway station. That she would be on board that train she saw from the top of the mountain, that meandering trail of quicksilver through the cane fields, heading south.

❧

'Welcome back, night owls,' said Graham Featherstone. 'If you've just joined us, I have Jacob on the line, and we're discussing ways and means of death. It is Jacob's conjecture that many suicides, for example, are committed by methods related to the employment of the victim. Namely, that you are likely to kill yourself in a manner befitting your work and experience. How Jacob knows this I have no idea . . .'

'A friend of my mother was a cleaner. She topped herself by drinking floor polish.'

Aurora heard another voice in the darkness. Two voices. An argument downstairs, outside the block of flats.

She turned off the radio and crept to the balcony and looked over. Waterbirds were crying over in the bay.

She couldn't see anyone in the fuzzy white light from the downstairs car park, but she heard voices. A shout drifted up to her. Bounced off the wall of the neighbouring apartment block. Came to her clearly. Her stomach clenched and she felt a trace of bile burn the back of her throat.

She ran into the bedroom, banging her arm on the old octagonal brass doorknob. She felt like vomiting. She reached down between the bed base and the mattress and pulled out the gun.

Shaking, she rushed into the bathroom, and squeezed herself down between the bath and the sink. She sat on the cold tiles in the dark and lifted the gun and aimed it out through the open bathroom door to the front door.

The gun trembled, and she held her breath. It was Wynter. He had found her.

SIXTEEN

THE RADIO HOST Graham Featherstone had been in the middle of his first holiday in eleven years – a short driving tour of Tasmania – when the Port Arthur gunman struck on that quiet autumn Sunday in April 1996.

Featherstone never took vacations because he feared he'd be replaced by the time he got back. It was a running joke in the media. Everybody was expendable. But it was more true for Featherstone, because his had been a career that began unspectacularly, though solidly, and continued on thinning ice. It had never approached the heights he had hoped for. Once driven by an invincible belief in his own talents, now he worked at shoring up and defending.

So he had booked a fortnight in Tasmania with his long-standing fiancée, Victoria, and the day before they were due to fly out she had found an excuse not to come, and he had journeyed on alone. He was disappointed but unsurprised at Victoria's absence, because he'd become used to her doing her own thing in the past couple of years – the sudden weekends away with girlfriends, the dinner cancellations, the staying out all night – and, as she told him, people needed their own space. When he was dumped onto the midnight to dawn shift he was worried about telling her. She had met him at a promotional function for the radio station when he was a new and unknown quantity, perhaps the next celebrity shock jock, his generation's million-dollar voice, but the crown had never come. Instead, he did as he was told, filled in for others, performed chores well beneath his age and experience. He eventually told Victoria of the graveyard roster, and she unexpectedly told him she was happy and saw nothing but positives in the move. They would, she said, finally appreciate his talents.

He took the fortnight off before starting in his new position.

Driving out of Hobart on that Sunday in April he heard on the car radio the breaking news of the massacre at Port Arthur. It took more than half an hour for him to understand that this might be the opportunity of a lifetime. He was at last one of those reporters who had found themselves in the right place at the right time. An instinct from his youth returned. Graham Featherstone would be one of the first journalists on the scene of this terrible tragedy, and as he sped towards the drama he was already rehearsing his reports, and awards and congratulations hovered at the edge of his thoughts. This guy Featherstone, he heard them say, why have you got him spinning discs in a dead air slot?

He got lost out of Hobart and was halfway to Orford in the north-east before he realised his mistake and turned round. Once on the Tasman Peninsula he accidentally found himself near Whale Beach before a local gave him directions back to Port Arthur. He'd tried to phone the station to tell them his plans and work out how he would get his reports back to Sydney, but he kept dropping in and out of mobile range.

The station's top reporters were already en route to Port Arthur when Featherstone arrived at the scene. He parked outside the gates to the historic site and waited in the car, trying to formulate a plan of operation. He had no idea what to do. He had no notebooks and pens and no recording devices.

He booked into the nearest motel. He needed time to formulate a strategy.

He phoned the station again. 'I'm here,' Featherstone told them. 'You're where?' the chief-of-staff asked. 'In Port Arthur.' It was suggested he track down the station's two journalists when they arrived later that day and give them a hand if needed. He'd never met either of them.

On the first night in the motel, unable to sleep, he went outside for a cigarette, then wandered down into the historic site. A cold breeze pushed across the bay from the Isle of the Dead. He saw a cordon of police officers and rescue workers, each of them only an arm's length apart, surrounding the Broad Arrow Cafe. It was like a strange, pagan ritual in the middle of the night.

Featherstone stood outside the ring, staring in at the blocks of light. Men in full body suits and masks passed across the window- and doorframes. It was silent, except for the intermittent howl of the Tasmanian devils in the bush on the edge of the light. He asked later, when he thought it was a dream, why the officers had stood shoulder to shoulder around the cafe, and was told it was to keep the devils away from the bodies.

He went back to his motel room and lay awake, staring at the stucco ceiling. By morning, the victims' bodies had been removed from the cafe.

He finally identified the two journalists from his station. They told him they'd give him a shout if they needed anything.

Featherstone walked and walked the site, trying to piece together the gunman's movements. He stood over pools of congealed blood on the concrete outside the service station near the entrance to the Port Arthur site. He examined the blood on the bitumen road past the guard's booth, and blood on dirt and leaves and bark, where the mother and her two children had been murdered. He stood outside the Broad Arrow, the windows now sealed with plastic sheeting, and tried to picture the scene inside, before white light had bleached it clean.

He stood on the roadway with other journalists at the house – Seascape – when the charred chassis of the gunman's hijacked BMW was taken away. Hours earlier they had arrested the killer. He had come to them, naked and on fire. Screaming like the devils.

Featherstone couldn't hold it all in his mind. Thirty-five people dead. He couldn't grasp the number. Thirty-five. At the daily press conferences at the site he stood at the back of the pack of journalists and counted thirty-five people. When he drove to the killer's childhood home, looking for information, he tallied thirty-five homes. Thirty-five trees. Thirty-five bricks. He couldn't get a fix on it.

He drove out to the pharmacy owned by the man whose wife and two children had been murdered beneath the trees on the road into the site. The pharmacy was closed. For a long time he looked through the front window. At the back of the dispensary he saw the drawings the two dead girls had done for their father – stick figures of children and houses and clouds in bright crayon. He couldn't stop looking at them, through the locked glass door, across the dead air of the pharmacy. He wanted to touch them. He put a hand on the glass.

We have lost our innocence, he thought, reciting phantom reports to himself. Here, this week, we became a part of the rest of the world. Or a modern madness has come to us. He wanted to speak on behalf of the nation, yet everything contracted inside his head, and he lost sight of what he was actually looking at.

By the following Saturday, when many of the journalists had left Port Arthur, Featherstone was still there, in the motel. He walked aimlessly through the ruins, the penitentiary, around the base of the turreted guard tower. He meandered about the asylum, and beneath the stands of English oak trees near the burnt-out ruins of the church. The dead leaves crackled under his boots.

Nothing came to him. No heartbreaking insights. No wise, compassionate pronouncements. Only the maps of blood on the roads. The crooked rays of sunlight in the drawings of the children. The fragile, rickety houses and dead dot eyes of the drawings. This insane opera in his head, underscored by the cries of the devils.

Perhaps if he could compile the most penetrating report into the mind of the killer, to answer the *whys* and not the *hows*, he might contribute something lasting, something important in this time of national mourning. So he went back, again and again, to the small suburb not far from Port Arthur where the gunman had spent his childhood years, and interrogated the same families until they refused to let him into their yards. He was told of tortured pets and a morbid fascination with fire. The boy, half-human and, sometimes, half-animal, disappearing into the bushland behind the suburb. Setting tracts of scrub alight. Waiting eagerly for the fire engines.

The station in Sydney never returned his calls. And still he stayed, catching sporadic sleep, trying to tear the boy out of the cool air of the Tasman Peninsula.

Near the end he had stopped taking notes in the pad he'd bought from the motel cleaner. He drew simple pictures and doodles of what he saw, or imagined he saw. A house, a tree, a parrot, a dog, a schoolhouse. Then the boy running through bushland. The boy squatting, striking matches. The boy waving from the top of the turret at Port Arthur.

'I can do it,' he told Victoria.

'It's over, Graham,' she said.

'There's more,' he said.

'Things happen, Graham, and then they're over.'

'But I was one of the first here.'

She hung up.

He stayed one more night then drove back to Hobart carrying that familiar heaviness of having missed one of his life's profound moments. It stayed with him, this feeling of ineptitude, on the pretty drive through Eaglehawk Neck and Dunalley and Sorell, and in the heated cabin of the small hire car the loss of confidence attracted other musings on other aspects of his life: the fiancée he no longer saw; the resentment he had for his entrepreneur brother Robert, the rich shopping mall designer; the graveyard shift which he worried, increasingly, represented the ceiling of his career.

Featherstone waited for his plane out of Tasmania. The flight was delayed, then rerouted. It took him seven hours, after a stopover in Melbourne, to get home.

As the plane descended over Sydney he looked out at the carpet of lights and tried to make out Hen and Chicken Bay in the inner west, where he and Victoria shared an apartment. He sucked a boiled sweet to clear his ears. It was after eleven pm and he didn't expect to see her at the airport.

It occurred to him that these were the last moments of his two-week vacation. He would report to work the next day. As for Featherstone and Port Arthur, it was like it had never happened.

SEVENTEEN

THAT FIRST NIGHT on the journey to Gippsland they set up camp at Gully Gap.

The four stockmen, Bill Lampe and his son, Wilfred, astride his small black brumby mare, had left Dalgety at dawn, the dogs looping and threading around the four hundred and seventeen head of cattle, and crossed the Monaro plains to the foot of the mountains and the start of the drovers' track.

They pushed through the lucerne and sassafras and occasionally looked up to the mountains which, at a distance, had started the day a deep violet then turned blue and had bleached pale yellow as old bone around midday. By late afternoon they were as russet red as the flanks of the Herefords, and were coal black just before the sun set.

It was a fine mob, the choicest the Cranks had to sell and some of the best animals on the Monaro. For a while on that first day, Bill Lampe felt the excitement of motion, of the journey, and marvelled at the baggy herd, the metronomic jut of bone beneath the loose hide of hips and rear legs, the tails switching at flies.

The cattle coughed and farted and salivated onto the

earth. They dropped pats and urinated on the move. They didn't know what was ahead of them, had only known the grass and clover of Crank's best paddocks, and cool streams, and the sometimes frightening hulls of their own shadows.

They were entering a new world. The thin, pure air of the Alps. The wild fields of feed up there, the un-expected explosion of stalk juice and flower heads on their rough tongues. Different textures. And with the water, too, and the sweetness of it.

Bill Lampe knew he would be tired and sick of the trip by the time they hit Ingeegoodbee in the High Country. That he and his men would be loathing the food and already pining for home, even before the climb at Black Mountain and down into Victoria. He worried for the boy, bumping and bobbing on his squat-arsed mare. The men hinted to the father that Wilfred was too young. Most of them hadn't done any droving until they were ten or twelve.

But it was his only boy, and he was glad of the com-pany, and he had an intuition that the trip to Gippsland was important, that they had to take it together. It was nothing he could put his finger on, but it itched in him, like you feel an itch, sometimes, deep inside the muscle of a leg, and can't get at it.

They got the cattle to Gully Creek just on dusk. Night had already fallen on the gully, and with the herd sucking noisily at the creek water the men built a fire and settled around it on rolled blankets and ate the food they had prepared and brought in the pockets of their shirts and trousers. They had no need, yet, on this first night, to take supplies from the packhorses.

The boy was saddle-sore and tried not to show it. He ate silently and tentatively sipped at his mug of tea and took a long time to drink it. He watched the men blow on their tea and he blew on his tea. The men rolled their cigarettes and when his father returned from the creek with the washed tea mugs he sat next to Wilfred and they all looked into the fire.

He nudged his father's arm.

'Will the cows be okay?'

'How do you mean?' his father said.

'In the dark. Will they run away?'

The bush moved around them and it was so dark outside the glow of the fire it was impossible to tell if it was the low ferns and trees or the dark shapes of the cattle shifting from hoof to hoof.

'Most times,' his father said, 'when you get a mob in just on dusk, they'll settle where they are for the night. Got to get the timing just right, though. They feel the night coming on. It's as good as any fence I know.'

'Oh,' Wilfred said.

'Don't worry about the cattle,' he said. 'You'll have names for 'em time we get to Bairnsdale.'

It wasn't cold enough for a fire but they settled around it, and in their nights across the Alps into Victoria and back again this was how they would settle, in identical order, the same points on a wheel, as if their place was as ordained as a configuration of stars.

The men were full of talk on the first night, surrounded by the shapes of cattle and the comfort of their velvet chewing. Their voices came into the circle and their thoughts and words passed through the fire, and back and forth, and as the night settled the voices seemed to come not from the rim of the wheel, but from deeper in the bush.

'Crank be gettin' excited at Lord Northcote comin' to town, eh Bill?' one of the stockmen said.

'I'd say.'

'New suit and hat and all, I reckon. Meelord. Meelord. Ole Cranky be sweatin' like a sow at Christmas.'

'Where they going to accommodate meelord?' another asked with a cheek full of plum.

'Buckley's, I suppose.'

'Hear a fart through the walls there. Won't do.'

'Mitchell'll need a lick of paint on the place for Northcote. Only time things get a lick around here, when a meelord shows up, eh?'

'Not our problem though, is it? What with them new councillors – that what they call themselves? Councillors? That's their problem, isn't it. What's the point of 'em? I don't need half a dozen blokes speakin' for me. I can speak for meself.'

The cattle dog crept into the firelight and nestled next to Wilfred, and licked the chop fat from his small fingers.

'That what this new road's for then? For meelord?'

'No bumps for meelady's backside.'

'Old biddy Corcoran be cookin' up a storm, won't she?' In the mountains, their mind turned to women and cast-iron stoves in home kitchens, and then just to women. There'd be nothing said about that other side to women with the boy around the fire, though it didn't stop them thinking about it.

'They gotta eat.'

They stared into the fire and saw plates of scones and rows of froth-headed ales and bunting draped across the dirt street in Dalgety for Lord Northcote.

'How's your old man, Bill?'

'Same.'

'Still angry as them bumblebees of his? I heard he wrote one of his write-ups and gave Carruthers a good hiding about the road workers comin' in.'

'They gotta work.'

'Told him to bugger off, they reckon. I'm with the old bastard.'

Bill said, 'He's a man of strong opinions.'

'Said we was being opened up to ruination. All brimstone he was, your old man.'

Bill Lampe coughed deeply and the cattle dog momentarily lifted its head from Wilfred's lap. The boy remained silent, having entered into an empathy with the dog and its affection towards him and that whole private world between children and dogs.

'Might be my last job for Crank,' Bill said, wiping spittle from his mouth.

'Eh?'

'Had a run in yesterday.'

''Bout?'

'Lately he's full of notions — not that he ever isn't. Don't like this and that. It's nothing we haven't been doing for years and all of a sudden he don't like the work.'

'Don't say.'

'New fence in the back paddock, he says no good, do it again. Dipping. Not done right. Do it again. The rabbits, he says. Get rid of them. I say to him, no matter what you do, rabbits going to be here sure as the sun in the morning, and he raises his crop at me.'

'The bastard raised his crop?'

'Went all red behind the whiskers and raised his crop at me.'

'You shoulda sit him on his arse.'

'I would've, he gone through with it.'

'He sits on that arse, I tell ya, he's not getting up for a long while.'

'Sooner than his missus.'

Bill coughed again and the fire collapsed slightly and exhaled a sheet of sparks. It ended the line of talk and the men sat quietly in the circle of amber wavering light, in turn enclosed by ring after ring of Crank's fat cattle, and then it was just them and the thick canopy of the bush in the gully through which they could see, if they stared long enough, the wash of stars.

'Reckon we might take some of old Dr Carter's hospitality when we get to Ingeegoodbee?'

All of them except Wilfred chuckled at the mention of Carter's name. Dozens of stories came to them, raced in like bogongs to flame, and at the thought of him they shifted in their places and relit cold pipes and rolled fresh cigarettes and the fire seemed to grow out of its momentary lapse. Carter was one of the mountain eccentrics. Some said a benign madman. Others a dangerous political mercenary. He was one of those people who emanated stories that grew far greater than the sum of his parts.

'Might be an idea to talk to Carter about your problems with old man Crank,' one of them said. 'He's the one dead keen on a revolution and all that. Last I heard.'

'Says them Russians got the right idea.'

'He still preachin' that stuff?'

'He's not just preachin', he's writin' a book.'

'Bullshit.'

The men laughed. Wilfred drowsed with the same heavy lids as the cattle dog.

'You know he wrote to the King.'

'Eh?'

'Carter did. Not about bringing them Russians out. He reckons he got some cure that'll fix everything wrong with ya. He thought the King might like to know.'

'Next time the King feeling poorly he can thank old Dr Carter.'

'That's it.'

'Mad bastard that Carter.'

'Yeah.'

The men snickered and simultaneously began preparations for sleep. They didn't want to exhaust the stories of Carter which, they knew, could sustain them right across the Alps.

Bill Lampe rested against the old log where countless stockmen had lain before him and stared at the dying fire beneath the lowered brim of his hat. He remembered what his father had told him – that mountains everywhere were strange things that attracted strange people. You'd think, he'd said, that each one had Edison's magnets deep inside them, whirring around and throwing out their electric fields and generating sparks. That people came to mountains because they were hiding from something, and most of the time it was from themselves.

He looked down at his sleeping child and for a moment the boy seemed thinner and longer than he had even that same afternoon. He noticed the boy's legs jutting out from the blanket as if he were a stranger. You blink and you miss things, he thought. Or you don't look hard enough. You get so familiar with something you don't see it. You just have an idea of it.

He heard soft snoring and couldn't tell if it was from the men or the cattle threaded through the darkness. The fire had fallen to a mound of deep red coals and gave off little smoke. He could feel the damp in the air and at the same time a residue of heat in the soles of his boots.

This pain in my chest, he thought silently. You come at night, don't you? You like sneaking in at night, and burning like the coals. He put his hand gently on the boy's tangled hair, as if to calm himself, and closed his eyes.

Wilfred pretended to sleep. He lay on his side facing the fire and he could feel the heat of the coals caught in the rough-hair blanket he'd pulled up to his chin and the curved spine of the dog against the back of his legs. Sometimes the dog shuddered violently and half woke itself and settled again with a sigh.

The boy had listened to the men and the stories of crazy Carter and he couldn't sleep, not because of Carter but the whole idea of the High Country. He had thought of it many times in his cot on the verandah at home, just as he had dreamed of finding the source of the river, which he would do one day. He saved all the bits of stories he had heard about the mountains and knew that the entire craggy range was full of caves – ten times bigger than the Imperial Hall – a hundred! – and that the mountains were full of bogong moths and some of them were so big they dragged in a lot of the blacks that used to live in the High Country and that's why there weren't any blacks left up there. Stan the Black, who sometimes worked with his father and sometimes had tea with them at the house, said his people used to go up there and feast on the moths and Wilfred could only think it was out of revenge for stealing all the men and women and girls and boys and eating them in the cold caves. He asked Stan the Black why the moths were so big long ago and Stan said it was just like the frilly-necked lizards on the boulders in summer which used to be dinosaurs, and just like the mountains which used to be taller, and somehow things got smaller as they got older but he didn't know why. Wilfred wondered how big the trout must have been a long time ago, and when he became King Trout of the Monaro he knew they must have been at least that big. Maybe the big trout ate some of the big moths, way back then. But it wasn't just the stories of the moths that made him wonder about the High Country. There were great packs of horses that lived up there, he was told, and whole families of children who were as white as the snow. There were hermits up there too. From what Wilfred could gather, hermits were made of bark and bits of possum skin and pond scum and you never saw them but you could smell them a mile away and their smell was worse than any dunny in the world. And there were mad men and mad women who wore their dresses and trousers back to front and lived on yellow wild-flowers. He knew they were the people who had gone

215

into the mountains to search for gold and when they didn't find any they went mad and ate the yellow wild-flowers because they thought they were gold. Not to mention the giant wombats who had dug the caves where the blacks were taken and eaten, and the leopards who spent their whole time tearing the bark off the snow gums which is why the snow gums never had any bark.

After he thought all these things he was suddenly very cold and standing at the edge of a tunnel that went deep into the earth.

He could hear his sister Astrid calling from inside the cylinder of blackness, shouting his name, and it echoed up to him and the echo was as smooth as water over river rock. By the time his name got to him through the darkness and broke into the cool mountain air it sounded like one word over and over – dead.

From somewhere he smelled burning wood and chop fat and toasted bread and the moths took flight in a sudden plume of wing-dust and he was left on his knees at the edge of the tunnel, his sister whimpering from the centre of the earth, and he, helpless, the tears dripping from his pointed chin.

'Boy?'

Wilfred opened his eyes and saw the shape of his father leaning over him, the edges of him sharp against the smoke from the campfire. He sat up and was surprised to find his cheeks wet and wiped them and stared for some moments at the dampness on the back of his hand.

'Tucker,' his father said.

The men had packed their swags and saddled the

horses, including Wilfred's little brumby mare. They ate standing, near the fire, their hats on, and did not talk in the blue of the morning.

They rode all day through the thinning scrub and after a while it became so monotonous to Wilfred that he saw it as the unending hide of an animal that they were riding across, the skin all pale dry earth and scratchy ferns and the trees rising up like thick hairs. And when they flowed up and over a rise and down into the cool of another gully it was as if the giant animal had breathed in and out. They were moving higher and higher, deceived by the gullies, and the men noticed the confusion and labouring of the cattle, bawling and bellowing against something they didn't know.

The track suddenly broke out into open sky and ran flat for a few miles and the cattle slowed, heaving like blacksmith bellows, and pressed together in the strange surrounds, and there were few sounds but the mass breathing of the mob and the chafe of their hides.

On the flat run, no longer having to lean into the necks of their horses, Bill and Wilfred bounced in their saddles, and the bouncing pushed conversation out of them.

'You gotta look after your sister,' Bill Lampe said. He had been talking in his head on the climb, and the long and unbroken internal dialogue had come out here, hours after it had started, on the flatlands.

'Yes, sir,' the boy said.

'Things don't always stay the same.'

Wilfred was watching the cattle, the tight swarm of them, all wild-eyed as they shuffled through grasses and flowers and odours they had never known, the horses and dogs suddenly new to them in new light, the shadows blacker and sharper. There was no more bawling, but a blowing of mucus and saliva through nostrils, and it was their own panicked breathing that made them more frightened.

'You remember Brinda?' his father said.

'Yes, sir.'

'Remember you woke up that morning and Brinda was lying in front of the fire? Her eyes were half open and she was breathing, but you remember she could hardly lift up her head?'

'Yeah.'

'She was an old dog anyways, but that morning you leaned over her and whispered her name into her ear and she'd open her eyes a bit but she couldn't get up no matter how hard she tried.'

Wilfred nodded and gripped the reins.

'Then she didn't move anymore. She was too tired and she just went to sleep with you whispering her name in her ear. Well, that's like all of us. We all going to get tired like Brinda one day and there's nothin' you can do about that. The way it is.'

Wilfred couldn't count how many dead sheep and foxes and rabbits and even other dogs he'd seen. Birds, too, and fish. But he'd never seen anything like Brinda, her eyes big and syrupy, then the syrup was gone and it was like she was asleep but wasn't because the eyes stayed open and even though he could still see his own reflection in them it wasn't the same.

'Grandfather Callistus, he'll get tired one day like Brinda. Same with Grandma Alice. And me too. Even you. The way it is.'

His father glanced down at him and they rode for another half an hour before they hit a small stream, edged with moss. They stayed on their mounts while the horses drank.

'You just make sure you look after your little sister. That's what I'm asking you to do.'

The boy felt tears smarting his eyes and he could barely see the rocks that mottled the floor of the stream, and the blooms of moss grew big and fuzzy, and before he knew it his father was lifting him off the mare.

'Buy your old man a drink,' he said, lowering Wilfred to the ground.

And they squatted together beside the stream and dipped their hats into the water and drank like the horses out of the wells of their hats.

'Bloody good,' his father said.

'Bloody good,' Wilfred said.

They both laughed and, still squatting, looked across the narrow stream and the open meadow to the fringe of bush that marked their next ascent.

'On the way back,' his father said, scratching his stubbled chin, 'how'd you like to catch a spot of fishin'?'

The boy watched the water drain through his hat.

'Just you and me. We'll try the Sally Hole maybe. Or the Rock Pool. Should be red ant time there, eh? Nothin' like red ant time on the Badja.'

The boy could see the wings. The wings of the ants. The blurred blood spots of the ants. In his head the wings beat furiously and became louder and even if he stared into the clear water of the stream nothing in that moment could soothe the growing hum of the ant wings.

EIGHTEEN

THEIR VOICES CAME to the old man like swarms of insects colliding in the dark. Drew him out of his sleep, although it no longer felt like sleep to Wilfred Lampe.

He remembered when, as a teenager, he had taken a dare to jump into the Snowy River in the middle of winter. The water was a rich, emerald green, low down on the banks at that time of year, and it flowed not with the recklessness of spring but begrudgingly, as if it were reluctant to leave its source in the mountains.

When he dived in, his head exploded with stars and his breath was struck out of him. He flailed in the water. Not because he couldn't swim, but the coldness tripped every latch and spring in his body at once, throwing everything out of rhythm. And when that was over, and he had numbed, there was a delicious slowing down of all things. He surrendered his concern not only over the cold, but of everything. He lost his care, and became a part of the grim momentum of the river.

They retrieved him. He lay on the western bank looking into the sky, and his body and his features looked like they'd been outlined in chalky blue pencil. His breath was shallow. The warmth in him took a long time to come back, starting, as he felt, with a small flame in the distant centre of himself, a place so far away he had never known it existed. Then the flame built into a fire, and soon it combusted, like the eucalypts he had seen during the bush-fires, their crowns spitting oil.

It was how he felt now, in the white room. It was just like being in the freezing river. He was at that place where care no longer existed, and everything moved with a grim momentum.

Had he slept? He wasn't sure anymore if and when he was actually awake. He could sense figures moving in and out of the darkness in the room. The air was so thick he could feel it being pushed across his papery skin. He sensed the disturbed air with his eyes closed, and when the figures came and went the treacle air they had displaced rolled over him minutes after they'd gone.

On the morning of the voices he lay still and found that if he opened his eyes a fraction, if he kept the lids trembling with their closeness, he could make out several silhouettes around his bed.

They were dark, square-shouldered sentinels, guarding the resting place of a dead knight.

'Whose idea was this anyway?' one of them said.

'The creative department, sir. It came out of there.'

'Ah. The entertainers.'

'Yes, sir.'

'One of their *ideas*.'

'Yes.'

'Ironic, isn't it?'

'What's that, sir?'

'That this poor fellow is expected to represent a century of Australian *life*.'

The rest of them were unsure whether to laugh or stay silent. There were some noises in throats that could have been a clearing, or an acknowledgement.

'Will he be – how should I say this – *with* us when the time comes?'

'The doctors report that for his age he is in remarkable condition.'

'He doesn't look so remarkable to me. What was he? Is he?'

'He's a gentleman from the country, sir. Down the Snowy Mountains way. He lived there all his life.'

'Is that right? A man from Snowy River?'

'Of sorts. He has a little property there. Gifted to him, to his family, by the adjoining landowners. His father worked for them, you see. General hand and rouseabout. Then he did the same. Mended fences. A rabbiter. Those sorts of things.'

'Who are the landowners?'

Wilfred could clearly hear the shuffle of papers.

'Family by the name of Crank, sir.'

'Crank. Like the Model T. Crank start, hmm?'

'That's right.'

'Have you found the niece? There is a niece, I'm led to believe.'

'A great-niece, yes. We have made contact with the girl's father. An interview is imminent.'

'When?'

'This week.'

The shapes of the sentinels were wavering now and the old man felt light-headed. He was too afraid to move. Had he heard the name Crank? He thought, for the first time in – what? Sixty, seventy years? However long it had been since he had taken to young Tom Crank with a stock whip, had sliced open the right side of the boy's mouth, and left him scarred and with an idiot grin. That day Wilfred had discovered a desire to kill another human being, and then immediately lost it. But he never forgot that he had it, and it stayed with him his whole life. It was like the distant flame that he felt after he nearly froze to death. The flame he knew was there, in a place where it was always dark, too far to get back to, to find, yet there, like it was in all people. Had they said niece? Or nice?

'Have the legals cleared this?' a voice continued. 'I mean, is this *permissible*? What if the press got hold of it?'

'Legally, we are providing him with care where no such care was forthcoming nor would have been, given his antecedents. You could argue that we are giving him a quality of life that would have been denied him. He is unquestionably nursing home material. We could provide that for him in the interim. Nobody else seems to care about him. It's an unexpected drain on the budget, of course.'

'You haven't answered my question. How would it look, to the public?'

'We would contend that our actions saved his life.'

'Would you?'

'Yes, sir.'

'Perhaps the most profound defence of all.'

'We would contend that, yes.'

'Very well.'

Wilfred Lampe could hear them breathing. He could hear a finch chirrup. It may have been a whistle from his own nose.

223

'And when they're done with him?' the man said.

'I'd have to check the figures, but care might have to be arranged. Until the Opening Ceremony. Then he'd be free to do as he wishes. It is a moral dilemma we had not factored in.'

'Look after him.'

'Of course.'

'Our man from the Snowy River. Dear God.'

Wilfred remained motionless for a long time after he heard the door click shut.

He had thought he was dead and now he wasn't so sure. Was it some form of purgatory? Had they managed to slip him into the nursing home at Berridale? How had they done it? Had he passed out?

The door opened again and he saw a shadow on the far side of the room. He heard running water and could smell mandarins.

Someone called from outside the room.

The shadow stopped and hurried out the door. He cautiously opened his eyes and could see the door was slightly ajar. He looked into the tall, thin rectangle of light.

He saw banks of neon, and the fuzzy diffused light of the neons reflected on the floor of the hallway outside the door.

Wilfred Lampe sat up in bed and pulled the drip from his arm. He pushed the covers back and swivelled his legs off the bed. He slowly lowered his feet to the floor. It was cold on the bottom of his old feet.

He stood. His legs felt shaky and weak. He reached out and found the back of a chair. He moved down the bed and found the metal rail of the bedstead and steadied himself.

'Astrid?' he said to the room.

He walked to the door and opened it.

NINETEEN

WYNTER SAID NOTHING to the driver in the warm and sour air of the truck cabin, and in those long silences he sometimes heard the throaty bawling of the calves packed into the trailers at the back, and hoof stamps, and whimpering that seemed almost human. It occurred to him that the cattle on board the rig weren't cattle at all, but all the demons that he carried with him in his life. And as the truck crossed the mountains towards the coast, he felt the engine roar with the load, and the grind of the gears entered his bones, and it was how he was now, straining against the haul of his own demons.

In Adaminaby, Wynter had returned to their room in the Snow Goose Motel and found Aurora gone. He looked down into the car park and saw the car wasn't there either. He sat and stared into the dark surface of the television screen and laughed. She had tried to leave him before but he knew, somehow, this was different.

He sat in the chair for a long time and could see a small reflection of himself in the television screen. He was surprised at how small he was in the reflection. He ran his hand through his hair several times and in the reflection his head and hand were so minuscule he could barely register the action. Wynter hated silence but he needed it now to think. About what to do with no money and no weapon, and he had to think about how to find Aurora. He stayed there for a long time and scratched his scalp at the back near the large nub of bone at the base of his skull, and then the ridges above and around the back of his ears, and he scratched until he broke the skin and the blood dampened his hair and gathered along the cuticles of his bitten nails.

Wynter lit a cigarette and let the match burn down to his thumb and forefinger and the flame nipped his skin before it died.

He saw himself sitting in the chair in the room with the black twisted remains of the match pincered between two fingers because he always pictured himself in a movie. He didn't know why. He just could. And here's Wynter scratching his head and there's blood on his fingertips. Cut to Wynter laughing at that bitch who's gone and tried to run away.

In the beginning she left him when he forced her onto the streets to earn money for the drugs. She had run again when he had brought a few old mates to the flat and ordered her to have sex with them in front of him. But he'd always brought her back and comforted her and become the whole protective world to her again.

Here's Wynter holding his woman and consoling her and telling her anyone touches a hair on her pretty head and he'll fucking do them. You got a line inside of you that you don't cross, he once said to Aurora. No matter what, you got that line.

He hated that about her. It made him hit her. It made him scream and spit in her face. Sometimes he wanted to split her mouth open at the hinge and reach inside her and pull that fucking line right out of her whore body.

It was also what kept him with her.

He thought about that line in the room of the Snow Goose Motel.

'You bitch,' he said, shaking his head and smiling. 'Sneaky little bitch.'

He hated the silence and even his talking to himself didn't fill it up enough. He had some drugs but he had no money. He could have used the drugs to close the door on the silence. But he had no money and didn't know when he'd next have some to buy more drugs so he'd have to ration what he had.

In the quiet room his head began to ache and he knew it was the silence pressing in. He didn't know where to go next, what to do once he stepped out of the room, and the silence held him and began to take over, and he knew then he would start thinking about his father and when he thought of his father he would think about his father's twin brother, Uncle Stan, and he didn't want to think about Stan again.

When he started the fires or felt his knuckles crack when his fist struck a human skull or when he winced at the needle going into that soft flesh between his toes or in the corner of his eyeball, he thought of Stan and he had to scream to chase the thought out.

Wynter took the last drugs he had and left the motel and started walking. He walked out of Adaminaby along the edge of the bitumen road and didn't know where he was headed and didn't care as long as he was free of the silence.

He talked to himself as he walked. With the wind through the pines and long, dry grasses on the verge of the road, and the crunching of the gravel under his boots, and the thin vapour trails of jets high in that winter sky above the brown sheep paddocks of the Monaro, it was enough to keep out the silence. He kept himself warm thinking of the great fires of his life. The groundsman's shed at school with the paint tins and kerosene bottles going off like bombs in a war movie. The next school he was sent to, the classroom window glass cracking and blowing out. The fancy car in Church Street that lifted into the air tail first with a *whoof* and threw a flaming mushroom into the sky. All small beer compared to the pine and eucalypt forests.

It was close to dark when the semitrailer stopped for him. Wynter had ceased putting out his hand for a ride, but the truck had pulled over fifty metres ahead, and twilight exploded with blood-red brakelights, and the dust the truck threw up on the verge hovered around the lights like steam, and as he walked down the side of the stationary truck he could smell wild animals and could see dozens of pairs of moist eyes staring out at him through the metal rails of the long trailers, and he climbed quickly into the cabin and shut the door and felt the hair tingle at the base of his neck.

It was dim and sour-smelling in the cabin. The driver looked at him and nodded without saying anything and jerked the truck into gear and pulled out onto the road.

The cabin rocked and shook before it struck the smooth of the bitumen. With the rocking Wynter saw that the cabin was suddenly alive with objects swaying from the ceiling and on the large front console. Surrounding him were crucifixes and shiny medallions bearing haloed saints and picture cards of the Virgin Mary cradling her child, the saviour of the world. He looked around him and there were dozens more little pictures of Christ nursing a glowing heart and the baby Christ and Christ dying on the cross, all of them affixed to the inside of the passenger's door and the front of the console and even the ceiling above his head.

Wynter thought again of his child. There was a moment, eventually, he knew it was dead. And only then, when it was too late, did the great emotional gravity of fathering a child dawn on him. It made him angry, to think of what had been denied him – kicking a footy in the park, camping and fishing, fiddling with cars, buying the kid his first beer at the local. But it made sense to Wynter, because the death fitted the pattern of his life. He was always being short-changed. Someone, somewhere, was always out to get him, to rip him off, to stop him attaining the simple things that other people took for granted. It fitted. His dead kid was just another example. And it was more fuel to his hate.

They drove for long straight distances through sheep country. The driver threw his high beams on and whole stretches of paddock rolled past them and they could've been on a ship the grasses flowed past so smoothly.

Sometimes the lights caught the eyes of a fox or a rabbit and the great wave of cold air pushed ahead by the prow of the semi rolled straight over those eyes and left them behind in the dark.

By the time they entered Cooma they had still said nothing to each other.

The truck rumbled through the main street. The driver looked over to the Alpine Cafe and as he passed he sounded his air horn and reached for a Thermos and unscrewed the lid and poured himself a hot coffee with one hand.

He drained the coffee and lit up a Winfield cigarette and wound down his window and the cold air bit into the cabin.

The air and the coffee and the smoke enlivened the driver.

'Set you down here?' he asked. 'Where you heading?'

'Over Bega way. That'd be good.'

'Suit yourself.'

The electric lights and the cars and the ski shops and fishing tackle stores and fast-food joints and the pub windows of yellow light with the silhouettes of drinkers inside, the life of it after the dark mountains and the pastures, entered the truck and started the driver humming.

As they left the town he pressed a cassette into the stereo and tweaked the volume knob and hummed along to some high-spirited church music that seemed to Wynter to have been sung in a big and draughty cathedral because he could hear the voices echoing all around the truck cabin and to him the echo sounded cold as stone.

When the voices grew thin and high he could hear the bawl of cattle and he wasn't sure if it came from the back of the truck or a poddy calf had found its way into the cathedral with the choir.

An hour out of town they pulled into a truck stop.

'Getting some tucker. You?' the driver said.

'No. Ta.'

'You look buggered. Grab some shut-eye in the back.'

'Thanks.'

'Suit yourself.'

Wynter crawled into the small bed at the back of the cabin and in the dark grabbed a pillow and rested his head on the face of Jesus, even though he couldn't see it, and he could hear the cattle moving about the rear of the truck. The sweet odour of cow shit seeped into the cabin.

He woke briefly to the sound of gears as the truck breached the range and he didn't know how long they'd been moving. He thought he'd lost the dangerous silence he felt back in the Snow Goose but in that small sleeping space, sandwiched between the driver and the dozens of Jesuses and the warm cows pressed against each other in the trailers, he was back at his Uncle Stan's in South Australia, the last time he spent Christmas there with his younger brother and several of his cousins.

It was the summer that fractured his life. It was like a chip in a car windscreen. It started there, a small and brilliant star. And that's the way it stayed, for a long time. So small you didn't notice it after a while. Then it started to fan out, that star, until it found a weakness in the glass, and when it found the weakness, which it always did, it began to travel. It travelled so slowly and secretively you never noticed it day to day. But after a month, or two months, you'd see with surprise that the fracture had moved a few inches. In the end it ran swiftly. It raced to the edge of the windscreen frame, to

232

the furthest borders of it, where it had nowhere else to go.

That was where the fracture of Wynter had happened. At Stan's.

When Wynter first fled Melbourne as a teenager for a new life, all those years ago, he had hitched his way to Bordertown in South Australia then over to Murray Bridge and down to Victor Harbor. He visited the penguin colony at Granite Island like any other tourist. He read the information boards at the tourist centre. In the heat of the day he saw no penguins but he could smell them. He peered into burrows like everyone else but saw nothing. He liked the penguins because they lived a lot like he did, only coming out at night, living at night, and disappearing into their otherworld an hour before dawn.

After the penguins Wynter made his way to his uncle's farm in the Inman Valley. He planned to see Stan for the first time since he was twelve, on that final summer holiday Wynter had taken with his ten-year-old brother Reece.

He knew what he had to do. Here's Wynter walking up the shaded drive to the verandah of the house, and stepping across the wooden boards of the verandah and rapping on the flyscreen door. Uncle Stan would come down the hall, a tall figure topped with a mass of wavy hair that reminded Wynter of a fluffy cloud. Stan, with that permanent querulous look on his face, the look that farmers brought in from the field every day, a look suspended, etched by the confoundedness of working with and against nature, with the stubbornness or generosity of the earth. It was the same face Uncle Stan wore to church. In the matter of God he had no doubt.

But the look there, in the church house, with its heavy marble bowl of holy water in the foyer, the streaks of grey marble shivering when the water moved, was not of doubt but of someone waiting a lifetime to be punished. At the flyscreen Wynter would see the face of the old man change with recognition, the lines of the face moving, blurring and altering with a smile, just like the distorted streaks of grey marble through the lens of the holy water.

Wynter might hesitate then. He would swear the man on the other side of the flywire was his father. It had shocked him at first during that summer visit, when Stan met them at the station. Wynter had left his father at the platform in Melbourne, and here he was again meeting him in Adelaide. It confused him that there were two of them, one at each end of a railway line. On the drive down to the valley in Stan's car Wynter kept studying his uncle for differences. In the end, he decided they differed in the exact thing that made them identical – their faces. Not the surface features. But there was something behind Stan's face that the boy couldn't grasp. A fluidness where his father was solid. Something like jelly that never set. Something that never formed properly when the rest of him grew up. When his father was angry you could at least read his anger. Its shadow was sharp-edged and defined. Yet Stan. He suffered without those hard shadows. He was all fluffy and grey-edged like his mass of hair. Couldn't move backward or forward. He was stuck in the middle of somewhere, some purgatory, some half-formed nightmare.

Wynter would see that face again at the flyscreen door of the farmhouse years later. They would go into

the kitchen, and sit around a wooden table. And Wynter
would rise, and grab that cloud of hair and pull Stan's
head back. Then he'd slit his throat.

These were Wynter's thoughts as the teenager hitched
from Victor Harbor to the Inman Valley. He had wanted
to make the trip to see Stan for years. He'd sat at
Spencer Street Station several times and thought of
returning to the farm. But something stopped him.

He knew what it was. He was frightened of Stan.
When he recalled that summer and his uncle he was
twelve again and scared by what had happened and
there were few fears greater than those you earned as a
child. Wynter had placed the muzzles of shotguns and
handguns to other people's foreheads, and woken in a
bed next to a dead junkie girlfriend with vomit caked
around her lips, and hit a man so hard he'd seen his eyeball literally pop from its socket and drop onto his
cheek. He'd done plenty of bad things in the six years
since that visit. Yet he could look at his father and think
of his uncle and he'd feel his bowels shift with fear. He
had brought it back with him to Melbourne when he
was twelve and had tried to run away from it with
everything he did and everything he became and it
wasn't until years later that he understood it sat inside
him all the time, wherever he was, and that it had to be
cut out of him like a tumour or something.

He told his father about the summer at the farm a
week after they got back. He told him about the barn
down near the creek. He told him how he and his
brother and the other cousins all went swimming in the
creek with Uncle Stan and then played a game Stan had
invented called Adam and Eve, and all the children went

235

into the barn, still wet and naked from the creek, and Stan had laid out some clean blankets in one of the horse stalls, and in the game some of the children became Adam and others became Eve.

Wynter remembered the smell of manure in the stables and the rich aroma of the hay under the blankets and a shifting plate of light on the surface of a water trough in the corner of the stall. He could hear horses elsewhere in the barn. The thud of a hoof. A whinny from deep within the belly of one of the horses.

Stan told him he was Eve and another boy was Adam and they were instructed to hug and play ponies and riders with each other. Feed husks drifted through the air of the barn and caught on their skin.

'You lose,' Uncle Stan said, pointing to two children, and they were ordered back to the creek. Pair after pair were banished from the barn, until it was only Wynter and the cousin he had to call Adam.

Then Wynter was laid gently on his back on the blanket and Stan held the head of Adam and pushed it into Wynter's groin and he remembered looking up into the rafters of the barn through motes of husk and dust and he heard the strike of hooves muffled by the sweet hay.

When it was over Wynter ran to the creek and at dusk refused to come out of the water. His skin pruned and he could see the lights on in the farmhouse up the hill. Insects cartwheeled above the surface of the creek and in the dim light he saw Uncle Stan sitting on the bank. It could have been his father.

'Where are you, champion?' his uncle called in the gloom. 'Where's our champion? You must be hungry by now.'

The cold penetrated Wynter's skin and crept inside him and felt as cold as metal on a winter day. He shook uncontrollably on the way back to the farmhouse.

In the morning he woke in his bed with his uncle standing over him. He thought he was home in Melbourne. 'Dad?'

'A big breakfast for our champion,' Stan said. 'Then a ride on the finest mare on the Fleurieu Peninsula.'

That first Sunday he took all of them to church at Yankalilla, and when the service was finished they played in the rose garden beside the church while Stan prayed on his knees in the front pew.

In the early morning of the day they left the farm to return to Melbourne, Wynter was woken by his brother groaning in his sleep and in the half-light saw Stan kneeling beside Reece's bed, his hands working at something, Stan hunched over his brother, pulling at him with such concentration that he didn't seem to notice the moaning. Wynter wanted to get up and hit his uncle then, to strike the back of that bowed head, but he pretended to sleep, and watched through eyes not quite closed, and when Stan left he sat up, shivering, his brother snuffling back into sleep, and through the window he saw a foal running and hopping crazily in the paddock down by the creek.

They had one last swim with their cousins. Stan stayed in the house. The children splashed and duck-dived and some of them shouted – 'I'm Adam! I'm Eve!' – and that night the two boys were on the train heading home.

Wynter told his father all of this at the kitchen table in their house in Melbourne. Why didn't he do anything? Why didn't he try and get rid of the hurt?

And so, six years later, Wynter went back to the farm to kill Stan. He was full of speed and bourbon and when he found the farm and saw the warm-lit windows of the house he lost his nerve and went down through the paddocks to the creek.

He sat by the creek until morning. He sharpened the blade of his knife on a rock at the edge of the creek. He figured that if he cut Stan's throat he'd have no more reason to hate. Or one less reason. He figured that extinguishing Stan would also eliminate a side of his own father that he hated.

He looked across to the barn and thought, yes, it started here. The origin of everything that went wrong. It started high up, something percolating through damp, spongy mosses, and gathered, and found a path, and grew, and trickled its way down through roots and wild-flowers, and grew again, and gathered strength, until it was strong enough to cut through rock, and bring down trees, until it had enough velocity not just to forge its own path, but to carry things with it. That's how it happened, from that moment in the barn all those years ago. A single act, perfumed with damp hay.

And his father had done nothing, and let the trickle become a river, and it had cut through the family, and dragged off bits of the family with it, and his mother had left, and his father had fled, and his brother Reece had disappeared. All because nobody did anything.

He peered into the barn that morning and saw that the stables had gone and it was a storage shed now for equipment and fuel drums and post diggers.

He crept up to the house, crawled like a commando

through the gullies of grapevines that he did not remember from that summer. The vines grew right up to the house. He could smell the tang of grape and the wood smoke from the kitchen fire. He heard voices. He heard the morning cry of a child woken too quickly from sleep.

Wynter moved silently to the back verandah. It was littered with toy trucks and green fluffy dinosaurs. He saw in the middle of the verandah a little blackboard on an easel. Someone had drawn a small, comical horse in white and blue chalk on the board.

Through the open back door he could see down the central hallway of the house all the way to the flywire door at the front. He saw the fleeting shape of a child pass back and forth across the hall. He saw a young woman in a floral dress and a plain blue apron moving in the kitchen. He saw a young man stand from a table and hold her from behind and return to his seat.

Wynter backed away from the verandah and returned to his nest amongst the gnarled vines. He lay on his stomach and could feel the shape of the knife in his pocket. He couldn't make sense of the young woman and the chalk horse and the cries of the child. Everything felt wrong.

It took him the rest of the day to walk into Yankalilla.

On the walk he reasoned that Stan had sold the farm. Wynter just assumed he would be there, always, in that farmhouse with its dark stained floorboards and old furniture and the dusty lace doilies draped over the armrests of the chairs. He didn't have to worry about what Stan looked like after all those years. He just had to picture his father.

The young family in the farmhouse had thrown him. Nobody had mentioned Stan since the summer when he was twelve. Whether he'd sold the farm. Where he'd moved to. Where he was in the world.

He thought, when he had told his father what had happened, that his father would take the first train to Bordertown, head down into the Inman Valley, and kill his brother.

But a year passed and nothing happened. Stan still sent an annual Christmas card and his mother still pinned it, with the others, to the drapes in the lounge room. Wynter always destroyed the card. He found the envelope in the garbage. He studied the postmark. He knew Stan was still at the farm.

Then, one year, the cards stopped. Wynter couldn't remember when that happened. But when the cards stopped he stopped railing at his father, stopped berating him for his inaction, and his anger turned inwards, and became much more dangerous, and it was then that the family began to fray. When he finally hit his father in that kitchen, that dead room with its ancient wood-fuelled stove always warm, always glowing with heat, that room where even the flies moved slowly in the drowsiness of it, where life slowed to nothing, that room where the family died, it all fell very quickly.

Wynter's father took the beating. When he fell from his chair he pulled himself up and sat again, as if nothing had happened. When he was hit again he did not even raise his hands to his split lip and damaged eye. He just sat with his head bowed, as Stan did in the church at Yankalilla.

The next day his father was gone. Dried drops of his

blood were still on the kitchen floor. A month later his mother moved in with her sister down on the bay. Reece disappeared. And Wynter hit the road with his knife.

He arrived in Yankalilla on dusk. He remembered nothing of the town until he saw the church. People were spilling out of the portico. There were a few cars parked on the gravel in front of the stone building. A priest in a white gown milled with his parishioners.

Wynter watched from the other side of the street. As the cars left he walked over to the side of the church. He was transfixed by the rose garden and how the last of the sunlight caught the rims of the petals and for a moment lit the pale pink and white flowers like small lanterns. The fragrance of the roses enveloped him and for no reason he felt his eyes sting with tears.

'Can I help you?' The priest stood behind him, his hands and forearms hidden in his white smock.

Wynter stammered. 'I'm . . . I'm looking for Stan.'

The priest studied Wynter for a moment. 'Stan?'

'My uncle.'

The sun dipped below a stand of blue gums and the light was blue and the lanterns of the roses had faded and it was suddenly very quiet.

'He's a parishioner here?' the priest said.

'He comes here sometimes, I think. He used to live near here.'

'Stan, you say? Does he have a surname?'

'Thomas.'

'Come inside.'

They went into the cool of the church. It felt so much smaller inside than it looked from the outside.

The priest pointed to a pew a few rows from the front. 'Take a seat. I'm new here. Six months. The name isn't familiar.' The priest disappeared through a door beside the altar.

Wynter could feel the sweat now under his arms and at the base of his spine. He could hear birds warbling and loop-calling outside.

His attention was caught by what looked like a stain on the wall beside the altar. Water seemed to have crept into the plaster and damaged the paint, bubbling the surface of the wall. A small spotlight was trained on the stain.

The priest returned with a large ledger open in his hands. He was reading the ledger as he sat down beside Wynter.

'We had a Stan Thomas as a member of the church several years ago,' the priest said. 'Very active in church activities, yes. Did many little odd jobs around here, so it seems. Held several committee positions, too. But nothing further.'

Wynter said nothing. He looked at the stain on the wall.

'You could contact the Bishop in Adelaide,' the priest went on, closing the book. 'The office there may be able to help.' He noticed Wynter studying the wall.

'Our famous Lady of Yankalilla,' the priest said. 'Do you see her? The profile?'

The priest explained how the image of the Virgin Mary had become a shrine to pilgrims from all over the world. That there had also been apparitions of her in the rose garden.

'Day in and day out they come to see her,' he said,

smiling. 'I've been woken in the middle of the night by strangers, just for a quick look.' He rose from the pew and nursed the book to his chest. 'Stay as long as you wish. I'm sorry I can't help you any further.'

Wynter sat for an hour in the church and wondered about the image of the Virgin Mary appearing and his uncle disappearing and he knew, then, that there was no balm for him here, no end to what burned inside him. He stared at the apparition, at the small shadows strong-lined and firm thrown off the bubbled plaster by the spotlight, and could not make out a face at all. He saw nothing but a pale stain on a white wall.

Then the church was filled with the sound of bawl-ing animals and the ring of struck metal and a great heave of compressed air and when he woke with a start he saw the shadowed outline of a man's head and shoulders looking above him, a silhouette edged with light.

Wynter sat up quickly, startled. He felt giddy and vulnerable and the crying of animals filled his head.

'Here we are then. Bega,' the silhouette said.

Wynter opened his mouth but nothing came out. The figure moved away and he could see through the open door of the truck cabin a single streetlight haloed with moths.

'Suit yourself,' a voice said.

Wynter realised he had wet his jeans.

TWENTY

THEY LEFT THE little outpost of Ingebyra with their bellies full of fresh home-baked bread and their minds, a day later, still carrying the image of the red, orange and cream strata of trifle served to them in triangular dessert glasses at the Black family's table.

It was Wilfred's first experience of trifle, and he looked to his father and the other stockmen for a sign of how to approach it, how to deal with this exotica that sat before him on the table like a magnificent trophy. The foreignness of it perplexed him – he had seen trifle, but its prettiness in this house was accentuated by the rough, calloused hands of the stockmen around the dainty glasses.

The boy had once glimpsed such glassware – on a long table in Mitchell's formal dining room at the Buckley's, at a supper for the new councillors of the area – and he had wondered, with the crowd of tall stemmed glasses and rows of silverware and serviette hats, how they'd fit any food and drink on the table.

In the mountains all was hardwood and granite and thick, scratchy underbrush, rough-hewn timber slab and bluestone. Yet sometimes, in these settlements in the middle of nowhere, you'd hear notes of opera through the tin flower of a gramophone, a trembling voice twisting and turning with the moths, or come upon a beautiful leather armchair in a shack of hand-cut grey wood and yellow lamplight, or find a ruined copy of Dickens on a boulder by the river.

It was the boy's first excursion into the world, and his father liked the way Wilfred didn't try and make sense of what he saw through constant talk, like other children, but tasted things and digested them slowly and quietly, as he did the trifle.

Decades later Wilfred would remember the trifle. The jelly and the sponge and the custard, unruined and steadfast, like the stripes in sandstone, still in that thick flute, lay on a shelf in the back of his mind for the rest of his life. This, rather than the long haul through rain at Black Mountain, and the three cattle that slipped off the high trail there and went over, uncomplaining, without sound, a clutch of upturned hooves and gone into eternity. This, more than his father's incessant coughing, or his noticeably diminishing appetite. Or how lonely he felt at night in front of the fire, away from Dalgety – how the fire went from being the lively, crackling heart of his adventure to the nightly ritual he dreaded. If he'd been asked to explain it, he couldn't.

There were only three families at Ingebyra, and a small graveyard. They were all family, in a way, united by the fenced cemetery and its wooden and granite headstones but more so by its empty plots. It made the community friendlier to near strangers. Maybe even gregarious. Brushed them, now and then, with eccentricity. They were only two-thirds up the mountains. A long way from the madness of the summit.

The families were pleased for the company when the herds passed through. 'What of the mainland?' they'd ask, as if the stockmen and the cattle were a rope-rigged frigate briefly resupplying at a remote port. Births and deaths. Politics and royal tattle. Descriptions of the great social events in those arcadias of Sydney and Melbourne and London, retrieved from the visitors like dated yet delicious morsels from a saddlebag. Nothing tasted stale.

It was what these people missed the most – ceremony. In the mountains they pined for ceremony in Sydney and Melbourne. And in Sydney and Melbourne, they similarly yearned for doings in London. It was their fate, so far away from civilisation. They were a people tinged with the disappointment of always missing out on something, somewhere, in the world.

Bill Lampe knew the Blacks through the Steersons and thus via the Corcorans. A stockman or two would be acquainted with another tenuous circuit of vague faces and handshakes and drunken bonhomie at the Buckley's or the oyster bars of Cooma. It didn't matter how ill-formed, this dot to dot. The men's arrival was an event and the families drew straws for the right to lodge them. And it was fortunate for all of them, especially Wilfred, that on this trip they had won the hospitality of Mrs Black, in whom was fixed, like a hatpin in antecedents that stretched all the way back to a cold stone kitchen in a manor house in Somerset, a mastery of trifle.

The dessert stayed with him, too, because it embodied home, and his thoughts from that first spoonful did an about-face, focusing on Dalgety and not so much on the sharp descent into Victoria, and the stretch to Bairnsdale, and the night in the hotel, the net of lace at the window no barrier to the wildlife of the street and where, peering out for the hundredth time and to the sinister music of his father's snoring, Wilfred thought he saw two people rutting in an alley, just as he had seen the bulls and the cows on the treeless plains of the Monaro, though not clumsy and silly with the foliage of clothing.

The job done, they headed back across Victoria without two of their stockmen. The men had hooked into other musters, flies to the sugar of opportunity, bouncing randomly through the countryside, falling into the abyss of a rosy-cheeked girl at the pub, or a fancy triggered at the brush of a gloved hand at the picnic races. Perhaps gone forever, like Crank's stupid cattle, perhaps not.

Without the herd the rest of Bill Lampe's team made good time to Swifts Creek and Omeo and on up to Corryong, following the same route they had taken in reverse. It may have been the speed of their unburdened travel, but the journey seemed different to Wilfred, and the landscape appeared new. It felt to the boy as if they were riding uphill on the trek back. It explained, in his mind, why the Snowy River moved south through Victoria and out to sea. The whole country was tilted to the south. He had solved a riddle of his river.

They pitched camp under stands of ghost gums and he marvelled at the fleshy quality of the trunks and the human-like wrinkles gathered under the branches and he thought of Grandfather Callistus bathing in the creek at the bottom of his orchard and even the big-bellied schoolmaster they'd discovered dead that time under the tree by the river at the Dalgety fair.

The party stopped again near Towong and struck camp on the banks of the Murray before the ascent to Suggan Buggan and up again to Ingeegoodbee, which they couldn't mention without word of Crazy Doctor Charlie Carter. They'd missed him on the way down. He'd been at Jindabyne for supplies. But one look at his shack and the adjoining horse yards and the single brumby in the corral with a calico sack sewed over its head and Wilfred knew why they called him Crazy Charlie. It was the way of madness; it had a habit of spilling away from its owner, establishing its own radius just as light, from a distance, grew its own halo. The whole of Charlie's fifty-acre spread throbbed with it.

At the Murray River camp they talked of Carter again. Perhaps his influence was wider than they thought, roiling down the western face of the Alps and rattling their fire.

'Lucky, in a way, he weren't there when we first passed through,' one of the stockmen said. 'You heard what he done to Harrison's mob around Christmas time.'

They all had. Harrison and his men had stopped for the night on the flatlands around Ingeegoodbee and grazed the cattle before the long descent. Early the next morning they'd found one of the cattle dead at the edge of the herd. When they rolled her over they saw someone had cut a neat square of flesh out of her rear flank. A small parcel of meat. Enough for a few meals. It could only have been Charlie.

'How he could cut a choice block out of her just like

248

that I don't have a clue,' the stockman added. 'That's about the strangest thing I heard in a long time, even for Charlie.'

'Is he still feuding with the Freebody boys?' another asked.

''Parently. He stinks up the creek with those bloody brumbies of his and out come the rifles.'

'It's not right. Those Freebody boys got a right to clean water.'

The feud had been going for almost two years. It was Charlie's brumbies, and his theory on breaking them in. He stitched sacks over their heads. Cream calico, with a little opening for the mouth. He kept the sacks on for weeks, and they stumbled around the property like men condemned to the noose. Sometimes they broke free of the ramshackle yard, tripped in underbrush, bumped into trees, or slipped into the creek and drowned. Then the Freebodys had bloated, hooded brumbies fouling their water downstream.

'That spat not over by a long shot.'

They could hear the movement of the Murray and feel the cool air over it and it gave them some relief at the camp. They all reflected on the long muster and saddle-soreness and how the boy Wilfred had broken himself in well and how there'd barely been a complaint from him on a ride that had busted plenty of grown men.

'Anyone know how Ernie Macintosh is faring?' Bill said at last.

And the men howled with laughter at the mention of Ernie Macintosh and not a small bit of their laughter carried the residue of relief that they'd soon be home and sleeping in a proper bed and didn't have to eat onions again for a month if they didn't want to.

'Poor Ernie,' one of the men said, wiping tears from his cheeks, 'won't be paying a house call to Dr Carter for a while.'

They hooted again and the crying stockman fell back onto one buttock and held a booted foot in the air.

'They say he lost a lot of weight,' Bill said, 'on account he can't ride for so long, he has to walk everywhere.'

'They sayin' worse than that. They sayin' he has to make use of women's methods so he don't go and have an accident after Dr Carter were done with him.'

They'd told the story many times, of the boil on Ernie's arse, and the poultice Dr Carter applied – some swore strychnine was part of the concoction – and then Ernie's screaming dash for the creek.

After a while their fading laughter became indistinguishable from the babble of the river. They dropped off to sleep, one by one, like kerosene lanterns blown out with a sharp and sudden breath, and the horses went quiet except for the occasional deep belly-sigh, and Wilfred felt again the desire to be back in familiar surroundings. He thought of his cot on the verandah back home and the trout suit still standing guard over him. He thought of the scent of the pepper tree at the front of the house and the dogs sleeping under it and their snapping at flies in their dreams. He wanted the warmth of his mother and the routine of the house and even the scratchy presence of Astrid. He looked at the Murray and wanted to be back at his own river, the Snowy.

When they finally reached Ingeegoodbee they saw,

immediately, that there were now at least a dozen hooded horses in Carter's corral. Blue smoke eased from the chimney of his shack. They remained mounted on their horses and stopped on the patch of muddied earth between the shack and the corral. Chickens with mud-splashed breasts and caked combs scattered.

'STOP!' someone shouted. 'Who be you?'

They looked around and eventually saw movement in a poorly constructed blind some yards to the rear of the shack. The muzzle of a gun poked from a confusion of dead leaves and branches.

'Settle down, Charlie,' one of the stockmen yelled. 'A few old friends, just passin' through.'

He half rose from his hiding place and lowered the rifle to waist level, but kept it trained on them.

'Who? Who be?' He squinted one eye trying to see the strangers and all his efforts and tension and madness seemed to conduct to the pink and blue cylinder of his tongue which trembled and darted about in his open mouth like that of a cockatoo.

Charlie was short and bandy. His close-cropped grey hair was a thorny mess of tufts and bald patches. His left eye permanently squinted, as if he always had his rifle raised and cocked. But it wasn't so, as the men knew. He had been kicked in the face by a horse years before, and the blow had collapsed his left cheek and smashed the bone of the eye socket, so to find the real face of Charlie you had to observe the right side, and replicate it, and fold it over in your imagination. But even for those who knew him before the accident it became impossible to do that after a while. Each half had over the years gone its own way. Wilfred was agape.

251

'Sent? Freebodys sent?'

'We ain't been sent by the Freebodys, Charlie. Put that bloody gun away.'

They set down their swags a good distance from the stinking horse yard and the shack, a hutch of hand-split boards and logs and flattened tins and warped and rusted sheets of corrugated iron. They noticed, from their horses and around the yard and their makeshift camp, the decayed and semi-decayed carcasses of dozens of wood pigeons and finches and the occasional magpie and crow.

Wilfred squatted by the little combs of ribs and feather. The more he looked the more he saw. The whole cleared property was a bird graveyard.

'Don't let that trouble you, boy,' his father said. 'It's just the man's way. He doesn't mean any harm.'

'Just don't go acceptin' Charlie's hospitality when it comes to them fresh vegetables of his,' one of the stockmen added, unbuckling a saddle.

At the rear of the shack was a bog of tilled earth that sprouted erratic clusters of vegetable heads – parsnips, turnips and carrots. To deter the birds and passing travellers, he infected the soil around certain vegetables with strychnine. Only Charlie knew what was edible in his little store.

'We'll rest the horses and head off at first light,' Bill said, tapping the crown of the boy's hat.

Only the knowledge that they were at the ceiling of the Alps, that the rest of the trip was a descent to home, kept Wilfred from being afraid. He thought again of all the stories he'd heard of the mountains and the giant moths and the skeletons of the cows and horses and the broken wagon wheels on the ledges of the bottomless ravines, and he knew as he was living it that Carter and the cemetery of the birds were becoming a part of that story. And by the time he came off the mountains the little skeletons with their tiny cages of ribs would reach as high as the foliage of the snow gums and whenever he looked up to the Alps from Dalgety he would think of the ribs as big as the frames of covered wagons and not a few of the boys of the town would see them too, the boneyard at the top of the world.

That night they ate from their dwindling provisions and politely rebuffed Carter's miserly offers of hospitality. He appeared on nightfall with a dead rabbit in one hand and a muddied chicken in the other, both without eyes or feet. In the end, he joined them at their fire.

'Lampe. You the Lampes.' As he spoke his good eye blinked rapidly and his head moved forward slightly with the blinking, as if to give the broken words enough velocity to leave his twisted mouth. His stubble was stained with tobacco juice.

Wilfred, huddled by his father, had difficulty understanding the old man. The words at first dropped to the ground like spat teeth. Then, as if a catch had been released, they flowed out quickly and smoothly until something at the back of his throat, the cog of a ratchet not as worn as the rest, suddenly caught.

'That's right, I'm Bill Lampe. I come through here last year, Charlie. You were planning on starting your own newspaper when I were last here, remember? Or was it that medical journal of yours? You run out of ink, if I recall rightly.'

253

'Ah,' he said, not quite sitting in the light of the fire. Half haunched, like a gargoyle. 'Brother your. Brother Berty, your brother Berty, he hell, he causin' hell and highwater Berty down at the Creel your Berty he been on the grog for a week down at the Creel and ohhhh Lord ohhhh dear Lord Berty he fightin' and cussin' and ridin' horses round the yard and fallin' off the verandah and no one can do nothin' about your Berty he ain't slept I don't think but I got a nice tonic for him and I tell 'em what to do but that Berty he's a cunnin' bugger and they say he stole a cleaver from the kitchen and now they don't know where he is where you Berty where you and they think he back in Africa stickin' it up them Boers and good luck to him I hope he gets a few but Thredbo down there at Thredbo they seen nothin' like it since that Russian come through with the pistols . . .'

Bill Lampe snapped a twig into neat sections by the fire and looked into the flames.

'Berty,' he said to himself.

'You put up that Russian feller for a while, didn't you, Charlie? Not a bad feller, you said.'

Charlie turned towards the stockman. Wilfred watched the shift of shadow on his face, and saw the normal, open-eyed side change to that other man inside Charlie, with the scarred divot in his cheek and the mean eye.

'Interesting feller. Marx it was we talked, Marx, big row we had over Marx you know Marx a big row I didn't agree with the man Marx a lot of his stuff good I like was good but all his theories on prices what was worth the prices how to relate the prices to the labour to the theories all wrong I see it all wrong it's in my book anyways in the book how the feller Marx was wrong and the church too we don't see we eye to eye we don't see on the church and materialisms material materialism and the church it must incul it must must inculcate cate cate materialism which has merit you know indeed ohhh lord yes there is merit in moderation which the Russian he the Russian ahh the Russian he did not agree with old Charlie no sir and I slipped him a little tonic of mine slipped it and well he went away and I ain't seen him since that Russian.'

'Is Berty okay?' Bill asked patiently.

It took more than half an hour for Berty's predicament to be outlined by Carter. When the owner of the Creel decided to get word to the police officer at Dalgety, Berty had disappeared. The next day a fisherman visiting from Sydney reported a naked man hacking at bulrushes out on the Badja. It caused great amusement in the dining room at the Creel that night. Then there were no more stories.

Bill Lampe sat and smoked by the fire and thought of Berty and hoped that, as before, the moment eventually passed and he had made his way safely back to the property and the solitude of his shed at the rear of the valley. But he knew the moments were becoming more frequent now and Bill couldn't help but think that his brother was wishing for death, was rushing to meet it, just as he had rushed death and somehow missed it in the war. He was still over there, in camp, planning the next attack, counting down the next rush to death, huddling from sniper fire, fixing his bayonet and waiting for the signal to ambush. He rushed and rushed at death and he missed. Men fell around him but not Berty.

He once told Bill of the ceasefires called when each side tended to their dead, and the ambulances came in quietly and the chaplain said prayers and the bodies were brought back to their own people and it was the ceasefires, Berty said, that were the worst. The ceasefires – no life and no death. Just the void. It was the void again when men like Berty came home. The great silence of the ceasefire. Life only existed, he wrote in a letter home, when it pressed cheeks with death. At that very moment of meeting.

Back home, with the river, and the endless quiet paddocks, and the huge, time-worn cathedrals of boulders leaning over the rock pools and rising from the earth of the Monaro, the ancientness of them, the unbearable slowness of ageing, Berty could not find the friction he craved. He was caught in the longest ceasefire of all – living.

Charlie was rambling on about his book, *The Reconciliation*. Bill Lampe had not heard a word.

'. . . you, you, fellers like you, you see, allow me to test my theories, these theories, in the book, the principles of life, it is you, see, it is all within you, Darwin, Mr Darwin you've heard of him probably not but he ohhh lord yes ohhh yes Mr Darwin I have in here up here in the brainbox and these mountains it is why I am here, it is why and that is so, the great glacial shifts the glaciers and the lakes and what we sit on here what you ride on and steer your cattle over up and down and up and down it is all here under you Charlie's theory the recipricocity don't expect you to understand the recip the recip here, re . . . cip . . . ri . . . coc . . . iteeee, my good fellers, ha, you sittin' on it and don't know it we're like a tree a vast tree us we as mankind you and me and the boy here and maybe his boys one day on and on and up and down you go over it all and don't see it not a bloody thing but we're it we're it we're it the branches and the leaves cannot live without the roots that is us is society, cannot survive without the roots and here we are then you sittin' on it all and don't even know it but that's the word from Charlie . . .'

A stockman belched. 'At least we're sittin',' he said. 'Not like poor Ernie Macintosh, eh.'

They heard a commotion in the horse yard and watched as Charlie took a lantern over to the rails and said something to the dozen or so brumbies that were lifting dust and swirling drunkenly around the pen. In the lamplight they saw the ghostly shrouds of the horses and the plumes of dust. The animals quietened down and bumped into the fences and into each other until they were still again, their hooded heads bowed.

'Bloody lunatic,' one of the stockmen said. And the other sighed, perhaps having arrived, in the sluice of silence after Charlie's babbling, at the exact moment where something inside him said the muster was over, that he'd had enough. That it ended here, on a plate of cleared land carpeted with tiny bird bones beneath the spectacular wash of the Milky Way.

The boy Wilfred had been watching the sky to keep his mind detached from the gargoyle, and the smell of decay at the camp, and had counted seven shooting stars. He said to himself, maybe these are the eyes of all the little birds that have died here. He offered them his good wishes.

The fire grew smaller and they could see from their camp the lantern burning in Carter's single glass window and they knew he would be reading and writing through the night with the loaded gun ready and resting next to the door just in case the Freebody boys decided to make a surprise move.'Old Charlie has it open the one the one eye always open it is,' Charlie had said, and by the fire Wilfred tried it, sleeping with one eye open, until the stinging got too bad, and he wondered if Charlie's strange face had grown that way over the years and adapted like the animals of Mr Darwin because of his method of sleeping with one eye open every night.

At dawn they packed up the camp quickly and Bill Lampe went to the door of the shack to bid farewell to the madman they knew as Charlie. He knocked quietly and looked into the single room of the shack and saw the old man asleep in an armchair made of sacking and packing cases. Shelves on the wall were buckled down with blue, green and clear glass bottles of his assorted medicines and concoctions. The shack smelled of smoke and sulphur and the myriad perfumes of an unwashed human body.

As they left the property the blinded brumbies gathered side by side at the rough-hewn rails of the horse yard and their hooded heads followed the leather creak and bit tinkle of the departing party. Wilfred looked back and saw the hooded horses, the sacks milky and terrifying in the blue light of morning. For a long while dry bird bones cracked beneath the hooves of his weary little mare.

TWENTY-ONE

GRAHAM FEATHERSTONE'S OFFICIAL job brief as the station's midnight-to-dawn host was to play music and take callers if absolutely necessary. They didn't anticipate many callers. He politely suggested that the brief was not exactly what he thought defined a late-night talk-back host. They said he could take it or leave it.

Two years into the position he played music and took callers when absolutely necessary. He was the Friend of the Sleepless. His colleagues privately referred to him as Mr Dead Air.

They had found a niche for him where the ratings would be nonexistent. They no longer had to tolerate him in the office, or pretend to be interested in his observations from Port Arthur and the 'stuff' that was never reported. And on the premise of the ratings, low as they were, they could quietly remove him at any time if need be.

Then one Saturday evening in late 1998, in the apartment at Hen and Chicken Bay, Victoria told him over dinner that their relationship was finished and it'd be better if he moved out. He asked her if there was another man involved and she said yes. He asked if there had been others over the years and she remained silent.

'Let's face it,' she said. 'It's been dead for years now.' He was Mr Dead Air.

Graham left. It was her apartment. He packed a bag and realised how little was his, how he left hardly an imprint on the apartment in Hen and Chicken Bay. It had been refurbished without him noticing. He was an old ornament.

'Who is he?' he asked at the door.

'Never mind, Graham,' she said, closing it.

He drove to a small motel he knew on Glebe Point Road and bought a bottle of Scotch en route and once there, in his room, he opened the Scotch and started working back through their relationship and joining dots that he suddenly saw as connected. The dots were everywhere. And the more he drank the more surprised he was that he hadn't seen all this earlier. Halfway through the bottle he was glad to be rid of her and considered it a lucky escape, and by the end of the bottle, early the next morning, he wept because he missed her.

He slept all day and went to work that night.

Over the next few months his two producers noticed that Graham Featherstone was growing prickly and argumentative. He offended the show's rare on-air guests. He was short with security staff and the early-morning researchers who came in at the tail end of his shift. When he finished work there were complaints that the studio, and particularly Graham's microphone, smelled of booze.

He rented a narrow, partially furnished semi-detached house in Rozelle, and ate most of his evening meals at the nearby Welcome Inn, and made a whole new group of friends there. There were plenty of them that didn't work so if he went to the Welcome in the early afternoon he'd find at least a few there, and he'd stay on until dinner then go off to the station. If none of his new friends were there it didn't matter, because he became good friends with the bar staff. He liked it at the Welcome better than his dark semi.

He liked the way everyone spoke their mind at the pub and by the time he arrived at work, still brimming with this bonhomie, carrying its afterglow, he spilled it into his radio show.

'. . . I still miss my ex-fiancée, you know,' he said one night. 'I can't understand why you left me after everything we've shared.' Pause. 'People tell me that's life. What does that mean, exactly? *That's life*. Can anyone tell me? If we know so much about it, to say *that's life*, to presume we have this complete understanding, then why do we use it to rationalise the unknowable?' Pause. 'That's life. That's shit, if you ask me.' Pause. 'Here's The Platters.'

He'd make himself a cup of coffee during The Platters.

'My brother Robert,' he said one night, 'he's a big businessman, the wheeler-dealer. Never been any different. Ran scams since he was a kid. Mr Big Shot. You've probably seen him down at Rockpool. The fat bastard in one of the booths near the front door. He likes to see who's coming and going. Robert. You've probably paid for a tile or two in one of his fancy bathrooms in one of his mansions. Everything about him's big, you know what I'm saying? Big house. Big car. Wife with big hair. Kid with a big arse. Are you with me on

261

this one?' Pause. 'He builds shopping centres. No, excuse me: retail facilities. He makes them big so you get lost inside them, can't find your way out. Spend some money on the way. That's Robert. The big guy responsible for the big malls you wander around lost in all day every day. Walk out with nothing in your wallet. The mall you let babysit your kids while you're off having affairs with other married people or blowing the monthly budget at poker machines or a crap table, too excited to leave for a piss. While your kids are lost in the mall scoring some dope. Let Uncle Bob look after them. You've probably seen him. You can't miss him. I'd love you to see his spread on the harbour. He's got this Greek Italianate thing happening, this boy from Green Valley. Where did it come from? You tell me. He likes haloumi and pizza. That's his pedigree with the ancient civilis-ations. He's got the big lions' heads happening, and the fountains. He's got a bit of Tuscany here and a bit of Santorini there, are you getting the picture? You mention Amalfi to him and he says – Bro, I don't like none of that green shit on my sandwiches. Here's a bit of Schubert. This'll put lead in your pencil.'

During Schubert he slipped out of the studio and picked up some Peking duck from BBQ King. He liked to have a beer and joke with the waiters while he waited for his food. They laughed at how he kept checking his wristwatch. Some nights it took ages to get his delivery, when the restaurant was full of tourists. Or he'd have to wait in the street by the door as they piled out of the restaurant and into a waiting minibus, headed for the Cross. He used to giggle with the waiters at the nutty taxi driver, Mr Harold, who ate his rice with a knife and fork. More often than not, Graham still had plenty of time to spare when he got back to the studio to arrange the sprigs of shallot just how he liked it inside the pancakes.

'Victoria never liked duck, did you, darling?' he said one night, eating the duck, on air. 'You see, with Peking duck you must eat it with your hands. Victoria never ate anything without an implement. In fact, Victoria didn't like touching food at all. I think that's decidedly odd. To Victoria, eating with one's hands was uncouth. It was not what one did at one's table when one was hungry, one ate with one's cutlery, that's what one did.' Pause. 'Now that I think of it, Victoria wasn't overly fond of touching anything. How curious. She certainly didn't touch me much. How peculiar. To live with someone and share their bed, and not touch them.' Pause. 'You may think that's not possible. I can tell you. It's possible. Poor Victoria. To go through life not knowing the pleasures of Peking duck. How monumentally sad. We're coming up to the hour. Here's a bit of Erik Satie.'

Satie always made him drift into a mild melancholia. He liked to play Satie after eating the duck pancakes. He felt Satie had an aftertaste, not unlike good duck.

'Ah, Paris,' he said one night, the duck oil still on his fingertips. 'Satie got it because he walked the cobble-stones, my friends. Hour after hour he walked those streets and boulevards. Step after monotonous step, like those beautiful notes of his, two, three notes, like steps, underlying his compositions. Have you noticed? The music. Like walking.' Pause. 'Unhygienic, though, poor Satie. The same corduroy suits, day after day. How Victoria would have loathed him. *Flinched* is the word.

How she would have *flinched* at the sight of Satie. All those beautiful notes out of such a dirty instrument. How could it be, Victoria? It makes no sense. Senseless Satie. Can you see him in Sydney? I don't think so. Never would have made it in Sydney. Never would have cut the mustard here, our Erik. And you can hear my big brother Robert, can't you? Satie? Satie? I *love* Satie, especially the peanut sauce. Here's the *Gymnopédies* for all you late night street-walkers.'

During the *Gymnopédies* Graham Featherstone left the studio again and walked around the block a few times to stay awake. He put some coins into a homeless man's empty styrofoam coffee cup. He avoided eye contact with the drunk and the drugged. He side-stepped the restaurant garbage on the footpaths.

'Back again,' he said one night after his short walk. 'Back from the land of Starbucks and Delifrance. I love sleeping during the day. Have I told you? I love shutting the blinds when everything goes on outside in the day-light. Schoolkids slipping knives between other kids' ribs during recess. Blokes abusing their children. People punching each other on television. Young guys smashing the skulls of old men over a bit of road rage. Old people mugged for a few bucks. Farmers going broke. Asians being spat on in the street because of some redneck imbecile in parliament. Australians going along, going along. Sportsmen like gods. Cricketers and footballers with too much time and money on their hands for their tiny brains to comprehend, acting like rude brats, in and out of court, ohh, it's okay, he's famous, he's a naughty boy. Morons that'd be in prison, most of them, if they weren't good at throwing or catching or hitting a little ball, feted by prime ministers, worshipped by punters, this little veneer of recognition that will pass, oh how quickly it passes, and fussed over like geniuses when there are men and women out there trying to save lives, cure cancer, eradicate diseases, and they're scratching for a penny. Mentally handicapped people forced onto the streets. Too expensive. Living in alleys and eating garbage. Stuck in squalor, raped, bashed, before the courts, back out again, picked up, before the courts again, and over and over we go. Chefs, *cooks*, like gods. Every move they make, the *cooks*, watched by the media. Millionaires and celebrities, because they can *boil an egg* just right. Because they satisfy the rich and the idle, fill their little tummies with yummies, so they can crap it out and do it all over again. And out the back some poor bastard's reaching into a garbage tin. Oh how the cooks sweat, oh how nervous they get, when the hats are handed out. Oh please God I promise I will be a better person I promise God please just this time give me an extra *hat*. Oh the hats, the *hats*. We hereby grant thee an extra hat for your *extraordinary* contribution to the sweet potato. *Thank* you, God. Houses locked up like fortresses. Neighbours taking each other to court over the price of a fence. Gamblers jumping into Darling Harbour trying to kill themselves after losing everything. Teenagers shot for a mobile phone. Young girls lured and raped by pack animals. Stockbrokers like gods. Bankers. People who spend every waking hour thinking about money, and every day play with what would take everyone else ten lifetimes to accumulate. Along we go, along we go. Row, row, row your boat, life is but a dream. Everyone for themselves. Manners lost. Kindness

265

gone. The coast given over to gated communities. *Gated*. To keep out the *riffraff*. Armed guards at corner stores. Black people in camps worse than the Third World outside Alice Springs and up in the Territory. A generation of them stolen and no apology. Movie stars like gods. Boofheads flickering on a screen for a few hours and we sweat on their solutions to world peace and poverty and strife. Gossip everywhere. Gossip in the press. Gossip the only dialogue. No unions for workers. Universities that can't afford to operate. The sea full of our own shit. No guts for a republic. Manners gone. Kindness lost. Australians going along, going along.

'What has happened to us, ladies and gentlemen? Two hundred years and here we are. What's happened to that good old-fashioned sense of humour we developed? Out there clearing scrub and tending sheep and growing food with our bare hands, all that wit and cheek and irreverence as we fanned out from the tents at Sydney Cove. When did we start taking ourselves so seriously, and lose all that? Where did it go? What's happened? *What's happened to my country?*'

Graham Featherstone did not know that his producer had cut his microphone and replaced him with *Rhapsody in Blue* shortly after the great weary sadness of Satie.

TWENTY-TWO

IN THE FREEZER of his old Kelvinator fridge Tick kept plastic bags of his own infected blood.

There had been a period when he felt the need to souvenir the blood and keep it close by. He had removed it from his body regularly with a needle and bagged it and soon it became an obsession with him and he filled bag after bag. He stacked the frosted packets of dark infected blood in the small compartment of the freezer. Sometimes he opened the swing door and fingers of frost fell out and he stared at the red blocks stubbled with ice in the rectangular space. When he had used all the space in the freezer he stashed other bags in the main vault of the fridge and in the blanket box under the window in the lounge room. Then he stacked the bags in the pantry.

For a while he thought he could drain the bad blood from himself and rid his body of the disease. He liked, in the early days, to take a frozen bag and hold it. It gave his enemy form and weight.

He was getting sicker.

The periods of lethargy grew longer and reached deeper into him. Tick felt the inside of his body was unexpectedly falling into a half-sleep. Drowsy. Gassed. If it had a colour he knew it would be the blue of a gas flame. Yet at the same time the ulcers in his mouth and the growing lesions and the sores on his scalp and the paper-thin skin between his toes that kept splitting open like dry earth and gaped without moisture, just fissures as red as meat, rendered his exterior self the opposite of the blue flame. He was all prickly and sore and sensitive outside, while the inside dozed and hissed silently with blue.

He lost three teeth in one ten-day period. He became fascinated with the teeth. One afternoon, staring at the teeth laid side by side on a small blanket of velvet under his trout lamp, he painted them with gold hobby paint. While they dried he prepared a small glassless frame of fake gilded gold and mounted the teeth in a triangular formation. He hung the frame next to the one that contained the slip of long hair from the days when he was Juliet.

It struck him, with the ruby bags in the freezer, and the hair and the teeth, that he might be experiencing a strange and artful way of death. A death that was the reverse of a simple child's puzzle. He was slowly coming apart, piece by piece. Like a completed jigsaw bumped and knocked, the pieces were easing away from the picture. A corner shape. An edge piece. You could still make out the scene despite the dark gaps between the pieces, and the missing elements. For the first time, with the teeth mounted in the frame, he saw that the gaps were becoming the picture. It was in the gaps that he could see his own death.

An idea came to him to make a work of art out of his collection of empty medicine bottles.

He had two hundred and thirty-seven small clear glass and amber bottles labelled with his name and the date of prescription. He had kept them from the beginning because he was a collector. They presented, in twos and threes, no overarching or comprehensible schema. He saw no specific use for them, just that they were tiny vessels with some vague future purpose.

Since childhood Tick had been compelled to document his life. He kept everything – teenage journals, tram tickets, concert stubs, letters, leaves and stones and shells and bird bones. He believed, one day, he'd be important, as would everything associated with him.

Contracting one of the late twentieth century's newest and most lethal viruses was not how he expected to become important.

In the cool, cramped flat he spread the bottles out on the rug. He sat quietly surrounded by the little glass vials and thought perhaps a large wall display would be arresting. But how to mount them? He could see them, too, arranged in neat rows in velvet cases. Or possibly a crucifix of bottles.

His nurse, Bibi, found him thinking in the nest of glass.

'That front door lock is sticking,' she said, placing her bags on the lounge chair. She was a slender woman and the thin white and blue stripes of her dress made her appear even more willowy. She was one of several nurses he knew from the clinic. He had asked for her. He didn't have the strength for a matron. For large arms and talcum. Tutting and the squeak of amply filled sneakers. He didn't want a mother. He wanted wire and edge.

'Have you eaten today?' She stood with her hands on

her hips. He looked like a child playing with a set of blocks on the floor.

'One lemon,' he said. 'And don't bother shouting at me. I'm creating, Bibi.'

'Oh hush, hush, everyone. The master's creating. Shall I hold my breath so as not to disturb the genius?'

'Bugger off.'

'Oh good. The lemon has done wonders for your temperament.'

'Let's see you in my condition and see how your temperament is.'

'A condition now is it?' She stepped onto the rug and nudged some of the medicine bottles with her left toe. 'Now it's a condition. Life is a condition, mate. Get used to it.'

'Do shush, Bibi. I'm working.'

She went into the kitchenette, sighed, and started cleaning.

'Such an artist,' she said from the small alcove. 'Too . . . occupied to even wipe his own arse.'

He smiled without opening his lips. He had begun practising the sealed smile since the problems with his teeth. He could hear her washing plates and cups in the sink and the crockery clinked dully beneath the water.

'How am I? Well, I'm okay, and thank you for asking,' she said. 'Old Wilberforce died last week. You were friends, weren't you? A lovely old guy. Mavis found him . . .'

Tick sat silently amongst the bottles and felt sadness for Wilberforce suffuse him.

During his last spell in the hospice they would sit out on the balcony every afternoon and play cribbage with

270

a deck of cards depicting the apostles. They took their same places at the large plastic picnic table, Wilberforce in his chrome and blue vinyl wheelchair, the table level with his chest. He would hold the cards up, the fan of apostles obscuring his thin face.

'In the Salon de Mort,' he would say from behind the fan, 'we played cribbage with picture cards of the twelve apostles.'

Tick phoned Harold for supplies, and they were ferried to the hospice in a taxi.

They played for hours, out on the balcony that overlooked Darlinghurst Road, and on some late afternoons a puff of wind brought to them laughter and shouting and the smell of exhaust and Thai food from nearby Oxford Street, beyond the trees.

Once, without warning, deep into a cribbage set, Tick felt a love for Mr Wilberforce that he did not fully understand and that he had no words for. He was unsure how a son was supposed to feel after all this time. He must have had that feeling once, when he was a boy, but he was like a child once heavily versed in musical scales and piano lessons and complex chords, immersed in daily practice and examinations and the great barbed complexities of sheet music who, as an adult, found he could not play a note. His life, at an early point, had eased away from the time-worn patterns and templates of everyday living and interacting with family and friends and the way the world operated day to day.

It was love that glued all of that together, and – he hated to think of it – he didn't have the glue. It was love, now, that unexpectedly arrested him. The sight of people holding hands, embracing or kissing had become so peculiar to him that it could stop him in the street. The sound of laughing children. It had all become a strange language to Tick.

He looked at Mr Wilberforce's freckled and lined pate and bushy eyebrows and moist and milky eyes across the top of the fan of cards and smiled to himself and the smile lit a warmth in his chest.

'As he drew on his Lucky Strike,' Wilberforce said in the gloom of the balcony, 'he once again won handsomely.' And he gently laid the apostles on the table.

Wilberforce occasionally gripped the armrests of the wheelchair as he looked to the city and Tick watched the fan of bones rise in his large hands, or the skin sink around the bones like the cloth of broken umbrellas, and counted how long he held the grip. He wondered what it was inside Wilberforce that took him so unexpectedly in these moments. What it was that pulled at him so powerfully, drew him in tightly, then released.

Maybe Wilberforce, too, was struck now and then with the cramp that was lost love.

Then just as suddenly he would turn back to the table, adjust the top of his dressing-gown, as elderly women constantly grasp at the tops of their blouses, and he would pull a cigarette out of the packet, light it slowly and thoroughly, hold the flame to the tip for an age, his eyes wide open with the lighting, and he would draw in the smoke with obvious pleasure, and the pleasure ran through him like a current, and he was Tick's pretend father again.

'No time for slackers in the Salon,' he would say, slapping the cards. 'Shuffle away, young man. Time's a-wastin'. And that's one thing I don't have to waste.'

They were two men playing cards. They were two men dying. They were in the same place.

When Tick was over his spell he left the hospice. He returned once to see Mr Wilberforce. He found him sitting alone on the balcony. They shared a whisky and looked out to the city.

'One thing I don't get,' he said to Tick. 'You're a young man. This isn't a young man's place. This is for old buzzards, like me. So what's a young man doing in and out of a place like this?'

They had never spoken of each other's illnesses or past lives, only of the moment. They'd just played cribbage with the twelve apostles.

Tick smoked. He couldn't look at Mr Wilberforce.

'Some mistakes,' he said quietly, 'you pay for more than others.'

When he went to leave, the old man grabbed his wrist, and then they hugged, and Tick prolonged the hug; he gripped old Mr Wilberforce. Afterwards he sat in the park not far from the hospice for a long time, until the food wagon for the street people arrived under the giant fig, and he walked home and sat in his flat in the dark and didn't know when he would visit Mr Wilberforce again because he didn't want to ruin the feeling of their embrace on the balcony of the hospice.

'. . . on the balcony,' said Bibi. 'Just like he was asleep. He'd been out there for hours and nobody knew he was gone. God rest his soul.' She made the sign of the cross in the little kitchenette. 'My friend Angelina, who went on the cruise two years ago? You remember? It happens there too, the old people, on the deck all day and dead, and nobody notices until the dinner bell.

273

But you don't want to hear this, because you are creating.'

He stared into the pool of glass medicine bottles.

It struck Tick, then, that he might make an effigy of himself with the bottles. They were him. They had his name on the outside. They had the exact dates of his decline. And inside they were empty. Nothing. Just a tiny pocket of air, cool and empty, and if that air had a colour it would be that of a blue gas flame.

TWENTY-THREE

THEY CAME DOWN past the still waters near Paddy's Corner and along the edge of the gorges of the upper reaches of the Thredbo River, arriving at the fishing lodge in the mid-afternoon.

The Creel was still so new they could smell cut timber as they crossed the small wooden bridge to the lodge. Bill Lampe and young Wilfred stopped their horses on the bridge and looked down at the rock pools and the swift passage of the brown river water and the frilly skirts of froth that pushed into the dark crevices of the wet boulders.

On the other side of the bridge was a small swinging sign attached to a freshly hewn post – THE CREEL AT THREDBO – and beyond it two stretches of white picket fence on either side of the entrance to the grounds. Just inside the property was a line of newly planted elms and poplars that reached no higher than the belly of a horse. They looked odd amongst the old red gum trees and great rolls of black-berry bushes that had been slashed back to the new fence line.

Bill noticed wood shavings in piles around the base of

the infant trees, and abandoned scraps of wood and wire across the stony ground.

'Fancy,' Bill said. Both he and his son noticed thick walls of bush close to the back of the hotel. It was the peak of summer and the dry bush held its own heat.

The horses stepped tentatively onto the crushed gravel of the driveway. They were dusted and scratched and their tails were flecked with dried shit and nettles and they both carried several yokes of sweat lines from their necks to their strong upper chest muscles and they trod daintily on the gravel like bemused pilgrims.

Bill and Wilfred were soiled too from the long muster. They had forgone bathing in the rivers and creeks on account of the exasperating temperatures, even for the High Country, which relegated any bathing useless. Face splashes and a damp hat had sufficed since they'd left old Charlie Carter's ghost camp.

As they approached the lodge, both felt suspicious and uncomfortable, as if they didn't belong in their own country. They had heard of the Creel, of course, one of the little jewels that dangled off Premier Carruthers' new road from Jindabyne to the foot of Kosciusko. They had been updated on its progress, and given it little thought. It blew through their conversation like a dandelion. They dismissed it as they dismissed Carruthers' road. They had used their own tracks and paths for a generation, just as the local Aboriginal tribes had beaten a network of tracks through the mountains to the summit during the seasons of the bogong. They had no concept of the purpose of the new road. It had no function to them, so it didn't exist.

Bill had brought Wilfred to the Creel to find out the

whereabouts of Uncle Berty. The story Carter had told of his brother running amok in this heat had burrowed into Bill Lampe's mind like a tick. He did not tell the boy of the incidents with Berty over the years. The day at the races with the pistol. The policeman and three graziers and Bill Lampe dragging his brother, in full military uniform, through the crowd, and the confusion of trampled hats and bonnets and the officer's broken jaw and Berty's deep wailing from the holding cell as wild as a trapped animal's. Nor did he tell of the spell in the hospital at Cooma, and the noose Bill Lampe had cut down and burned at the back of the valley, and Berty's sniper runs through Crank's hills. The boy didn't need to know. It had been a while since the last major 'turn', and Bill Lampe had been waiting for it.

The horses and the father and the son had never seen a grand semicircular city carriageway before, and they proceeded slowly to the lodge, all raw timber and stone and clinging uncomfortably to the earth, with the wonder of entering a great cathedral, filled as it was with the incense of recent labour and wood shavings and just-dried paint alongside the familiar perfume of pine needles. They could hear the babble of the river down to the right of the entrance.

The lodge was long and low and a verandah stretched across its entire facade. There were two motor vehicles parked near the front stairway. They stopped near the cars and the horses leaned forward and smelled the tyres and the leather seats. Fishing lines were drying on small pegs along the verandah. They lifted and lowered in unison like hair in a breeze.

'You wait here,' Bill said, dismounting. He looked

uphill past the sharp edge of the verandah roof. 'Take them up there and let them feed for a while.'

Bill Lampe's boots reverberated on the timber of the balcony. He could see the shapes of wash stands and brass bedheads in the bedrooms.

'Hello?'

He found a passageway about halfway along and peered into the gloom.

'Anybody there?'

Just inside the passageway he noticed a flyscreen door and hesitantly entered a large dining room with long tables. On the wall beside the door was a noticeboard for recording the names of fishermen and any catch over three pounds. In the gloom, pressing his face close to the board, he noticed it carried a single name. J. Carrington: 4 lb 6 oz.

'Anybody?'

The room was pungent with the smell of cooked bacon and fish and burnt butter. He walked to a square of light at the far side of the room, another flyscreen door, and through it could see a huge stove, even larger than that in the kitchen of the Crank homestead, where he had been invited to dine on two occasions in fourteen years' service. He would, he knew, never be asked into the formal dining room, in the cool centre of the house, which was as big as the entire Buckley's Crossing Hotel.

Even though it was newborn, this lodge, to Bill it felt old and worn inside, as if already gathering breathy stories of heroics, of fish lost, of dangerous eddying currents and sudden, life-threatening rises in the river, all of them already soaked into the dark wall timbers.

He returned to the front balcony and was momentarily blinded by the afternoon sunshine. The river glinted through the scrub and the gums and he figured the guests of the Creel were trudging out for the dusk rise. Suddenly he was hit with exhaustion. Perhaps it was the residual odour of the food, or the sight of neatly made beds through the crocheted lace curtains, or the thought of having to mop up whatever catastrophe Berty had left in his wake this time.

What is it with this family? he thought, scratching his chin. They have a habit of going missing.

Wilfred sat quietly between the feeding horses. He could see his father leaning against the railing on the verandah, the silk fishing lines wavering away from the rail and out towards the shiny motor cars and the circular drive of gravel. In the centre of the circle were the beginnings of a garden. It looked to Wilfred, from his spot on the hillside, like a giant keyhole. A funny big keyhole carved into the rock above the river.

He, too, saw flashes of the river, and wondered if he and his father would fish after all, with Berty missing.

The boy, Bill thought. He ain't going nowhere. He's here for good, like those fat and heavy boulders across the plains of the Monaro. He thinks he's the King Trout. Still goes on about the night of the opera disaster, and the missing teacher, the German. What was his name? Schweingill? He didn't have the heart to tell the boy they'd found him up at Pretty Plain, swinging from a tree. The dogs had been at him, jumped up at the corpse and taken his feet.

Bill observed the motor cars. Again he was

overwhelmed by the smell of young cut timber and shattered rock.

Lighting a cigarette, he sat down on the steps of the lodge and coughed deeply and felt the pressure of the cough behind his eyes. He needed to get home, yet he wanted to keep his promise of the fishing to the boy. Berty would turn up. He always did. He had survived the Boer. A few jars of grog or a wander in the bush weren't going to kill him. Though Bill Lampe tried not to think of the pistol that day, and the knives, and the noose. They rested in a dark drawer in the back of his mind.

On the way down the mountains Bill Lampe had thought of rigging up some willow poles for fishing. He'd caught some of his best fish with a pole. The Creel, though, might loan him a couple of rods for a day or two, so long as Berty's indiscretions hadn't been too excessive.

He whistled and the boy came over with the dog.

'How you like to stay here the night so we can hit the river first thing in the morning?' his father said.

'Here?'

'Why not? Sleep in a proper bed and all.'

'You can sleep here? Like at the Buckley's?'

'They got beds so I suppose you can sleep in them. Make a nice change from Mother Earth, wouldn't it?'

'I guess,' Wilfred said. He was confused by the proposition. 'It looks a bit fancy.' He had remembered his father's word, and had rolled it around in his mouth like a boiled sweet.

'Looks fancy to you, does it? I guess it is a bit fancy. But we're fancy, ain't we? Two fancy old boys staying at the Fancy Lodge.'

Wilfred giggled. His father raised his head, winked, and blew out a thick, straight plane of smoke.

'Just two fancy fellers,' he said. 'That's the Lampe boys.'

'Yeah. That's us.'

Later, the lodge's small fishing party returned and after a long and sometimes jocular discussion with the new proprietor, Wilfred and his father were assigned a room off the verandah where they washed up before joining two other guests in the dining room. The smell of fried trout pushed through the flyscreen door of the kitchen.

They sat together at one of the long dining tables and were soon joined by Jack the proprietor. Through the flyscreen they could see his wife working at the giant black stove.

The guests – a school principal and a lawyer, both from Sydney – discussed the day's fishing with Jack and quizzed Bill about the best local holes and rivers. Wilfred listened quietly to the talk of fishing and the smell of the trout drifting in from the kitchen made his mouth water. He sat on his hands and watched the bow of the woman's apron jiggle as she manoeuvred the pans on the stove.

In exchange for the night's board, Bill Lampe agreed to take the men out fishing in the morning. He planned to leave them on the Thredbo, then disappear with the boy to the reliable holes he knew of. He did not warm to the school principal or the lawyer – at how they dressed for dinner, all jackets and starched cuffs, with the sawdust of the lodge still fleshy and raw in the corners of the rooms, the light fixtures incomplete, and the cleared gums still stacked at the back of the property with ants encased in bleeding sap. He could not penetrate the dialogue of the city men. Found no moments of intersection. He tethered himself to the crack and creak of the settling building.

And thoughts of Berty who, he learned, had not been anywhere near the Creel, but had in fact taken an axe to the other newly built hotel, the Kosciusko, over near the Plains of Heaven, and absconded into the bush before arrest.

They finished their drinks. The city men talked of schools they had attended and Jack had a whispered word to his wife at the flyscreen door.

'I'm sure you won't mind waiting a few moments longer for dinner,' he said on his return. 'Our other guest has just returned to his room and will be with us shortly. You may have heard of him – the scientist, Clement Wragge?'

The city men nodded uncertainly.

Bill did not react. But he knew of Wragge. When Mitchell the publican added some rooms to the back of the Buckley's, he brought over Arthur Mawson, a builder from Cooma, and they had shared some beer, and stories. Mawson had built a weather observatory for Wragge up at the top of Kosciusko in '98. Wragge was a meteorologist, Mawson said. They called him 'inclement rag'. A likeable fellow. Made an arse of himself out in western Queensland, firing cannons into the sky to break the drought. Straight shooter though, Wragge. Except for the cannons.

The lure of the mountains, Bill thought. They all come through at one time or other, scientists and fortune hunters, thinking to change the world. Here, where nothing changes. Granite doesn't shift too fast. But they don't see that. Till they get here.

'He has just come back from the summit of Kosciusko,' the proprietor said with some pride. 'For reasons I'm sure will be made clear in the course of the evening.'

'An explorer,' the school principal said, in a voice as reedy as a child's. 'How tantalising. I have come across him in the newspapers, I think . . .'

'He's the weatherman, is he not?' the lawyer said, happy to outpoint the principal. They were youngish Sydney men of position and on the rise. It, the outpointing, was expected of them. 'Was he not called upon for a long-range prediction of weather conditions for the opening of federal parliament? I believe it's the same gentleman. There was some fall from grace, I seem to recall.'

'Ah,' the principal said. 'Of course.'

'A firebrand, I remember reading. In his younger years. They called him the Prophet, I think. Or he called himself a Prophet. One or the other.'

'Let us hope we hear it all,' Jack said, 'from the horse's mouth.'

He disappeared into the kitchen and the city men continued to gossip about the notorious Clement Wragge until they heard heavy bootsteps down the adjacent corridor. A tall, thin man entered the dining room and stopped inside the doorway, as if adjusting to the light. He played nervously with his strangely old-fashioned jacket collar and cuffs.

'Good evening,' he said in a loud, stony voice. 'Professor Wragge.'

He stepped into the yellow haloed light from the lanterns, his hand already extended for shaking, and formally greeted each person at the table, including Wilfred, with a small bow.

Taking the seat opposite the boy, he continued to adjust the bothersome cuffs as he carefully studied each of the guests without self-consciousness and without blinking. His face was long and narrow and two large identical furrows ran down from just beside his nostrils and into his red-grey beard. His mouth was hidden by an uncombed moustache.

The chin jutted, not by natural design, but by the way Wragge kept his head perennially tilted back at a slight angle. The beard on the chin was pointed and not dissimilar in size and texture to a clump of hair at the centre of his scalp, so it was a face that looked identical top and bottom, a face capable of being swivelled around without noticing, and it was this feature that attracted Wilfred. The boy theorised that if Mr Wragge was smiling, he would be frowning if you turned that face upside down, and vice versa.

'I trust I have not delayed your meal, and if I have I offer apologies,' Wragge said. It was a voice Wilfred recognised – Mr Schweigestill had it, so did Grandfather Callistus. It was too big for a dining room the size of the Creel's, better suited to lecture rooms or halls, or the great empty auditoriums of nature. 'But as I indicated to you earlier, Mr Ferguson, I am not one for the formality of mealtimes, and you were free to adhere to your agenda without me.'

He kept his pointed chin directed at the proprietor.

'We noticed you coming in, Professor Wragge, and felt the other guests wouldn't—'

'It is of no further consequence,' he said. 'I am here now. Please continue as before. I won't be dining long.'

Wilfred studied the sharp, darting shadow of the upraised chin on the tablecloth. It prodded and retreated like trout fry around the sugar canister and salt shaker.

The school principal wriggled his horn-rimmed spectacles. He beamed at Wragge with the trained official smile of all heads of school, one that replicated the smiles of the many hundreds of fat, pink-faced boys he guided into life.

'We were discussing, Professor Wragge, your work for the opening of parliament. In Melbourne,' he said. His voice had developed a quaver since the professor had arrived. The principal hesitated. He had hoped to trump the lawyer by being the first to engage the famous man.

'What of it?' Wragge said.

The lawyer interjected. 'What is your business here, if I may ask?'

'You may,' Wragge said, interlacing his fingers on the table. 'It is a journey of nostalgia. I have visited, on this day, the weather station I established at the summit of Kosciusko. Or remains of it, if I'm to be accurate. It was a pleasure for me those many years ago, having set up a similar facility on Ben Nevis as a youth. I find, at this moment in my life, an impulse towards such things. Specific places. I never gauged myself as nostalgic, but there you have it. May I ask, Mr Ferguson, what is the substance of this evening's menu?'

Bill Lampe picked at a piece of blistered skin on his palm. He liked Wragge immediately. The professor's lined face, though tanned, betrayed patches of windburn on the forehead and cheeks, and perhaps it was this that endeared him to Lampe. He was all edges and angles, a man of the outdoors, unlike the city men at the far end of the table. But it was more than that. Lampe worked out in the heat and the cold because that was all he could do. Men like this, with books in their head, who were driven up mountainsides, who sought out storm and gale, hail and lightning, possessed something that men admired, and feared. For most, it was too frightening to imagine. Men like Wragge. He strode into life without fear, and it was this that made him fearsome.

Jack poured more wine once the menu was recited, and Wragge brought the glass to his lips. He sipped, and his moustache wriggled rapidly like the snout of a rabbit with the tasting. Wilfred suppressed a laugh.

'Local?' Wragge inquired of himself, studying the yellow wine in the glass. 'Very fine. It is not a stretch of the imagination to taste the region's geology within it.'

He looked around the room and settled the point of his chin on Bill Lampe.

'You are the fishing guide?' he asked of him.

'For one day only. Tomorrow. Then the boy and I head home.'

'A local, too? Like the wine?'

'Down Dalgety way.'

'I figured as much,' Wragge said. Wilfred thought he noticed a grimace behind the thickety moustache. 'I, too, have a son,' he continued. 'Clement Junior. He was in charge of the station, up on the mountain, until we were closed down. Lack of funds, you see. Lack of foresight, to be precise. But my opinions no longer have any

286

value in this country. We shall be moving, across the Tasman. It is why I came here, for one last look at the mountain.'

He picked over his fried trout and, like all men used to eating alone in remote places, gazed into the plate as if it were a porthole to another world. Of his past. Or the future. Yet he ate the jelly and suet pudding quickly, and Wilfred noticed the quivering raspberry was there one minute and gone the next.

They were treated to grapes, and Wragge savoured them.

'It was once my pleasure to be in the south of Italy, amongst the vineyards, studying the havoc of their hail-storms,' Wragge said, returning his attention to Bill. 'The theory was to divert them from the vineyards with the Stiger Vortex. Are you familiar with it? A cannon, of sorts, that blasts air into the atmosphere. It was my belief that we could utilise such a weapon, a weapon of weather, to draw rain from low cloud cover. We attempted it outside Charleville. That's in Queensland. But I left the operation in charge of the local mayor, and the fool nearly wiped the town off the map. How we as a race draw forward quite often amazes me.'

Wilfred, his belly thumping with the cold jelly, stared wide-eyed at Wragge.

'You shot the cannon into the sky?' he asked.

'Correct. I still believe there is some merit in it. As for Charleville. Well. The dogs of Charleville disappeared under beds and houses for a week, or so I'm told.'

The boy laughed. He, too, liked Mr Wragge.

'Mr Lampe, will you join me on the verandah for a

smoke?' Wragge stood. 'Thank you, Jack. Gentlemen, good evening.'

They stood together leaning against the verandah railing with Wilfred quietly loitering beside them and Wragge accepted one of Bill's cigarettes. Bill could see, in the flare of the match, details of the face he had not been able to detect in the dim dining room. It was a face etched with regret. With dashed ambitions.

They drew on the cigarettes and looked out into the darkness. They could clearly hear the rush of the river.

'I say, with apology, that I may be responsible for this,' Wragge said.

A dog howled further down the valley. Wilfred sat quietly on the steps.

'For what?' Bill asked.

'When we first opened the station, on the summit, we had a single goal. To retrieve all the data we could from the highest point in the country, compare it with our coastal data, and see what patterns we could pull from that information. Simple enough. I'd done it all over the world. At the end of that first winter they started to arrive. You may recall it. The treks of tourists. The pack-horses. We were there for scientific observation alone. It was not intended as an invitation. Yet up they came. Like teenagers to their first ball. We were there, that was all. It was because we were there. And it is human nature, isn't it, to follow.'

'You were doing your job.'

'The lodges, like this. The hotels. They follow the packhorses. Everything follows something else. Even the weather, for a time. One pattern shadows another. If you know what to look for, you can see it.

Unfortunately, this was all I knew to look for. And while I was looking at the sky, life went on.'

'Why New Zealand?'

Wragge sighed in the dark, his chin pointed up at the stars beyond the low fringe of conifers down near the front gate.

'I should have been head of the new federal weather bureau, you know. There is nobody more qualified. Do you know the only area of cooperation between the states before Federation? Thanks to my work, the weather bureau and record stations. The weather was federated long before the nation.' He grunted in the dark. 'I will always wonder if my naming cyclones after women annoyed them. Or more so, some of the lesser storms after my male enemies. They say this country is full of humour. I wonder nowadays.'

They smoked in silence for a while.

'We have all weathers here, in the mountains,' Bill said.

'Perhaps it is what has always attracted me to the place,' Wragge said. 'It's the great rain tank of the nation. Better than a thousand Stiger Vortexes. After only one season at the Kosciusko station I came to the strong belief that the water here could be diverted across the ranges and down into the farmlands of the west. My superiors showed little interest.'

Bill was puzzled. 'But how would you catch it? The rain?'

'Dams. And a piping system, one of such dimensions I have yet to get my mind around it. But the project was scuppered.'

'Pipes.'

'Big enough to drive a motor vehicle through. They laughed at the thought, of course. As they did with the Stigers. But it is nothing I am not familiar with. It will be the ruination of this country, I'm afraid, Bill. Thought here is not directed outward, but inward. It is far more comfortable nattering at the parish pump. Present company excluded.'

Bill chuckled.

'It has taken me a lifetime to realise that there is always a price to pay for such ideas,' Wragge continued, picking at the end of the cigarette with a thumbnail. 'The utilisation of nature. You tamper with it, you take the best from it, and you unlock the seeds of its destruction.'

'Destruction?'

'You alter the natural order, and its death is certain. It is, regrettably, what I have found. It is my rule of un-natural order. You build the dams and you attract people like ants to sugar. And it is the ants that devour the very thing that attracted them. That is what you will have here, Bill. It has already started. We are living witness to it, here, on this verandah. Just stamp your boot and it will resonate on this timber when, a year ago, there was nothing but earth. How very simple a notion it is, how obvious and unoriginal, when said out loud. But how often we do not see what is at the tip of our noses.'

Bill felt he understood the eccentric Wragge. He was not sure about damming and piping the mountains. It was as vague as the business in Our Lady Star of the Sea church back in town, or the unfenced expanse of Berty's madness.

'It is why I am turning my back on it all,' Wragge said.

'A terrible thing to say. But I am beginning to wonder if my whole life has not been wasted.'

They were silent for a moment. Bill Lampe felt he had been caught inside a man's private emotions and thoughts without permission.

'I apologise for the dramatics,' Wragge said quickly.

'My boy,' Bill said, 'wants to explore the source of the Snowy River one day. Isn't that right, Wilfred?'

'Yes, sir.'

'He thinks there's something magical up there.'

'And there most definitely is,' Wragge said. 'I will not ruin the surprise for you, but a great river like yours, well, a great river . . . its source is . . . is life itself.'

The father and the son both looked to Wragge in the dark. It was the first time all evening they had heard him hesitate, or his voice change pitch, and in that split second he was heading back inside the lodge.

'Good evening,' he said. The door clacked shut behind them. They listened to his heavy boots recede down the hallway.

TWENTY-FOUR

'TELL ME WHAT you've come up with,' the Olympics official said.

'Have you read the submission?' the ceremonies official asked.

'I have, but I want to hear it from you.'

'What did you think?'

'Just explain to me how you see it.'

'In reference to the old man?'

'Yes.'

'There are several instances where we can slot him into the performance. The opening sequence, as you are aware, involves the stockhorses and the theme from *The Man from Snowy River*. Although not finalised, we see it as a sort of horse ballet—'

'A *sort of* horse ballet.'

'A dance sequence with the horses. Formations. Choreographed to fill the expanse of the "stage", or to the full perimeters of the playing surface of the Olympic Stadium. We feel the horse is an enduring symbol of—'

'Yes, get on with it.'

'They, the horses and riders, will in the end form the Olympic rings in the centre of the stadium floor.'

'At the end of our *sort of* horse ballet.'

'Yes. The riders will be dressed in the Snowy Mountains costume of Drizabones, hats and boots, and will be carrying stock whips, and will suggest the pioneering days of yesteryear.'

'Yesteryear.'

'Yes.'

'Go on.'

'We view this as a prologue for the rest of the drama which will take the narrative structure of a dream sequence.'

'A dream.'

'That's right.'

'So where are the horses?'

'They have left the stadium at this point.'

'So how do we get from horse to dream?'

'A little girl. At the beach. She spreads out her towel on a typical Australian summer's day and initiates the dream.'

'She has a dream?'

'She falls asleep, and the ceremony becomes her dream.'

'From the mountains to the beach.'

'Correct. The full panoply of the Australian experience.'

'Panoply.'

'As part of the dream, the history of the nation unfolds in loose chronological order. Pre- and post-European settlement. The Aborigines. The arrival of Captain Cook. The—'

'I'm sorry to interrupt, but where does our old man come into this?'

'I'm getting to that. Following Cook, we have the opening up of the country. The Land Sequence, as we call it. Before Industry, and the Happy Immigrants, and Modern Australia. In our opinion, the old man would dovetail nicely into the Land Sequence.'

'Because he's a man of the land?'

'Yes, he's our man of the land. The great unflappable and resilient face of the country. The pioneer spirit. The sheep. The building of a country from the soil upwards . . .'

'He's from around the Snowy River region, our old man, is that correct?'

'From what I understand, yes.'

'Then why wouldn't he be in the – what did you call it? – the *horse ballet*, with the other men from the Snowy River?'

'I think we'd all agree his age would have to preclude him from this segment of the Opening Ceremony. It is quite *vigorous*.'

'I see.'

'Besides, he is our Living Symbol of twentieth-century Australian life, and to put him with the riders in the prologue would, technically, be chronologically inaccurate. In the context of the spirit of the narrative.'

'The spirit.'

'We would suggest that, in the Land Sequence, he be displayed, for example, on the back of a dray. Or on a sulky. With little effort, and in deference to his age, he could, say, be transferred from the dray or sulky to a modern-day motor vehicle. This would encapsulate the narrative theme of a modernising nation, the rapid shift from old to new. With the subtle change of the mode of transport.'

'Are we still dreaming all this?'

'Yes.'

'Go on.'

'In lieu of that, we see another window for him with the Woodchoppers.'

'You want to have him chopping wood in front of a billion people?'

'We see him, in this segment, as more of a symbol of the labour of rural life. Wardrobe is toying with the idea of a giant axe.'

'A giant axe.'

'Or Merino. This is all in gestation. We have to take into consideration, too, that he may be confined to a wheelchair come the Big Night. We have yet to work out how to integrate him if he is in a wheelchair. A wheelchair would be problematic. A wheelchair might send a negative message in what is ostensibly a positive endeavour.'

'Has it occurred to you that the old man could possibly be excised from the dream?'

'It has occurred to us.'

'That perhaps he *should* be?'

'Our writers and choreographers have considered the possibility. There is indeed the probability that he is, without being unkind, the weak link in the chain.'

'The weak link in the chain.'

'Yes.'

'The nightmare in the dream.'

'That's very good. Yes.'

'Fix it, will you?'

'I'll try.'

TWENTY-FIVE

'THEY'VE BEEN BANGING on your door all day.'

Aurora had the key in the final lock at the door of her flat and was startled by the woman's voice in the empty corridor. She turned and saw a small elderly woman silhouetted in the open doorway of an apartment down the hall.

Green light filtered in from the frosted glass at the end of the corridor, the giant fronds of a *Monstera deliciosa* outside pressing at the pane. The fronds were blurred and fleshy against the glass. The light caught what appeared to be a lacquered hat on the woman's head.

'They were making a frightful racket,' the woman continued. 'I instructed them to shove off, excuse my French.'

The old woman's voice was deep and rich and had the velvety edges of a heavy drinker, or smoker, or both. Aurora could not tell her age but could smell an old sweetness and stale cigarette smoke issuing from the flat and she noticed a burning cigarette in a holder in the woman's left hand. The shape of her head seemed elongated by the hat, held at a slight angle to the left, and as Aurora's eyes adjusted to the light of the corridor the details of a beehive revealed themselves, the straw-coloured hair layered and lacquered and folding in on itself. Throats of roses were scattered across the thin material of her printed dress, and below, thick and veined calves and ankles, the feet, as blotched and spotted as blood sausage, pushed into a pair of old-style high heels. The heels were so high the woman appeared to hover in the soupy green light reflected off the linoleum hallway.

'Thanks,' Aurora said, returning to the lock.

'I've made tea,' the woman said, drawing on the cigarette, turning, and the heels clacked down the hall, the smoke from her cigarette faintly swirling where she had been in the doorway. It was not an invitation but an order.

For a moment Aurora held the key in the lock, then turned and moved slowly to the open door. From the entrance she saw down the far end of the hall into the flat a window of illuminated lace and the edge of a thick brown sofa. On a small table in front of the sofa was a potted aspidistra, its leaves edged with silver. The woman of the beehive suddenly emerged from a door off the lounge room, and lowered a tray onto a coffee table. The cigarette in the holder jutted from her mouth.

'No use standing there,' she said loudly, the words slurred around the black holder, and disappeared back into the kitchen.

Aurora closed the door behind her and entering the brilliantly lit lounge room she was overwhelmed by the bric-a-brac that covered every surface — even the window ledge behind the lace, where she could just make out a conga line of small elephants and hippopotamus, zebra and giraffe. The giraffe looked out onto the streets of Rushcutters Bay, a calf beside it.

'Sit, sit,' the woman said, bearing a saucer of biscuits. 'I am Lily May Prescott. You can call me Dot. They've always called me that. I have no idea why. Too late to care now, anyway. Sit, sit. You're making the place look untidy.'

Aurora took a seat beside a huge orange and black lamp. The base was the carved head of a Negress, the lips full, the nose prominent and rounded, with thick hoop earrings and a headpiece of painted fruit. The lamp woman's eyes were closed modestly against her own beauty. The shade was flecked orange cloth.

The room glowed like a stage, the animals and Jamaican lamps throwing strange, diffused shadows over the furniture and the carpet, and the other little profusions of framed photographs and commemorative cake tins and polished stones and snuffboxes and hair combs encrusted with mother-of-pearl.

It was a clean flat but with the cigarette smoke and the aged furniture and the clutter it was tight with old air. It had the feeling that nothing had been moved from its designated place in years, and that nothing new had been added to the landscape for just as long.

Dot poured two cups of tea and added milk to both and placed one in front of Aurora and sat back in a reading chair beside which was a small table. There was no room on the table for the cup and saucer, crowded as it was with spectacles and magazines and books and packets of cigarettes and a heavy glass ashtray filled to the brim with old tan butts.

'I told them you weren't in,' she said, sipping daintily

at the tea. 'I didn't know. But gathered. Have your tea before it gets cold. I said, It's pretty obvious, isn't it, gentlemen? The apartment is unoccupied at present. Take your noise elsewhere. Eat, eat. You're a rake.'

She fitted another cigarette into the holder and lit it theatrically.

'I have been in the hospital,' she said to the room. 'Nothing too serious. That's what you hear at my age – nothing too serious. It has been the last thing some of my friends have heard in their life on earth. Oh, it's nothing too serious, and that's that. They want me in a nursing home. No, I apologise. They don't call them that these days. A retirement village. Who do they think they're dealing with? Be careful when you get to my age; they speak to you like you were a baby. Come along, Mrs Prescott, do you want some nice cowd cwustard? Bah. Nothing Too Serious, that's what they should call the retirement village. This is my village. I've been here at Rushcutters since my late twenties. They can carry me out in a box. Or a bag. Or a bucket. Whatever. A friend of mine, an elderly gentleman passed away in her unit block, gone, and was there three weeks before they found him. Rest his soul. In the old buildings, you know, the lifts are too small, a lot of them. They forgot they might have to bring out dead ones once in a while. This old gentleman, they brought him out in a plastic bag. Not a nice thing. Not dignified. But what else to do? Bring him down with a crane, like a piano? I shouldn't laugh. So I'm back, from the hospital. There was an unfortunate gentleman in your flat, before you. Forever three sheets to the wind. Always falling over. People get involved in the silliest accidents, don't they?

We came home from a show one night. Spring. Delightfully warm. And there was old Ken Slessor in the gutter again with the most gruesome graze on his head. As drunk as a lord. Do you know him? I often said to my husband, He'll die that man, falling down the steps to that castle of his on the harbour. I thought the stairs might get him. My husband turned to me that night, when we saw Ken Slessor, and said, That man, he's always having silly accidents. I've been here forever. When it's all over, and they open me up, they'll find little bits of Sydney inside. Perhaps a tile, from the Opera House. Or a trinket, from Foy's.'

After the first cup of tea, the woman retrieved a powder compact from the side table and patted at her face in its small mirror. Satisfied, she snapped it shut.

'I was, contrary to current ravages, a great beauty. Once.' She smiled at Aurora, her face waxen in the afternoon light. 'One simply doesn't account for getting so old.'

She poured more tea. 'So, neighbour. Tell me of you.'

Aurora had a sudden and profound desire to leave the smoky flat. She had no facility, she realised, to communicate with the old woman. For months she had been in dialogue with herself, and through that had become fearful of the most elementary human transactions. A question directed at her – in a supermarket, on the street – now made her jittery, and struck her dumb. She only now realised, sitting uncomfortably in the room, that for weeks she had not looked out at the park.

The old woman sensed her reticence. She held her swollen feet a few inches off the floor and studied them. 'I used to dance until I could barely walk, at your age.

Reginald – that's my husband – on more than one occasion was forced to carry me home over his shoulder. But it's all gone. How sad to think. There was a particular hairdresser I used, many years ago, a sweet woman, plain, from the suburbs, but a magician with her hands. A dear little salon, and always with fresh flowers. I had a taxi cab take me there only last week. And in its place, a ghastly store that sold Indian food. I came straight home. I reeked of the tandoor. Only yesterday did I realise I had not been to that salon in more than twenty years. Yet the flowers. And that sweet woman's little hands. I can see them now.'

She pointed to the only photograph in the room. A framed black and white picture of a dark-haired man in a military uniform.

'Reginald Percival John Prescott,' she said. 'My husband. He passed away in October, 1961. In the lavatory, where most men's lives seem to end, funnily enough. Even Reginald would have laughed at that. Had he not died, naturally.'

She explained that they had lived their married life in the inner city, first across the park at Darling Point. They had entertained the bohemians of Sydney, the artists and poets and composers, and had gone to Africa, 'when it was fashionable, dear, to go to Africa', and had traversed Europe for its music and art, and had met the great people of their day, and then their life together ended, with a swift and fatal stroke in a downstairs lavatory.

They had had a child – Oliver. Born into a life too busy for children. They had packed the boy off to boarding school at six years, 'and by eighteen he was dead at the blades of a harvester' on a property outside Yass. 'At

301

least dead of the soil,' Dot said matter-of-factly, 'and not of the outhouse.'

Aurora thought briefly of her own dead child, and felt squeamish in the stifling room.

The old woman continued with her stories and alluded to some lost chimera of vast wealth, to long hallways with wooden aspidistra stands and formal dining rooms and Middle Eastern rugs, libraries and diamonds, fountains and gravel driveways. And that this all connected back, somehow, to vast landholdings and fatted stock and towers of wool bales.

She talked of her and Reginald's house in Darling Point, and his 'selfish' death. 'Bum ticker,' she said, lighting a cigarette off the still smouldering one in the holder. 'But who's to know? My sister said for years I had murdered him with my Yorkshire pudding. I had cooked it, that day, for luncheon, and Reginald had cited constipation. And thus, the fatal blow, so to speak, in the lavatory.' She paused, and studied the crackling cigarette and its long arc of ash. 'Who ever heard of Yorkshire pudding killing a man? Who can know what leads from one to the other? I told my sister to get stuffed, excuse my French. But now. She may have been right.'

The Darling Point house, she said, 'went to seed', and had to be subdivided as the years passed – into two flats, then four, then six. A retirement village was suggested by nieces and nephews. 'They, too, went and got stuffed, at my request.'

The old woman had tired herself out. The flat was turning darker. 'You'll want to get going,' she said, in a dry voice, as if just roused from sleep. 'A beau, I imagine, and the opera. How I miss it. But the body is not willing. I am not one of the elderly who complains.'

She sniffed here, a single inhalation that dismissed the rest of her generation. A lamp was turned on, and Aurora studied the old woman's face, and the hair, lifted into a tremendous vase-like structure, was partially transparent and strafed with silken threads, held by a scaffolding of hairspray. It seemed to absorb some of the lamplight, and had a dull glow about it, as if it contained a cooling ember.

The old woman closed her eyes and appeared to wince, not in pain, but perhaps at a memory that had suddenly pulled at her, and in the dim light she seemed much smaller, as if the memory had retracted her, and she reached out for a cigarette and her lighter with her eyes still closed, dispensing with the long holder, and only with the cigarette lit did she seem to breathe again, and return to her natural size.

'Over there on the shelf,' she said, pointing again, 'is the belt buckle of a Turkish soldier. Cut off and souvenired by my brother, at Gallipoli. Cut off from a dead Turk. I hold it, sometimes. Just as he held it. My brother. How he wept for the dead man. But the buckle is here. A survivor.' She held the cigarette and did not draw on it and a cone of ash dropped silently to the floor beside her chair.

'He said to me once,' she said, 'Dotty, it is the curse of this family. Survival. Now I see what he means.'

Aurora had had a total absence of elderly women in her life. Women who were supposed to be there, always, sitting quietly in a reading chair in the light of a lamp. She had had no grandmother to teach her what it was like for women to grow old. And her own mother, gone in circumstances described as 'not suspicious' and well and truly buried by the time she had made one of those rare, crazy, nonsensical phone calls to her father from nowhere during her flight with Wynter.

'How rude of me,' Dot said, pulling herself up from the chair. She returned from the kitchen with a bottle of brandy and two small glasses. 'An aperitif?'

She poured herself a full glass, and then seemed to forget that Aurora was in the room. She stared into the shadowy shapes of the bric-a-brac, and hummed between sips.

'Can you tell me about my visitors?' Aurora asked eventually.

'I'm sorry, dear?'

'The people, banging on my door today.'

'I told them to shove off,' she said, sitting up in her chair. 'Two of them. Men. In suits, of dubious quality if I can say that without sounding snobbish. Suits of a country bank manager's quality. They weren't from Harvey, at David Jones, I could tell that. Three, four times they were here.'

'Did they say what they wanted?'

'A young woman by the name of Aurora Keck, or Fleck, they said. Had I seen her, they said. I don't stick my nose into the business of Miss Aurora Fleck, I said. I have better things to do with my precious time, I said.'

Aurora hesitated. 'The police, do you think?'

'Too wet behind the ears.'

There was a heavy layer of cigarette smoke in the room now, a ghostly tide line that Aurora could see stretching through the lounge and into the kitchen. It wavered and wobbled with each new exhalation from the old woman. It had already submerged them both.

'I pleaded with him to come home, but he never did,' Dot said. 'He wrote to me, said that he was *of the country*. What rot. He was as much country as my little finger. *Dear Oliver*, I wrote back. *Your father is ailing and, as a son, you have responsibilities*. And into the soil he went, for good.'

Aurora heard the shrieks of the evening birds and knew the bats would be making their way from the Botanic Gardens in the city to the trees of Rushcutters Bay Park and across to Centennial Park. The great, twisting airborne river of them, of leathery wings and bead eyes and rust fur.

She watched the orange pilot light at the tip of the woman's cigarette, the only thing alive in this dead flat, the African animals all milky and stillborn on the ledge lit now by a streetlight outside the window.

'They leave us,' the woman said. 'And then it is only us. The women. Gathering dust. Like the Turk's buckle.'

The blanket of cigarette smoke triggered a memory in Aurora. Back in Murwillumbah. A walk, with her father, on a morning where everything seemed damp, and Mount Warning had disappeared behind cloud, and the clouds were not ordinary clouds, but towering columns bigger than any buildings in the world, columns that rose straight up and boiled with thunderheads as they had done forever, when there were no patchwork farms and thread of rail lines and tiny cluster of sticks and tin that was the town. She had walked with her father along the edge of the cane fields, the hem of her white nightie wet with dew, and she had seen it, the plate of fog, and then they had entered it, and she pretended to swim through its clinging greyness, and her father's laughter had echoed off the walls of spectral cane.

Aurora stood. The old woman didn't seem to notice.

'*Come back*, I told him,' Dot said quietly. '*We are your family, Oliver Prescott*.'

The coldness of the remembered fog crept into Aurora. She needed a hit of something. Anything.

She started walking towards the hallway.

'Family,' Dot said. 'Does it mean nothing to you, child?'

The tip of the cigarette slowly pulsed in the gathering dark.

'I'm sorry,' she said. 'I have to go.'

'Please don't leave,' the woman said. 'It's nice. To talk. To another woman.'

It was precisely what Aurora was thinking as she left. It was what she wanted and needed, the old woman's gravel voice and the memories shovelled into the room without logic or respect for time. It was comforting and frightening and it had prised a small opening into a large and empty reservoir in Aurora, a vessel of her loss.

'Don't leave.'

Aurora entered her flat and deadlocked the door and rushed to the small balcony. She tried to draw in the cool air. Bats crashed into the fig trees down in the park and she saw people moving through the balloons of light along the pathways.

She felt Wynter out there, moving closer, and not far away she sensed Tick, whom she could not think of now without hearing the sounds of the beautiful little music box, and she felt the shift of pewter ash and the heaviness of the smoke in the lonely woman's flat down the corridor, and the cold of the belt buckle on the cabinet of life memories, and the wood grain of the tiny hand–carved animals on the window sill, and the seared and burnt ridges of the stripes and patches of their lifeless hides, and the fusing of the child of her dream and the rich soil under the pine trees in the abandoned cemetery of old Adaminaby.

She doubled over on the balcony, her eyes wide, and patted uselessly at her chest for breath. She was suffocating. Righting herself, she drew in spoonfuls of air, then more. Her heart beat furiously and she continued to flush with panic, now over.

Inside, Aurora threw up in the kitchen sink. She vomited over and over until the bile stung the back of her tongue. Then she splashed water on her face, regaining the rhythm of her breath, and steadied herself against the sink. She had been here before. She had done all this before. It would never end. Being pursued. It was never going to end.

She was the last of her family line. It ended with her. Just as Lily May Prescott's line ended with her, inside her flat down the hall, behind an old door less than an inch thick. Lily May Prescott, and the slow, dim, unseen pilot light of her cigarette. With Oliver of the soil. And the dull, beaded eyes of the animals looking out at the life of the world. But unlike the old woman, she still had family.

I have to see my father, she thought. I have to see my father.

She didn't realise the tap was still running. The water thumped against the steel drum of the sink. The water thumped and swirled and gasped in the drain. She listened to it and then after a while she heard a voice in it and was convinced it was her father, calling her home.

TWENTY-SIX

WILFRED LAMPE SHUFFLED past the vacant nurse station and found himself in the television room of the hospice.

He had seen television in the front bar at the Buckley's Crossing Hotel and remembered when Mitchell had taken an age to install it high up on its brackets above the fly-soiled photographs of the trout club members, and when he'd flicked the switch – snow. Here, he stood at the back of the room and looked at the fake walnut box mounted similarly on the rear wall. Chairs were arranged in front of the screen and he saw the backs of several heads. Beside some of the chairs were various drips with their bladders and clear tubes. The heads didn't move. The thatches of hair caught the blue light from the television.

In the room he smelled death. The scent of it was pushed back behind a tangy surface odour of antiseptic and deodoriser and night breaths. Wilfred caught the aroma as he had, many times, in the paddocks back on the Monaro. The whiff of a sheep or calf carcass across the folds of hills, the invisible streamer of it that passed over you if the wind was right. But death wasn't like this, Wilfred knew. It didn't wait in hiding, or lurk, or set traps. It was the natural end of things, and dressed itself not in dark cloaks and carried no scythes. It was there, that was all, like worms under a log, or the granite reefs embedded in the river, or a freckle on your face.

On the television Wilfred saw men floating weightless inside a spaceship. He remembered sitting at the bar of the hotel at Dalgety – when Mitchell had, after two days, finally tweaked and tuned his fancy television – watching the first man land on the moon. Wilfred had fenced that morning and installed rabbit traps around the granite boulders at the far western corner of the property and set fires at the base of other boulders not far from the homestead, where old Mrs Crank had suddenly decided, a week earlier, to build a bed for the growing of gardenias.

Lighting the fires that would burn for days and heat the rocks, he caught a glimpse of the pale moon through the early smoke off the wood, and told himself that there were men there, at that moment, on its surface, and yet the thought made no sense.

They didn't need to go all that way to the moon, he said to himself. They could've just come here. To the Monaro.

It was a strange day, not just because a man had landed on the moon. Sitting on the buckboard of his old Buick, his smoko had been interrupted by two men from the local newspaper. They asked to take his photograph, and for his thoughts about the man on the moon. They were writing a story on what locals were doing, and what was in their minds, on this great day in history. He'd ignored the men and driven to the Buckley's to watch the event on Mitchell's television. The river was low and the town was quiet. He could feel the cold as he crossed the bridge above the Snowy.

He had expected everyone to be there, but only three men sat in the bar. He took a beer and watched the grainy spaceman step onto the surface of the moon. It looked cold on the moon just as it was cold outside in the main street and down by the river, and Wilfred hoped the fires were catching well and the wood was burning cleanly out at Mrs Crank's new gardenia plot. He heard the spaceman say that it was one giant leap for mankind, and as the man walked on the surface of the moon and left his boot prints in the powdered surface Wilfred thought of the volumes of ash from the burnt wood after three or four days and knew the ash, worked into the soil, would be good for Mrs Crank's flowers.

When it was over, he tipped his hat without a word, and went back to the boulders and their fiery nests.

Nobody moved in the television room of the hospice, just the astronauts on the television, tumbling in the zero gravity of their spaceship, and Wilfred, in bare feet and a pair of navy pyjamas with a white pinstripe, moved back out past the nurses' station.

A man and a woman – visitors – waited in front of the lift. He stood with them.

Inside the lift, the woman, dumpy in tweed and heavily perfumed, her ankles like creamy marble in a pair of shiny stockings, studied Wilfred's hoary, knuckled white feet as they went down. Her companion studied the floor indicator lights above the door of the lift. They got out on the ground floor, the woman first, and then the man, who nodded at Wilfred and issued a thin 'Good evening' before stepping out of the compartment. Wilfred followed.

He turned left, away from the manned security desk, and wandered down a dark corridor and into a small unlit cafeteria. Behind the counter he found an open door and then, through the shadowed shapes of hanging pots and ladles and skillets, another door that opened into a stairwell. At the bottom of a short flight of stairs there was yet another door, and through it, the side garden of the hospice.

His feet felt cold on the dewy grass. He stepped cautiously, leaving footprints on the lawn. It gave way to a car park that opened onto the street. He stopped and leaned against the wet duco of a car. The metal was cold and it was then he felt the sting in his right arm where they'd kept the drip and his stomach clenched.

A few hundred metres to the left he could see the tall, shadowed spire of a church and beyond it a stream of traffic. Buses, motorcycles, cars. Past the traffic he saw shopfronts illuminated with electric light. ART SUPPLIES. CAMBODIAN RESTAURANT. TOOL SHED. TAKE AWAY. Someone was beating a drum.

Wilfred walked away from the traffic. He passed a small park bordered with concrete, and in the centre of it a glassed-in rotunda, and on the sloped grass he saw what could have been the shapes of sleeping human figures.

The cold of the bitumen was beginning to creep up through his feet and into his ankles and shins. Cars tooted their horns and words were shouted out into the dark and were snatched away. At the corner of the park he

312

stood alone at the intersection. He saw a red shape at eye level across the street and then heard a sharp call, like a whippoorwill, and the red light flicked to green. He stood for a moment and watched the configuration of the changing lights.

He crossed the road when there was no traffic and shuffled close to the steel fencing and ratty gardens of a string of terrace houses before he reached another crossing of roads and then another. Two young men in leather jackets passed him in the shadows and shouted something after him and their laughter faded to nothing. He walked past a long, narrow cafe full of people eating and drinking and he stood for a moment staring in at them. It looked warm inside and he could feel their talk through the large panes of glass, and many of them turned to look at him with puzzled faces and faces that creased with laughter and faces that were pale and fixed and expressionless and wouldn't have changed if a wild doe had found itself there, in the yellow light at the intersection, and caught their eye.

A man in a large black apron holding a tray began to move to the front door without taking his eyes off Wilfred, but the old man was crossing the street by the time he came outside, and the man in the apron was left on the footpath, the tray still held at chest height, watching the barefoot old man in the pyjamas progressing deeper into Darlinghurst.

As he shuffled past a hotel and then more eateries, his eyes were bombarded with reflections and knife-flashes, with bursts of blood-red tail-lights and raw yellow filaments on a palette of milkwash. All the different grades of light came to him from small balls of steel pierced in human lips and ears, from studded belts and oversized buckles, from rings and handbags, teeth and hair. He grew frightened. He'd been amongst large groups of people before, at the Bombala show and Dalgety races, but these were different, either blurred and out of focus, or too sharp and animal-like, and they came in unending surges, packs of them, then mobs, then a single dark figure and the packs again.

Hands seemed to paw at him and he knew his feet were cut and the noise became disorienting.

Wilfred reached a huge intersection. Side roads drew in from every direction and he was ushered onto an island of concrete footpath with the crowd and was suddenly unable to move any further. He looked to the west and for the first time saw the great central business district of Sydney. He reached for a railing and leaned against it, out of breath, and worked hard to suck in air before the glowing edifice of the city, the heavy, impenetrable cluster of high-rise towers that rose before him, the space-age Centrepoint fixing it all together, the centrifuge of it, like a maypole.

William Street roared below him, and it took him some moments to realise he was standing on an overpass. The crowds came and went, staring after the old man in navy pyjamas looking into the city. The cars flowed and the light dashed like swarms of flying ants and he gripped the cold railing and could feel a deep tremble in the metal and it conducted into him.

Then he was at the morgue in Glebe in 1937, on his first-ever trip to Sydney, and he was standing in the cold room of watery green light, and they had pulled the sheet back from the body resting on the metal table, and revealed the white face of the dead woman and asked him, Is this your sister, Astrid Lampe? He had stared at the face and said no, it was not Astrid, and had taken the next train to Cooma. On the train he had not even removed the coat of his only suit, worn to weddings and funerals and picnic races alike, nor had he loosened his tie, and he had looked dolefully out the window and seen nothing but the plain, dull, simple-faced reflection of his own face, and he had been relieved that the woman on the metal table in the green tiled room was not Astrid, but he wished he had never seen the dead woman. In time he associated Sydney only with that face, and the useless hair pulled back from her forehead, and the slight gap between the unclosed lips and the darkness of it, the horrible darkness of the aperture of a dead woman's mouth.

Forever after that, he could not visualise Astrid's face. He had been able to, at will, until that moment in the cold room of the morgue. And on the island above William Street, he saw the dead woman's face everywhere, and he turned away from the lights of the city, and above the people that jostled past him, the multitudes of them, bumping and brushing each other like the sheep back home, he saw and was instantly transfixed by a huge neon sign.

Coca-Cola. It swarmed before his eyes, ebbed and flowed, pulsed and swirled. Coca-Cola. The red of the lights washed over him and tinged pink his face and hands and feet. The sign strafed him and bathed him and doused him in blood red. His skin flickered pink and his pyjamas throbbed with a purplish light.

Coca-Cola.

He stood before it, staring, cars roaring past under him and in front of him and on either side of him, and wondered if this wasn't the end of the world.

Enjoy. Coca-Cola.

TWENTY-SEVEN

BEFORE DAWN BILL and Wilfred were shaken out of
sleep by a motor car grinding up the drive of the Creel
and an explosion of light through the windows of their
guest room off the front verandah.

The boy sat bolt upright in the bed and was lost, the
light sending shadows of lace patterns and distended
water pitchers and the brass cage of the bed base wheeling about the room. Then all the shadows retreated and
the plate of yellow light was reefed from the room and
became just a glow outside, jolted and halted by crunching gears and a screech not unlike a black cockatoo
heralding a blizzard.

Bill snuffled and looked out towards the light. There
was a deep rasping in his chest and he turned his
shadowed face to the frightened boy. 'Hmmph,' he said.

It had been an uncomfortable night for Wilfred. He
had slept with his parents before, when he was younger,
in their little house down on the plains. And he had
nestled into his father's broad back on the muster. But in
the fishing lodge, there was no deep and hidden inner
tick. Home, at least, had a heartbeat.

On the muster, the strange noise of his father's chest

had been hardly detectable in the open air, the cattle farting and snorting columns of warm, grass-sweet air out their nostrils, the fire murmuring.

Here, at the Creel, in the fancy room with its large and terrifying blackwood wardrobe, and the lip of the water jug high on its stand protruding like a sulky child's, and the polished brass globes at the corners of the bedstead, the room eerily still, the stillness so foreign to Wilfred, a night stillness he had never experienced at home, or anywhere, here the boy was held in thrall by the amplification of his father's peculiar internal rattle. It was like a dog scratching a gauze door. It was the only sound he had in the room all night, grating away inside the smell of fresh paint and cut timber and new nails.

The boy was, in a way, glad to be awake.

'Hmmph,' his father repeated, scratching his head, and then he was up and out of bed, the farmer's curse, this rising into the world, unthinking but automatic, with the weight of a day's labour already on the shoulders.

Wilfred saw the outline of his father against the illuminated lace, and watched him delicately pull aside the curtain. There was vibration of boot now, on the verandah, and voices outside in the near dark.

'You up?' his father said, and coughed. The coughing reached into the room like branches, drawn back by a wet and ugly inhalation of breath.

'Yep,' the boy said.

'There's a pot under the bed, if you need it,' his father said, looking out at the commotion. 'Then you're best to check the horses.'

His boots still unlaced, Wilfred crossed the verandah, studying the new motor vehicle in the gravel drive. He noticed a large caboose of leather luggage strapped to the back.

As Wilfred approached the horses in the side paddock the dog slipped beside him and licked his hand. The sky was as rich as wet bluestone beyond the pines and elms. Smoke eased from the kitchen chimney and long angled rectangles of light as warm as butter stretched out across the grass and wood piles at the back of the lodge.

The boy rubbed his arms but there was something cold now inside him, so deep he did not consciously know of it. It was the rattle of his father's chest, a tremor from the centre of the earth, from the heart of his creation, which had somehow entered the rhythms of the boy's own sleep and become a part of him. The dog's tongue was warm against his hand, but it only acted to make the rest of the boy feel a new coldness.

He returned to the lodge and found his father smoking a cigarette on the verandah.

'All okay?'

'Yep,' Wilfred said.

His father gazed at the car.

'Drove all night from Sydney, probably,' he said, stabbing the cigarette at the machine. 'For the dawn rise.' He shook his head. 'Madness.'

The music of metal pots and pans crept out to them through the dining room and foyer.

'You know what day it is?' his father asked.

'Nope.'

'Saturday. I think it's Saturday.'

They both contemplated the shiny car as if it were a strange dinosaur fossil that had inexplicably broken, whole, through the surface of the earth.

'You got that good fish feeling this morning, Wilfred?'

'Yep.'

'That's good enough for me. Let's get some grub.'

It was exactly the same as the evening before in the dining room. The lamps. The view into the kitchen. The long tables and the sawdust in the corners. It was a room of perpetual evening.

At the table the school principal and the lawyer sat in the same places as they had done for dinner, but both were dressed now in their best fishing apparel, probably purchased from the same stores in the city, and Bill smiled at the cumbersome tweed and multi-layers of shirts and vests. He had never failed to be amused by the propensity of city people to dress for moments in life. He saw no connection between tweed and fishing. You fished, and you ate.

'Morning,' he said to the two men, and they raised their pasty faces and nodded and he saw about them that curious misalignment of people unused to rising in the dark, a fractional blurring at the edges, and invisible burrs catching at their responses and simple morning actions, bringing teacup to mouth, or buttering toast.

Jack came in from the kitchen with a second large pot of tea and a scallop-edged plate heavy with a pyramid of lamb chops.

'The Lampe boys,' he said, smiling. 'Those rainbows don't know what they're in for, eh?'

At that instant Professor Wragge blustered in with a rolling tangle of greetings. He was sprightly and physically animated and a younger man than the previous evening. Now the morose lethargy of nostalgia had been shucked off by the start of another day, and Bill again felt a kinship with the meteorologist. They were both men whose lives started afresh each morning.

'I have already investigated the Thredbo,' he said to the table, pouring himself tea and taking a mouthful of dry toast in a single action, 'and there is a high probability, in my educated opinion, that it may contain some fish on this day.'

He plonked the pot on the table as if punctuating himself, and he smiled at his own humour, and some laughter followed. The chin, tilted high, wriggled with his mastication.

'And the weather, Professor?' the lawyer ventured.

'A light breeze, from the south-east,' Wragge said, chewing like a rabbit, 'and a perfect high plodding towards the coast. Not a hint of rain, and clear conditions for the duration of this fine day. Temperature? I would guess in the early nineties, though temperature has never been a forte. Certainly not the conditions to be encased in heavy, fibrous materials. Hmm?'

He smiled at the boy as he buttered more toast.

'You'll be joining us?' Bill asked.

'I have been pondering this overnight, Bill,' he said, gazing into a far corner of the room, 'and I have concluded that an introduction to fly fishing may be useful prior to my relocation to New Zealand. They have, as you are probably aware, some very fine streams and lakes. To dip a toe into the sport may be just the ticket.'

He took three chops from the plate and ate them with his hands, gesturing with floppy strips of gristle and gnawed bones fringed with flags of meat.

'Besides,' he said, 'it is a mountain unclimbed. And I

should at least venture into the foothills. It is my nature.'

'Good on you,' said Jack, standing with a dish of fried eggs.

'And one should never deviate from one's nature. As I've always said, basalt cannot pretend to be a streak of opal, hmm?' He directed his pointed beard to the principal and the lawyer.

'We have a fourth member of the party, if that's all right, Bill,' Jack said. 'A Mr Singleton, who arrived just this morning. He is familiar with the area, and more than competent. He may wish to go his own way.'

'Do we have enough rods and reels?' Bill asked.

The professor tore at a chop bone. 'Please, enlighten me on the equipment,' he said, his eyes wide.

'I have a selection of rods I made myself,' Jack said. 'Several from spotted and grey gums. A few greenhearts. And some excellent cane rods with steel centres just in from Sydney. I picked them up from the Cooma Post Office only last week. I have yet to test the weight, but by all accounts they perform with deadly accuracy. They come highly recommended in Eastway's catalogue.'

Eastway's Australian Angling Depot Trout Catalogue & Guide had been a focus of intense interest at the Buckley's the previous summer, and several of the locals had sat around it in the gentlemen's smoking room and peered into its pages as scholars might study ancient Egyptian papyrus. Their fishing lives had been one of equipment pulled and honed from nature, and knowledge self-taught or passed from mouth to ear, and of intuition. But now that the city men were arriving with their minted and manufactured gear, it was all changing. The catalogue was as startling as Gale's written account

322

of his fishing trip on the Goodradigbee River, and a copy had been passed from shack to house to shack, and read slowly by firelight, until the copy was limp with use, and smudged with lard, and freckled with tea splash and fly dung.

'What about flies?' Bill asked. He suppressed his excitement about the cane rods.

'A decent selection from the House of Hardy, of course,' Jack said, 'and some untried specimens from Inglis – a Bredbo, as he calls it, and a Snowy Favourite. Eastway's also sent out, for trial, some new designs by Howard Joseland – do you know him? The architect.'

'Indeed,' the lawyer said, pipping the school principal with his societal connections.

'We have samples of Moonbahs and Bougongs, the former a startling rendition of a grasshopper. I have never run into him, Joseland, but he is apparently quite familiar with the area. He will wash up here one day, no doubt.'

'What a delicious little secret society you have,' Wragge said, licking his fingers without a care for propriety. He could have been sitting in his hut on Ben Nevis, finishing off a roasted badger. 'I'm going to enjoy this.'

'Justice O'Connor speaks very highly of Mr Joseland,' the lawyer interjected. 'Justice is president of the NSW Rod Fishers Society. I'm awaiting membership.'

'Is there a special handshake?' Wragge said.

The lawyer winced. 'I have had the pleasure of using Mr Joseland's Red and Black Wasps, and they were more than serviceable. In his flies, he is fond of the Chinese feather duster.'

'I don't have a single clue what you're talking about,' Wragge said, balling a napkin, 'but look forward to a swift education.'

The lawyer went to rebut, half raised an index finger, then caught Wragge's unblinking gaze and stopped short, his scalp prickling.

'Then we should get moving,' Bill said. 'Me and the boy will take the gear by horse.'

'Excellent,' Jack said.

'We'll start at the Gutters. An easy walk. And the gentlemen can fan out from there at their leisure. See you out the front in half an hour.'

Wragge, Bill saw, wrapped some leftover chops in a napkin, dabbed his mouth with the bundle, then tucked it in the pocket of his coat.

'I should like to ride with you, if I may,' he said to Bill. 'I have an inflamed left knee, the rheumatoid.'

'You can take my son's little mare if you like, down to the Gutters.'

'If it's no bother,' he said. 'The bung knee is splendid for predicting rainfall. Makes me wonder what I dedicated my life to, when in old age a knee can be just as wise. But there you have it. Splendid. See you on the drive.'

On the way down to the Thredbo, Jack and the principal and the lawyer walked ahead, with Wragge looking delightfully comic astride Wilfred's runt mare brumby, the saddlebags spiked with rods and heavy with wrapped luncheons from the Creel kitchen. The boy and dog followed.

They moved off the cut road and onto a track through low grasses. The track was littered with flinty blue stones that must have once belonged to the river. Droplets of grass dew caught on the bellies of the horses.

'You should see a doctor,' Wragge said to Bill quietly. 'It's nothing I need to tell you.'

Bill could see the man's pointed beard in his peripheral vision, jutting like a blade.

'It's under control,' he said.

'At least before the advent of winter, Bill. Just an observation, meant with kindness.'

Bill turned to check on Wilfred, following them down the track, scything the snake flowers and thistles with a stick.

'I appreciate it,' he said.

'It is one thing I know. If you accurately detect an early disturbance, the full force of the storm can be prepared for. I apologise for the meteorological analogies, but after a lifetime I have learned they bear an uncanny parallel to elements of life. Not to speak of the human body. Make no mistake.'

Bill watched the men trudging ahead. They could see the silver flash of the river, and at the sight of it, the principal and the lawyer seemed to pick up pace.

'But this,' Wragge said, chin jutting at the party in front. 'This I have not encountered in a recreation. It's nothing less than an addiction.'

'True. It can take some men.'

'They spoke, the dullards, of Howard Joseland,' Wragge said, swaying steadily with the mare, his boots nearly touching the track. 'I know him well, but didn't want to say. We met through our mutual interest in choral music. He is, you might not know, heavily involved with the Sydney Liedertafel. But that's beside the point. He designs the most beautiful homes, the style known as Federation. So austere. So stripped of pomposity. He too is a mad fisherman, and I have always seen it as an oddity in his character, truly. But now it makes a little more sense. And possibly more so by the end of the day. I have watched him tie these silly little flies of his, after dinner, a pastime he attends to with absolute rapture, just as some men savour a good cigar. Precision, too. It is amusing to me, to see the man work so daintily with those big hands of his, and derive such pleasure. He couldn't have been happier if they'd invited him to design Parliament House.'

They had reached the lower flats of the Thredbo, and Jack and his guests stood in muffled discussion, pointing up and downriver.

'To successfully trick the fish,' Wragge went on. 'I can only suppose the joy resides there. In the deception.'

They headed towards the reach where the Thredbo met the Snowy.

'We've always made our own flies,' Bill said as they proceeded. 'Held us in good stead.'

'Addiction,' Wragge muttered, in his own head again. He looked with some distaste at the school principal and the lawyer, the former picking thistles from his heavy trousers. The latter strode beside Jack, his jacket removed and pegged by a single index finger over his right shoulder, his swagger rendered ridiculous by the height to which his trousers were pulled. 'Even addiction can become fashion.' Wragge tsked and shook his head, as if confounded by the world at ground level.

They reached the junction of the two rivers and the party held a waterside conference.

Wragge stayed astride the short-legged mare.

'What would you suggest, Bill?' Jack said.

'Cut across the corner of the paddock there,' he said, squinting in the river light, 'to the tea trees, and you'll find the Gutters. Between the granite reefs. That's the likeliest spot. The channels are deep. I've taken my share of four-pounders out of there. If she's bare, head a few hundred yards downstream. There's a nice little pool between the river edge and the sandbank. It's a high bank. You might want to test it with a dry fly for starters. But the Gutters shouldn't disappoint.'

It was heavy work once they were through the corner of the paddock, but there were narrow passages through the blackberries and tea trees, and beyond them the promise of the gentle willows.

Wilfred and his father unpacked the gear and marvelled at the new rods from the city, and the variety of brass and wooden reels. The silk lines were well oiled. It was the fly boxes, however, that staggered them.

'Never seen the likes of it, hey, boy?' Bill Lampe said, turning over a Claret and Teal in his stubby fingers.

Wilfred held up a Moonbah and squinted at it.

'But can they match the Bonza Bluey?' Bill said, winking at his son. 'We'll see, eh?'

Jack and the two city men moved further up the bank while Bill set up the rod and reel and fly for Wragge.

'How beautiful it all is,' the meteorologist said. 'I had no idea.'

He practised casting and both Bill and the boy were

surprised at how quickly he caught on, the silken line rolling out and back in neat waves.

'Look,' Wragge said, unembarrassed by his infantile delight. 'Like isobars.'

'Nip the water,' Bill said. 'Nip it and back.'

'My goodness.'

'You're getting it.'

'Goodness.'

'Keep the rhythm.'

'How metronomic,' said Wragge between casts.

'Good.'

'Gracious.'

In a fit of exuberance he snagged the line on a roll of blackberry bushes several feet behind him, and frowned the frown of a child denied a jelly, but was buoyant as a feather again once released.

'I shall confound them on the Awakino.'

Jack and the lawyer brought in two modest rainbows within the hour, sending the school principal's casting askew, and he hit the water awkwardly, his rhythm now like a broken clock, short and long of his target, and dashed the fly against the fins of granite, and tossed and retrieved with great labour.

Wilfred fished down from Wragge and without focus. He was deep inside the effects of the new equipment, and happy to be there, the reels and rods relinquishing to him fresh possibilities.

Later, with the other men lost to the fishing, even Wragge, Bill tapped his son on the shoulder and they set off with their gear through the willows and headed for the Moonbah stream. The Gutters party would be occupied for hours, even when the trout had abandoned their morning feed, and Bill wanted to fulfil his promise to Wilfred, a spot of fishing, together and alone.

'Might be a little late in the year for the Moonbah,' he said as they walked. 'But it always gives you something, hmm? Even if it's only a little peace.'

They studied the Moonbah then ventured a short distance along its tributary, Rendezvous Creek, where they set up amongst the thick tussocks like two water-birds. They knew the chance of a fish was slim with the sun starting to climb, but they automatically fell into the pretty quiet and the murmuring of the low water. A red Hereford watched them through a curtain of willow.

'We don't do this enough,' Bill said eventually.

'We could,' said Wilfred, 'if you became a fishing guide.'

His father laughed. 'There are better fishermen than me. You're as good as I am. Why don't you become a guide?'

'I'd like to.'

'Very well.'

'I'd like to guide people like Professor Wragge.'

'Would you now.'

'He's funny.'

'He is funny. There are lots of different people in the world, that's a fact.'

The Hereford grumbled through the willows.

'You could be a guide, and I could be your assistant,' Wilfred said.

'The Cranks have been good to us, you know that. One has to stay loyal. They helped me and your mother through the Depression, in the late '90s, before you were born. Loyalty will always see you through. As good as money in the bank.'

The boy mulled this over.

'We can always fish, then.'

'That's right. We can always fish. The river's going nowhere.'

They stared into the mottled water and beyond the reflected pins of tussock and to the shallow base of the creek, the brown and pale cream stones clear through the water coloured weak as tea.

There were no strikes. No disturbance on the water's surface. No hint of grasshopper or flying ant or any insect. Just the odd, ethereal singing now of the shadowed Hereford.

'It's not the prize that matters,' his father said quietly.

'No.'

'It's every little moment in the seeking.'

'Yes.'

They let the dry flies drift slowly with the current.

'It's in the silence.'

Their lines slowly began to converge downstream.

'You're a good boy,' his father said finally.

And Wilfred beamed quietly, and the lines touched out of sight behind the shoulders of tussock.

They reeled in, and cast again, and again. They reeled in always at the moment of convergence, which they knew, instinctively, beyond their vision. It was how it was. They fished together, and their lines drew in the same direction, at the same pace, with the current. But the flies always came in separate, and alone. It was how it was.

TWENTY-EIGHT

WYNTER CROUCHED IN the shadowed alleyway between the canvas annexe and the side of a neighbouring caravan, the ropes zigzagging around him, and from his hide, which reeked of dishwater and potato peelings, he saw, across the gravel lane, his father sitting in the glow of a gas lantern.

He heard, somewhere behind him, the great thudding flume of the blowhole at the edge of the sea, and it boomed like thunder through a clear sky.

You filthy arsehole, Wynter thought, looking at his father. The old man could have been dead in the fold-out chair. His slack, open mouth. His reading glasses crooked on his nose. His face blotched pink and white. In the lamp's glow Wynter could not tell if he still wore that moustache of his, a thin line trimmed to the lip, fanning out like the geometrics of a moth wing, Continental movie-star style. It was how Wynter last remembered him. A middle-aged man preparing to leave his family and re-enter the world, shaping and clipping, primping once more for the mating game. He would have his wedding band cut off in favour of a pinkie ring of onyx.

From across the lane he looked small and pathetic to Wynter, and his feet were marbled blue and white and scabrous, his legs peculiarly hairless. He could have been an old woman, there in the dim light.

The small, striped annexe of the van was filled with a huge cedar wardrobe that belonged in a house, and tea-chests with wood panels swollen from rain, and a card table buckling under piles of newspapers, and buckets and fishing rods and a small bar fridge pitted with rust. There was a fan on a tall stand, an empty birdcage, and two pairs of rubber thongs placed neatly beside each other at the edge of the concrete apron. Around the trailer ball of the van, propped up with three besser bricks, was the ragged suggestion of a garden, and a gnome peering out of the weeds.

On the card table beside the sleeping man was a transistor radio and a tall amber bottle of beer.

The blowhole thudded again, and Wynter could hear the soft giggle of children somewhere in the caravan park.

He moved out of the alleyway and stood on the gravel in front of his sleeping father.

I could slit your fat guts open with that fishing knife in the bucket, he thought.

A woman wearing a dressing-gown shuffled past. She had a towel over her shoulder and a washbag under her arm, headed for the shower blocks. She snuck a glance at Wynter and moved quickly into the neon. Steam rose through the louvres of the block and poured out of the roof vent. A man's watery whistle lifted up and out with the steam and came to Wynter in snatches.

He had forgotten what it was like. The deep bass of

the blowhole, and the unceasing music of van-park living laid over it -- the snores and underwater clink of dishes, the drone of televisions and radios, the muffled voices and scuffled feet in the laneways. It was the whole pathetic clattering machinery of life, all amplified by canvas and thin, studded sheet metal, layer after layer of it, an orchestra with everyone playing a different tune, and then, at night, the only tune they shared, the farting and coughing, the snoring and the cries in their sleep.

It was the music of his father's life. Of loners and drifters and strugglers, and it had been Wynter's music, and he hated it because he knew it was still inside him. It was the only thing his father had given him.

'Get up,' was all he could say.

The old man stirred.

'Get up.'

'What?'

'It's me.'

His father wriggled helplessly in the chair and adjusted his glasses and stared at the figure before him.

'What do you want?' he said. His voice was croaky and high-pitched, and he held the open newspaper across his chest as if to protect himself.

'It's me, Wynter.'

'Wynter?' The old man's eyes were huge through the thick lenses of his spectacles. The ragged, moth-wing moustache seemed to quiver.

'Yeah, your worst nightmare,' Wynter said, 'popped in for a cup of tea and an Arrowroot.'

The old man's eyes were glassy. 'I ain't done nothin',' he said.

'You done plenty.'

'Don't hurt me.'

'Can't I drop in and say hello to me loving dad?'

A man passed in the laneway, his cropped grey hair slicked back with shower water.

'Evening,' he said to the annexe, and kept walking.

'You gonna let me in?' Wynter said, stuffing his hands in the pockets of his jeans. 'Not that you got a front door or anything.'

'Yeah,' he said, rising slowly to his feet. 'Come in. I haven't got any money, just so you know.'

'Jesus Christ.'

'Just so you know.'

'As fucking warm and friendly as ever.'

'Mind your language, there's kids live round here. Get inside, if you have to.'

He disappeared into the van.

'Nice to see you, son. How you been?' Wynter said, shaking his head.

His father stepped down into the annexe with a bottle of beer and two cups.

'Here,' he said. 'Pull up that chair over there. I ain't got nothin' to eat, if you're hungry. I was gonna go down the club.'

'I'm not hungry.'

'Here, pour this. We'll have a beer.'

Wynter poured the beer into the plastic cups and they sat.

For a long while the two men said nothing. All the sounds of the park came to them in the stuffy annexe. Beyond the line of tents and vans and crooked and rusted television aerials was the inlet, and as they sipped

334

the beer the fishermen were preparing the trawlers for the night's work. Behind the jetty was the little grid of the town with its takeaway cafes and Chinese restaurants and rotunda and a war memorial near the roundabout. And the houses that carpeted the hill behind the town. And beyond the red tiled roofs the valley of dairy farms that ran all the way up to the base of the range.

It was a town known for nothing but the blowhole. It thudded as they drank, like air being thumped out of a body.

'How you been?' his father said, a fringe of froth on his moustache. He stared into the laneway.

Wynter looked at him without blinking. He could have laughed. At the two of them, sitting like old mates in the floral fold-out chairs in the light of a gas lantern, enjoying a beer and shooting the breeze.

'That's it?' Wynter said.

'What?'

'How you fucking been? That's the lot?'

'What you want me to say? It's been years.'

'Who's counting?'

'It runs both ways, you know.'

'Is that right? All this time to hear that? It runs both ways.'

'I got a life, whatever you think of it or think of me. Just tell me what you want and let's be done with it.'

Wynter sipped the beer and shook his head. 'Then piss off, that's what you're saying, isn't it?'

'I don't want any trouble is what I'm saying.'

'Too hard for you, isn't it? Life. Too fucking hard.'

'You could talk civil. That's not much to ask.'

'You hear from your brother Stan?'

The old man adjusted his glasses and stared into his cup. 'I keep to meself.'

'That's handy.'

They were silent again. A child flashed past on a bicycle and was gone.

'How about Reece? Where is he?'

'You'd know better than me. I told you. I keep to meself.'

Someone was cooking meat and a fatty aroma came to them and Wynter suddenly felt very hungry. He poured himself more beer and stretched out his legs. With the smell of the meat he began, too, to feel weary. His father was right. He needed money. He needed to score. He had to get to Sydney and find Aurora and put everything back the way it was. If he had to he'd wait till his father was asleep and take whatever was in his wallet and the transistor and maybe the fishing gear and offload it and at least score. He wished he still had the gun. He could get rid of that, no problem, in the local pub. The gun could've seen him through to Sydney.

He saw the old man's hands trembling.

'You just a retired old gent, now, hey? Enjoying his retirement, he is.'

His father said nothing.

'You just an innocent old bloke doing his crosswords and throwin' in a line now and then, eh?'

'I made a life here.'

'Kinda small, isn't it?'

'It's enough for me.'

'You go to the RSL, do ya? Chat about the war with your old war buddies.'

The old man looked away.

'Pity you weren't in no fucking war, isn't it? What you do? Headed for the hills was how Mum saw it. Went prospectin' in the bush, wasn't it? Make your fortune while everyone else was away fightin' for their country.'

'You don't understand.'

'No, I don't know nothing. It was you who always told me that, wasn't it? That I was a fucking idiot?'

'What's done's done.'

'It ain't fucking done by a long shot.'

'Just tell me what you want.'

Wynter watched the steam issuing from the shower block.

'How about another beer for starters.'

The father retrieved a second bottle.

They sipped again in silence, then the old man said, 'I can only spare a hundred bucks.'

Wynter belched lightly.

'It's all I got at the moment.'

'Well that'll have to do, won't it.'

He studied his father's profile and saw Stan in the jawline and the fall of hair, a Stan buried deep in the twin brother, retreating with age, erased by it, when people started to look the same closer to death, just as babies looked the same at the start, and the features that were yours alone fell away, fell into you, behind the hatching of wrinkles and the jowls and the enlarged ears and the false teeth and the hair that grew yellow and thin, the whole of it worn down, weathered away, even though you could still see yourself, who you were, in the mirror every day, and what you witnessed in the mirror was different to how everyone else saw you, always, throughout life. Stan was disappearing into his father. But he was in there somewhere. Just as Wynter was in there. He used to see flashes of himself, in his father. A glance. An expression. He was proud of that before everything fell apart. Now he saw bits of himself as an old man, and it fanned the fire in him, and set the surface of him tingling, because hate was his fuel and had been for a long time, hate came off him like shower steam. He could gut the old bastard with the rusted fishing knife and kill off that part of the hate inside him. Just as he wanted to kill Stan. He could end all that tonight, he thought, in the dark curved space of the caravan that his father called home. He could end it all now.

'We could end it tonight,' he said.

'End what?'

'Nothing.'

The old man's left foot tapped nervously. 'I could maybe get a hundred and fifty.'

'I'm gettin' richer by the minute.'

'You staying in town?' the old man asked.

'Yeah. At the fucking Sheraton.'

His father pulled a handkerchief from the pocket of his shorts and removed his glasses and dabbed at his brow and top lip.

Wynter looked at him and thought, You're not so big now, are you? Tough guy belting everyone you could, the standover guy, tough as a brick shithouse, busting heads and breaking kneecaps, big tough Reg with an iron bar for a spine, and look at you now – weak as shit like any other old bloke, those fists behind you. Does it hurt? Being like everyone else?

After a long while the old man took off his glasses again and rubbed his eyes with the heel of his hand and said, 'Sometimes things don't work out how you want 'em to.'

'Yeah.'

'Some blokes, they don't grow up till it's too late. Some of 'em not at all. I know what I should've done, now I know, but I didn't back then. That's the price I gotta pay.'

'Don't give me that price-you-gotta-pay bullshit.'

'You can think what you like. I pay every day. Always will. You make a choice and you live with it.'

'You're weak as piss.'

'Sometimes you run into a part of yourself that you didn't know was in you. Like it's waiting for you, up the road. You don't know what I been through.'

'Don't wanna know.'

'You got a right to be angry,' he said, turning to Wynter, 'but if there's anything I can tell you, you got to let it go in the end. You got to. Everything turns to shit if you don't.'

'I didn't come here for some bullshit lecture from you.'

'You got to live your life. I fucked mine. Doesn't mean you have to.'

'What do you mean "have to"?'

'Blame me if it helps you. But it ain't the way to go.'

'I'll be the judge of that.'

'I got nothin' else to say.'

'Give me the money,' Wynter said.

The old man pulled his wallet from his pocket and handed over three fifty-dollar notes.

Wynter stood. 'You're a sad, selfish fuck like you always been. You're dead to me.'

He left the van park and wandered down to the inlet and sat on the wall and watched the pinlights of the trawler fleet heading out to sea. He'd lost his hunger but his hands shook and, although the briny breeze coming in off the ocean was warm, he felt freezing all over.

The sprinkling of the trawler lights grew dimmer and slipped behind waves. They seemed to wink and Wynter looked up and there were no stars in the sky and watching the trawlers winking it seemed, for a moment, that the stars had fallen and were bobbing on the surface of the sea.

It was such a place. Where the stars fell down. And everything turned to shit.

He scored at the local hotel and injected himself in the park near the war memorial and the rotunda and he lay back in the soft grass and felt every blade of it growing around him in the dark. A stone soldier cradling a rifle looked down on him. Salted dew was gathering on his slouch hat.

At dawn Wynter went back to the caravan park. His father's annexe was zipped shut. The crescent heels of the old man's thongs jutted out from the base of the canvas.

He padded silently to the rear of the van. The small window was closed and the single sheet curtain pulled. He pressed his palms against the aluminium and put his ear to it. The metal was cold. Wynter thought he could hear the old man breathing.

Across the bluff the blowhole sounded and it was so loud in the still morning with all the static of life gone, with just the quiet shift of dew on the canvas, that Wynter could feel the vibrations deep in the aluminium.

That's my old man breathing in there, he thought.

The blowhole sounded across the town like a giant kettle drum.

My old man, that's him breathing.

The drum seemed to enter Wynter and disturbed the rhythm of his heart, which raced in his chest, and even when he reached the highway at the back of the town his heart still pounded, and when he couldn't get a ride straight away he started walking to get away from the town, and he passed the old stone cemetery and the train station that ran along the front of the cove and still he kept walking.

When he breached the hill at the northern end of the town he didn't look back, he just kept walking in the gravel at the side of the road and didn't even put out his thumb, he just kept walking.

He could still hear the drum.

He felt the short fish-gutting knife in his pocket and kept his head down and freight trucks passed him and milk trucks delivering milk to the doorsteps of families all through the hills and down on the coast and bread trucks with their beautiful golden loaves in trays passed him and he kept walking to try and shake the drum but he couldn't.

The knife was cold and sharp and as he walked he ran his thumb back and forth across the blade.

By the end of the day, he knew, he'd be back in Sydney. And he'd find Aurora and they would be a family again.

She's mine and I'm going to take what I want, he said to himself.

He thought of his pathetic, decaying father in the caravan shaking with the beat of that funeral drum. By nightfall he'd be in Sydney. And he was going to take what was owed him.

As he walked he remembered the bumper sticker on a car he'd lifted in Dubbo a long time ago. It read: I WANT IT ALL.

TWENTY-NINE

A MONTH BEFORE the third anniversary of the Port Arthur massacre Graham Featherstone sent a lengthy memo to the newsroom chief-of-staff arguing for his return to Tasmania to do some 'colour' reports and interviews with survivors. Graham had, after all, been there at the time of the event. He received no response, just like the last two years.

The rejection continued to hurt Featherstone. His initial reaction was that of almost all reporters around the world – the people in charge didn't know what they were doing. Didn't know a story when it stared them in the face. But deep down it struck a familiar chord with him. One he had heard intermittently throughout his career. He would always be someone who just made up the numbers. Who, in the race of things, stood off the winner's podium every time. He ignored this when he was younger, but he was no longer a youthful 'firebrand', as they liked to say, and with age he heard the striking of the chord with greater clarity.

Featherstone went about his business, while the real heart of his profession beat somewhere else.

After work, at daybreak, he crept into the BBQ King

restaurant round the corner from the studio and shared thimbles of tea with the waiters and cooks. He sat on a stool near the huge warm stoves in the basement kitchen and let their Cantonese and Mandarin flow over him and it spun a cocoon around him in those early hours, removed him from the sharp edges of his own language. And against going home to the loneliness of his rental in Rozelle.

In the restaurant kitchen the staff made him the butt of their jokes and teased him, but he was allowed to stay because they were men who had worked to survive and were broken too, and in those times the best place to be was among people where the dialogue of human beings was not close and clear, but a long way away. It was at that point of distance, at the rim of human noise, where you could be most alone and not suffer true loneliness.

For Featherstone, the gaggle of incomprehensible Cantonese and Mandarin, and being in the vicinity of people working quickly, crowded together, arms and elbows scissoring, pans and woks breathing fire, the staccato of knives on wood, and the fleshy vegetables there amongst blades and cast iron, soothed him. He did not have to tell them of the comforts of a large kitchen, and the blue flames of the stoves flickering and burning unceasingly like religious candles, and the smell of cooking fat and all the ingredients that had passed through it. He positioned himself so he could peer over to the room of golden roasted ducks, hanging in rows from the low ceiling.

Behind the chatter of the men he could hear the cleaning trucks up in Goulburn Street and the water hissed by like the surf. He knew the sun was coming up, yet down there in the basement of the restaurant it was always night.

His life was out of synchronicity with the rest of the world. Once, in the early evening, he would wind down with a few drinks in the city or up at the Courthouse Hotel on Taylor Square or at the Goldfish Bowl at the Cross, and that would flow into dinner, but now, sometimes foggy with the drinks from the Welcome Inn before his midnight shift as well as the Scotch during, when he emerged from the kitchen of the restaurant, the sun was still weak and fresh and the streets were wet and there was the beautiful smell of coffee and pastries that seemed new to him when it hovered over the footpaths, and people were going to work. He was getting used to this – being tipsy at breakfast.

He liked to stroll down George Street to Circular Quay and have coffee and watch the crowds coming in on the ferries and spilling onto the wharves to be instantly sucked uphill and into the city.

He could sit there on one or two coffees and feel like he was part of something. He loved the rush hour, and the great grey blocks of people funnelling in a single direction, and their watch-checking and quickened pace in tune with the cogs and springs inside the watches, and the purposefulness of their walk and their faces, pale and grim and determined, as if the day ahead was to be wrestled with, to be broken down with a sledgehammer. Their determination knitted brows and cast mouths and eyes in different ways. The muscles and skin and hair and fluid of them were pinched and tugged at by invisible wires that stretched from some problem that the day, the future, was to present. Featherstone knew part of that determination was the residue of what they'd just left behind – bills pinned by magnet to fridge, a baby with colic, an unmade bed, dishes in the sink, the perfumes and secretions of a new lover, a faulty shower rose, the news of the world on television. All this, too, pulled at a face. Featherstone saw this keenly, because it was the life he had left behind.

Everybody seemed to have somewhere to go, at rush hour. This is what it is to be alive, and part of a community, and a race, and the world, Featherstone thought. Living is about having somewhere to go. It happened that he would do anything not to go home.

After the rush hour Featherstone would trace the markers on the ground that revealed the contours of the original shoreline in 1788. He became fascinated with it. How it had shifted, and become something else. When he came down to the quay he always tried to imagine 1788; to see the ships anchored offshore, and the investigating parties rowing in, and the trees and shrubs that stretched down to the waterline, and he tried to visualise them stepping from the boats, and the harbour water swelling their leather shoes, and the spines of the small wooden boats scarring the gritty sand and soil of the shore, and the view of the forest ahead of them, the low crowns of trees and the darkness they held. He liked to think of the embryonic grids of streets the settlers laid out, the tiny herringbone tracks of order that would become the city centuries later.

At other times he liked to sit on the lawn in front of the Museum of Contemporary Art and look out at the water. It was Port Arthur. Then it was Circular Quay again. Then Hen and Chicken Bay. If he looked at the water long enough he returned to thoughts of Victoria.

It still irked him that she had left so quickly, at the first signs of trouble. Was it really as an old family friend had confided to him when he was a teenager: when soldiers go to war, women find another soldier?

It disturbed him, too, that at thirty-seven he knew nothing of relationships and the subtleties of them and how to attend to their delicate mechanics. But how was he different from anyone else? Who could know this?

He always wanted to be a reporter and put things down honestly on paper. His father never had two cents to rub together, and here was his brother Robert building the biggest shopping complexes in the southern hemisphere and living in a mansion in the correct suburb and banging his callgirls in the Toaster. And Graham on the fringe of these orbits, the orbits of a city with infinite orbits of celebrity and bullshit and A-list and B-list and C-list and all the other fucking lists and all the suburbs turning into little villages of wealth or influence or bohemia or anti-wealth or neo-bohemia or post-baby-boomer-Gen-X-faux-punk-camp-intelligentsia fucking horseshit. All this, glutting the city, choking it. Cosmopolitan. How small we become when we think we're big.

And what difference does it make? Fuck all. Do you want to be influential? Is that it? There are enough 'influential' radio announcers in this city. Fuck them.

He didn't want to go home. He was so tired, but he couldn't face the long, dark, pictureless hallway of the house in Rozelle.

When he was feeling drowsy he walked around to Mrs Macquarie's Chair and sat under the giant fig trees and continued to look out at the water. He kept his back to the Woolloomooloo wharves and the new apartment development at the Finger Wharf because he hated what this city had done to the wharf, the place where young Australian men sailed away to the First World War now an enclave for those of the city in one of the higher orbits, a finger of ostentatious wealth where the only history that mattered now was a nearby pie cart.

Under the figs he became melancholy too because he looked over the harbour and thought of his youth and of all the wonderful women he had known and the moments they had had at various points around the harbour. The apartments he had woken in at Cremorne, or Watsons Bay, and the picnics at Balmain and Glebe, and the time he had made love to a woman on the rocks above Shark Bay and held her hips and taken her from behind and had a full vista of the city as the sun set, and the light shafts between the skyscrapers were thick and golden and the harbour water lapped against the sandstone and the bats were threading across the sky in great squadrons from the gardens, and while he was making love the city relinquished one of its moments to him, and it was why he stayed, and loved it, because of these things it offered him.

Sometimes he went back through the gardens to the city and had more coffee in Hyde Park and watched the men play chess with the giant pieces in the shade of the trees. He had loved chess, once. Then he began to think of all the things he had loved when he was a child – collecting rocks, making small electrical circuits with batteries and light bulbs, watching cartoons, swimming in creeks, reading books on bushrangers, drawing – and wondered where all those passions had gone. How such things could evaporate. Is life so long that we leave such things behind completely? Or is it so short and fast that they fall away?

Then Graham Featherstone would be reporting on himself again, and he would realise how tiring they were, these fractured thoughts of himself, and how wearisome it was to be wandering the city and thinking these self-indulgent things.

His mobile telephone rang and for a moment it did not occur to him that it was his phone. Nobody rang him anymore since he had started living out of synchronicity with the world.

He finally took the phone in his hand and stared at the number. It was the office.

'Yes?'

'Graham, this is Maureen from the switch.'

'Hi.'

'I have a gentleman called David on the line for you.'

'David? David who?'

'He won't give his surname. He wants to talk to you personally. He won't say what it's about.'

'Okay.'

'Go ahead, David.'

'Hello, Graham?'

'This is Graham speaking.'

'Graham, hi. I'm a big fan of your show. I work night shifts, you know, and it gets me through.'

'Thanks.'

'Listen, I've got a story here, and I didn't know who to call.'

'A story?'

'I don't want to get anyone into trouble, you understand? I don't want to lose my job. But it's just not right.'

'Where do you work, David?'

'I'm a nurse. A night nurse. You know I listen to you every night and you're the first person I thought of.'

'Sure. I understand.'

'We're off the record, right?'

'Yeah, sure, off the record.'

'This is going to sound a bit crazy to you, all right? But they got an old guy stashed away here in the hospice, some top-secret stuff to do with the Olympics . . .'

'The Olympics?'

'Yeah. The Opening Ceremony. That's what I've been told. This guy, he's going to turn a hundred in time for the Olympics and they're going to wheel him out, you know, a century of Australia, in the flesh, something like that. Can you hear me? Graham?'

'Yeah.'

'I'm no nutter, okay? But it seems they kidnapped this old bastard and now they're just keeping him hidden to make sure he's dancing around and happy as a pig in shit come ceremony time.'

'That's months away.'

'I'm just telling you what I heard.'

'Have you seen him? The old man?'

'Yeah, I check on him at work. I've seen him plenty of times.'

Graham Featherstone looked over at the chess

players. An old man in a tweed cap was wrestling the knight in both arms and dragging it to a fresh square.

'Like I said, I didn't know who to call. But it's not right.'

Over near St James Station the people of the city were starting to head home.

'Thanks, David, I appreciate it.'

'Love your show, man.'

The dusk came quickly in the park and he watched the men packing up the chess pieces, hugging and lifting the kings and queens and castles, until the board was clear.

He sat with his phone in his hand and stared at the board. A few of the chess spectators were still in their seats, looking at the board, as if a game was in progress. The slow, cunning march to the king. Forwards. Diagonal. Sideways. Backwards. He felt an old excitement flicker to life.

'David?'

'Yeah?'

'You free for a drink? Off the record, of course.'

THIRTY

IN THE WINTER of 1914 Astrid Lampe had found her father's body face down on a thin sheet of ice and snow in the back paddock, not far from the Cranks' secondary dam. A frozen rose of blood issued from his mouth and nostrils. They had to wait for Bill Lampe's body to thaw before they could lay it out on the wooden table in front of the fireplace.

His right arm and bunched fist were iced to his belly, his left arm extended out at near right angles, and when they brought him in on the homemade sleigh the stiff, outstretched arm quivered and seemed to point accusingly at something, or someone, in the distant trees, or high up on the ridges of the snow-covered mountains.

One eye was frozen shut, and the other lazily half open, and there was nothing you could read in the eye about Bill Lampe's last moments; it did not express horror, or surprise, or even confusion. If anything, the half-closure of the lid betrayed an indifferent resignation. So, you have come at last. Let's get it over with.

But they had seen enough death in the mountains, and they knew that the look of the dead was one you could interpret whichever way you wished. If you feared death, the fear was there. And vice versa.

Astrid had gone out to explore the snow which came swiftly in the night after a mild beginning to winter, as if shovelled by a maniac from the mountains and onto the lower plains. It dusted the horses in the corrals out by the shed, and caught in the red eucalypts, and suddenly the country changed and they were no longer on the Monaro. Nothing had moved, of course, but the snow erased the khaki paddocks and the purple hills and it was the change of colour that made it another country. The giant granite boulder at the back of the house wore a powdered conical hat.

Bill Lampe had gone out early that morning, apparently for more wood – though there were questions, later, about why he didn't go to Uncle Berty's for wood. Berty had wood all year round, and he kept the fireplace alive day and night, even at the height of summer, because Berty liked a warm house, liked it hot, as hot as he remembered it that summer in South Africa. The trees around Berty's shack at the end of the valley were down to stumps in a large, almost perfect radius fanning out from the shack, and he'd already started to nibble into the forest at the foot of the valley's hills. Berty had plenty of wood, and some of the locals wondered why Bill didn't avail himself of his brother's supply the morning after that unexpected snowstorm.

In fact it was the snow that drew out Bill Lampe. It teased him out every year, be it a stream of flakes blown down from the Alps, lost instantly to the heat of the earth, or a solid fall. It was the surprise of it, and then the quiet of it. How the snow hushed the bush which, even when you were used to it, was maddening. For much of the year it ticked and clicked and creaked incessantly, and layered over that was the monotonous hoof-music of sheep and cattle, and encasing it all the hidden ringing of the heat that could have been in the air, or inside your head, or both.

The snow altered the pattern of work on the Monaro. It broke the unending blandness of it all; the miles of fences and grazing paddocks – the dun-coloured ocean of them, on which bobbed mobs of sheep; the paddocks of which, after a time, you knew every foxhole and rabbit colony, every formation of rock and boulder. It was, Bill thought, like a human face. When you took in every freckle and hair and crease and expression over years, how blandly infinite it became with familiarity, despite a wish to the contrary.

Bill Lampe had taught himself not to feel the cold. Fences and farm machinery still needed mending in winter. And on that morning of his death, he noticed, as he pulled on his boots, that the hacking cough that had become a part of him was eerily absent. He felt a coldness in his chest where the cough usually came from, and when he tried to cough he felt a strange dryness, as though something had disconnected inside him overnight. He put it down to the storm.

It was not fully daylight. The whole valley seemed to thrum with a blue light, and the new snow was clean and almost pink-edged. There were icicles on the shingled eaves of the house, and several on the rim of the shed roof, and the crown of the pepper tree out front had elongated under the weight of the snow caught in its branches. Its trunk and branches were so fine against the snow they could have been drawn with a sharp lead pencil.

Bill noticed a single pair of fox tracks in the powder between the shed and the hen house, and checked the hens, then saddled the horse in the shed and whistled for the dog. When he reached the fence line at the end of the paddock a flurry of flakes spun out of the sky and pricked his face and the horse lowered her head as she walked. There were kangaroo and brumby tracks amongst the sally trees.

He rode up onto the ridge and caught sight of Berty's shack, a tiny box of grey hardwood and a smudge of smoke in the centre of a wheel of dead stumps. Perhaps it was another reason why he liked the first snows. From the right distance it made everything simple and child-like. Berty's toy house. The ploughs and water windmills and iron tanks small and fragile on the sheet of white, as though scattered out of a Christmas stocking. He saw the shape of everything again, its definition renewed by the snow. The essence of it all, clear and immutable, drawn by the hands of children.

He wished the boy was with him, because he knew Wilfred would love the brumby tracks in the fresh snow. He was a gangly boy now, messy as they were at that age, growing out of step with the mind, the arms and legs lolloping and swinging towards the man, yet the head still mired in bomb-diving off the Dalgety Bridge, and practical jokes, and the foreign language of algebra.

Bill Lampe thought of his son as he followed the tracks of the horses and the roos. He found where they'd penetrated the fence, the ground broken and scarred with hoof crescents, and he made a cursory repair to the shattered rail.

He continued along the fence line then down into a small gully of thin scrub, the horse gingerly seeking footing. At the bottom it drank iced water from the rivulet, the dog too, and all three of them were encased in the rich exhalations of the eucalypts, the odour so thick it seemed to cling to Bill's flannelette shirt and drill breeches and exposed skin, and to the hair and hides of the animals.

He stopped the horse and loosed the reins. He saw to the east a great whorling flurry of cloud towards the tops of the Alps, and he knew it was the source of the snow, the living, moving soul of it.

With the white whorl behind him, he looked down on his valley and felt at the origin of things. No matter that the sudden whitening of all he saw meant it was an illusion and that the white would eventually disappear into the earth, and that he would be once more William Joseph Lampe, husband and father, farmhand and machinery fixer to the landowners Crank and sons, rabbiter and fence mender, occasional drover and fisherman, citizen of Dalgety, the Monaro, Australia. In moments like these he took great comfort in his place in everything, knowing that the chuff of smoke from the chimney of the small house beside the giant volcanic boulder was from a fire first fed by him that morning and now fed by the hands of his wife or his daughter Astrid. That across the ridge, in the wooden house surrounded by orchards at Berridale, was his son, Wilfred, and his own father and mother. That in the farmhouses he could see across the plains, and further, lost in the foggy breath of the snowstorm, were men and women whom he knew and could rely on, in whose heads and hearts were similar feelings and sentiments towards him and his family. That everything, the memories and the faces and the hands and the roads and tracks and the river were all interconnected and a part of a fabric, a community. That was the best you could ask for in life.

The sun was coming up and it made the heavily misted valley glow like a giant lantern. Bill Lampe struck his hat against his thigh and droplets of water sprayed to the ground. He could hear the Snowy. He thought of the boy, and the good fishing to be had in the river's cold waters. He headed down to inspect the secondary dam.

At that moment Wilfred was standing at the kitchen table with Grandfather Callistus in the house in Berridale. Laid out on the wood was a damp three-and-a-half-pound rainbow.

Wilfred had sought the old man's counsel on the art of taxidermy. He wanted to know how to preserve and mount trout.

'Go see your grandfather,' Bill had told the boy. 'He did a few ducks, when we lived at Paupong. He's been around forever. He might have done a bit on himself. You never know.'

Wilfred had arrived mid-morning the day before, a Saturday, and had hoped for an afternoon of instruction. He had brought, in his saddlebag, two freshly caught rainbows. But the old man was deep in thought in his study, composing an essay for the *Mercury*. When he broke from composition, he smoked a pipe and circled the house. He paced the rows of his experimental growing beds. Checked the menace of the clouds.

He took tea on the verandah during another break.

'Snow,' he said, the tea steam tickling his long nose hairs.

And silence.

'In my article,' he said, without being prompted, 'I am arguing for the rights of women. The debate they have provoked. The vote, and pay equal to men. I am supporting this.'

He opened his mouth on relighting the pipe and released a thick, slow-moving plate of smoke.

'It appears to me an entirely reasonable proposition. I have known many women smarter than the average fellow. It is everywhere in nature. I don't need to remind you of the queen bee and her slavish male troops. Don't get me started on the magnificently simple and complex society of the ant. But I cannot reconcile the ladies' argument with this new passion for the music hall and its vulgarities. It strikes me as working against the flow of debate. It is this I am attempting to resolve in my essay.'

He longed for discourse. It was, at times, as if he spoke to his shrubs and flowers and orchards for resolution on matters that vexed him. As if they were contemporaries in a London club, or in the smoking room of a fine home, nodding assent or shaking their heads in disagreement.

Out here, whole verbal volumes of his work were picked up by the mountain mistrals and thrown down towards the sea. In the early evening, at the dinner table, only the clock spoke.

After, Callistus said: 'The trout. Tomorrow.'

So they found themselves on that cold morning in the kitchen of the house at Berridale, with milky light pressing against the side window, standing before the trout laid out on the wooden table. The fish had been wrapped in damp newspaper, and now, on the nicks and knife cuts of the table, more than half a day after being taken from the river, their colours were already fading, and they held an aura not of something that had lived at one time and now was dead, but of objects that had never lived at all.

The old man studied the corpses.

'How quickly the life drains away, hmm?' he said. 'There is barely a vestige. Yet it is that vestige we have to recapture. For a successful mounting.' He stroked his beard. 'Your father will remember. A long time ago, when we first moved to the mountains, I preserved, not so well, a magpie. They fascinated me. I thought them very exotic, and still do. The most beautiful song. Have you listened? An exquisite, watery warble from the back of the throat. And here? Considered so common. I rate them highly against any European bird you care to mention.

'But the fish. It's a difficult thing to get right, in terms of taxidermy, a complex art at which I am a mere amateur. It's the skin, you see. The lack of pronounced scales. Now a carp you can hollow out and dry and it will retain its original shape, more or less. It stiffens nicely.

'A trout, though. The skin is thin, and will warp and wobble every which way on drying. As if willingly throwing away its original self. I like to think that of the trout. That if you have outwitted it and brought it ashore, it denies you the satisfaction of the catch. That it becomes anything but itself. Even in death it works at this. Denies you its soul. A noble endeavour, you think?'

Wilfred nodded.

'We can see here,' Callistus continued, 'that the colours have faded almost entirely. The spots are pale. The soul is gone. I don't need to tell you. You can only hope for a caricature of its former self. Life is not easy to reproduce.'

The boy continued to nod, staring down at the trout that, before his eyes, seemed to diminish in size and grandeur as his grandfather spoke. Wilfred began to feel very foolish.

'May I ask of your sudden interest in taxidermy?'

'I thought,' Wilfred said, 'that I might make some money. Off the city folk that come up here to fish.'

'Go on.'

'That I might mount their catches. For them to take home.'

'A souvenir. A memento. Of their fishing trip.'

'Yes.'

'Wilfred Lampe. Taxidermist.'

'Sort of.'

'You are familiar with the mineral borax?'

'No, sir.'

'It is a modern marvel. Your grandmother has employed it very successfully in preserving some of her flowers. And it should do the trick for your trout skin. Pay attention.'

He produced a knife from the cupboard drawer and sharpened it, all the while staring down at the dead trout.

He rested the knife on the table and then doused a tea towel in water. He folded the towel neatly, lifted a trout, and placed the towel beneath it.

Then he slowly rolled the trout over, back and forth, inspecting each flank.

'You will need to choose the side you wish to show to the world, the prettiest,' Callistus said. 'Which is it to be?'

The boy shrugged.

'As we had it seems best,' the old man said. 'Now, on the side we do not wish to show, cut a long lateral line, thus, from gill to the base of the tail. Here, come closer, you will need to cut the bone beneath the gill cover. There. Now, at the tail base, again a short cut perpendicular to the lateral.'

He reached into the drawer and produced a second knife, but did not sharpen it.

'Using this blunted blade, careful, careful, we can peel away the skin.'

The old man leaned over the fish, his beard touching the wood of the table, and slowly and delicately lifted the tissuey skin from the body of the fish.

'Hand me some scissors, will you? From the drawer.'

With the skin removed, he took the scissors.

'Gently cut the dorsal and anal fins,' he said, snipping, 'and here, the dorsal bone. Now the ventral and pectoral fins.'

He cut with singular snips and they could hear the crunching of cartilage and bone.

'Following the same process,' he said, turning the fish over, 'we can remove the skin on the other side thus. Be careful here. This is our precious side. Now a quick cut of the vertebrae, and the body and gills are gone.'

The sheet of skin, still attached to the head and tail, was much larger than Wilfred had imagined. The old man carefully scraped away the little scraps of flesh still clinging to the inside.

'Remove the ventral and pectoral fin bones thus,' he said, his old hands as sure and still as a surgeon's, 'and we are ready to work on the eyes.'

Callistus washed his hands in the bowl near the stove and wiped them dry.

'Are we clear so far, Wilfred?'

'Yes, sir.'

'Don't say yes if you're still not clear.'

'No, sir.'

'Good.'

Callistus rested both hands on the edge of the table and looked down at the separated body and the spread skin.

'How different life looks,' he sighed, 'when we choose to pull it apart.'

Wilfred was fixated on the head. It was simply too much for him to imagine the rest as having any relationship to what he had caught and brought to Berridale in his saddlebag. The disconnected fins. The useless gills.

'Take your knife,' his grandfather went on, raising the head of the fish, 'and cut behind the eyeballs. Thus.'

He then fingered the eyes out of the sockets and they dropped silently to the wooden surface of the table. They sat there like moist buttons.

'Now use a piece of wire,' he said, 'to take out the cheek flesh through the sockets.'

The boy did not feel ill. But he was startled to know that trout had cheeks. His own were apple red in the warmth of the kitchen.

Retrieving a box from the kitchen shelf, his grandfather sprinkled borax crystals onto the table. Spreading out the skin, he then pinched borax from the pile and rubbed in the grains.

'Ensure a complete and even coverage,' he said in a whisper. 'In ten years, we would not want the good judges and politicians to notice their prize trophies springing leaks, would we?'

Looking at the splayed fish, Wilfred recalled the trout suit he had worn at the Christmas pageant when he was small. He saw his father fashioning the frame of the body with wire and slivers of timber, out in the shade under the pepper tree, and later the stretching of the hessian skin around the frame. He remembered the miracle of the trout shape that for a long while was not evident and then was suddenly there. A twist of pliers, a small adjustment to the hessian, and there it was. The shape. The shape of the trout, in a blink, transcending the sum of its unlikely parts.

When the eyes were fitted, it came alive.

'This must be left for at least half a day,' his grandfather said, putting finishing touches to the skin, inspecting it closely, holding his beard off the table with one hand. 'Before the stitching.'

It looked cold outside. The clouds were low and heavy and grey yet the light was incandescent and there were pale shadows off the back shed and the clipped and sleeping rose bushes.

Callistus wiped crumbs of borax off his hands and examined his handiwork.

'Thus, with some close stitching along our original incisions, it is the river sand on which we will rely. To return our specimen from the dead. Tea?'

He lit a pipe to go with his brew and chuffed away in the chair beside the window. Fumes issued from the tea in his left hand and the pipe in his right.

'It's fitting,' he said, pointing the pipe at the table, 'that what will return body to our friend there is some tightly packed river sand. I somehow like the symmetry of that.'

The boy said nothing. He had been filled with a sudden and unidentifiable gloom.

'Wherever our friend may end up, on a wall in a home in Sydney or Melbourne, on a mantel in a city office, there he'll be, big and bright and proud under glass. And inside him? The very grit from whence he came. His outside world. Now inside.'

They could hear the muted clock in the dining room.

'The final touches, of course, the oil paint, is not something I can help you with,' his grandfather puffed. 'You may have to call on the expertise of Pritchard, here in town. A detestable bore, but tonally competent. His specialty seems to be the willow. You will see how fitting that is when you make his acquaintance. A longer and more melancholic hour you will not spend than with our Pritchard. I guarantee it.'

Wilfred could barely make out his grandfather now in the darkened kitchen. Only the pipe smoke fixed him in the room. From his own chair near the stove he tried to locate the drying eyes of the fish on the wooden table. They seemed to have vanished.

'It is the final illusion, the paint,' the voice in the room said. 'It would be my advice not to replicate to the finest detail the colours and markings of the rainbow or brown or that which you bring to life. An exact reproduction of anything, in my experience, is often too real. I'm not sure if this will make sense to you. But in life, we are happier with suggestion. We all have our own interpretations. And our own memories. It is these you must leave room for.'

The boy was only half listening. Through the window he saw a man approaching the house on horseback.

He stood at the window. 'It's Tom Crank.'

The clock sounded the hour in the dining room. It was ten am. The chimes were loud and cold and tremored through the still air of the house and when they were done you could still hear them, absorbed in the furniture and the doorknobs and the heavy window lace.

Tom, hat in hands, was greeted on the front verandah. Wilfred could see his grandfather talking to the boy.

At twenty minutes after the hour, they were riding back to Dalgety, behind the black hooded sulky of the doctor.

Wilfred later learned that Astrid had found their dead father beside the dam on a patch of stubbled white tussock grass, an axe not far from his open hand, the axe welded with ice to the earth. The horse stood nearby, its leather rein loose and hanging forward, a clutch of crystals clinging to its forelock, its eyelashes sugared, staring dully down at its master. The dog shivered beside the body.

The Crank boys brought the body down to the house on the sleigh. Tom Crank was dispatched to Berridale to fetch the doctor. And Wilfred.

The blood that had coagulated around Bill Lampe's nostrils thawed quickly in the small house, and Wilfred's mother surreptitiously wiped it away with a handkerchief.

They sat silently with Bill Lampe in the house and waited for the doctor.

On the ride home, behind the doctor's sulky, Wilfred's eyes and nose ran in the cold. He could see the distant snowfall as they crossed the hills on the way to Dalgety. The Alps had vanished.

As they rode through town a few locals stopped and removed their hats and stood silently to observe the procession. Word was filtering out, from the heart of the town and out over frozen paddocks and into the warm homesteads of the district. The great machinery of death was swinging into motion. Families were already assuming their roles in what would come. The procession to the cemetery. The funeral. The wake. The provision of food for the Lampe family. Clothing for the children. Repairs to the Lampe house. Odd jobs for Widow Lampe. The parts were moving automatically, as they had done many times before.

When Wilfred observed his father's body on the wooden table by the fire in the small house he saw not death, but his father by the stream on that day of fishing after the muster, and his father's broad back as he rode ahead of him through the forest of snow gums on top of the Alps, and his father shaping delicate flies with his thick, scarred fingers, and his smile at the completion of a Bonza Bluey, and his father all hemmed in and uncomfortable in his tweed coat in the audience on the night of *The Trout Opera*, the sweat sheening his forehead and cheeks. It was as Grandfather Callistus had said: life can overcome death, if you give it the room.

He stepped out onto the verandah and the dog nosed at his shoes and ankles. Through the flywire of the door, he saw his father on the table. And he knew where he had seen this before.

On the night of the performance in the Imperial Hall. The trout suit. Resting on the back of the dray down by the oval. The fallen knight in the shadows.

It was his father. The fallen knight.

THIRTY-ONE

THE TRAIN FINALLY left Sydney behind and clattered towards the Hawkesbury River. Aurora still carried the residue of the city and could not see beyond the panes of carriage glass, milky with human hair oil and hand prints and the film of travellers' breaths. Instead she anchored herself to the rail map fixed to the wall beside her seat.

The map was a maze of thin, coloured piping. Sometimes the pipes met at a black hole. The pipes made up a map of New South Wales. There were no coastlines or mountain ranges or flat and dry interiors. It was the shape of New South Wales in cold, angular tubing.

I'm moving along one of those pipes, she thought.

When she had shut the door of her apartment behind her, she'd wondered: what if she left it with the double deadlocks as it was, forever, and it became a time capsule of her life at twenty-six? What if she started a new life, clean, and came back to the flat one day with her husband and children, and took the old keys out of a handbag and opened the door and led them into the small lounge room and showed them how she was, all those years ago, in that black hole that was her life?

I'm heading towards the next black hole, she thought. The clean, certain, immovable grid of the map gave her comfort. After everything that had happened, it was a relief to know she was moving forward and that there were definite black holes to meet, and that she would alight at an exact point at the top of the map. Somewhere, in that coin of blackness, was her father. She reached up and touched the final hole with her index finger and started to see through the carriage windows to the rushing landscape.

Two youths entered her carriage. They wore outsized pants, the crotch at their knees, and outsized shirts, and over the shirts white perforated singlets, and American basketball team caps and huge padded sports shoes. They both looked at her in the back corner of the carriage, and dropped into their seats.

They were dressed for the street, two teenage boys, and she thought nothing of them. She had seen their type before, in shopping malls, and on the main streets of country towns, and milling around train stations and congregating at city cinemas. When it got late, and they got bored of sitting around looking tough and saying nothing, they went home. And went to school the next day. Or packed tinned food at the supermarket. Or slipped on their overalls, smelling of Mother's sweet lemon washing powder, for work at the mechanic's bay.

She'd lived on the street. It wasn't an idea to her. She wasn't frightened of their type. They were the kids who kept the cops busy every Friday and Saturday night across the country, but it was dress-ups. Sometimes the role they played forced their hand, and a gun muzzle or blade flash turned the pantomime, in a millisecond, to reality, yet in ten years, she thought, most of them will be in some three-bedroom prefabricated house with a child wailing out the back, under a hoist of flapping laundry.

After the Hawkesbury the motion of the train and the green-blue blur of the trees and the creamy rock sidings dislodged pictures of home and friends and family from her memory like someone shaking out a photo album.

Strangers passed through the carriage. A ticket inspector. The bored and agitated. There was the ceaseless, drilling drone of music through a pair of headphones.

All these things stopped you from ordering your life, pulled you away from the view out the window, and drew you back into the small, stuffed carriage in which you sat in that moment in time.

A robotic voice came over the carriage speakers: 'Next stop, Dungog.'

Aurora had taken this train more than nine years before. So much had happened since, so much life between then and now. The gulf between girl and woman. And her mother, who'd let death come and live in the family house.

She was angry with herself, frustrated at not being able to link her memories to seem as clean as the map. She was convinced that deep inside those black holes were the connecting pieces to her life. Who was my mother, really? Who is my father?

It was part of the reason she was heading home, wasn't it? And the other, which was for herself. She had to get to the edge of the gravity of Wynter and Tick and Sydney and the drugs. A tiny moon trembling at the furthest reaches of its orbit. Aurora wanted to feel what that was like. She wanted to see the defining edge of this orbit of hers.

The train announced its next stop – Gloucester.

She remembered Gloucester from the first trip. She had fallen asleep at Nambucca Heads on the way down, and woken just before Gloucester, and she could have been in another country. Somewhere, during her sleep, she had crossed a line. Mist cloaked the mountains that day. The mist and the ranges and the little town seemed so foreign to her, from the subtropical landscape of Murwillumbah, that for the first time she truly realised she was a long way from home.

And the quality of light. Even when Mount Warning was wrapped in cloud, and thunderstorms rolled over the town and out to sea, the light was not heavy and deadening but a brilliant lemon, and all the colours of the cane fields and the soil and the clapboard houses and ox-blood red roofs screamed their pigments. But in Gloucester that afternoon, the forests were almost black and the clouds grim and leaden and she was chilled to the bone, even inside the train.

She'd run away to a life she'd only seen in magazines and on television, and in each moment, until Gloucester, she'd thought that her friends were watching her hurtling towards a glamorous and exciting existence, as if they were spectators sitting on the rickety wooden stand beside the sports oval on the river at school. That was how she thought then, just turned seventeen. That life was like the end-of-year pageant. That everything was a performance.

That was how Aurora felt. Until Gloucester. At

Gloucester, a light had gone. And there were no crowds of friends in the bleachers. And she was just cold and alone in a train.

She had felt that loneliness with Wynter. It shrouded him. She knew it. Even in summer his skin was cold. She shuddered at the thought of his fish skin. His dead eyes. The cold, cold mouth, like a wound from a box-cutter. She suddenly remembered the shape of his penis when erect. Curved. Like a hook.

She closed her eyes and was cradling her child again on the faded red coverlet of the double bed in the motel room in Adaminaby. Crows skipped in the stubbled grass outside the room and the sun streamed through the tissue of white curtain and lit a cheap amber glass ash-tray and a longneck beer bottle and her packet of Peter Jackson cigarettes and her lighter. The room smelled of tobacco and vomit and takeaway food and she had not washed for two days. She had been on the red bed-spread, holding the child, since they arrived at the Snow Goose.

She thought she heard a banging on the door but it went away. Then Wynter was standing over her with his black eyes and the blackness of two missing teeth in his mouth. The crows cried and the pounding came and went and then he'd be there again, one sleeve of his checked shirt rolled up and his blue bandanna tied tightly around his bicep. He'd crazily spin the handgun, then he'd be gone and leave the gun glowing on the table beneath the window. She heard crying in the corners of the room and wondered if it was the crows. Or the child.

The room shook when four-wheel-drives and trucks

and utes passed on the road outside the red-brick motel, and when they'd gone the glasses and loose shelves in the small fridge tinkled and shuddered to a stop.

She could have been in any cheap motel room in Australia, with its fake walnut table and vinyl padded chairs and broken air-conditioner and bright neon light over the bathroom mirror, both ends of the tube clotted with the carcasses of insects. Anywhere, with the cut-glass water tumblers and plastic shower curtains and small pink cold tiles around the toilet where she kneeled and vomited.

Aurora and Wynter had meandered through country New South Wales, in flight. He had convinced her, somewhere along the way, that they were driving towards a future. It had always been the same since she'd met him on that night years before in the great empty late-night womb of Sydney's Central Station. He had been there, as if waiting for her, leaning against a colonnade, with the echo of pigeons, of their wing shift and claw scratch, high up in the spans of the roof, and he had offered her the warm glow of a cigarette. In that second, she was his.

As they drove from one town to the next she saw, in the drowsiness brought on by the motion of the stolen car and the scent of crushed eucalypt seed, the country as a mass of veins and ventricles, and each place they stopped, when they became still, a place to inject in the vein. Each town meant nothing, and everything. It was where they could, at last, be still.

They avoided the highways and crept along dirt roads and partially sealed arterials through canopies of gums

and strange, unexpected stands of poplars and yellow
walls of wild wattle. She would casually rest her forehead
on the cool of the car window and gaze out at the landscape. Sweat and oil from her skin smudged the glass. It
was like a drug in itself, the vast, unending monotony of
the Australian country. A dull khaki canvas with
moments and movements thrown against it – veils of
grasshoppers, pink galahs, tottering sheds the colour of
driftwood, rusted tractors and skeletal ploughs.

Wynter railed against it, between towns, between
their moments of stillness. A foul, prickled torrent of
words issued from him and it heated the air in the car.

'I'll take what I fuckin' want when I wanna take it
you know why? you know fuckin' why? because these
cunts have got it and if they've got what I want I'll
fuckin' take it don't you fuckin' worry about that they're
not going to miss it eh they're not going to fuckin' miss
it but if it's somethin' I want it's mine and I don't fuckin'
care because this country's fucked it's fuckin' dead
it's fuckin' dog-eat-dog and you gotta survive am I
right? am I right? and who gives a shit anyway . . . am
I RIGHT?'

And on he went until he was dry in the throat and
the heel of his hand was puce from thumping the steering wheel. Aurora reached over to the back seat of the
car, half conscious, and felt the hand of the child sleeping in a nest of blankets and she played with the child's
fingers and scraped the boy's tiny crescent fingernails
on the bottom of her thumb, one by one, over and over.

They had left Yass, and scored more gear in Tumut,
and the drugs had set him alight again, and flared his old
argument with the country, with the effort of living and

breathing, and this time for no reason his vendetta was against the mountains, the Great Dividing Range, and he gunned the car recklessly up and over them, the roads icy on the lower reaches. At dusk they drove into snowfall. He didn't seem to notice anything outside the furnace of the cabin. The car fishtailed up and over the range.

Aurora had never seen snow. She didn't want to stop looking at it, being in it. It blanketed the fields at the top of the range and nestled in the crooks of the gum trees and gathered into the edges of the windshield. It absorbed the last of the sunlight and everything, for a moment, was flooded pale yellow, and then blue. The most beautiful shade of blue, the blue of cold, a blue she had seen on television, the blue at the waterline of icebergs in the Antarctic.

It was the blue, too, on the rim of her child's lips and eyelids. She drifted into sleep to the static of Wynter's hate.

The car overheated, and they limped into the town, Adaminaby, and parked outside the pub adjoining a motel. She got out of the car and checked the baby in the back seat. The snow had stopped.

The Snow Goose Motel. She peered out the window at the low pine-covered hills. She kept looking out at the hills and the pines, and it became dark and the pines were blacker than the sky. She felt she had been here before. That she knew this place. The feeling nudged at the small of her back.

She looked towards the main road and saw the giant concrete statue of a trout. There were grains of snow on its flared tail fin. She stared at the towering, pale fish, and

375

tears smarted her eyes. The trout made her feel for a moment that she had stepped into a child's fairytale.

In their room in the Snow Goose Motel she squeezed her baby and could not warm it. Wynter came and went with a slamming of doors, and laughed hysterically, and poked her with the muzzle of the gun, or put it in his mouth and tried to make her laugh. He stood outside the motel room door and studied the cage of the insect zapper, littered with ant-hollowed insect carcasses from another season. Or he genuflected by the bed, the weight of his elbows shifting her body to him.

'We'll go clean this time, I promise,' he said. 'We'll stay with me father by the beach and go clean, I promise. No more runnin'. I'll do me time and we'll make a home with me father by the beach. We don't fuckin' need anyone else, we'll be a family there, by the beach, like I always promised, eh?'

And when she didn't answer he slapped the bed and shouted, 'Well fuck ya,' and left the room and gunned the engine of the car and she heard the hissing of the radiator and a shower of gravel and he was gone.

If she looked out the window she could see the illuminated concrete trout.

After two days she was shivering without the drugs and she carefully arranged the heavy limbs of the child and wiped its brow and tucked the red bedspread up beneath its chin and rocked it to sleep. When she shivered so violently that she thought she'd wake the child she whimpered and held the child even tighter and eventually the tremors passed and she became convinced that the child now had eased her pain and it was this that she clung to and that comforted

376

her as she slept for minutes or hours at a time.

She knew her baby was dead and understood that if she stayed with it for three days, if she survived the three days, they could get away.

On the night of the second day he came into the room drunk with another man and a woman, and tried to inject her as she lay with the child. She took the gun she had hidden beneath the bedspread and held it with both hands and aimed it at his chest.

She saw him now as she had never seen him. The blood-red rims of his eyes, and the sharp, hard cut of his mouth, one side of it hooked in a perennial smile that was not a smile, but an invitation to what the world set against him. The violence of the mouth.

'Whoa,' he said, raising his hands, stumbling back into a chair, and the man and woman left, and he looked over his shoulder – 'Oi, oi!' – and snorted a laugh and followed them outside and slammed the door.

She heard the crunch of gear changes and woke in the dark and saw crows on the fake walnut table looking at her and the baby and crows perched on the backs of the vinyl chairs staring at her and crows skittering on the tiles in the bathroom and dozens of them hopping across the worn carpet towards her.

Nothing was right from the start with the baby. Inexplicably it had been there, inside her, pushing under her ribs, struggling, sending gentle waves across her stretched belly. When she got big and could find no comfort, she'd inject herself and stare at the huge sphere of it and see it not as a part of herself but as a huge stone that was pinning her to the earth. She had little recollection of giving birth. Just leaning against a strange bed on her knees, wailing at an infected cut on the palm of her hand, and wondering why the cut was on fire and drawing everything from her. Something was screaming, then; it was a part of her, but not her. She saw it outside of her body, attached by a branch. She thought for a second the little bloodied baby was the innocent part of herself she'd left behind in her other life, before everything.

Then she was in the back of a taxi, alone, heading back to Wynter's place, picking at the dry, raw wound in her palm.

Weeks passed before she saw the baby again. She went back to hospital. Three older women handed it to her in a windowless room. They talked at her and chastised her like a naughty child and she was there in the white light and peculiar smell for a long time before they gave the baby to her, this totem of doom, of bad luck, and she felt instantly the child was not right.

One of the women from the hospital visited each week and taught her new things about the baby and sometimes there was a second person who jotted in a notebook while Aurora and the woman washed the child and fed it and rocked it to sleep. After a while the second person didn't come, and then the older woman stopped coming too.

Wynter came and went and shot up and slept and raged and brought strangers in and out of the flat and disappeared and reappeared as he had always done, and the child did not exist.

With the heroin inside her Aurora pretended it was a normal child and she dressed it and held it and talked to it and went through what she thought were the rules of living the life of mother and child. Just as the older women had taught her. Tried to pretend that it was not brain damaged from the heroin she had delivered to herself each day when it was inside her. It was waiting for death from the day it was born. Aurora, and her life, wrapped in a blue blanket covered in little white horses.

At the Snow Goose she carefully tucked the blanket around the dead child and sat by the window looking out at the ghostly trout. She believed it changed colour at different times of the day, and thought it moved, fractionally, on its stone plinth in the middle of the small pond. She noticed the shift of its shadow across its border of grass and hedge, the elongation of the torso and the contortions of the inky tail.

It did, in the end, draw her out of the room and into the town. She dressed the baby in a bright velveteen jumpsuit and slippers and a beanie with muffs that covered the child's ears, and held it close to her, and walked to the base of the concrete trout and studied its gills and scales and the garbage glutted in the pond.

She sat at the small white metal table near the trout and rocked the baby in her arms. She examined the fish. The oversized tail curved to give energy to the sculpture, to render movement, upward, a leap. A trout, lured by insect, broken through the plate of the river's surface and captured in the open air, free of all it knew. She looked at its thin mid-afternoon shadow, and its narrow body and extended gill fins threw the shape of a cross over the grass.

Aurora knew as she walked through the streets of the town with the baby, talking to it, patting it on the back, kissing its cold left ear, that she could bury her child here, that it would be safe to do so, and that half of the burying was in the assurance of place, and it had to be somewhere she could remember agreeably, all her life. She convinced herself this was such a place.

In a shopfront opposite the hotel she saw displays of old sepia streets from another time with advertisements for A. W. Foley Newsagent and C. J. Yen General Storekeeper and Importer and Goldenia Tea, and read that there had been another Adaminaby, Old Adaminaby, flooded in 1957 as part of the Snowy Mountains Hydro-Electric Scheme, drowned by Lake Eucumbene.

She examined the photographs of the town as it had been. The petrol pumps. The Alpine Cafe. The farmland. And a hill behind the town crowned in pines and flecked with rows of headstones the size of rice grains.

When she returned to the room in the Snow Goose she planned her escape. She knew Wynter was out there. Knew he was watching her, waiting for her move. The car was not parked out the front of the motel.

He was gone fishin'. That's how he said it, no matter what city or town they found themselves in. I'm gone fishin' for a while. He disappeared, for hours, sometimes days, looking to score. A town was full of tiddlers, or enough bream for a decent meal, or marlin, he'd report. If it was out there, he'd find it. Ingratiate himself with the locals, weed out the big talkers, the bluffers, until he pushed through to the edge of the infrastructure, soft with bullshit and rumours and facial gestures, and through even further, past the kids and messengers, the small fry, to the second layer, the suppliers, and there he fished long and hard.

In the small towns he honed his skills. He learned the perimeters of danger, how far he could venture into it, and return. They had blown off the little finger of his right hand in a car park in Coffs Harbour. He disappeared for a while after that. But it burned in him, that they'd done that. And he'd come back, and torched their fucking clubhouse with three of the cunts still in it. They'd gotten out, but one's hair had caught fire, and he ran around like a fucking farmyard chook, screaming like a little girl. Suck on that, gentlemen.

How he loved fire. Wynter stole a new car once a week. Set fire to the old ones. Loved fire. Always fucking loved it. Set fire to two of his schools after that summer with Uncle Stan. 'Cause they gave me a fucking hiding, the cunts. Burned the fuckers down.

In summer, when they'd first gone on the run, he'd thrash the car down fire trails, his eyes blood-rimmed, a cigarette in the crook of his hooked mouth, and leave her in the car while he wandered into the bush. Little pigs! he'd shout into the forests. Little pigs! She'd drowse in the passenger's seat, surrounded by the clicking of the bush.

He'd come crashing through the undergrowth, laughing, and they'd be gone, and she'd smell the burning before they shot out of the forest, and at night, in a motel, she'd notice the hairs on his hands and forearms singed off. He'd bat her away, studying the television news. Look. Look! he'd shout, and he'd bring his knees up in delight, and roll back into the chair, and slap his thighs.

On the news she'd see men in yellow firefighting suits battling blazes, and huge columns of smoke from above, and the great orange and red rim of the fire front, and she'd look at Wynter, and he'd be rubbing his forearms like a maniac.

He'd put the fire into his veins then, and his eyes would roll back in his head, and if he passed out, she'd creep closer to him, and study the inflamed stump at the end of his right hand.

On that last day in the motel she opened the curtain and saw the great metronome trout shadow was long now and had fallen across the hedges. Below, in the street, was their car. He was back. He was somewhere close. In the pub next door to the motel. Perhaps the fishing was bad here, in Adaminaby. No bites. He'd want to be going soon. Hit the road. She had to move now.

She checked her face in the bathroom mirror. Teasing and touching her hair, she noticed the underskin of her arms was mottled like marble.

She gathered her stuff into the baby's bag of clothes and blankets and disposable nappies and bottles. She checked inside the nappy bag, and the roll of money was still hidden there. She neatly rewrapped the baby in its blanket of blue and white horses, and held it over her shoulder, and slung the bag across her other shoulder.

In the car, with the baby in the passenger's seat, she brought the two exposed wires beneath the steering column together and started the motor. The red temperature light came on. She ignored it, and slowly backed the car onto the road in front of the motel, and drove past the trout and turned left onto the main road. Her teeth chattered and she gripped the wheel until her knuckles were white. She saw, not far out of town, a sign to Old Adaminaby, and she drove there, across cattle grids and past farmhouses until she came out at the edge of Lake Eucumbene.

She drove down to the lake. She expected, for some reason, to see the old sepia town, but there was nothing but a caravan park, and a boarded-up church, and a tourist sign with the same picture of the vanished town she had seen in the shopfront in new Adaminaby.

There was nothing to recognise. No landmarks that correlated with the old picture. Just water and dead trees rising out of the lake.

She went into the office of the caravan park and asked an elderly woman behind the counter about the cemetery.

'Got relatives you gotta visit?'

'Yeah,' Aurora said.

'Other side of Eucumbene,' she said. 'Back out where you came, few kilometres, you'll see the fishermen down on the water. Four-wheel-drives. Follow that road down and around, you'll see it on the hill, across the way. Where the pine trees are.'

She followed the woman's instructions and ended up on a dirt road that traced the edges of the lake. Some fishermen were already there early for the dusk rising, their vehicles clustered a few hundred metres apart. Men were waist-deep in the water. Others stood at the edge, whipping lines back and forth. They did not even notice her.

Aurora looked across the lake and could see the darkening cluster of pines on the far hillside. She followed the road around the lake. Rocks thudded the undercarriage of the car. Sheep flowed up and over the rise as she approached. Fingers of steam clawed at the front of the car bonnet.

She stopped the car outside the cemetery gate and sat still behind the wheel. The hissing of the wind through the pine trees roared like the ocean.

It was an old cemetery built for a town that no longer existed on a hill that had overlooked the town, so that the townsfolk could look up during the day and see, yes, their loved ones were closer to God. It was a big cemetery, only a third occupied, with enough space for another century of the dead. Until the town disappeared beneath the water of the lake.

She took the baby from the car and the car's club lock device from the front passenger well and unlatched the rusted gate and walked through the rows of graves. There were some with little low fences of laced iron that had fallen in and sunken graves and cracked granite and everywhere broken vases, some filled with plastic flowers. There were German names and Polish names and Italian and English and Hungarian and Dutch names and others she did not recognise, all covered in scattered pine needles.

She spoke to the baby as she walked to the back of the cemetery.

'I love you,' she told it. 'You can sleep now.'

She chose a shaded spot beneath the giant lower arm of a pine. She rested the baby on the damp grass and cleared away pine cones and needles. Suddenly she was very cold and she got down on her knees and took the club lock in both hands and struck into the earth and the wind roared past her ears and whistled through the trees.

Her heart pounded when she was finished and she threw the tool aside and stared into the fresh hole, its

384

sides whiskered and damp. The grass hissed around her.

She picked up the baby. 'I love you,' she said. 'I love you.'

She kissed its smooth, cold forehead and placed it into the open grave and sat at the end of the grave and stared into it. She instinctively reached for a pine cone and held it in both hands. Her eyes watered in the cold wind coming down from the mountains and she picked at the hard spikes of the cone.

Reaching over, she swept the soil into the grave with her forearms and packed it down and the soil lodged underneath her fingernails and caught in the fine hairs of her arms. When she was finished, she sat up and placed both open palms onto the surface of the grave and the soil felt warm.

'Goodbye, angel,' she said, and wiped her eyes, and streaked her cheeks with dark red soil.

As she walked back to the car, the wind brought to her the mewling of distant sheep, and human voices. The sun had lowered behind the hills, and she latched the cemetery gate and in the gloom she could not see her baby's grave beyond the grey-blue broken headstones.

She drove back past the lake in the gathering darkness. There were several dozen fishermen there now, knee-deep in the great empty expanse of the lake with its copper surface and its drowned crucifix trees, and she saw them working their lines, the water rippling out around the legs of their waders. She slowed down and for a moment the lake was alive with insects, blurred with them, and the water rippled where the fish rose and concentric rings moved out and out from where they had broken the surface and the rings intersected and tried to push through each other below this haze of insects and the fishermen levered their rods and lines back and forth into this with their flies of coloured feather and it was all there, this life and death, before the darkness erased the fishermen.

Wynter would be looking for her now. Turning over the motel room. Putting his fist through the cheap plywood door of the bathroom.

She turned on the car headlights, limped out onto the road to Cooma, and kept driving.

Aurora opened her eyes and saw stands of cane rushing by in the yellow light from the train carriages. They looked soft and beautiful.

The train began to slow and she looked into backyards littered with old tyre swings and car shells and children's tricycles and tin boats.

She couldn't see Mount Warning. It was not marked on the tubular map and she had no view of it from the carriage but it was there. Its old and cragged face, still looking down on her.

She was exhausted on waking and her eyes were gritty and quickly watered. In the stark neon of the carriage she felt a false hope, that this was a fresh beginning, a clean white slate, because she knew that whenever she closed her eyes her child might be there.

The train stopped, and she stepped onto the platform.

Home.

THIRTY-TWO

Wynter sat in the foyer of Joe Panozza's office, next to a seven-foot inflatable soft drink bottle. The bottle was green, and you could see through it, and on the other side was the distorted head and shoulders of the receptionist.

He had been waiting for twenty-five minutes. Occasionally the receptionist peered around the side of the green bottle and said: 'He won't be much longer.'

She looked like a monster, or the victim of a hideous accident, through the blown-up bottle.

He had been back in Sydney for twenty-four hours and had not slept. He went straight to Kings Cross and took a corner table in the old Piccolo Bar where he sat for ages on a single black coffee. In the early hours of the morning a friend of a friend from his past came into the bar. They talked. The friend of a friend said if he wanted some quick cash a businessman called Joe from Leichhardt needed someone for a few odd jobs.

Later that morning Wynter cleaned up in the toilets at Town Hall Station. He smeared pink liquid soap under the armpits of his shirt. He wet his hair and finger-combed it. He made the short bus trip to

Leichhardt and walked to Joe Panozza's office behind Norton Street. His stomach rumbled at the early morning aroma of the coffee and pastries that hovered around the front of the cafes.

If he hadn't been going to Joe Panozza's office he might have had to resort to some of his old tricks and jump a few old ladies for their handbags down in leafy Elizabeth Bay or Woollahra. There were a lot of old ladies there. Or lift some CD wallets or shoes or anything he could hock from cars parked on the street. Or a whole car.

He could wait until nightfall, and head down to Rushcutters Bay Park, and wait for the faggots on the bench seats under the big trees. He could enjoy the salty breeze off the harbour and the soft sounds of the yacht rigging and the pock-pock of the tennis balls from the courts behind the trees while he waited for them in the shadows. But he hadn't done that sort of work for years, when he was really desperate, and it was the dance before it, the luring in, and the low talk prior, the game of it, the whispered queries, the attempt at tenderness before the strike, that made him feel sick to the base of his stomach, not for what he was about to do, but that feeling coming off his victim, the tangible desperation and need for affection that tightened every muscle and sinew in Wynter's body, and the effort it required to hold back his violence, his rage, that so exhausted him, and that minute between the stranger taking the bait, and doing what he had to do, always felt endless and painful and something hot howled through him until his fist crashing on a forehead or a jaw stopped it and cooled everything down like jumping in the surf on an autumn morning, and he could walk away, his heart belting in his chest, with a calfskin wallet in his hand.

There was always Central Station, too, tried and true, with its wide-eyed youngsters emerging from the trains and into the big smoke, as innocent and soft in the underbelly as freshly hatched turtles on a beach. There were always the innocents of Central. But you needed an infrastructure for a good haul at Central.

Joe Panozza's office didn't look like an office. It was on the ground floor of a Victorian terrace on the end of a row of terraces. There were retractable security shutters on all the windows. It was the only terrace without a front garden.

He pressed the buzzer and said he was there to see Joe Panozza. The door automatically clicked open and he entered a small dark cubicle with a security camera in the corner of the ceiling. Another door clicked open, and he was in the reception, with the giant soft drink bottle.

He studied the bottle because there was nothing else to look at, except the disjointed face of the receptionist. The label had in its centre a perfect circle surrounded by rings the colour of the rainbow. It looked like a target. Written in the middle of the circle was ETERNAL LIFE. And under it: THE WORLD'S FIRST THERAPEUTIC SOFT DRINKS.

He picked up a pamphlet on the coffee table next to his chair, and read about Eternal Life.

There was a quote on the front of the pamphlet from someone called Chia Tao. *I asked the boy beneath the pines/He said, 'The master's gone alone/Herb-picking somewhere on the mount/Cloud-hidden, whereabouts unknown.'* He didn't know what that was about.

Inside, there was a photograph of a man and a woman and two children running through a sunny meadow. Under the meadow were little pictures of soft drink bottles. The Re-Energizer, made with licorice root and dandelion root and milk thistle. The Fat Buster with *Garcinia cambogia*. There were other drinks with *Ginkgo biloba* and sarsaparilla. He recognised sarsaparilla. He remembered his mother used to love sarsaparilla, all those years ago in Melbourne. It was one of the only words he understood. The rest was a foreign language.

'He won't be much longer,' said the monster in the bottle.

Wynter needed a hit. He had to get back to the Cross. He recalled finding smack on the street once, a tiny red rubber balloon and, inside that, the chip of heroin wrapped in foil. Just lying there, in a crack in the road in the middle of a pedestrian crossing. That was Sydney. Horse littering the streets.

He returned to the picture in the pamphlet and thought again of Aurora. If she was here he'd find her. The photograph of the family in the meadow made him sad. He missed her. He wondered about their child. If he could get some quick cash out of Joe Panozza he could clean himself up and he and Aurora could start over again, and he could come around to her place with flowers and take her out for a nice dinner, and they could go down to Farm Cove for picnics on a Sunday or out to Peats Ridge and ride horses or run together through a meadow. Then, just as quickly, the pamphlet made him angry, and he'd take her by the fucking throat when he tracked her down, and punish her, because she'd left him. Taken the gun and the car and his child and his fucking money and left *him*. Nobody left *him*.

'Not much longer now,' the receptionist said.

He'd have to be real smooth with Joe Panozza. He'd do what the man asked and take the cash and score and get a meal. He looked up at the looming bottle. Maybe I'll be selling soft drinks at the football, he thought. I'll have a tray over my shoulder and a little cap and I'll be flogging Eternal Life in the grandstand. Fuck me, he thought, and laughed at himself.

He heard voices behind the office door and then the door opened and two men walked out. The green bottle of Eternal Life shivered on the spot.

The men who walked through the reception looked like brothers. They were not tall men but they were huge. They were Tongans or Fijians or something and both had short-cropped black hair. Wynter could see shoulder muscles straining the cloth of their shirts. One had a tattoo on his forearm. They looked at Wynter and nodded and left the room.

The man at the door to the office was speaking on a mobile phone. He waved Wynter towards him.

'He's ready to see you now,' the receptionist said.

Wynter could smell the man's aftershave leaching into the reception area. Panozza kept talking on the phone. The door closed behind them and he pointed Wynter towards a couch, still on the mobile phone. He had another in his other hand.

'. . . Sure, sure, speak with Johnson in Mexico, get a feel for how much they might need and we'll check the warehouse, get it on a plane by tomorrow . . . Sure, sure . . .'

The other phone rang.

'. . . Hold on a sec . . . Yes, yes . . . How much? Listen, I want to know how many fucking cars that bastard leased and get me an exact figure on the billboard advertising . . . Exact . . . *Exact* . . . Then we'll take it from there.'

He snapped the second phone shut. '. . . John, get back to me as soon as you know.

'Sorry, sorry,' he said, extending his hand to Wynter. 'Madness. Crazy. I'm having a fucking heart attack here. Sit down, sit. Let's talk. You're Wilder . . . Wynter. Wynter. Sorry. Of course. Sammo tells me you were referred, by our friend in the city . . .'

'Yeah.'

'Good. Good. Here, have a soft drink. Try this. You like grapefruit? Here, try the grapefruit. It's my kids' favourite. Try it. Tell me what you think. Now. Open it now. Try it. You'll like it. My kids love it. Go on. Have a sip. Like your opinion.'

Wynter tasted the soft drink.

'Good, isn't it? Excellent. Taste the herbs. You can taste the herbs, yeah? Got a hangover, that'll fix you right up. Not too sweet. Taste it. Taste it. The citric acid. Good, isn't it? Six months ago I'm an accountant and now I'm a world fucking expert on the healing properties of herbs. No shit. True story. I'll tell you about it. You live here? Staying in town? Need a place to stay? I know a nice place in the city. Know the people there. They'll look after you . . .'

One of the phones rang again. 'Yes, hello . . .'

Wynter saw in the harsh light of the office that part of Joe Panozza's face was covered in a pale rash. His hair, too, was muddy brown and grey and there seemed to be tufts of it missing across his scalp. He could have been forty years old, or seventy. He was dark around the eyes and the eyes themselves were rheumy and red-rimmed. He wore a black suit and an open-necked white shirt. In a certain light his whole face was ashen.

'. . . I'll have someone on it in a matter of hours, yes, correct, correct . . . I thought I'd wait to see if we achieved *resolution* to our problem before we called them in . . . No, I haven't but I will, yes . . . How do you think after all I did for that cocksucker . . . No, yes . . .'

Wynter's attention was drawn to the long fish tank against the far wall of the office. It was clean and a filter bubbled furiously. Coloured pebbles littered the base and there was a cave made out of large rocks and a ship-wreck and reeds and through it all swam a swarm of fish that looked exactly like bumblebees. They were striped black and yellow and they swarmed around the tank. He'd never seen anything like it.

'. . . I'll call in an hour . . . Sorry, Wynter, sorry . . . I should turn the bloody things off. Ruin my life. Too much stress. It's killing me, this. All this. How was the grapefruit? Good, isn't it. Ironic. A drink for people's health. Eternal Life. Be the death of me.'

Joe Panozza scratched at the top of his left hand.

'Six months I've been developing this. Got ware-houses full of the stuff. Pallet after pallet. Got billboards up and down the east coast of the country. Big. Huge. Got a brilliant product. Nothing like it. Anywhere. You tasted it. It's good. No shortcuts. Pure quality. Water filtered seven times. Water so pure you could use it for fucking eyedrops. And where is it? Stuck in the ware-houses. Every fucking bottle. Nothing on the shelves, in the fridges. Nothing. Zip. Fuck all. Got orders from round the world. Mexico. Philippines. America interested. Got the supermarkets begging. Got six airlines that want it inflight. Eternal Life at thirty thousand feet. But not a single bottle out there. That one. There. In your hand. Travelling down your gut. You're one of the only people on earth to have tasted Eternal Life. Can you fucking believe that? It's my problem, but I need you to help me. Not one of my people. A stranger. No offence. In and out. Simple as that. I'm told you can help – an in and out person. That's what I need.'

One of the phones rang again. The bees swarmed all over the shipwreck in the tank.

'. . . half-day? What's that? They're here? On their way? Sure. Send them in. No problem. Yep. They've eaten? Good. No problem. I've got no time for shopping. Janet can take them. Call Mamu for me. Get him over here. Yeah. I don't care what he's doing. In half an hour. Good. Yes. No. Okay.'

He pressed a button on his desk phone. 'Janet, kids are on the way. Send them in. Ten minutes. Then out. Take them shopping. Good.'

Joe Panozza scratched at his flaking cheek.

'This is killing me, Wilder. Wynter. Early grave – that's where I'm headed. I wanted out. Trust me. The fast life. Deals and deals and deals. I got two kids. Wanted to enjoy them, you know. While they're kids. Then I come up with this idea. I'm worried about my kids' health. Same as any parent. Want them to have the best, live a clean life. Not much to ask. My wife and I, we're at a club. One of mine. Over in Stanmore. We're having a party. Lots of friends and relatives. The kids are running around like kids do. I say to my wife – look at them running around. Look how they run. Full of energy. Full of beans. And they're drinking cola. Full of sugar. They're running around like lunatics, fuelled on sugar. I say to my wife, Remember when we were teenagers? Hippy shit, right? Goat's milk and peace and fucking love, man. That was us. Organic vegetables. Organic pot. That was us. And look at this. Look at our fucking kids, flying around on chemicals. This ain't us, I said. What happened? How we let our kids eat and drink this shit? There's got to be something better. Got to be an alternative. Something they can drink I don't have to worry about their teeth falling out or getting fat. Having a heart attack at twelve. That's when I came up with it. Eternal Life. World's first therapeutic soft drink. Hardly any sugar, pure water, natural herbs. Away we go. I should've stayed crunching numbers. Construction. People said we couldn't do it. Been tried before. Big companies won't like it. They'll crush you. Fuck them, I said. This is for my kids. Spent millions. Got it on the therapeutic goods list. You know how hard that is? Really, do you know? You couldn't know. I could tell you now and still you wouldn't know. I got the taste right, the herb balance, the water. Got on the therapeutic goods list. Then one miserable little cocksucker takes advantage of me. I'm too generous. Always have been. People take advantage. I helped his fucking father. I saved his family home. I gave him a fucking job. And he does this to me. The arsehole rips me off. Fucks off my distributors. Sells thousands of bottles in advance and takes the money. Doesn't tell me so everything is still sitting in the warehouses. All that work. Millions of dollars. No sleep. Stress. Losing my fucking hair. Eternal Life. Wynter, you can help me with this problem. In and out. In and out . . .'

The door to the office opened and two children ran into the room.

'My princesses. This is them. Miss Universes, both of them.'

The children grabbed at their father's legs and waist. He kissed each of them on the top of the head. The older child was about ten, the younger seven. They wore designer jeans and chunky high sandals. They wore bright T-shirts. Wynter swore the older one was the girl in the pamphlet, running freely in the sunny meadow.

They didn't even look at Wynter.

'They didn't have half-days when I was a kid,' said Joe Panozza. 'Half-days. I sleep four hours a night. Even then I don't sleep. Not real sleep. Been like it since I was a child. Dozing. That's what I do. I doze. Don't know what real sleep is. Never had it. Never will. When I'm in a box. That'll be my first sleep. Janet's taking you shopping. You're as bad as your mother. Settle down. Where is your mother? You're coming back here later. Correct. We'll have dinner at Enrico's. You don't like? Too bad. We're going there. Daddy's got business. What happened to the money I gave you last week? Can you believe this, Wilder? Still in nappies but they know about lay-bys and fly buys and whatever the shit buys. There. Look in the drawer. Yes. That's enough, Evangeline. I won't say it again. Put half of that back. Take it. Get out of here. I didn't see it. See? I'm looking away. I didn't see anything. Go. Go. It's bread and water for you tonight. Go. You're giving me a heart attack. Get out of here. Shoo. Go.'

The girls ran from the office and slammed the door behind them.

Joe Panozza pulled a handkerchief from his trouser pocket and mopped his brow.

'You got kids, Wynter? Don't bother. They're good kids. The oldest one. Marianna. She's talented. An artist. And music. Loves music. Plays the flute. Beautiful. Real creative. I bought the club. In Stanmore. That's for her, when she's old enough. Marianna's. That's what it's called. Sits there empty the whole time waiting for her to grow up. Fully fitted bar and restaurant. Beautiful. I got a grand piano in there. I tinkle. Helps me relax. She gets it from me. The music. I write songs. To relax. Helps me. I don't write them down. They're all here. In the head. Anyway. You're an in and out man. I think you can help me. Here. Try the Re-Energizer.'

Joe Panozza took several more phone calls. Wynter was anxious to get out of the office. He was tired. He was hungry. He began to smell his own body odour through the rich aftershave of Joe Panozza. He began to lose concentration. He focused on the fish tank, and the hovering of the bumblebees.

'. . . so Wilder. Wynter.'

'Yeah.'

'This is the name and address.' He handed Wynter a business card with details written on the back. 'Gino Spina. That's his old man's place. We've been told he's there. Pay him a visit. Explain what I'm trying to do here. This is good, Wynter. I'm trying to give something good to the fucking world. I can't be held back by some two-bit junkie. Explain that to him, Wynter. Can you? You can. In and out. He has to make things right. Tell that to him. I want my money back, Wynter. I want to get my distributors back. Every day I'm losing. Eternal Life can't sit in the warehouses. Has to get out on the street. Tell him to make it right. Convince him. You can do that. Now I don't know you. You don't know me, Wynter, I don't know you. Wynter who? Right. Joe Panozza? Never heard of him. Here. A down payment. Appreciate it. Do your best. If he's high be careful, he's a crazy bastard sometimes. But this is the craziest thing he ever fucking did. This is too big. He doesn't know what he's done. He has no idea. A cockroach, Wynter. In the palace of the mighty. Thanks for your time. Thanks for coming over. Fix it. In and out. Give me a call. Number's there on the card. Ring any time. Let me know. Good work. Good stuff. Thanks, Wynter. Appreciate it.'

One of the phones rang again.

Wynter walked out into Leichhardt with a thousand dollars cash in his pocket.

He caught a taxi to the Cross. No buses for Wynter. He was king shit. He had a grand in the kick. He had a screaming headache after the visit to Joe Panozza. It was like the bees in the fish tank had slipped into his head and were hovering through his blood and swarming behind his eyes. He'd score. That'd chase the bees away. Then he'd get a room in Macleay Street, have a shower, get a meal, and go pay Gino Spina a visit. He wanted it over and done with, the balance of the cash from Joe Panozza, and then he could track down Aurora.

I'll find her, he thought. This is a small fucking place.

Nowhere to hide for people like us. When you have a need like we do. Friends you can trust? None. Everyone can be bought, when you have a need. No privacy like normal people have. You seen him? Sure, what's it worth to you? Where you drink. Who you talk to. Where you're living. Sure, no problem. Courts have got your records. People got you in their memories. You have to be clean and straight to hide properly.

Someone will have seen her. For sure. Someone in this filthy shit heap will have the information I need.

He scored some heroin in Springfield Avenue and shot up straight away in a urine-drenched alcove. It was still mid-morning and the world was beautiful and he went and bought two burgers and some fries and a strawberry shake. He threw up in the bathroom and forgot about the hotel room and went straight to the Goldfish Bowl where he ordered a schooner of VB.

The twenty-four-hour bar was in that transition period between the late-night revellers and the daytime regulars. Wynter pulled up a stool at the end of the bar where he could watch the street while he drank.

You're here, aren't you, Aurora? he asked himself. He watched the life of the street. He expected to see her walking past with the baby in her arms or in a stroller. Where would she get money for a stroller? She'd probably found some sugar daddy cunt who paid for everything and fucked her when he wanted and fed *his* child in the mornings and tucked *his* child to sleep at night. Some fancy apartment she lived in, probably, overlooking the harbour. Probably went to the hair-dressers at the same time each week and ate in restaurants while a nanny looked after *his* child. Maybe she was pregnant to him. Setting up a nice little family.

He hated the man who was looking after Aurora and had made her pregnant. He'd find the man and let him know the score. He'd take him out and put everything back to normal.

After four beers he studied the crowds that passed the glass windows of the Goldfish Bowl. There were men in suits carrying expensive leather satchels and gay boys holding hands and dressed in trendy pullovers and jeans and women so fancy they simply didn't belong here, in the Cross, as he knew it. At one point in the afternoon he saw a man wearing a cap walk past the bar with a huge leather golf bag over his shoulder. He thought he must be seeing things. He could not reconcile the vision of the golf bag with the Cross. The place had changed. Who the fuck did they think they were? What was going on? He wanted it to be night so it wasn't so confusing. At night it went back to normal.

Wynter sat in the bar all day. By late afternoon he struck up a conversation with another drinker. Wynter noticed the green-blue prison tattoos on his wrists and asked him when he got out. He'd been let out of Long Bay three days before, and produced his release card. He'd been drinking for three days.

They watched the street like two predatory birds.

'Can you fucking believe that?' Wynter said, raising his index finger from the beer glass and gesturing to the footpath outside.

They both watched the man in the giant fur coat pass the windows of the bar. His hair was pulled back in a ponytail. His eyes were huge and his cheeks sunken, like he had no teeth. He walked with his hands in the pockets of the coat and its circumference was so huge pedestrians had to swerve around him. Thin shins comically held up the furred spectacle of him.

'Fuck me,' the drinking companion said.

'What was that?'

'I've seen him around. Last couple of days.'

'Junkie.'

'What else.'

Wynter shook his head.

An hour later he watched as a three-wheeled motor-cycle puttered past the glass. It was towing a small trailer, and on the trailer was a seven-foot green inflatable soft drink bottle. It quivered and jiggled on the trailer. ETERNAL LIFE was written inside a target on the side of the bottle.

'Hey!' Wynter shouted. People in the bar looked at him.

'What?'

He half lifted himself from the stool and watched the bottle before it disappeared. He knew it from some-where. 'I know that,' he said.

His companion lifted his glass. 'Here's to eternal fuck-ing life,' he said.

Wynter bought his new mate drinks. He shot up again in the toilets of the bar. He didn't know where the drugs had come from, or where he was.

At around one am he woke up on a bench near the El Alamein Fountain. He splashed the fountain water over his face. It took him fifteen minutes to orient him-self. He checked his pockets. He had less than a hundred dollars in notes and change. With relief he found the two hundreds he'd stashed beneath the filthy inlay of his

401

right shoe. He also found the crumpled business card with Gino Spina's name and address on it.

Fuck, he said to himself.

He could see the lights of the police station across the square. There were other bodies on benches in the park.

It was a clear night. Construction cranes hovered over the trees. He noticed one towering above a nearby gutted hotel, then he made out another, and another. The pale skeletons of the cranes. The place was being torn down. All the old hotels were disappearing, making way for apartments.

Everything was slipping away. He felt, for a moment, that he was lost. That there was nothing left to hold onto. It was all moving too fast.

For the first time he wondered if he really could find Aurora. He was stranded again. The times between being stranded were growing shorter. He couldn't keep his feet.

At the bus shelter he read the address on the card in the light of an advertisement for TAG Heuer watches.

Wynter had to find Spina. Get the job done. Earn the rest of his money. Find Aurora. And get out.

Put the kettle on, Mr Spina, I'm on my way, he said to himself. And he started walking towards Surry Hills.

THIRTY-THREE

WILFRED STOPPED THE horse just above the tree line on Summit Road.

The cold bit his face and his eyes watered. Cloud pushed over the escarpment of the Main Range and it looked like the mountains were on fire despite the long tongues of snow and ice that ran down into the valleys.

His horse, Bodalla, once his father's, was breathing quickly in the thin air.

From the crushed gravel road he could hear the music of the thaw. It was under him, and all around him, and he saw chains of pools amongst the dark bog moss in the valley, and water snaking swiftly in the meandering gouge the river had cut into the valley floor, and there was a muted trickling and gurgling that played under the hum of the wind.

Where the snow had melted were thousands, millions, of rocks and shards, cairns and sprays of rock, crowds of them rising out of tufted sedge, and he could have been a traveller heading into an ancient city built on the flanks of a mountain. A place from the Bible, with huge bazaars and narrow cobbled laneways and houses cut into the earth, dark and cool inside, where donkeys laden with baskets passed open doorways. But they were only rocks. A mile away. Not a distant city. Just the detritus of a volcano, and the trash of glaciers, and the water, still doing its timeless work.

He had come in search of the source of the Snowy River.

Nobody knew he was there. Not even Grandfather Callistus.

Wilfred had waited three months for the thaw. His father was dead. Now he was astride the horse Bodalla, in the Alps.

Wilfred had decided to make the journey the day they buried his father in the Bolocco Cemetery, a few miles out of Dalgety. He and his mother and Astrid were returning to town in the pastor's sulky after the service. They travelled in silence. Wilfred sat with his back to the pastor, facing the bowed and shrouded faces of his mother and sister. Intermittently he noticed Astrid's pink tongue poking out at him behind her black veil.

The sulky passed their front gate and kept heading towards the town and the wake at the Buckley's Crossing Hotel. As they crossed the span bridge over the Snowy, he had already decided to seek its source in the spring.

Wilfred thought of little else after the burial. He did not return to school. He stayed with his mother and sister, and did repairs around the house, and then Tom Crank rode into the valley one cold morning and asked Wilfred to help him fix some fences, and the boy quietly filled his father's place and became a property hand for the Cranks, and nothing had to be said of it.

Wilfred waited for the thaw. At night, exhausted in his

cot, he thought about it, and every day he kept a sharp eye for the little signs of the breaking of winter, and every morning he studied the old thermometer nailed to the wall of the kitchen.

There, astride the horse on the granite road, the constellations of stones swam in front of him, his eyes freely weeping, and when he saw the landscape clearly again the rocks and sedge reminded him of headstones in the cemetery.

How many millions of stones, he thought. Perhaps they are markers for everyone who ever died in Australia. Stones, big and small, to remember each and every soul. Now Father is here. And I'll be here one day too. He leaned forward in the saddle and placed a hand on the horse's neck to feel the warmth of blood and a heartbeat.

Wilfred felt his skin goose bump. It was why it was so quiet here, he thought. This place felt as though it was the beginning and the end of everything.

For a moment, he wondered if his journey was a mistake.

He felt the horse shivering beneath him. He dismounted and unpacked his bedroll. Removing the saddle, he slung the roll over the horse. The roll draped down both sides and almost to the horse's belly, and he felt embarrassed for the horse, dressed in this skirt or strange coat or something. He rebuckled the saddle and it pinched the roll up under the horse's quivering flanks.

Wilfred had talked to the horse all the way up the range.

'Soon as we hit the river you'll get a good drink and feed,' he said. 'So none of that complaining.'

He took a small notebook out of his swag and leafed through the pages. Tapping it with his forefinger, he said to the horse, 'You see? A mile or two and we cross the Snowy. Then up to Rawsons Pass, if you got the energy, and North Rams Head. That's where the source'll be. Stop your shivering. How do you think I feel? You're the one with the fancy coat.'

He pulled himself up into the saddle and they moved on slowly and he detected mint on the wind. It made his stomach grumble, smelling the mint.

The road rose gradually and the gravel crunched under the horse's hooves. He thought of the fireplace back home to try and keep warm, and when he did that he could see his father in his chair in the room, and hear his reprimands for riding into the High Country before the thaw proper. The horse's ears switched back at him and he wondered if Bodalla could hear the cussing too, even though it was in Wilfred's head.

'He didn't mean nothing,' the boy eventually said to the horse. They rode on.

The road swung to the left and at the turn they came upon a new vista of the mountains. Ahead the road cut across the valley and lifted sharply up the side of the range. At the bottom of the valley was a stream that ran at right angles to the road and across it a small wooden bridge. He knew the ribbon of water was the Snowy.

He exhaled at the surprise of it.

'Like them old philosophers say,' he could hear his father, 'you never put your foot in the same river twice.'

For some reason he had always thought of it huge and roaring, even this high up. Yet here it was, not ten feet across at its widest point, its banks bordered with pale boulders and dark, small-eared bushes and mosses, and in it, huge rocks as smooth as eggs.

It was like going back in time. Like being a grown-up, and being able to see yourself as a kid, and then a baby. All connected, like one long life.

Wilfred knew, then, why he had waited for the thaw, and gone off without telling anyone. He understood it, with just him and the horse and the wind. Not that he could have put it into words, right then, if someone had been there to ask. He clicked his tongue and they went down into the valley. He rode onto the bridge and they both looked down into the clear, rushing water.

'No whinin',' Wilfred said, and he walked the horse over to the far bank. 'Go eat.'

The horse nosed at the verge of the road. The boy removed the saddle and placed it on a boulder at the edge of the water. He knelt down and scooped the cold water up with his hand and drank, and he wished he had someone else to talk to aside from the horse.

'I'm goin' for a walk,' he said, adjusting his hat, and with his hands in his pockets he headed upstream, leaping from rock to rock. He sat on a granite tor that pushed out over the stream and watched the horse tearing at the tussocks and herbs way down at the crossing.

For a long while he stared into the water and at the wobbly shapes of the stones on the bed of the stream and he remembered the gravestones of the children at Bolocco the day they buried his father.

He'd gone into the paddock that was the cemetery as soon as they'd arrived and, while the pastor and his mother waited for the procession to converge and dismantle and for horses to be hitched to trees and carriages and carts to be emptied and for the mourners to adjust their hats and put on their Sunday-best jackets and quietly mouth greetings to each other in the silly silence that shrouds death, he wandered amongst the graves.

They were clustered according to family, and in some places the clusters were dozens of yards apart, and some were pushed into the far corners in shade or open to the sky. One of the first through the gate was the Corcorans, and later he found the Johnsons, way down the back, which seemed right, because just as it was in life, they were two families that chose to keep well away from each other.

Near the centre were the Cranks. Their cluster was the biggest, and the tallest, and that seemed right too because they'd been here the longest, and had more kin to add to the cluster. They had the biggest homestead, and the biggest spread, and the finest cattle and sheep. And the biggest memorials to their dead. Still, Wilfred thought, dead is dead.

There were tall headstones for the men, the fanciest for Aaron Crank. Native of London, it was written under his name. Wilfred didn't know whether to laugh or bite his lip. He didn't know that there was a native in the Crank family.

But it was the small graves that shocked him. All the little Crank children who had passed away – Edward and Evelyn and Victoria and Roland. Cyril and Reuben and Stanley. He had never been much good at maths, but he made some calculations there at the graves. Some were one month old, and others seven, and there was a girl who was his age.

He thought about this as he trudged around the cemetery, keeping the empty grave of his father in the corner of his eye. There were sheep grazing between the clusters of marble and iron, and wooden crosses, and the winter grass was almost blue, and littered across it, caught in the tough grasses, were white and grey bird feathers.

He couldn't stop thinking about the children. There were enough here in the Bolocco Cemetery to fill a school. And it was like the schoolroom, it occurred to him. All of them buried in neat rows and facing the east. Correct spelling on the headstones. Maths to be done. The only difference was there were grown-ups at this school too.

My father is the latest grown-up in this school, he said to himself.

While they buried William Lampe some feathers skipped across the tatty grass. One caught on the raised mound of freshly shovelled soil. If he were superstitious Wilfred would have made something of the feather. But he wasn't. There was no Almighty principal presiding over this classroom. No resurrection when the sun rose over the hills. Things lived and then they died. Sheep and people and trout. It was all the same.

He dashed to the pastor's sulky as soon as the grave-yard service was over and watched the townspeople milling in the cemetery. Tom Crank had his arm around Astrid. Tom was sixteen. They'd played together, Tom and Wilfred, when they were younger, but now Tom had dark fuzz on his top lip and on the point of his chin and he was a foot taller than Wilfred and he wore proper riding boots and a hat with a pronounced singe mark on the brim from some distant campfire in the mountains. The style of his hat would mark him and be with him from start to finish. You saw the hat and you saw Tom, just as Wilfred had his life hat.

Tom had changed since he brought Wilfred's father's body down to the house with his brother on the wooden sleigh. It made him bigger, bringing the body, and in the house Wilfred felt the act itself had given Tom Crank some sort of authority over the family.

It wasn't right that he had his arm around Astrid.

The horses and sulkies began their silent journey back to the town, leaving Berty in the graveyard. He had appeared, out of nowhere, at the back of the mourning party around the grave, in full military regalia. Medals. A feathered hat. Even a brass bullet belt. The bullets and medals glowed warmly in the dull light of the day. He stood to full attention, his hands closed and straight at his sides, and he looked not to the people of the town, or the pastor, or the coffin of his departed brother, but through them and beyond them to a point in the distance. Wilfred had seen this look before on Berty's face. He was seeking that place, the boy thought, where all soldiers are laid to rest.

They left Berty alone in the graveyard, exactly where he stood, and as the sulky pulled away Wilfred could see him saluting repeatedly to that distant place, over and over. By the time they'd reached the bend in the road to Dalgety, he was small as a tin soldier amongst the gravestones.

Later, at the wake, Wilfred noticed Tom Crank bringing Astrid cake and lemonade, and standing near her in the big dining room of the Buckley's Crossing Hotel, where they'd drawn back the curtain that usually divided the landowners and visiting dignitaries from the farmhands, and he saw that Astrid was affected by it, and tried to imitate in little ways the other ladies in the room, and it was this that worried Wilfred even more.

In the months leading up to the thaw he worked under Tom Crank, and at first they were like mates, shooting rabbits and mending the machinery together. Then Tom Crank suddenly steered clear of him, and for whole days at a time they didn't talk. Then he ordered Wilfred to do things and sent him to the far side of the property on his own, and in the afternoons rode in to check on Wilfred's work. Later, during an altercation, he went to take his whip to Wilfred but stopped short of drawing it off the saddle.

That night Wilfred was quiet at dinner and took to his cot early and thought long and hard about Tom Crank and remembered overhearing his father tell the story on the muster of when Crank Senior had raised the whip to him, and the boy felt no different from the workhorses up in the Crank stables, even the dreary mobs of sheep that crawled over the hills like lice, and he didn't know what to do about it.

Maybe finding the source of the river might yield a resolution.

As he sat on the tor, his thoughts were broken by a long, clear whistle. He looked up, and where the road disappeared up on the ridge, towards Rawsons Pass, was the shape of a man. Then it was two men, or a man and a child. The child seemed to have snuck out from behind

411

the man's silhouette. Wilfred stood and waved his hat. There was no response so he returned to the horse.

'Maybe they're in trouble,' he said to Bodalla. 'Let's go see.'

He resaddled the horse and rode up to the ridge, noticing the temperature drop suddenly though they were less than half a mile from the stream that was the Snowy.

The road rose sharply. The man played with the child's arms. Then Wilfred realised it wasn't a child at all, but a tripod with a black box on top. The man leaned down behind the box.

'Gidday,' Wilfred said. The horse sniffed at the black box.

'Whoa, whoa, careful,' said the man. 'Hello, sir. Would you mind moving your mount away from the equipment? Appreciated. Much appreciated. I'm Mr Bell. A bit further. Much appreciated.'

Wilfred tangled the reins in the densely packed leaves of a hebe shrub.

'Much obliged, much appreciated,' Bell continued from behind the box. He held his hand out to the side, on the point of blessing Wilfred. 'Be with you in a moment. It's the light, you see. It's almost with us. And now that I have an empty valley, we can proceed . . .'

'It's a camera, isn't it?' Wilfred asked.

'A moment, sir, many thanks.'

'I seen them in my mother's magazines.'

'Yes, thank you, sir, we're almost there . . .'

Bodalla watched the man's poised hand. His nostrils flared.

'*Annnnd* . . . done,' Bell said, lowering his hand in a

single swoop. The horse's ears twitched at the sound of the equipment. Bell removed his hat and patted his brow with a red handkerchief. He seemed exhausted.

'That's good. That's nice. Many thanks.'

'I'm Wilfred Lampe.'

'Wilfred,' the photographer said, puffing. 'A pleasure. Pleasure. Phew. That's nice. That's good.'

It was mid-afternoon, and the pale sunshine that had illuminated Bell's valley had been swallowed again by cloud. It grew dark very quickly.

'A moment,' Bell said, disappearing over the ridge. He returned with his packhorse.

'You best come along, Wilfred Lampe,' he said, carefully packing his equipment. 'There is a storm on the march.'

'I'm heading to North Rams Head.'

'You won't be heading anywhere tonight, sir. We have a camp down below Charlotte. You're welcome to join us.'

He watched Bell load the gear onto the horse with extraordinary speed. The horse's haunches were covered with all manner of specially made leather bags and sheaths, and when he was done the poor animal looked rear-heavy and ridiculous. It stared implacably through a ratty fringe.

'Come along now, Mr Wilfred. These squalls will catch you as quick as a wink.'

The photographer moved off accompanied by much leather creaking and had crossed the Snowy before Wilfred wheeled Bodalla around and followed.

'Probably right,' he said to the horse, checking the fast-moving scuds of cloud over his shoulder. 'And you with my bedroll and all.'

He caught up to Mr Bell and they rode silently back to Charlotte Pass and down again into the deep scoop of its valley and alongside the Snowy once more, a different stream again. It oozed quietly through swampy grassland.

Wilfred could smell burning wood, and a mile or so north of the pass Mr Bell left the road and headed into a lightly treed gully. The smell of the fire was strong and a gossamer of blue smoke clung to the treetops.

The gully narrowed and soon they were riding through a half-canyon of granite tors and slabs covered in the long, narrow fingers of tree roots and wheels of lichen, and the air was still and the gully was protected from the mountain winds.

'Heyyup,' Mr Bell called, and his voice was loud and muffled in the narrow canyon.

Beyond Bell and the broad rump of his packhorse were two neat canvas tents stretched tight to external frames of grey snow gum branches. A man was lifting a billy can off the fire with a stick. A girl sat near him on a rock.

'You know how to time it, Charlie,' the man said. 'Get what you want?'

'As good a soft light as I've seen.'

'Good, good.' The man lowered the boiling can onto the trampled grass and looked up.

'We have a guest. A Mr Wilfred.' The girl craned forward to see the boy. 'Making for Rams Head, if you please, with his horse better rugged up than Amundsen.'

Bell dismounted, as did Wilfred, and they looped the reins of their horses over a makeshift rail at the back of the camp.

'This is Mr Henry Chauvere,' Bell said, introducing Wilfred. 'And this here is Miss Dorothea Chauvere.'

Wilfred pinched the brim of his hat.

They settled down to tea. The two men talked as Wilfred and the girl sipped at their mugs. Bell and Chauvere stood near the fire, and occasionally Bell, still talking, reached down and threw some snow gum chips into the flames.

Dorothea was no more than twelve. The same age as Astrid. Her light brown hair was cut like a boy's. She wore boy's boots and trousers and a huge grey woollen coat. He couldn't tell how big she was, inside the wrapping.

It was getting cold but Wilfred didn't move from the log. Dorothea stared at him. Eventually he spoke, her stare forcing the words out of him.

'I ain't seen you round the Monaro,' he said.

She didn't move, or lower the mug. 'I went there once,' she said.

'So where you from?'

'We live on the Geehi Flats. At Towong.'

'I don't know where that is.'

'You been to many places at all?'

'Not really.'

'You haven't been many places if you don't know where the Geehi Flats is. It's just over the border, in Victoria.'

'I might have been there, on a muster. But I don't remember anyone calling it the Geehi Flats.'

Dorothea rolled her eyes.

The men cooked chops and onions and continued to talk as they worked over the fire. The wind howled in the distance but there in the gully the sounds of the sputtering chops and the sizzle of the onions bounced back off the walls of granite and traced in and around the words between Bell and Chauvere as sure as the sparks that rose up off the shifting logs in the fire.

Dorothea prepared the bread and put on more tea.

After dinner, they sat around the fire. The food had temporarily plugged the men's talk.

Dorothea cleared the plates and fed the horses.

'What's your interest in Rams Head anyway, Mr Wilfred?' Bell asked. Wilfred noticed him pouring a measure of whisky from a flask into his tea.

'I'm looking for the source of the Snowy.'

'What on earth for, may I ask?'

'I dunno.'

Dorothea returned to her place at the fire. 'You don't know?'

'A man has his reasons,' Chauvere said. 'Charlie, you've probably got a picture of it somewhere, hmm? Mr Bell's been photographing these mountains for quite a while. Not much here that's escaped the eye of Mr Charlie Bell. Isn't that right?'

'That's most certainly right.' Bell poured some of the liquor into Chauvere's cup.

'Mr Bell here,' Chauvere continued, 'learned from the great Charles Kerry out of Bombala, isn't that right, Mr Bell?'

Bell snuffled behind the mug.

'Mr Bell here was the master's apprentice, he was.' He kicked Bell's boot.

'Thought we might go one trip without mention of Kerry.'

416

Chauvere laughed and nudged the outstretched boot again.

'Why, Mr Kerry—'

'Should've brought more whisky if I'd known we'd be fixating on Kerry.'

'We'll let it rest there, shall we?'

'We shall.'

Wilfred looked puzzled. He saw Dorothea smiling in the firelight. He had been accidentally snagged in a joke amongst friends.

'My daddy's a geologist—'

'Amateur,' said Chauvere.

'Amateur . . . and Mr Bell is a photographer, and Mr Kerry's a photographer too, but he's rich and he lives in Sydney, and we come to the mountains twice a year and talk about Mr Kerry at night around the fire.'

Bell pretended to hold his head in agony but he was smiling, and Chauvere roared and his laughter boomed through the gully.

'Mr Bell doesn't like Mr Kerry's pictures, especially since Mr Kerry beat Mr Bell in a snow race from Kiandra when they opened the hotel and all the famous people were there and Mr Bell came in last when it was dark and they all applauded Mr Bell . . .'

'Thank you, Dorothea.'

'. . . and they put his butterpats up above the entrance to the hotel and called it Charlie's Place after that.'

'How rude to exclude Mr Wilfred from such a marvellous anecdote, don't you think, Mr Bell?' Chauvere fed the fire.

'Which hotel?' Wilfred asked.

'Kosciusko,' Dorothea said.

417

'My uncle Berty tried to chop it down when they was building it.'

'*Were* building it,' Dorothea said, rolling her eyes again.

'You see, Mr Wilfred,' said Chauvere, stroking his bearded chin, 'it was a fine and clear day . . .'

Charlie Bell moaned.

'. . . when our young Charlie lined up with some of the most well-known personages of his day. The photographer Mr Hurley, and the author Mr Charles Bean. And how well Mr Bell started, flying through that thin powder on his old butterpats . . .'

Wilfred was confused, and Dorothea caught it.

'They're skis.'

'Oh.'

'Yet it was Mr Bean who beat them all, stout fellow that he is, solid, in life and on the page. He beat them all, even Mr Kerry, who knew these mountains back to front. And then there was Charlie . . .'

'Then there was Charlie,' Charlie said. He looked drowsy from all the tea.

Wilfred saw Chauvere and his daughter looking at each other and smiling and their faces were beautiful, warm little lanterns in the sheltered gully that night, and he felt a deep sadness at the loss of his father for the first time since it had happened, since seeing the body laid out on the kitchen table in the house, since the funeral. The whole phenomenon of it, which he'd chosen not to see or feel.

But it was the firelit faces of the father and daughter that delivered to him the full impact of his grief, shearing through him like a split through granite.

He told his story then, unbidden, of his dead father, then left the fire and went and curled up in the frosty grass near Bodalla, and when he woke the next morning he was inside the tent with a snoring Charles Bell.

There were voices out by the fire and Wilfred emerged from the canvas as if into a new life. The air was crisp and his skin tingled. He could smell fresh tea in the billy and Mr Chauvere smiled at him and wished him a good morning and he felt connected to everything in that camp that day, and bigger than he was the day before, and stronger, and even wiser, as if the answer to any question rested on the tip of his tongue. And the people he was with were not strangers and he felt some sort of love for the Chauveres, and that he had known them since before he could remember.

'Tea, Mr Wilfred?'

He took the mug and every minute that morning was like a beautiful, elongated hour.

'You may join me on my peculiar quest for basalt today, Mr Wilfred,' Chauvere said. 'Or partake of the hospitality of my daughter. I believe she would like to take you skiing. Up at Carruthers Peak.'

There was a moan from Charlie Bell's tent.

'I would appreciate it. If you'd accompany her, Mr Wilfred.'

'Yes, sir.'

He had forgotten about the source of the Snowy.

'I ask her what she would like more than anything in the world,' he said, as if talking to himself, 'and she tells me – to be the first woman to ski the western slopes of the Alps. The first *woman*. How extraordinary she is, Mr Wilfred.'

'Yes, sir.'

'My wish is that I live to see it.' He stared moment-arily into the smoke of the fire. 'The world is changing, young man. We must make the most of it while we can.' He slapped Wilfred lightly on the shoulder. 'And here she is, the snow queen of the High Country.'

Dorothea emerged from her tent. She hugged her father and poured herself some tea.

'Can you ski?' she asked Wilfred.

'Nope,' he said.

She rolled her eyes, and her father imitated her, and they all laughed.

'Then I'll have to teach you,' she said, smiling.

And Wilfred had no fear, and already he never wanted the day to end.

THIRTY-FOUR

THE OLD MAN woke with a dry throat.

When he opened his eyes the room was bright and he was lying in his pyjamas on top of the cover of the hospital bed. The first thing he saw was his feet bound in white bandages. It was the pain from his feet that woke him. He couldn't understand what had happened to his feet. He tried to remember.

Lights came to Wilfred, strings of coloured bulbs, and streams of motor cars, and crowds, and he remembered visiting Bombala years ago. They had a big intersection of two streets in Bombala, unlike Dalgety. They had a saddler and a picture house and several pubs. They had young women who dressed up and promenaded through Bombala, and a photography studio where ladies posed in front of potted ferns.

He had taken Astrid to the Olympia Theatre in the town not long after it had opened, and while she had thrilled at the local players, and the excitement of a crowd, he was reminded instantly of how different it was to be in the audience rather than on the stage, like he was in *The Trout Opera*. From the outset he found he took in little of the shenanigans on stage, unable to get around the idea of so many people sitting in ordered rows in one large building, and the noise of them, and the warmth and odours when you collected human beings in a single place, knowing that outside a frost was settling across the Monaro, and foxes were padding across thousands of acres of paddocks, and pushing through the milky fog were tens of thousands of sheep. Above it all was a wash of stars, and in the dark of all this infiniteness was the tiny yellow-lit theatre house in Bombala, and he sitting beside his sister, feeling the brush of her arm every time she laughed, or gasped.

Old Wilfred remembered, too, returning to Bombala to see the Men from the Snowy River on their recruiting march for the war. It was hot, the middle of January, and he had stood with a mate as the men marched by. Later, alone in a back paddock near home, he had practised his marching with a weapon of snow gum branch, trying to regain the spirit of what he had seen in the main street of Bombala, the sense of marching towards something great and true. But the march in the quiet paddock, to an audience of sheep and crows, had the opposite effect. It ended with him as self-conscious and foolish as a boy.

Then there was the Bombala carnival on the bank of the river that cut through town. Had he hurt his feet at the carnival? When he rode over the hill not far from the town he stopped his horse and saw below the cluster of violet and red and yellow lights all shining on that clear winter night and reflecting on the surface of the river. The shadows of people moved about beneath the spectrum, and the steam from their bodies and breaths smudged the lights of the carnival.

In the immensity of the Monaro and the black winter night it was like he'd stumbled across a happy part of his heart. As if a source of life had unexpectedly risen out of the earth, and the folk of Bombala and surrounding properties had flocked to it, and it awoke something in them that had gone to sleep, or been shut down by the winter. Wilfred walked the horse slowly towards the glowing carnival.

There he had seen Dorothea and spoken to her, but he couldn't recall what was said. Nor did he remember the ride home very late that night. He only thought of her, the blonde waves of her hair, gathering all the coloured lights, and in the gully of the curls, pools of lavender.

'Mr Lampe?'

He had burned his feet badly in a bushfire. The cinders had eaten clean through the soles of his father's boots. And he was marching well by then. It was no longer the silly practice of a boy. But he hadn't been able to walk for months. Had missed the ride into Cooma where his mates enlisted. He couldn't walk.

'. . . you hear me, Mr Lampe?'

There was someone at the side of the bed. Someone sitting in a chair, and two people near a door.

'. . . very important contribution to your country,' a voice said. '. . . have you fighting fit for the big event, Mr Lampe . . . worry about that . . .'

He tried to swallow but his throat was dry and constricted and his eyes watered with the attempt.

'. . . seen by billions of people around the world, Mr Lampe . . . Opening Ceremony . . . do you understand?'

At the carnival by the river he did remember the

smell of the damp straw they had spread onto the ground, little laneways of straw, between the attractions and tables of food, beneath the archways of light, and in the distance, for a single moment that was imprinted on his memory, he saw Astrid and Tom Crank together. She was nursing a sprig of lavender, and he was pressing his face into her hair. It was one of the last times he ever saw his sister. At the carnival in Bombala. And later, he wondered about the warmth of her arm in the Olympia Theatre that one night, and the trembling lavender in her white hands at the carnival, and why these moments in life happened elsewhere, away from where they should happen, disconnected, their importance only recognised when it was too late.

'. . . a proud representative of your nation . . . a century of history . . .'

He saw the man in the suit sitting beside his bed. Two men in suits stood behind him. But Astrid was still with him, in a halo of yellow carnival light. She was lost in the light. She was fifteen. She had left school and was helping their mother clean the local school and the police station, and sometimes washing the linen at the Buckley's Crossing Hotel. They had to do everything they could after Father died. Wilfred had specially made the clothes line props and rigged the wire and on some days, when all the sheets and pillow slips of the Buckley's were hanging out to dry behind the house, riffling in the wind, he could see them from the town and it was like great sailing ships were passing through stubbled fields of the Monaro.

Then, overnight, Astrid disappeared.

'Mr Lampe? . . . understand what I'm saying?'

424

He was very tired. He was as tired as the day he had fallen in the grass amongst the moons of dandelions. He thought he had died then. Now he wasn't sure. The voice murmured somewhere in the white room. Was this death? There had been the lights and the cars. And his bandaged feet.

Give me some water, he thought.

'. . . soon be joined by your great-niece, Aurora . . .'

Had someone said Astrid? She was always fifteen. When he was asked to come to Sydney to identify her body, which wasn't her at all, he thought of her as fifteen. When their mother eventually died, and he sat on his stool in the bar at the Buckley's at exactly the same time each Saturday night for his two beers, he would look out to the river, his hands liver-spotted and fingers around the glass lumpy with arthritis, and he would see her coming towards him across the bridge, a fifteen-year-old girl, clutching a posy of wildflowers.

'Thank you, Mr Lampe . . . in touch.'

The man in the chair patted the end of the bed, and then the room was empty.

Am I dead, or simply dreaming?

THIRTY-FIVE

THE TAXI PUSHED through the low setts of cane as smooth as a motorboat.

Aurora had avoided looking at Mount Warning since she alighted from the train, but she could feel it. On the way to the old house they drove past the Royal Hotel in town and she kept her eyes averted from that too. She didn't want to see her father in there, framed by the window. These immovable totems. She began to think she might not be ready for any of this.

The cabin of the car was no refuge. The driver reminded her of Tick, with his ponytail and receding hairline. The skin where the hair thinned looked pale and tender compared to the rest of his narrow and lined face. 'Where to?' he asked, and he had the stained and deteriorating lower teeth of an alcoholic. His cheeks were pitted. He could have been an old junkie. She didn't think junkies got old.

She felt the pain of coming off the drugs. She felt a deep need for them, but when it overwhelmed her, she thought of the child in its grave in the old Adaminaby cemetery. The dead child. The circles of dark skin around its closed eyes. The way death had defined its features at the end, pencil-sketched its lips and the cavities of its tiny nostrils and the crinkled skin of its ears. The drug she desperately wanted had taken the shape of the baby. She saw it behind her eyes, buried in the dark raw earth of the grave and floating in the universe. The shell grit and quartz chips in the soil were the stars.

Aurora studied the driver again. She remembered, for a moment, the endless rides in stolen cars with Wynter, and her with the baby in the back, watching the sharp edge of his face from exactly the same position. Several months after fleeing Adaminaby, she could not even make out Wynter's face in her mind. He had returned, somehow, to the featureless human being that he had always been. He was nothing to her. Maybe this was what it was like – the beginnings of recovery.

The taxi pulled up in front of the house. She got out and walked up the front stairs, avoiding the mountain, and she realised the house, too, had its own gravitational pull.

There was nobody home. The house was shabby and neglected. She found the spare key. The brass of the key was dull and weathered from lack of use.

Aurora stood in the dark inside the empty house with her bag still over her shoulder.

It smelled of old cooking fat and human sweat and the damp. It was the middle of the day but with the gathering clouds it seemed like night. She stood in the lounge room and rain tapped then belted the tin roof and the roar kept her gaze fixed on the old imitation Persian rug in the middle of the room.

The furniture had been moved, and she knew it was

one of the final acts of her mother before she had hanged herself, because her mother's life had always been a calendar of furniture moving.

It was like walking into a museum, but the pieces on display were objects from Aurora's life. She recognised a chair or an ornament or a magazine rack with the slow surprise of someone being reintroduced to their childhood toys. It was both wonderful and awful.

She dropped the bag and walked into the kitchen. There were crumbs on a breadboard on the table, a small china cup with dregs in the bottom. The tap dripped, but she couldn't hear it behind the pounding of the rain. Ants streamed back and forth from the breadboard, a small organised river of them flowing out of a crack in the tile behind the cold water tap. There were three drowned in the teacup.

In the enclosed balcony off the kitchen she saw a cot and a loose blanket and a full ashtray on the floor. She smelled the soil coming up through the floorboards and she could smell her father mixed in with it.

He was obviously living on the narrow balcony. Clothes were piled on the floor. His small transistor radio was near the head of the cot. An empty beer bottle. Work boots and thongs. He had removed himself from the house they shared. Left everything as it was when she died.

Aurora checked what used to be her parents' bedroom. The bed was neatly made. Her mother's combs and mirrors were still on the dresser. There were grey, wiry hairs caught in the soft teeth of the brush.

In her own room the single bed was undisturbed. Her crayon drawings of the mountain, yellowed and buckled, were still fixed to the tongue-and-groove wooden wall with rectangles of old sticky tape the colour of weak tea.

She sat quietly on the end of her girlhood bed and heard rain falling. Someone had removed the curtains and the closed glass louvres were milky with grime. Through the glass she saw the shape of a tree in the backyard, shaking with the rain.

She looked up at the drawing of the mountain. The outline of it in jagged brown. The sun an imperfect disc. And a girl, in a triangular dress with orange spots, leaping in space, half as big as the mountain, a wide grin, her arms open.

Aurora sobbed then. For the little girl in the spotted dress. For the hair caught in the bristles of the brush on her mother's dresser. For the boots placed neatly together on the balcony. For the tarnished key. For all the time that the drawing of the mountain had been clinging to the wall of her old bedroom up to now. She sobbed deeply and with absolute awareness of her grief.

The rain eased and it was night when she came out of her bedroom. She went into the kitchen and filled the silver kettle. She turned on the front burner and struck a match and lit the gas. She took a cup down from the shelf and found a tea bag and poured the boiling water into the cup. The milk in the fridge was fresh and she poured some into her tea. It was comforting to see the expiry date on the carton and to know it was fresh. She sat at the table, her stomach muscles sore, and sipped the tea.

Her father came up the front stairs shortly after ten pm.

He moved cautiously into the doorway. She looked up at him from the table. He was smaller than she remembered and his hair was grey. Not with the ash of the fields, but a grey that had moved out from the scalp and chased away the original black. His face was covered in white stubble.

He knew, of course, that this was his daughter, but he couldn't make sense of her sitting there at the kitchen table. How many times, near the end, had he seen his wife waiting each night in that exact chair? And how many times since had the chair been empty when he came home?

'Hi, Dad.'

He'd been drinking, but wasn't drunk. His cheeks were flushed and the white stubble accentuated their redness. He tried to speak but nothing came out. She went over and hugged him, then resumed her seat. She did not feel emotional about seeing him. The sobbing had drained all that out of her.

'Tea?' she finally said, and again boiled the kettle. They said nothing to each other during the ritual of the tea.

If he'd looked he would have seen that her hands were trembling. It was close to midnight, and she knew what the trembling meant. It didn't concern her that he might see it. He wouldn't understand it. She'd been gone nine years. Things had happened that he couldn't have imagined. It was a lot of life, time to develop your own codes, secret language, tics and signs that signified an expatriate existence. He'd just been here, alone in the dead house, surrounded by cane fields. He knew the signs of when it was time to burn, and to harvest.

'I got laid off at the mill,' he said to her at last. The

plain statement was like a cooling breeze through the room. 'They got machines can do what I do now.'

'How long?'

'Two years this Christmas. Got work pretty much straight away, over at the nursing home. I'm the odd jobs bloke.'

'Sounds good, Dad.'

'People ask me what I do, I tell them I got an odd job.'

He smiled at her and fidgeted with his teacup.

'Your mother . . .'

'I can't talk about that right now, Dad.'

'Sure.'

She leaned over and put her hand on his wrist.

He said, 'You staying long?'

'For a little while, if that's okay.'

'Course.'

She squeezed his wrist. It stopped the trembling in her hand.

'There's a lot to catch up on,' Aurora said. 'We can't do it all tonight.'

'That's right,' he said. He could hardly look at her, for fear she might suddenly not be there.

She lay awake for a long time in her old bed. She felt like a stranger in the room. She had yet to connect to everything around her, though the wardrobe and the dressing-table and the walls were familiar. She tried to hear her father breathing in the house but the rain was still heavy on the roof.

The storm had taken ages to pass and in its wake was a stillness and the sound of the settling water. The river would be high now, and even more so in the morning with the rain coursing its way off the mountains.

In her mind she saw the ancient boulders at the base of Mount Warning dark with the rain and the water that was feeding down through the canopies of the rainforest. Everything washed clean. Bird tracks erased from the forest floor. Nests flushed out. Leaves and mulch shifted. The whole forest coming to life again in the morning.

In the morning her father made bacon and eggs. His hair was still damp from the shower and neatly combed, like he was going to church. Aurora kissed him on the cheek.

'Odd jobs man *and* a chef,' she said, pulling up a chair. There was a large brown envelope in the centre of the table, next to the salt and pepper caddy. They ate.

'I have to go to work for a few hours,' he said. 'I want you to read this.' He pointed to the envelope. 'Then we can talk about it. Or we don't have to. It's up to you.'

They had always been like this. Some people didn't need to speak to communicate. Others never ceased and still couldn't connect − her mother had been a bit that way. Spun words around things, like fairy floss on a stick, until the whole conversation was so huge and unwieldy it collapsed. He walked behind her and pecked her on the top of the head as he passed.

'Be back early afternoon.'

She heard the old Toyota come to life. Then he was gone.

She made a second cup of coffee and took the envelope down into the backyard. The weeds were knee-high. She sat on the old bench that looked out on the river. The river was muddy and ran swiftly, full of leaves and small branches. The air was humid and still.

Aurora removed the documents from the envelope. They were sealed inside a clear plastic sheath.

The top sheet was her mother's death certificate. It carried her name typed in a crooked line inside a black box. It said she was born in Sydney. It looked strange to her, the word, in the Place of Birth box. She put the certificate to the bottom of the pile.

There were a handful of old greeting cards, from her father to her mother. Bouquets of flowers on the front. Baby bears holding red love hearts. An idyllic river bordered with willows and a man and woman in a punt. The man wore a boater and the woman a large sun hat. *To my darling Theresa, from your loving husband.*

From a separate envelope she retrieved half a dozen old black and white photographs. One was of a woman walking purposefully in a city street. She wore a smart skirt and matching jacket and a short-brimmed hat slightly tilted to the left. She nursed a handbag under her right arm. There were other pedestrians in the picture. Men in baggy suits and felt hats. Women in old-fashioned dresses. It looked like the 1940s or '50s. The sun was on the woman's face, and the photographer had caught her half smiling. It was nothing more than a glance. She didn't look like she belonged in the picture, but was passing through it. There was another of the same woman, but younger, nursing a baby on the back steps of a house. And another of her dressed up as if to go to the theatre, with her arm linked through the arm of a man in a black suit and hat, his face square and ruddy. He was an ugly and unpleasant-looking man, with a pug nose and a smirk. He could have been an old-time gangster, a tough who wore all of his limited intelligence on his pocked face. Again, the woman was half smiling. Her face was taut with the effort of it. The last picture was small, the size of a credit card, and it showed a woman standing on the bank of a lake. The figure was too small to make out any facial features.

There were other documents. A letter signed by a Sister Williams from a nursing home in Lilyfield. It read: *Dear Theresa, Your mother Astrid was received into the arms of God shortly after 3 pm on Thursday. She passed away peacefully and with dignity. I can say on behalf of all the nursing staff that she will be greatly missed.*

There was a badly deteriorated marriage certificate dated 8 August 1925. It stated that Astrid Florence Smith had married John Stanley Littlejohn in a church in North Sydney.

Wrapped in clear plastic was a small handwritten note folded into four. It said: *Edmund, the game is up and there's nothing to hide from you anymore. I'm sorry it had to happen this way and I have decided to go away. It's best for you and the children. Tell them I love them. A.*

There was a 1928 newspaper clipping of a dance troupe in Sydney's Kings Cross called La Belle Époque. A picture showed a line of can-can girls kicking their right legs up. They wore frilly skirts and black stockings and their lips were black. Someone had underlined one of the names of the girls, A. Crane, in the picture's caption.

The last item in the envelope was a King James Bible. It was worn and well read and as Aurora started leafing through the pages items fell out, prayers and poems and even a death notice from the *Sydney Morning Herald*, as well as a small, flat crocheted cross.

There was no name in the front of the Bible. But Aurora could see that there were annotations all through the pages, passages underlined or highlighted with ink stars in the margins.

Some of the heaviest markings were in Revelation. Aurora studied the highlighted passages. *And I will kill her children with death. And the second angel sounded, and as it were a great mountain burning with fire was cast into the sea; and the third part of the sea became blood. And they had hair as the hair of women, and their teeth were as the teeth of lions. Fear none of those things which thou shalt suffer: behold, the devil shall cast some of you into prison, that ye may be tried; and ye shall have tribulation ten days: be thou faithful unto death, and I will give thee a crown of life.*

And there was a passage of John that someone had enclosed in a neat inked box: *For all that is in the world, the lust of the flesh, and the lust of the eyes, and the pride of life, is not of the Father, but is of the world.*

At the back of the Bible, written on the thin end pages, she found in the same hand some incomprehensible lines of verse. Around the lines were childish drawings of bees, their flight trajectory marked by dots, and daisies, and a crudely drawn fish with an X for an eye.

Aurora could barely make out the lines. *Oh the rivers and the streams. Witness the new race, for generations to come. Set sail have we to the southern oceans, to the free land. Deliver we the eggs of the sacred trout. As God intended, for eternity.*

Inside the brown leather sleeve of the Bible she found another photograph. An old car parked on a bare hill.

Sitting on the running board of the car, with his chin in his hands, was a man. He wore a grubby rabbit-skin hat and his hands were soiled. His large boots, too, were filthy, and both laces were untied. She could barely make out the man's face in the dark shade beneath the brim of the hat. She turned the picture over. Someone had printed the word WILFRED on it with a ballpoint pen.

She placed the Bible and the documents back into the envelope. From her seat by the river she could smell the rich and sticky odour of processing sugar. For the first time that she could remember it smelled good.

She walked down to the general store where she had worked all those years ago. Where the armed robber had entranced her, and stuffed a fresh ten-dollar note into her brassiere. She picked up some bread and ham and cheese. She didn't know the kids who were working there now.

When her father got home she already had sandwiches on the table. They took them out the back, under the jacaranda tree.

After a while, Aurora said: 'I don't know what the documents mean. The old pictures. I don't know who the people are. Astrid. And Wilfred. And the Bible. The name in the front is Astrid Collins. On one of the papers, the name is Smith, then Crane.'

He ate half a sandwich and looked out at the river.

'Astrid was your grandmother. Your mum's mum.' He said it matter-of-factly, between bites of the sandwich.

'I thought her name was Therese, same as Mum.'

'Sometimes she used different names, when it suited her. There was trouble. It was a long time ago.'

'I thought my grandmother died before I was born.'

436

'She died a year before your mum.'

Aurora studied his whiskered face. His checked flannelette shirt had spots of dried paint on the shoulders.

'Mum said she was dead.'

'Well she wasn't.'

'Then why did she say she was?'

'She was dead to your mother. That's how she felt.'

'You're telling me I had a grandmother up until a couple of years ago?'

He looked at her. 'Yes.'

'I don't understand,' Aurora said.

'They never got along. You met her, when you were very young, too young to understand. We all went down to Sydney, where she lived. Your mother wanted to make amends. It never happened.'

'What was wrong between them?'

He drank from a stubbie of beer.

'It's a long story.'

'I've got time.'

'She wanted to tell you. She kept putting it off. And then . . .'

'I left.'

'You left,' he said.

The murmur of the river was there, somewhere, behind their conversation.

He went on. 'Your grandmother, Astrid, had an unusual life. Or perhaps it wasn't as unusual as we think for the time. She had your mother late. She was well into her thirties and something like that, a child, she couldn't handle. She adopted out your mother.'

Astrid looked across the water to the far bank. She

could see the tall weeds half submerged, and the heads of the weeds pulled over with the rushing water.

'Mum was adopted.'

'Your mother, she found Astrid when she was in her late twenties, just after we met. They saw each other, on and off, for a while, and then it stopped.'

'My mother was adopted.' A door had opened, and Aurora stood beneath the architrave, and couldn't make sense of what she saw in the room.

'It had happened before, you see. Astrid, your grandmother, had fallen pregnant when she was a young girl, to a local grazier. She was a country girl. Only fifteen or so. She ran away. To Sydney. As far as we know, she never saw her family again.'

She continued to stare across the water. 'Go on,' she said.

'It is no reflection on your mother. Astrid adopted out that baby. Before your mother. She married. She had another two children to her husband. Then that fell apart, too. There was an affair. She walked out of the marriage, and was with another man for a while, until that ended too. It was too much for her, all of it. It was what your mother grew to resent. It was why she never told you.'

'Why?'

'She was afraid you had it in you. What she had.'

'Which was?'

He finished the beer. Her father didn't speak for a few moments.

'She turned away from her own blood and thought nothing of it. She did it over and over again. It frightened your mum.'

For a second Aurora thought this was some form of practical joke. Or a long made-up anecdote that would have an amusing ending.

'We don't know the half of it,' he continued. 'But your mother knew enough. She was the best to judge. That's how I saw it. Some families are like this. Most of them. Strangers over a little argument at the dinner table. Twenty, thirty years. Sometimes forever. These things are magnified in families. Something that means nothing in the outside world, it can break up families. We're all bits of each other, and people don't like seeing themselves in somebody else. And they either want to kill it, or ignore it. It's what your grandmother did. She could ignore it. But sometimes that's the same thing as killing it.'

They sat in silence. The sun dipped low over the cane fields.

'Who's Wilfred?'

'That was Astrid's only brother.'

'My great-uncle.'

'That's right.'

'Great-uncle Wilfred. And what happened to him? Did he bang up the wrong people too?'

'Wilfred is still alive.'

She started tearing at the grass around her folded legs. 'I can't believe this,' she said.

'I was telephoned last month, about Wilfred. A man. Some family tree society asking about the whole family. Then I get another call the next day. Someone else. They wanted to talk to you because you're Wilfred's next of kin. They've been trying to find you.'

'Me? For what? The family tree?'

'They want your permission for something. They need you to sign some legal things. He's in Sydney. He has been chosen to perform a task, and they need your signature.'

'What task?'

'They only said it was something in the national interest.'

'In the national interest? Is he a spy? He'd have to be a thousand years old.'

'It's to do with the Olympics. Something about the Olympics. They couldn't say too much. Said it was secret and all that.'

Aurora stood and looked down at her father. He might have gone senile.

She walked to the water's edge and made her way slowly along the bank. It was an elaborate plan by the cops, perhaps, to bust her on something new that Wynter might have done, or something old that she had done. Or it might have been Wynter himself, luring her into a trap.

Aurora's hands shook. The sun was gone and a gossamer fog was settling on the surface of the river. It was all fucked.

She faced the mountain, its great silhouette black against the sun. She looked into the blackness, and for a second she could see that the mountain was vanished, not a mountain, but the night sky through a tear in the blue.

Aurora had come home, but beside the river she heard that familiar howling in her head, and she wasn't sure where she was at all.

THIRTY-SIX

TICK SAT SHIVERING inside the blanket in the park beside the harbour. The water was grey and choppy and slapped against the sandstone harbour walls. A sea bird hovered about a bobbling buoy, dipping and retreating, unable to secure landfall. Sitting next to him on the bench, his nurse, Bibi, rubbed his back, and her palm ran bumpily across his sore ribs.

'You ever sailed boats?' she asked. 'It looks nice, to sail boats.'

He was thinking of Mr Wilberforce as he stared at the water, and he could see his friend's cavernous grey face, and the smoke from a Lucky Strike curling from his nostrils and mouth and up into his hair, massaging its way through the dull waves.

'A girlfriend of mine, her man drives the ferries, but that's not a real boat in my mind. A boat, he's got to have sails.'

Then there was Harold, arriving day and night with his bowls of cold chicken soup and bottles of lemonade. Poor, sweet Harold.

'We could watch the sail boats at Watsons Bay, have fish and chips,' Bibi said. 'Nothing like eating fish and chips and watching the sail boats.'

He pulled the blanket tighter.

'It's salty, the air today,' she added.

'The different curios that I obtained,' he said, looking at the water.

'Don't start your silly talk again,' she said.

'*They arched their mackerel-backs and slapped the sand.*'

'I'm gonna put my hands over my ears if you keep talking the silly talk.'

'I need to get my affairs in order, Bibi. I want to be remembered.'

'Remembered? I see.'

'Fondly.'

'Ha! Fondly, he says. Remember me fondly.'

'I'm serious.'

'People can't remember what day it is, and you want to be remembered.'

'Is it too much to ask?'

'I'll make sure I remember you, how's that.'

'Bibi.'

'I'll try and remember to remember you.'

'Ha bloody ha.' He was trying to be serious with her, but they had set the design of their friendship from the outset – it was cheeky, and humorous, and mocking – and the apron had set firm. The design was at its sparkling best when his energy surged and the drugs lifted him almost to the point of flight. When he came down, as life ebbed, he thought about things like his 'affairs'. 'I want to set things right, but I don't have anyone to do that with.'

'Set things right, get your affairs in order. Now I see. You want to go out nice, not nasty.'

'I wouldn't have put it so crudely.'

'You want to make up for all those naughty things, all the pain and suffering you caused, and sail away all sweet and cute. Well, brother, let me give you the drum. It don't work like that.'

He turned away from her. He didn't want to hear it.

What he wanted was to be benevolent. Suddenly. Completely. In the way an addict needed to become something else. Perhaps it was a conversion he was looking for. But not to a god. To goodness, and giving. At his lowest point in the erratic drug cycle he loathed everyone, including Bibi. The only person he didn't was Aurora Beck – his adopted sister. She stayed constant to him, high and low. It was not his doing. It was how she was.

He had not told Bibi about the incident that had triggered his new thoughts, his need to repair.

Harold called it Tick's *closure*. Harold watched too much daytime television.

The *closure* had come a few nights earlier, on the steps leading down to Woolloomooloo. He was tired of the stuffy flat, and decided on a walk. Once, he had loved to walk. He felt good. Better than he had in weeks. His body was at the top of an oscillation. He put on his fur coat and walked.

Near the sandstone steps down to Woolloomooloo he had an overpowering sense of déjà vu. Not just that he'd been there before, at a similar time of night, when he was Juliet and plying his trade all over the Cross and Darlinghurst, but a déjà vu of want. A desire for something he thought he'd left behind. The thrill of the lure. The exposure to danger and physical harm. He felt it again, at the top of those steps.

443

A stranger walked past. Before he knew what he was doing, he offered the man sexual favours, in the voice of Juliet. He wanted to be her again for just a moment. And to his surprise the man slowed, stopped, and circled back.

'Come on,' the man said, and proceeded down the stairs. Tick followed. At the bottom, the stranger, hands in pockets, stood to the side of the stairs, near the straggly pine trees, and waited. It was dark. The shadows smelled of urine.

The next second Tick was on the ground, his ears ringing. His head was struck again, then his ribs. He lost consciousness. He didn't know how long he was out. He had pine needles in his hair and coat. When he opened his eyes, he saw across the road the twinkling lights of Harry's Cafe de Wheels. The pie cart. It was incandescent.

'I saw the little *pie* stand glowing with warm light, and people gathered around it, like children at the gates of heaven,' he said. 'It struck me . . . it struck me as something so simple and profound. The freshly baked food. The people eating together. The halo of lights. At that moment, it was what I had been seeking my entire life. It was my epiphany.'

'Don't start your silliness again,' Bibi said.

'Some go to Lourdes,' he said. 'I find mine in a *pie* cart at night.'

'What's this Lourdes bullshit?'

'I'm running out of time,' he said. 'I'm serious, Bibi. One gesture. I want to make one last gesture. To someone.'

'You got no family,' she said. 'And as far as I can tell,

you got no friends. Except for your taxi driver mate.'

'I used to have a family.'

'You gave up that asset a long time ago, my friend,' Bibi said. 'Can't go back there. That's a nut you're never going to crack. You best direct your gesture somewhere else.'

He only loved Aurora, anyway. His favourite one. He wished she was there with him. He wished he had his sister Aurora by his side, rubbing his aching back. He was cold. He knew what he had to do, but not yet how to do it.

THIRTY-SEVEN

WILFRED AND THE rest of the four-man Dalgety delegation stood with their horses and the cart at the side of the Cooma railway station, away from the crowd, behind the wooden fence and the platform. The men smoked in silence, the smoke easing out of the shadows beneath their hat brims.

The station verandah sent down the same angle of shadow. The line crept down the brick walls and long, narrow windows and wooden doors of the station. It cut through the waiting crowd and pieces of them – gloved hand, ankle, coat button – glowed in the sunlight. Dozens stood on the platform, and still all you could hear was the faint sound of watch chains, the scuff of shifting shoe leather, and the odd cough. It was what Wilfred would remember, later – the mournful crowd, the silent tracks and cinders, and the horses grazing along the fence line.

On the platform were the mayor in a top hat and other important men of the town in frock coats, and two trumpeters from the local high school band. There was a priest and the stationmaster and a reporter from the *Cooma Express*. Young boys loitered at the fringe of the party. People with luggage waited for the train. They were civilians, part of the everyday, of the world that woke to go to work or washed clothes for the family or delivered mail or caught trains from one place to another, not of the black mourning crowd.

At Cooma station they waited for the body of Vince 'Spud' Baker, who had died on a battlefield in France, and was coming home. He was the first casualty of the Great War from the Dalgety region.

On the ride to the station, Wilfred trailed the cart, its dusty tray and cargo of ropes and strips of calico. As they were heading out of town early that morning, Mitchell's wife from the Buckley's Crossing Hotel had rushed to the cart with a maroon velvet cushion, for they had dealt with transporting the dead in town and from the surrounding properties prior to the handiwork of the undertaker, but not with the body of a war hero, and they were uncertain of the protocol.

They rode all morning across the hills towards Cooma, and Wilfred thought of Spud Baker, and the memories came to him as large and evenly spaced as the clusters of green and grey granite in the fields on either side of the road.

He was the ship's urchin, the face-soiled cabin boy in *The Trout Opera*, because he was small and nuggety for his age, and Wilfred saw again clearly the boy's awkward opening recitation of sailing to the land of the free, and the distinct tremble in his left leg, and the way he pinched his knees to hold an electric bladder. He would always remember Spud as that boy, alone, terrified, in the heaving room, who would never again place himself in a position of singular attention, but be part of the

447

pack, and even in the pack, the dog deepest in the cave.

They were friends, he and Spud. Their families both did it hard. Just Spud and his father. He was never tall, Spud, but strong, and two years older than Wilfred. He had the semblance of a beard when the other boys were willing whiskers. Thatches of hair on his legs and wrists. As he hurriedly became a man, his father withered. Spud Senior loved a jar. And soon, each Saturday evening, it was young Spud who carried his drunk father home across the beam of his shoulders. If you ran across them on the tracks that fed out of town, you always marvelled at the sight of Spud hefting what looked, from a distance, like a dead ram or a wooden yoke. He was created to be a farmhand, which he was, and left school early, and his strength, irreconcilable with his height, became what people recalled of him. This silent brawn formed his personality, and as he grew into a quiet man it seemed the natural way of things that his size spoke for him, and hid a lisp and a slow mind. When the word 'Spud' was mentioned, you thought of the granite tors on the Monaro.

When his father died, Wilfred tried to teach Spud how to fish, but his fingers were too thick, his wrists too rigid, for any delicacy with the fly. Their dead fathers kept them together, though. And Spud without a mother, not long after. He lived on rabbit, bread and potatoes when he wasn't eating at other folks' tables, which he did often, because all the mothers loved him, and his clothes were the best darned in the district.

On the day he and Wilfred took off to Bombala to see the Men from the Snowy River on their recruiting march for the war, Spud didn't return home. He joined there and then, and filed straight in, waving his hat and laughing. That night Wilfred rode back alone to Dalgety. It was moonless and dark and he heard rabbits in the fields. The rocks clicked like rifle hammers after the heat of the day, and Wilfred knew it would still be warm in the rabbit burrows, in the thousands of tunnels beneath the earth, and that they would be looking towards him and the horse, twitching and with quickened heart, still as stones in the blackness.

Halfway back to Dalgety Wilfred boiled his billy by the roadside. It was so still even the horse was alert to the unseen hordes of rabbits and the crackling of the fire twigs. At the edge of the fire light, with the tea mug cupped in his hands, Wilfred thought of Spud Baker at the volunteers' camp outside Bombala and their march towards Goulburn. They got guns so big they turn night into day, Spud told him on their ride that morning. Better than fireworks. Wilfred had heard the men of the area talk of this on the verandah of the hotel, and Grandfather Callistus, who hated the war, and the giant guns, ranted in his study and in the orchard and even in the main street and outside the general store in Berridale with a look on his face that Wilfred had never seen before.

Not long after they had buried Wilfred's father, Callistus's face divided, became a combination of men. It was the left side that had changed most, the eye narrower, the mouth mean and pinched, the sinews in the neck taut, and it was this side that hated the guns and the slaughter the most. The villagers had thrown eggs at his grandfather's house, and cut the heads off all of his roses, and he stayed inside, the half that was afraid

449

keeping the angry half in the house. It was Wilfred who had to check the hives by the creek when he visited, stepping through the rotting fruit of the neglected orchard. In the spring of 1915 the old man's Cyprus bees simply disappeared. The boy did not have the courage to tell Callistus until the middle of summer.

Wilfred continued to work for the Cranks, and Tom Crank continued to order him around, and assign him menial and sometimes dangerous tasks, and to hang around the Lampe house, and Astrid, while he was away. On two occasions, bringing sheep in for shearing, Crank had stood in his saddle and fired his rifle within feet of Wilfred, citing a fox. On a dawn rabbit shoot, Wilfred found a single bullet hole in his swag. When he asked Crank about it, he just said, 'Accidents happen.'

With all the thoughts of Spud Baker fighting on the other side of the world and his grandfather's mad sermons of death and dismemberment and the wayward bullets it occurred to Wilfred that one day he might have to kill Tom Crank. The reason had yet to define itself. But he knew it was on its way, just as he knew that day waiting for the body of Spud Baker at the Cooma railway station that the vibration from the train would be heard and felt through the rusted tracks well before you saw the smoke smudge from the engine.

At Cooma station, Wilfred sat in the shadow of Bodalla and stared at the dry grass and stones between his feet and thought of Spud dying in a cold and muddy field in France while he had been mustering some of the Crank cattle down into Victoria.

Over in Europe, Spud Baker and his brigade

wallowed in a plateau of cold mud near Flers. For weeks they slept in barns on wet straw and couldn't get their clothes dry. They burned sodden fence palings and sat around the smoking fires and in the smoke they could smell death.

Wilfred sat around the familiar campfires along the route into Bairnsdale. He did not know Spud Baker was knee-deep in mud and shivering in wet clothes and huddling in a trench lit up with coloured flares in a place called Flers on those nights in the mountains and on the plains of Victoria, as he drifted into sleep to the honking and farting of the cattle.

When Wilfred thought of Spud he saw an urchin in *The Trout Opera*, and the pattern of the boy's cumbersome and rhythmless dancing feet on the stage of the Imperial Hall, and the wink of coloured light from the jewelled headdress of the Queen Lure of the Monaro, and the mad flutter of Spud's coat-tails on the ride into Bombala to see the proud ghosts, and one of his hats left by someone on a peg in the Buckley's, untouched, awaiting his return. This was what Wilfred Lampe saw as he drifted into sleep, the images carried away by the eucalypt-smelling campfire smoke.

He wondered many times about Spud's decision that day in Bombala to change his life in an instant. Wilfred could not get past that impulse.

There had been talk at the Buckley's of this. A debate over conscription. There were mutterings of eligible young men of the area and, in some cases, their sudden enthusiasm for the land and stock. Talk, too, of Tom Crank, and an ill-defined medical condition that had suddenly come to light. Dr Fingal knew nothing of it. If he doesn't have a medical condition now, someone said, he'll soon have one.

But Spud went to war as though he and the war were two ideas that met at the perfect time and place. Spud joining the rear of that parade through Bombala, back of the pack, and winking at Wilfred before he disappeared.

While Spud was meeting his death, Wilfred delivered the herd into Bairnsdale, left the other two ringers in town, and began the long ride home. He felt empty and lonely on the journey. It confused him. He had never been this way in the bush, or on the muster to and from Victoria. The bush always felt crowded to Wilfred. There were voices, sounds, and the memories of his father on that first trip. Each campfire on the route had a name, as if the pits filled with the charcoal of countless fires were evenly spaced baubles on a well-loved necklace. And the bush couldn't have been more alive as it approached mid-summer.

It was quiet, though. He wasn't imagining it. It was as if all the noises of the continent were drawn into the northern hemisphere and to the war. As if any extraneous sounds were sacrilegious. It was the same feeling he'd had at the Bolocco Cemetery when they buried his father. It was a state of mourning, only this time it applied to the whole nation.

As he approached the border, he turned east for Corryong. He'd take the Khancoban way, so he could at least ride past Dorothea's house.

He did not know, then, that he and the horse were laying down a tradition that would continue through most of his life. A pilgrimage. To the grand two-storey red-brick house on a hill at Towong, with its short gravel

452

coachway and nub of rose bushes in front of the entrance stairway. The place stood like a dark, solid vase on a clean square tablecloth, the surrounding paddocks thick with lush feed and neatly bordered with white rail fencing.

The back of the house faced the southern buttresses of the Snowy Mountains. It was an architectural decision made not out of disrespect to the panorama of the mountains, but out of humility, a gesture towards their grandeur, and so the house appeared smaller than it was with the backdrop of the Alps, and the property neater against the dramatic escarpments, and everything was in its place, and shared a harmonious perspective.

It was how Wilfred felt about Dorothea. She was in perspective. She calmed him. And he felt the same, too, about her father, Mr Chauvere the amateur geologist. They had a relationship with the earth, both of them, which the boy could not define but liked to think about, and know existed.

He recalled that day on the slopes down from Carruthers Peak, not far from the summit, where she had taught him to ski. Astride Bodalla, he had followed her and the solid black rump of her mountain horse up the slope. Dorothea was slight but she managed the muscular horse deftly, and powder kicked up from its hooves in front and clung to its long tail. She half stood in the stirrups, and he watched her long tawny ponytail sway with the horse's gait. She went with the changing pace of the animal, let it trot or walk as the terrain determined, and soon they were high above the valley, a great bowl of rocks and stones and herb bushes and stains of moss and the grey scythe of the Snowy.

Wilfred could only just see the veiled Rams Head across the valley, and as they got closer to the top of Carruthers the nearby range and the foliage and the river became as pale as watermarks. It was snowing lightly when she stopped the black horse and dismounted. He did as she did. Dorothea unlashed the butterpats.

'Well, come on,' she said.

She was standing in her skis before he reached her.

'Let's start you on this short run,' she said, pointing into the flurry. 'It's only a hundred yards. You can get a feel for it.'

He looked into the swirling white. 'It's a long way down,' he said. His lips were blue.

'There's a line of rocks at the end, silly. You'll see them before you get there.'

He squinted in the direction of the rocks. 'I can't see any rocks.'

'I can't either. But they're there.'

And with that she was gone, hissing away in a wide S-figure, and soon she was shapeless, and just a bundle of colours, and then no colour at all, but a smudge. Then she vanished.

He struggled fitting the skis. The two horses stood silently and watched as he tangled himself in the apparatus.

'Very funny,' he said to the horses. He could hear her shouting in the wind.

'I'm coming, I'm coming,' he mumbled, pushing himself up off the dusted boulder, and with that he hurtled towards her voice, and the horses' ears twitched at a clack of wood and a loud thump of breath, and for a moment a girl's giggle fluttered with the snow.

They'd arranged to meet only twice since their adventure, at the carnival in Bombala, and at Foley's Circus in Cooma the previous August, where they had strolled together and inspected the animals, and she was captivated by the Indian elephant. Wilfred had seen the same elephant the year before, and the tired tiger, and the clutch of monkeys.

'I'd like to go to India,' she said.

He was a foot taller than her, courtesy of a recent growth spurt, and he studied the white rose in her hair and the blonde down on her cheekbone.

'What for?' he said.

'Don't you want to see the world?' she asked.

'It's a long way to go, just to have to come back.'

'Perhaps I'll live in Paris.'

'What for?'

She studied the deep lines around the elephant's eye. 'To experience things.'

He shrugged. 'That elephant's travelling. He don't look happy with all his experience.'

'We're going away,' she said quietly. 'To my uncle's house in Melbourne. Until the war's over.'

Wilfred watched the metronomic movement of the elephant's trunk.

'My father's joined up. To study maps.'

He looked at the crazed etching across the elephant's hide. It looked like something you could read, but he made nothing of it, and the elephant stood before him, huge and heavy and incomprehensible. Wilfred just stared at it and said nothing.

'You can write to me if you want,' she said, moving

away, and his legs felt like lead and he didn't immediately follow.

That evening in the summer of Spud Baker's death, Wilfred pulled up his horse in front of the shuttered red-brick house at Towong and again it was something that took on the shape of his grief and longing. He dismounted and sat on the front steps for a long time. The circular bed of roses had grown wild in the middle of the carriageway. He could just see the skeletal limbs of the rose bushes through the weeds. There were no flowers.

Later, he walked around the house and peered into windows looking for traces of Dorothea. Inside were chairs and cabinets draped in sheets. A dark stairway leading to the upstairs bedrooms. On the lower steps was carpet stained with red roses. The kitchen was yellow with the sunlight through the windows. There was a wooden table and six chairs in the centre, and a huge fireplace with a black kettle hanging from its hook, and a black cast-iron stove. The shelves were all empty.

He saw, just inside the door off the kitchen, a single rabbit-skin hat on a wooden peg.

Wandering out the back again, he came across a patch of lawn, the grass as dry as straw, and sat on a small bench that looked out towards the southern end of the Alps. The fields were clean of livestock. The horse yards empty. Nothing moved in the chicken coop at the bottom of the garden except for a few quivering feathers caught in wire.

He looked up at the mountains. You're right, he said to them in his head. I was wrong. You're always alive. The mountains change. They're constantly moving one way or another. The tiny glaxias will be swimming up in the waters of the Snowy near the summit. A rock will shift. A fissure will widen. The bogongs will live and die and others will replace them. A fire will break out and the wide, open arms of snow gums will be aflame. Brumbies will thunder off at the snap of a twig. The trout will rise at dusk, and see both their darkening world of black reeds and shadowed pebbles, and through the surface of the water to the orange sky and the descending, silhouetted squadrons of insects. And the river. Always the river, looping like a giant question mark past Jindabyne and Dalgety, and pushing out to sea.

On the ride home he kept seeing in his mind the rose in Dorothea's hair the day they stood before the elephant. It was the ivory throat of it that, for a moment that day, seemed to contain all the happiness and hope of his adolescent life. Then, in an instant – *we're going away* – it was gone.

One moment you have a rose in a girl's hair. Across the plains, an old man has beds of thorny rose bushes but no flowers and broken pieces of eggshell stuck to the screen door. A hand gives you one thing, and another, out of sight, takes something away.

He rode through the night to Dalgety. A few weeks later, he was accompanying the empty dray to Cooma station to meet Spud Baker's body.

THIRTY-EIGHT

WILFRED LAMPE WAITED alone in the room and studied the children's crayon drawings on the walls.

There were space rockets with little dorsal fins pffutting blue smoke. Stiff-legged dogs floating in zero gravity. Big oval heads with pin eyes and huge grins. Brown, boxy elongated cars with black tyres, and the letters DAD with an arrow pointing to the driver. There were wizards with crooked wands, lone trees, and oceans flecked with crayon crumbs.

The old man's attention was caught by the violet fish. It was suspended in mid-air over a small pond. A green line extended out of its closed mouth to the bank of the pond, where a stick boy wielded a rod as thick as his arms and legs. The stick boy had a smile that was wider than his coin-sized face. It reminded him of the secret fishing holes of his youth. Then the stretches of the Snowy River where he brought the tourists, as a trout-fishing guide. He could always find a rainbow or a brown.

Wilfred stared down at the tan slippers on his feet. He'd never owned a pair of slippers in his life. The blue and white striped pyjamas. The bare room where he slept. The corridors lit with watery green. Now this room, with its table and two chairs, and the drawings of the children.

He wasn't dead at all. The day he collapsed in the yard, the suited men, the helicopter. It was all coming back to him.

He felt stronger than he'd been in a long time. He was right now to fix the dam out the back, and the water mill. The generator, too, could do with an overhaul. And his Humber Vogue. He needed to turn the motor. Replace the spark plugs. Fit a new oil filter. He had a lot to do. He had to get home from wherever he was.

There was a light tap at the door. A woman walked in wearing a caramel suit with large, creamy buttons and carrying folders under her arm. She smiled and nodded at him, and quietly closed the door.

Her heels clacked in the small, empty room. The chair barked as she pulled it out from the table. She sat with the folders in her lap.

'Good morning, Mr Lampe.'

He didn't know what time of day it was. His watch with the brown leather clip-over cover had disappeared.

'Good morning,' he said.

'I'm Dr Morrison.'

Wilfred laid his large, speckled hands on the surface of the table. 'I think I saw a doctor yesterday.'

'I'm a psychologist, Mr Lampe.'

'I'm feeling good.'

'I'm pleased to hear it.'

'I need to go home.' He again checked the freckles and sun spots where his watch face used to be.

'Well . . .' She put the folders on the table and tidied

them. Her hair was short and dyed deep red like the under-fur of a fox tail.

'I got things to do.'

She smiled. 'That's very good to hear, Mr Lampe. But I'm here today to ask you a few simple questions. To assess you.'

'What for?'

On the wall behind her was drawing after drawing of wild grins and floating cows and volcanoes spitting out thick torrents of yellow and orange lava.

'I'm here today to evaluate your current state of wellbeing.'

'I'm well. I told you.'

'Not your physical wellbeing, Mr Lampe. You look fighting fit to me. It's your mind I'm interested in.'

'I'm the same as I've always been.'

Dr Morrison opened a large writing pad. She took a pen from inside her coat and clicked the top. 'This shouldn't take long at all.'

She wore small, black-framed spectacles and she glanced at him over the tops of the rectangular rims.

Wilfred looked at a picture of a rickety house with a crooked chimney and it occurred to him, too, that the old place might need some minor repairs after the winter. Then he wondered, What season am I in? He'd never not known the season.

'You're a widower, Mr Lampe?'

'Pardon?'

'A widower? You?'

'I never married,' he said.

'Never married,' she repeated, writing in the pad. 'So no children?'

460

'No children, no.'

'Siblings?'

'You mean brothers and sisters?'

'Yes.'

It was cold in the room and he felt it around his exposed ankles. The pyjamas were too short, and his toes were frozen even encased in the tan slippers. He rubbed the top of his left wrist where his missing watch had been.

He finally said: 'No.'

'All right then,' Dr Morrison said, underlining something on the page of her notebook. 'You maintain a healthy diet now, do you, Mr Lampe? Any smoking or drinking?'

'I eat what I always ate,' he said.

'Smoke?'

'Sometimes.'

'Drink?'

'Sometimes.'

'Moderate, then. Medication? High blood pressure? Diabetes?'

'I guess not.'

'Was there a point, Mr Lampe, where you began any form of social disengagement? Reducing societal contact?'

'I don't know what you mean.'

Dr Morrison removed her glasses and brought the tip of the left arm of her spectacles to her bottom lip. 'I'm sorry. Lawn bowls or golf. Things like that. Was there a point where you ceased participating in activities like that?'

'I never played them.'

'Anything similar? Something recreational, involving other people? Friends?'

'We'd go down to the pub after the crutching.'

'Nothing else?'

'Fishing. I always fished.'

'With others?'

'Only when I had to.'

'I see.' She scratched something out on the paper. 'Do you suffer moments of depression? Are you largely cheerful? I need to find out a few things about your history. Do you see what I mean?'

'Yeah.'

'For example. When you retired, was it a difficult experience for you, and if so, did that difficulty stay with you for a long time? The feelings of uselessness. Of no longer being productive to society.'

'I just work when I feel up to it.'

'You have employment in your retirement?'

'If I feel good in the morning I'll do things,' Wilfred said.

'I'm sorry,' the doctor said. 'You have a hobby? A recreation?'

'I do what I always done.'

'And what's that?'

'I go rabbiting or I fix things up. And fish.'

'But what did you do when you were younger – you know, prior to retirement?'

'I keep telling you. I caught rabbits and fixed things up. And fished.'

There were voices somewhere outside the room and for a moment it seemed like the big, round-headed stick people on the walls were mumbling to each other.

'Mr Lampe, there are a number of psychological categories established for people of your age and I'm here today to try and find which category best suits you. This can tell me a lot about your mental disposition.'

She leafed through some papers and Wilfred thought of Charlie Carter up in the High Country and this time it was Wilfred's turn to smile. It didn't take a thousand questions to work out Charlie was as mad as a March hare, as his father used to say. Poor Charlie. He'd dropped dead in the scrub and it was a week before they found him and by then he was all bad smells and not much else after the animals had got to him. They buried him in his vegetable garden, with the strychnine-laced carrots and turnips, and not even a headstone to mark his time on earth, just a few heads of lettuces gone to seed.

'There are people who hold on, Mr Lampe. They cling to the success and vigour of their middle age. There are others who drop the ball altogether, at the very early stages of old age, and are constantly in fear of what ageing entails. Others rely heavily on the support of others, Mr Lampe, be it friends or family. And others enter an almost vegetative state, and no longer see a purpose in life at all. I am trying to ascertain to which of these categories you belong, Mr Lampe.'

When they let crazy Carter's brumbies go, Wilfred was told, the animals stood around that vegetable patch for a while like they knew he was buried there. One even urinated on the freshly dug soil. Or so Wilfred was told. They still laughed at that in the Buckley's fifty years later.

'Mr Lampe?'

'Can you tell me when I can go home?'

Dr Morrison placed the pen on the table and rested her glasses on the folders. She looked at him with an idiot grin similar to several that adorned the walls. 'I'm afraid I have no idea. It is not up to me.'

'Can you find someone who can tell me?'

'It is why I am here,' she said. 'To produce an evaluation which will let us know exactly what you can and can't do, Mr Lampe. What we learn today is the key to the question you're asking me.'

'Then I can tell you. I feel good and I want to go home.'

'Your file says you were recently at a point where you were happy to die, for want of a better term.'

Wilfred ran both hands along the striped thighs of his pyjamas. 'When I fell over? In the backyard?'

'I don't know the precise details, but it clearly says here you expressed a willingness to die.'

'Course I was happy to,' Wilfred said.

'To die?'

'I'm not afraid of death.'

'I'm not suggesting that you are, Mr Lampe.'

'I was tired. Had enough. Then they brought me here.'

'You'd had enough then, but not now?'

'Now I feel good.'

'Now you want to keep going, to live, because you feel good.'

'Sure. You feel good then everything's good.' He couldn't see what she didn't understand.

'You live day by day?'

'What other way is there?'

She hurriedly jotted notes in her pad. 'Tell me about your religion. Do you have any?'

'Religion?'

'Yes.'

'Never saw a need for it.'

'No faith?'

'Sometimes I got faith and sometimes I don't.'

'That's not quite what I mean.'

'You want to know if I ever went to church.'

'Did you?'

'Plenty of times. For funerals. One time I fixed the gutters. My mother used to clean the church back home, before she passed on.'

'But no worship for you?'

'I liked the bluestones and the river rocks they used to make it. But they come from the hills, and the river bed. I knew where it all come from, that church, so what's the point of worshipping? I could see the big stones in the water from the bridge. Why would I worship some big stones? It was the same to me.'

'So you're an atheist?'

'I don't know what that is.'

'You have no belief in a higher force, in God.'

'I used to think there was something up in the mountains. Something special, at the source of the river. But I never got there to see it. That ain't God, though. I just wanted to see where the river come from.'

'Some might see that as a metaphor, Mr Lampe.'

'I don't know what that is.'

'A symbol. For God.'

'Are you asking me do I believe in God?'

'In a manner, yes.'

'Why do people always ask that same question?'

'It's one of our fundamental questions.'

'I never saw the sense of that question, and I never saw the sense in people keeping on asking it.'

'I'll take that as a no, then.' She wrote on her pad.

'You can take it whatever way you want. It makes no difference to me.'

'Mr Lampe,' she continued, 'how much contact do you have with your niece?'

He stared at her. 'I don't have no niece.'

'I'm sorry – your great-niece.'

He looked blankly at her.

She checked the file, lifting it off the table and closer to her face. 'My records indicate that you have a great-niece.'

He didn't understand what she was saying. He could see the stick children leaping, suspended in space, all around the room. The dogs and houses and fences and cows and trees and moons and stars surrounded him. Fish with crosses for eyes. Rivers that didn't move.

'Ms Aurora Beck, twenty-six years of age,' Dr Morrison said.

How could he have a great-niece? He had no siblings, as she put it. When Astrid disappeared, it was only Wilfred. It had always only been Wilfred. Wilfred out in the valley. He was the old bloke who caught rabbits and fixed things. And fished.

'Mr Lampe.'

'I don't know what you're saying to me.'

'Let me ask you candidly, Mr Lampe: did you have a problem with that side of the family? A rift, perhaps?

Please, don't be ashamed to answer. What we say here is between us only.'

'What was her name?' he asked after a long time.

The woman checked the page. 'Ms Aurora Beck.'

He felt nauseous and light-headed. He gripped the table with one hand. He tried to focus to stop the room from rocking like a ship in a swell.

He locked on to one of the pictures on the wall. The drawing of a small red balloon. He tried to hold the string with his mind. Tried to stop it from floating off the edge of the paper and out into the world, from rising up, a ball in the sky, then a speck, then a pinpoint, until it disappeared.

THIRTY-NINE

THE MORNING AURORA and her father climbed Mount Warning there was a heavy mist over the surface of the river. The cane fields to the west were bright and sharp, as were the highway posts and signs and bitumen that ran alongside the river to the east. The mist clung only to the water, replicating its loose winding to the sea.

Both of them knew, then, the view from the summit would be clear.

Her father had dressed as if for an occasion. She glanced at him as he drove the old car out of town to the base of the mountain. He had ironed his checked shirt, too warm for this burst of spring, and buttoned it to the neck. His hair was wet and shiny with Brylcreem, his face clean of whiskers.

He had prepared a backpack of water and sandwiches, and a tin of dusted sweets. 'For energy,' he said. Small racing binoculars were tucked in the front pocket. Handkerchiefs. A compass. 'You never know when you might need it.'

She was amused by his fastidiousness.

It was one of several changes she'd noticed in the past few days. He'd moved back into the main house and his old bedroom. He stayed away from the hotel. They sat at the kitchen table and ate meals they cooked.

He'd changed, too, since the police car arrived out the front of the house three evenings earlier. Two officers came to the door and he spoke with them on the verandah. They were just passing and thought they'd see how he was getting on, they said. He knew one of them, from the death of his wife. They shared that. The body at the end of the rope under the house. The horrible, undignified bringing down of the body.

The police were looking for Aurora Beck. And when she got home that night, and he mentioned the visit, they sat at that old kitchen table in the yellow light and she told him everything. The baby. Wynter. The drugs. That since she'd returned she'd been taking a bus to Tweed Heads and the drug clinic.

He focused on his hands during the telling, wrapping one over the other, forming the steeple with his fingers, wringing them. He nodded and did not interrupt. When he scratched his chin you could hear the rasp of his stubble.

Late that night she heard him sob, in the yard behind the kitchen. Not even the hard glass of the louvres repelled his pain. He had heard her throwing up in the bathroom, seen her shivering under a blanket on the couch, noticed her hands shaking at breakfast and dinner, and her attempts to hide it. He hadn't known what was happening to his daughter.

The next morning he was sitting on the end of her bed. His eyes were puffy and red-rimmed. She sat up and he stroked her cheek. 'The first place in the country to see the sunrise,' he said.

They drove to the mountain, passing old farms and cow paddocks and banana plantations. She saw, dotted throughout the foliage, the bunches wrapped in protective blue plastic bags.

Her father cleared his throat. 'You can't run anymore,' he said. 'If there are things to face, then you have to face them.' He cricked his neck. A quiet emphasis.

'You're right,' she said.

He stared at the road ahead, but he was watching her. 'It's best. We can sort something out.'

It was pretty, the blue through the ragged banana trees. Like cornflowers, she thought.

'Do you hear me?' he said. 'I'll be with you. We'll sort it out.'

His definition had returned with Aurora around. She had tethered him again. It made her sad to think of him alone in the house for all those years. People needed purpose. They needed someone to care for. It was the small gestures of that purpose that formed them, that held them up, like the hidden cross-beams and joins of a roof.

'Thanks, Dad,' she said.

It was feeling less strange to say the word – Dad. She liked saying it. He was coming back to her, not the man she had left, the defeated man who came home each night flecked with ash from the cane fires, his hair seemingly grey, the ash blurring him at the edges, but the man with the strong hands and curly black hair that she gripped, aloft on his shoulders, walking through town.

She, too, had been as ill-defined as her father when she left home. Embryonic. All instinct. Reacting to everything like a sensitive chemical.

Her years away had taught her that people didn't always collide with life at all. They did everything to avoid it.

Something had pushed her from home. It was the fear, still forming, a tangle of cells and atoms, of becoming an adult, fully formed, the mental pathways set, as clearly laid down as a street map, and emerging as her own mother. It had pushed her to a place with no friction under her feet, without landmark. A place where people like Wynter waited.

You could not avoid who you were, she knew now, and where you came from. She shared a line with her mother and grandmother, and whoever else was in the queue beyond them.

Aurora had come home for a reason. The news of her great-uncle Wilfred and her father's strengthening and the arrival of the police were all happening for a reason. The drive to Mount Warning. The long, painful hours in the clinic. All of it. It was time to turn around now. To grab that line that disappeared into the past. To infinity. It would take her into herself. It would make her understand. She had no future without it.

'We're a bit late for the sunrise,' her father said, driving into the car park at the foot of the mountain.

'Hmm?'

'The sunrise. We've missed it.'

'Next time,' she said.

There were several other cars parked at the base. The pre-dawn climbers. She liked to think of it. People sitting at the summit. Others making their way down, returning to the world.

'Righteo,' he said, slinging the backpack across his shoulder. 'We're off.'

She let him take the lead. It was her father, carrying the provisions for both of them.

They said little on the climb. They stopped at intervals and had some water. They passed three other parties on their way down, and each made perfunctory remarks about the steepness of the mountain and the clarity of vision from the top. It was slow going near the summit. He was getting older. It struck her, fully, on the side of the mountain in the sunlight. The missing years, how we age imperceptibly in each other's presence. But dramatically, with absence. I've aged too, she thought. I have the stretch marks of a lost child. The wear and tear of the drugs, the metal-on-metal years with Wynter.

At the top they sat and stared at the view and said nothing until her father's breathing had returned to normal.

He pointed towards the sea. 'There's talk,' he said, 'of these big gated suburbs, right along the coast.'

'Gated?'

'Self-contained. With restaurants and shops. No reason to leave them. Everything you need, right inside the gates. Like the old villages in Europe, protected by a wall.'

'Prisons.'

'For the rich people. People are scared nowadays, maybe.'

'Mum might have liked it.'

'She would have loved it, I'm sure. It might have made her . . . less scared.'

They ate the sandwiches he'd made.

'I wouldn't like it,' he said, chewing, stabbing a crust at the coast. 'Too much like the nursing homes where I work. What's the rush? We're all going to the same place in the end.'

They could see the steam from the sugar mill, and the neat grids of cane around it. The river was shimmering in the midday heat.

'Terrible,' he said quietly, looking down at the toy town. 'How it goes so fast. Will you stay?' he asked.

'Yes,' she said.

'That's good.'

She trained the binoculars along the length of the narrow river.

'There's something I need to do first,' she said.

'Whatever you want.'

'Some loose ends to tie up.'

She handed him the binoculars and he carefully fitted the black caps over the lenses. He smiled.

'What?' she asked.

'It's still funny to me. How grown up you are. Having loose ends.'

'That makes me grown up?'

'Loose ends make you grown up.'

She punched him lightly on the arm.

That night he fell asleep in his chair in front of the television. She sat curled up on the couch.

They had talked on the way down the mountain. Without the exertion of the uphill climb, and with a stiff breeze cooling them, the talk flowed and their words and laughter disappeared into the rainforest. They were rising as they came down the mountain.

Dizzy and exhilarated. Drugged with the moment.

On the couch she felt the heat of the day held in the tin roof. Her father snored.

Aurora was, for the first time in years, at the quiet centre of not just where she belonged, but of who she was, as a woman. A woman who knew what had to be done, and was capable of doing it.

PART II

FORTY

IT WASN'T UNTIL the end of the seventh day that Wilfred and Percy came out of the scrubby skirts of the Alps and returned to familiar trails, set up camp by the river, and struck a proper fire for a warm meal.

Wilfred settled the horses for the night while Percy prepared the supper. They ate the chops and sucked on the bones and grease glistened at the corners of their mouths. They sipped the hot tea and then Wilfred rolled them both cigarettes.

Nearby the river flumed through a narrow gorge. Wilfred wasn't sure if it was the memory of the chops and then the cigarette that was giving him satisfaction or the sound of the river. They'd been riding in elevated country with just the wind for company. He'd never found the wind good company. The river, though . . .

When Astrid disappeared, almost a year to the day after they buried Spud, and he'd ridden to Cooma, this time to check the railway station for her, then down to Bombala to look inside the picture palace and the fancy ladies' dress shops in the main street, then covered every square inch of the Crank property, he simply rode into the hills. He'd made no decision. He could have left that to the horse for all he cared.

Somewhere along the way Percy appeared on horse-back beside him. Only when they reached the camp by the river did Wilfred realise he was saddle-weary, and hungry, and that he might have been away somewhere and come back.

A few fat bogongs played at the edge of the flames.

'Moth,' Wilfred said. It was the first word between them that day.

'Yeah, bogong,' Percy replied.

Wilfred couldn't stop thinking of Astrid in those last few days back at the house. She broke a china teacup. She dropped to the floor to retrieve the shards and the loop of handle, and held the handle, the rough and clean china, the bone of it inside the glaze exposed for the first time, and on her knees she wept inconsolably for the broken cup. She fought for breath between the sobbing. And still she held the piece of handle with her trembling fingers, as if someone precious had died. They knelt with her, Wilfred and his mother, confused by the grief unleashed by the pop of worthless china. Her whole bent body shook. They led her by the elbows to bed, and her muffled whimpering came to them through the timbers.

Mother and son said nothing. But both knew Astrid's sorrow came from a place much further away than the next room.

The next night he stepped in from the paddocks and before he'd taken off his boots she'd grabbed him and hugged him out on the verandah. It was a moment like the breaking of the cup. Where strange, unexpected emotions were summoned without context. It was like a death, but with no body.

'What's this for?' he'd asked, his arms wide in surprise, though it wasn't only surprise. Caught by the moment, a boot half-dislodged, he reeking of sheep and with fine galaxies of blood spots across his shirt front and sleeves, he was taken aback by the embrace and unable to react. It diffused him.

He could see her on the day before she disappeared as clearly as the perfect strands and patterns of a feather. She sat on a patch of exposed granite, the one they imagined, as children, was the tip of a giant subterranean dinosaur egg, near the old pepper tree. Her arms held her knees.

He went up and sat beside her. She didn't look at him. She failed to notice he was there. He studied her face and was taken aback by what he saw. This is my sister, he thought. She's almost a grown woman. This is my sister. How could you live with someone all your life and miss these moments? Where was the little girl who'd gone missing once before and been brought into town on horseback with soiled cheeks and a fistful of wild-flowers? Where was the child who'd danced, as if in a trance, below the stage during the performance of *The Trout Opera* all that time ago?

Wilfred never felt he was grown up. When he saw others around him, close to him, getting older, it always left him confused.

The amber sunlight illuminated Astrid's face that afternoon on the egg, and her eyes were large and red-rimmed and trembling with tears.

The next day she was gone.

Again, the town searched for Astrid Lampe. But this time it was not infused with that electric dread that comes with looking for an innocent child in a forest. The thoughts of the infinite ways of death driving the parties to exhaustion. That cold, coin-sized pit of fear in everyone, lodged firmly in the child they had been. Not a few of them thought that night, their lanterns held aloft, how death sometimes came with titanic struggle, and also how it came quickly and without effort.

Astrid was almost a woman. She was a Lampe. She'd known hardship like the rest of them, and hardship equipped you with certain skills. She had not wandered off to pick wildflowers.

Then word got through, days later, that someone had seen her at Cooma railway station. She had no luggage. The Lampes didn't have luggage.

Wilfred rode to the railway station. It was where they'd picked up the body of his friend Spud. (He knew the casket had not really contained his body. Only his hat and boots. But that had been enough.) And now it had swept away his sister. Percy would have said it was a place of bad spirits for Wilfred.

Then Bombala. There were no coloured lights on the river this time, but there was a picture that kept recurring to him, an image from his memory so small it could have fitted into a locket. Astrid and Tom Crank, at the carnival.

Later, in the bush, before he hooked up with Percy, he woke in his swag early one morning surrounded by a curious mob of brumbies. He was still half asleep. He thought he heard loud breathing all around him, and when he partially opened his eyes he saw them — the long-haired maliima women, the spirit women, that Percy had told him lived in the bush. Wilfred screamed. The shaggy-maned brumbies took flight.

Coming back from the bush to the river he knew two things. That he would never find Astrid. She had crossed into some new world. She was gone, yet she would be all around him forever, like the maliima women. And he knew that Tom Crank was somehow involved in her disappearance.

At the pub he learned that Crank had suddenly headed down to Orbost to buy some cattle for his father. Wilfred had heard nothing of the urgent trip. None of the shearers and farmhands had mentioned a word about it.

He'd deal with Crank eventually. But the image of his long-haired sister Astrid standing on the platform at Cooma haunted him.

'Here,' Percy said. He held out several wingless, roasted moths in his pale palm. They were small and shrivelled.

'I tasted them before,' Wilfred said. He nudged at a smooth, veined rock around the fire with the heel of his boot.

Percy studied the pellets of moth.

'I ever tell you about the Moth Men?' he asked.

Wilfred emptied the dregs of his tea onto the river sand.

He'd known Percy for years. They were the same age. They wouldn't let Percy go to school in Dalgety. Some of the parents had complained. Written to the school board. Didn't want a dirty little blackfella in the school with his hygiene problems. So he'd worked around the district since he was a kid, bringing in cattle strays and hacking down blackberries for food. Worked for almost every family in the region on and off. Left one property a boy and came back years later a teenager. Left another a teenager and came back a young man. Nobody ever saw Percy grow up. He didn't stay in one place long enough. Left with baby cheeks and reappeared with whiskers on them.

He worked for the Cranks several times, swung around them like the moon. He was the best rider Wilfred had ever seen, and he'd won a few bob at the buckjumping down at Bombala.

Some said he was related to old Biggenhook, the last fullblood Monaro blackfella, but Percy said it wasn't true. He said there were other fullbloods still around, down south and over near the coast. He didn't know his father anyway. He moved around too much to know things like that.

'You told me a lot of things but I never heard of the Moth Men,' Wilfred said.

'That's what I call 'em, the Moth Men, but there's three of them, see. There's the Moth Man, and the Bogong Man, then there's Caterpillar Man.'

'Spirits.'

'Not spirits. This sacred ceremony stuff – you don't know much.'

'How am I supposed to know about the Moth Men when you're telling me something for the first time?'

Percy caught one of the roasted moths with his tongue. 'You know about the moths?'

'How could I not know about the moths? I seen 'em every year. I live here too, don't I?'

'When you seen 'em?'

'On the musters I seen 'em.'

'You never do the muster in spring.'

'What's that got to do with it?'

'You missed 'em, see, if you reckon you saw 'em outside spring. Sometimes they come early, but not most of the time. You don't know much.'

'Why do you keep on saying that? I know you lot used to go up there as skinny as snakes and come back down fat as barrels. I know that much.'

'You want to hear about the Moth Men?'

'Go on, tell me about your bloody Moth Men.'

'Sacred ceremony. The Caterpillar Man, he has the big long things on his head, like this, see.' He cleared a patch of sand with his palm and drew a head and two wavy lines. 'The things on the caterpillar's head. The Bogong Man, he has this on his head, see, like the jacket for the moth, and the eggs.'

'The jacket?'

'Yeah, like my jacket.' He tugged at the lapel of his old coat.

'The chrysalis.'

'Yeah. And the Moth Man, he's the daddy insect, when it's grown up.'

'The life cycle of the moth.'

'The life, yeah. This one, this one, then this one.' He stabbed at the sand with his finger.

Wilfred removed his hat. He went down to the water's edge and washed his face and came back to the fire. He stood in the glow of the flames, the droplets of water running down his cheeks to the point of his chin.

483

'You joking with me, Percy?'

'What's wrong with you?'

'If you're joking with me . . .'

'Why joke with you? This the sacred ceremony for the moths, see. Keeps them coming back every year. More and more every year. You don't know much if you think I joke with you about that.'

Wilfred resumed his seat by the fire.

'You heard of *The Trout Opera*?'

'Trout, yeah.'

'No. *The Trout Opera*. It happened over in the old hall, years ago. It was a ceremony, too. For Christmas.'

'Nah. I never heard.'

'It was about the trout coming to Dalgety.'

'The trout. Yeah. I like 'em.'

'We dressed up, too. All the kids in the school did. Some of them were just like your Moth Men. The life of the insect. We had that too.'

'You had the moth's jacket too?'

'Yeah, Percy. We had that too.'

'Not secret, though.'

'No. Not secret.'

They didn't speak for a while, and Wilfred lay back on the cold sand and put his hat over his face. Something about the Moth Men had disturbed him. Made him melancholy. Percy settled down for the night.

Wilfred's eyes were open, peering into the pitch-black bowl of the crown of his hat. Insects clicked around him. He felt the cold coming off the water, creeping over the rough river sand and chilling the right side of his body, away from the fire. The river's like a life, his father told him. Birth to death. Plenty of twists and turns in between. Shallow parts, swift drops, deep holes. One minute it's as wide as the world, and the next it's squeezed through narrow passageways. Slow. Steady. Fast. You'll see, one day.

He thought of the story Percy had told him. Had Mr Schweigestill known about the Moth Men? He couldn't have. A big Kraut, tall and skinny and half blind and white as a lily. But somehow they were connected. The blackfellas and their sacred ceremony, the caterpillar and eggs and chrysalis and moth. Probably been doing it for hundreds of years, he thought. Thousands even. Then *The Trout Opera*, less than twenty years ago. Were there Ant Men in the Amazon who had the same ceremonies? Butterfly Men in Africa? It was Jesus's story too. The baby in the manger and the death on the cross. And the river – the source, the twisting and turning through the mountains, and the push into the sea at Orbost.

Maybe Mr Schweigestill hadn't been that stupid after all.

Wilfred remembered the night like it was a fairytale someone had told him a long time ago. Moments were in focus and others not. He saw the old judges on the verandah of the Buckley's, and the great spheres of their bellies beneath vests and watch chains. He could hear the crying children dressed as bulrushes on the dray, and see the little curling willy-willys of dust from the rear wheels. He remembered the necklace of electric bulbs on the Imperial Hall and how pretty they looked from the bridge, and the racket of the steam generator.

Then he was inside the hall, standing beside Maggie Corcoran, and Mr Schweigestill was just a black stick insect behind the side curtain, his face distorted with nerves and anxiety. He recalled the smell of sweet toilet water coming off Maggie, because it was the same as her mother wore and he was familiar with it from the local store and at the cake table at the show.

But most of all he recalled the whole town in the audience, and as he grew older that view from the stage was no longer a living thing in his memory, a hive of coughs and murmurs and giggles, of big and small heads and different-shaped hats as exotic as assorted flowers, of tweed and cotton and silk, of beards and clean chins and small and large ears and grey and auburn and blonde hair. It froze. It froze into a photograph. And he could look at that photograph now, and see his whole life.

There was little Astrid, kneeling on the bare boards at the front of the stage, her hands clasped tightly, just as they would be one day in the kitchen of the house before the broken china cup. There was Dorothea in there, somewhere. There was his father, his jacket too tight for his shoulders, his arms too short to be folded, the whole of him bunched up and straining against himself, proud as punch, a lifetime of fishing and grand-children ahead of him. The Cranks were there, standing along the back wall, too good and too rich to sit with the ordinary folk, agitated, there to take a look at what the town was up to, chewing together, as if to say we have better things to do than to be here. Outside, out of the photograph, down a grassy stretch to the willows, was the old river. It was his whole future in that picture, too.

Maybe, somewhere in a jungle on the other side of the world, people were dancing as caterpillar and chrysalis and moth. Maybe, in a small amphitheatre of bamboo in Asia, the ceremony was being performed. Maybe it was daytime there, and night here, and dawn somewhere else, and thousands of these rituals were being played out in different light, as the earth spun round against the never-ending wash of the universe.

Before he realised what he was doing, Wilfred reached out and gripped a handful of pebbly sand as if to hold himself down. Percy snored on the other side of the fire. It was comforting to hear Percy snuffling in his sleep.

'Your sister, she'll come back, like the moth,' he told Wilfred.

But Wilfred had been to the station at Cooma, and just seeing the railway tracks extending forever filled him with loss and dread.

His mother continued to work cleaning the pub and the police station and the lockup and the Star of the Sea church on the hill, her days a cosmos of suds. The family was down to two, and the house was not bigger with the absences, but even more crowded, filled to the corrugated tin roof and earthen floor with everything they didn't say and everything they worked to avoid.

It all felt changed after they'd buried Spud in the Bolocco Cemetery, when the last post was played and echoed across the plains and drew querulous looks from the trembling sheep. Spud made the war real. His hat on the hook in the pub was a sphere of hope until they brought his casket home. Then no one wanted to touch it, and it stayed there, misshapen, a cursed totem of the future.

Dalgety had been brought into the wider world, and the weight of that unexpectedly pressed down on all of them. When the dead Australians came back, or remained on foreign fields, irretrievable, then the grief descended over the High Country and the Monaro via a gossamer web of connections – friends of friends, cousins, acquaintances – to the dead.

That was when Astrid disappeared. That was when Wilfred took a whip to Tom Crank and held a rifle under his weak chin. That was when he moved out from under the debt he always felt he owed the Cranks. There were no repercussions. Old man Crank never mentioned it. Tom kept to himself. The town knew, though, and Tom had to move away. Crank thought he owned Dalgety. Only when Wilfred put the muzzle of the gun under his son's chin did he understand the town would operate anyway, with or without him.

Wilfred had half thought of heading to Canberra to work on the construction of Parliament House. He knew a few blokes who'd ridden up on spec. He reasoned that any man from Dalgety who asked for a job on Parliament House would get it, just beaten by a whisker for the site of the federal capital as they were. He still had one of the original surveyor's pegs in the backyard behind the shed.

Astrid's disappearance put paid to that. That event opened the earth beneath him. He had seen this many times across the valley. Cracks and subsidence. He could not know that it would continue opening through his life, this maw, and keep him company.

Unless, of course, he found her. He knew, from the war, that people didn't come home. He felt like that about his sister. That she was some sort of casualty of the war.

He hoped she'd just turn up in the main street one day, in one of the motor cars they were seeing more and more of these days. You could hear them a mile off, coughing and lurching over the cart ruts, and they had a devil of a time getting across the bridge.

They were as fast as the river, and the river had always been the measure of pace and time in Dalgety, and to see the motor cars hurtling along and kicking out barrels of dust was not natural and made little sense and the men at the pub shook their heads at the puzzle of it. They figured the motor cars had something to do with the war, and they didn't trust them.

But Wilfred knew the cars would bring people down from Canberra. The Parliament House people. Even from Sydney. And those people would need a fishing guide. He was putting together the rickety architecture of his future.

He lifted his hat off his face and sat up. He saw, beyond the camp, the white flares on the horses' heads. Something broke the surface of the water. The coals in the fire shifted. Percy was curled up and no longer snoring. His knees were all bunched up and he held his head like he was protecting it from an explosion. All tight and snug in his old jacket. In his chrysalis.

Maybe she will come back, like the moths, Wilfred thought. If I built a fire big enough, she might see it from wherever she is. If I set the Alps on fire, surely she'd see it and fly home.

He eased some twigs onto the coals and watched them flare.

Astrid was a different sort of insect, though. She didn't move with the swarm. She had to be traced, and caught.

He lay back down and again put the hat on his face. Why didn't you tell me? he asked his father. That I'd reach the rapids so soon?

FORTY-ONE

'SHE JUST CLOSED her eyes and was gone,' the matron said. 'It was like someone blew out a candle. That's the way it is sometimes, if you're lucky.'

Aurora stood with Matron Pearce in the doorway of the room where her grandmother, Astrid, had died. The room had at the far end a window, two bedside tables, two lamps, two chairs, two water jugs and glasses, and two beds. There was a woman dozing in one.

'That was hers.' The matron pointed to the empty bed. Its sheet and coverlet were pulled tight as a drum skin. On the side table was a plastic jug of water, a cup, a small vase of plastic flowers, and a Bible. 'Number twelve. That's Mrs Dunleavy's now.'

The woman in the other bed was no bigger than a child, and had the blanket tucked beneath her chin.

'It's all right, dear,' the matron said, turning to Aurora. 'Not nice to talk about d-e-a-t-h in front of them. Let's go back to my office.'

Aurora followed her through the maze of the nursing home, caught in the slipstream of her overpowering fragrance. They passed down corridors that opened into little square sitting rooms then funnelled back into corridors. At the entrance to each corridor was a brass nameplate – BANKSIA WING, WATTLE WING, EUCALYPTUS WING – and each arm off the hubs of sitting rooms was decorated in different colours, the walls ochre and aqua and yellow, the carpets navy and burgundy and grey. From above, the layout would have appeared as a rudimentary system of cogs and levers. A piece of farm machinery drawn by a child. Designed for death.

On the walls were framed watercolour and pencil-sketch prints of botanical specimens, parrots, daffodils, seascapes, outback scenes, Depression-era terraces, old-fashioned general stores, sandstone banks, children rolling hoops, women hanging out washing on props. It was an attempt to make the place Olde Worlde, to position the residents in former lives, when they were a functioning part of society. The terrace houses. The hoops. The butter churns and laundry coppers. But these fragments on the walls were as meaningless as photographs of other people's children, and couldn't disguise the business of the place, which was dying and death, nor could they distract from the parade of needles, oxygen tanks, bedpans, drips and heart monitors, ferried ceaselessly past the cheap frames.

Aurora followed Matron Pearce, and the woman's perfume fought and wrestled with the scent of antiseptic and urine and boiled vegetables and shit and the sourness of old skin that waited at the open doorways they passed.

In Matron Pearce's office you could just see through the wide window the tip of Sydney's Centrepoint Tower above a line of fig trees.

'I understand you want to speak with Mrs Cave,' the matron said, easing into her seat behind the desk.

'I'm told she was my grandmother's room mate. Before she died.'

'Can I be honest? I don't see much point in speaking with her.'

Aurora had shaken the matron's hand when they first met and the perfume still clung to her fingers and palm. In the office, it caught at the back of her throat. Hours later, Aurora would still be tasting it.

'It's a family matter,' Aurora said.

Matron Pearce patted a folder on her desk. 'Your grandmother, Astrid. She had Alzheimer's, as you might know, for some time. And her records indicate probably years of undiagnosed postnatal depression. If this is a legal matter . . .'

'It's personal.'

Matron Pearce leaned back in the chair and looked up to the far corner of the room, as if there were imaginary faces there, and behind the faces the files of the men and women who had been shunted through her machine.

'She was a dear thing,' the matron said. 'She meant well. It happens that way, time and again, in my experience. The softening. The surrender. She was tough, yes, but a lamb at heart. An innocent little girl, when the time came.'

The speech had the airless monotone of one that had been recited many times before. Aurora studied the matron's meticulously set short hair – burnt orange, and trained to a neat seam that ran down the centre of the back of her head. She wore no rings, no watch or bracelets, just a large single pearl on a gold chain that sat against her navy jacket like a small frosted light globe. She was trim, compact, and moved incessantly with nervous energy.

'You were there, then,' Aurora said. 'At the time of death.'

'No, I wasn't.'

'Then how did you know what she was like when she died?'

Matron Pearce's face shifted into a broad smile that exposed a neat line of small discoloured teeth. The change was so sudden you could almost hear it click. She was used to speaking to people like they were children, and was not accustomed to being questioned or contradicted.

'It was reported to me by Sister Williams, who was present.' She cradled her hands. 'Be that as it may, death can be routine, dear, just like most other things.'

'You understood she had a daughter, then.'

'I don't see your point.'

'I suppose there was morphine involved, for the pain.'

'Of course.'

'Then who gave permission for the morphine?'

'My dear girl, her physician had authority.' The smile had flagged, held up tenuously by the net of wrinkles beneath her heavy make-up. 'I don't see how these questions are serving any purpose. With respect, you're a little young to understand. My supposition is you've received some conflicting news about your grandmother which you seek to resolve. Her death is not the answer. You're looking in the wrong place for what you need.'

The matron was right. Aurora was trying to fill in the grey areas all at once. The nursing home was her first port of call because at least, here, something was fixed. Astrid's death was on the map, at precise coordinates, marked by a black-headed pin. She had to work back from the pin. There was nothing beyond it.

'What I'm saying to you is that the information you receive may not be . . . wholly reliable, if you understand me.'

'I understand,' Aurora said. She understood, too, what unnerved her about Matron Pearce. The woman rarely blinked.

'Good,' the matron said, standing again, her hand outstretched. 'It is not for me to lecture you. You have your reasons.' They shook. The queer rose smell was nauseating. 'You are not the first and won't be the last.'

She clucked her tongue as she steered Aurora to the door. 'Family puzzles. We look to solve them after death, only to find, more often than not, that they are unsolvable. Nurse Levett will take you to Mrs Cave.'

They found the old woman in the garden at the back of the nursing home. She sat alone on a bench seat. An elaborate silver walker stood in front of her. Mrs Cave wore a dark brown wig of large, lopsided curls. The whole set of her face was off-centre. It could have been the wig tilting everything, or something in the old woman's face, an incident, an accident from the past, long healed. Her mouth was a wound of crumbed lipstick.

'Mrs Cave,' the nurse said. 'Mrs Cave.'

The old woman stared at Aurora.

'This lady's here to see you about Mrs Crane.'

'Who?'

'Mrs *Crane*. You remember Mrs Crane?'

'Mrs Crane.'

'That's right. I'll leave you to it.' The nurse went inside.

Aurora pulled up a small fold-out chair.

'Mrs Cave? I'm Mrs Crane's granddaughter. You were her room mate.'

'Mrs Crane.'

'Astrid. Her name was Astrid.'

The old woman smiled. 'Oh, Astrid.'

'That's right.'

'She was a lovely dancer. Always dancing.'

'That's right, Mrs Cave.'

'Dancing, yes. Poor Mrs Crane.'

'She died.'

'All alone. She was from the mountains. She lived there for years with her husband. Yes. He passed away a long time ago. They lived in the mountains.'

'They did?'

'Wilfred. Her husband Wilfred. They lived in the mountains. There was a picture of him next to her bed. They had a farm.'

'I don't think so, Mrs Cave.'

'The farm was in the mountains. It was . . .' The old woman's mouth contorted with the effort of memory. She spoke silently to herself. Then nodded. 'I think it was Dalgety. They had a farm in the mountains, at Dalgety.'

Mrs Cave looked across the yard to the mandarin tree in the corner. Small, inedible balls of fruit hidden through the dark foliage.

'I think that was her brother.'

'They had no children,' Mrs Cave said. 'So poor Mrs Crane died alone.'

Beneath the mandarin tree was a circle of bare earth almost the precise circumference of the overhead foliage. It had been raked and cleared of fallen fruit and leaves. If you glanced at the tree, or stared into it long enough, the circle of dirt became one with the tree, a part of its dark mass. And the globes of rough-skinned mandarins, the crescents and triangles of them just visible through the scissor leaves, teased like memories.

'She was calling for her husband – Wilfred – behind the curtain. It was like a song. *Wil*-fred. *Wil*-fred. Then poor Mrs Crane passed away.'

That afternoon, Aurora talked to several other men and women at the nursing home. A Mr Jenkins sat with her in the music room and remembered the dancing Mrs Crane. He nodded, repeatedly, towards a small upright piano by the windows. The sunlight through the glass caught the rich burgundy flame in the wood of the closed lid.

She had been some sort of professional dancer when she was younger, Mr Jenkins said. Could dance to anything. Foxtrot. Tango. Waltz.

'I think she was famous once,' he said. 'With Mo McCackie and that mob at Her Majesty's. I saw them once with the big pool and the seals. Marvellous. I think Mrs Crane was with that lot.'

A Mrs Bird said old Mrs Crane was 'the one who always went missing'.

'Never had a visitor far as I knew,' the woman said, chewing constantly on nothing. She wore a large straw gardening hat, and fidgeted, bent over in her seat, as if shelling peas into a colander. 'I never spoke to her. She was in Wattle, wasn't she? I think she was in Wattle. I've always been in Eucalyptus. But she'd cause a ruckus. Few times they had to get the police. She liked to wander, you know? She was a wandering type. I saw her dancing around in the courtyard one night in her nightdress, no shoes. There were all sorts of drama when they tried to bring her in. Said she wanted to dance in the snow. Snow. That's a funny thing to say, isn't it?'

Later, in her room in the motor inn at Elizabeth Bay, Aurora lay on the bed with her hands as a pillow and tried to make sense of the testimonies of the old people in the home.

She fell asleep and when she woke it was dusk. She didn't know where she was for a moment, and through the half-open window of the kitchenette she heard a long, loping line of bird call, and it reefed her out of her fug and she stood giddily in the darkening room. From the kitchenette window she could see her old block of units, the flat she had abandoned when she fled north, and the neat rows of windows.

She wondered who was in her flat now. What they'd done with her boxes of meagre possessions. There was nothing she regretted leaving behind. She tried not to think of the child's blanket with the prancing white horses, stained here and there with the soil of Adaminaby. Then she remembered. She didn't have the blanket. She'd buried the child in it.

A bit later she sat in the dark on her small balcony.

She debated whether to leave her room and go down to the street. With her father's money she had arrived in Sydney by plane and taken a taxi to the nursing home in Rozelle and another cab to the motor inn near the Cross, which was familiar at least, its alleys and court-yards and darkened porticos known to her. But since she'd returned, her feet had barely touched the city streets. She knew how easy it would be to step into that orange pool of light and disappear.

After five weeks attending the clinic in Tweed Heads she felt strong enough to return to Sydney to tie up loose ends. The counsellors told her to expect a sequence of challenges, and that resistance to one would lead to the next, until she was free. Stand in the centre of a challenge, they said, and if you can survive that, you'll be strong enough for another. It was the lot of the addict. A willingness to face self-destruction, already there, embedded, even before the drugs came along.

One girl at the clinic had said to her, 'You got to put your head in the lion's mouth.'

She didn't share with them something she'd learned on her own. A greater need eliminated a lesser one. Aurora was tired of being a prisoner in her father's house. She hid from the police. And periodically cars containing men in business shirts and ties, with jackets swaying off hooks in the back seat, slowed and cruised past the yard. Her greater need now was to settle this business of Astrid and Wilfred on her own terms. She found, in her new clarity, that logical paths opened before her in her mind. That she could make firm decisions and reason her decisions several steps ahead. She thought in ways she never had. As an adult.

So she found herself back in the lion's mouth, in Sydney, and at about 10.30 pm on that first night she rang Tick. She'd avoided the rash of messages he'd left on her mobile phone when she'd fled north.

But she needed to show him she had changed her life. She needed to show herself.

Within forty-five minutes she was at the door to his flat round the corner off Billyard Avenue. The moon was back in its familiar slingshot orbit.

'Darling!' he said.

A wave of Tiger Balm and incense hit her at the door. He looked as small as a child in cheesecloth pants and a singlet. He opened his arms and they hugged awkwardly. His head was shaved. He was skeletal and in the dim light of the hall she was not sure what she was seeing – a man who'd obsessively driven himself beyond fitness and into dangerous vanity, or a man close to death.

'Sit, sit,' he said, waving her to a couch. She settled in the light of a lamp with three cast-iron trout forming the base. 'A drink,' he said, patting her knee, and disappeared into the kitchenette.

Schubert was playing at low volume on his stereo.

'*Sooo* much to catch up on,' he called, returning with a bottle of chilled wine and two delicate brandy glasses on a tray. 'What an unexpected treat.'

He poured the wine into the thimble glasses and sat in an armchair opposite her.

'I only hope you've come for a skerrick of my company, and not the other,' he said, raising the glass in a toast.

She sipped. 'I'm off it. Clean.'

'Good for you.'

'I'm serious.'

'You could run a pack of hounds through here, darling, and they'd turn up nothing. To put it your way, I'm off it too.' He tried to plug a dry cough with a bandana he held permanently scrunched in his left hand. 'Both of us. A clean start. Except for my trailer load of pharmaceuticals – all prescription, of course. You've caught me on a good day. As the surfies might say, I'm atop a thundering barrel.'

'Yes.'

'Well, well, well,' he said, clucking like a hen. 'I thought I'd never see you again, to be honest. I came up with two scenarios – you'd taken a little vacation, or were in the clutches of that horrid beau of yours. What was his name?'

'It doesn't matter,' she said.

'But Harold was convinced you'd be back. It's the taxi driver in him, darling. The eternal hope of a return fare.'

'I'm just visiting,' she said. 'I'm using you actually, as a test. Part of my recovery.'

He smiled kindly and leaned forward in the chair. 'Now that's interesting, because now that you're back, I have every intention of using you too.'

'Is that so?'

'As part of *my* recovery.'

She didn't understand. They stared at each other across the short space between the chairs. The room was a crowded grotto of knick-knacks, paintings, wall hangings, drinks trolleys, antique cabinets, ornaments and books. On the long window ledge that looked out over

Billyard Avenue were hundreds of small medicine bottles, an amber forest of them.

In the dim light of the apartment his head looked like a skull. There was no illusion. He was dying. His eyes were huge, his cheeks sunken. And there was something different to the set of his mouth. It was no longer his mouth.

'A friend of mine in the dental trade made these delicious falsies for me – see, top and bottom at the front.' He partially removed each set as proof. 'But I'm still here, Aurora. I have left the best doctors and specialists scratching their heads. I am what they call a medical *marvel*.'

'I didn't mean to be cruel, before. About the test.'

'My darling prodigal sister,' he said. 'I understand precisely why you rang and it has nothing to do with tests or being polite or wanting a good old-fashioned catch-up. You had to touch a bit of your past, to see if it was real. It's a seminal part of recovery. Not a step from your clinic manual, but real. There is nothing you have to explain to me. This bushwalk? I've done every trail. Backwards.'

He sipped the wine with an extended pinkie finger, and crossed his thin legs.

'You're not dealing? Honestly?' she asked.

'Nope. Struggling by on the pension. I'm a pensioner. The bainmarie of life is open to me, at a discount.'

'You're not bullshitting?'

'This city. It has become impossible for the industri-ous solo trader. For the small businessman, no matter how enterprising. They build a Woolworths, and your friendly neighbourhood butcher goes bankrupt.

Besides, I lost the energy to keep up with who ran what, and who worked for whom. So many toes to be trodden on nowadays.'

He tilted his head back, closed his eyes, and waved his left hand to the cushion scales of Schubert. 'You will notice,' he said, eyes still closed, and smiling, 'how European I have become. My sentiments always lent themselves to that side of the globe.'

She saw as he conducted the music a line of black tattooed spots on the thin flesh of his inside upper arm. The ticks.

'So here I sit,' he continued, 'a medical marvel, fading from the planet.' He hummed a few notes and sat up. 'Still, these old ears are as sharp as a schnauzer's. You have been asked after, you know. Dear Harold, he hauls back snippets of gossip, tales from the street, like a magpie for my pleasure. As my chief scout on the ground I let him loose on your trail, Aurora, concerned as I was for your safety. Harold asked around. Kept his ears open. Dropped you into conversations. Anyway, men have been calling for you. Cops. Harold can pick them a mile off. And another, particularly nasty. One of those *junkies*, darling. I can only presume it's your former beau. And good riddance, by the sounds of it.'

'What do you mean?'

'Vile, Harold described him as. His behaviour has been noted up and down Darlinghurst Road, and that's saying something. I don't need to tell you that side of the Cross is a community too, darling, with its own standards, as louche as they may be.'

She drained her wine, poured another and toyed with the stem of the glass. She felt sick in the stomach at the thought of Wynter. She had naively presumed, having expunged one side of her life, the side involving him, that he too would disappear. But she was not free yet. She realised miserably she was a long way from free.

Tick seemed to read her thoughts. He smiled broadly and his new teeth glowed. 'Just as well you're as safe as a church mouse with Tick and Harold around, hmm? So. What can the new, improved me do for the new, improved you?'

She explained long into the evening the story of her return to Murwillumbah, her mother's death, the grand-mother Astrid and the missing great-uncle Wilfred of Dalgety.

After, Tick sat with his hands in his lap in lengthy contemplation. She thought he'd fallen asleep. He stood and relit the little candles on his Buddha shrine on the side table. He returned to the chair and his hollow face creased up with a huge smile.

'Did you know when I was a child I pined to be a detective?'

She was a bit drunk. 'Who doesn't?'

'A Hardy boy. And you? A Nancy Drew?'

'Who's Nancy Drew?'

'Never mind. Anyway, those boys, the Hardys, taught me one valuable thing.'

'And what's that?'

'Always start at the source, dear girl, and work your way out from there.' He held his forefinger up in the candlelight. 'Your lost uncle Wilbur . . .'

'Wilfred.'

'You say he's from Dalgety.'

'Dalgety.'

'Then wouldn't any good and decent detective begin there? The source?'

She giggled and closed her eyes. 'That would make sense, Nancy.'

'Dalgety it is, then.'

'Dalgety it is.'

'Just one question,' he said, settling comfortably into the chair. 'Where the hell is Dalgety?'

FORTY-TWO

WITHIN VIEW OF the Hotel Kosciusko, Wilfred stopped the horse on the Jindabyne Road and could feel her rapid heartbeat through his legs. He had pushed her hard up the range and there were faint tide lines of sweat on both sides of her neck.

He dismounted and stood with the heavy-breathing horse. The air was cool and thin. Behind the hotel stretched the Grand Slam ski run, and he saw toboggans being worked across odd-shaped drifts of snow up the side of the mountain.

It was inconceivable to him that folk would drive their motor cars all the way from Sydney to come play on the shrinking snow patches. But a lot had changed in the seven years since the war ended. He heard that at night they dressed up in expensive gowns and black suits and bow ties and danced in the dining hall to the latest music. That they drank wines and liquors into the early hours of the morning and had snowball fights in the dark and later dried out in front of the hotel's huge stone and tile fireplaces. These were the stories that came to him down in Dalgety, like the pieces of wood that the Snowy carried under the bridge in the spring thaw.

Sitting by the lake, Wilfred suddenly felt a cold stone in the pit of his stomach. The letter from Dorothea was warm in his jacket pocket. On the ride up, he'd tap his left breast just to hear the paper crackle. He swivelled on the bench, turned his back on the hotel and retrieved the letter to reread the few short sentences, the neat black ink on paper bordered with cornflowers.

He'd committed them to memory. Could have closed his eyes and described everything else about the letter – the geography of the single sheet with its pulp flecks and ink splashes. The hint of a thumbprint. He marvelled that the heel of her hand had brushed back and forth across the paper.

The letter was soiled with dust and soot from his own hands. He had carried it everywhere for twenty-three days, since he'd picked it up from the Buckley's. He'd read it there and then, on the verandah at dusk, and after had to go back inside and ask Mitchell the exact date. She'd suggested they meet at the Hotel Kosciusko for 'morning tea' on the seventeenth of the next month. He had no calendar. After the letter, he'd strike the days in pencil on the door of the shed, and count the inch-long lines each morning and evening.

As the strokes began to build across the door, a little crooked fence, he experienced a raft of new emotions that wobbled within him like the ever-shifting shapes of the spring snow patches. He had not seen her since he was a teenager, during the war. Yet she was with him each day. He might be riding, or sitting by the river with a line out, or lying in bed after a day's shearing, and he'd see her in his mind. The small Dorothea disappearing into a flurry of snow powder. And later, at the carnival, the young lady Dorothea with cream gloves. The fresh and beautiful Dorothea, turning her face to him in front of the dry and wrinkled hide of the elephant that day at the circus in Cooma. Or the Dorothea he imagined now, wearing an outfit drawn from the hats and dresses and shoes he'd seen on young women who'd passed fleetingly through Dalgety in their open-topped motor cars, or the pages of his mother's old magazines.

He had hoped he might spot her one day as one of those ladies in the motor cars. But they flitted in and out of town, year after year, in dresses and skirts with hems of varying lengths, and hair that seemed to change and shift in never-ending modes of cut and style, loose as clouds, and she never came.

Then the letter. Stuck on the board inside the pub doors beside the handwritten results of the last Dalgety race meet, a faded and curled newspaper clipping on the results of the selection for the national capital, and half a dozen old flies hooked into the cork, wizened as wasp carcasses.

On the bench by the lake he felt the eyes of the entire valley were upon him.

He felt overheated in his borrowed jacket. It was too tight on the shoulders and across the chest. He was unused to the scratchy tweed. It had vexed him, the equation of the hotel and the 'morning tea'. The protocols. They were something he never had to think about. Only two evenings before the final pencil stroke for their meeting day the problem hit him. He was too embarrassed to ask his mother, so had quietly sought the help of Mrs Mitchell, and she had produced the coat – a forgotten remnant left by a guest at the hotel – and a pair of her husband's leather lace-up shoes.

In the shed out the back he had modelled the outfit, and was relieved. He woke early the following morning and took breakfast with his mother at the small wooden table. Through the window in the kitchen the world was still etching itself out in the blue light. Dressed in his customary dungarees he kissed his mother farewell, and slipped into the shed and the borrowed clothes. He took off cross-country through the back paddocks, past the charred and collapsed frame of Uncle Berty's shed, and into the thin tree line, before tracking back to the road to Jindabyne. It was an awkward ride from the outset. He couldn't strike a rhythm with the animal, banging his tailbone on the saddle, his feet slipping in the stirrups. It felt like he'd never ridden a horse before. He blamed the clothes.

Things returned to normal on the ascent, but sitting by the lake in the orbit of the fancy hotel and the gleaming cars and the neat industry of maids and gardeners and ski attendants and porters, the jacket again was maddeningly tight, and the shoes chafed his heels, and he found it awkward to walk.

He had run through their conversation, over and over, and he had a surprise. An offering. He was set to become a professional fishing guide. Since the letter, he'd set up a string of rudimentary camps south of the town. He'd hacked down tea trees and bulrushes and hauled river stones for the fireplaces up to the flattened grass. Each camp was less than half a day's ride to the other. He'd chosen different parts of the river to give variety to the camps. One was in the shelter of a wall of granite, where the fat edge of the river was quiet and the surface smooth as glass. Another was surrounded by thick tussocks on a flat, shallow stretch of the Snowy where the water rippled and bubbled against a jagged plate of granite.

They were chosen, too, with a mind to the different types of fishing his father had taught him. If he was going to be a successful fishing guide, he had to give his customers their money's worth – rapids, deep holes, flat stretches of warm water, gentle stream.

He had pinned a handwritten advertisement to the board in the Buckley's Crossing Hotel. *Wilfred Lampe. Fishing Guide.* But there were no reciprocal queries left for him at the hotel. No cards of introduction.

His fingers were still sore from hand-stitching the special saddlebags and tying hundreds of flies in advance of his business venture. The stitching and the tying took his mind off Astrid, still with him, however fleeting, each day, despite being gone for years.

Wilfred knew by the position of the sun he was early for their meeting. He'd ridden frantically and, even though he'd stopped, the many rehearsed moments in his mind rolled and tumbled still with the momentum of the ride.

He wondered why he had not told his mother about the meeting. She could have helped him with his problematic attire. Offered advice and suggestions on what to expect in the hotel. Shared her knowledge on the thoughts and actions of young ladies. But deep down he knew the answer. It was because of his missing sister, Astrid. He was meeting a woman the same age as Astrid would have been. A woman taking her first formal steps into the adult world, living that brilliant cornucopia of rites of passage – the attention to appearance, the touches and glances from the opposite sex, the manners and rituals. As Astrid might have experienced. Behind Wilfred's single meeting was the weight of all those incremental moments that had been stolen away from his sister. She may be living them. They both silently thought that, mother and son. In a parallel existence. In the city. In another country town. They only nursed the notion because the alternative was that she was dead. As the months and years rolled on, though, the life they imagined for her became harder to see. Death, though, was never obscured.

There were plenty of young women in the district. Women Wilfred had known from school. Cousins of families on the Monaro visiting from the other side of the world. Cartloads of them brought in for the annual races or the Peach Blossom Ball, as delicate and bright as pallets of flowers. And still he looked at them from a safe distance, and did nothing.

He clung, though, to his memories of Dorothea. They'd only met a few times. The encounters years apart. Still he marvelled at her transformation. Thrilled at her life cycle, as he would that of a butterfly. And the time between each stage felt like nothing. Passed as clearly and instantly as the shooting stars. He was still that boy who gaped at the Milky Way. The boy on the side of the riverbank opposite to where life happened.

He didn't know what it was that he felt. He knew that machinery worked or it didn't. If it broke down, you fixed it. He knew the texture of timber. The sound a bullet makes when it strikes a rabbit, or penetrates the skull of a horse or cow with a broken leg or a sickness.

He knew the noise a sheep made when you cut its throat. The feel of trout skin. The whimper of his mother at night.

He knew all these things. Love, though? He knew family love. It was just there, inside you. But how he felt for Dorothea . . . It was shapeless. You couldn't take it in your hands. You couldn't smell it on a breeze. All he knew now was that he had to go around the lake, and hitch the horse, and walk under the hotel's stone entrance, shaped like the old-fashioned plough yoke of a beast of burden, and meet Dorothea for morning tea.

The round-edged stone in his gut was more real than anything.

He walked the horse towards the hotel in his ill-fitting shoes. The hotel sat heavily on a low, treeless hill, and Wilfred didn't take his eyes off the main building, as if stalking an adversary. It looked out of place. Years after the grand opening and still it hadn't settled into the landscape, this place of sharp-angled roof gables and rectangular window frames, themselves divided into smaller squares of glass panes. It was designed out of a city head, thrown down amongst the ancient rocks and herb shrubs. It didn't belong. Never would. It couldn't survive. The mountains, they wore things, and people, down.

Coming in on the arched road, he saw what looked like stable houses and several empty sulkies at the rear. He secured the horse, straightened his jacket, adjusted his hat, and walked around to the hotel entrance.

He was startled by the sudden laughter of three people sitting on the deep-set balcony. His attention fixed on the stone entrance, he had failed to notice them

512

in the shadows. One managed a 'Good morning' at the tail end of a laugh, and he nodded.

He passed an empty motor car with its engine idling. Under the stone arch he almost collided with a young man in a white shirt and jacket struggling with armfuls of suitcases. The man dropped a hat box and Wilfred retrieved it.

'Thanks,' the man said, sighing.

Wilfred stood with a strange woman's hat box.

'Over there, if you could,' the man said, nodding towards the car, and Wilfred went with him to the vehicle's luggage rack.

'Thanks, mate,' the man said. 'She's not damaged, is she?' He turned the hat box over. 'Me wages if she is.' Satisfied, he put the box in the car.

'You here for the job?' he asked Wilfred.

'No.'

'What can I do you for?' The man clapped imaginary dirt from his hands. He had no trained manners and drilled niceties for Wilfred. They were of the same station and nothing was required for that understanding.

'I'm here to see one of your guests.'

'Who might that be, mate?'

'A Miss Dorothea . . .'

'Oh, Miss *Dorothea*,' he said. Almost sang. He winked. 'I know for a fack she just come back from a spot of skiing. Here, come with me. You can wait in the reading room.'

He followed the short, oil-haired man and was grateful for it. He had an accidental guide into the hotel, and a place to wait, and a myriad of awkward encounters, in his mind's rehearsals, had been avoided.

They passed along the edge of a dining room crowded with rectangular and oval tables, and into the reading room. It was dark, except for diffused light through two oval windows on either side of the fireplace. He could have been on a ship. The room was divided into two sections: the first had studded leather couches on each side and a small writing desk in the centre; the second, closer to the fireplace, was filled with long-armed squatter's chairs and a couple of round side tables. Underfoot were giant patterned rugs.

'You make yourself at home and I'll let the princess know you're here, righteo?'

The young man winked again and produced a double click out the side of his mouth. Wilfred dropped too quickly into a deep squatter's chair near the fire and had to pull himself up. The fire was small and fresh, and he detected the familiar scent of burning snow gum branches. It reminded him of nights in the High Country with his father and the fishing trips with Percy.

As he waited he heard footsteps overhead and the weight of people shifting the floorboards. He wondered, for a moment, if it was Dorothea against the shellacked hardwood, and he looked up, just as someone issued a light cough at the end of the room.

He struggled to escape from the squatter's chair and stood, a trouser cuff caught in a sock. It was the oily young man and, beside him, Dorothea. The man extended a theatrical hand, presenting her to Wilfred. She was a half-foot taller than her chaperon, and was biting her lip against laughter.

'Excuse me, sir,' the young man said, his voice completely changed now, as polished as the fender on the car in the drive. 'Miss Dorothea Chauvere.'

The valet stood to attention, turned, and left the room. She smiled broadly and strode towards him across the rug.

'It's wonderful to see you,' she said. He extended a hand but she gathered it up and held it.

She had come fresh off the snow and wore jodhpur skiing trousers and a cream heavy-corded jumper and matching scarf. A small brace of blonde curls showed beneath the line of her short-brimmed bell hat. Her cheeks were ruddy.

'Let's go straight to tea,' she said. 'I'm famished.'

She led him by the hand into the dining room to a small round table close to the fire. She pulled out her own chair and sat before the waiter could reach her.

'Wilfred, sit by me,' Dorothea said. She lifted a serviette from a drinking glass and placed it on her lap. 'Tea, please,' she said to the waiter. 'And the scones. Thank you.'

Other groups were wandering into the long room with its heavily beamed ceiling and serviette blooms. Music was being played somewhere. It was as if, by her presence, the whole place came to life. That was how he saw it.

'Dear Wilfred,' she said, pinching his wrist. 'I have to be sure it's really you.'

'It's me,' was all he could think to say.

'I wasn't sure if you'd got my note. Or had the time to come up here. I know how busy it can get on the land, this time of year. It's terribly sweet of you to take the time.'

He had learned a lot about time in the past

twenty-three days. How stubborn it can be, when you want it to fly. And now the opposite.

'I've so much to tell you,' she went on. 'How long has it been? You look wonderful. You never change. You are one of the only things I can rely on in that regard, Mr Lampe.'

He saw the girl in her then. But things had quickened about her, the way her eyes took in each movement in the room, the arrangement of the table, his old second-hand jacket too short at the sleeves, and the flow of words. It was not unpleasant to him. Nothing could have been. But it was a manner used to things at a faster pace, and here, exposed in the thin and drowsy air of the Alps, against the invisible thaw of ice and snow, it seemed even more urgent. They said you picked up an accent if you lived long enough in another place, and the same was probably true about the speed of life.

He, though, moved at the same setting of the metronome.

'It was a surprise,' he finally said. 'Your note.'

Was she aware it sat, soiled and damaged, in a pocket behind a thin layer of cloth, between them?

The waiter brought a large silver teapot and a plate of warm scones on a tray, and two small jugs of cream and milk. He went to pour but she took the handle of the pot. 'Thank you,' she said, filling Wilfred's teacup herself.

He watched her as she poured the tea. The blush of her cheeks had faded. He still thought he saw a trace, on her red lips, of that happiness to see him, of being at that table in the Hotel Kosciusko at that exact moment. She looked up and caught him staring.

'How handsome you've become,' she said. He fiddled with the hem on his napkin.

She prepared the two halves of a scone and placed one on his plate. He knew already that the scone would supplant his memory of the trifle in the High Country when he was on his first muster with his father. Now he would dream of this. Not just the scone, and the raspberry jam, and the fresh cream, but the taste of it as he watched her eat, and the gentle movement of her left temple as she chewed, and the small crumb on her lower lip.

He was grateful for something else on that morning. He was a man of long silences. That was the Monaro, and the mountains. And she was a woman who could fill in those silences. He was satisfied just listening.

'When did we last see each other?' she offered, and coloured in the years. Her father had distinguished himself in the war and they travelled through Europe before settling, for the remainder of her schooling, in Florence. (Where, she said with affection, her father had spent much of his time studying the properties of marble.) On their return to Melbourne he had been encouraged to enter politics, and had won a federal seat. They moved back into the house at Towong, but returned to Melbourne almost immediately because of her father's parliamentary commitments. Now it looked like another move, to the new city of Canberra.

'I am hovering around you, you see,' she said. 'South of the range, and now north.'

They had already visited the capital and inspected the construction of Parliament House.

'A fright,' she told him. 'Like a big wedding cake in the middle of nowhere. Men crawling over it like ants.'

She picked scone crumbs off the plate with her left index finger.

Now, she just wanted to get back to Towong, with its view of the southern escarpment of the Alps. She had skied all over Europe, and still she missed her own mountains. They were, she said, the mountains that would always be inside of her. She flattened a gloved hand across her breasts.

'I'm talking too much,' she said, pouring more tea. 'Tell me everything about you, Wilfred.'

It was brighter now in the room, and the staff discreetly prepared tables for lunch. A car horn sounded out on the drive, and a group of men and women carrying tennis racquets moved noisily through the dining room. Two of the men struck at imaginary balls and knocked into a table.

Dorothea did not take her eyes from Wilfred.

'Everything,' he said, 'is much the same.'

'No need to be shy with me, Wilfred.'

He was in the empty wake of her stories of the art of Florence and the skiing in Schruns and lunch with famous politicians and their wives at the Australia Hotel in Sydney. The young, smart people with the racquets had momentarily broken something between them.

Once more she rescued him.

'Tell me of this past winter,' she said, laying a hand on top of his. 'I heard it was a beaut.'

They were still talking as the lunch crowd began filling the room.

'Are you hungry?' she asked.

'Not really.'

'Me neither,' she said, tweaking her nose at the room, dismissing the diners. 'Let's walk by the lake.'

He retrieved his hat and she took his arm. Together

they walked through the centre of the dining room.

'Don't they know it's rude to stare?' she whispered, and held her head higher, exaggerating even more the regal stride of some Italian princess, attached firmly to her tweeded count, and the moment they hit the cool air on the drive they burst into laughter, unable to continue the walk. Dorothea composed herself and again held out her arm to be taken.

'Sir.'

'M'lady,' he said, and they strolled down to the lake. Seeing the mountains, with the air in his lungs and her arm pinned to his ribcage, he felt truly comfortable, at last, and for the second time since he'd known her he was exactly where he wanted to be and could not imagine a greater happiness.

Being outside quelled something in both of them. They walked silently. Things were real again. They circled the lake, and sat on the same bench where Wilfred had agonised several hours before. She took his hand and held it with both of hers as they looked across the lake to the hotel.

She said, finally: 'This is me here, you know. Not over there.'

He did know. He felt the warmth of her through the cream gloves. Cars came and went, clattering and kicking dust. Smoke lifted from two of the hotel's three chimneys. Huge plates of cloud pushed overhead and it grew very cold. Lights came on in several of the hotel windows. He heard her sniffle and turned to see her crying.

'Is everything all right?'

'Yes,' she said. They disengaged hands. He gave her a handkerchief, and she dabbed at her eyes.

'Are you sure?'

'Yes. Let's head back.'

She was chatty on the return walk but he remained perplexed by the tears.

He thought that soon she would be in one of those brilliantly lit rooms. He tried to picture the dresser, and the arrangement of her mirrors and brushes. The dresses in the wardrobe. The luggage trunk on a stand, and the nicks and scuffs the trunk had accrued on its journeys. The latest magazines on her bedside table. The stationery on the writing table, and perhaps the cornflower paper, a piece of which he had in his left jacket pocket.

He knew he'd try and picture all this until his head hurt on the ride back to Dalgety.

At the hotel entrance she stood and looked into his eyes and squeezed his hands. Her eyes were rheumy but he wasn't sure if it was from the cold air tearing up from the lake.

'I'll write again soon,' she said, and embraced him quickly but firmly. He thought he could smell roses.

She walked into the shelter of the stone entrance, and turned. 'Don't forget,' she said.

'Forget what?'

'Your promise. To take me to the source. Remember? The Snowy.' She looked, for a second, to the crushed rocks of the drive, and then was gone.

⌦

On the ride back he saw the mane and ears of the horse and the shapes of trees and lines of fences in his peripheral vision but nothing in detail. By the time he walked the horse up the road to the shack in the valley, small and dark with his mother not yet home, he knew what troubled him. He brought a hand to his face. It smelled of the leather rein and, buried behind that, roses.

That night, in bed, he lost sight of Dorothea. He had carried, in his mind, a clear picture of her face for years, and now, half a day after seeing her in the flesh, after feeling warmth from her actual hands, and hearing her voice, he could summon nothing of her.

He got up and sat on the steps of the verandah and smoked a cigarette. It was a clear night and the river thundered over near the town. He looked to the hills and in the direction of the hotel where she would be, sleeping in a warm room. She was in his part of the world, breathing the same air, and then she'd be gone, and ahead of him were years of familiar paddock and earth fold, fresh-cut lumber and the monotony of sheep.

In the early hours of that morning, the Snowy River sounded unnaturally heavy to him, a great leaden weight pressing down on its bed and the banks and the town and the neighbouring paddocks. It had always sounded like freedom before.

He brought a hand to his face and it was gone, the perfume of the roses. He smelled nothing on his fingers but burnt tobacco.

FORTY-THREE

WYNTER DIDN'T REALLY want to hurt Gino Spina.

He was still half drunk and sliding into that temporary purgatory between fixes when he reached the house in Surry Hills at dusk. He felt sore to his bones. His finger stump ached. To break an arm or crack a kneecap required, at that moment, more energy than he could muster.

He crept into the lane behind the house and stood for an eternity in the empty backyard without a plan. He owed Joe Panozza. He had a job to do.

There was a garden shed to his left, an old chair by the fence to the right. A canopy of grapevines sheltered the rear of the house. The limbs of the bare vines twisted against pale brick.

Wynter broke into the shed and felt around. A light bulb brushed his hair and he flicked at it in a panic. He fumbled at a workbench. Ran his fingers over a vice. There were loose nails, and wood shavings. He found the head of a hammer. Holding it, a familiar feeling came over him.

Could this be his last moment on earth? He tried not to think of it.

In prison he'd thought on and off about death, and the ways of it, and he'd heard many stories, usually embellished, and some not. The body did spectacular things when lured away from its dreary patterns. One time in Goulburn he'd seen a bloke with a knife in his right eye, up to the shaft. His tongue dangled from the corner of his mouth like a cartoon character. And it wasn't the homemade knife you remembered and the pink jelly of the ruptured eyeball, but the funny tongue. As a kid, Wynter had held a kitten underwater and saw its eyes widen beneath the surface and the thin little quivering stamp of its tongue. He just wanted to see how death worked. Again, it was not the drowning of the kitten that occupied him, but the dark, wiry hairs at the base of his own wrist he noticed for the first time, a clutch of them, like a man's, refracted and magnified through the bathwater.

Dead people and dead things weren't frightening. The living were scarier.

Would Spina's old man be in the house, and cause a problem? Maybe if he killed the old man Joe Panozza would hand over a bonus. Maybe the old man already had cancer, and Wynter would be doing the old man a favour, delivering him from this shit hole and his hopeless cunt of a drug addict son, Gino, and this life.

He didn't know the intricate relationships of the Italians, of Panozza and the old man. Perhaps it was some Godfather-style shit where the old man came from the same village as Joe Panozza over on the Boot, and helped Joe Panozza's parents during the war, and the Panozzas owed old man Spina a lifelong debt, and that was why Joe Panozza gave the useless Gino a job, as a favour to old man Spina, and it wasn't the old man's fault that the son was such a lowlife drug-fucked waste of space, and that's why someone like Wynter, from outside the ancient and intertwined vines of family, was brought in to give Gino a bit of a hiding. Nobody would be dishonoured. No branches would be severed. Godfather shit.

He was too tired to think about it anymore.

He broke through the back door and heard a television in the downstairs front room. Fuck it, he thought, as he made his way slowly and quietly up the narrow staircase off the kitchen.

At the top he peered into a small room where a young man was laid out on a dishevelled bed. His mouth was half open in the light from a lamp. Wynter instantly noticed the heroin kit on the table beside the bed. He lowered the hammer, and smiled.

The kid was out of it.

Wynter sat in a chair facing the bed, the hammer across his knees. The steel head of the hammer felt cool in his hands. What am I going to do with you, Gino Spina? He studied the young man's face. Black curls fell over one eye. What a sweet place you're in, and here I am, a few feet away, with a hammer.

'Fuck it,' he said to himself, retrieving Gino's gear. He shot up. Poor Gino. Stupid fucking kid fucked up. We all do, don't we?

Wynter woke in the morning still sitting in the chair.

'Who the fuck are you?' a voice said. It was Gino, standing near the wardrobe at the side of the bed.

'Ginooooo.'

'Who are you?'

Wynter sat up and groaned. 'Be cool, kid. I'm a representative of Eternal Life.'

Gino stared at Wynter. 'You're fucking what?'

'A friend of Joe Panozza,' he said. 'Eternal fucking Life, mate. You got something of theirs, I believe.'

Wynter picked the hammer up from the floor and tapped the steel head in his left palm.

Gino Spina was silent.

'You fucked up, kid. Joe's not happy.'

Gino looked over to the spoon and needle and small black satchel on the floor next to Wynter's chair.

'Help yourself.'

'I did.'

'I can fucking see that.'

'Just hand over the cash, mate, and you'll still be able to walk like normal people, understand?'

Wynter stood. He was shorter than Gino, but you could feel, in the small bedroom, the menace that came off him. Wynter was a junkie, too, but he had the furnace in him. When he wasn't high.

Gino sat on the bed.

'We can do this another way,' he said quietly. He could hear his father snoring downstairs.

'And what way would that be, young Gino scallopino?'

'I got plenty of good gear. You can have it.'

'Yeah.'

'And some cash.'

'How much?'

'About six grand.'

'Six.'

'Yeah.'

'Joe's not happy.'

Gino lowered his head like a chastised child.

'Joe says you failed to grasp what he's trying to do with his fine product. Eternal Life, Gino. Eternal fucking *Life*. How can you mess with that, man?'

'Fuck Joe.'

'Fuck Joe?'

'You heard me,' Gino said.

'You already fucked him. That's why I'm here.'

'How much is he paying you?'

'Enough to put you in a wheelchair.'

'Take the gear. And the cash.'

'Am I fucking getting through to you, Gino?'

'My father'll square it with Joe.'

'Fucking wops. You're always squaring things. Square this. Square that. You're in a fucking *hole*, Gino. Wake up.'

Gino stood and retrieved a carry bag from the top of the wardrobe.

'Always the top of the fucking wardrobe,' Wynter snorted. 'Why is that?'

'Here,' Gino said, pushing it across the bed. 'Take the money.'

Wynter leaned over and opened the flaps of the bag with the head of the hammer.

'Hmm.'

'The gear. Here. It's good stuff.'

'Hmm?'

'First class. Try it. We'll both try it, just to show you.'

Later, Wynter left the house through the back door with the carry bag over his shoulder. The vines, he noticed, were not bare at all, but carried hundreds of small green shoots. They glowed. Wynter stood, transfixed.

'Spring.' It was the old man, sitting in a chair in the sun in the yard.

He startled Wynter.

'Yeah.'

'New life.'

'Eternal life.'

'Who you?'

Wynter dropped the hammer into the old man's lap. He looked back at the vines.

'Mr Eternal Life,' he said. He tapped the carry bag. 'And it starts today.'

'Who?'

Wynter stepped into the back alley. He drew in a huge, exaggerated breath. Across the lane was the rear wall of a factory. Spray-painted on the wall in huge black letters was ANGLE OF DEATH.

Below it, in green paint, someone had added: 180 DEGREES.

Wynter roared with laughter. 'You got that right,' he said to himself.

He left the alley and headed for the Cross.

Before Wynter had even woken in his cheap motel room in Springfield Avenue that afternoon, Joe Panozza was hearing about how sad Gino had been ripped off by a junkie.

Old man Spina sat with Joe Panozza in his empty nightclub in Stanmore and relayed the story. Old man Spina sipped from a chilled bottle of Eternal Life.

'I don't know who this man is, I never seen this man before,' the old man said. 'He took everything. He put a gun to my head and said "Fuck Joe". I say you can't take Joe's money. He say, "Fuck you, too." '

'How much?' Joe Panozza asked. He paced the stainless-steel dance floor.

'Thousands, Joe. Hundreds of thousands. It was your money, Joe. Me and Gino was just about to bring it to you when this junkie come to the house.'

Joe Panozza sighed. 'You were just about to bring it to me.'

'Yeah, Joe. That's right. This junkie. He laughing all the time. He says, "Fuck Joe." '

'Is that right.'

'That's right, Joe,' the old man said.

Joe Panozza resented the interruption. He had gone to the nightclub for some peace and quiet. He was trying to work out how he might hire someone to put to music the fairytale he had been telling his daughters since they were babies. Or put it down in a book. He was not creative but he valued creative people, and he had, at his age, started thinking of the past, and the importance of putting things down permanently, for posterity.

The fairytale began with Joe Panozza's recollections of fishing in the skiff with his father when he was a child, back in the village. One day he was permitted to join his father, and they headed out of the little crescent harbour, past the church on the point and the light-house, with the other fishing boats.

At dawn he loved to look back at the village, and see the sun strike the cupola of the small church. To young Joe Panozza the light on the dome always meant home. He could look at the warm light and think of his grandparents still sleeping in the downstairs room and the pitcher of milk on the stone step and the smell of bread from the kitchen and the shadowy figure of his mother opening shutters.

He'd return home with his father arm-weary and sunburnt and have salt crusted in his ears, and after they tied up the boat and cleaned their catch on the long marble-topped gutting and filleting tables on the waterfront they always went around to the church and offered their prayers of thanks for a safe journey and a good catch, even when the catch was not particularly good.

There was a painting of a fish inside the church. It was a golden fish, as he remembered it, though it was most likely brown with grit and dust, just as the whole fresco on the side wall was dulled with age. It was like looking at the world through a gauze curtain.

Joe Panozza could close his eyes in that dim empty nightclub and see the golden fish leading a long trail of skiffs out to sea. The fishermen wore robes from a long time ago and there was no lighthouse on the point of the bay. In the picture of his village there were horses and mules near the waterfront and people in robes tending to the animals. It was a long time ago, even before his grandparents. He liked to think that one of those men in the robes on the waterfront was his great-great-great-grandfather.

But it was the golden fish he always recalled. It was there swimming around in the back of Joe Panozza's head, and it was this fish that he saw when he started to invent the fairytale for his children.

In the story there was a fisherman who went out every morning in his wooden skiff with his two daughters. The elder daughter had long golden ringlets like the sun hitting the copper dome of a church. She was wise for her age, and practical, and helped her father navigate the skiff. The younger had special powers – she knew exactly where the fish were under the water and she could always tell the good creatures from the bad creatures, and sense danger, be it deep in the sea or in the weather.

Drawing in the nets one morning, they all struggled with what felt like a very large catch. After much effort, they found only one sea creature at the bottom of the net – the golden fish. It was as big a fish as you could hold in both hands, but it was so heavy that it weighted down the back of the skiff to the waterline.

They sat around it in the boat, and watched it gasp for air. Its skin was as rich and shiny as their mother's wedding band.

I have never seen such a fish, their father said.

After a while, the younger girl got on her knees beside the fish and put her ear to its mouth.

This fish says, the small girl recounted, that he is from the painting in the church.

How could that be? her sister asked.

Sssh, the small girl said. He's still talking. He says that if you do not believe him you just have to go to the church itself and see that he is no longer in the painting. He says he is hundreds of years old, and for all those years he has lived on the wall of the church, guiding the fishermen in their wooden boats. Watching over the village.

But why is he all the way out here, in the deep water? the older girl asked.

He says that he has been called, like many other fish similar to him all over the world, to travel the currents of the oceans and deliver messages of peace and happiness to as many towns and villages as he can. He says the meaning of love and family is being forgotten, just as he, when he was in the painting on the wall, was becoming invisible behind dirt and salt.

What does he want us to do? the elder sister asked.

He says he is very old and heavy and tired and he is pleading with us to take him to where he has to go so that his message may be heard.

But why us?

Because, the little girl said, this message is for the children everywhere, and if they do not hear it now then their children's children will be even more lost, and then *their* children even more so, until eventually nobody will know where they came from, or why they are here on earth and what they are here for. Nothing will have any meaning, and each person will just live for themselves. No one will have any memories of anything, except what they need to do to survive. Everyone in the world will be separate, like the stars, and will spin around the universe, alone, forever.

When Joe Panozza opened his eyes in the empty nightclub he was momentarily startled to see the old man sitting in front of him, watching him. Dim pinpoint halogen lights in the ceiling reflected on the polished surface of the dance floor.

The grubby business of Gino Spina and his old man

and the junkie Walter or Wilbur or Wynter had thrown his whole day out of alignment.

'I'm sorry, Joe,' the old man said.

Joe Panozza picked at the sore on his hand. There was another, a stress boil, forming on his neck.

He tried to recall Wynter's face. He couldn't. Wynter was the same faceless nobody scum that populated that other part of his life and, as his own father once told him – scum, it all looked and smelled the same.

'You know where this junkie is?' he asked.

'No, Joe.'

Joe Panozza raised his hand in the air and one of his men strode out of the shadows at the back of the club and Joe said to him: 'Find out everything you can about the fucking junkie piece of shit from Mr Spina here. When you've checked it out, take Sam with you. Find this fucking arsehole and bring me my money.'

Joe hugged the old man and they kissed on both cheeks.

'Go home,' Joe Panozza said.

What would he tell his girls tonight? The old and wise golden fish would tell them about loyalty. That if you looked at the stars, they didn't have to be separate at all, but could exist as a family, and what lay between them and held them together was not the black infinity of space, but that thing called loyalty.

He put two fingers to the hot swelling on his neck.

FORTY-FOUR

THEY SECRETLY ASSEMBLED the Dream in an old railway depot in Redfern in inner Sydney, and in factories to the west, and at hidden locations up and down the coast. They worked night and day stitching, forging, welding and painting the symbols of Australia that would be seen by billions of people around the world.

Anonymous workers fashioned the giant billowy canopies and long tendrils of the jellyfish that would swim around the bowl of the Olympic Stadium. Others pieced together the spiny-backed fish with their wide eyes and puckered mouths, the plankton, the gropers, and the shimmering schools of pilchards that would course through the aquarium.

As trains carried people through the city and to the outer suburbs and across the state and into other states, and trucks crossed borders with their refrigerated meats and mail bags and livestock, and giant container ships left from the major ports on the east and west coasts, and planes flew out and across the world, they toiled away on fins and gills and eyes and tails in the illuminated light of the brick depot.

They worked on the great botanic puzzle of

Australian flora, shaping hundreds of pieces of desert peas and banksias, wattles, waratahs, waterlilies and eucalypts. Patiently they constructed stems and leaves, petals and pods. They were making nature.

Somewhere else they erected a huge mechanical horse with a head like a skull, screwing and bolting and welding together what seemed like the detritus of old machinery, the flotsam and jetsam of discarded parts from farms right across the country, the junk of farms, the cogs and cranks left to become a part of the soil, exhausted, tired, and reborn into a fire-breathing horse.

Others made two-dimensional Ned Kelly figures, oblong heads, letter-box slitted, dark knights brandishing strange weapons, the flat, bodiless outlaw, the menace, the black shape in the black bush at night, the bogeyman, the monster children feared, the armed robber, the shape of the hooded terrorist, the universal terrorist.

Elsewhere they carefully brought to life the cartoon explorer ship, a penny-farthing imagining of a lunatic. A birdcage with a rabbit inside. A ship log and quill. An innocuous, brittle perambulator, a wiry contraption that had, in history, hit the land like a giant fist.

They worked on little pieces of a country town, and drays, and boxes that would represent sheep. The sheep of the Darling Downs and the Monaro and the upper Victorian pastures. The dull, comical, jumping box sheep of dreams and nursery rhymes. The calculus of sleep.

In front of the sewing machines they sat, stitching costumes for the explorers and the outlaws, the hayseed farmers and the construction workers of the Modern Age. And the bright outfits of the Islanders and

Asians and Europeans, the happy migrants, who had arrived and continued to arrive in this lucky country. The riff and the raff cast off from civil wars and personal tragedies with the dream of clean water or a bed beneath a roof, or food to mouth more than once a day, or medicine for ailing children, the fugitives from misdemeanour or death, the seekers of love and the players of chance, the deserters of their own histories, fleeing from lives that didn't work out, from pressures not foreseen, from decisions gone awry, and the conquistadors with a nose for gold, all of them surrendering themselves to the great whirlpool of the dream of Australia.

In another part of the depot they carefully worked away on the Aboriginal spirit of creation, the giant, mouthless head of it with eyes as black as tar pits. The head of a monstrous moth.

Under a secret roof in the heart of Redfern and in aircraft hangars and long tin sheds and anonymous workshops, they stitched and painted and forged and bolted and sawed and nailed and filed and polished and oiled the entire history of a nation.

FORTY-FIVE

Aurora and Tick stood in front of the old Lampe shack outside Dalgety.

Tick was breathing heavily. They had walked the half-mile from the red front gate along overgrown tyre ruts towards the canopy of a huge pepper tree. Behind it was the shack.

From a distance it looked like there were people at the house. Cars were parked at all angles beneath the tree and down the side. Closer, they were just the abandoned wrecks of an ancient Plymouth, a Morris, and a Special Deluxe Chrysler. The tail of a Humber Vogue poked out from a nearby shed.

The shack itself looked like a sad old face. Wind shook the pepper tree. All along the track to the house the grass hissed and Tick started at any movement in the under-growth. By the time they reached the tree several baby hoppers had attached themselves to his Indian cheesecloth shirt. He grimaced as he pulled them off.

'Wilfred actually lives here?' he said. There was sheep dung and death on the cool breeze. 'People exist like this?'

'He was born here.'

'How ghastly for him.'

They were being watched by a straggly flock of sheep on a low rise to the right of the shack. The sheep were stained with dust but their faces were as smooth as hewn bone. They were scattered amongst a clutch of dead snow gums. The stumps and fallen branches were the colour of the sheep's faces.

'I don't wish to whine, darling, but this is freaking me out,' Tick said, rubbing his arms.

'They're just sheep.'

'It's something else.'

Aurora felt it too. They'd been fine on the train out of Sydney to Canberra, like two children on a school excursion. They made an odd couple. The petite and pretty Aurora, in jeans and sneakers and a bright back-pack, and the hollow-faced Tick, with his bead necklaces and metal amulets and death skull ring. He carried with him a leopard-skin travelling make-up case. 'The pharmacy,' he'd say, patting it.

Out of Canberra, aboard the Greyhound bus to Cooma, he longed for the National Gallery and an exhibition of Renaissance masters. 'In another life,' he said matter-of-factly, 'I was a religious iconographer. I adore the crucifixion. In the afterlife I want one night, just *one*, with Caravaggio.'

The bus rocked through dry plains studded with granite. Low, bald hills. The monotony of it was hypnotic. When Tick saw a creek, a homestead, a cluster of buildings at a bridge, it loosened him out of the reverie, and he'd announce a thought, as unexpected as the civilised intrusions in the land-scape.

'When I die I'd like to be turned into a diamond,' he

said. 'They will have the technology, in a few years. I want my ashes compressed – we are only carbon, after all, aren't we? – into a quaint little carat. Mounted in a tie-pin. Gold, of course. I should think, after being turned into a diamond, that the gold would be quite warm, like a little cardigan.'

Aurora grew silent and sullen as they neared Cooma. She was thinking about Adaminaby, and the great crucifixion-like figure of the concrete trout outside the window of that room in the Snow Goose Motel. Walking the baby around the town. The cold. The sharp-toothed crowns of the dark pine trees. The carpet of needles in the old cemetery.

You have to put yourself in the lion's mouth, she remembered again. And here she was, free of drugs, with a former dealer, on a bus. She had been a child when she met Wynter and had entered the strange parallel world of heroin, and emerged from it, from its jacket, a grown woman.

On the outskirts of Cooma they picked up a ride in a half-full cattle truck.

'Thought you was two sheilas,' the driver said, staring at the road.

There were long silences between scraps of conversation.

'You married, mate? Got a sheila, have ya?' Tick said in an affected twang.

'Yeah, in Yass. Two kids.'

'Lucky old you.'

'Pretty lucky, I reckon. What about you?'

'I have antiques,' Tick said through a paisley scarf.

'You're not from round here then.'

'No,' Aurora said.

'Just visiting?'

'Family,' Aurora said.

It felt good to say it. For the rest of the ride she nursed a fantasy of Wilfred greeting her on the front verandah of his house, and a long hallway of photographs of relatives, and a cosy kitchen. But she knew he wasn't there.

She remembered what Tick had said on the train – you are a sleuth of your antecedents. He was right. Perhaps it was the way of some families. That someone, at some point, needed to penetrate the accumulated stories and myths and lies and diversions and tricks and the sheer weight of talk.

It was late afternoon when the truck driver dropped them off in Dalgety.

Tick brushed dust off his make-up case. 'So where's the town?'

'I think this is it,' Aurora said. 'Dalgety.'

'Your family comes from *here*?'

She produced the crumpled photograph of a man sitting on the buckboard of a car, and on the back in pencil was WILFRED. 'So I've been told. Dalgety.'

'I suppose everyone has to come from somewhere.'

They walked cautiously down the road towards the bridge and the river.

'We'll ask in the pub.'

Two utes were parked out the front of the Buckley's Crossing Hotel. A cattle dog, ignoring them, chewed at a rear rubber mudflap.

'Why don't you wait out here,' Aurora told Tick. 'I'll be out in a second.'

'I'll set myself down on the step, like a real jackaroo. I wish I had a rollie – you know, to roll.'

Three men sat at the bar. They turned and stared at her.

'Afternoon,' she said.

The oldest man of the group nudged the brim of his hat.

It was the same as any country pub across Australia. Laminated tables and stools. A long narrow towel on the bar. Black plastic ashtrays. She noticed an ancient, wizened hat on a peg just inside the door.

'Mitch!' one of the men shouted, and returned to his beer.

A man emerged from a side door. 'Can I help you?'

'I'm looking for the Lampe place.'

The men stopped talking and turned towards her again.

'Lampe?'

'Yes.'

'You mean old *Wilfred*?'

She felt disconcerted by the staring men. The building groaned and clicked. Outside, the sun had dropped behind the hills.

'Yes.'

The barman glanced at the men and back at Aurora.

'Who are you?' he said.

'I'm his great-niece.'

The barman retrieved a towel. He wiped his hands repeatedly, watching Aurora, sizing her up. He went to the wall telephone at the end of the bar and dialled.

She stood there awkwardly. The men mumbled something to each other.

'Pete?' the man called Mitch said. 'You want to get over here. There's someone here looking for old Wilfred Lampe . . . Course I'm sure . . . Yep . . . No worries.'

Through a partition at the end of the bar Aurora saw the shape of a woman standing in the dark corridor. He had looked suspicious of her, the barman. Now he stared at her as if he'd seen a ghost.

'Got a fella coming over, he'll be able to help you out,' Mitch said.

'Thanks.'

For a moment nobody knew where to look or what to say.

'Get you anything?'

Tick was whistling some tune outside.

'Okay,' she said. 'Two middies, thanks. VB.' She produced a note and put it on the bar. 'Could we have it outside?'

'No problem.'

She pulled up a plastic chair on the verandah and Tick joined her.

'Beeyoootiful spot, love,' he said. He fingered the scarf that he'd knotted at his neck.

From the verandah they looked down the hill to the span bridge and the Snowy River. A single streetlight at the intersection flickered on. It was here, waiting for the beers, that they first felt like they were being watched. Tick held out his forearm. It was covered in goose bumps.

'Ghosts,' he whispered. 'I have always been a ghost-ometer. Have I told you? Oh yes.' He tapped his nose.

At that moment she was willing to believe him. It was a dead town, but she felt that a lot had happened there.

It had seen a lot of life. It was too quiet. It was quiet in a way places abandoned by generations were quiet.

The barman set the beers on the table. 'Bloke's name is Peter Crank. He'll help you out.'

'Thanks,' Aurora said.

Tick sipped delicately at the beer. Soon, another ute rattled across the wooden sleepers of the bridge and pulled up outside the pub. A large man in his fifties got out of the car. He wore a soiled Akubra.

'Gidday,' he said. 'You the ones looking for Wilfred?'

'Yes,' she said.

'You had any tea? Let's go inside.'

They sat at a round table near the fireplace in the dining room at the back of the hotel. The woman Aurora had seen earlier in the shadows now stood in the doorway of a kitchen off the main room. The man introduced himself as Peter, removed his hat and placed it carefully on a spare chair at the table.

'Steaks do?' the woman said from the kitchen.

'Thanks, Ella.'

Peter Crank's cheeks flamed red in the dining room. His hair was flat to his head and creased with the ring of his hat. He had a kind, lined face, and he kneaded his thick-fingered hands on the table. A tiny plastic rose in a vase in the centre trembled with the kneading.

'Aurora, is it?' he said, finally.

'That's right.'

'You say you're Wilfred Lampe's niece, Aurora?'

'Great-niece.'

He smiled and stared at his hands. 'Well, it's the damnedest thing, Aurora. As long as our family has known Wilfred we never heard of any great-niece. I can tell you,

542

us Cranks has known Wilfred his whole life, and his father too, and this the first time we heard of such a thing.'

Tick rearranged the lace-edged serviette.

'It was a surprise to me too, Mr Crank.'

'There's been some strange things going on, I know that, with Wilfred disappearing and all. Now a great-niece. I don't mean to doubt your word, but I come here to get a few things straightened out for myself.'

'I know it must seem strange. I'm still trying to sort it out too.'

'Entire town's been perplexed by the whole thing, Aurora. One day he's there then a helicopter comes out of nowhere and he's gone. Jean went straight out to check on him, and he's vanished, with his lunch still on the table. We rang the police and all and the hospitals and National Parks and everyone we could think of. Sent out a party ourselves. Old man like that doesn't just disappear off the face of the earth with his lunch still on the table.'

He looked at her squarely. His brow was creased. His fingers were white-knuckled. The ruddy cheeks aflame. Voices travelled to the dining room from the front bar.

'We've all been worried sick, Aurora, to be honest,' he said.

He seemed resigned to news of Wilfred's death. She might have been the bearer of that news. This, she understood, was a meeting on behalf of the entire district, and the revelations that came out of it would reverberate throughout Dalgety and the surrounding properties. Threads weren't left hanging in the country. It wasn't like the city. Here, threads were important.

He shook his head and stared at his hands. 'The

Lampes. They been around forever. Wilfred's pa, Bill, he worked for my great-grandfather. When Bill passed – quite young, younger than me now – our family give them lodging in the house indefinite like. Old Wilfred then worked with my grandad, Donald. He's been there ever since. Old bugger refuses to die.'

He looked up at Aurora, inviting the news of Wilfred's death.

The woman from the kitchen brought three plates to the table. Each was covered in a huge rump and a little cairn of boiled vegetables.

'Thank you, ma'am,' Tick said, doffing his baseball cap. It had BOY stitched on the crown in thick white cotton. She stared at him as if he were a new and unclassified insect.

'Thanks, Ella, ta.'

'Welcome,' the woman said. She glanced at Aurora and, for no reason, touched the girl lightly on the shoulder as she returned to the kitchen.

A few moments later Mitch walked in from the bar and put an open bottle of red wine on the table.

They ate quietly in the old dining room. It was shabby, the plaster flaking from various parts of the ceiling. The huge marble-topped fireplace was too big for the room. It belonged in a grander building. Aurora got the same feeling about the room as she did about the town. This was where the business of decades, of generations, had been transacted. Sheep and cattle sold. Property sales negotiated. Race meets organised. Council matters decided. Feuds dismantled. Here, passing dignitaries were entertained. Scrutinised. It had been the epicentre of the dialogue of a town.

After dinner, Peter Crank waited for Aurora to speak.

'Please excuse me,' Tick said. 'I must stroll, to aid the digestion.'

When he'd left the room, Pete said, 'Your friend doesn't look well.'

'He isn't,' she said, sipping the wine.

'As we were saying . . .'

'Mr Crank,' she said, 'I'm here to find out as much as I can about my great-uncle, and in particular his sister – my grandmother.'

'That'd be Astrid,' he said.

She dabbed her lips with the serviette. Instantly, and confusingly, she felt close to tears. 'Yes,' she said. 'Astrid Lampe.'

They talked for almost two hours. When it was over, the big landowner stood and they embraced as gently as father and daughter. She was saddened and relieved by what he had told her about the family, and when the tears arrived at that table by the huge empty fireplace they stemmed from both emotions in equal part.

Her confirmation that Wilfred was still alive would reach most kitchen tables in the area by breakfast.

On a used envelope he drew her directions to the house on the Crank property. She was free to investigate it the following morning.

By the time they had stood and hugged, the woman from the kitchen had already prepared a room in the hotel for her and Tick. Aurora asked for separate rooms. They were the only people staying overnight.

Before dawn, Aurora found Tick curled up in her bed. She hugged his bony frame. He breathed laboriously. In his sleep the chain of his silver crucifix had swung around, and the cross rested between the sharp wings of his shoulder blades. She felt it, the cross, cold against her left breast.

Tick found her, a little after sunrise, down on the riverbank.

'Where is that colt from old Regret anyway?' he said.

'Got away,' she said.

They looked into what was little more than a creek, heavily silted and barely moving. You could clearly see the old gouged banks of the original river, tens of metres either side of the remaining water flow. It was no longer a river.

'Dead. Like the town,' he said.

'No,' she said. 'It's still there. Somewhere.'

She wasn't sure if she'd slept. She was too excited about seeing the house. The mewling sheep and the odd cattle honk came to her through the night. She'd got up for a pee at some point and stood, lost, in a back room of bare boards and wash tubs. She thought she saw figures moving in the dark, in the gloom of the long corridor and through internal glass windows.

By the river she felt connected to the place – hotel, river, bridge. In her back pocket, she had a map to her own past. She couldn't be sure if she really felt it, or desperately wanted to feel it.

'Breakfast?' she asked Tick.

'Love, I'm still full of cow.'

'Then let's go to the house.'

Wilfred's shack. It seemed here that all the bits and pieces of a century of a life had fallen from the sky. A lopsided work shed and hen house stood to the left, as did a wooden outhouse with no door. The ground was littered with old car wrecks, steering wheels, rotted car tyres, bumper bars, car batteries, boot soles, the cannibalised shell of a Wilkins Servis washer. Between the hen house and the shack was a small concrete grave and headstone, and fixed into the headstone a His Master's Voice emblem. A dog, passed on.

They peered into the work shed and in the gloom made out a long bench covered in rusted tools and strips of leather and jars full of nuts and bolts. There were dismantled generators and even an old pram. Hanging from a hook on the wall was a tool belt and nail bag. The leather was stiff and cracked.

'He was neat and tidy, our uncle Willy,' Tick said.

At the top of the stairs was a pair of weather-damaged boots, still side by side. Aurora opened the door.

The smell of bird shit hit them and they were startled by the thud of small wings in the dim living room beyond the kitchen.

'Jesus!' Tick tied the scarf across his nose.

They stood in the kitchen. It was eerie. It was exactly as Wilfred Lampe last left it.

'Too much, darling, too much,' Tick said, adjusting the scarf. 'Fresh air is required. I had forgotten the array of country aromas. I'll leave the curating to you.'

She stood alone in the kitchen. There were still pots on the Canberra stove. Enamel tins – Flour, Rice, Tea – in descending order on a high shelf. An empty meat safe. Dishes in the sink, a tea towel hanging off a peg above it. A mitten on a hook. Indecipherable, cramped handwriting in pencil on the wooden wall. Beside the

547

writing a box of matches pinned with a tack. A thermometer. On a nail beside the thermometer dangled a pair of horn-rimmed spectacles.

Stepping into the adjoining room she heard birds shifting in the roof. On the small wooden table in front of her were sugar and jam canisters. There were two chairs pushed back from the table, and a single white bread plate.

Twigs of light shone in the fireplace hearth. Two dirty hens were carved into the wooden mantelpiece.

You were here, she said to herself. Then you were gone.

She tried to see the man sitting on the buckboard in the picture eating lunch at the table. It could have been 1937 inside the house. Or 1916. Or 1958. He had lived here, quietly, in the same way, with the same rituals, all his life. It wasn't just his home, it was him, worn down to the barest essentials, pared back to the rawest functionality. Water, fire, table, chair, roof, bed. It was a child's drawing of a life.

She stood in the doorway to the single bedroom. There were two pillows on the bed. The pillows and plain eiderdown were covered in crumbs of bird shit. There was still a head indentation in one of the pillows.

Newspapers covered the floor. She walked in. The window was filthy and cracked. Feathers edged the broken glass in the window. Two old pictures were mounted on the wall above the bedhead.

Aurora's heart pounded. Skipped. The photograph on the left was of a stern-faced woman, probably only middle-aged, but she looked old. Her hair was parted precisely down the centre of her skull, and gathered in a bun. The picture to the right was of a little girl sitting in a wood-carved chair. Her booted feet didn't touch the Persian rug. She sat alone in the big chair, her hands in her lap, clutching a posy of wildflowers. An aspidistra frond arched above her like an umbrella.

The girl had curly brown hair. The outline of her eyes, her nose, her fine mouth, had been touched up with paint. She was smiling mischievously. Her left foot was slightly blurred in the picture. She stared at Aurora through the dusted glass.

Aurora knew it was her grandmother.

She brushed bird shit off a small chair in the corner of the room and sat there looking at the picture for a long time. When Aurora was born, it was here on that single hook. When Aurora was drawing pictures of Mount Warning and being carried through town on her father's shoulders the picture was here on that single hook. When Aurora's mother changed, and Aurora took the train and stepped into the cold auditorium of Central Station with the pigeons scratching high up in the rafters, and shot heroin into her veins with Wynter in room after strange room, and passed through the warped and frightening Australian countryside, and hid from her old self in a room overlooking Rushcutters Bay, and made it back to the mountain, and felt the heat and hate of hell finally leave her body, the picture was here on that hook.

A single hook. The ancient hook tattooed forever on her belly. The hook of Wynter, of Tick, of addiction, of family, of the past. The hook.

'Astrid,' she said to the room.

A vehicle approached the house. Through the window she saw a young man in work pants and a singlet talking to Tick near the shed and the pale blue boot of the Humber Vogue.

The young man left.

In a box in the wardrobe in the bedroom, and in the sideboard, she found reams of papers and photographs, some stained and eaten, others fused with mice shit. She sat at the table going through the material, sorting it into separate piles, reading, laughing. The light grew stronger in the hearth. The wooden chickens stared at each other across the front of the illuminated ashes in the fireplace.

She finally emerged onto the verandah. The sun blinded her. Tick leaned against the boot of the Humber.

'Taxi's waiting,' he said.

'Who was that before? In the ute?'

'Young Mr Crank *Junior*. And what a specimen of a sheep man was Junior. Came to make sure we got what we wanted.'

She clutched the backpack stuffed with papers and pictures.

'So did we?'

'Yes.'

'May we return to civilisation?'

'How do you propose we do that?'

'In this, of course,' he said, stepping away from the little box-shaped sky blue Humber.

'It works?'

'Like a Swiss timepiece, darling.'

'You got it to work?'

He feigned modesty and flicked his scarf dramatically over his shoulder.

'You think I've been like this all my life? You're looking at one of Victoria's finest apprentice mechanics, once upon a time. Like riding a bicycle.' He sniffed, got into the car and started the engine. It puttered and coughed exhaust as he backed it out of the shed.

'Shall we go?'

She closed the door of the shack and with difficulty opened the passenger door. He revved the engine. 'She'll warm to the task. Old things usually do.'

'I don't believe this.'

'Who could resist something called a Humber *Vogue*. We shall *motor* all the way home.' He gripped the wheel. 'That is where we're going, isn't it? Home?'

'Yes, Tick.'

'Thank you, Lord.'

The little car shook violently as it crossed the bridge at Dalgety and sent him into a fit of giggling. She stared quietly out the window. The Humber lurched towards the intersection and coughed its way past the Buckley's Crossing Hotel and onto the road to Cooma.

Aurora turned in her seat and through the back window saw Mitch in a gritty haze standing on the verandah of the pub.

She sat, clasping her knees, and rocked with the jerking motion of the little Humber.

'I smell mischief,' Tick said, rabbit-tweaking his nose. The car passed into open country and soon they were flying along the thin stretch of bitumen, through shadows thrown down by the big, lichen-covered, round-headed volcanic boulders stacked at the roadside.

'No mischief,' she finally said. 'It's just time.'

'For what?'

'To take back my family.'

Sheep stared after the Humber and its tumbling wake of gum leaves and eucalyptus seeds and burnt oil. Then they resumed feeding, the streak of blue a shooting star, instantly forgotten.

FORTY-SIX

FEATHERSTONE WAITED FOR his police contact at Balmoral Beach.

He was beginning to feel silly, with the story of the old man from the Snowy River. He had met his informant, David the male nurse, in a bar in Kellett Street at the Cross. David repeated what he had told Featherstone on the phone, then asked at the end how he might get a job in radio. Suddenly the story seemed trivial. It embodied what he had become – trivial.

'Excuse me, are you the fellow wearing a white carnation?' It was Wiley.

Featherstone turned. 'You still look like a copper.'

'That's because I am a copper. And you still sound like an opera singer. In the high range, you know, with the pretty little voice.'

'How you been?'

'You never ring. You never call. You never send flowers. I'd listen to your show but I like to be asleep at three am, like normal people.'

They walked together with their hands in their pockets to the small island off the beach.

'How's business?' Featherstone said.

'Good, mate. I enjoy not having to have eyes in the back of my head. It slows the ageing process.'

'Bullshit. You miss it.'

'I miss you buying the drinks.'

Wiley lifted his head and sniffed at the air. He was not old enough to be Featherstone's father but he had the gravitas of one. He had a solid, square face, feathered with light scars from his years as an amateur boxer with the police force, and a slight overbite. He had loved the street work, and been good at it. Then they promoted him, and still he went out with his men as often as possible. He loved the street. He was permanently incredulous at the things people did, to themselves and each other. He was new to the human race every day.

Wiley was a year and a half off retirement. They had seconded him to Olympics security. Part of your personal closing ceremony, they told him. Get fucked, he told them. He had another desk, and all manner of national and international law enforcers and spooks and sunglass-wearing hot heads he had to share it with. He'd have been happier busting shoplifters at Chatswood Mall.

He finally asked: 'What am I here for? Let me guess – Olympics.'

'Yeah,' Featherstone said.

'Even *you* I can't help on this one, my friend. It's not worth my pension.'

'I'm not interested in security.'

'How refreshing.'

'Let's get a coffee.'

They bought two flat whites in polystyrene cups at the nearby cafe and returned to the bench in the park facing the beach.

'What do you need to know?' Wiley asked, staring out to the Heads.

Featherstone told him the story of the old man and his forced incarceration and the Opening Ceremony of the Olympics.

'You got any names?'

'Nope.'

They both watched a giant container ship easing towards the Heads.

'I know a couple of guys looking after ceremonies,' he finally said. 'There's all sorts of security shit going on you wouldn't believe. SWAT teams guarding factories and warehouses all over town. It's the most hush-hush school pageant in history.'

'I just need to know about the old man.'

'Your source good?'

'Not bad,' Featherstone said.

'Will I make an arse of myself over this?'

'No more than usual.'

They finished their coffee.

'Thanks for the breakfast,' Wiley added, thumping Featherstone on the back. 'You keep those ratings up. What are they, ones? Twos?'

'Ha bloody ha.'

'I'll be in touch.' He moved towards his car then stopped and turned. 'Shouldn't you be home in bed? Night shift and all?'

Ten days later Wiley called him.

'You got your pencil?'

'Fire away.'

'Your old man checks out.'

'You're kidding me.'

'I'm not. My little birdie tells me that they've had him on ice for more than six months.'

'Shit.'

'He's an unknown. A nobody. Picked him from some sort of national statistical ballot. Pot luck. Born in 1900. Do the maths. Turns one hundred just in time for their little Olympic shindig. Australian centenarian. Man of the land. Man from Snowy River, that sort of crap. You writing all this down?'

'Yep.'

'My little birdie was involved from the get-go. Turns out our centenarian, one Wilfred Ernest Lampe, was just down the road, outside Jindabyne, so they go pay him a personal call. He's got no phone. No nothing. Living in a shed with a dirt floor. Never seen a tall building. The original Dad and frigging Dave.'

'Christ.'

'They turn up. Courtesy call. You've been selected, blah blah blah. You'll be performing a national service, blah blah blah. You get my drift?'

'Yeah.'

'My squealer's one of the courtesy callers. They arrive. It's like a bloody time warp. The land that time forgot. And lo and behold if the old bastard isn't laid out in the yard, collapsed, on his way to heaven. There's our national icon, adios, see you in the next life. You there, Featherstone?'

'Yeah.'

'They don't know what to do. Scared as rabbits. This is top-secret stuff, you've got to understand. Forget

556

about national security and bugging embassies and spies and all that shit. This is the Olympic frigging Games Opening Ceremony, biggest show on earth, seen by billions. They shit themselves. They might get the blame for the poor old bastard carking it. Lived the whole century and dead in the backyard courtesy of the Olympics. They call in the cavalry. Bing bang boom, he's airlifted to Sydney for emergency treatment. You still there?'

'Yeah. Go on.'

'So our man from the Snowy's all laid up in hospital. Out to it. Lights out. Just when they find him, their prize, he's had enough. Now they got him hooked and wired up in hospital, and they have to keep him alive. You see the irony here, Featherstone?'

'Yeah.'

'Can you imagine the ramifications if he does pop off and this gets out?'

'What about his family?'

'The first question they ask. They have to talk to the kids, grandkids. Let them know what's happened to Pop. They start asking around. There was a sister, but no one knows what happened to her. They've got to find his family. He's their responsibility without any family. They do a bit of sleuthing on the quiet and finally get a hit on the sister.'

'She'd be pretty old.'

'She's actually pretty dead. From there they trace a daughter up north.'

'So he does have family.'

'What do you know? She's deceased too.'

'Great.'

'But wait,' said Wiley. 'There's a great-niece. Alive and kicking. Ms Aurora Beck, formerly of Rushcutters Bay. They call her daddy in Murwillumbah. He either doesn't know where she is or he ain't saying.'

'They're not ecstatic? That the old geezer is about to be a part of history?'

'Don't seem to be. Family troubles. You never can please some people.'

'Can I run with this story?'

'You're the journalist. You got a threat to national secrecy. You got embarrassing headlines. You got shit and nonsense flying all the way to the top. Everything you guys love.'

'It's got it all. Where can I find Aurora Beck?'

'Jesus, Featherstone, you want me to do your job for you?'

'Your source reliable?'

'What do you think?'

'Your little birdie? I've got to be certain on this.'

'He is no longer a part of the Olympic family.'

'Resigned?'

'Sprung diddling his expenses.'

'Ah, an axe to grind.'

'They're the best sources, Featherstone, you know that.'

'It's a start.'

'As they say in the classics, it's a start.'

'It's a mess, Wiley, is what it is. A soap opera.'

'You're really going to do this?'

'What?'

'This story.'

'It's a great story.'

'It's a sidebar, Feathery. A news brief. A filler. Did I get my terminology correct?'

'It'll get people's attention.'

'Come Games time and no one'll give a shit,' said Wiley.

But it was Featherstone's story alone. It was all his.

FORTY-SEVEN

ONE NIGHT NEAR the end, two field hands found Callistus walking naked on the dirt road out of Berridale towards Dalgety.

It was the late winter of 1928. Temperatures were still dropping to zero, and he was brought back home draped over a horse's rump like a sheared sheep. He was still shivering hours later, his toes and fingertips blue.

It was his last excursion into the world. He contracted a cold that became pneumonia and was confined to bed, his wild tangle of hair and beard as stark as dead snow gum branches against the pillow.

The doctor told Wilfred and his mother the old man would not make it to the summer, so they stayed with him in the house in Berridale.

The orchards were overgrown there, and in the evening the smell of rotting fruit carried into the house. Parrots and starlings gambolled amongst the apricot and apple trees, and rolled and staggered drunkenly in the weeds. Grandfather Callistus, too, seemed giddy with fermented fruit.

For hours everything in the house centred around the loud ticking of the clock on the dining room mantel, and was abruptly shattered, sent into chaos, by the old man's incomprehensible rantings. He was seemingly fighting the clock, trying to shout it outside. His soliloquies permeated every corner of the house, spilled through the archway of wild roses out the front, roiled over the caked manure in the flowerbeds out back. Exhausted, he'd fall into slumber.

Wilfred and his mother sat with the doctor one morning in the kitchen.

'Can you explain . . . his condition,' Mrs Lampe asked, 'the night the two boys found him?'

'Obviously distraught,' the doctor said, nudging his spectacles with a thick white forefinger.

'I think my mother wants to know why Grandfather was discovered without clothes.'

'Ah,' the doctor said. 'Dementia, I would confidently say dementia. There is this fixation, too, with the poor lad they found last week, the American, Mr Seaman.'

Everybody in the mountains knew of the fate of Laurie Seaman, frozen to death in a blizzard up near Etheridge Range. His skiing partner, Hayes, was still missing. Seaman was the first skier to perish on the Main Range.

'But I think it's natural enough,' the doctor went on. 'A life is cut short in dramatic circumstances. Your grandfather feels his time is coming to an end. He's latched on to it. It's a portent to him, it seems. One death as a natural companion to another.'

Planes had joined the search for Hayes. Parties arrived from Sydney. You couldn't have a conversation without theories offered on the tragedy of Seaman and Hayes.

It bewildered Wilfred, how death drew these new

crowds to the mountains. Bill Hughes nearly perished in the rescue mission, along with his brother Bob. The rhythm of the mountains, the natural way of life and death, had all been thrown off-centre with the rush of outsiders.

Wilfred couldn't stop thinking about the schoolboy who'd found Seaman's body sitting up, frosted, waiting for Hayes, not far from where Wilfred had abandoned his quest for the source of the Snowy, all those years ago, and skied with Dorothea, the shape of her just visible through the snow flurry. He was a boy then, too, in love for the first time without knowing it.

'My advice?' the doctor said quietly. 'Keep him away from the newspapers for a while. He needs to rest.'

During the days at Berridale Wilfred chopped wood and cleaned up the garden and orchard. Sometimes, at the woodblock, he'd hear the stream of splintered words coming from the house, and he'd still the axe, stand motionless on the carpet of fresh woodchips, and try to pull some sense from the diatribe.

He stayed outside from daybreak to dark, weeding his grandmother's grave down by the creek near the relics of the bee boxes, and poking at the crumbling hives. His thoughts were as jumbled as his grandfather's final sermons.

One night, at dinner, his mother said something that pulled the knots free in his mind, and brought the line taut.

'When he goes,' she said, 'you will be the last male with the Lampe name.'

She had identified the source of his agitation. The line ended with him. The thought greeted him with the satisfaction of its clarity, but the pain of its truth.

In bed that night Wilfred, too, thought of the American, Seaman, the frozen corpse surveying the valley, the eyes dull as ditch water. They were similar in age. They were young men. Yet the future of Seaman, the sons and daughters he might have had, and their children, were snatched away in a sudden blizzard at the bottom of the world.

It had taken this stranger to die on the Main Range for Wilfred to think about the arc of his life. He was like everybody else. He took each day at a time. He set rabbit traps, mended fences, repaired machinery, oiled saddles. And the sun set and rose again. A day was just a day.

For days, pruning the plum trees, wielding the axe, sitting quietly by the creek at the back of the Berridale property, he thought about these connections. He thought especially hard about Dorothea.

It seemed only a fortnight ago he'd taken tea with her at the Hotel Kosciusko. It had been two and a half years. Her most recent letter describing the opening of Parliament House in Canberra seemed to have arrived just the other day, but it had been ten months. He still laughed at her description of nearly gagging on the turtle soup at the fancy luncheon, and the way he heard her tell the story to him in his head.

It was there, in his head, that they lived a life together. They had a past reaching back to childhood, and their subsequent meetings of which he was able, quite easily, to run every detail over and over in his mind and stretch out. He taught himself to ration. The letters put more visions of her in his head and were also there, to be touched at any time. That was the present. Then there was the future, which he found a limitless space to fill, and happily did, with children and shared meals and community dinners at the Buckley's and work around the house and the annual school pageant where he sat, with his wife Dorothea, just as his own mother and father had in the Imperial Hall, and saw, with absolute clarity, a son, a daughter, performing on the stage.

Sometimes it was all so real he'd come in from the fields at night, remove his boots on the front verandah, and wonder where the children were, and be flushed with panic at the absence of Dorothea in the kitchen lamplight. Then he'd eat at the table, once more, with his mother, in silence.

Grandfather Callistus deteriorated rapidly. The incomprehensible shouting stopped. Wilfred kept chopping wood. He stacked enough for two winters against the wall of a house that would soon be empty.

One day his mother brought him sandwiches and they sat together in the frilled shade of the orchard.

'It won't be long,' she said after a while.

'Yeah.'

'You're a man now,' she said. 'When we get home, you should start thinking about what you're going to do.'

'I got work, and I look after you,' he said. 'That's what I do.'

'You're a young man,' she said. 'There's your own family you got to start thinking of.'

He felt embarrassed. It was as if she'd snuck a peek inside his head, and seen the pictures.

'It's the natural way of things,' she said. 'You can't be

responsible for me, then your own life. That's two lives you got to carry. You have to look forward, and make your own the best it can be. Your children, they do the same. No looking back. Everything has to fold forward, or it doesn't work. It mucks things up. It's the way it's been, since dot.'

He picked at the grass.

'A good girl and some children,' she said. 'Nothing else matters, really.'

Some of his mates were taking brides, it was true. And there'd been Maggie Corcoran at the last Rabbiters' Ball. Big, round Maggie, who'd been his Queen Lure in *The Trout Opera* and at the Rabbiters' offered him a scone by the urn of boiling water, baked by herself, and it was every bit as good as her mother's. She'd been away, and come back with airs and graces from some- where, and a worldliness that pricked at him like a barb. But there was nothing that interested him in Maggie's big, doughy cheeks and furtive looks, because every- thing for him was traced back to the little girl with blonde curly hair on the snow run above Charlotte Pass.

He'd met another young woman by chance one Saturday afternoon at his private trout fishing hole. He'd been casting without result for more than an hour when he heard voices. Downstream from the Buckley's on a busy afternoon you often picked up snatches of conver- sation, broken words and phrases carried along the surface of the river. He cocked an ear to the water, and was soon startled to find a party of six staring down at him from the grassy ridge above the bank.

They were dressed as city people dressed in the bush – starched khaki, new woolly socks, an array of blemish-free boots, even a pith helmet. They were comically decorated with various water bottles and knives and shoulder bags. A few brandished walking sticks.

He discovered, later, they were members of the Sydney Bushwalkers' Club. They shouted down hellos and queries about the weather and the fishing, overly curious about everything now that they'd stumbled upon a native. One young woman scrambled down to the bank and filled her bottle with river water.

'Is it sweet?' she asked him, kneeling delicately at the water's edge.

Wilfred was taken aback. He watched her dip the water flask, and the water runnel down her wrist.

'Is it sweet?'

He had never seen a woman in trousers, and caught the curve of her buttocks as she squatted in the sand.

'They say,' he said, in a voice not his own, 'you could get addicted to it.'

When the group was gone, and he was left with the memory of the khaki crescent and his own strange voice, he flushed with a delayed embarrassment that prickled his scalp.

Sitting at his grandfather's bedside in those final hours, he thought of what his mother had said in the orchard and the sightless eyes of the dead Seaman, as he held Callistus's cold right hand. His mother sat on the other side of the bed, holding the left. The doctor dozed in the corner of the room.

'He must not die alone,' his mother had said that afternoon. 'Let us be there to see him across to the other side.'

Wilfred said nothing, just nodded, because the awful,

lonely death of Seaman was in his mind. So, too, the death of his own father in the icy paddock. He was tired of death and its monotonous regime.

Callistus died in the stuffy room in Berridale and Wilfred studied the lines and crags of his grandfather's face. The doctor approached the bed and held a small mirror to Callistus's open mouth. He nodded solemnly. The edge of Callistus's lips and the rims of his eyelids changed colour, from sallow to a powder blue. Wilfred saw then the wonder of death. His grandfather's face, where it had a few seconds before carried the gravity and torment and joy of a long life, was now free of the cross-hatchings on his forehead and the long and deep lines of the cheeks and the accreted wrinkles around the eyes. The face was smooth and shiny, and it was no longer his grandfather, or the old man he'd always known, but a younger Callistus, from a time before Wilfred was even born.

He and his mother still held the dead man's hands. They felt, both of them, something depart the room. A presence. A weight. Then it was just a room again.

'I'll leave you with him for a while,' the doctor said, taking up his bag.

Later, on the ride back to Dalgety, his mother asked him about the moment of Callistus's death.

'Did you feel it?'

'I think so,' he said.

'What was it?'

'Like something rising up, and then it was gone.'

'His soul. It was his soul that left the room.'

Wilfred was not sure if it was his grandfather's soul he felt or not. Again his mother read his thoughts.

'If we both felt it, then we felt the same thing.'

He did not tell her that at the moment of death and shortly after, his thoughts went directly to the mossy bogs high in the mountains that formed the beginnings of the Snowy, and the busy little galaxia fish that swam in the forks and rivulets that were the true headwaters of the great river.

He decided to join the search for Seaman's partner, Hayes.

They buried Callistus next to his wife, Alice, near the old bee boxes.

The old man had left nothing but enormous debts. He'd invested in harebrained schemes across the Monaro and beyond Cooma and Adaminaby and even, they discovered, on the other side of the world. The biggest was a final importation of the Cyprus bees. He'd sent money to a man he'd read about in the *American Bee Journal*. The money vanished. The bees never arrived.

So the house in Berridale was sold to pay creditors. The clock on the mantel. The sulky with the Singer sewing machine. Even the bed in which he had died.

Wilfred rode home with his grandfather's pipe and a hand-crafted fly rod and a knife. His mother had a photograph and a clipping from the rose garden.

Early that summer he and his mate Percy headed into the mountains to look for Hayes.

In the pub, Wilfred heard all the theories about the missing skier. After Seaman was found they'd recovered a camera, and there was much conjecture about two of the pictures it contained. They'd made it to the summit of Kosciusko, but by then only one member of the party had skis.

If Seaman had walked back down to Rawsons Pass, then what of Hayes? How had they become separated? It wasn't difficult, in a sudden blizzard, to lose a man ten feet away. They knew that. And they knew how quick the weather changed up there. The slap of God.

They reckoned Hayes had become disoriented, despite his expertise on the skis. In the white-out he'd dropped off a precipice. Not enough to kill him, but break an ankle in those conditions and you can start planning your funeral.

They'd already found Hayes' gloves and scarf. And ski tracks near Merritts Lookout. Yet no Hayes.

On the ride up, Percy said: 'I think the tree line.'

'Why?'

'You not going to leave the tree line in the big snow.'

'Why not?'

'Have to be crazy to leave the tree line. Maybe he was crazy.'

They rode to where Seaman was found and ate quietly, looking down into the valley.

'You think you can find any tracks?' Wilfred asked. 'You're a black bloke.'

Percy chewed a sandwich. 'You think all black blokes can track?'

'I dunno. Can you?'

'You don't know much.'

'I'm just asking you.'

'If you knew anything you don't need to ask if I can track. Course I can track. My mother could track. My sisters, they track. It's nothing special to track. Just a way of getting food. Taught when we're little. If you knew anything you'd be able to track.'

'Just asking,' Wilfred said.

'Can't track when the snow's gone, can I?'

'I suppose not.'

'You don't know much.'

They searched the ridges and tree line for two days and found nothing. Back at Rawsons they decided to return home.

'Should've brought the dogs,' Percy said.

'We'll come back with the dogs.'

'Maybe,' Percy said.

'At the end of summer.'

'Maybe I got things to do at the end of summer.'

Wilfred simmered as they left the cool of the range and dropped down into the proper heat of December.

'We can't leave him up there,' he said eventually.

'He dead, ain't he?'

'Yeah, he's dead, but it's not right.'

'He not going anywhere.'

'That's not the point.'

They rode silently above the gorge down from Jindabyne.

'Why you need to find this bloke so hard?' Percy asked.

'I don't.'

'This bloke, he got under your skin somehow.'

Percy was right, but Wilfred didn't want to admit it. The link back to Callistus, and being the last of the line.

They never went back to look for Hayes. Sometimes, out in the back paddocks, Wilfred caught a glimpse of the Alps and thought of the young man still lost up there. Entombed. Preserved.

Two stockmen eventually discovered the remains on New Year's Eve the following year. They were tending cattle on a grazing lease above Merritts Creek when their dog came across poor Hayes' corpse.

When the news reached Dalgety all anyone was talking about in those first weeks of January was young cricketer Donald Bradman's record 452 not out against Queensland at the Sydney Cricket Ground. Some idiot, they learned, had carved the bloke's statue out of table salt. But Wilfred didn't forget about Hayes. It seemed to him a bad omen.

They'd built a solid stone two-room hut up at Rawsons Pass in honour of Seaman. They called it Seaman's Hut. His parents, from New York, put up the money. Wilfred knew exactly where the hut was and he didn't need to see it. It looked out over the little stream of galaxias that would later become the Snowy proper. Wilfred often sat on the verandah of the Buckley's with a beer and watched the river and thought of it winding all the way back to the Alps, getting thinner and thinner through the High Country, to the steep ridge and the little stone hut. Once he thought of the river only flowing in one direction. Down. Time and again now he was tracing it back, upward, against the flow.

Months later there was more talk of New York and stocks and shares and well-to-do men in suits jumping from windows and exploding like melons on concrete, along with the cricketer Bradman, and it all seemed to fit with the gloom that the death of Hayes cast over Wilfred that year, and his thoughts that pushed upstream.

By now he was working just for food, and fishing at night for eel to put on the table. He was swapping fresh trout for a lamb leg. Around town they grizzled about the Hungry Years, and swagmen came and went, and kids' breeches and shirts were patched with tablecloth. Still, everyone came to work like they'd always done even though nobody had any money for fuel or a new saddle or cream cakes at the general store, not even for the poor box in the church up on the hill.

Then the passenger plane the *Southern Cloud*, part of the Australian National Airways fleet founded by aviators Charles Kingsford-Smith and Charlie Ulm, vanished in the Alps and the search parties went out all over again. There were men who claimed to have seen Ulm's Gypsy Moth buzzing the Main Range like a giant bogong, all crazy and out of kilter and too early for the migration. They found no trace of the plane or passengers.

So somehow it made sense when Mitchell handed Wilfred a letter at the Buckley's one Saturday afternoon. The envelope, crinkled and soiled and much travelled, bore a sprig of cornflowers in the left-hand corner.

He read that Dorothea was to be married in Sydney the next spring and it seemed the most natural thing in the world to feel nothing. He screwed up the letter and the envelope, and walking home, numb, his head instantly pictureless, threw the ball of paper over the railing of the steel-scalloped bridge, and did not even watch the river carry it swiftly past the bend of bulrushes and out of his life.

FORTY-EIGHT

FEATHERSTONE WAS DRUNK on air.

The producer had missed it. Featherstone was late and had slipped into the studio a minute before the show started. He'd waved to the producer through the glass and sipped from a large mug of coffee. He lit a cigarette in the small recording booth. Did it instinctively. The producer was flailing his arms. It might as well have been a bushfire. There'd be alarms. Sprinklers. Featherstone clenched the cigarette between his teeth and saluted the producer.

'G'evening scumbags and reprobates,' he said into the microphone. 'Is ole Graham back again to fill yer useless boring lives with some stuff 'n' nonsense till sunrise.'

He ashed in the black coffee mug.

'Few ales at the tavern,' he said. 'Jus' round the corner. You know the one. Irish something. Paddy friggin O'Lepreprabloodycaun or something. Full a pissed tourist backpacker gits and Pommy chicks bombed outta their friggin' heads – but hey, what's new eh? Thas what we are, ain't we? Friggin' playpen for the rest of the bloody world?'

The producer stared through the dark glass. He sawed at his neck with his right hand.

'Sorry, no need to be narky and all. Don't want any calls tonight, ya hear? None. I'm sick of hearing all your crap. Oh boo bloody hoo to you too, ringin' in with your chronic fatigue syndrome and your repeti . . . repetit . . . repetitive strain injury whatever the hell it is and your sleepless bloody nights and let's stop givin' money to the Abos and keep the bloody refugees out and . . . if they gonna come here they gotta learn to assimilate, you know? They gotta be like us . . .

'Well what the bloody hell are you that's so good they gotta be like . . . hmmm? Sittin' in your little boxes with your little patch o' grass watching the interest rates like it was your child and meantime your real kids are out there getting whacked out and killin' themselves in cars and screwin' their life up 'cause Mummy and Daddy got more important things to watch . . . What'll we make on the property . . . Oooh, let's sit and do nothing and contribute nothing to anything and watch the pile grow and hey . . . we mighta sat and waited for twenty years but we tripled our money on that place . . . Well bugger me, good on ya mate . . . Car's leased, mortgage to the hilt, holiday on the credit card, let the kids do what they want, world going to shit, people starving, Aborigines out at the Alice living on friggin' dirt floors and not even a bloody freshwater tap to drink out of but you close the gate and water your friggin' bonsais and study those interest rates like it's a bloody heart monitor . . .'

He lit another cigarette.

'Ooops, not allowed to smoke in here but I'm smokin'. Stuff all of youse. Can't smoke anymore 'cause a bit of smoke might waft your way and give ya health problems and you don't want that 'cause you got to be alive twenty-thirty-forty years to make your fortune on your little suburban shitbox . . . Fiscal management, that what they call it? Fiscal this and fiscal that.

'Gotta hack the forests down so you can read your finance pages and know how the nest egg's goin' . . . Fiscal management . . . Privatise . . . Me me me . . . I can see the board lighting up but you're not getting through . . . You're not talking to Uncle Graham because I'm sick of all of ya . . . Selfish, self-interested bunch of bloody bores . . . Can't have an opinion anymore? Nooo. Have an opinion nowadays and you're a bloody lunatic . . . Must be the only place in the world . . . So long as it's an opinion you agree with . . . Stuff debate . . . What's debate? . . . Something that only happens 'tween vendor and buyer . . . Ah, you know those two words, don't you . . . What sort of place we livin' in when real estate agents are celebrities? Hellooo.

'My producer's going nuts . . . Very funny . . . This may be the last you hear from Uncle Graham . . . I'll be glad to see the back of youse . . . I hope you get old real fast and see how helpful your nest egg is then . . . Got grannies and grandpas out there stuffed in these asylums they call nursing homes or retirement villages. Got people out there trying to live the end of their lives with some sort of dignity packed in with mentally disabled kids because we got nowhere else to put them . . . Can't look after our own because we're too busy worshipping cricketers and real estate agents . . . too busy keepin' an eye on the egg . . . too busy putting refugees in prison camps, people who've risked their bloody lives for a fair go, in the land of the fair go, and we whack 'em behind the razor wire for a few years while we do their bloody paperwork . . .

'Stuff you. I'm talking to my producer. *And* you out there. But we got the Olympics . . . Ooooh, won't we show the world then . . . how bloody sophisticated we are . . . how international . . . arse end of the world. Not us . . . we as good as the US of A. We with the big fellas. Get all the homeless people and the blacks out of town so we look all nice and purrrrty for the visitors . . . No problems here . . . No poverty and racism and child prostitutes and drugs and violence . . . We da happy country Down Under, all shiny and purrrrty . . . We welcome the world here . . . Y'all come down and have a lovely party wid us friendly folks . . .

'And before I go, a little scoop for ya from Uncle Graham . . . Got a surprise for ya . . . about the Opening Ceremony of the 'Lympics . . . Yeahhhh . . . that big secret nobody knows about 'cause it's a big happy purrrty surprissssse for all da whole wide world . . .

'Well d'ya know, dear reprobates, that the creeay . . . creeyative folks behind the shindig got an old bloke stashed away in a 'ospital in Sydney . . . had him there for months . . . ta wheel out on the big night when the whole wide world is watchin' us . . . D'you know that? Old bloke. Kidnapped. On a drip. Keep him healthy and happy. A hunnerd years old for the ceremony. Get it? A century of Orrstalian history. Living history, folks. There he is. There he goes. On with the show. Maestro.

'Groundbreaking stuff. You heard it here first from Uncle Graham . . . Should hold your attention for a fucking nanosecond between who's screwing who and who's got the biggest house and who's gone to bloody rehab this week.

'Hang on while I light another fag . . . Can I say fag? Ohhh, I forgot. Cigarette. I can say cigarette . . . I can say whatever I fucking like . . .'

Someone banged on the other side of the locked door.

'I . . . cannn . . . saaaaay . . . what . . . everrrr . . . I . . .'

Graham Featherstone had been dead air for seven minutes.

FORTY-NINE

TICK AND AURORA sat on the small balcony of his apartment overlooking Billyard Avenue and sipped iced tea. The sun was setting and the stream of bats from the Botanic Gardens filled the sky.

On their return to the city Tick had canvassed his many contacts. He paid an unexpected visit to the hospice to see his old carers. They greeted him warmly. They didn't say, when they looked at him, that they'd expect to see him back soon.

The cleaner, Norman, told him what he needed to know.

'Tell me about the hospice,' Aurora said now.

Tick had been in the Salon de Mort, as he called it, more times than he could remember, and each time he'd expected to die. He waited for death. The building personified death. You get to know a place when you've got time to die. But he'd come out each time, paroled. He knew the building's layout, its angles, its hidden rooms and concealed stairways like he knew his own apartment. He knew the staff roster, and many of the nurses and orderlies by their first names. He knew the hospice from its rooftop to its morgue. When the garbage was collected. Who snuck a smoke in the garden. Who was lifting medication on the side. The lot.

'Darling, what *does* one wear to a kidnapping?' Tick looked drawn and pale. It had taken them more than fifteen hours to drive from Dalgety to Sydney in the old blue Humber Vogue. Like Tick, the Humber had coughed and spluttered the closer it got to Sydney. Tick had repaired a hole in the radiator with a wad of gum. The car still had seeds and dead insects from Wilfred's valley embedded in the grille. The car overheated three times and had limped into the city in the early hours.

'He's already been kidnapped,' Aurora said. 'We're just reclaiming a relative.'

'Oh, to have a relative one wished to reclaim.'

Strong winds ripped up the harbour and buffeted the giant pine tree in front of Tick's balcony. A clutch of cockatoos flashed past, all odd angled wing and crest in the unstable air. Shrieking echoed off the brick blocks of flats.

'How's Harold getting along with the car?' she said, sipping the tea, going over their plans, looking for the birds in the pine rungs.

Tick grimaced. 'He is what you would call a man who has tools. I can find my way around a rocker cover gasket, but Harold is a motor surgeon. Three days and it'll be as good as the day it rolled off the showroom floor. Don't tell Harold of my admiration. Mustn't set a precedent.'

She had grown fond of Tick. They were co-conspirators, and she had not hesitated in accepting his hospitality and a bed in his cramped flat. For your protection, he said, and she bowed to his superior street cunning and experience. Wynter was still out there.

Aurora studied Tick's profile. He looked sicker and older than she'd ever seen him. He was dying. And it was death, perversely, that had saved him from himself. He had rolled up his sleeves and she saw the old tattooed ticks on his forearms.

They had stopped to let the car cool on the edge of Lake George, just outside Canberra. It was empty of water, a huge pan of green and yellow grasses stroked with vehicle tracks. A small herd of cattle floated in a distant haze.

He said, 'During my career as a water pump salesman, I came through here all the time.'

She looked at him with surprise.

'Oh yes, sister. My little patch stretched between Sydney and Melbourne. I drove back and forth twice a week, and became quite a familiar figure on the Hume. I made some very interesting friends on the road. As the road is wont to yield.'

He ended the sentence with a theatrical flourish of the hand, staring into the empty lake, glancing at Aurora, waiting to be encouraged.

'The truckies. That wonderful transient group of men in their big rigs. We became quite chummy. One afternoon I simply couldn't go on. Fatigue. A catnap was in order. When I awoke, my little jalopy was surrounded front, back and both sides by semitrailers. The dears had *sheltered* me, so I could rest in peace. They understand the rigours of the road. We often had some ad hoc cricket games at rest stops. Delightful people, with more grace and manners than any dames of Double Bay. They got to know my vehicle, of course, and we'd toot each other up and down the highway. There is nothing nicer than a trucker's friendly toot. Just as I love to hear the wail of the ships on the harbour at night. It's the same sensation.'

Back in the Humber he talked in brilliant, manic bursts, until the telling exhausted him and petered, sometimes mid-sentence, into a breathy nothing. Between Gunning and Goulburn he spoke about his illness. He had a name for it. Leo.

'Leo is getting stronger,' he said, tsking. 'Once, I *hated* Leo. He was very easy to hate. Then I fought him. Not so easy. But I had some success. I beat him back and kept him quiet for a long while. But he grows, you see, like those wonderful firestorms you may have seen on television in the summer. How they explode with fresh oxygen. How they *roar*.

'Well, that's Leo. He feeds on my oxygen, and I wait for the explosion. That's him now. He is taking my breath from me, is Leo. I have no option but to respect him. Which I do. I have learned to respect Leo.'

Aurora drove on in the noisy Humber. She felt an unexpected twinge for him, a stitch in her side. 'There are very good drugs now. The medical advances, the technology . . .'

He laughed, and followed it with a small cough into his left hand. 'Sweet Aurora, they have yet to apply their *technology* to good old-fashioned death.'

'They can prolong your life.'

'There comes a point,' he said, 'when one wishes to go. I am trusting Leo will at least grant me some grace when his work is done. It is my greatest fear, now, that loss of grace. That makes no sense at all, does it? I saw it all the time, in the hospice. Some of them were not afraid of death, oh dear no, but *soiling* themselves. Vomiting. Pissing the sheets. Even messing their hair. It was *this* they fretted about. The loss of dignity. They would rather have died, so to speak, than die without dignity. That's a little line I used once, and thought funny. Not anymore.'

Aurora felt tears sting her eyes, and was suddenly surprised at her emotion. She had been removed from it for so long, this clear interaction with another human being. The exchange of feelings. There had only been her father, since the clarity, and now Tick.

'It is the real reason why,' he said quietly, 'I retired from my . . . business. The business that brought us together.'

She glanced at him and he was still gazing out the passenger window.

'It is why I am strangely in debt to Leo,' he went on. 'He gave me a little vision, though I loathe the religious vernacular. Love the art, detest the language. Yet there's no better word for it. It was the opportunity for restitution. Now, thanks to Leo, I am a *restitutionalist*. Do you like that?'

'I like that,' she smiled.

'I'm *glad*,' he said. 'I am a man of the restitutional cloth.'

They were silent for several kilometres.

'It is why I am here with you now, at this instant, on our little planet, in the giant cosmos. I am here to aid and assist in the saving of your dear old uncle Willy. I trust if we are successful my small gesture will *reverberate* through history. Ta daaa. It is my mission. My final act of generosity.'

She couldn't help but laugh. 'It will reverberate. Through my history.'

'One history. Is it not all history? So endeth the sermon. And please pull over at the next snackerama, Aurora. Leo and I are famished.'

The night before they planned to snatch Wilfred Lampe, Tick and Aurora strolled past the hospice. Just a couple taking the night air.

They slipped into the shadowy wings of the figs in the park that abutted the hospice fence. They looked through the wire and into the dark garden, sizing up the place like two international bank robbers. At the back of the building they lingered by the gates.

'He's up there,' Tick whispered. 'Third window from the left.'

They looked at the yellow cube of light.

'We'll bring him out here,' he pointed, 'to the service gates. Harold will have the Humber running.'

'Will there be security? At his door?'

'Nothing.'

'How come?'

'The dying don't need armed guards, my love. And he's a secret. Nobody knows he's here. Without being rude, your Uncle Willy Wonka doesn't exist.'

They turned and walked back to Tick's flat. 'What about cameras?'

'Oh yes. We'll be captured gloriously on film. But by the time they get to review our performance, Willy will be long gone, consumed by the big city. Poof. Vanished. A thin man, into thin air. They can interrogate me all they like, but I will be impervious. You shall wear one of my wigs, my sweet. And if they recognise Harold? Well, how easy is it to find someone without a single recognisable feature?'

That night she slept on Tick's couch. Her mind was still racing with the plan.

She had a disturbed sleep. The shadows of his detritus played at her – the knick-knacks on every shelf, the brass trout lamp, the African heads and dead butterflies under glass, the painted mannequin in the corner, its torso consumed with flames, the head like Munch's scream.

They stayed in the flat all the next day.

At eight pm Tick said, 'Time to get ready for the ball, sister.' He emerged from his room more than an hour later, dressed in his 'cat burglar' outfit – black loafers, jeans and skivvy. He opened his arms and pirouetted. 'Is it too much? The all black? I'd hate to be mistaken for a poet.'

In the yellow light of the lamp Aurora studied the old photograph of Wilfred sitting on the car buckboard.

Tick called Harold. He checked his face one last time in the large gilt-framed hall mirror.

'Aurora,' he said. 'It's time to give the great Wilfred Lampe his freedom.'

She wondered what Wilfred might look like. Whether she might see, straight up, any trace of a family line, a facial gesture or ear shape that she knew, even a turn of phrase. She wanted that recognition. She was desperate for the line of family.

FIFTY

IT TOOK TEN minutes for Wynter's father to get to the phone in the office of the caravan park.

'Hello?' he said.

'I'm calling from a fucking phone box here.'

'Wynter?'

'Listen carefully. I need to get in touch with Reece.'

'Wynter?'

'Jesus Christ. I need to find Reece. *Reece.*'

'What for?'

'What do you mean, what for? It's none of your fucking business. I just need to get hold of him.'

'I don't think that's such a good idea.'

'He's my fucking brother, isn't he?'

'No, no, I don't think that's the right thing to do.'

'What the fuck do you mean? He's my brother and I want to know where he is.'

Wynter could hear people talking and the sound of a fax machine. He stared at the handset then brought it back to his ear.

'Dad? Dad?'

'Yeah.'

'Where is he?'

'When did you last speak with him?'

'I can't fucking remember, Dad. Years.'

'Why now?'

Wynter banged the earpiece against the green metal phone box.

'Hello?' the old man said.

'Listen, I need a place to stay for a few days, that's all. I'd like to see him.'

'He has his family.'

'I know that. I know he has a fucking family.'

'It's best you leave him be. With the family and everything.'

'I cannot fucking believe this. Dad. Listen. I'm in a bit of trouble, okay? I just need a quiet place to stay for a little while. That's all. I haven't seen Reece in ages. Or the kids. I thought it might be nice. Kill two birds with one stone. See my nieces and nephews, and that wife of his.'

'Karen.'

'Yeah, Karen. I just need the number.'

'What sort of trouble?'

'*Fuck*, does it really matter?'

'I think it'd matter to Reece, with a family and everything.'

'Are you going to give me the number?'

'Son, I don't think it's a good idea.'

'Son? Did you call me *son*?'

'What?'

'Fuck you.'

'He's got a life now, his own family, and I don't think—'

'You're telling me about family?'

'I don't—'

'What the fuck do you know about families?'

'Just settle down.'

'Where the fuck is Reece?'

'I told you, it's not a good idea.'

'Am I getting through to you, you stupid old prick? This is my fucking life here too—'

'I'm sorry, Wynter.'

He smashed the earpiece repeatedly. He got out of the booth and kicked the glass. When two men on the other side of the street called out for him to stop, he ran back to the car he'd boosted from Newtown.

Fuck you, he said inside the dark car. He punched the dash, drummed his fingers on the wheel, checked the rear-vision mirror, the side mirrors. Fuck, he said, and headed for the Pacific Highway.

Wynter drove through the night to Queensland.

During the ten-hour drive he was photographed four times by highway speed cameras. At Coffs Harbour and Grafton he bolted without paying for petrol, and was captured by their video surveillance system.

By the time he crossed the border he was a priority target for the highway patrol. Just after five am he dumped the car by the beach at Coolangatta.

He had $1273 of Gino Spina's money left. He figured it might last him a week, ten days at the most. He needed to find his old mate, Hammer. He'd heard Hammer was on the coast. He fixated on Hammer. He could crash at Hammer's place for a week. Get his head together.

Wynter hadn't been to the coast for years. Not since he'd lived in the squat at Main Beach and worked with Hammer on the building sites. They were a good little team when the contractors and developers needed some muscle and there were unions to worry about, in the days when unions mattered.

Hammer knew all about the unions in Melbourne, where he'd worked on the docks. He'd pissed off the wrong people, and drifted to the Gold Coast at the same time as Wynter. They found each other like a melody and lyrics. Hammer wore a ball-headed hammer in a custom-made holster on his belt. He was handy with a hammer.

Then they spent six months together in the Arthur Gorrie Correctional Centre after they fractured the skull of a local councillor. Prison hardened Wynter like steel but it sent Hammer the other way. Hammer came out Mr John B. Citizen.

The coast was booming. Housing estates were spreading into the hinterland and north of the city to Brisbane. Hammer put the hammer to conventional use. He lived in one of the houses he built, with young families either side. Planted daisies and mondo grass on the weekends. Took his kids to netball and swimming lessons. Had a little wooden wine rack next to the wall phone. A pine outdoor setting on the back deck near the Barbecue Meister. Smiley faces and Simpsons fridge magnets with notes underneath that read: *pay electricity, lumber quote for Smythe, toilet rolls, T-bones, Jason camp money*.

He had his neighbours over to watch the AFL grand final. Had the wives in the kitchen making coleslaw.

None of them had a clue about the old Hammer. That there was a building in Surfers Hammer couldn't look at and not think of the body in the foundations below the car park. He was a regular Joe, Hammer.

When Wynter turned up at Hammer's L-shaped three-bedroom brick veneer house in Nerang, his old friend answered the doorbell. It played *Greensleeves*. Through the flyscreen he looked all soft and out of shape to Wynter. You could hardly recognise him. Hammer took a step back from the screen.

Wynter stood on the WELCOME mat. He opened his arms. 'Hammer, you old bastard. It's me, buddy.'

Wynter stayed two nights. Hammer and his wife Sharon put him in the kids' room with its blow-up dinosaur and Star Wars quilts and mobiles. The kids slept with their parents in the main bedroom.

Hammer and his wife fought behind the thin pine doors. Wynter heard them in the dark room.

His friend took Wynter aside on the first night. 'You use in this house and I'll break your fucking neck, are we clear?'

Wynter just grinned with that slit of a mouth. He'd scored in Southport. He'd passed a neat little park with coloured swings on the way to Hammer's house. He'd go there if he had to.

'Sure, Hammer,' he said.

While Wynter was staying, Hammer didn't go to work. He watched his every move. Wynter thought it was nice, his buddy taking a sickie to spend time with him.

'You got it nice here, Ham,' Wynter said.

'Yeah.'

'Decent roof over your head. Little family. Got it all worked out. I admire that. Gonna get some of this myself soon.'

'That right?'

'That's right.'

'Plan to settle on the coast, do you?'

'Might just do that. I like the sunshine, you know? You can't beat the sunshine. Gonna get a nice joint close to the beach. Like the old days.'

'Good for you.'

'Great place to bring up kids, the coast. With the sunshine and the beach. I got to hand it to you, Ham. You done real good.'

'Yeah.'

'Forget the beach. You could build a house for me. In suburrrbeeea.'

'You think so?'

'Sure. It'd have to have a big yard, though. For the kids. How old are your kids?'

Hammer stared at him. 'Five and three.'

'Five and three. My little boy, he's four now.'

'Is that so?'

'Be coming up with his mum soon. Get set up. Gonna be real nice. We could have barbecues at each other's place, you know, every weekend.'

Hammer said nothing.

Wynter got warm with the fantasy of his new life, and house, and barbecues with Hammer, but just as quickly the warmth was gone, and he looked at his old friend across the room and the warmth became a blaze, and he hated that Hammer had come from the same place he had, and they'd done time together, and reentered the world around the same time, and Hammer had all this and Wynter had nothing. He hated that he couldn't understand how come their lives were so different. He hated Hammer and his blonde wife and his kids, and the street with its neat fences and cars in the drives and ordered numbers on the letterboxes, and the lights in the windows at night, and the laughter of children.

Wynter stared at Hammer. He was glad to see him, and at the same time wanted to smash in his skull.

Sharon didn't understand why Hammer had let Wynter stay. On the second night Sharon and the kids went to her parents. She couldn't see that to have turned away Wynter would have been like pulling the pin from a grenade. She didn't understand people who were capable of erupting at the slightest provocation. She didn't know what desperate people would do to survive.

In the presence of Wynter, Hammer, too, had to draw on those old instincts, those abandoned skills, the wile and cunning and brutality that he had lived with a long time ago. Men like Wynter didn't just blow in and out of your life. From the moment he turned up at the door, Hammer had to work out how to get rid of him permanently. Wynter had found somewhere to feed. Hammer had to cut off the feed source.

On the morning Wynter was due to leave they had coffee at the kitchen counter.

'You got someplace to go?' Hammer asked.

'Sure. Plenty of places.'

Hammer lazily turned the pages of the local newspaper.

'Here's a guy I know,' he said nonchalantly, pushing a piece of paper across the bench. 'Might be able to help you out with some work.'

'Is that so? Construction?'

'Maybe.'

'You're a good man, Ham.'

'He can help with temporary accommodation, you know, if you need it. Till the wife and your boy get up here.'

'He can do all that?'

'Sure.'

'You're a fucking champion.'

'I'll drop you into Surfers,' Hammer said, and left the kitchen.

Wynter pulled the newspaper towards him and started browsing. He loudly sipped his coffee. On page nine a headline caught his eye. OLYMPIC ICON GOES MISSING. And the subheading – OPENING CEREMONY CENTENARIAN VANISHES. He read about the man called Wilfred Lampe who had disappeared from his Sydney hospital bed without a trace. The article claimed Mr Lampe was to have been part of the Olympic Opening Ceremony. It finished by saying his closest relative, Ms Aurora Beck, was unavailable for comment.

Wynter read the article over again and again. He tore it from the paper, folded it and tucked it in his back pocket with Hammer's contact.

'You ready?' Hammer said.

He finished his coffee noisily and banged the cup down on the bench.

'You okay?'

'The world, Ham. It works in mysterious ways, doesn't it?'

In the car on the way to Surfers, Wynter thought of nothing but Aurora and the old man. He had come here to sort his head and it had been sorted for him. It reignited Aurora in him. This woman. Mother of his child. The wife he would take unto death. He had lost his purpose. Lost Aurora. Now he was back on track.

He wanted to be alone so he could again read Aurora's name in print.

'Miracle on Cavill Mall,' he said suddenly.

'What?'

Wynter sat quietly with that hard and dangerous mouth set in a self-satisfied grin.

He didn't know of Hammer's friend Steiger, one of the last, old-fashioned standover merchants on the coast. Nor that Hammer had briefed Steiger, and Steiger would make sure Wynter was politely removed from the city.

Neither of them knew that Steiger had made a few calls. That phone lines were working overtime, texts were being sent on mobiles, contacts hooked up with other contacts. It would have surprised even Hammer that an insignificant junkie scum like Wynter could cause such a conflagration, and that the fire would reach all the way to Joe Panozza's bedside phone in his mansion in Gladesville, wake up Panozza and his wife, and send their terrier into a paroxysm of barking.

By the time Joe Panozza finally turned off his bedside lamp, two of his employees were preparing for an un-expected trip to the Gold Coast the following afternoon for a quiet chat with a man called Wynter.

Wynter sighed as they crossed the Southport Bridge.

'Paradise,' he said.

'Certainly is,' Hammer said.

'You know, I can see myself setting up here. Getting old in the sun. Playing bowls and shit.'

'Why not.'

'Yeah. I can see old Wynter's going to settle in real nice here.'

'It's a free country, man.'

'Yeah. Free country.'

'Might be a bit slow for you. After Sydney and all.'

'I'm gonna get a degree in slow. That'll be me. Mister Slow.'

'That's the way.'

'Wynter in paradise.'

'Here we come.'

'Here we fucking come.'

FIFTY-ONE

THE OLD MAN saw his sister Astrid standing at the end of the bed.

She held a straight finger up to her mouth. Wilfred felt wide awake but he knew she must be part of a dream. Nothing surprised him anymore in the small white room with the cubed window and closed blind. He had been placed in some sort of institution, and recently he'd hoped that a familiar face, someone from the town, would visit and explain everything that had happened. Instead there were the men in suits, and talk of getting him better for some big event, and how proud they were of him. He was too tired to work it out. At least he had Astrid. She'd come to him many times in his dreams, as a little girl, and as a young woman. The age he last saw her. He could never visualise her as a middle-aged woman, or an old lady. Her age and looks were preserved to him, forever, like that poor boy Seaman had been frozen up in the Alps.

He'd pictured her on steamships, or waving to him from the window of a moving train. Sometimes he'd be browsing through an old magazine over at the Buckley's, and he'd see an advertisement for a car or a watch or an airline, and behind the cars and watches and aeroplanes the picture of a building – the Empire State Building in New York, or the Eiffel Tower in Paris – and he'd bring the page to his face and try to find her in the building windows or on the tower platforms.

Now she was in the white room, gesturing him to be quiet.

'Astrid?'

'Ssshh.'

Her hair was loose and fell over her narrow shoulders. He could not remember seeing her eyes so clearly. They were brimming with tears like when Maggie Corcoran's headdress engulfed her at the end of *The Trout Opera*, and she was retrieved from beneath the grand hive of feathers and baubles, and when they stood her on her feet and brushed her down she was close to tears, eliciting the sympathy of the adults fussing around her. But her mouth betrayed something, a secret joy, a deception, that always belonged to that moment.

She lowered her finger from her mouth and smiled. He smiled back.

'You've come to take me home?' he whispered.

She nodded.

'Are you coming home with me?' he asked.

Again she nodded.

He sat up in the bed.

'You'll go away again, like all the other times.'

She glanced at the door and back. 'No.'

His mouth was grimly set. He bunched his fists on the surface of the coverlet.

'How do I know?'

'You're coming with me. We're leaving together.'

'Where have you been?'

'Ssshh.'

'Tell me where we're going.'

'Home,' she said, but the word came out as a sigh.

'I wanted to die.'

She nodded once more.

'Am I dead?'

'No.'

'I think I died. But I don't feel dead. I got pulled back.'

'Sssh.'

'I feel stronger than ever.'

'Good.'

'Astrid?'

'Yes.'

'Is it really you?'

'Yes.'

He smiled. 'I can go home now.'

'Yes.'

'Where were you?'

'We'll talk later.'

He pulled back the cover and slowly swung his legs out of the bed. He didn't take his eyes off her.

'I was tired, but I'm not anymore.'

She helped him to his feet. He felt her grip around his upper arm. He looked down at her and felt the shock of his sister's touch. He staggered with it. She held him firm.

'Astrid.' He wiped his eyes with his pyjama sleeve.

'It's okay.'

He composed himself. He put on his slippers.

'I'm going home,' he sniffed.

As she led him to the door she said, 'That's right.'

'With my sister.'

'Sshh. Keep quiet now.'

'Okay.'

She opened the door and checked the corridor. She swung it open fully and the green–white neon of the corridor light bathed the old man.

She held out her hand.

'Come with me.'

Wilfred took her hand.

I'm going home, he thought, with my sister, and he went deeper into the dream. He could feel her young skin, and the delicate bones of her hand.

Together they left the white room.

FIFTY-TWO

IT WAS EARLY autumn on a Thursday. Wilfred had taken his standard two jars at the Buckley's. He'd just returned from Cooma on an errand for the Cranks, and felt electricity in the air on the ride back to town. The hills were cold and brown, crouched as if tensed for a blow. Steady, bitter winds strafed the Monaro, and the sheep stood huddled and bemused at the season's first real portent of winter. It blew away the pleasure of the ride, the chill, and there were voices in the wind that had made the horse jittery.

At the Buckley's Harrison said something was not right with the river. The trout were acting funny. They were breaking the surface without the draw of insect or fly, snapping at ghosts. Or they were refusing to rise, gathered in little schools as if exhausted, resting on the sandy beds in the shallow holes. They seemed stunned by some distant detonation.

After the jars Wilfred crossed the bridge for home. Halfway across he saw the big, dark beetle shape of a stranger's Buick.

'Howdy,' a voice said to him. Wilfred had heard the word before, but only in the picture theatre in Bombala.

'I seem to be in a spot of bother,' the voice said. A man emerged from behind the car. Wilfred stopped the horse. He looked down at the suited man. A river mist was tickling at the reeds and swirling around the bridge's riveted pylons.

'What's the problem?'

'Flat.'

'You got a lamp?'

'No. No lamp.'

'Mitchell. At the hotel. He'll lend you one.'

The man clapped his greased hands. 'I seem to be stuck in a culvert. As well as the flat.'

Wilfred looked back across the river and already the yellow squares of light at the hotel were pale and hazy around the edges.

'You could take a room for the night,' Wilfred said. 'Best I could suggest. Fix her in the morning.'

'Yes,' the man said. 'You're right. Thank you.'

Something kept Wilfred there, high on the horse, looking down at the stranger. It was now pitch-black. He could only see the smudge of the man's creamy face and hands and the collar of a shirt.

'Businessman?' he asked.

'Pardon me?'

'You here on business?'

'No, not really,' the voice said. 'Heading to Jindabyne. Well, yes, on business of a sort.'

'What sort?'

The man began fussing around the driver's door of the car. 'Engineer. I'm an engineer.'

'What sort?'

'Bridges. Dams. Weirs. That sort of thing. You think

they'd have a room available? Now?' His voice had changed. It was harder. Impatient. As if his throat had clenched in the gathering cold. It was a city voice. He poked around in the car cabin.

'Always a room there,' Wilfred said. 'Evening.'

He thought of the faceless engineer all the way home. It was the disembodied voice that disturbed him most. The shift in tone. Bridges. Dams. Weirs.

For days after, he asked about town if anyone had met the engineer. Mitchell said no one in a suit had come looking for a room that night. Nobody remembered seeing the stranded Buick on the far side of the bridge. Jasper the baker and Billings the milko could not recall any strange vehicle the following morning.

It bothered Wilfred, the phantom engineer.

This deep, agitated feeling was still with him when the two canoeists arrived in Dalgety.

He was convinced, by then, something terrible was happening with the river. First the engineer, now the canoeists. He was especially wary of the canoeists. The night they packed into the Buckley's to celebrate the adventurers, Wilfred sat quietly in the corner and watched. He felt a burning in the pit of his stomach.

There'd been a lot of talk and hoo-ha about the adventurers launching out from Jindabyne. Some snickering about a watery Burke and Wills, traversing the length of the Snowy River. Water or desert. You could die at the hands of both of them.

Half the district seemed to be crammed into the pub to greet the intrepid Hanson and Hunt. Beers were shouted. There was much chin-scratching and imparting of local knowledge.

They were not aloof, the canoeists, but they seemed separated from the crowd by an unmistakable glow of foreignness despite being hemmed against the bar. He knew most of the locals thought they were buying beers for two dead men. It was this that contributed to the adventurers' peculiar remove.

Fear can colour a man, Wilfred thought, looking at the two pale slickers beyond the hats and the smoke. They didn't know what they were in for. But the skin and heart did, in advance.

Everyone had tidbits of advice. Grim warnings. Verbal sketches of various stretches of the river. Ravines. Overhanging boulders. Rapids. Narrow funnels where the trees joined like the roof of a cathedral, and it was permanently night. Reefs that could gut a steamship. Great granite buttresses that could crack a head like an egg. The river was relayed to Hanson and Hunt in pieces as the men of the town knew it from their own experience or stories they'd heard. Though they lived with the Snowy, none could present a cohesive picture. They dished up a broken plate to the nervous explorers, and glued it willy-nilly, and as the night wore on gorges inexplicably rose out of nowhere, the river wound back on itself, meadows hit forests, mountains stood where they shouldn't have been.

Hanson and Hunt nodded and smiled at the barrage. Not an insignificant few of the men in the pub that night studied the living skulls of Hanson and Hunt, the hairline, the temples, the bone structure around the eyes, for any clue that they might survive a good dashing against the river rocks downstream. It gave men a keen sensation, looking at other men set to embark on a dangerous, or deadly, adventure.

Wilfred listened quietly to all the stories. It had been his dream, as a boy, to travel the full length of the river in the suit from *The Trout Opera*. To go with the current and be washed out to sea and then to sail the oceans of the world. His dream had changed from wish and possibility to a longing that folded inside of him.

These two men were living part of his dream. They were taking it from him. If they reached the sea at Marlo it would be gone from him forever. It was the same with Dorothea. He had lost Dorothea to someone else living his dream.

This consistent pattern of loss disturbed him. Life rolled through, wave after wave of it, and passed him by. He could not believe he was almost forty years old. He felt like the boy who gathered wood and mended fences and shot rabbits. His freckles were fixed, like a wash of stars, on his ears. He still ate every day at six and twelve and six, and woke before dawn, and fished the river. It roared with the snow melt and lost its strength and energy in winter, and he knew it as well as he knew his mother. But there was a huge difference between them that he finally understood. The river kept moving while he stayed stationary.

Wilfred was sick at heart. He'd been so for a long time. When it caught up with him he went riding alone and camped up in the mountains and did his old trick of trying to trace the source. One morning, watching the galaxias in a pool way up in the High Country, he went cold with the thought that it all began by just being born, this sickness. Maybe he'd come into the world with it, and it was this, the weight of sickness, that prevented him from moving.

He did not discuss any of this with his mother but she sensed the malaise in him and urged him to go to mass at Our Lady Star of the Sea. He didn't think there was anything he could learn at church that he couldn't discover for himself from the mountains, or the river.

If he had any religion at all, it was cause and effect. You used the wrong fly at a certain part of the river or time of year and you caught nothing. You take it too quickly down Jacobs Ladder and you'll lose cattle to infinity. Ringbark a tree and it will die. Cut yourself and you'll bleed.

He was beginning to see, though, that his belief was like any other. Something he thought he knew, which gave him comfort and a place in the world. Wilfred knew nothing of the cause and effect of things on his heart. Knew nothing of an inner life. Everything with him was external.

Once, he had the memories of Dorothea, and they made him feel strong and confident. But they had disappeared, they'd gone downstream, and left him vulnerable. What he thought was his solitariness had turned into loneliness. He was at an age where he was starting to bruise on the inside. He was feeling the bruises. He didn't know when the blows would come, let alone how to stop them.

Something was happening to him, just as it was happening to the river. He thought he had a big life. But he'd never had to compare it to anything. Now the world was coming into Dalgety and doing it for him, whether he liked it or not, and it didn't seem so big anymore.

In the house one night his mother said, 'It's just idleness.' He was finishing a plate of mutton stew. He didn't register she'd said anything. It was the way it was between them, together so long. Just the two of them. It was just a noise. A log shifting in the grate. The starlings in the roof.

'It's why you're this way. The idleness. Your father went through it and he was the same.'

For years he'd had little work to do for the Cranks. Everyone had battened down the hatches after the Depression. Families bartered for food. There'd been some mending fences for vegetables and fruit. Singh the hawker gave him half a dozen oranges for repairing a cartwheel spoke. He'd even butchered a sheep one night in a rear paddock, and brought it home dismembered in his saddle bags. In the morning the horse's hindquarters were streaked with dry blood. They burned the bones in the fireplace.

And there were always trout.

In late 1938 there was word of some work up at the Hotel Kosciusko. Wilfred winced at the mention of the hotel. It was, to him, like one of the great, bottom-less ravines off the track through the western end of the Alps and into Victoria. It was a place where you lost everything. But weeks later he found himself working for the Department of Main Roads, laying rock and bitumen between Smiggins Hole and the hotel. It was good, physical work he could lose himself in. He kept to himself for the first week and set his swag a short distance from the other road men's tents. It was like a little town. A lot of the men had brought their children and wives.

One late afternoon, returning to his swag, he found a boy sitting on his bedroll. The boy was studying the homemade fishing rods Wilfred had brought to the camp.

'You like fishing?' Wilfred said. He was pale with crushed gravel dust.

The boy froze and half stood.

'You can touch 'em, it's okay,' Wilfred said. 'How old are you?'

'Six.'

'What's your name?'

'I'm Sid Kelly.'

'I'm Wilfred Lampe and I used to be six too.'

A woman approached, shaking her head as she walked. 'There you are,' she said, and the boy ran to her. 'I'm sorry,' she said to Wilfred.

'No problem,' he said. 'He likes fishing, your boy.'

'Fishing?'

Wilfred gestured to the rods.

'No fishing in Chippendale,' she said, smiling. He didn't know what she was talking about. She asked him to dinner. It was how he came to befriend the Kellys.

He ate with them just about every night. Seamus Kelly was about the same age as Wilfred. They both had hard faces from working outdoors. Kelly had worked for six years on a rivet crew building the Sydney Harbour Bridge. It was, Wilfred learned, how these men related to each other. The jobs they'd done and the crews they'd worked with. It wasn't unlike the drovers and shearers he knew.

'He's been all over the shop,' Seamus Kelly said, nodding towards the boy. 'Newcastle. Down to Wollongong.

Cut some cane for a season in northern New South Wales. He never seen the mountains before. Now he can say he seen the mountains.' The boy sat crouched by the fire like a large grasshopper ready to take flight.

For weeks Wilfred joined the Kellys at night and grew accustomed to the patterns and rhythms of the young family. He watched Mrs Kelly cook the supper and attend to the child. He took in the order of their camp and the little touches she brought to the tent and its surrounds. It got to the point where he washed up quickly and arrived at the Kelly tent before Seamus, and helped her around the camp.

'You got a wife, kids?' she asked him one evening.

He was building the fire. It had become an unofficial duty. He was a bushman, and they noticed it, and he built an excellent fire.

'No,' he said finally. 'My mother. And a sister.'

'Fit young fellow like you?' she said. 'You should be thinking about your own family.'

'So I been told,' he said.

Each day the road crew got closer to the Hotel Kosciusko. Each night in the swag he pictured it, built into the hill, the pretty lake, the bench seats under gums around its edge. He dreaded the hotel coming into view.

He realised, one evening, that since he had been with the Kellys he felt a different sort of loneliness. The small and infinite movements and gestures and interactions of the husband and wife and child had drawn this new solitude to the surface and given it sharp relief. Wilfred tried to keep it at bay with his own industry. He taught the boy and then the father some rudimentary bushcraft. One Sunday, he took Sid Kelly fishing.

They set down by a small stream not far from camp.

He felt nervous alone with the boy. 'You been fishing before?' he said, tying the flies.

'Nope.'

'You think you'll like it?'

'Nope.'

It was the wrong time of day and a slight breeze disturbed the surface of the stream. The boy looked into the water for fish.

Sid Kelly brandished the rod like a cricket bat. His tongue poked out of the corner of his mouth and the line and fly hit the air in crazed loops.

'That's good,' Wilfred said. After a while Sid tried to imitate Wilfred's graceful casting. There were no fish, but it was pleasant to be by the stream with the boy. The sun was warm. In the distance was the incessant grinding of the gravel-crushing machines.

'You know what snow is?' he asked the boy.

'Nope.'

'It's cold and white and falls from the sky in flakes.'

'It's hot.'

'Yes, it's hot now, but in winter it's cold. That's when you get the snow.'

After a while they sat and ate the sandwiches Mrs Kelly had packed for them. He watched the boy chewing. He wondered what he was thinking, looking across the stream. About a ferry on the harbour in Sydney, perhaps. Or the coast at Wollongong and the tall stacks of industry. The burning cane fields up north. Or just his mother's face.

Wilfred remembered sitting by a similar stream with his father when they'd stayed overnight at the Creel. He wanted to be back there again, to be in the orbit of his father, and to have nothing more to worry about than not getting his line caught in the blackberries.

How relentless, this thing called life. Everything going forward, getting faster. He was glad the boy did not yet know this. That a day still stretched out forever.

Wilfred worked through Christmas and the New Year with the road gang. In the early weeks of January the temperature soared. It was impossible to sleep at night. Wilfred didn't feel right about the heat. It had been a dry summer. They'd lost a lot of stock down in the valley. The grass was so brittle it crunched underfoot.

That Monday night Wilfred knew what was coming. He lay awake on top of his swag and could smell the burning eucalypt oil and snow gums from miles away. By the early hours he noticed, without surprise, the faint orange glow of distant fire.

Late Tuesday night the smell of the fire was stronger, and by dawn ash and dead leaves began appearing in the sky. The morning was unnaturally still. He went to the Kelly tent and took Seamus aside.

'It might be a good idea to send Mrs Kelly and the boy ahead to the hotel,' he said.

'Why?'

'We've got a bushfire coming.'

'What?'

'Across the Main Range.'

'You've heard this?'

'Don't need to hear it. I can smell it. Look at the ash. They'll be safer at the hotel.'

He sat silently with Seamus Kelly at the camp that evening. It was strange without the woman and the boy. The fires glowed strongly now from the direction of the Snowy River Valley. The smell was pungent. Not just the burning snow gums, but pine now, gorse bush, peat. In it, too, Wilfred recognised the odour of burnt flesh.

They sipped sugary black tea and finally Kelly asked, 'Is it bad?'

'Yeah,' Wilfred said.

'How bad?'

'We'll know tomorrow.' But he knew already it was very bad. With the north-wester, and the size of the discs of light across the hills, it might be the one they had predicted for decades. The Big One. The one that razed the mountains to bare earth.

Plenty of graziers clean-burned at the start of the year. The hotter the fire the sweeter the shoots for the stock. But one day the perfect combination of wind and heat and dry bush would create the maelstrom that got away from them. They joked about it, as they often did in or about adversity. They quipped that it'd rain ash across the whole country if it ever happened.

Holding the mug of tea, Wilfred thought for the first time in ages of Grandfather Callistus's sermons about the Great Inferno.

'Why tomorrow?' Kelly asked.

'If it crosses Pipers Creek we'll have some work to do,' he said into the tea. He didn't want to alarm his new friend. Wilfred could already tell it had jumped the creek.

'Try and get some rest,' he said to his friend. They wouldn't be sleeping for the next few days.

At dawn Wilfred rode over to the hotel. The air was hot and thick and pale pink, flecked with ash and debris. The horse coughed and shook its head as they cantered up the drive. Dozens of the hotel horses were tethered in small groups on the carriageway. Above the main entrance was a sign -- HAPPY NEW YEAR 1939.

He was told a group of men had headed off to the Pastures of Heaven to build a firebreak. Staff were mounting fire hoses and clearing debris around the powerhouse and garages. Two boys stacked empty kerosene tins at the side of the hotel. It stood, implacably, facing the lake, as people crawled over it clearing gutters, watered the earth around it, locked down its windows.

A tall, thin, balding man in a black suit strode through chaos, waving his arms like some mad conductor – pointing, scooping up imaginary water, hammering fist into palm. Long strands of his hair rose up at the back of his skull and quivered like broken instrument strings.

'You,' the conductor said, pointing at him as he strode past. 'See what you can do about the oil dump.'

Wilfred checked on Mrs Kelly and the boy and helped around the hotel until late afternoon. It could have been night, with the ash and the strange filtered light, then when night did fall it was like dawn, copper-glowing. Kangaroos and wallabies broke through the bush from all directions and stood, puzzled, around the lake and over near the tennis court.

Wilfred tried to join the men up at the Pastures, but met them coming back to the hotel, sooted and reeking of the burnt bush. The wind was roaring now, howling up the valley, alive with glowing cinders.

Back at the hotel he found Seamus Kelly and the rest of the road gang smoking and whispering out the front. Some of the men's hats were dotted with burn holes.

The fire had driven an odd array of people to the hotel. Through the night and day they straggled out of the bush – stockmen, fence menders, even a hermit from Sunrise Mountain. Volunteers emerged from the Monaro. Police from Jindabyne. All swept into the open grounds of the Hotel Kosciusko. Strangers washed themselves in the lake, escaping the heat. Birds wheeled through the cinders, screeched crazily overhead.

The hotel's portly chef, in white apron and tall white hat, bustled through the front doors and onto the carriageway. The crowns of distant trees were watery in the fiery winds.

'*Die Apokalypse!*' the chef cried, and scampered back inside.

It struck Wilfred how quiet everything was in the face of disaster. There was a lot of movement, burlap sacks piled, kerosene tins filled with water from the lake, stock calmed, but hardly any talk under the strange sky. They were left without speech, disoriented, needing to be told what to do. Seamus Kelly was like a stricken animal, his shirt and trousers singed. At one point he seemed not even to recognise Wilfred.

Later on that black Thursday a Balmain Brothers bus came thundering along the road to the hotel. It was scorched and bubbled. It was surreal to see the bus parked amongst the terrified horses. The two men in the bus had brought news. It looked like the Creel would be lost. When Wilfred heard he wandered down by the lake and the winds rushed at him off the water as hot as a blast furnace and his eyes teared up, swollen. Cinders bit at his bare arms.

By the next morning the whole hotel compound was surrounded with walls of flame. The men broke into small groups and fought it back with the water tins and damp sacks. Cinders showered the lake and the hotel roof and the outer buildings and were pounced on by waiting staff with extinguishers.

As Wilfred threshed at the flames between the lake and the carriageway he saw a pine tree explode behind the hotel, a flash of white flame. Across the lake a small summer house erupted and sent black smoke into the gritted air. He saw a screaming pig, on fire, dart across the Grand Slam and career into the bush.

He beat at the scrub and talked to his dead father at the Creel, then he talked to Dorothea on the bench by the lake, and he kept talking and talking until he could no longer lift his arms and his grimy face was streaked with tears. His eyes felt like they were boiling in their sockets. One moment he looked to the sky and thought it was the lake. And looking at the lake he wondered if it was the sky alive with sparks.

Shortly after midnight rain fell and by morning steam rose off the surrounding hills in huge, unnatural plumes.

Wilfred rode home alone through the blackened country. For miles he saw hundreds of burnt sheep carcasses against the fence line, some hanging off the wire, others piled on top of each other. Charred teeth, shrivelled tongues. Many of them smouldered like peat bogs.

He didn't stop at the pub. He didn't even register the great towering columns of smoke off the mountains, the fierce sunset. At his gate a small curl of smoke issued from the chimney of the house.

He had been to the outside world and it had been destroyed. The white gums were black and twisted. The dead sheep grimaced, their brains cooked in their skulls. Granite boulders as big as houses had fissured in the heat with cracks loud enough to shake the earth.

He tethered the horse and walked slowly up the stairs and onto the verandah. Through the flyscreen his mother saw him, a middle-aged man, freckled with hundreds of small singe spots. He was as speckled as the skin of a brown trout.

FIFTY-THREE

THAT NIGHT, WHEN he woke in the strange grotto of Tick's flat, with its crucifixes and weeping Christs, Wilfred thought of the time they found Uncle Berty dead in his shed at the back of the valley.

They hadn't seen Berty for days but that was nothing new. He often disappeared on what he called his little 'bivouacs', and could be gone for days or weeks. But this autumn they had not once heard the ring of his axe as he got the wood pile ready for winter, and one morning Wilfred's mother had found Bert dead in his army cot inside the shack. He was laid out, neat and straight, on the narrow bed, dressed in his old uniform from the Boer War. The cloth was stretched tight at the buttonholes.

After they buried Berty they went through his belongings. Wilfred had not set foot inside the shed since he was a teenager. He remembered only simple sticks of furniture, a bare earth floor, the cot, a kettle. It was like Berty was camping, the way he lived, ready to pack up and move on in an instant. Or living light, ready for a quick and uncomplicated vault into death.

As they went through the single-room shack, the

whole place took on for Wilfred the feel of a shrine to his uncle's war. It was the epiphany of Berty's life, the moment when all he believed himself to be came together and formed a perfect apex. The war had both made and destroyed Berty.

On the wall opposite the bed stood a homemade wooden hutch with shelves and two lower cabinets with hinged doors. On the shelves of the hutch were his military hat, belts and buckles, his pannikin and water bottle, a revolver, a sheathed knife, a compass, a watch, and a pair of field-glasses. They were all neatly displayed on the shelves, just as his mother displayed the china ballerina and the good plates and the crystal sugar bowl in the glass-fronted cabinet back at the house.

On the rough-hewn wall beside the cot Berty had affixed several large maps. From the front doorway they looked like water-stained sheets of wallpaper but closer they proved to be extraordinarily detailed, revealing shaded hills and spurs and names and coordinates and hairline rivers and streams and coded figures in pencil.

Mounted on the wall next to the door were several saddles, so polished and well cared for they caught any skerrick of light in the shack and reflected it as soft crescent moons on the rich leather. Belts of brass bullets hung from nails beside the saddles.

In the little cabinet of the hutch they discovered several of Berty's wartime diaries and more maps and dozens of unsent letters.

They had to bring the Chevrolet to the front of the shack to remove all the material. Wilfred never questioned why his mother wanted Berty's place cleared out. He saw no sense in it. Berty had never received

616

visitors and nobody would be occupying the shack. He liked the idea of the shrine left as it was, a museum, and sheep and wallabies and wombats wandering in at their leisure. If you left it as it was, it was like Berty was still out the back. Then he wondered if his mother intended that he move into the shack.

Wilfred swept out the place when it was empty and sat on a stump outside and read a few of the letters that he'd secretly pocketed. They were written to Wilfred's father. The words were very straightforward and clear and described weeks camping in the rainy season and how the muddy black loam was dispiriting and later the sounds of pom-pom guns and a long description of the death of the regimental trumpeter, and the funeral they conducted for him in open terrain, the Boers watching respectfully from distant hills.

Wilfred wondered why the letters had never been sent. He wondered, too, why Berty's voice sounded so different, so normal, compared to the Berty he had known who used words like he'd put them in a sack and shaken them up and pulled them out at random. The letters were from a different Berty. The one that had been left behind in South Africa. Perhaps the shrine had not been to the war, but to the person he was before he'd gone mad.

There was no one at the funeral but Wilfred and his mother and the pastor, and Mitchell's kid from the hotel. He was dressed in his boy scout's uniform and he stood at the side of Berty's grave and blew a slew of odd notes from his dull brass trumpet when the pastor gave him the signal. It was supposed to be military sounding, the trumpeter's tune, but it plopped and barked in accordance with the small boy's limited lungs, and ended with a comical and relieving fart. The jumble of notes caught in the pine trees.

Now, in the strange room, Wilfred felt he was again inside a shrine. This one, though, was to something he could not recognise or comprehend.

On the wall next to the couch where he rested was a large framed photograph of a muscular man's torso. No head and no lower body. On his powerful right upper arm, which dominated the picture, were the letters HIV? tattooed in black ink. Hanging at the end of a chain from the ceiling was a dome-topped birdcage. Inside the cage was not a bird but a pink plastic doll, a naked baby, on the perch. The baby held up a syringe in its right hand.

A mannequin stood in the corner, its head and face horribly disfigured, as if it had been caught in a fire. Syringes were embedded in the torso. On the window ledge were hundreds of medicine bottles. There were framed locks of human hair, statuettes, vases, books, antique cabinets, music boxes, feathered African masks. There were gold-leaf icons of Christ and Mary and in each the faces had been disfigured. A gold-painted skull rested on the lid of a gramophone player. There were contorted insects in jars filled with amber fluid, and the wall space above the window was crammed with deep-framed dead butterflies.

A lamp stood on a wooden table at the end of the couch. The base was formed by three brass trout.

From the couch he detected the hiss of water, and the

gear change of motor cars. He heard whistles and jack-hammers. Muffled voices came through the wall.

It was so unlike the white room. This room was crowded and full of movement and sound. He didn't like this room. It was a shrine to something he didn't understand. It frightened him.

He drifted into sleep again.

Hours later he woke with a face hovering over him. The eyes bulged and the cheeks were sunken. A large, dark rosette bloomed on the left cheek.

'Wake up, wake up, Uncle Willy,' the skull said. 'Your taxi's waiting.'

FIFTY-FOUR

It was the nature of being downstream. Stories from the outside world, details of births and deaths, events in the big cities, stock auction results, ribbon winners at the Royal Easter Show – things took a while to get to Dalgety.

Men carried news in their saddlebags. Or exchanged it over a beer in Jindabyne or Cooma or Adaminaby. Then it was brought back to town, often polished beyond recognition with the telling en route, or jiggled and altered on the long horse ride.

So nobody quite believed the two shearers from over at McHugh's when they relayed the story of the six German hunters they came across one morning a dozen or so miles outside Cooma.

It was only early at the Buckley's, so the men weren't drunk – not all of them – and the story sat on the bar as strange and out of place as a glass of milk.

'They was wearing funny pants,' one of the shearers said. 'Looked like they was made of leather.'

'Bullshit.'

'I'm just telling ya what I saw.'

'You see it too, Ringer?'

'I saw it.'

'They was blasting away at rabbits like no tomorra. There was so much blasting you could hardly see 'em for the smoke.'

'I asked Peel when we got to town and he said them Germans all arrived last week and first thing they done was clean him out of ammo.'

'Bullshit.'

They had all heard about the coming of the dams but that night in the Buckley's they could make no connection between the dams and the German hunters. All most of them thought about were the newsreels from the war they'd watched down at Bombala and sometimes up at the new Hotel Kosciusko.

The war was over but here, downstream, it was still fresh. The vegetables they'd grown for the war effort down on the silted river flats were still yielding decent cabbage and carrots. Many of the sheep that produced the wool for diggers' uniforms still grazed the Monaro. The locals lived prudently, continued to ration their fuel, sat silently in the Buckley's and listened to news of Europe and Japan on the wireless.

When Harrison dropped off the mail and told of a busload of Norwegians turning up at Jindabyne, and a group of Italians in shiny suits spotted in Adaminaby, the villagers finally connected the invasion with the dams.

For weeks it was all men talked about, in the shearing sheds and out in the grazing paddocks. The Eyeties and Squareheads and Balts. The makeshift camps on the outskirts of Cooma. The whole world washed up against the mountains after the war.

Tales of foreigners and their strange dress and customs and language rippled through the Monaro, tilted it up and put everyone on edge. The lacquered hair, different skin complexions, tangled patter – the sheer numbers of them being trained and bussed into the bowl of the valley – it blinded the locals to the monumental size and scope of the dams. They couldn't see, through the blur of newness, the arrival of the machinery, the teams of drillers and hydrologists, the monsters these men were assembling. Nobody and nothing could level mountains and redirect rivers.

It's just what happens after a war, they said. Got to give people something to do. They'll be gone in a year with their picks and shovels.

But it burrowed into Wilfred like a bush tick. The mountains had always attracted great visions. Not just here, but everywhere. Moses on the mount. Noah's ark caught on Ararat. Christ on Calvary. There was talk of a New Zealander hoping to scale Mount Everest. There was Crazy Carter and his book of philosophy and the shrouded heads of the ghostly brumbies.

There'd been Mr Schweigestill, too, and his epic opera. And Clement Wragge at the Creel. Wilfred thought of the eccentric weatherman on and off throughout his life. When they'd first met he was an oddball, so attractive to children. Later, Wilfred saw him as a folly, an egoist, his life's work secondary to official appointments and public acclamation. Yet in recent years he felt admiring of Wragge again, this loner dedicated to pulling information and patterns and knowledge out of the sky. It was this, the grasping, that softened his memories of the man, despite his prophecy of the coming of the dams.

Wragge had known that dreams were okay. But he realised that dreams were not enough to hold up a life. They had to be informed, and tethered to action on the ground.

Wilfred decided to go into Cooma on the pretext of buying supplies. He wanted to see what was happening with his own eyes.

He rode into town at dusk on a Friday. On the rise he stopped the horse and saw the long, broad ribbon of Sharp Street that cut through Cooma. It all seemed the same at first. Then it slowly revealed itself to him in that fading peach and blue light; the shapes and shadows of something new. It reminded him of the many times he found himself transfixed by the low grasses of the summer pastures up in the High Country, when the wind gusts changed direction, and the millions of blades that were silvery were suddenly dark green, and he was looking at a totally different thing in the blink of an eye.

In the Cooma twilight he first saw the big rounded metallic hulks of the buses angle-parked along Sharp Street, and groups of people moving up and down the footpaths and from one side of the street to the other. As he watched, the electric lights broke into life. The thoroughfare twinkled almost constantly with the dim flare of matches, disappearing into cupped hands. A mile or so to his left he noticed clean white columns of camp smoke.

Continuing into town he was forced to stay close to the edge of the street because of the motor vehicles. Six months ago a car had to negotiate its way through the horses and sulkies. He noticed some of them tied up down the side alleys. Now Cooma was congested with metal and glass, with rubber wheels and silver grilles, mean or happy like people's mouths, and the headlights round and perfect like trout eyes, except they had no colour or life.

Wilfred's supplies were there on the front verandah, bundled up and left, as usual, by the store owner. From his mount he saw groups of men in suits and ties in the dimly lit store. Peel, in his old apron behind the counter, was rushed off his feet. His two daughters were helping to serve. For more than thirty years he'd been greeted by Peel out on the verandah, his hands resting flat not on his hips but the upper portions of his rump, accentuating the substantial curves of his chest and belly. But not on this night.

Wilfred secured the horse beneath the trees in the municipal park and walked over to the Prince of Wales for a beer. It was smoky and crowded and the din was still a din, but thick with sharp points and rolled *r*s and a music the likes of which he had never heard. No recognisable words leapt out of it.

He made his way over to a cluster of familiar graziers' hats in the far corner, the local cockies herded together and staring out at the population of the bar, wide-eyed and uncertain, as if peering from beneath the canopy of a tree, waiting for a storm to pass. Wilfred nodded to a few of them and they nodded back. He bought a beer and took in the spectacle.

A skirmish spilled onto the street. It was nothing new to the Prince of Wales, but it wasn't a source of good humour and laughter to the strangers. They tried to placate the boss and his staff and the locals huddled in the corner. They smiled and apologised with their hands and it seemed, to Wilfred, they were addressing an audience far greater than the contents of the Prince. They were apologising to Cooma.

That night Wilfred slept in his swag beneath the trees in the park. All night he heard whispered voices amongst the hissing of the leaves. At dawn he saw several dew-covered bodies curled up throughout the park.

He rode out early to where he'd seen the columns of smoke and came upon the workers' camp, the white canvas tents neat and tautly rigged in long straight lines, one after the other, and a mess hall, and latrines. It was like a military bivouac. It was there, perusing the camp, that he knew the men back at Dalgety were only half right. An army of men from all over the world was setting up in the foothills of their mountains, men who were once at war against each other, would have killed each other on sight, men who had seen incomprehensible horrors, lost parents and wives and children, men who carried death and cruelty and the handiwork of evil in their heads and their hearts, and had been brought over on the clean plate of the ocean to join a new army in the Snowy Mountains, and start their lives afresh.

This was bigger than anyone could have imagined. There were similar camps being prepared over on the Snowy at Jindabyne, at Adaminaby and Talbingo and Geehi.

The size and order of the camp, the volume of men compressed into such a small place, it was confusing to a man whose entire life had been paddocks and pastures. This was what frightened Wilfred – this tightly wound spring of men.

Back in town he had bacon and eggs in a cafe and by eight am was securing the supplies to his horse. Strangers in crinkled suits and ties tipped their hats to him and muttered things he didn't understand. One man stood watching him load the horse, then shook his head and moved on.

Wilfred went inside Peel's store and the old man made him a cup of coffee. They sat on two upturned boxes just inside the storeroom. Peel brushed back the few long strands of hair he owned across his bald and freckled pate and cleaned his round spectacles on his apron.

'Business is good, yes,' he told Wilfred in his gravelly voice, and sighed. 'Seven days straight. That's not what I'm worried about. It's . . . the other.' He tilted his head towards the back room.

'The other?'

'You know.' He gestured again towards the back room, where his daughters were sleeping.

'Oh.'

'Like bees to honey.'

'Hmm.'

'I can't keep my eyes off them for a minute. Don't get me wrong, it's not my girls I'm worried about. But twenty, thirty of them in here at once, every afternoon and night and, well, you know, they being the age they are . . .'

'Yes.'

'It's not what I expected, at this stage of life.'

'No.'

They sat silently as old Peel's brow creased with worry over his daughters' virtue. A pale scum formed over the top of his coffee.

Wilfred asked about the German hunters.

'Cleaned me out of bullets and rifles in a single swoop,' said Peel. 'They missed their hunting, from what I could gather. Fox and the like. I told them there was plenty of rabbit. Then I hear they're bringing back galahs and parrots and cooking them up. It's a crazy world when you got people eating parrot.'

They would not believe Wilfred downstream, at the Buckley's. They would not believe the stories of the plucked and boiled parrots.

He checked the rigging on the horse one last time and was ready to ride for home when he was stopped by a man wearing braces and rolled-up shirt sleeves and a short-brimmed hat. The man was puffing on a big-bowled pipe.

'Excuse me,' he said, stepping closer. The pipe stem stayed on his lips. He puffed and studied the horse and supplies and saddle. 'Could we talk?'

They went back to the cafe where Wilfred had had breakfast and sat opposite each other in a booth by the window. They both put their hats on the table.

The man had introduced himself as Jack Dunphy, and had a habit of smacking his lips to punctuate a question or the end of a sentence. He brought the pipe back and forth to his mouth which, for a while, quelled the smacking. His face was pink-skinned and smooth, and his neck was a fierce red. This was an indoors man. From an office in the city. Already the Monaro had gone to work on him.

'What do you want?'

The man smiled and sipped from the big white thick-lipped cup. He had an honest face as far as Wilfred could see but his wrists were hairless and as pink as his cheeks and he looked like a giant grown baby there on the vinyl seat in the cafe.

'Mr Lampe, we need someone with local knowledge. The assembling of the men and the equipment is not a problem for us,' he said, 'and we have some of the finest engineering minds in the world at our disposal. But we can gather the best brains and machinery that money can buy, and it means nothing without knowing the land we have to work with.

'This project is about the land. What's on it and under it. Its idiosyncrasies. How it changes with the seasons. It's as individual as any single person, wouldn't you agree?'

'It can be.'

'We have to find a way into it. That's our problem.'

He sipped more coffee and habitually reached for the pipe. It had extinguished itself, and his lips sucked desperately around the thin stem.

'The pay is very generous,' he continued, flustered by the dead pipe. 'You'd be a guide, of sorts, for some of our crews. Through the more inaccessible parts of the mountains. There are regions, I am told, that have never been examined by human beings.'

'Not white.'

'Pardon?'

'Not by white blokes, anyway.'

Dunphy nodded vigorously as he relit the pipe.

'Mmm. I understand. Very true. It will be − is − important work for the nation, Mr Lampe. Imperative. And men like you, Mr Lampe, men like you can lead us in.' He smiled broadly and his cheeks lifted and ballooned.

That evening Wilfred sat with his mother by the fireplace and shut his eyes and thought about the dams and the armies of men gathered upstream. The pink Dunphy had given him a sheaf of brochures and documents about the dam projects and he'd tucked them into his saddlebag and ridden out of town.

'We need men like you, Mr Lampe,' Dunphy had yelled at him as he left.

Across the granite plains he felt sick to his guts. He had glanced at the illustration on one of Dunphy's pamphlets before he slid them into the leather saddlebag − a curved wall of concrete holding up an ocean.

Wilfred burned the pamphlets on the side of the dirt road before he arrived back in Dalgety.

At home by the fire his head swarmed with what he'd seen in Cooma − the silver buses, the strangers in the Prince of Wales, the white canvas bivouac, the harried and ageing face of Peel, and the skin of Dunphy, sanded and sheened by the Monaro sun and wind.

One Thursday in September, Wilfred came in from the paddocks for lunch and found his mother dead on the floor beside the fireplace. The kettle hissed in the grate. Two plates of corned meat and cold potatoes sat in their right places on the table.

He didn't touch his mother and sat quietly in the chair by the fireplace with her for much of the afternoon. As the sun set he watched fissures of orange sunlight move over the picture of the prize bull on the far wall of the lounge room. The shack creaked and groaned as soon as the sun sank behind the hills, and his mother dissolved in the darkness.

They held a full mass for her at Our Lady Star of the Sea. He sat nonplussed in the front pew and with his head down he studied the flagstones. As the service continued around him he looked and looked at the stones, at their creases and ripples and folds. They were fashioned from the bluestone of the region, and for a moment he became so dizzy with his staring that he felt he was under Dalgety and in the earth and that he was tracing his hands along the seams and veins of bluestone that held up the town and all the gently rolling paddocks and all the sheep and cattle and human beings.

Outside, he walked with his hands in his pockets to the back of the church and from the knoll – the highest point in town – he could see the arc of the river. It was full and wide and strong, as it had always been. He felt, once again, just as when his father passed on, that he had to ride up to the summit and see the galaxias and hear the sweet sucking of the peat moss and bogs and try and piece together the whereabouts of the web of underground streams that formed the source of the Snowy.

He clenched his fists in his pockets.

He looked upstream.

FIFTY-FIVE

NOT LONG AFTER Graham Featherstone was suspended for his drunken rant at the radio station, and featured in the gossip pages for forty-eight hours, and had the transcripts picked over on air by other radio talk show hosts for a day before a footballer's love affair made him yesterday's news, he found himself sitting in a back room of the BBQ King restaurant at 2.40 am opposite a taxi driver called Harold.

It was nutty Harold, the man who ate rice with both a knife and a fork, to the endless amusement of the waiters.

Featherstone had been unable to break his work and sleep pattern, even without the midnight shift, and despite his embarrassing celebrity decided to eat at BBQ King and see his old friends in the kitchen. He missed the Peking duck.

It was crowded on this morning, and he found himself queuing next to the dishevelled taxi driver, Harold.

'You're him,' Harold said to Graham, biting on the knuckle of his right hand.

'Sorry?'

'You're the drunk guy on the radio.'

Graham looked at the floor.

'Aren't you? You're the drunk guy.'

'Sure. Whatever.'

'The Snowy River man.'

'Yeah, that's me. You got me.'

And Harold nudged him in the ribs. 'You want to know a secret?' he said, and that's how they ended up dining together in the BBQ King at 2.40 am.

Featherstone sipped on a Tsingtao beer while he watched Harold eat a plate of beef in black bean sauce and rice. Harold ate close to the plate and revealed only the crown of his large head during the eating. Featherstone was mesmerised as the man consumed the rice in small portions off both the tip of the fork and the knife, turning his head slowly and attentively from one utensil to the other. It was the moments of the knife that fascinated Featherstone.

'Good?' he asked.

'Yeah,' Harold said.

He could smell Harold from the other side of the table, even in the poorly ventilated room which captured all the odours of the restaurant and the kitchen in the basement and the ceiling of a hundred golden ducks on hooks and the toilets on the landing between the first and second floor. Harold smelled sour and of the street. He was in his late forties yet he had the manner of a child, exemplified by the performance with the knife and the rice.

'Would you like a beer?'

'Coca-Cola, please.'

'You sure?'

'Coca-Cola, please.'

Less than thirty-six hours after Graham's suspension a small item had appeared in the Sydney *Daily Telegraph* detailing his bizarre antics and the peculiar story of an old man incarcerated for use in the Olympics Opening Ceremony.

The following day in the *Sydney Morning Herald*, buried amongst tidbits about how much beer would be consumed by spectators at the Games, the number of condoms issued to athletes in the village, the average height and shoe size of American basketballers, the history of abattoirs at the Olympic site at Homebush and the endangerment of a frog species in western Sydney courtesy of the twenty-seventh Olympiad, was a similar snippet on the mysterious old man from the Snowy River. It was accompanied by a cartoon showing a man in a wheelchair rounding up brumbies.

An official with the Olympics committee had telephoned Featherstone's station manager threatening to rescind all media accreditation to the company's reporters if Featherstone's 'drunken rant' was not repeatedly apologised for as a publicity stunt and a fiction. The station manager emailed staff with a summary of the telephone discussion.

The email was leaked to the press and they looked for Featherstone. The story crept forward in the papers, made it as far as page four of the *Sydney Morning Herald*, with a photograph of an old geezer in a paddock, the 'alleged' Wilfred Lampe.

The station told Featherstone to disappear. He was informed he was on his final warning and that if his antics resulted in the station being stripped of its

Olympics coverage he'd best start thinking about permanent emigration.

At the restaurant table Harold sipped his Coke noisily through a straw.

'I fixed the car.'

'You fixed the car.'

'The Humber.'

'The Humber?'

'Vogue. I fixed the car for the bust-out.'

Featherstone leaned closer to the table. He was stripping the label off the Tsingtao. 'Harold, listen to me. Who helped the old man escape?'

'My grandfather had one.'

'Had what?'

'Humber. But his was black, not blue. Peter said, "Fuck the colour, Harold, just fix it."'

'Peter who?'

'Peter said he'd take me out for a dinner if I fixed the Humber.' He checked his watch.

'Who's Peter, Harold?'

'He's my friend but sometimes he gets cranky with me and doesn't speak to me but that's when he's Tick – that's his other name – but I like him better when he's Peter. He was best when he was Juliet.'

'You fixed the car?'

'Peter said I had to fix it for the old man and the girl because they had a long drive ahead and I had to make it run like a cuckoo clock from Switcherland. Can I have another Coke?'

'A girl? Was it Aurora Beck? Harold?'

'Peter said he'd take me to dinner if I made it run like a cuckoo clock and then Tick said he'd never be my

634

friend again if I didn't make it as good as a Switch cuckoo clock because the girl had a long way to drive.'

'I'd love to speak to Peter, Harold. Can you tell me where I can find Peter?'

'Yeah.'

'Where is he?'

'Can I have another Coke? Then I can take you in my taxi, but it's only a short fare so you'll have to pay for my dinner and the Cokes.'

'Of course, Harold.'

'But if it's Tick when we arrive you can't tell him it was Harold who dropped you off in the taxi.'

'I think I understand.'

'I got to be in the taxi in seven minutes.'

'We'll get you a Coke to go.'

'Peter says Tick is going away but I don't believe him.'

Featherstone raised his finger to the waiter. 'Peter says Tick is going away?'

'Yeah.'

'But you said they're the same person.'

'They are, but there's the nice one, that's Peter, and the sick and angry one, that's Tick.'

Featherstone slipped the notes in the black bill folder. 'Whatever. You've been a great help, Harold.'

Featherstone sat on the marble step of the unit block until 4.45 am when a frightening figure in a huge brown fur coat stopped in front of the building.

'Tick, I presume. Or should I say Peter?' Featherstone said, standing.

'Detective? I didn't catch your name.'

'How about a coffee?'

PART III

FIFTY-SIX

THE EMERGENCY MEETING was held in a conference room at Olympic headquarters. The walls of the room were papered in fake timber, and the dark knots stared in on the long and shiny table. In the centre of the table, behind the water jugs, were the new stuffed toys of the Games mascots. There was Millie the echidna, who lived in a burrow beneath Millennium Park. Olly the kookaburra, who resided in the park's tallest tree. And Syd the platypus, whose energy, vigour and personality reflected that of the Australian people.

The three animals stared dumbly through the beaded water jugs.

'Explain to me again how, after years of work and millions of dollars, we're the laughing stock of the Western world.'

The official flicked a sheaf of news clippings down the centre of the table. They tapped the feet of Syd, who fell slowly forward onto his bill.

'Can anyone help me?'

Nobody spoke.

'Come now, children. I want answers. Remind me who this man is and how he managed to fuck over the best minds and talents in the business. Clark.'

Clark sat up in his chair and cleared his throat. He didn't look at the chairman, who was pacing back and forth behind his chair at the head of the table.

'He's called Wilfred Lampe.'

'I know that. Tell me something I don't know.'

'He is . . . was . . . to play a small part in the Opening Ceremony. A stockman. A bushie from the Snowy Mountains.'

'Yes, yes, yes. The Old Man from Snowy River. Who was the genius behind that masterstroke . . . Christ . . . What else?'

'Mr Lampe was to represent twentieth-century Australia. A living symbol. A motif of modern Australia.'

'A motif of modern Australia. Did you write that, Clark? What does the press know?'

'Not much more than has already appeared in the papers.'

'And how would you know that, Mr Clark?'

'I don't, sir.'

'You don't, sir.' The official clutched at the back of his neck. 'Is it true? What they're writing? That this man from the Snowy fucking River was *incarcerated* by us, against his will? Please tell me it isn't so, Clark. Anyone.'

'The plan,' Clark continued, 'was to give Mr Lampe the best medical care and then to provide him with comfortable lodgings befitting a man of his age and circumstance, perhaps a retirement village, until he was required for the ceremony. He was making tremendous progress when . . . he disappeared.'

'I see,' the official said. 'Has the gentleman, by chance, returned home, wherever that may be?'

'Dalgety, sir. On the Snowy. Not that we're aware of.'

'Has anybody bothered to knock on Mr Lampe's door to find out?'

'Not that we're aware of.'

'Are you aware of whether the press knows the details of Mr Lampe's place of abode?'

'Not . . . no.'

'Then, Mr Clark, why don't you take a drive down to Dalgety and find out.'

'Yes, sir.'

The official sighed and rested both hands on the back of his chair, surveying the table.

Clark gingerly put up his hand.

'Yes, Mr Clark.'

'What do you suggest we adopt as the official line if there are further press inquiries, sir?'

The official clicked his tongue. 'The official line? The official line.' He smiled. 'We may not have to worry about that, Mr Clark. When I sack the entire media fucking relations unit there'll be nobody to answer their calls, will there? But if I were asked, Mr Clark, I would say this. Details of the Olympic Opening Ceremony are strictly confidential.

'Did we ever have any plans to roll out a living symbol of twentieth-century Australia? A – what did you call him, Mr Clark – a motif? All aspects of the ceremony are confidential. That is what I would say, Mr Clark. If I were asked.'

'And if he speaks to someone? Mr Lampe? What if he sells his story to the current affairs shows?'

'Give them something else. Something to replace this

Lampe. Let them think it's a leak. A scoop. An exclusive. Whatever they call it these days.'

'Any suggestions?'

'Something. Anything. For Christ's sake, Clark, use your imagination. Gymnasts. Fire-eaters. Any fucking thing. The media, they're like goldfish, Clark. One lap around the aquarium and they've forgotten what just happened.'

He paused. 'Are we clear?'

They nodded their heads around the table. They left the room. Someone corrected the prostrate Syd.

FIFTY-SEVEN

THEY HEADED OFF in the Humber before dawn. Wilfred was still sleepy and his joints ached. He wore strange clothes that the man with the cadaverous face had given him in the dark flat crammed with antiques and crucifixes and medicine bottles.

The skull man had led him down a set of stairs to the street where the car was waiting. The girl was already behind the wheel. Just an hour before she had sat him down, held his hands, and explained to him that she was his great-niece, the granddaughter of Astrid. But so much had been happening, and so much foreignness continued to swirl around him, that the only familiar thing he had to hold on to was his belief that the girl was his lost sister. It was what his heart wanted, not what his head knew to be true, and he thought this must be what people meant when they talked of faith. Then Wilfred saw his old Humber, and the gentle tail wings, metal windscreen shade and chrome double headlights made him feel the nightmare was almost over.

'Now don't forget to *revive* and *survive*,' Tick said, helping Wilfred into the passenger's seat. Tick closed the door and Wilfred looked at him through the window.

Flare from a streetlight exposed a watermark of suds across the glass.

'Farewell, angels,' Tick said. He was bulky in his fur coat. A big, dying animal with a small head. He waved at them like a child. As the car pulled away he disappeared in the shadows of a plane tree. By the time the Humber turned at the corner Wilfred wondered if he'd imagined the strange animal.

The streets were wet and empty and the Humber cruised quietly down to the Woolloomooloo wharves past the little red eternal flame where the Australian troops left for the First World War. Wilfred was too disconnected to link the flame and the wharves and the war and Spud Baker from Dalgety whose casket was brought back home on the back of a dray. He had seen the wharves in newsreels and magazines a long time ago but he didn't think, in the cramped Humber at dawn, that these were the same wharves.

A short time later the car hissed around a large park at the foot of the towering city. It loomed at Wilfred and then was so big and imposing he could not see the tops of the buildings through the curved windscreen and the next minute they passed under a sign that said HARBOUR TUNNEL and then they were in a neon-lit tube that went down and further down and for no reason Wilfred thought of the story of Jonah and the whale.

The Humber then climbed until it shot free of the tube and the gears whined up past another cluster of skyscrapers and one carried a light that said 5°C and they were suddenly in a labyrinth of roads and flyovers and bridges, all sketched out in peach light.

The freeway narrowed to four lanes and soon they were cruising past endless car yards and petrol stations and furniture and lighting stores and restaurants and schools and electrical shops and everywhere there were signs that competed for Wilfred's attention, that flickered and moved or were stationary under lamplight. He didn't understand them. Signs for things called mobile phones. Signs for cars as sleek and silvery as fish. Signs for home loans and for aeroplane companies and for beer in small green bottles. The huge faces of beautiful men and women smiled at him every few hundred yards, it seemed, and some of the men and women of the signs wore hardly any clothes, and others were elegant in evening dresses and smart suits. He didn't understand LOW FAT and SMS and FREQUENT FLYERS and S-SERIES and INTERNET and DIGITAL.

It was impossible to take in, and it amazed him and frightened him – the glass-fronted stores packed with chairs and tables and lamps and clothes racks and gleaming cars and bicycles and suitcases and picture frames and shoes and everything you could imagine in the world all stacked and folded and hanging and illuminated behind the glass.

It was getting light when the Humber turned north onto the freeway. Wilfred sat quietly with his hands in his lap. He studied the walls of rock where the hills had been cut through for the freeway. It took him back to the early days of excavating for the hydroelectric scheme at home. The teams of diamond drillers. Their stories around the fires at the camp at night. So many stories.

He had so many questions firing off in his head they

tangled and tripped each other. The answers were right there, in the cabin of the Humber, held by the young girl behind the wheel, her fingers long and pale like his sister's, so too the way she gently chewed at her bottom lip, folded strands of hair behind her ear, raised a left eyebrow for no reason. But he'd been thrown back to the beginning by the revelation – Astrid had had a life, after all – and in his mind he had a long way to go before he caught up with the living, breathing great-niece sitting next to him in the car.

The tyres sounded like rushing water in the quiet cabin.

Then the girl suddenly said, 'How about some breakfast?'

He turned to look at her and she was half smiling, as if they had crossed a border somewhere along the highway, a field of danger that radiated from the city, and were now safe. She no longer gripped the wheel. He felt the release of tension.

'Yes,' he said.

They pulled into a service centre and she bought him a bacon and egg burger in a small cardboard box and coffee in a styrofoam cup. They sat at a bench outside the roadhouse off the highway. He studied the burger, then lifted the top of the bun to check its contents.

'Where are we going?' he asked, closing the lid of the cardboard box.

Aurora sipped her coffee and drew on a cigarette. 'North. Home. To Murwillumbah.'

'I never been to Murwillumbah. What's at Murwillumbah?'

'Home.'

'Your home.'

'Yes,' she said. 'My home.'

He didn't touch the coffee. Cars and semitrailers pulled in and out of the car park. He had never seen so many vehicles together in one place. The sides of the trucks had more incomprehensible words and symbols. BIG W. TNT. KIT-KAT.

'And your home, too, in a way,' Aurora added. 'Or it could be.'

He watched the steam coming off the pale brown coffee. 'Is it far, this place?' he said wearily.

'Maybe ten hours' drive,' she said.

They passed through Newcastle and were, for a while, taunted by a carload of youths on the stretch to Hawks Nest. The young men yelled incomprehensible things at the Humber and darted in front and behind the old car before disappearing in a puff of grey exhaust.

'I imagine everything's changed for you,' Aurora said eventually. 'You know, the country.'

The highway ran through a man-made forest. Wilfred stared at the perfectly spaced rows of young trees.

'I didn't get to see much of it,' he said. 'Until now.'

'What do you think so far?'

'I don't know what I think.'

She was trying to get him to talk. To find a way into his real self. She glanced at his liver-spotted hands. His thin legs in the baggy nylon trousers Tick had bought from a thrift shop at the Cross.

'You must think something,' she said.

They passed what looked like a huge red elongated boulder with two petrol pumps out the front.

'I think it's not my country.'

Beyond Taree he observed sporadic grazing paddocks and clasped his hands tightly at the sight of cattle huddled in the shade of trees.

At Kempsey they refuelled and Aurora parked the car in a rest stop by the river. They sat at a picnic bench and ate toasted sandwiches.

'What river is this?' he asked.

'Don't know. Sorry.'

He chewed slowly and his dentures clicked.

'Doesn't look like good fishing.'

She laughed.

'Sometimes you can tell, just looking at the surface. Sometimes you can't. That one you can tell.'

'You were a fisherman.'

'I was a fisherman, before the river went away.'

They could smell the eucalyptus trees and split bags of garbage and something sickly sweet from the small red-brick lavatories nearby.

'Did Astrid like to fish?'

He continued to stare at the water and chewed although he'd finished the sandwich. 'She liked the flies.'

'Flies?'

'The trout flies. She liked the feathers and the bright colours. Sometimes I'd catch her with my fly box and she'd have them all laid out in a circle like a necklace. She'd put them up to her ears like they were earrings. She'd prick her fingers and her earlobes and cry. She never saw the hook. Just the feathers and the colours.' He smiled. 'She was a clever girl, but she never learned that. About the hook.'

'What else was she like?'

They discussed Astrid all the way to Coffs Harbour.

Wilfred told of the disastrous evening of *The Trout Opera*, and Astrid's propensity for going missing. He told of her wanderings at night, even in winter, and how he'd have to bring her in from the far end of the paddock and warm her feet by the fire. The stories stopped the night before she disappeared, as fixed in the earth as the great granite boulder in front of the old house in the valley a few miles out of Dalgety. They had sat, brother and sister, on its exposed egg tip, and then she was gone.

Wilfred feigned interest in the oyster beds they could see from the highway at Nambucca.

'Can I stretch my legs?' he asked. They stopped again and the old man walked alone by the water's edge.

He fell asleep immediately when they started off again. He was cramped and awkward in the small passenger's seat. It had taken a lot longer than she expected, the drive. The Humber Vogue belonged to a different time, had its own pace, and she learned that beyond a certain speed it began to shake and shudder as if in fright and she had to ease back on the accelerator. She was worried about the old man and it was getting dark and she fought the steering wheel in the air flow when the huge semitrailers thundered past.

That night they stayed in a roadside motel. Aurora hardly slept. She pressed her ear to the wall to hear noises, anything, from the adjoining room where she'd put him.

She telephoned her father and told him to expect them at noon the next day.

Just before seven am she tapped lightly on his door. It was unlocked. She found him sitting on the bed, fully dressed, just as she'd left him the night before.

Aurora made them tea and they sat together on the edge of the bed.

'It was guilt,' he said suddenly, 'that kept her away from her family.'

'Astrid?'

'Different times,' he said. 'It was simpler. I suppose you've heard that before. But it was.'

'I suppose.'

He toyed with the tea. 'She broke a china cup, just before she went away. You would've thought it was the end of the world. She was tough, like our mother. She could wire a fence. Break a horse. Had no fear most of the time. It can be scary, to see someone without fear. Then she broke the cup and she couldn't stop crying. It took me a long time to understand.'

'Listen,' she said. 'I've been thinking about things and I can take you home whenever you like. Today. I'm sorry. We can just turn around and get you home.'

He sipped his tea.

'Seriously,' she said. 'You don't need this. You've been through enough.'

'You broke something too,' he said. 'I can tell.' Wilfred got up from the bed. 'Best fix it now while you're still young.'

She sat with her head bowed. She had taken the cup from him and cradled it with both hands. She had tears in her eyes but didn't want him to see them.

'So you think I could get some more tea before we head off?'

He waited in the car while she checked out of the motel. In the foyer there was a bundle of newspapers.

The Humber's motor kicked over on the third

attempt, and it crept onto the damp highway heading north.

Inside the bundle of papers, in each edition, at the bottom of page six, was a small story about the Olympics' Man from Snowy River and his great-niece, both missing now, and a photograph of an old man in a hat sitting on the buckboard of a car in an anonymous paddock.

FIFTY-EIGHT

ON THE FIRST day of the rest of his life in paradise, Wynter lay out on the banana lounge by the pool and when he wasn't asleep stared up into the crown of a palm tree.

Hammer's friend Steiger had, as promised, installed him in a small one-bedroom flat at the back of a block of three-storey townhouses on the fringe of Surfers Paradise. Steiger said he'd call when he had work. Wynter said don't rush.

Before settling into the flat he went over to the Southport Courthouse and milled around the front entrance where the defendants and their families gathered to smoke between hearings. Within an hour he'd scored and was back in the flat, shooting up in the lounge room with its cane chairs and cushions patterned with bamboo shoots, and as he lay back pastel-painted fish stared at him with googly eyes and puckered mouths from all over the walls. Ooo–ahh, the bug-eyed fish said.

I should have come here years ago, Wynter thought later, on the banana lounge. These hicks and amateurs, he reasoned, must have heard of the big shot from

Sydney and Melbourne and places in between. Must have got a whisper about his reputation.

Looking into the head of the palm tree, its wind-tattered branches exploding out like a frozen firework, he had a very good feeling about the Gold Coast, and his future in it. Soon he'd have his own pool and his own spread on one of them canals, and a boat out the back. He'd take the fucking town by fucking storm.

'We'll have something for you in a couple of days,' Steiger told him. 'Relax. Have a break. Go swim with a dolphin or get laid or something.'

He stretched out on the banana lounge without a shirt and his professional and prison tattoos swirled and screamed across his pale skin. He was punctured and bruised and scarred. But there was gear in his bag and food in the fridge and a cold beer in a foam holder beside the lounge and he felt like a king.

'Too fucking easy,' he said to himself, his eyes closed behind his black sunglasses.

The day before he was down to nothing, and today he had it all. Piece of piss. He'd taken pity on Steiger the moment they met. He'll be working for me in a month, Wynter thought. Shaved head and Maserati and all. These hillbillies didn't know what the fuck was gonna hit them.

The sun and the beer and the drugs made him drowsy. He wriggled his toes and took a pull on his stubbie.

I told you, he said to Aurora. I told you we'd have a place on the beach and be a real family. But do I want you anymore? I'll be able to get any blonde-tanned piece of arse I bloody well want in a few weeks and we'll see how you feel then, hey bitch? You'll be on your fucking knees before you know it. Begging. You'll always be the bitch that dumped Wynter, top dog, Mr Fucking Gold Coast.

He'd get his father up on the bus, pick him up at the transit terminal in his new Jaguar – he'd always liked Jaguars, classy – and bring him around to the house where his housemaid, Mitzy or Miho or Kiko or whatever the fuck her name was, would open the door for them and have booze and snacks ready on the balcony, and he'd show his father around the place and run him through his media centre and projector screen and sound system, then he'd show him the bedrooms and all the spare rooms, each and every one of them fucking empty, then he'd show the old bastard the door and tell him to find his own fucking way to the bus station. He might even shove a hundred-dollar bill into the top pocket of his filthy shirt and as his old man walked away with his old grey-yellow hair all shiny with oil and gleaming in the beautiful Gold Coast sunshine he'd say, See you in the next fucking life, if you're lucky.

And he'd hang out at the fancy restaurants in Tedder Avenue and they'd be lining up to join him at his table and the boss'd bring out some special treats made just for him, Wynter, compliments of the chef, and the girls'd wiggle their G-stringed arses at him as they walked past and he'd know by the end of the night he'd have one of them or three of them up in that giant bed with him in the bedroom that looked over the ocean. He'd have Hammer begging to borrow some money from him, or to do a job, anything – You gotta help out an old mate, we started out together, didn't we? You and me? Come on, throw something your old mate's way, please – because it was Christmas time and he needed to buy the kids presents. And generous Wynter would give him a tidbit and then he'd own poor old Hammer. And some of his old mates'd visit from down south and say shit and fuck, Wynter, you done all right for yourself, mate, anything we can do for you? And he'd say yeah, wipe my fucking arse.

I'm a lucky guy, he said to himself. Just one of those guys that always lands on his feet. He stretched out, contented.

He woke again in the early afternoon and a block of shadow had fallen across the pool. He looked up. The head of the palm tree was motionless.

He went back into the flat and was fixing a sandwich behind the kitchen counter when the two men entered the lounge room and sat quietly in the cane chairs.

'Hello, Mr Wynter,' one of them said. They were both wearing khaki trousers and Hawaiian shirts. Palm trees bent every which way like brackets across the shirts.

'Who the fuck are you two goons?'

'You like a little deep-sea fishing trip, Mr Wynter?' the man said.

'Complimentary. Courtesy of Mr Panozza. He say, Do something special for my friend Mr Wynter.'

'Mr who?'

The men stood. One walked behind the counter and put his arm around Wynter's shoulder.

'Mr Wynter,' he said, smiling. 'Let's go fishing.'

FIFTY-NINE

SIX WEEKS AFTER the funeral of Wilfred Lampe's mother, and having not seen or heard from him, Mitchell the publican was delegated to drive out to the house in the valley. The lucerne was so high from the front gate to the house that Mitchell was forced to drive through a straw-coloured tunnel, the stalks arching over the vehicle. Inside the open house, on the kitchen table and resting under the sugar canister, was a note: *Back next year.*

It was grief, they concluded quietly at the Buckley's. It did strange things to people. Grief could crowd out an empty house. Send you into unmapped terrain.

'He's gone fishing, probably,' they said. It was their age-old euphemism for the cure to all life's ailments – death, depression, money problems, diseased stock, even sin.

Wilfred had told the Cranks nothing. It was days before they noticed his absence, and then it was only mentioned as brief and passing news at the dinner table in the big house, in between discussions on the perennial problem of flyblown sheep and the titillating findings of the recent royal commission into the sly grog rackets.

There were more than a few who thought Wilfred had gone, yet again, in search of his missing sister Astrid. His only sibling, and now the mother passed on.

As the town theorised now about the whereabouts of Wilfred Lampe, he was in fact less than sixty miles away, as the crow flew, leading a team of drillers and surveyors into deep, mountainous scrub near Geehi. He had become a bush guide for the hydroelectric scheme.

He had indeed viewed his mother's death as portentous, entangled somehow in the activity upstream. She had tried to loosen the grip his heart had on his logic for years. He thought he understood, now that she was gone. The detonations upriver helped dislodge things. And her death, which she'd taught him to embrace, and learn from. Fold forward, she'd said.

He had gone fishing, for three days after the funeral, and landed a few slender browns which he cooked 'there and then, over an open fire, on the gravelly bank. There was always something satisfying about cooking and eating a catch beside the river.

At the end of the third day, as he was packing his gear, he noticed a man's black felt hat swiftly carried by on the surface of the river. He stood with creel and rods in hand and watched the hat glide past. Within seconds it had disappeared around the bend.

The next day he rode into Cooma and found the pink-cheeked Dunphy and signed up with the scheme. He didn't care about the money, though they immediately provided saddlebags and supplies and even a new pair of boots. He had to see, first-hand, what they planned to do with the river.

That night he drank beer in a pub crowded with

newly arrived scheme workers. Dunphy, across the bar, tipped his pork-pie hat at Wilfred. Men were playing cards and backgammon at the tables. Wilfred's boots felt tight and ill-fitting.

Someone tapped him on the shoulder.

'Herr Wilfreed. No. *Meester* Wilfreed. I am pleasured to make your acquaintance.'

Wilfred turned and faced a short, sandy-haired man in a black suit and tie. The man held out his hand in greeting, his elbow pinned to his ribs.

'Mr Wilfreed. I am Boris Hintendorfer, sir. I will be your accompaniment to the camp tomorrow.'

They shook once, firmly.

'Mr Dunphy is informing me that you are the expert of the Australian boosh who will take us to our camp site, sir.'

'Yeah,' Wilfred said. Dunphy was beaming across the room, his cheeks aflame, and touched the brim of his hat again.

'Very good, Mr Wilfreed. A beer for you, yes?'

For more than an hour Hintendorfer sat with Wilfred and asked questions about the terrain and the river and creek systems. Each time the German struggled with his English his eyelids fluttered uncontrollably.

'I am accustomed to the forests around Hamburg, sir, but familiar I am not with this they call the boosh.'

'You'll be familiar with it soon enough.'

'Yes, Mr Wilfreed, thank you, but can you illuminate on the animals of danger that we may encounter? As team leader I am to be aware of all possibilities, for the men's good being.'

He jotted down pertinent facts in a small black

flip-top notebook – wild dogs, the brumbies, snakes, and above all the bush itself, which could take you in the blink of an eye – nodding and fluttering as he scribbled with the pencil.

'I had a German teacher once,' Wilfred said, almost to himself. 'Mr Schweigestill.'

'Schweigestill. *Ja. Das ist Deutsch.*'

'He created an opera.'

'So, Mr Wilfreed. You are to say there are none of the wolves.' Hintendorfer licked the tip of the pencil and looked up eagerly.

The following day Wilfred met Hintendorfer and the team at Jindabyne, and they headed over the range to the proposed camp site at Windy Creek, north of the Geehi River. They were mainly surveyors and drillers of several nationalities – Poles, Balts, two other Germans and three Norwegians. Two Italians commandeered a Land Rover that followed the team. Hintendorfer rode in the vehicle as far as the eastern foothills of the range, then saddled up and joined Wilfred.

A fresh and steady wind funnelled down from Kosciusko.

'This is not the boosh, as they call it?' Hintendorfer said.

'Not yet.'

'Is beautiful in its own way,' the German said, 'this that is not the boosh.'

They crossed the range and into the lightly wooded scrub below the snow line. Wilfred followed an old brumby track into a steep gorge. The horses' ears twitched at the grinding of the Land Rover's gears.

It was mid-afternoon before they reached the site for the proposed camp. Hintendorfer dismounted. He inspected the thick carpet of ferns at his feet and the tree canopies. 'Is quiet, Mr Wilfreed, like the cathedral.'

Wilfred unpacked the horse and set up his swag for the night. The grinding of the Land Rover made him clench his teeth. He was irritated after the long ride and tired of Hintendorfer. This small man of sharp angles and precise movements. He was a shiny piece of fresh-cast metal here in the scrub.

The next day they cleared the site and erected neat rows of tents, a mess and rudimentary lavatories within view of the camp. Wilfred built the central fire. Hintendorfer erected a portable outdoor office for himself beneath a large gum. He sat there going through his paperwork, oblivious; he could have been in a building by the Hamburg docks. He brushed seeds and insects off his papers as he worked.

For the next few weeks Wilfred led several teams of the men into the bush for surveying and retrieving soil samples. He took two of the Norwegians down to the Geehi, where they performed several tests on the river. He sat quietly and watched them on the riverbank. These Norwegians – with their boxes of instruments standing knee-deep in creeks and rivers all across the mountains – were measuring and pinching and scratching at the whole place.

Wilfred had not been able to get out of his head the news, from Hintendorfer, that huge aerial photographic maps of the region were being prepared in Sydney.

'I am told,' Hintendorfer quipped, 'that your big river,

your Snowy, looks like the giant – what do you call – question mark, from the air. You know it? The question mark?' He drew a loop in the air with his index finger.

It niggled at Wilfred, the thought of the photographs taken from an aeroplane. And now the teams of men scraping at the earth.

He had had a picture in his mind of the Snowy River from Omeo up to its source since he was a boy. A secret map. His own personal topography. Now he was being told it was shaped like a question mark. A question mark?

In the evenings, around the fire after dinner, the men talked in several languages and drank rum and now and again communicated with Wilfred in broken phrases that crackled like dry wood.

Late one night Hintendorfer checked his watch and clapped his hands twice. 'Schlafen,' he said. 'Big day for tomorrow.'

One of the Poles – Wladyslaw Drabik – drained his tin mug and stared across the fire at the camp leader. He held the cup out to the man next to him for more rum.

'Go to hell,' Drabik said. The group fell silent.

Hintendorfer stared back, tensing his jaw. 'Was?'

'It is not the war anymore,' Drabik said, nursing the cup again with two hands and returning his gaze to the fire.

The young Hintendorfer fell silent and after five minutes repaired to his tent. The two Poles muttered to each other. The talk around the fire resumed.

〜

Later that month, Wilfred guided Drabik into the bush north-east of the base camp for surveying work. They were gone for three days. At night, at their makeshift camp, they achieved a sort of dialogue. Wilfred liked Drabik. He was a man not uncomfortable with silence. His black hair was dusted grey at the temples. A heavy, black-blue shadow of a beard made his face look permanently soiled.

'You farmer?' he asked Wilfred at the fire on the first evening.

'Not really.'

'Farmer. Crop. What crop?'

'Sheep.'

'Ahh. Sheeps.'

'You?'

'I? Engineer.'

'Engineer.'

'For the Polish Army, I engineer. Was engineer.'

'Oh.'

They shared a jug of rum. Drabik rolled them both cigarettes.

'Married, you?' he asked. He lit his cigarette with the end of a burning sapling he pulled from the fire.

'No.'

'I married. Was married.'

He fell quiet again. The heavy silence of the bush dropped over them and they detected the encroaching dew in the air. They stayed anchored to the dying fire for another half-hour before retreating to their swags.

The next night they assumed the same positions around the fire and repeated the ritual of the rum and the rolled cigarettes.

'My wife I lost. In the war,' he said, handing Wilfred a rollie.

'I'm sorry.'

'You see the war?'

Wilfred shook his head. He picked at the eyelets of his boots. He looked up and saw the orange light playing across Drabik's lined face. For long moments he wouldn't blink. It struck Wilfred that his eyes, his whole face, looked different in the night. He became a much older man, the man he would be in fifteen or twenty years, his shoulders rounded over, the cheeks sunken and defined by sharp crescents of shadow. He was like a flower that reacted to sunlight, and closed in on itself in the dark.

'We was in Lublin. We was. She was died in Majdanek.'

Wilfred drew quietly on the cigarette.

'You know Majdanek? Concentration camp near Lublin.'

Drabik ran a hand down one side of his face. He leaned forward and shifted the wood on the fire. The cigarette dangled from the corner of his mouth as he squinted at the spark rise and smoke.

'I was in Majdanek also. For four years in Majdanek, but I did not see her after the first year and someone told me she was died.'

'I'm sorry.'

'I was strong. That's why I was not died in the camp.' Drabik adjusted the stew pot at the side of the fire and sat back on the damp earth. He threw his butt into the flames and immediately rolled another cigarette. 'What is it, the place you kill the sheep for their meat?'

'Abattoir.'

'Abattoir,' he said, licking the cigarette paper and looking at Wilfred. 'That was Majdanek. It was just the place for the killing. Is all. Russian soldiers. And the Greeks and the French and many others more. And us Poles, too. Of course, us. I was in control of the tractor, yes? The tractor. To take the bodies to the Krembecki Woods. At the woods I was one of them who took off the bodies to make the bonfire. You know bonfire.' He jabbed the cigarette at the campfire.

'It was like the making cake. One level, layer, layer of the bodies, and the planks, and another layer, up and up and up.'

He picked a grain of tobacco from his lip and stared at the wet flake on his index figure. 'The light of it, of the bonfire, you could see many miles away from Lublin. You know?'

Drabik rubbed his hands vigorously. 'Getting cold, no? Me I like. The cold.'

Wilfred looked away. He could see Drabik's surveying equipment at the extremity of the firelight, and the wall of bush.

That night Wilfred stayed awake for a long time staring at the stars through the treetops. He looked across the fire at Drabik in his swag and could make no shape of the man in the dark. He wasn't sure if he was there or not. He made no sound in his sleep.

Wilfred pondered the aerial maps Hintendorfer had told him about, which showed what his world actually looked like from above. He wondered if his shack in the valley would be visible in the photographs. Or the Buckley's. Or the Bolocco Cemetery where his mother and father and Berty rested under granite. He wondered where he was when the picture was taken from the aeroplane.

Dew had settled on his swag. The dying fire held a faint glow, and no warmth came from it.

He didn't want to see the mountains from the air. He didn't want to be able to trace the meandering route of the Snowy River. He didn't want to look at it and know that he was in there, somewhere, so small that not even a magnifying glass could find him.

But the other matter had most unsettled him. First a question had occurred to him as Drabik talked beside the fire, but it was one he could not ask. What had happened to Drabik's wife? Had Drabik, as driver of the tractor, transported the body of his own wife to the giant flaming cairn of human beings near the forest?

He was here, in the bush at night, with one man, a stranger who lived with unimaginable horror, one that would not touch Wilfred in a dozen lifetimes. How many Drabiks there were now, in the mountains, holding horror in their heads as they laboured away, day after day, at a foreign landscape.

Wilfred wondered about Dorothea.

He held himself in the envelope of the swag, and in the dark he listened hard for signs of Drabik's breathing.

SIXTY

AFTER HE VANISHED, Graham Featherstone's brother Robert and ex-fiancée Victoria entered the Rozelle terrace half expecting to find a body. Instead, they discovered a house barely lived in, the rooms sparse and half full of someone else's old furniture, the fridge empty save for an old carton of milk and an open container of curled and hardened ravioli. They found, in the backyard, a small pile of empty beer, wine and spirit bottles. But otherwise there was virtually no sign that this was Featherstone's home. He had made no impression on the place.

As Robert and Victoria stared, confused, without a clue as to his whereabouts, Featherstone was negotiating his hire car through the back streets of the tiny township of Dalgety, crawling up and down its hillside grid of ghost streets, feigning the lost tourist. He was heading out to the house of Wilfred Lampe.

It had taken only cursory sleuthing, some minor personal misrepresentations on the telephone, careful questioning and a little-boy-lost routine to trace the location of the property.

Driving up to the shack he almost expected to see

Lampe sitting on the front verandah in a checked shirt and braces and baggy work pants. He parked the car under the giant pepper tree and approached the front door with a dictaphone in his hand.

'Arrive at Lampe property 4.27 pm,' he said. 'Car bodies and rusted machinery and shit everywhere. Old man's boots still on the front step. Door padlocked.'

He rattled the lock and wriggled open the louvres to the left of the door.

'Pots and pans in the sink. Thermometer nailed to the wall. Pair of spectacles hanging from another nail. Dark inside. A kitchen table and chair. Picture of a beach and palm tree on the far wall. Have to get in.'

With a piece of scrap metal he tore the whole side bolt and padlock off the old door.

'Like going back in time,' he said into the dictaphone, walking into the house. 'Fireplace and kettle. Armchair. Light through cracks in the wood slab walls. Simple life. Clock stopped on the mantel. Cabinet with ornaments and pieces of crockery. Smells like . . . smells old.'

He unlocked the door off the back room and peered into the overgrown yard. 'Weeds a metre or so high. Sheep on the hill. An apple tree. Rotting fruit.'

Back inside he took a stiff tea towel from the rack in the kitchen, wiped down the single armchair, and sat in front of the sooted fireplace. The shadows of starlings flickered across the narrow beam of light down the chimney. Ash gleamed in the grate.

After a while he whispered into the dictaphone, 'Funny, a house abandoned. Suspended. A whole life here. Many lives. Begun and ended inside these four walls. So thin, the layer between inside and out.'

The house grew dark. He went around to the front and took his cigarettes out of the glove box of the car and sat on the front steps. He smoked and watched the sun set, taking small sips of bourbon from a flask.

He tried to get a feel for the man Lampe in the sharp-edged ranges in the distance, the same serrated landscape the old man had seen every day of his long life. He tried to imagine Lampe in each of the rusted car bodies scattered around the pepper tree, when they were roadworthy, Lampe in the '30s and '40s, driving into town for supplies, or to an agricultural show.

There were no pictures of the man in the house. No photographs at all, except the two framed women on the bedroom wall.

Featherstone had contemplated his story on the drive down from Sydney. Had a handle on it by Cooma. Was writing it in his head by Dalgety. He'd made up his mind he was right by the time he reached the Lampe gate.

The life of Wilfred Lampe. Simple country gentleman, generations on the land, up at dawn, hard worker seven days a week, good Christian and church on Sunday, pillar of the local community, salt of the earth. A good, plain Australian.

Perfect for the Olympic Opening Ceremony and how we would represent ourselves to the world. It was what the Olympics gave you – a couple of hours to express the national character, a single moment in a choreographed pantomime.

Then again he was not sure any longer he could readily describe the national character. He was the master of the tabloid radio quip, of condensing grand events, tragedies and entire lives into minutes, but he could not readily editorialise his own country. Port Arthur had defined his abilities. It had been hard for him to accept that the light of his talent did not shine far.

He might have had a crack at wrestling the national character when he was younger, and his vision was limitless. The working-class ethos that was driven into him as a child. Blue singlets, white collars, us and them. The suburban block, food on the family table. Relatives of English and Irish descent, carving out a living on the land, sheep and cattle. And back even further, to that small camp at Sydney Cove. The bush ballads and jigs and rum and muskets and gum leaves and mountains crossed and songs around the billabong and lawmakers and scallywags. The woodcutters and road builders. The blokes that stuck together. The great tangled mess of mateship. The Aussie bloke who'd die for his mate. Die of thirst for his mate. Take a bullet for his mate. The unspoken, unexplained riddle of mateship that covered this country like a creeper vine. The mass of blokes bound in mediocrity, and the aggression and fear this place exuded when anyone stood apart from the mob. The thundering subterranean river of alcohol that trembled the surface plate of Australia's history, there at the start at the Cove, the cork-stopped ceramic jugs locked up and precious as gold, and still flowing under and through and over the place, forming amber lakes across the nation, that held a population splashing and playing, and bound by the tepid waters of mateship. And beyond the gambolling, the real world kept turning.

How will they show this in our national opera?

Featherstone thought. How do you define the so-called 'fair go' you never stopped hearing about from the day you were born, a place of equality, tolerance, co-operation and respect?

What exactly *were* we now? They might do the indigenous people and the land and the European settlement and the agricultural and mineral wealth and the birth of cities and the immigrants and the obsession with sport and the mateship and the larrikinism. But what of the line crossed when much of that disappeared? How could they show that?

And beyond the line. How do you represent greed and apathy and self-interest and a nation of kids whacked out on chemicals and racism and the evaporation of culture and materialism and celebrity obsession and narcissism – how do you show that with pots of paint and a sprinkling of sequins?

It was these many unanswerable questions Graham was left with as he drove into Dalgety.

At the Lampe place he began to doubt himself. Had he needed to come to the house at all? He checked his mobile phone. There was no service.

He went back inside the house for a final look. In the washroom at the back he noticed an old wooden cupboard. He pulled open one of the two doors. Nothing. He pulled at the second door. It was stuck. He reefed it open and the timber squealed.

That was when he saw the thing that would keep him in Lampe's house all night.

Featherstone laughed at what he discovered in the cupboard. It was ludicrous. He wasn't sure if he was seeing things. It didn't belong in the house. It was at odds with everything he had seen of Lampe. It didn't fit with the prewritten narrative in his head.

He lit a fire and sat in the armchair and studied the fragile object he'd placed on the floor between himself and the mantel.

He fell asleep in the chair and woke again in the early hours of the morning. He stoked the coals and put on more wood. The object took shape again in the brightening light.

It was quiet in the house. He could not remember ever being in a place so quiet.

He looked down at the strange object and thought for the first time in years about the summers he'd spent as a boy up at The Entrance, and the first girl he ever kissed, and all the beautiful things when life was simple and the family was together. Before his brother's ambition. Before the mad race for car and mortgage, for promotion and the right woman on your arm and opening nights and bars and restaurants where you could be seen and see others. That whole mad dream that always ended with his shoe soles sticky with night-before booze.

He thought about all this for a long time in the quiet, and he thought about the last thing the dying man Tick told him when he'd left the apartment in Elizabeth Bay on his quest for Wilfred Lampe.

'Do you get sick of it?' Tick had asked.

'Sick of what?'

'Watching life, rather than living it?'

He leaned over and looked more closely at the object. It was just over a metre long. Inside an ancient cloak of torn and frayed hessian was a skeleton of roughly cut pieces of wood and wire. There were discs of rusted tin attached to the fragile cloth.

At one end the thing opened out like a sack. And at the other – and this puzzled him the most – was something that resembled a head. He clearly saw it. The conical shape. A slit that could have been a mouth. And above it, a single loose-hanging eye. It rested at his feet, bathed in the soft light of the fire. He laughed to himself and settled back in the chair.

You're a fish, he said to himself. I do believe you're a fish.

SIXTY-ONE

'I WAS ADDICTED to drugs,' she told Wilfred.

They sat in the garden of the Indian cultural centre in Woolgoolga, just north of Coffs Harbour, and ate sandwiches from the nearby service station. Wilfred marvelled at the huge replica elephants standing in the long grass of the overgrown garden. The highway traffic rushed by.

'What do you mean? Drugs?' he said.

Aurora looked over to the roundabout and the Sikh temple on the hill. She lit a cigarette. 'Heroin. And a few other things. I was an addict. I went to a clinic.'

Wilfred studied his sandwich, turning it around. 'A clinic? What for?'

She looked at him. 'To get clean.'

'Clean?'

'You don't know what I'm talking about, do you?'

'They used heroin for pain in the war.'

She shook her head and bit her lip. 'I'm sure they did, but that was a long time ago. You can use it for different things now. It's been used for different things for a long time.'

'Were you in pain?'

'I suppose so.'

'And you couldn't stop taking it? Because of all the pain?'

'That's right, Wilfred. I wanted to take it. I couldn't think of anything else but taking it. It was my whole life. If you could call it a life.'

'You wanted to take it.'

'Yes. I took lots of it. Here, here, here.' She slapped at both her wrists and ankles and feet. 'Between my toes. Here and here. I shot up everywhere I could.'

'Shot up . . .'

'Shot up. *Shot up*. With a needle.'

'A needle?'

'Fuck,' she sighed, holding her head. 'Yes, with a needle, what else? A fucking chopstick?'

She stood and walked back to the car. They drove for an hour without speaking. The highway ran through long, dull stands of bush towards Grafton. Several cars passed honking their horns and flashing their headlights.

Speed trap, Aurora thought.

He needed to use the bathroom. They stopped at the first petrol station in southern Grafton. Not far out of town the highway ran by the Clarence River. Wilfred couldn't take his eyes off it. It was broad and beautiful and he loved the way some of the houses backed right up to the banks.

'Could we walk?' he asked.

She was frustrated with him. She pulled into a rest stop and reefed the handbrake.

'Walk,' she said. She continued to grip the wheel.

He pulled himself out of the little Humber and made for the water's edge. She stayed in the car and watched him through the grimy windshield. He seemed a little unsteady. He stopped, put his hands on his hips, breathing heavily, and continued. He'd disappeared behind a stand of trees.

'Fuck,' she said, banging the wheel, and went after him. Wilfred was sitting on the grass looking over the water. Aurora dropped down next to him.

'I just wanted to be honest with you,' she said, 'about a few things in my life.'

He nodded. 'I'm glad you feel you can tell me things,' he said.

She explained about leaving home, the encounter with Wynter and how her life went out of control. She told him of the child.

He placed his big hand onto hers. It was the only thing he could think of doing. He felt there was nothing he could draw on in his long life on earth to console her.

He fixed on at least something he knew – the view of the Clarence River. His river, the Snowy, used to be like this. Bigger. It took you all the way to the ocean. It claimed lives. Provided food. Sustained the crops and grazing pastures all along its banks. It swept away people's livelihoods. Slaked the thirst of horses and cattle. It was all of life and death.

Then they built the dam up at Jindabyne. Sank the old town. Drowned it. He was there when they blew the bridge, and filled up the valley like a bathtub. There was so much water nobody could think of anything else. Water everywhere. It tricked their minds, all this water. Flooded their logic.

Downstream, the river grew weak. Downstream, all of

a sudden, there were stretches of bank that had never not been caressed by rushing water, never been exposed to the sun and the air. Trout leapt onto caked earth.

The fanfare of the great dam still played in everyone's heads as the breath was squeezed out of the river, downstream.

'This,' he said, gesturing to the river. 'It was always enough for me. Sometimes too much.'

'Is that when you'd go fishing?'

'It was a part of me. Nothing else to say about it.'

'You can teach me one day, like you taught Astrid.'

He squeezed her hand and released it.

'Tell me why you never got married,' she asked. 'Come on. You must have been a bit of a ladies' man, hmm? All those country girls lining up for a dance with young Mr Lampe.'

'It just never happened,' he said.

'There must have been someone.'

'Some things are meant to be, and others not.'

'So there was someone. What was her name?'

He tried to stand and she helped him up.

'Come on,' she said. 'Tell me what happened.'

'Wilfred Lampe was too cautious in life,' he said, brushing off his trousers. He walked slowly back to the Humber.

In Byron Bay they parked in front of the Beach Hotel. He waited beneath a giant hoop pine while she called her father from a public phone.

'We're about an hour or so away,' she told him. 'He's fine.'

Wilfred stood, in awe of the ocean. He looked down the long yellow arch of Clarks Beach. Men and women with hardly any clothes on lay on towels with their feet pointing to the shore. Children flew across the waves on small coloured rectangular planks. A huge orange kite, more a funny cut-up parachute, dragged a man across the water.

'Say that again?' she said into the phone.

A young man with ropes for hair was playing a narrow wooden drum near the rocks. Under the pine trees were some Aboriginal people sitting on the ground talking and smoking. Wilfred could never have imagined his old mate Percy anywhere near the beach.

'You're kidding me,' Aurora said. 'What'll we do?'

A group of young people came up from the beach. They wore T-shirts with NIKE and DKNY and FCUK written on them. A woman in black skin-tight pants and a singlet ran along the beach pushing a three-wheeled pram. He saw another woman wearing similar clothes with wires coming out of her ears.

'Okay, okay, we'll come the back way,' she said. 'Christ.'

Then he saw the mountain.

'Sure, Dad. See you soon.'

It stood blue-grey in the middle of a cluster of other volcanic plugs, strange and alluring with a bent peak like a crooked finger. It looked like the beginning of the world.

'We've got to go,' she said, taking his arm.

'What mountain is that?'

'That's Mount Warning. Come on, we have to get out of here.'

'Warning.'

'That's where we're going. I'll tell you about it on the way. Please, let's get back into the car.'

They took the turn off the highway to Mullumbimby and began the climb into the rainforests of the mountain range. Two cars on the highway and a third in Mullumbimby tooted their horns and waved at the blue Humber. The car strained on the steep roads.

'What's wrong?' he asked.

'I just found out why we're so popular with our fellow motorists,' she said. 'You're a celebrity.'

'What?'

'It's on the news. The kidnapped old man from the Snowy River driving north in the Humber. Seems like everyone's trying to find you.'

'There must be some mistake. Why would anyone be interested in me?'

She ground the gears and worked furiously at the clutch. The car breached the range and disappeared into a cool, scented tunnel of trees, towards Mount Warning.

'Welcome to the end of the twentieth century,' she said.

SIXTY-TWO

FEATHERSTONE WOKE AT dawn hunched in the armchair in the old house. For a minute he didn't know where he was. It looked different inside the house now light was streaming into the room where he sat in front of the fireplace.

The sunlight caught the glass in the little wooden hutch and laid a strip of rainbow on the packed earth floor.

He went into the kitchen, turned on the single tap, splashed water on his face. The water was cold and smelled of copper. He found some dry tea leaves in a canister. He hefted the black kettle out of the grate, half-filled it and rebuilt the fire.

He lifted the brittle fish suit onto the table and delicately laid it out like it was an archaeological relic. As he sipped his tea he studied the fish. It was ragged and dusty and rusted, but it was beautiful.

That morning he cleaned up the house. He swept it out and wiped surfaces and scrubbed away countless piles of calcified bird shit. He went over the windows with damp newspaper and removed the soiled coverlet from the bed and soaked it in the laundry tub. He polished the soot from several kerosene lamps and cleared out the grate of old ash and removed the dust from the pictures of the two women in the bedroom and the painting of the prize bull in the main room. He turned the kitchen calendar to the right month.

Then he found an axe in the shed beside the house and replenished the wood pile. It was hot in the sun and he removed his shirt as he chopped. Tingly blisters formed on his hands but he kept chopping.

In the early afternoon he scythed the tall lucerne and weeds around the house and raked the scraps and deposited it in the red rusted 44-gallon drum that was the incinerator. He burned the dry clippings and stood and watched the flames, and on the hillock not far from the house several dozen sheep stared at him.

He unscrewed the front door latch with the padlock and wedged the door open so fresh air funnelled through the house. It was mid-afternoon when he stopped and had a smoke on the front verandah.

The sun drew down, just as he remembered it the day before. His arms ached deep inside. He was dusted pink from his work in the sun. A single calf mewled some-where over the hills.

Again he sat in that chair by the fire until late into the night. If he looked over at the table he could see the fish staring at him with its single silly eye. And the next morning he waited for the light to strike the diamond pane of glass in the hutch. It did, right on cue.

Later, he drove into Dalgety and on to Berridale where he picked up supplies. When his mobile phone came into range it told him there were three voice messages and five text messages. All of them but one were from Robert and Victoria asking him to call and demanding to know his whereabouts; ordering him to get back to the old terrace in Rozelle and get his fucking life in order. The final voice was that of Wiley, telling him that the blue Humber Vogue had been sighted in northern New South Wales.

Featherstone sat in the car for a long time and wondered what Lampe was doing up north. He erased all the messages.

Back in Dalgety he stopped and had lunch at the Buckley's Crossing Hotel. He was the only one in the pub. After his first beer the publican asked: 'You another one of those newspaper dickheads looking for Lampe?'

Featherstone looked into his beer. 'I was.'

Mitchell wiped down the bar, though it didn't need it. 'Some idiot rings me and asks if there's any place to land a bloody helicopter in town. I told him to shove his helicopter up his arse.'

'Good for you.'

'I've been waitin' for them, but none of them have showed. Must have sniffed a juicier rabbit on the breeze. Haven't had you lot around since Federation, and we ain't missed much I reckon.'

'I'm with you.'

'You sure you're not with the papers?'

'Radio. I'm officially retired.'

'You're a bit young to be retired.'

'I feel old enough.'

'Bit like that, is it?'

'Yeah. It's a bit like that.'

'How do you have your steak?'

'Medium.'

Mitchell watched him eat and cleaned away the plate and salt and pepper shakers.

'I still can't make head or tail what they wanted out of old Lampe,' Mitchell said, unable to refrain from talking with a human presence in his landscape of stools and tables. 'And now they're talking about him on the radio like he's a bloody fugitive. The bloke never did nothin' his whole life, never bothered nobody.'

Featherstone smiled. 'An exhibit. He was to be an exhibit.'

'Now *he's* old enough. To be in a museum.'

Featherstone looked out at the river. 'He was to be our everyman. He's us.'

'Every man. I don't know about that. He just been here forever, if that makes you an every man.'

He sat in the Buckley's all afternoon and talked with Mitchell. After a while the publican's memories and observations about Wilfred's life flowed easily. Graham learned the story of Wilfred and Dorothea. Mitchell told the tale succinctly and matter-of-factly and without adornment. It had been told many times to Mitchell by someone else, and to that person before them, and it was only sad to Featherstone because it was his first hearing.

'Course, he'll be coming home,' Mitchell said.

'You think?'

'Nothing bloody surer. Last time he left town was to see Jindabyne go under in the sixties. Rode up there in his Sunday best like he was going to a funeral. Hasn't travelled further than to town and back home since then. Those Lampes, they never were the travelling type.

Featherstone drained his beer.

'Except the missing sister, of course. But we knew the reason for that,' Mitchell said. 'Those Crank boys still randy as hell so they must have got it from somewhere back in the family. People are people, they don't change much when it comes to the sex thing, eh?'

'I guess not.'

'We have fun with him, old Wilfred,' the publican said. 'You got the ultimate journey ahead of you, mate, we say. The big one. That'll get you out of town. And he always says, Down to Bolocco Cemetery? It ain't that far.'

Featherstone went out to the car and unlocked the door but stopped and looked down the slope to the bridge and the river. He walked down to the water and stood on the edge of a small cliff near the base of the bridge. The earth dropped a few feet to a flat level of weeds and cracked soil until it frayed into pools of algae and greener weeds and finally the thin stretch of what was the river. It was narrow enough in places to jump across.

He realised that he was standing at the edge of the original river width. The true, natural edge of the river, carved in line with the first major pylon of the bridge. The ghost template. For a moment the sunlight caught a small wheel of insects above the murky river water, and it was this that Featherstone later thought of in front of the fire back at the Lampe shack, with the fish looking at him from the table; the halo of insects that had come to him like an image that travelled to astronomers from light years away.

He had no idea why he decided to stay. He was beyond all known limits of his life. He had an abandoned house in Sydney, and no job, and his mobile phone was outside any signal. He had drifted from his own time and space.

He fell asleep in the chair in front of the fire, waiting for Wilfred Lampe to return to his centre of gravity.

That night he dreamed he was trekking through a valley of stones. He had crossed a treeless range and could see down into the grand scoop of the valley and although he was breathing heavily he didn't stop trudging forward.

He was weighted down with layers of clothing and a huge snow jacket and old-fashioned hobnail boots and he struck his single wooden skiing pole into the stony earth as he moved forward and could hear the pole shift the stones on the mountainside.

It was freezing and he heard the clear, crisp air scratch against his throat and contract the wings of his lungs. Occasionally he glanced through his own frosted exhalations and saw a winding stream at the base of the valley and up the top of the next range a small square stone hut. He imagined a glow of firelight in the window of the hut.

With each step he focused on the hut and it never seemed to get any closer. He could hear the drone of aircraft engines overhead and men's voices shouting after him, calling his name, and he tripped and clambered upright and tripped again. His whole body ached and his hands bled and although he could clearly see the warm light in the window of the hut, it never got any closer.

Featherstone knew, even as he was dreaming it, that if he could just get to the stone hut, if he could only peer through the little window, he would see, inside in the warmth, all the answers to the problems and disappointments of his life.

SIXTY-THREE

Even as the 36-foot launch passed through the Southport Bar, Wynter, his hands taped behind his back and his ankles strapped together, knew he was not going to die. Not on this day.

They sat him in the downstairs cabin across from a small rectangular porthole on the starboard side of the boat. If he bent down he could also see, through the open hatch, the men's legs on the back deck and the long white ice cooler for drinks and bait. At the rear of the boat there was a perspex live bait aquarium with a single clear panel. There were small fish darting around in its soupy water.

Wynter's porthole was close to the waterline and through dashes of spray and the giddying swell he glimpsed the huge granite rocks that formed the bar. People fished off the rocks. At the end of the finger of granite was a small lighthouse. Once they passed the lighthouse the boat accelerated, lifted, and the cabin filled with the roar of the outboards. The porthole blurred with seawater. Through it the high-rise buildings of the Gold Coast fused into the droplets.

Earlier, on the drive to the Southport Yacht

Club, Panozza's men had told him about their skipper.

'You gonna like him, Mr Wynter,' one of the men said. 'He does the deep-sea fishing, yes. But for his other job, he gets up before the sunrise and checks the shark nets and drum lines all along the coast. Is drum lines, yes?

'That's a noble job I think, Mr Wynter. To rid the beaches of the danger. Of the predators. The mamas and nonnas take their children to the beach for the day, see, and already the terrible sharks have been removed before everyone has put on their sunscreens.

'His name is Mr Black. I like that name for him. I like that there are these peoples, removing the danger and the scum without anybody knowing. They just do their job, yes?'

The other man said, 'There are more than just the sharks that get caught in the net, too. That's what Mr Black says. The turtles and the dolphins. Life's innocent creatures, minding their own business. But because of the shark and the nets they must have their lives lost.'

'Yes,' the other said. 'Mr Black believes it is very unfair on the innocent creatures. Don't you think, Mr Wynter? It breaks Mr Black's heart. But the scum, it is the oldest story. They take the good with them.'

Wynter was manacled at the hands and he watched the backs of the heads of the two men in the front seats of the car. They drove down a street of restaurants and there were people enjoying a late lunch and others smiling and talking on their bar stools and an old woman retrieving mail from a post office box and two young women pushing prams, side by side, and a giant tourist boat on wheels and shaped like a duck cruising the boulevard. It was just another afternoon on the coast.

You'll wish you'd never met me, Wynter thought inside the cabin as the boat skipped and thumped to the horizon. There'll be knives on board. Hooks. Strong fishing wire. I'll take out the two goons first. Get them overboard. Then deal with this Mr fucking Black.

He needed a hit. He felt like throwing up the beer he'd been enjoying only an hour earlier, on the sun lounge, plotting his future. He tried to wriggle his hands free from the duct tape. The stump of his missing finger throbbed like a drum.

The boat started to slow and he peered up to the deck. He could hear the men laughing. The air was rank with diesel. For a second he relished the familiar smell of it.

Panozza's men came into the cabin. 'Up we get, Mr Wynter, it is going to be a beautiful sunset.'

They dragged him onto the back deck and sat him on the long white central cooler that formed a bench.

'Mr Black,' one of the men said, 'he believes we are perhaps at the wrong end of the day to get the good deep-sea fishing. He say the mornings are better. But it is lovely, yes?' He waved towards the horizon.

They were a few kilometres offshore. You could just see the tiny clutch of high-rises and the curtain of hinterland. The men's shirts flapped with the gusts coming off the water. The surface of the water looked calm but the boat heaved slowly and steadily to the deep swell of the ocean. Wynter scanned the men for any sign of concealed weapons.

For the first time he felt fear. The coastline tilted.

Specks of light were appearing in the tiny buildings. The sun hit the distant range and lit the underbelly of great pale scuds of high cloud. The whole world was pink and orange.

Wynter vomited down his shirt front.

'Oh, Mr Wynter,' one of the men said. 'Now Mr Black has to clean up after you. You mess his lovely clean boat.'

Wynter spat out the vomit and a tendril of saliva dangled from his chin.

'Lucky Mr Black is a professional, and is used to the mess of the deep-sea fishing,' the man continued.

Wynter watched the men pull on pale medical gloves they had retrieved from their pockets. The surface of the water was almost fluorescent. The two men smiled at Wynter.

'You see the shit on the water, Mr Wynter?' one of them asked.

He looked out and noticed long stretches of brown scud on the surface. They stretched like twisting roads as far as he could see. He nodded to the men.

'You know what that is? No. How would a dumb fuck redneck cowboy junkie like you know what that is? Mr Black, he tells us it is the spawning season, Mr Wynter. You know spawn? It is the fishes' eggs.'

He watched the man they called Mr Black produce a leather package from the tackle cabinet. Mr Black did not look at Wynter. He had a beanie pulled down low on his brow. Deep ridges lined his sunburnt neck. His large, scarred hands were flecked with salt.

'All of life, Mr Wynter,' the man went on. 'It is a wonderful thing, nature. The natural selection. It gives the balance to everything.'

689

Mr Black unfolded the leather package and arranged several dark-handled knives across the suede sheath. Wynter struggled against the ankle and wrist tape. He was losing circulation in his hands.

'Let me tell you one thing that I have observed about our mutual friend Mr Panozza,' the man continued. 'At the dinner in the restaurant, he has the whole family there. His wife. His kids. His mother. His sisters and brothers. It is chaos, Mr Wynter. The children running around. The family all talking at once. The food and drink coming and going. And there is Mr Panozza, in the middle of it all, grinning like the cat with the cream on his whiskers. You see, he is at perfect peace, he has the balance, when he is surrounded by the chaos of the family.

'It is something a fucking scumbag junkie like you can never understand. You only care about feeding your belly. Feeding what it is you need to feed. You are self-ish and alone. You cannot see very far. All you can see is what you want to take at that minute. Even for an animal, Mr Wynter, you are very sad and pathetic.'

Wynter spat again. He thought, Fuck you, dickhead.

Mr Black presented the knives to the two men then moved to the side and took the deck hose like it was a gun.

'You see what I say? Here is the beautiful sunset. Here is the miracle of the fishes and the eggs. And you see nothing.'

The man stepped forward and reefed Wynter's head back over the edge of the perspex cooler. His partner pressed down on his abdomen.

Wynter could see out of his left eye the wash of

orange sky. To his right the live bait tank. He could just make out the frenzied yellow-tailed fish darting through the murky water.

Then the serrated knife was pressed to his throat. He tried to twist but the other man pinned him with his body weight. Bile rose in Wynter's throat. He could barely breathe. He recognised a momentary, light-headed euphoria.

The man holding back his head leaned down to Wynter's left ear.

'Mr Panozza, he want me to say two words to you,' the man whispered. Wynter couldn't swallow. His mouth was open. The fish tore around the tiny tank.

'Eternal life,' the man said, and ran the knife across Wynter's throat.

There was the sound of running water and a coldness around Wynter's upper body and it felt warm below his waist and there was the smell of shit and piss and salty sea air and he tasted the copper sky and felt his eyes engorge and there were white lines tilting upward and the shapes of human heads and something black splash-ing across his arms and hands and he heard the ripping of tape over and over and a huge weight strapped to his chest and then the wild coils of orange rope curling across his vision and gone and corkscrewing again and pain in his wrists and ankles and more weight and he was lifted up and he heard the deep groan of men and when he hit the water millions of eggs caught in his hair and funnelled into the hinge of his throat and coated his eyes.

Wynter felt himself falling and then there was nothing.

He left a comet trail of bubbles and blood and spawn in his wake as he sank into the darker, colder water.

SIXTY-FOUR

AURORA AND HER father left Wilfred alone in the house with the documents and photographs that had belonged to his missing sister Astrid. When they returned two hours later the old man was sitting on the front verandah looking over to Mount Warning. The cane was tall and vivid green and hissed loudly.

They didn't know what to say to him.

Aurora made tea and brought it onto the verandah.

The air was sticky with humidity and still Wilfred wore his checked shirt buttoned at the cuffs and collar and his heavy brown shoes and socks. Aurora and her father were flushed and perspiring from their walk by the river, yet he looked cool and comfortable nursing the teacup, his once tanned face having paled over the past month. Splays of countless freckles were emerging across his face, ears and neck, like secret hand–writing revealed.

After a long while he said, 'It's nice to know she had a life. Astrid.'

He was not sure whether he preferred the life he had imagined for her to the one he had just pieced together from the scraps of information. They certainly posed more questions. He might have discounted her newly discovered life as less real than his own version, if it hadn't been for Aurora, sitting a few feet away from him, real and breathing.

There were no pictures of the illegitimate child that had initiated Astrid's flight from Dalgety when she was just a girl. He felt sorry for that child, always a fugitive from shame and guilt, smuggled out of the Monaro by its teenage mother. When he thought of that child he felt ashamed of Astrid. Then there were the other for-gotten children, spidery lines of life radiating into the world, and one of them leading here, to Aurora and her father in the cane fields.

Wilfred was tired, too, of talking about his own life. He had recounted it, wearily, for the sake of Aurora and her father, the night before over dinner. Aurora, again, had questioned him about his mystery love, Dorothea.

'My world was not big enough for her,' he said. 'She belonged to something more. More than what I could offer. It wasn't her fault. She was born to that.'

'People can change,' Aurora had said.

'It can be a comfort to know what you're born to,' he said. 'And a burden.'

'You never thought of her?'

He took a long time answering. 'I think of her every day.'

'What do you think of?'

'Everything people like me think of. A life we're not born to. I can see the big old house we might have lived in, and children and grandchildren. A stupid young teenager. That's me.' He paused. 'But there's you, now.' This unexpected gift, from Astrid.

They finished the tea on the verandah.

'It's just a matter of time before they turn up looking for you,' Aurora's father said. 'I don't know what you want to do.'

'I'd like to go home,' he said flatly.

'They might be there, too.'

But he could already hear the Humber rattling the wooden slats of the Dalgety Bridge, always loose as old piano keys, and he'd give his customary glance down at the river, wizened now, the water barely moving, its memories lost without the movement, without the music of the flow. It was just like him. Just like the old blood in his veins.

'They'll forget about me soon enough,' he said matter-of-factly.

'What would you like to do, Wilfred?' Aurora asked him.

'Dalgety,' was all he said.

SIXTY-FIVE

THE MEDIA HELICOPTERS never arrived in Dalgety.

Instead, the nation's newspapers and radio and television became fixated on other matters: in the Sydney Olympics Athletes' Village, 15,000 beds would be made 396,000 times, equal to 271 years of bed-making for an average Australian family; one of the designers of the Australian athletes' outfits for the Opening Ceremony said if he had the choice he would dress the nation's representatives in platform thongs, sheepskin ugg boots, blowfly-wing capes and football-shaped hats; the NSW Taxi Council lobbied for a twenty per cent increase in fares during the Games; New Zealand police claimed to have uncovered a terrorist plot to blow up Sydney's Lucas Heights nuclear reactor during the Olympic Games; Australian police were concerned terrorists might send a fully loaded aircraft hurtling into the Opening Ceremony in front of the entire world; and Olympic officials announced that at the Games a pie would cost $3.50.

Graham Featherstone returned to Lampe's shack and lit the fire after talking all afternoon with Mitchell in the pub in Dalgety. The roof creaked, and he heard animals moving out in the paddocks. The house smelled of bird shit and wood smoke, despite his fanatical cleaning efforts.

In the dim light the strange hessian fish on the table was sketched out in shadowed points and black cavities and clots of wire and broken ribs. It looked battered. Savaged. Dead.

He had bought a bottle of J&B from Mitchell and now he drank it neat from a small empty Vegemite jar he'd found on the sink. The whisky was for clarity, not obfuscation. To blur the intrusions of his own ego, the distractions his personal crisis had accrued. He drank the J&B convinced he could see through it all, to a clear purpose, in Wilfred Lampe's shack.

Halfway through the bottle he went out into the yard. It was a cloudless night with a three-quarter moon. The tussock grass was damp beneath his feet. He stood and stared at the great feathery head of the pepper tree, flickering with silver like a shoal of tiny fish. He breathed deeply and took in a bouquet of soil and pepper and manure and rusted tin.

Swigging the whisky, he walked unsteadily past the tree and the outlying sheds and the rounded human shapes of granite and pushed south, up the side of the hill that formed half of Lampe's little valley, convinced he had to get a higher vantage point to see things, to see himself and his place in it. He hit the invisible wires of a fence and was thrown back. On the ground he laughed at himself, stood up, and checked the level of the whisky against the moon.

He struggled through the wires and forged on through the long grass, glancing over his shoulder for the amber window of the house. At the top of the ridge he sat down heavily, his chest aching.

Using the glowing rectangle of the shack as a compass point he made out the distant nest of pinpoint lights that was the town and a few neighbouring properties up the valley towards Jindabyne. But he kept coming back to the light in the Lampe house, imagining black lines radiating out from it, blacker than the paddocks and the sky, lines on an infinite map, which stretched across the world and fitted it precisely in the age-old grid of longitude and latitude, the gossamer net of them that encased the planet.

Hearing a movement behind him in the dark, he turned. His heart beat quickly. He smelled the whisky on his own breath. He stumbled back to the house, half-jogging, and lit a kerosene lamp with an unsteady hand, and sat at the table with the old fish. Then he took out a notebook and wrote the start of a story that would never be published or broadcast.

The next morning he talked again with the affable Mitchell and radiated out to surrounding properties to speak with several old locals. He studied photographs retrieved from wooden sideboards. He was sent from one property to the next, tracing lines of gossip, snippets of story, half-remembered facts. He wrote it all down.

In the course of his investigation he heard how Wilfred's father had died of a horse kick to the head, a tractor accident, pneumonia. How his mother had a heart attack cleaning the stone floors of the church, an asthma attack, a broken heart. How the girl Astrid had thrown herself into the Snowy and been swept out to sea; had perished as a field nurse in the Spanish Civil War.

Featherstone delighted in each contradiction, in changes of hair colour, temperament, mannerisms. It was impossible to capture a person, a life, and it was nonsense to suggest you could. Lives were mercurial. They slipped and shimmered and darted. Then they were different again, in one person's memory, and then another. And in the next layer, with the stories and memories relayed to another and removed from direct observation and experience, life became something else, part of the life of the person doing the telling, and away it went again, altered and imbued with another's moral and actual perspective of the world. Hills became mountains. Rivers shrank to streams. Cowards heroes. Ugliness beauty. It pleased Featherstone to finally understand this. It was liberating to be amused by his own folly. To have what he had liked to think of as his entire reason for working, for being, totally upended.

On the morning of his second day of investigations, one thread led him to a big house across the Victorian border, down a gravel driveway of ragged pines, to an unkempt carriageway and its centrepiece rose garden. Through thick weeds he could see the dark dead arms of old rose bushes.

Featherstone had telephoned ahead from the local Corryong post office, and announced, to his own surprise, that he was a historian. The man at the end of the line spoke slowly and deliberately and punctuated the conversation with long, excruciating pauses.

'Best to be here around midday, if you'd like to come by then,' the man said.

The man greeted Featherstone on the front verandah. He was in his sixties and had a full head of black hair that grew in odd-angled tufts, some of them tipped with white, like he'd been walking in a snowfall. His blue cardigan was unevenly buttoned and had the same askew geometry as his hair.

'Tea?' he said, and led Featherstone into the house. Once, it would have been a grand mansion. Featherstone peered into the large formal rooms on either side of the central hall and they were filled with tea-chests and piles of old newspapers and stacked furniture. Fireplaces were hidden behind the bric-a-brac, the stately overhead lamps just frosted planets hanging in the gloom.

'This way, this way,' the man said. 'I'm Daryl. D-a-r-y-l.'

Featherstone negotiated his way with difficulty down the hall, an obstacle course of coat and umbrella stands and stacked books and sheets of salvaged roof iron and timber. The whole place felt abandoned, except for the kitchen. It brimmed with yellow light. In it sat a huge black cast-iron wood stove. An old refrigerator clicked and hummed. The kitchen table was covered in newspapers, crossword books, coffee mugs filled with pens, and several bottles of tablets. This was where Daryl mostly lived, he told Graham.

It was some moments before he even noticed the old woman sitting by one of the windows in the corner.

'Mama? This is the historian who rang earlier.'

She turned towards Graham.

'His name is Mr Featherstone.'

Daryl filled an electric kettle and switched it on. 'Isn't that a funny name, Mama?' He hitched his pants up and retrieved three cups. 'Feather at the start and stone at the end.'

Featherstone took a chair at the table. He glanced at the bottles of medication.

'Mama comes here every day, from the home,' Daryl went on. 'Mr Digby drives her out and I drive her back. Sometimes we sit in the garden and look at the mountains. You can see the southern slopes of the Snowy Mountains from the garden. They're Mama's favourites. Mama was the first woman to ski down them, weren't you, Mama? She says the mountains are more home to her than this house, which is her home and was my father's home and is my home.'

The old woman's face was crazed with fine lines and wrinkles, and the pale glow through the window lit her like a painted portrait. Her hair was held in a style from another age, drawn back from her face by a stained-glass clip near the back of her head.

Featherstone thought she smiled at him as Daryl filled the small room with his fumbling tea preparations and incessant talk.

'We have a thousand head of cattle and maybe four thousand sheep, that's what Mr Strelow says. Mr Strelow is the property manager, he's been here for years. The property goes all the way down to the Murray River. Grandfather built the house here last century and then Mama was here with her family until she moved away to Melbourne and Europe, and then Father died in the war and she came back so she could look at the mountains. You wouldn't believe seeing how small she is but Mama knows those mountains like her own hand, or the back of it I should say, and she was the first woman to ski down them. She's already in the history books, Mr *Feather*stone. Mr Feather*stone*.'

She was small in the wooden chair by the window and thin in a nylon dress patterned with white and yellow roses. Her veined hands were clasped in her lap. Featherstone couldn't see her traversing the mountains in winter, even as a young woman, but her grey and violet eyes told him something. They were eyes that had not kept pace with the ageing of the rest of her. She turned to the window and her right eye caught, behind the iris, an amber chip of light.

Daryl left the room but before Featherstone could speak to the old woman he was back with some sheets of paper and a pen. He hummed a song to himself, took his seat at the table, and began work on one of his unfinished crosswords, scratching sample words on the blank paper. It was as if Featherstone wasn't there.

'Grind brackets teeth, five letters.'

'Daryl,' Featherstone said.

'Grind brackets teeth.'

'Daryl.'

'Oh yes, the tea. White? Black? Sugar?'

'Could I speak to your mother in private?'

'Private?'

'Yes.'

'You can speak to my mother in private if you need to have privacy, Mr Featherstone.'

'Thank you.'

'Mama, Mr Featherstone wants to speak to you, in *private*.'

She slowly got up out of the chair, straightened her dress, and touched her son on the shoulder. It surprised Featherstone. She seemed fixed there, by the window, in the yellow light. He wasn't even sure if she could hear, let alone speak. She entered the hallway and walked towards the back of the house.

'You can sit with Mama outside, on the bench that looks over the mountains. That's where she always goes when she wants to be *private*.'

Featherstone followed her into the back garden. He could hear Daryl in the kitchen: 'Grind brackets teeth, five letters.'

Featherstone could see now she was not as small as she appeared in the chair. She was of average height and thin and walked with an assured elegance. It was a walk, he knew, she had probably carried all her life. Something age had not meddled with. She went to the garden bench and ran her hands briefly beneath her dress hem as she took a seat.

He could see now the full artistry of the hair clip. A butterfly in small, exquisite multi-coloured leadlight panels.

Together they looked over to the imposing buttresses of the Alps, at once a tall and rugged mass with sheer drops, and yet the longer you studied them the softer they seemed, in purples and blues and tipped with pockets of snow.

A chilly breeze pushed across the river flats and rolled up to the old house which stood on what seemed to be its own hillock, a pedestal, high above rich grazing pastures flecked with livestock.

He turned to her. 'You are Mrs . . . you are Dorothea, aren't you?'

'Yes,' she said, looking at him.

'There was a boy. A man. From Dalgety.'

She straightened her dress over her knees and again clasped her hands and seemed to look into the bright, fresh petals of the white and yellow roses on her dress.

'Yes,' she said quietly. 'His name was Wilfred.'

SIXTY-SIX

THE INSTANT THEY blew the Bailey bridge at old Jindabyne in 1967, Wilfred, astride his horse, felt the shock wave pass through him and knew, before the shower of water returned to earth, that the river was dead.

They had come in throngs to watch the army bring down the bridge. There were gasps and cheers when the explosives detonated. Cars parked in rows shone in the winter light like beetles, their headlights trained to the cleared valley and the old town. Soon, it would all be under water.

Wilfred wore his old tweed jacket and his only tie. He could have taken the Humber but he had wanted to go by horseback. He tracked the Snowy River from Dalgety as best he could, almost to the base of the new dam wall, and was surprised by the carnival-like crowds.

On the grass hillock, he tried to imagine the town submerged in the new man-made lake. Old Ted's Snowy River Cafe. The hotel with its worn bench on the verandah. The church. He thought of people's living rooms and kitchens and bedrooms deep down in the murky water. The backyards, the lanes where children played, and the trees they stole fruit off, and the gates of the old cemetery, the empty shelves of the general store cold and silent under the water.

There would be no fish straight away, he thought. But they'd introduce them, and they'd be swimming in the spire of the church and in and out of houses where people had eaten together and through rooms where they'd made love and women had given birth and children had fought and hugged and slept. It would all belong to the fishes.

He'd seen for himself the damming up at Island Bend two years earlier. Yet downstream nothing seemed to be affected by the dam. Wilfred checked the river regularly, as you would tend sheep after rumours of the grass staggers. There were no changes he could detect. He still fished and caught some decent trout. It was this, the unaltered rhythm of the fishing, which made him wonder if he'd been worrying about nothing.

One afternoon, wading to his knees at one of his favourite spots at Iron Mungie, he saw something he'd never before witnessed in all the years he'd fished the river. He'd only caught a single brown in two hours when a small cloud of red dragonflies appeared above the surface of the water. Out of nowhere dozens of rainbow leapt up into the blur of insects, the water boiling with their attack, the sky alive with trout. And just as quickly the dragonflies were gone, and the river surface smoothed.

This moment quelled his concerns. Men had burrowed into the mountains, poured untold tons of concrete, scratched out roads where there had never been roads, and diverted streams and creeks and rivers which had remained undisturbed for thousands of years, maybe millions – he had seen much of it with his own eyes – and still the river could produce something that surprised him. An intense flash of life.

When they finally blew the bridge, though, and the aftershock passed over and around him and the horse, and they were left in that horrible vacuum of silence and nothingness in its wake, he knew in his soul that the river would never be the same.

It didn't make sense. With so much water around, how could the river be killed? That day he watched the new lake rise an inch an hour after the explosion. It was like the spring thaw happening in fast motion, even though it was only July. They were filling the valley with water.

The closer the hydro-electric scheme got to completion the more confused Wilfred became. The locals were told the summer grazing leases would not be affected. Nothing would change. Australia was thinking big at last. This would be one of the greatest engineering feats of the world. They debated it in the front bar of the Buckley's. The closer the scheme got to completion, the less the talk.

Old Alf Brindlemere's son, Jack, with the same velvety rattle in his chest as his father, couldn't see the point.

'We done without it all these years and we did all right,' he said. It became his mantra.

'It's progress, mate.'

'The way I see it,' Jack said, and his companions groaned, 'they just wanted to keep the war goin', with all the dynamite and stuff. Couldn't let the war go.'

'How you think they gonna dig them tunnels for the pipes and shit, with toothpicks?'

'Country thick with bloody Yanks and Eyeties, like we haven't got the blokes here to do the job. Building a bloody nation, my arse. We got hands to do it.'

'I seen your new water tank, you silly old bastard. You couldn't build a billycart for your kids. Three wheels and facin' backwards, that's you.'

'I built plenty of billycarts in me time.'

'You're a stone's throw from the biggest source of 'lectricity in the bloody country and you still scratchin' around with candles and kerosene out at your joint.'

'That'll do me.'

They cheered in the bar. They'd been waiting for it. *That'll do me.*

Sitting on the stationary horse on the day the bridge was blown, he watched crowds mill about the old town like it was an open-air museum. Folks having one last look at their homes, sightseers and strangers strolling through it, hands clasped behind their backs, like it was already the ruins of Pompeii.

He made his way around the back of parked cars and the straggly crowd and headed for home. He heard a single car approaching from behind, and moved to the gravel verge of the road. The car stopped in front of him and a woman in a straw sun hat with a scarf around her neck and wearing large black sunglasses emerged from the passenger's seat and held up her hand, motioning Wilfred to stop.

He jerked on the reins of the horse.

'Excuse me, but would you mind?'

He looked down at her as she foraged in a shoulder bag. She pulled out a large black and silver camera.

'Just one photograph?'

SIXTY-SEVEN

THE HUMBER SKIRTED Canberra and struck the low, yellow hills of the Monaro with its cold sentinels of granite and clusters of leafless trees, but Wilfred felt too tired to take any comfort from the familiar landscape.

The journey from northern New South Wales had taken them more than four days. Aurora and her father had mapped a crooked, fractured route that kept them off the New England Highway as much as possible, away from the attention of popular thoroughfares.

They had urged Wilfred to leave the Humber in Murwillumbah, under a tarp, or send it home by rail and take a hire car, but he'd insisted. He did not want to abandon it.

They looped and zigzagged their way from town to village to town, ate takeaway food in the shadows of bridges, shuddered down fire trails, crept into rest stops.

It reminded Aurora of her life on the road with Wynter. This time she knew where she was going, what awaited her on the far side of a range or in the crook of a valley. In the long silences during the drive with her great-uncle she thought about Wynter constantly. Once she imagined that the shape of Wilfred beside her was in fact Wynter as an old man, no longer full of fire, rage, the hatred that came on as suddenly and violently as a shift of air could trigger a car alarm, and that he had made it through, and left that self behind. But men like Wynter didn't get old.

She had felt him close, many times, in the past few months. Now she felt nothing at all. But no matter how strong she'd become, she knew he could take this fresh start from her in an instant. It was what most attracted men like Wynter, the opportunity to destroy something they could never have. She didn't know if she'd ever stop wondering when he would suddenly step out of the dark.

Despite their attempts to go unnoticed, the Humber Vogue had, in fact, been spotted on the first afternoon of their journey back to the Snowy Mountains. They had got no further than a roadside rest room in the hills behind Byron Bay. While Aurora waited for the old man, a VW Kombi van pulled onto the gravel verge. The driver, a middle-aged man with grey dreadlocks, leaned across to the open passenger window.

'You okay there?'

'Sure.'

'Is it really him?' he said, motioning to the Humber.

'Don't know what you're talking about.'

'Here,' he said, disappearing into the back of the van. Moments later he produced a plastic bag full of oranges, apples and mandarins. He passed them out the window.

'Organic,' he said.

Aurora stood holding the bag.

'Good luck to you,' he said.

On the first night they stayed at a caravan park

711

outside Lismore. She reasoned it was better than a motel. It was the unwritten code of the van park, to respect privacy. You could be anyone in a caravan park. Aurora had stayed in enough of them over the years.

That night she barely slept, cramped in the Humber beneath a thin caramel-coloured blanket retrieved from the van. Aurora could sense that Wilfred was sullen and tiring. When she offered the van to him exclusively he didn't argue.

In the car, as the dew lowered over the duco and the windows fogged with the warmth of her breath, she thought of him in the bed in the van and wondered again about the women in his life. She could not accept, now that she had family again, that he was alone in the world.

What of Dorothea? A great hurt, she reasoned. Big enough to change a life, or stop it dead.

Was it Astrid's fault that he felt destined never to be with any woman – because he already had a woman missing in his life? That until she was found, it was not right, not permissible, to fill the void with someone else? The notion seemed to fit with his simple code of living and the quiet acceptance of his lot. Or was this part of his problem? This timidity? This impenetrable aloneness which, over time, might become an addiction in itself?

Still, in his eyes, he had been Astrid's guardian. He had failed in his guardianship. He didn't deserve even the basic principles of human companionship and happiness.

But Astrid had had a life. Marriage. Children. She'd at least had that.

Aurora woke from her half-slumber before dawn and sat in the car and smoked and felt sick over what Wilfred thought now, at the end of his life, knowing the fate of Astrid. It might have been kinder, even merciful, to have denied him the truth, not to have dragged him through it all. They had given him something that only lent shape to his loneliness and loss.

All this, at the end of life. He had managed his hurt. Now it was back again.

They slipped through Tenterfield. 'Birthplace of Federation,' she said as she drove.

'Federation,' he said after a while. He remembered, for the first time in ages, that he still had the surveyor's peg somewhere in the back shed.

At a roadhouse outside Armidale they ate in the small flyblown dining area and when they returned to the car they'd parked out the back, they found a truck driver inspecting the Humber.

'Gidday,' he said.

'Hi.'

'Thought you might need some help.'

'What for?' Aurora asked.

The driver smiled. 'Get your famous cargo here to where he's got to go.'

For the rest of the drive to Lake George they were shepherded, closeted, fed and hidden by a string of semi-trailer drivers who formed part of the great twenty-four-hour river of interstate trucking through western New South Wales and down into Victoria en route to Melbourne.

The truckers kept each other informed via their CB radios, speaking in code, enjoying the espionage of it all. Wilfred became known, for several days, as The Big Fish.

After the protection and refuge of the truckers she no longer cared about keeping out of sight. They were so close to home. She drove down through Cooma, past the flags of the nations of the world, and was about to make for the Monaro Highway when he said, 'Turn here.'

She slowed the car, confused. 'Shouldn't we—'

'Here, turn right here.'

He had said nothing in the previous few hours. She had expected the opposite, close to home. They wound their way through the low, stubbled hills.

Then suddenly she knew, only a few kilometres along the Snowy Mountains Highway, why he had made the detour. They were less than forty-five kilometres from Adaminaby.

'I don't want to do this,' she told him, gripping the wheel with both hands.

He looked out the window.

'Do you hear me?'

He rubbed his cramped knees.

'I don't have to do this if I don't want to,' she said.

She reached into the console and foraged for her cigarette packet with her left hand but he reached out and held her wrist fast.

'Why are you doing this to me?'

He released her and stared ahead at the broken white line on the road.

He said, finally, above the hissing, 'They drowned it, Adaminaby, just like Jindabyne.'

She was angry with him, and saw nothing but the blur of line.

'They moved the houses to the new town on the backs of trucks, what I heard. They put down the new town away from the lake. It never took. No roots.'

She could turn the car around. Go back to the right road to Dalgety and get him out of the car. Leave it with him. Walk back to town. Hitch her way out of there, away from the ghosts and the dead river and the steel bridge and the willows, and turn her back on him forever.

'That lake, it took everything away. You say people got their memories, but memories are only the half of it. Memories got to be attached to something, or they fade away. A house. An old tractor. Smell too. Like the skin of a rainbow. Those beautiful pinks and blues and greys, and all the spots in amongst the colours. They fade real quick when that fish is out of the water. They're only beautiful when the fish is in his proper home, you know what I'm saying? Take him out of that and he's not a rainbow anymore.'

'Is this some grand life lesson you're trying to teach me?'

'I'm just telling you something.'

'I don't need to hear it.'

'It's just something I know. The new town, it died. It had a lot of the same people in it. Same folk from the old town. Didn't take. Everything those people had together, it was at the bottom of the lake before they even knew it.'

SIXTY-EIGHT

BY THE TIME the Olympic flame was halfway through its hundred-day journey around Australia, the country had forgotten about Wilfred Lampe. The flame was carried off the plane, flickering inside a little lantern, and transferred to the first official torch, and it flared there in the dead centre, near the great red leviathan of Uluru.

It headed due east for the coast, via Dalby and Longreach, held aloft by local businessmen and councillors and schoolchildren and celebrities and old people and war veterans and sports heroes and charity workers and Christians and atheists and unknown suburban men and women.

The moving caravan of officials and safety vehicles followed the torch to Coolangatta, through Mermaid Beach, Palm Beach and Main Beach to Surfers Paradise, and up to Brisbane and the beginning of the flame's counter-clockwise journey through the nation.

It was applauded at Dicky Beach and Bli Bli and Coolum Beach and Noosa Heads. It visited Cairns in the tropical north and cut across to Darwin and through the heat and flies of the Northern Territory to the west, where they welcomed it in Geraldton and right down the coast to Fremantle and Perth, and over the desert it went to Kalgoorlie, then across the border into South Australia to Clare, and Yacka, and Adelaide, then Mount Gambier.

They lined unsealed roads waiting for it near Ararat and tooted their horns as it made its way to Swan Hill and Echuca and Bacchus Marsh. They gave it a hero's welcome in Melbourne before it skipped the Tasman Sea and was watched with wide-eyed delight by crowds in Queenstown and Hobart and the old penal colony at Port Arthur.

And back it came to the mainland, cheered in Cockatoo and Sassafras, Glenrowan and Violet Town, and up to Mount Beauty, and over to Greta and Jerilderie.

They waved Australian flags at it in Wagga Wagga, Young, Cowra, Parkes, Broken Hill and Lightning Ridge, and staged lunches and little ceremonies for it up through Tenterfield and Byron Bay.

Then it came, south, through Coffs Harbour and little Frederickton, Kempsey and Nambucca Heads, to Aberdeen, Scone, Willow Tree, and out to Orange, Emu Plains, and back again to Medlow Bath, then Bowral, then Bundanoon, then Wingello, and on to the capital, Canberra.

They greeted it warmly in Cooma and took it up the mountains, to Thredbo, before bringing it back to Cooma again.

Mitchell from the Buckley's drove over to see it before it disappeared towards the coast, and up to Sydney, and the Olympic Stadium at Homebush.

It was day ninety-two of the torch's hundred-day

journey around the country. It was the end of the first week of September.

Mitchell remembered that day. Not because of the little flame, and the local dignitaries who trotted with the torch in their baggy shorts and tops, and the flashing lights and cameras and general hoo-ha, but because when he returned to the pub early that evening he noticed through the window, as he was wiping out some glasses, what he thought was Wilfred Lampe's powder blue Humber Vogue crossing the Dalgety Bridge.

SIXTY-NINE

WILFRED AND AURORA saw a flicker of light through the tall lucerne as the little Humber puttered across the paddock towards the house at dusk.

A mob of sheep on the hill stopped and stared down at the car. Their fleeces were dirty and indistinguishable from the earth, but from the road that cut through the valley their long, creamy faces looked like a crowd at the theatre, all blank and the same in the glow of limelight.

They rounded the dark shape of the pepper tree and parked beside a white car. Aurora cut the engine and they both sat in the silence, looking at the strange car. Her first thought was of the police. Detectives. Wilfred observed it indifferently. It could have been a whale hauled onto the grassy shoreline – he was beyond surprise.

He pulled himself out of the Humber and walked around the front of it. He felt the heat thrumming off the radiator under the bonnet. Aurora stayed in the car.

Looking up at the house he stopped. He teetered a little on the soft grass. He was confused. He looked around. It was his house with the rusted roof, the shed, the homemade electricity generator, the giant boulder in the growing dark beyond the pepper tree. But something was different. The light was strong and bright and streaming through the clean louvres. And in the light there was a grey-haired woman sitting in a chair on the verandah. Her hair glowed like a lamp.

Someone filled the doorframe of the house, just the shape of a man through the flywire. 'Mr Lampe,' the man said.

Wilfred fiddled with his spectacles, made a tentative move towards the house and stepped into the sharp-edged corridor of light thrown onto the clipped lawn. He hooked his spectacles behind his ears but he still couldn't see details in the old woman's face.

He walked up the three steps, gripping the old steel rail as he went, to the wood-slatted verandah, stopped, and looked down at the old woman.

Her eyes were large and violet. Her face was lined and powdery. Her lips were pale pink with lipstick. Through the scent of burning snow gum and roasted meat and the freshly cut grass he detected roses. The old woman wore a clip in her hair, and from where he stood, it looked to him like a beautiful bogong moth.

She got up out of the chair, pushing her weight onto a cane, and stood before him.

She was, until then, only familiar. A face he might have known. Or someone who resembled somebody else he knew. The recognition was a great distance from him, a shape in a blizzard. Then everything aligned, and he took a sharp breath.

'Welcome home, Wilfred,' the old woman said.

Dorothea rested the cane on the chair, took Wilfred's hands in hers, and for a long time they just stared at each other.

A LONE HORSEMAN rode into the centre of the Olympic Stadium. He wore a Drizabone and tan bushman's hat and brown trousers and boots. As the horse reared, the rider cracked a stock whip and it echoed around the bowl of the stadium.

'From the outback, and from the mountains . . .' a voice said.

At that moment, in the last of the day's light, Wilfred and Dorothea walked together along the Old Kosciusko Road, towards Seaman's Hut and the summit, high in the Australian Alps. The sky was pink and grey. As they descended along the gravel road to the beginnings of the Snowy River in the valley of stones, they saw snow patches on the ridges and these too were pink but darker and edged with blue and looked like pieces of cloud caught on the rocks.

On the coast, one hundred and twenty stockhorses flooded into the stadium and circled before filing to the centre. The mob slowly dispersed and the horses formed the interlinked Olympic rings.

'Immortalised in the poetry of Banjo Paterson . . .' a

voice said. '. . . the stockhorses . . . a vital part of the nation's development . . .'

Featherstone and Aurora followed the old couple down to the river. Featherstone carried two unlit kerosene lanterns. As he walked the tin handles of the lanterns squeaked and the glass clinked in the metal frames.

'What wonders and excitement we've still got to come tonight,' a voice said. And a small girl in a pink dress skipped into the middle of the giant bowl. You could hear gentle surf and the tinkle of seagulls. The girl put on sunscreen and lay down on a towel.

'. . . meant to encapsulate the evolution of Australia,' the voice said. 'It is now, and always has been, a land of dreams . . .'

At the river, Wilfred and Dorothea stopped on the small concrete bridge and looked towards the mountain ridges. They could hear the gentle gurgle of the Snowy River beneath their feet. Its pure, meandering surface was orange in the dying light, almost metallic, quick-silver against the dark sedge and herbs and peat, stretching back into the mountains.

He was thinking: I am ready now, to find the source.

Hundreds of galaxias dashed and darted through the orange-plated water.

On the coast, giant jellyfish and plankton and big and small fish moved into the arena that was suddenly an aquarium, an ocean. It was the dream of the small girl. Deep-sea dreaming. She suddenly flew up into the air. She swam and spun and twisted amongst the pilchards and the gropers.

'Thirty-six thousand, seven hundred and thirty-five kilometres of coastline,' a voice said.

Near the roof of Australia, Featherstone and Aurora joined the old couple on the bridge and Featherstone lit the two small lanterns. Great blocks of snow-chilled air moved down the valley. He handed the lamps to Wilfred and Dorothea. Their eyes were dewy with the cold. Together the old couple moved off the bridge to the riverbank, the lanterns throwing wobbly circles of light across the stubbled grass.

The two feeble flames were safe inside the glass of the lanterns. Featherstone and Aurora watched as the couple moved off. They both noticed a moth playing in the lamplight.

'This is an awakening . . .' the voice said, as the Aboriginal women moved across the floor of the arena in Sydney. '. . . calls visitors to listen to the sounds of the earth.'

In the Olympic Stadium, three hundred women from Central Australia suddenly became one woman. Thousands of cameras flashed inside the bowl and it was like the birth of a galaxy. The mass of women expanded until they formed what appeared to be a huge human head, or a womb.

'The rebirth has started,' a voice said. Songmen cleansed the air with smoke. The spirits awakened. High up, bogong moths dashed themselves against the brilliant stadium lights.

The old man Wilfred held the lantern in front of him and followed the trembling circle of pale light. He and Dorothea walked slowly and carefully along the riverbank. At the edge of the light Wilfred saw the shapes of boulders and the heads of spring wildflowers and the veil of dusk was suddenly gone and in the starlight everything looked like it was just forming, and the two of them were there in it, in the moment of creation.

From the bridge Featherstone and Aurora tracked the two lanterns. They could no longer see Wilfred's or Dorothea's hands and wrists attached to the lamp handles. Just two points of light.

In the stadium a bushfire swept from one end of the arena to the other. 'Australia can be a hard land,' a voice said. 'The blackened earth nurtures life . . .'

And suddenly the eruptions of flame and kerosene and cinders gave way to a carpet of greenery. The bowl was an effusion of desert peas and banksias, wattles, waratahs, waterlilies, eucalypts and swamp daisies. Orchestral music looped around the segmented flowers, drew them together, forced them to bloom out of season.

After the floral Eden in the stadium came the *Endeavour*, a strange penny-farthing ship with two small sails, a rabbit in a birdcage, a periscope, book, quill. The blue-coated explorer looked innocuous, silly, a clown on the spindly contraption. A transparent sketch, a thatch of twigs and bird bones, the flap of his swallow-tail coat unheard in the gruel of sounds that swirled around the arena, his lethal impact reduced to that of a cycling child.

Then came the fire-breathing mechanical horse, huge, frightening, head like a skull, and the outlaw Ned Kelly, many of them, replicated, the heads a narrow window into insanity and murder. They played fiddles and fire sparked from their rifles and they lurched like drunken death masks, warriors not of a lawless history but of wars yet to be fought. They strode like

724

choreographed terrorists. And the giant horse writhed, its guts all cogs and farming implements and scrap metal.

'. . . made out of agricultural material,' the voice said. 'New technology . . .'

Water tanks rolled in. Sheets of corrugated iron were strewn across the arena. Metal struck metal in a tin symphony. A town materialised. Men chopped wood. A water mill was erected in the middle of the bowl. Men played two-up. A machine produced a herd of box-shaped sheep.

'The sheep days . . .' the voice said.

In the Alps, Wilfred felt the bogong moths in the air, brushing his hand, dusting the spots and the vein ridges and the creases on his knuckles and fingers. He recalled their nutty flavour. Millions of them sheltered in the mountains' crevices and folds, thick cantilevered blankets of them seeking the cool.

The grass sighed beneath Wilfred's and Dorothea's feet. They could have been the only people left on the earth, and still the place was alive around them in the dark, filled with countless eyes, carpeted with star-shaped flowers, the river edge lined with breathing moss, the granite rashed with lichen. They both felt everything was softer now. The river a stream and it grew narrower. Its music not a symphony any longer but a hymn. Beneath them, soon, the great ancient cathedral of the source.

Into the stadium, down on the coast, flowed the new arrivals, the people of the world. Humanity, bright and beautiful. From the South Pacific and China and India and Germany and Eastern Europe and the Middle East and South-East Asia, new arrivals for a new, tolerant, welcoming nation. Australia, the cradle of a future civilisation. Its arms wide open. Happy, accepting Australia. Safe Australia.

The people of the world formed a human map of the country. Their linked arms the shoreline. They felt each other's pulses through their joined hands, this coastline of beating heart and warm blood.

'Now the workers are summoned to build a new Australia of concrete and steel . . .' the voice said. There was scaffolding. Construction. A bridge. They were building a bridge.

Featherstone and Aurora kept an eye on the lamp-lights. They stood on the little bridge across the Snowy River and peered into the darkness. The two lights were not solid now, but winking, twinkling, being absorbed by the night.

A bridge. The men were building a bridge in the Olympic Stadium. And the bogong moths, blown off course on their way to the Snowy Mountains, were great balloons of wing and antennae and eyes and feet around the light towers.

Wilfred knew he was close. The ground was soft underfoot. They were at the edge of the subterranean catchments, the bogs and springs. The river was there but it fed underground. They heard nothing, but Wilfred could feel the life of the source deep inside of him.

He and Dorothea did not even notice that the little flames in the kerosene lanterns had gone out.

Wilfred Lampe stopped and stood beside Dorothea. One second he was back on a tiny wooden stage in Dalgety, watching from inside the trout suit the dance of the eggs and the larvae and imago and pupae. Another second and the Moth Men were dancing for him, and it could have been now, or thousands of years ago.

They stood beside each other, Wilfred and Dorothea. They were, finally, at the beginning.

And a long way away, down on the coast, where the moths that had lost their way were forming frantic halos, striking hot glass, blinded, colliding, removed from the paths of their ancient migration, a single word was unfurled to the world.

Eternity.

ACKNOWLEDGEMENTS

Many people have contributed to *The Trout Opera* over several years of research and writing, and my debt is substantial.

I would like to express my extreme gratitude to the Literature Board of the Australia Council for the senior fellowship that allowed the novel to be brought to completion.

The origin of the story arrived courtesy of a brief meeting with Mr Ray Reid, a real man from the Snowy River, at his home outside Dalgety on the Monaro in 1996. On assignment for the Sydney *Sun-Herald* with photographer Dallas Kilponen, and examining the state of the Snowy River and calls for a partial return of its flow, we managed a half-hour interview with Mr Reid en route to the airport at Cooma. Unexpectedly, that encounter would dominate many years of my life, and I salute the memory of Mr Reid and the generous co-operation of his surviving family.

I am grateful to the people of Dalgety for their warmth and hospitality, in particular Jo Garland of the Snowy River Alliance, Charlie Roberson and Don Wellsmore. The characters of Dalgety as they appear in

The Trout Opera are products of my imagination, although many names and events have their basis in the actual history of the town and surrounding district.

I wish to pay tribute to Andrew Clark, my former editor at the *Sun-Herald*, for his enthusiasm for the Australian High Country, and for that original Snowy River assignment, and subsequent stories he shared about his periodic visits to the mountains.

Thank you, also, to writer Meg Stewart, who pointed me towards the epigraph penned by her father, the late poet Douglas Stewart, and for allowing me into her home to examine her trove of his fly-fishing equipment, providing a copy of his wonderful memoir – *The Seven Rivers* (Angus & Robertson, 1966) – and for extensive notes, illustrations and photographs pertaining to the Creel fishing lodge near Thredbo, long since burned down.

My heartfelt love and thanks to family and friends for sustaining me in so many ways during the writing of the novel: first and foremost to my wonderful wife Kate, for your warmth, patience and understanding, and to that other great love of my life, my son Finnigan, who deserved more attention from his father during those early months in the world; to Mum and Dad; to Marsha, Phil, Ryan, Fraser and Jordan Pope; to Gillian Morris, Geof Hawke, Gary Morris and Jo Gaha; and to the memory of the late Troy Davies.

I would like to thank my publishers, Random House, for their patience and support of the book. I especially owe a deep gratitude to Carol Davidson for the friendship and professional nurturing that were crucial in bringing the project home; and unqualified thanks to

the novel's sublime editor, Catherine Hill, and to Ali
Lavau. And thank you to Jane Palfreyman.

I owe my appreciation to the following newspaper
and magazine men and women for support during the
long gestation and writing of this book, particularly
David Fagan, editor of the Brisbane *Courier-Mail*,
the late James Hall and Murray Waldren, both of the
Weekend Australian, Steve Foley of the Melbourne *Age*,
Christopher Pearson, formerly of *The Adelaide Review*,
Ian Jack of *Granta*, and Julianne Schultz, editor of the
Griffith Review. Special thanks to Christine Middap,
editor of *The Courier-Mail's Qweekend* magazine, for
understanding and latitude granted beyond the call of
duty. I would also like to pay tribute to Des Houghton,
a wonderful newspaperman and friend.

Portions of the novel have appeared in various books
and periodicals over the years, including *The Adelaide
Review*, *Best Stories Under the Sun* (Central Queensland
University Press, eds Michael Wilding and David Myers,
2004), *Sunset* (Penguin, 2005), *Granta* (Issue 72: *The
Overreachers*, ed. Ian Jack), the *Griffith Review* (Autumn
issue, 2006, ed. Julianne Schultz), *Meanjin* (Winter 2006,
fiction ed. Carmel Bird) and *Best Australian Stories
2006* (Black Inc, ed. Robert Drewe).

Several texts were essential to the novel, especially
Searching for the Snowy by George Seddon (Allen &
Unwin, 1994), *The Snowy* by Siobhan McHugh
(William Heinemann Australia, 1989), *The Aboriginal
People of the Monaro*, compiled by Michael Young with
Ellen and Debbie Mundy (National Parks and Wildlife
Service, Sydney, 2000), *Trout Fishing: A Season on Monaro*
by John Hedge (Abbey Publishing, 1968), *People of the*

Australian High Country by Klaus Hueneke (Tabletop Press, 1994), *Tales from the Australian Mountains* by Niall Brennan (Rigby, 1979), *Before We're Forgotten: The Spirit of Snowy River* by Mike Hayes (ABC Books, 1999), and *Australia's Alps* by Elyne Mitchell (Angus & Robertson, 1942).

I was lucky enough to meet Elyne Mitchell, author of *The Silver Brumby* and other fine works set in and around the Snowy Mountains, shortly before she died, and she was an extraordinary inspiration to me and to the direction of parts of the novel.

The Obscure Logic of the Heart

Priya Basil

From a stunning new story teller with a razor-sharp eye for the drama of human relationships across cultures.

LINA HAS ALWAYS been the apple of her father's eye. When she meets Anil, a wealthy, cultured and decidedly liberal student of architecture from Kenya's Asian community, the intensity of her feelings for someone so different takes her by surprise. She is political and he is not; she is of modest background and he is not; she is a Muslim and he is not . . .

While Lina's parents still dream of a suitable boy for their eldest daughter, she engages in an intricate game of deceit to hide her blossoming relationship. When Lina's mother chances upon a suitcase of their love letters, a moral chasm threatens to tear the family and the lovers apart.

> 'A searing love story . . . burns and scorches with wry conviction about love that refuses to say die'
> *INDIA TODAY*

9780552773850

Six Suspects

Vikas Swarup

There's a caste system, even in murder.

SEVEN YEARS AGO, prominent playboy Vivek Rai murdered Ruby Gill simply because she refused to serve him a drink. Now 'Vicky' Rai is dead, killed at a party he had thrown to celebrate his acquittal. Six guests are discovered with guns in their possession. Who are these six suspects? And what were they doing at the party that night? Vicky Rai had enemies, and many had wanted him dead – but only one had the nerve to pull the trigger . . .

Audaciously and astutely plotted, with a panoramic imaginative sweep, *Six Suspects* is the work of a master storyteller, from the acclaimed author of *Q & A*.

'Unusual, witty, quirkily, cleverly plotted, intelligent . . .
a rollicking good read'
MERCEL BERLINS, *THE TIMES*

9780552772518

The Poet's Wife

Judith Allnatt

It is 1841.
Patty is married to John Clare:
Peasant poet, genius and madman.

TRAVELLING HOME one day, Patty finds her husband sitting, footsore, at the side of the road, having absconded from a lunatic asylum over eighty miles away. She is devastated to discover that he has not returned home to find her, but to search for his childhood sweetheart, Mary Joyce, to whom he believes he is married.

Patty still loves John deeply, but he seems lost to her. Plagued by jealousy, she seeks strength in memories: their whirlwind courtship, the poems John wrote for her, their shared affinity for the land. But as John descends further into delusion, hope seems to be fading. Will she ever be able to conquer her own anger and hurt, and reconcile with this man she now barely knows?

'A fascinating, compelling novel about the wife of John Clare,
and the bewildering effects of her husband's madness'
Clare Morrall

'A subtle and sympathetic portrayal of losing a loved one to
mental illness . . . at once homely and poetic'
Times Literary Supplement

'A beautifully written, poignant novel, lyrically descriptive of the
landscape, detailed in the country life of the time and reminiscent
of the gentle style of the genius peasant poet'
Choice Magazine

9780552774437

The Boat to Redemption

Su Tong

Winner of the Man-Asian Literary Prize 2009

DISGRACED SECRETARY KU has been banished from the Party – it has been proven he does not have a fish-shaped birthmark on his bottom and is therefore not the son of a revolutionary martyr, but of a river pirate and a prostitute. Secretary Ku and his teenage son, Dongliang, leave the shore for a new life among the boat people on the Golden Sparrow River.

One day a feral little girl, Huixan, arrives looking for her mother, who has jumped to her death in the river. Huixan sows conflict wherever she goes, and soon Dongliang is in the grip of an obsession for her. He takes on Life, Fate and the Party in the only way he knows . . .

'Restrained and merciless, Su Tong is a true literary talent'
Anchee Min

'A picaresque novel of immense charm'
Colm Toibin

'Su Tong is delusional almost to the point of illness, as if wearing a black lacquered jacket, stubborn but elegant'
John Updike

9780552774543